I0714210

THE
MENACING RED DRAGON

GOD OF WAR

RYAN KING SCALES

Printed in the U. S. A.

First Printing, January 2022.

Library of Congress Cataloging-in-Publication Data has been applied for.

ISBN: 978-1-7342346-1-9

DEDICATION

To Shanice, because you are the reason I got up.

REVENGE: to exact punishment or expiation for a wrong on behalf of, especially in a resentful or vindictive spirit

"I WILL DOUSE THE WORLD IN
THE BLOOD OF MY ENEMIES
UNTIL I HAVE MY REVENGE..."

TABLE OF CONTENTS

PREFACE

THIS BOOK WAS written with the integrity that I hold for myself and my family. I will never forget the death of my little cousin, Timothy "lil Tim" Johnson Jr., for his murder was why I answered the call of heroism. The details of this book do not necessarily reflect the events of real-life situations; however, I'm sure that some readers may be able to understand and relate to some of the more heinous situations that occur.

This story is more than a decade in the making, with its motivation about as long as my life. I've always suffered from what I refer to as a "heroes complex," as I was always the boy who wanted to save everyone. I learned early on that I wasn't into the normal, admirable heroes, but I was meant to be a dark hero. My early inspiration was of course Batman, but taking me further were the works of Todd McFarlane and my favorite dark hero, Spawn. They each fought for what was important to them, but they had lives that came from the shadows of darkness along with a graphic, untamed edge that set them apart from all the others.

The Menacing Red Dragon was birthed on October 18, 2003 as I sat in my 9th grade English class. It was a manifestation of my depression turned into a hellish rage without discrimination. I hated everyone and everything, even wanting death to find those I hated the most, but I knew that I couldn't live my life enraged about the things that I couldn't control. I channeled that anger into creation and became everything I wanted the Red Dragon to be, thus creating the worst version of myself. It took a few more years, but I eventually found that I wanted to fight for good. But forgiveness wasn't a concept I was too keen on, as it allows the forgiven person an opportunity to do wrong again. I live my life occupied by two spiritual entities; one I refer to as King and the other is Red Dragon, and I view them as my energies that have conjoined from my past lives.

I thank my big brother, Kermit Brower, for waking me up to the truth of my ancestry while I struggled to find myself. His teachings are what encouraged me to tell the story I actually believed in instead of the story I thought people wanted to hear. Ardre Orie and her team at 13th and Joan Publishing paved the way for me to tell this story with her literary initiative *100 Seeds of Promise,* something that Kermit actually made me aware of. Without the two of them, this might not have been possible. I also want to thank the great ancestor and my favorite singer, Barry White. His music is what got me through the long hours of writing through the night trying to make this dream come true.

In the times we currently live in, we all have all been given the call of heroism and are also given the choice to answer. Whether we say "Black Lives Matter" with the roar of our fallen ancestors or vow to "Protect Black Women" as if they were all our own, there is a hero that lies within all of us. Ase...

PROLOGUE

THOUSANDS OF YEARS *ago, the Great Battle of Vengeance was fought between Heru, God of the Sky, and Set, God of Disorder. Years before, Asar, father of Heru, fell victim to the mischief of Set, paying the ultimate price for his mistake and allowing Set to take control of ancient Kemet. The hostile takeover came with years of death and destruction, leaving the future of the Kemetic people hopeless until one day Heru rose to power and opposed him. Heru reigned victoriously over his uncle, ending the decades of misfortune.*

Heru worked diligently to restore the sanctity of the kingdom, reinstating his father's legacy throughout the lands. In time, peace filled Kemet with laughter and joy, refining the unity between the gods and the humans that dwelled in the lands with them. The gods taught the laws of Ma'at to the people, ending disorder and strife throughout the kingdom.

It was said that the reason for Set's disorder was because of his inability to reproduce, a theory that was later proven to be fictitious.

There came a day that Heru was not awakened by the light of the Sun but by the cries of mercy from the people of Kemet. He transformed and summoned his spear, quickly heading out to defend his kingdom. He screeched his powerful war call from his beak to summon the other gods for battle, but only a few came to his aid. Upon arriving at the scene, Heru laid eyes upon his greatest fear. Before him stood the three illegitimate children of Set. The evil demigods had pillaged the kingdom, destroying all forms of life within their reach.

The gods fought several heinous battles against the evil three but failed to vanquish the villains. The random attacks depleted their numbers tremendously, leaving the gods to lay to rest the lost humans along with some of their own. Heru held each fallen god closely to his chest to keep them calm, bravely watching them as they took their last breaths.

The tyrants sought to vanquish all of the gods but had no interest in ruling the kingdom. Their desire was to gain control of Duat, the Realm of the Dead. Learning this, Heru changed his war strategy. To avoid losing more innocent followers, he flew through the lands and ordered the Kemetic people to abandon their homes as they were falling victim not only to the tyrants but also war and chaos from invaders of the north. He vowed to Ra that one day, peace would fall upon the lands again and they would all return, free of despair.

Heru warped into Duat to join Anpu, God of the Dead and Keeper of the Spiritual Gates. The two desperately worked together to conjure up an offering to the ancestral gods for aid to defeat the evil three, but the tyrants grew privy to their plot and located the Spiritual Gateway. They moved the sacred Gateway Stones to bring forth the chamber that concealed the lock to the three Realms. They locked the realms so that the souls of the fallen might enter Duat but could never exit without first surrendering their souls to do deeds of evil. The tyrants also used Duat as a means to feed on the fallen souls as all were denied their rite of passage. The lock also prevented Heru and Anpu from leaving Duat in their natural forms.

Now trapped in Duat, Heru and Anpu continued to battle the fiends viciously without victory or defeat, losing souls in the crossfire of battle. Heru's curiosity led him to discover that he was only able to reenter the Life Realm in his spiritual form, and he took on the shape of a golden falcon to scope the lands, seeing all that changed across the world. He later discovered that he could still transport his full body to the Spirit Realm. With the blessing of the ancient ancestors, Heru tried to reach out to future descendants, catching them in their dreams and showing them the way, but his calls went unanswered as the ways of the world changed.

Ancient African societies that had fallen began to be covered up with lies and falsehoods, mocked by those who chose to follow the ways of the evil tyrants. Heru swore to his people that a day would come when another god would realize their destiny and free them all, and until that day came about, he would continue to put his life

on the line to protect the fallen souls.

CHAPTER 1

THE MOVE

WITH LESS THAN 24 hours to go until she became Mrs. Harrison, Camille rushed home from work to deliver the sudden news to her family. The happiest moment of her life was turning out to be a leap of faith as moments of exaggerated passion would lead two people down the path of matrimony at the county courthouse tomorrow. She cruised down I-20 with no music playing, her thoughts creating an uneven tempo in her mind.

"I can't believe I'm really going to do this, I can't do this," she panicked. "Come on, Camille, you know you gotta do this."

The sun moved behind a cloud with its rays shining brightly over the top as she looked out the window into the sky. Camille wanted to believe she was marrying a man that loved her and her son for the right reasons, ignoring the doubts following her into her apartment complex. She slowly drove to her building neglecting to check the mail, her mind racing at the speed of light. She parked and sat in the car trying to calm her nerves as she stared at herself in the mirror of her sun visor. With nothing else to distract her from the pending confrontation, she conjured up the confidence to face what awaited her in the three-bedroom apartment.

Visions of her son's reaction plagued her mind as she made her way down the stairs to the bottom floor. She stepped on the doormat and took a deep breath, exhaling as she inserted the key into the lock. The deadbolt echoed loudly through the breezeway and rattled her heart like the sound of prison cell doors closing. She slowly opened the door and fixed her voice to greet everyone.

"Hey, everybody, I'm home!"

Ryan sat at the kitchen table diligently working on his latest drawing. Camille's mother, Alpharetta, was in her room lying on her bed eating a piece of leftover chicken as she gawked over her favorite evening gameshow.

"Hey, Mama," Ryan shouted.

"Hey," Alpharetta hollered from her room.

Camille walked into her room and tossed her purse and keys on her bed and began to pace around her room, lost in her thoughts. She worried heavily about the effects of bringing this sudden change into her son's life considering it would be the seventeen-year-old's senior year. She took another deep breath and walked out of her room, trying to leave her doubts in the closet. As she walked through the living room, fear rumbled through her belly at the sight of her son, his eyes glued to his sketch pad. Camille continued to her mother's room, where the door was already open.

"Hey, Mama," Camille said.

Alpharetta looked over at her while chewing the savory bite.

"Hey, darlin'," she mumbled. "How was work?"

"It was a pretty okay day today." Camille sat on the bed. "Today is the day I tell Ryan the news, and I've got some more stuff to tell y'all, too, so could you come into the living room, please?"

"Yeah, I can, but I gotta ask you—" Alpharetta sat up. "Are you sure that you really want to do this?"

Camille closed her eyes and released a deep sigh.

"Yeah...yeah, I'm sure." She nodded. "You didn't tell him, did you?"

"No, I didn't tell him, now come on." Alpharetta shifted out of bed. "I wanna know what else you gotta tell us."

Ryan switched pencils, adding color to his creation, the vibrant red giving life to his work. Just as he prepared to place the finishing touches, Camille and Alpharetta approached the table. He looked up at them strangely, Alpharetta happily scooting a chair next to him while Camille grabbed the remote from the table and muted the television. Alpharetta grabbed his hand and winked at him, causing Ryan to grow suspicious of what the two were up to. Camille nervously tapped her foot on the floor as she prepared to deliver the news.

"Okay, well, I have some news I have to tell you all, some already known, and also some I have not told anyone yet. This is good news, of course. I'm not dying or anything like that, it's—it's just important for everyone to know," Camille said.

She looked into her son's eyes as he gave her his undivided attention. She cleared her throat and clasped her hands together, trying to hide her nervousness.

"Okay," she sighed. "Last week Saturday, Reginald and I went out on a date, remember?"

"Yes," Ryan replied.

Camille wiped her hand across her non-sweating forehead.

"Well, a little later we went to a party. You know, everyone was dancing, and so after the dance, Reginald went up to the stage and said a few nice things about me. Then he asked me to come up to the stage, and he got down on one knee and... he asked me to marry him... and I said yes."

Ryan looked down at his incomplete drawing, causing Camille to shudder with fear from his awkward silence. Alpharetta squeezed Ryan's hand and looked at him, but he gave no facial reaction.

"So you're gonna get married now?" Ryan asked, staring at his drawing.

"Yes." Camille trembled. "I am, and Reginald's gonna be your stepfather. We're gonna get married—"

"So when is the wedding?" Alpharetta interrupted. "That's what I want to know."

Camille's stomach dropped, and her knees began to buckle as the question echoed in her mind. The room suddenly felt like a sauna as she desperately clung to whatever pride she had left.

"Well, that's what I wanted to talk to you both about," Camille said.

She took a seat next to Ryan and looked off into space, trying to find the words while avoiding her mother's eye contact, but the ever-wise Alpharetta knew there was something that Camille was hiding.

"It's a simple question, darling," Alpharetta prodded.

Camille planted her eyes on Ryan's drawing, desperate to find something to avoid feeling trapped. Unable to run any further, she leaned back in the chair and closed her eyes.

"Tomorrow."

"What?" Alpharetta exclaimed.

Camille scrunched up her face and lowered her head, preparing for the scrutinizing tongue-lashing her mother was about to deliver.

"Camille...Scales." Alpharetta scowled. "I know you're not marrying this man tomorrow. I know this has to be a joke. It had better be a joke!"

Camille's silence sent Alpharetta into a mouthy fury.

"Camille! How could you? You haven't even been engaged a week!" Alpharetta shouted.

"Mom, I really just need you to be supportive right now," Camille calmly begged.

"Hell no! I don't support this! Did you even think about this before you decided to do this? I mean, did you really utilize rational thought?" Alpharetta yelled.

Accustomed to the constant back and forth between them, Ryan shook his head and quietly went back to drawing. It was just another day in Apartment 402.

"It's not that bad, Mama, you're overreacting," Camille uttered.

"The hell if I am!" Alpharetta rose from the table. "With all the sh—crap you've been through! I bet you haven't even considered relationship counseling. Clearly not, there seems to be no rational thought here!"

The years of Alpharetta's deleterious judgment forced Camille to constantly fight for support behind her decisions, no matter how trivial or delightful they were. Their ear-numbing arguments had warranted complaints from their neighbors in the past.

"Well, being irrational isn't going to make things better either," Camille defended.

"I'm not being irrational!" Alpharetta slammed her fist on the table. "Clearly, I'm the only one who cares about the child in this house!"

Camille twisted her face at her mother, her words triggering her anger.

"How dare you say something like that to me?" Camille scowled.

She rose from the table, and the angry women competed over the next spiteful line to say to the other. Lightly dusting over his skillful piece, Ryan focused on his drawing, trying his best to drown out the shouting before him.

"I expected better from you, Camille, I really did." Alpharetta crossed her arms.

"Well, unfortunately, I'm not living my life for you, Mama, and that's not all I have to say," Camille replied.

The two stared at each other, anger rising between them like a tragic house fire. Ryan continued to ignore them, shading in the dark color to his drawing.

"You mean there's more to this foolishness?" Alpharetta placed her hands on her hips.

"Yes, there is. Since we're getting married, Reginald and I decided to get an apartment together, and we're moving next Saturday." Camille curled her brow.

Ryan lost his grip on the color pencil and nearly destroyed his drawing. He quickly turned his head and looked at his mother in disbelief.

"Next week?" Alpharetta shouted. "This is the same crap your sister pulled, and even though she made well, when was the last time we've heard from her? Did you even think about Ryan in all this?"

Ryan leaned back from the table and looked over his drawing, failing to disguise his face.

"Reggie and I have been talking about this for a while," Camille said.

"And you're telling us only a week before you go? Not only that, but Ryan's not even ready to move yet!" Alpharetta yelled.

"And that's why I'm telling him now so he can get packed during the week."

Camille looked at Ryan, who continued to stare at his drawing. He had straightened his face, but the grit of his emotions showed up in the grip of his color pencil.

"You like Reginald, don't you, Ryan?" Camille suggested.

Ryan rolled his eyes up to his mother and witnessed her desperation for acceptance. He peeked over at his grandmother, who was anxious to hear his answer to Camille's question. He then looked back down at his drawing and quickly decided to give her some words that would ease the tension of the argument.

"Where is this new place supposed to be?"

Camille quickly gathered herself before she spoke to her son, strategically hiding the trembling in her voice to keep Alpharetta at bay.

"So we were trying to find a place that was close to both of our jobs, and we agreed to get an apartment in College Park," she said.

"I gotta change schools again?" Ryan scoffed.

"Well, you always complain about school as it is. Maybe a change of scenery will do you some good," Camille encouraged.

"I think not," Ryan bluntly replied. "It's not the school I don't like, it's the people, and I don't think changing the school is going to fix the problem."

The conversation began to go more and more south as Camille desperately tried to defend herself. The never-ending delusion of her decision-making loomed over her head as she struggled to find the words to remedy the situation. Refusing to be troubled with Camille's actions, Alpharetta chose to pull away.

"You know what, I'm done. You got my blood pressure going through the roof! Between you and your sister, I don't know what the hell I did wrong, but I declare today, y'all are not going to be the death of me! I'm just saying, you could have said something about this a long time ago. Can't stand when people say stuff at the last minute, and what about our lease? We got another two months!" Alpharetta grunted.

"I will still give you my half for the next two months, I promise," Camille agreed.

Alpharetta flung her arms into the air and disappeared into her room, slamming the door behind her. Camille took a seat at the table and placed her hand on her head, releasing the tension in her shoulders with a deep sigh. The room was quiet with the sounds of Ryan angrily shading in the dark coloring to his drawing. Camille looked over to her son, frightened by the curl of his brow. She feared his true feelings, but she knew she had to face him to gain his acceptance.

"I know this isn't the most ideal situation," Camille said.

"No, it's not," Ryan snapped, looking up from his drawing.

Camille lowered her head in shame as she prepared to drag her son into her latest situation.

"Look, I'm sorry. I didn't mean to spring it on you like this, but I didn't know how else to tell you," she said.

"I'm starting to understand why Grandma gets so mad at you," Ryan snarked.

Camille looked away, hurt by his stinging remark.

"Okay, I know I deserved that. I know I haven't made the best decisions over the years, but I'm doing my best to try to right the wrongs of the past. I just...I just really need your support right now. You've been the only thing helping me hold it all together, and I only want to do what I think is best for you," Camille said.

Ryan gave his mother the side-eye and scoffed as she turned away. He went back to his drawing, trying to suppress his anger. Camille could feel the cold shoulder of his emotions but continued trying to coax him into her plot.

"We're gonna be moving to these apartments called Garden Crossing. The main reason why we're moving there is because my job's office is moving to Stockbridge, and his job is in Forest Park, and we found an apartment that's kinda between those areas. Can you help me out by getting everything packed this week?"

Ryan closed his eyes and tossed the color pencil to the side as his blood boiled over. He took a breath, trying to conceal his rage as his malicious thoughts consumed his mind.

"Yeah," he sighed.

Camille scooted next to him and gave him a tight hug, disguising herself as she wiped a tear on his shoulder.

"You know Mama loves you, right?" she whispered.

"Yeah, I know," Ryan grunted. "I love you, too."

Ryan frowned as Camille rocked him back and forward. She quickly gathered herself before releasing him, knowing that his transition would not come easy.

"You know, Reginald's nice, and he's very clean. I think you'll like living with him," Camille said.

"I guess we'll see," Ryan replied.

"Good. He likes you, too." Camille smiled. "Well, I gotta call him now, so if you have any questions, just come and talk to me, okay?"

"Okay."

Camille walked back to her room and plopped across her bed. As she stared at the ridges in the ceiling, she let go of her strife and focused on the thought that everything would be all right while anticipating round two with her mother.

Meanwhile, Ryan had gone back to trying to finish his drawing but eventually succumbed to his frustrations about the move. He had lived his life doing everything to please his mother, but he had finally reached a point of yearning to be left alone. His unsettling thoughts of Reginald complicated his compliance, though his history with Reginald wasn't particularly unpleasant. He never felt that there was anything special about him, nor did he understand what his mother saw in him. As the next few days passed, Ryan walked through the neighborhood with his best friend Byron. With each passing day, the anxiety Ryan felt grew stronger.

"So where did you say y'all moving to again?" Byron asked.

"Some apartments my mom found in College Park. I really ain't tryin' to go," Ryan scoffed.

"Man, y'all movin' over there? Why there and why now? We graduate next year," Byron asked.

"I don't even know, bruh, and what makes it so bad is I ain't gonna see where we're moving to 'til we actually move there. I hate this shit! Like, I don't want to live with Reggie! I was hoping they'd pull this shit after graduation," Ryan groaned.

"Damn, I wish I could go with you," Byron said.

"I wouldn't wish this on you, bruh, though I can say I appreciate the loyalty. We need more brothers like you," Ryan said.

They laughed, fist-bumping as they crossed the street.

"I thought you were cool with Reggie, though?" Byron asked.

Ryan's uneasy expression said nothing positive about his true thoughts. He fixed his face, looking for a feasible answer.

"I guess, I mean, I—my mom has been with him forever off and on. I've never really spent a lot of time with him. I just tolerate him because she's with him."

"That's how things started with us." Byron shrugged. "I mean, it was a little bit different, starting out at least."

The boys looked into the sky at a golden falcon cawing as it flew by.

"When my mom met Chris, I thought he was cool, too. He used to do stuff with us when we were younger, but after they got married, he changed. He just started actin' all crazy toward me and my sister. Him and my mama always be arguin' 'n fightin' over stupid shit, and they went to jail one time cuz the neighbors heard them arguing through the wall," Byron said.

"Yeah, I remember that. You stayed at your grandma's house for a minute," Ryan said.

The two found their spot on the bench near the playground and observed the other kids playing basketball as they continued their discussion about their unfortunate situations.

"I wish she never met that fool. My sister don't even come visit, and my mama just acts like she don't care." Byron frowned.

"I swear our parents make marriage look so undesirable." Ryan shook his head.

"I ain't ever getting married. My sister's getting ready to graduate from college at the end of the summer and said I can stay with her until I go to the Army. I'm glad she got out of the house cuz I got tired of seeing her cry every day."

"Shit, I need to come live with y'all," Ryan said.

Byron's cell phone rang with his mother's ringtone, and his mood immediately changed.

"Hey...okay, here I come," Byron scoffed as he hung up the phone. "I gotta go, bruh."

"Aight, I'll see you later," Ryan said.

They performed their secret handshake, and Byron jogged off toward his building. Ryan remained at the playground observing the men playing basketball until golden hour sent him walking back to his apartment. He worried about his best friend, trying hard not to dwell on the story he'd heard. He looked over to the top of one of the buildings and stared at a golden falcon perched on a satellite dish, similar to the one he'd spotted earlier. The bird seemed to follow his movements as he passed the building, the two linked by eye contact. He thought of the freedom to fly the falcon possessed and wished he had the ability to fly away from his anguish.

Vivid memories of Camille played in his mind of when she would talk about how she wanted to be married, how her face lit up when she envisioned her dress, the ways she described how elegant the ceremony would be, and how strongly she expressed who she would and would not invite. The ending of summer would commence his senior year, and the seventeen-year-old planned on finding a job and spending the majority of his time working. His only hope was that this move would finally make his mother happy.

The countdown continued with depressing thoughts eating away at Ryan's happiness. Alpharetta revealed that she would be moving once the lease was up, leaving him with nowhere to stay if he wanted to visit his friends. He attempted to find enjoyment in his art but instead found himself drawing pictures of the evil figures that haunted his mind. On the day before the move, he succumbed to accepting the sudden change on the strength of his mother's word that everything would be all right, once again sacrificing his happiness and silencing his true feelings to see her smile.

Deep in the shadows of Duat, the Realm of the Dead, trillions of souls roamed around aimlessly, unsure if they had reached hell or if they were trapped in a blood-curdling nightmare. The ancient practice of the heart being weighed against a feather had been long neglected as the sacred gateway between the Life and Spirit Realms had been locked by the three nemeses that had plagued Heru and Anpu thousands of years ago. As a result, souls entering Duat after death weren't able to fulfill their rite of passage, bringing an end to their reincarnation on their spiritual journey. As ancient tribes died out from being attacked by northern invaders, famine and plagues, so went the bloodlines of their heritage. Never dwindling in his duties, Anpu steadily maintained order over the souls through the millennia. He along with Heru would speak to the souls, informing them of their ancient ancestors and heritage. The souls spoke with their emotional expressions because their voices did not carry over into Duat, but their screams could be heard by the gods if they were in distress. Troubled souls who had lived their lives terrorizing others would try to avoid the sight of the gods, knowing their true judgment would eventually come. Though the dynamics of Duat had been brought to order, there was still no shred of resting peace among the realm.

The three savage gods didn't stop their reign of terror, as they now controlled access between the Life Realm and Duat Spirit Realm. They would whisper to the weary souls, offering them passage to the Life Realm in exchange for doing their bidding on Earth. Periodically they would launch vicious attacks upon Duat, feasting on souls to strengthen their abilities for battles fought against Heru and Anpu. These battles brought great suffering to the souls, eventually bringing a bizarre distrust from some souls desperate to escape from Duat. Sadly, neither of the gods were able to detect when the trio would return.

Another day had passed, and Anpu found Heru again trying to force open a portal between the realms. There was a neon blue aura forming before Heru, who strained as he fought against the crushing power of the locked gateway. Veins bulged from his neck and arms, beads of sweat dripping from his forehead as he struggled with the blowback of the repelling energy against him. The aura began to fade into tiny sparks that popped with charges of energy until finally, Heru dropped to his knees, gasping for air, frustrated in his defeat.

Anpu knelt beside Heru and placed his hand on his shoulder. "I think it's time, brother."

Heru slammed his fist to the ground and groaned with anger.

"No, I just need to figure out what they did," he said. "It's not supposed to be blue; it's supposed to glow gold."

"I know that, but—"

"We've got to unlock the chamber!" Heru interrupted. "I've got to get it open! I know there has to be another way!"

Anpu grabbed Heru by the shoulders and shook him.

"You know the other way! You know the other way, and you've denied trying again," Anpu pushed.

Heru broke away to gain control of his frustration, revealing his stressed eyes to Anpu. He took a breath and looked around the endless space in despair.

"I refused to stay in the sky, knowing Set's children were killing off the villages around our kingdom. Our people have suffered tremendously," Heru sulked.

"The gods did what they could to stop them," Anpu replied sorely.

"The things I've seen out there over the millennia, Anpu. They have demolished our legacy of peace and virtue. Our men and women are treated as inferior beings worldwide. They worship false gods, using our history as if it were their own, making a mockery of what we stand for. They even have us fighting each other. It's disheartening," Heru wept.

"Are they afraid of us?" Anpu asked.

Heru wiped the pain from his face and masked his emotions, looking off into the distance and feeling the energy of the trillions of souls around them.

"There are some that know their history, possibly the ones that escaped when they promised those other three that they'd carry out their task, but they are treated like fools. Our history is evident, yet they call us a myth. I know I can beat them, Anpu. They know we can beat them." Heru balled his fists.

"I know we can beat them, Heru, but there is more that we need to do," Anpu stated.

"We can beat them, Anpu, and we will," Heru declared.

Anpu placed his hand on Heru's shoulder to comfort his falling tears as images of the disheartening destruction flashed through his mind. The cold shudder of souls lost in the wars over the millennia rocked them through each grueling year of captivity.

"Gather yourself, Heru. We must do what is necessary to stop them, but we've been unsuccessful for generations. We've survived because they've continued to flee, but we aren't free! The others here in Duat aren't free! The fallen gods before us, their legacies, they are not free! It is time to try again," Anpu urged.

He looked around the darkened corners of Duat, awed by the lights of the infinite shining souls in the distance. The harrowing sight was the closest they had come to the sight of a star-filled sky in ages. The shining lights seemed to fill the boundless realm as if they were in outer space.

"This is where I belong, where I have always been, but this is not the place for you. You fought to protect the people of the land from the savages. You are an example of leadership, and more importantly, you've fulfilled your duties as the God of the Sky. You have a higher calling, Heru. We both know this!" Anpu stated.

Though he couldn't deny the truth in Anpu's statement, Heru's heavy emotions wouldn't allow him to receive Anpu's message. The thought of trying again brought him no hope after the countless failures over time.

"We've done that so many times before, a few times within the last few hundred years, and each attempt has been unsuccessful. They're afraid of me, afraid of us. Our monuments have been altered, and some have been destroyed. It's like our enemy wants to erase us from history," Heru grunted.

"What other option do we have? The ancestors taught us to never surrender in the face of defeat. At some point, there will be one who is ready to accept it. We know not what is going on entirely; however, each time you visited, things were different. Now might be the time to find the one," Anpu advised.

Heru looked out among the gleaming souls, remembering that some had been trapped for as long as he had. He felt that he had failed them in his fight for their freedom and was unable to understand how he and Anpu were unable to defeat a threat that couldn't beat them.

"It killed me to see them that way. The troubles they endured daily. They spoke to me in fear. The whole world changed. I don't know what Set's children created, but I refuse to search again until the realms have been reopened," Heru said.

"This is no longer our fight! What happened to us, to them, it is tragic, but their suffering will be in vain if you fail to awaken the new savior. I know it seems grim, my brother, but it's going to get better. It will! We can't allow our focus to distract us from what we know needs to be done," Anpu charged.

Suddenly, the shrieks and cries of the souls could be heard in the distance. The two gods snapped into formation with their eyes scanning the space for a threat.

"They've returned!" Heru pointed.

"Go, Heru! I will cover the souls and join you when I can! Show no mercy!" Anpu shouted.

Heru curled his arms, and his golden aura began to form around him. He charged his energy, releasing a vicious battle cry that shook Duat. The dark sands whisked through the air, forming a golden dust storm as golden jolts of energy plunged down from above, surrounding Heru as his body transformed. Great wings with thick gold feathers quickly formed from his back, flapping wildly as his transformation continued. His thick hair turned to gold, and from the roots, feathers began to grow. His mouth and nose protruded and curved into a falcon's beak with a razor-sharp tip. Finally, Heru reached his final form, and his aura flared like a golden blaze around him.

With the souls of his people in mind, the transformed god released a soul-shattering shriek. He spread his wings and raised his right hand, shooting out golden sparks before him. The sparks shaped themselves into a long golden spear with hieroglyphics etched all around it, telling a story older than time. Heru took hold of his weapon and whipped it to his side, and with one flap of his majestic wings jolted through the air toward the evil three, ready for war.

The souls screamed in terror as they tried to escape the fiendish attack. One desperate soul attempted to dash away from the scene, putting his all into every step. A long, black tongue cut through the air like a whip, chasing him down and wrapping around his head. The soul was snatched through the air, his muffled screams silenced by the grip of the tongue. Waiting for its prey on the other end was a large scaly mouth equipped with rows of razor-sharp teeth. As the soul drew closer, acidic saliva dripped from the mouth, anxious to devour its meal. The soul flew into the mouth of his captor, and the large chameleon jaws clamped down on its meal, viciously thrashing its head around. The light of the soul faded away as the dark god's saliva burned through the soul, creating steam as it swallowed its prey.

Twisting through the air were the three dragon-like heads of a hydra playing with its food. It had snatched a soul from the fleeing crowd and began to toss it around like a volleyball. Frantic screams from other souls rang out as they scattered from the attack. The game quickly came to an end as each head latched on to a different part of the soul's body and ripped it limb from limb, fighting over the last remaining piece of the expired flesh. The light of the devoured soul faded to darkness as the pieces traveled down the dark god's throats.

Helplessly stranded amidst the attack was a soul locked on to the eyes of its doom. The soul had found itself entangled within the giant coil of a viperous snake that stared back at him with the features of a beautiful woman as it squeezed away the essence of his being. The dark goddess flicked her tongue and rattled her tail as she descended upon her victim.

"You shall serve as a divine meal for me." She grinned.

Her eyes began to glow green, and she revealed her hellish fangs dripping with toxic venom. She steadily moved in on her victim, opening her mouth and revealing thousands of smaller teeth that traveled down her throat. The drained soul could only watch as he was taunted with the fate of eternal death, for the souls that die in Duat never return to the cycle of life. She hissed and rattled her tail, readying herself to strike. She launched suddenly at the fading soul, but to her surprise was met with the taste of Heru's spear. She hissed in pain, raising her hands to her face as the razor-sharp tip had severely cut the corners of her mouth. She released the lucky soul as her black blood dripped onto the ground like thick ink.

Heru landed and stood with his wings spread wide as he pulled his spear from the dark sands. He followed the path of the injured snake as she fearfully tried to slither away from his mystic glow. She hissed and rattled her tail to keep him away, but Heru marched forward with fury in his eyes.

"I told you not to return to this land!" he charged.

He lowered his wings and raised his spear to throw it at her once more but was interrupted by the arrival of her brothers. They jumped in front of her, hissing at Heru, but the threats quickly turned to laughter. There they were before him, Mabaya the Hydra, Wivu the Chameleon, and Lamia the Viper, the three evil triplets of Set. Emboldened by her brothers' protection, Lamia peeked over Wivu's shoulder and hissed at Heru as her blood dripped onto her robe. Heru grunted and clenched his spear, fearlessly staring down his nemeses. The three had disowned their Egyptian heritage and were cloaked in ancient Grecian robes. They were minacious, their eyes filled with the hatred their father had instilled within them. They sought vengeance upon Heru and Anpu through torment, their goal to make them their pawns for enjoyment.

The three necks of the hydra retracted to its human-like body, swaying from side to side like a venomous cobra.

"Why haven't you died yet, Heru? Aren't you tired of fighting with us? The souls will be freed if you surrender," Mabaya said with his three heads.

"I will fight you to the death, and I will never surrender until we are all freed," Heru grunted.

The triplets laughed, mocking Heru's heroism.

"What has your leadership done for you in the last few millennia? You've been trapped down here for ages, so long that the Life Realm practically belongs to us. You've failed at every attempt to defeat us, much like you failed to save the gods we killed," Wivu boasted.

The blood-curdling statements sent Heru's aura into a wild flare, brushing a wave of energy across the noses of his foes. He whipped his spear to his side and spread his wings as he focused on their unsightly grins.

"I will not argue with any of you! Leave now or I shall do worse to you than I did to your father!" Heru threatened.

The grins of the triplets turned back into threatening hisses of offense. Heru sharpened his eyes, positioning his body to attack, his spear thirsty for the blood of his enemies. Lamia slithered in front of her brothers, coiling herself into her strike position as she wiped away the blood on her chin.

"I'll kill you for what you've done to my faccccccce! Your sss-soul is mine!" she shouted.

Lamia lunged at Heru, her mouth wide and ready to deliver her venomous bite. Heru whipped his spear around and dipped into a diabolical spin, creating a cloud of dust with his wings. He knocked Lamia across the jaw with his spear, sending her into a daze as she crashed to the ground. With no time to waste, he dashed toward the other two, continuing his attack. Mabaya struck his three heads at Heru, the necks growing longer and longer as Heru dipped and dived around him. Heru whisked his spear in the air and struck each of the heads, sending them crashing to the ground, leaving Mabaya unable to regain his bearings as Heru stomped on his necks.

Suddenly, Heru's left forearm was engulfed with the malicious burn of Wivu's tongue. The beast showed off his teeth as he planted his feet and thrashed his head around, trying to pull Heru in. Heru tried his best to pull away but succumbed to the hellish burning of Wivu's toxic saliva. He screeched in agony as he was yanked toward Wivu when suddenly, the transformed Anpu darted toward Heru with his golden staff in hand. The jet-black jackal slammed his staff into Wivu's tongue, breaking off the piece holding Heru. Wivu whipped his injured tongue back into his mouth and groaned in pain as his black blood spilled from his mouth. The broken tongue unraveled, and Heru shook his arm free. His arm smoked from the toxic burns on his skin as he quickly tossed the dark sands on his arms to dry up the burning saliva. His golden blood dripped from his elbow, but he ignored the pain and focused on the battle before him.

"It'll heal. Let's finish this," Heru said.

The sands of Duat went into a frenzy as the two charged their Ki. Once at their max, they stood back to back, ready to strike as their enemies reassembled. The evil three pulled themselves together, hissing and growling at the gods.

"Leave now! I won't warn you again!" Heru screeched.

"Never! The Spirit Realm shall be ours!" Mabaya declared.

Mabaya growled and locked his six eyes on Heru, his three heads drooling like a rabid dog. Heru spread his wings and peeked at Anpu, who nodded his head as they put their strategy in motion.

"If you want our souls, you're going to have to kill me first!" Heru shouted.

Heru dashed toward the evil three and aimed his spear, causing Mabaya's heads to charge toward him with his mouths wide open. Just as the two were about to collide, Heru dashed upward into the air, daring Mabaya to follow. Mabaya engaged, and a chase ensued as Heru dashed in several different directions, twisting and turning in the air.

Lamia summoned the dagger she had stolen from Heru's kingdom, and Wivu summoned the bladed whip he'd stolen from a god he'd murdered years ago. They rushed toward Anpu, anxious to quench their thirst with his golden blood. Anpu swung his staff around and took a stance, ready for their attack. The two split up and surrounded Anpu on both sides, attempting to intimidate their prey, coupling their sinister grins with hisses as they showed off their fangs.

"We don't have to fight, Anpu. Just let me kissssss you," Lamia hissed, her fangs dripping with her toxic venom.

"I'll hold you down while she does it," Wivu grunted.

Wivu whipped his weapon toward Anpu's head, but Anpu dipped down just before the blade clipped his ears. Just as he rose to his feet, he was forced to lean back to miss the stabbing blade of Lamia, who lunged at him. The two evil gods rushed at Anpu, violently swinging their weapons along with kicks and punches. Anpu answered their attacks, swinging and blocking with his staff. Meanwhile, Heru kept Mabaya busy still dipping and dashing, avoiding his vicious bite. He taunted Mabaya by slowing down and allowing his heads to catch up so that he could swat at them with his spear.

"You'll never have what it takes to defeat me!" Heru proclaimed.

"I have everything it takes to kill you. It takes a god to kill a god, just like we killed your wife." Mabaya's heads swayed.

Heru's expression transformed into a wave of furious anger. He released a tremendous battle cry, and his aura violently flared up. He gripped his spear, looking at Mabaya's heads with fire in his eyes and charged at them with a mind-blowing power. He slammed his spear into the top of one of the heads, sending it into a daze as it fell toward the ground. Heru then darted toward the second, raising his spear as Mabaya roared and launched toward Heru with his two remaining heads. Heru threw his spear, but the fast-acting Mabaya quickly dodged the weapon. He quickly turned to follow the spear in hopes of catching it but discovered that the spear found its mark, passing straight through Mabaya's third head as it fell lifelessly to the ground. Before he could react, Mabaya was met with a barrage of punches and kicks to his remaining head as Heru dashed up, down, left, and right, unleashing his fury.

"You'll bleed for what you've done to my people!" Heru screeched.

Heru delivered an awesome hammer fist to Mabaya, causing him to sway in dizziness, but Heru refused to let him fall as he continued his onslaught. Back on the ground, Anpu continued to find himself barely escaping the edges of Wivu's blade whip. He dipped and dodged Lamia as she violently struck at him with her dagger. Wivu flipped through the air, swinging his weapon and forcing Anpu on the defensive. The blade whip wrapped around the center of the staff and locked on. With all his might, Wivu yanked his weapon and successfully pulled Anpu's staff from his hands. At that same moment, Lamia sprang headfirst toward Anpu, toxic venom burning into the dark sands as it dripped from her fangs. Anpu fearlessly charged forward, thrashing Lamia with a stupefying sucker punch to her face. He continued with another punch to the other side of her face and then dipped down and went into a jumping spin in the air. Anpu howled and caught Lamia midair with a swift kick to her scaly torso that sent her flying to the ground. She bounced across the sands like a skipping stone on water.

Landing on his feet, Anpu dashed behind Wivu and swept him off his feet with a surprise kick. As Wivu flailed his arms, trying to catch himself, Anpu darted into the air and howled as he flashed toward Wivu and bashed him with a catastrophic elbow that caused him to spew his blood upon crashing into the dark sands. Anpu continued his assault, kicking Wivu into Lamia, who was still struggling to get up. He dashed toward the beaten dark gods and grabbed Lamia by her rattle and Wivu by his ankle and commenced a violent spin. He swung them around and around as they growled and hissed, unable to break free. Anpu howled and raised his arms into the air, crashing the two together and then slammed them to the ground with all his might. The force of the slam rocked their brains, rendering them defenseless. Anpu then threw them at Mabaya's staggering body, succumbing to the might of Heru.

Heru uppercut Mabaya and finished him with a back-spinning punch. Mabaya wailed as his head swayed widely from side to side.

"NOW!!" Heru called to Anpu.

The two began to make mystic hand motions, and a golden light began to form in their hands. They began to chant simultaneously.

"MAAAN-SAAA-MUUU–"

The light forming in their hands grew brighter, drawing in energy from the spirits surrounding them.

"SAAAAAA!!" they roared.

They thrust their hands toward their enemies, unleashing a large, golden energy blast. The blast met and joined, creating a gigantic explosion of energy and sending the dark sands flying into a whirlwind. Heru quickly landed and stood with Anpu, ready to attack as the cloud of dust cleared. Anpu quickly summoned his staff, but the two were quickly made aware that the conditions of the battle had changed.

"I can't sense their energies," Heru said.

"Neither can I," Anpu seconded.

The dark dust settled, and the evil three were gone.

"They've escaped again!" Heru shouted. "How could they have gotten away so quickly?"

"It has been so long since either of us has opened the portal, I've forgotten how quickly it can be done," Anpu said.

They powered down their energies and transformed back into their human forms. Heru sighed as he walked toward where their bodies had once been and picked up the sand, observing grains fall from his hands.

"This is driving me insane." He drooped.

"This isn't a fight we're going to win, Heru. Even if we do defeat them, that doesn't mean we will be free. The answer to our freedom is not here in Duat; it is somewhere out there in the Life Realm. You must find them," Anpu said.

Heru looked around and witnessed the fear in the eyes of the glowing souls scattered across the realm.

"All of our fates are now in your hands."

CHAPTER 2

THE ILLEGIT FAMILY

P OLICE SIRENS BLARED in the distance with echoes of stray dogs barking in the alleyways. The voices of lost dope fiends and prostitutes faded into the shadows as the light of day lit up the city streets. Traveling westbound in an unmarked police car on the outskirts of I-20 were Detectives Porter and Simmons. Dressed in plain clothes to tend to their morning routine, they first went to war with the morning rush hour.

"I will never understand how the damn fast lane gets backed up with traffic. It's the damn fast lane!" Porter groaned.

"People just don't know how to drive," Simmons said. "I'm just glad it's not raining. None of these out-of-towners know how to drive in the damn rain."

Porter swerved in and out of the lanes, carefully maneuvering inches in front of or behind slower cars. The impatient detectives were anxious to get to their destination, for the missed calls and text messages would equate to mass frustration because of their tardiness.

"I tell ya, Porter, I wish we could use a squad car for this," Simmons said.

"Me and you both, but it is what it is. Hell, I wish we could have gotten him sooner so we wouldn't have to fight through this," Porter said.

"Yeah, but you know how Swain is. Wants us to get stuff done during business hours and only business hours. Gotta inspect and detail everything from back to front—what kind of crap is that?" Simmons said.

"C'mon, go, lady, damn!" Porter hollered.

"Little road rage there, buddy?" Simmons laughed.

"The exit is literally right there." Porter pointed. "It's every day with this shit!"

The traffic inched along for a few more minutes until Porter finally had a clear shot to his exit and zoomed up the ramp. The two traveled down a double-laned road that later turned into a single as they escaped the city limits. The surrounding trees hid the lively wildlife, although exposed deer watched the passing vehicle as Simmons made finger guns and aimed at a buck in the distance. The rooftops of homes began to appear through the trees as they pulled into an unmarked subdivision. They traveled uphill on a street that dead-ended into a cul-de-sac, and the men straightened themselves up as they approached one of the homes with a thuggish-looking man standing at the end of the driveway.

"Aw shit, he's got one of his boys out here waiting for us," Porter said.

"Crap. Think he's mad?" Simmons asked.

"Shit, I don't know. We're already late." Porter giggled nervously.

"Maybe he'll be more forgiving because of what we're bringing," Simmons said.

"Yeah, let's hope," Porter said.

They pulled up to the large home, and the waiting man approached them. Porter rolled down the window quickly, cleared his throat, and put on a smile as he greeted the man.

"Top of the morning to you, good sir. We're here to make a delivery," he said jovially.

The thuggish man mugged Porter as he did everyone that pulled up, then walked around the car, looking through the windows and underneath for anything unusual. He made his way back to Porter's window, still looking at him in disgust as he pulled out his walkie talkie.

"All clear?" Porter smiled.

"They're here," the man said into the walkie.

After a brief moment, an aggravated voice came over the walkie, sending a wave of fear over Porter and Simmons.

"Send them to the back immediately," the voice grunted.

"Aight." The man looked at Porter. "He wants y'all to go to the back."

"Thank you," Porter said politely.

The man kept his eye on the car as Porter and Simons traveled up the driveway with security cameras tracking their every move from the front to the back of the house. A few armed men were lurking around the property, ensuring that no unwanted visitors made it onto the premises. As they arrived at the back of the house, the detectives were stunned to see a few of the extra cars that were already in attendance. They were immediately scrutinized by the guards waiting for them by the garage.

"Shit, Sims, we might have messed up for real this time," Porter said nervously.

"Yeah, this doesn't look too good," Simmons replied.

The men quickly tucked their pistols and exited the vehicle. Simmons got a few dirty looks from the drivers waiting in the cars as he gawked at the high-end vehicles. Porter punched him in his arm, urging him to stay focused while he schemed on how to work his charm to get himself and his partner out of hot water.

"Dammit, Sims, hold it together," Porter urged.

"Sorry, sorry. Any idea what we're gonna say?" Simmons asked.

"We just need to be honest and keep it real with him," Porter said.

"I hope he believes it," Simmons replied.

"Just let me do the talking," Porter said.

The guards watched them as they walked up to the stoop, alerting someone over the walkie-talkie. Overhead cameras locked on to their movements as they approached the door. The detectives looked at each other and took a deep breath. Just as Porter raised his arm to knock, the door flung open, and a dark figure stared back at them.

"Face," Porter shrieked. "Good mo-"

"You're late," Face flared.

Porter dropped his eyes and smiled.

"Face, brother, you know it's damn near impossible to rip through this morning traffic."

"Then you should have left earlier! I told you not to be late for this meeting," Face growled.

Thinking quickly on his feet, Porter quickly brought up another subject to free him and his partner from the rising wrath of their boss.

"Not only that, but uh, it ain't always easy 'attaining evidence' from the precinct. Sometimes you just gotta wait for the right time to come." He grinned.

Face was a slim, untrustworthy-looking man who always wore black. He kept no facial hair, as he was always hidden by his notice-able disguise. He covered his face with white face paint along with chrome aviator shades and one of his many black hats that covered the roots of his long locs. Face stood in the doorway, exhaling his frustration as he stared at the detectives. Simmons remained quiet as Porter attempted to win over Face with his charming smile. Face groaned and tightly gripped the door handle.

"Back the car into the garage," Face grunted as he slammed the door in their faces.

The detectives exhaled a sigh of relief and quickly made their way back to the car.

"I can't believe that worked." Simmons released the tension from his shoulders.

"I told you, Sims, it works on men and women," Porter laughed.

Simmons quickly backed the car into the garage while Porter regrouped with Face and his guards inside. The guards pulled out their guns and aimed them at the trunk as Porter proceeded to open it.

"No need for the guns, fellas," Porter said.

Inside lay an unconscious man who appeared to have taken a minor beating. His hands and feet were bound together behind his back, and there was a bag over his head. Face laughed with a sinister grin, releasing the frustration he'd initially had with the detectives.

"Snatched'em up as soon as he stepped outside, didn't even have to go get him," Porter giggled.

"Take him to the basement. I'll deal with him once my meeting is over," Face commanded his guards.

The guards roughly grabbed the man out of the trunk and proceeded to carry him to the basement.

"And tie him to a chair. I'm gonna have fun with this one." Face grinned. "Detectives, there are some people I need you to meet."

The men walked inside the house and down a long hallway that led to Face's office. The house was newly bought and yet to be decorated, their voices echoing in the open space. Anxious to get back to his meeting, Face quickly briefed the detectives to catch them up on what had been talked about.

"I probably should have told you who would be at this meeting, but I'm sure you saw the cars outside," Face said.

"Heh, pretty hard to miss," Simmons said.

"Sorry for the tardy, dear friend, but to get this one we couldn't break protocol without being noticed. I.A.'s been running through the department lately, and we had to make sure nobody was on to us," Porter advised.

"I can only be so understanding. Next time you better communicate with me. I swear if you had messed up this deal, you'd be in a worse predicament than the one in the basement," Face said sternly.

Porter and Simmons looked at each other and shuddered. They continued down the hallway until reaching a guarded set of French doors at the end. Face stopped and turned to the detectives to give them their final instructions before they entered the room.

"You two were late, so it's already bad enough. I need you on your toes while you're in there. You already know who's here, and you know what's going on. Porter, lay off on the jokes, and Simmons, try not to look so tough. These guys ain't particularly fond of White men. I really don't want you in here, but I've already mentioned you, so they want to see you. We're putting everything on the line with this one, so act like you've got something to live for. Got it?" Face instructed.

The men nodded.

"No jokes," Porter agreed. "Let's do this."

Porter mimicked Face as he turned around to open the door to the room. A quick breeze from the air conditioning greeted the men's faces as they walked into the room. Before them sat two men at a large, round table with a couple of their own guards on each side. To the left was Al-Qadir Nassar, one of the area's most notorious arms dealers from the Middle East. The elder was dressed in a dishdasha with a turban wrapped tightly around his head. Just below his jawline was a scar from a failed assassination, a constant reminder of the importance of always hitting his mark. On the other side of the table was Jin Hong, a young Asian mob boss who had come to power a few years before to take over the family business. Hong had long hair, which he constantly played with for the sensation, accompanied by a sinister look in his eyes.

"Gentlemen, I greatly appreciate your patience." Face nervously grinned. "It appears my package has arrived."

Nassar quickly sat back from the table, prompting Hong to stand, both of them, with their eyes zeroed in on Simmons.

"Who is this fool?" Hong pointed at Simmons.

Hong's and Nassar's men reached for their weapons and aimed at Simmons. He stood stricken with fear looking away from the six cocked and loaded barrels aimed at him. Face quickly turned to his men, signaling them to stand down.

"Relax, gentlemen." He turned to his guests. "These are the inside men that I told you about. Detective Porter and his trusty sidekick, Detective Simmons."

Face grinned at the men, hoping his risky introduction had not ruined the meeting. Simmons lowered his eyes, trying not to make direct contact with anyone aiming at his head.

"Boys, introduce yourselves to our guests, please," Face said coyly.

Porter looked over at Simmons and chuckled as he stepped up to the table.

"Good morning, everyone; I'm Antwan Porter." He pointed to one of Hong's men. "I like that .45; that's a good brand."

Porter cleared his throat and, with a cheesy grin, peered over to Simmons, who stood motionless. His throat had dried out, and his skin was pale with fear.

"Uh...I'm Rick Simmons. Just trying to...Nice to meet you all," he squealed.

Nassar stroked his beard and looked Simmons up and down.

"You trust this man as a member of your organization?" he asked.

Face looked at Nassar with a straight face and nervously cleared his throat. He rode the fence of regret, thinking bringing Simmons into the meeting might not have been a good idea, but he refused to lose the progress he had made with the men.

"I can assure you both that we have absolutely nothing to worry about," he said calmly.

Hong took a step toward Face and ran his fingers through his hair, his eyes still locked on Simmons.

"Then I assume he must know I will slit his throat and extend the invitation to his family should he ever decide to betray us?" Hong cruelly stated.

Face locked on to Hong with a serious look.

"They both understand that they will have their throats cut, their tongues ripped out, and their bodies fed to the gators in Florida if they ever decide to cross *me*, so I can assure both of *you* that there is absolutely nothing to be worried about." Face smiled. "So please, gentlemen, put your toys away. We're having a meeting."

The two locked into a stare until Hong grew tired of looking at his reflection. He grunted and eased back into his seat as his men stood at ease. As the detectives remained standing, Porter grinned at Simmons, and Simmons glared back with daggers in his eyes.

"So, Mr. Nassar, where did we leave off?" Face asked as he took his seat.

Hong looked at Nassar and with a serious face, nodded with confidence. Nassar took a puff of his cigar and slowly exhaled the thick white smoke.

"The way business was conducted in the past was to be a means of protecting ourselves and the communities we serve; however, today it seems that the meaning of protecting *our* people has changed. It is our belief that some of the people in control need to change, too," Nassar stated.

Hong fiddled with his hair and grinned as he loved to hear the story of how their businesses were established. Face listened attentively, doing his best to keep his composure before the leaders.

"Back in the years when all of this began, we used to only look out for our own communities, but society can be quite unkind when you don't look the way *they* want you to. I'm sure you understand that." Nassar glared at Simmons.

Face nodded in agreement, ignoring his scrutinized aid.

"We saw the way *they* treated our people, your people especially. It was so bad that we all found ourselves nearly living in the conditions that we had been trying to escape from. Finally, a day came where we all realized we shared a common enemy, and instead of trying harder to join them, we chose to beat them. I, Hong Sr., a man by the name of Alonzo Jackson, and lastly Adrian Diaz came together and made a pact that we would all help each other so that we could thrive against our enemies," Nassar said.

"Alonzo Jackson? Aw wow, he's a legend where I'm from! I had no idea he used to be involved with you guys." Face smiled.

"Ah, yes. Alonzo was a good man, my friend." Nassar nodded. "We divided the playing field into four districts around town in order to make sure we had equal access to the necessary resources we needed, and whatever we didn't have we shared. The area you say you are from is also the area that Alonzo covered; however, because of the ignorance of racism, your people's community seemed to always be under siege. The years between the '60s and the '80s proved to be the most trying time for your people when Alonzo was with us."

"Yes, I remember the stories the elders in my neighborhood would tell me from back in the day," Face said.

"Unfortunately, things did not get better for a very long time as we were all taking losses in our communities from the obstruction of the authorities. After a while, our dealings with Alonzo became an issue. They didn't want us working with him. One day we all had a meeting, and before we could get started, Alonzo told us that he would be resigning from our union. Two days later he was killed in a sting operation by the APD," Nassar said with sorrow.

"Yeah, the big bust in '89. I've heard a lot about that one," Face said.

"I believe that his death doomed your side of town. He did a great deal for the community that no one will ever know," Nassar said.

"It was pretty hard to miss growing up," Face said.

"Well, now we have a new problem." Hong stroked his hair. "In more recent years, things have changed a little with politics and the alleged *wars* this country seems to want to fight. We've all been affected, to a degree, but what has happened has ultimately destroyed our communities."

"What happened?" Face raised his brow.

"Betrayal." Hong angrily flicked his hair.

"Adrian Diaz." Nassar puffed his cigar and exhaled. "He has broken the trust that we've established, and we've once again found ourselves in the same situation as before, only this time the enemy is one of our own."

"He's keeping resources from us, saying that we owe him for all the things he has done for us over the years as if we have not all sacrificed to keep this union together. I believe his insolence is what triggered my father's failing health." Hong fingered his hair.

"Sounds like this Diaz guy got himself a little money and forgot his roots," Face concluded.

"Precisely, my friend. It is as if our decades of struggle have been forgotten. This society has turned his morality. It is tragic," Nassar sighed.

Anxious to break away from his nervousness, Face shifted the spotlight onto himself to get to the bottom of their story.

"So what is it exactly that I can do for you?" he inquired.

Hong flicked his hair and grinned.

"Ah yes, I had long heard about you and your brother during the years when my father ran the business. I believe it was you all that unknowingly aided my father's associate. By the way, I'm sorry about his arrest," Hong said.

"I appreciate it. He's being well taken care of in there," Face replied.

"I'm sure. As I was saying, in learning about you, I found myself intrigued with your work." Hong twiddled his hair. "Your brutish leadership has made it possible for your generation to overcome corruption in your area. Even the name is invigorating—*Illegit,* I love it! You've grown your organization to the masses, and though I don't agree with one of the choices you've made"—he glared at Simmons—"I felt obligated to tell Mr. Nassar about you."

The men shared a laugh as Simmons held his tongue and backed into the wall.

"I must say, my friend, you have built quite the resume for yourself," Nassar said.

"Why, thank you. You all have been quite the inspiration, and please, call me Face. You're family here," Face responded.

"Ah, yes, certainly, but I must ask you, Face, what is it exactly that your friends can do for us? We've already got our own protection for our businesses," Nassar questioned.

Face grinned as he leaned back into his seat, preparing to flex his abilities with the detectives. He sensed that his answer to Nassar's question would gain his acceptance.

"My apologies, I thought they told you already. Porter, I don't exactly remember your job description. Could you please tell these gentlemen exactly what it is you do?" Face said sarcastically.

Porter grinned and chuckled his way up to the table with his hands in his pockets.

"Well, I'm sure you are aware of the roadblocks in certain areas, highway patrol, and such. I specialize in getting that kind of information ahead of time, but not just locally. I can get it anywhere across the US," Porter said confidently.

"Anywhere?" Nassar raised his brows.

"Yes, anywhere." Porter smiled. "As an example, let's say Face has a transaction that's taking place across state lines. He calls me, I look into the area, see what the local authority is, and then I do a little hacking to finagle the systems at the other departments so that we can travel virtually undetected."

Hong tightly gripped his hair, and his eyes widened.

"Impressive," he said, "but what can we do about the police already on patrol?"

"Simple." Porter pulled out his badge. "How hard is it to become an undercover cop with this thing?"

Nassar puffed his cigar and chuckled as smoke exited through his smile. He straightened his face as he looked over to Simmons, trying to go unnoticed against the wall.

"You, White man, what do you do?" Nassar asked.

Simmons kept his head down and approached the table, feeling the burn of Hong's and Nassar's stares. He continued to look at patterns on the floor, hoping to avoid making eye contact.

"Uh, well, I-I'm more of an inside guy–"

"That's not telling me what you do," Hong interrupted.

Simmons cleared his throat and strengthened his voice.

"Of all the things I can do, my biggest thing is finding people," he said.

Nassar looked at Simmons and laughed.

"So, what, you just type in your computer and search names? We can do that ourselves. We don't need you for that," Nassar said.

"True." Simmons nodded. "But you can't find everyone I can find. Even the ones that seem to have disappeared."

Hong flicked his hair back, curious about Simmons's statement.

"Disappeared?" Hong inquired.

"Hold it right there, Sims." Face motioned to Simmons.

Hong glared at Simmons, fiddling his hair with intrigue as Nassar leaned closer to the table, stroking his beard.

"Gentlemen, we are all gathered here today for a reason, and because I know that you are both very busy men, with all due respect, I'd like to know exactly what I can do for you," Face asked.

Hong looked at Nassar and nodded with assurance to ease the elder's defense. Nassar took a long puff from his cigar and relaxed in his seat.

"We've been talking about you, and Hong has made it clear to me that he approves of your business. From what I have heard, I can say that for the majority I am on the side of Hong, but this White man on your team brings me much concern," Nassar said.

"Thank you." Face grinned.

"Well, with that being said"–Hong happily flicked his hair–"we'd like to make you an offer. We want you to run the third district and be a part of our community. Join us, and you will be among the true elite. You'll have access to all the resources you need within our circle."

"And ultimately reclaim what's rightfully yours for the sake of your people," Nassar added.

The two grinned with acceptance, causing Face to sit back and chuckle a bit. He looked down at the table and smiled, for this was the moment that he and his brother had long hoped for.

"Well, of course you know I accept." Face grinned. "But I also know how these things work. You've all worked very hard to establish yourselves over the last few decades, so I wouldn't expect to so easily gain acceptance into your circle. What do I have to do?"

Hong again looked at Nassar and nodded with assurance. Nassar took a long puff of his cigar and exhaled the thick white smoke from his nose, nodding his head as he closed his eyes. Hong looked into Face's shades with seriousness in his eyes and stopped playing with his hair.

"We want you to kill Adrian Diaz," Hong said bluntly.

The room was hit with an awkward silence. Face sat back in his seat and exhaled, contemplating his response as Porter and Simmons looked on in awe.

"You want me to kill him? But how?" Face asked.

"We need to know for the sanctity of our communities and everything we have fought for that we can entrust the leader we bring into this family," Nassar said. "Even though you have magnificent credentials, many people have given their lives to ensure the future of what we have created, and I need to know that I can guarantee the same from you."

Face adjusted his shades and rubbed his chin, trying to think of how to approach this challenge. Though the Illegit Family was on the rise, he didn't possess the manpower nor the necessary artillery to go after a major crime boss.

"I know it's a risky task, but think of it this way," Hong advised, "you'd be taking over the area that he is over now. Force out the things you don't want, replace them with your own touches—"

"Yeah, I'm well aware of how the process works," Face interrupted. "I'm thinking about something."

A sudden knock at the door brought the meeting to a halt.

"Pardon me, gentlemen." Face signaled his guard.

The guard cracked open the door and whispered to someone outside the room. He then turned to Face and brought a shift to the discussion.

"They said he's ready," the guard stated.

An evil grin slowly appeared below Face's shades, accompanied by an evil laugh.

"A question, gentlemen. Do you believe in ghosts?" Face asked.

The two men looked at each other, confused. Nassar was beginning to feel uneasy about their recruit. Face chuckled and rose from the table.

"If you would all please come with me, I have something I would like to show you."

Face's men opened the door and walked out, followed by Porter and Simmons. Hong and Nassar looked at each other once more, curious as to where this walk would lead them. Nassar grabbed his cane, and the men proceeded down the hallway after Face.

"As Simmons mentioned before, there are people that can be found and the ones we think can't be found. Now I'm no witch doctor, but I can definitely tell you that I believe in ghosts," Face said.

"You speak in parables. What are you referring to?" Nassar demanded.

Face stopped in front of the basement door and turned to the men with a big grin on his face.

"Does the name Enrique Consuelo ring a bell to either of you?" Face asked.

The men thought for a moment but were ultimately still confused.

"I think I know him. He worked for Diaz. If I understand correctly, he died in a car accident," Hong said.

"Oh, is that what they are saying about him?" Face said sarcastically.

He grinned and opened the basement door, leading the others down.

"Well, gentlemen, it seems we have a common enemy." Face exaggerated a country accent. "You know I find it absolutely amazing the things you can find in the archives of the living dead, you know? It's like the dead are dead, but they don't stay dead, so they are the living dead."

The men reached the ground floor of the basement, where a few of Face's men awaited. At the center of the room was a man bound to a chair who appeared to have been roughed up a bit. The groaning man rolled his head from side to side. Hanging above him was a work lamp with the cover taken off. Face walked around to the backside of the man as Hong gripped his hair tightly with his eyes wide open. Nassar took another long puff of his cigar to calm his nerves.

"You see, the funny thing about ghosts is that they have a history," Face said. "There is always someone that cares enough to say something about a dead man, but I found it particularly strange that this man didn't have any kind of farewell ceremony."

Hong and Nassar looked at Face with increasing intensity.

"As I said before, I know you two are very busy men, so I understand that you may not pay much attention when certain people die, but I do. You see, there were several people involved in a shootout that took place some time ago. Each of these men had some form of farewell service, a funeral, cremation, a got damn cookout, whatever, but there was one person who had absolutely nothing. Not even an autopsy photo."

Face reached behind the bound man's head and began to untie the bag.

"They say curiosity killed the cat, but I simply could not resist the urge to satisfy my curiosity because I felt like it would lead me to a kill. So I spent a little time with Simmons here, and after hours and hours of searching with Porter and coordinating the correct route, we found a ghost! I gotta say he's not a particularly friendly one," Face said.

The men's eyes locked on the bound man's head as Face gripped the top of the bag.

"And do you know who this ghost used to be?"

Face slowly removed the mask from the man, revealing a beaten and bloody Latino male, instantly smacking Hong and Nassar with bewilderment. Nassar dropped his cigar, failing to catch it before it fell onto the concrete floor. Hong released his hair, realizing he'd seen this man before.

"Enrique Consuelo! The same Enrique Consuelo that was working for Adrian Diaz when he messed up my deal that ended in a shootout which landed my brother in federal prison, so as I mentioned before, gentlemen, we have a common enemy," Face said, throwing the mask into the man's face. "And if it weren't for Simmons' tenacious efforts, we may never have captured this ghost."

Face looked toward Simmons, who played coy to hide his grin. Hong looked Simmons up and down as he slowly approached him in wonderment.

"You found this man?" Hong asked.

"Yes," Simmons replied.

"And now you see why he's on the team," Face mentioned.

Hong turned toward Enrique, who was too groggy to fight away from his bondage. He closed his eyes and took a deep breath to maintain control of his emotions.

"Face, I don't think you realize what this means," Hong said.

"It means we have a common enemy that needs to be extinguished." Face grinned.

"No." Hong shook his head. "It's deeper than that for me. This man was there the evening my father announced his retirement and I took over."

Hong pulled out his cell phone and looked at the date. He quickly turned to Face, bearing a shred of terror.

"That was over two years ago. This can only mean that Diaz has been plotting to take us down for a while," Hong said. "This man was in my house!"

Hong looked over to Nassar, who was being aided by one of his guards to stand.

"Get 'em a chair," Face ordered one of his men. "You good?"

Nassar began to breathe a little heavier as the room spun around in his head. Face's guard quickly delivered a chair to Nassar and helped ease him into the seat. His guard picked up the fallen cigar and reached into his coat pocket for Nassar's cigar case. He opened it and put out the burning ashes and pulled out a new one. Nassar reached for it and put it in his mouth as his guard lit it for him. The troubled man inhaled deeply and coughed out a thick cloud of smoke, breathing slower and slower, still struggling to regain his composure.

"I...I need...a moment," Nassar said.

"Take your time," Face replied.

Porter walked over to Simmons and nudged him with his elbow, and they both retreated up the stairs.

"Well, it looks like you gentlemen have some business to handle, so we're gonna get out of your way. Just call us if you need us—and gentlemen, it was a pleasure meeting you," Porter stated.

"Aight, I'll see you later," Face replied.

He turned away from his guest and again focused on Enrique. He cracked his knuckles, ready to have fun with his resurrected foe. He tightly gripped Enrique by the hair and yanked his head up. Enrique groaned in pain, unable to pull away from Face's might.

"Look at me," Face said. "Open your eyes, dammit!"

Enrique slowly opened his swollen eyes, staring back at his reflection in Face's shades.

"You," Face grunted. "Do you know how long I've waited to find you? Do you have any idea the kind of pain you've caused me?"

Enrique continued to stare at Face, speechless.

"Well, don't just look at me, speak up! I know you know English," Face yelled, turning Enrique toward the other men. "Do you know these men? Did you and Diaz plan on thwarting their plans, too?"

Enrique continued to remain silent and began to look angry as blood dripped from his mouth. He did what he could to maintain his composure, experiencing the feeling of being the victim firsthand. Face shook with anger from Enrique's defiance. His heart began to beat faster, and his legs began to jump. He reached into his pocket and pulled out a large black cleaver pocket knife with the word "Buddy" engraved on the blade. He moved in closer to Enrique and locked eyes with him.

"If you don't start talking now"–Face flicked the knife open– "you're going to get real familiar with my Buddy."

Face intimidated Enrique, sliding the dull side of the blade under his eye and across his swollen cheek, but still, Enrique refused to utter a word. His patience already worn, Face's energy jolted from calm and collected to deranged and deadly.

"Still don't want to say anything, eh?" Face smiled. "Good, I was hoping you wouldn't."

Without warning, Face raised the knife in the air and, with all his might, jammed the Buddy into Enrique's thigh, leaving only a very small portion of the blade hanging out. Enrique screamed in agony, thrashing in his chair as tears formed in his eyes. Face delivered a swift kick to Enrique's side, knocking him to the floor and laughing cynically as he stepped over him.

"Get up! Oh wait, you can't," Face sarcastically stated. "Here, let me help you up."

Face grabbed the chair and the base of the knife and slowly sat his victim back upright. Enrique screamed for mercy as the blade sliced through his flesh. His heartbeat trembled as he struggled to catch his breath. His exhaustion wouldn't allow adrenaline to produce, making the pain in his leg unbearable. Meanwhile, Hong's hands were all over his cell phone, texting at a mile a minute, informing his men about his father's protection. Face knelt down and locked eyes with Enrique, grinning as he watched the blood leak from his pants.

"You know my brother may not see another day outside of that place?" Face slowly twisted the blade.

Enrique thrashed, unable to escape torture. Face's expression turned from angry to infuriated as he softly spoke to Enrique.

"Do you know what it's like losing the last shred of family you've got?" He continued to twist. "Do you?"

"I have informed my father, and as a thank you for his capture, he has also offered our assistance with removing Diaz if needed."

Face looked up and grinned.

"Tell him that I graciously appreciate his offer, but before I kill this fool there are some things that I think we all want to know," Face stated.

Face rose to his feet and yanked his bloody Buddy from Enrique's thigh, spattering drops of blood on the floor.

"Gimme my knife." He laughed.

Enrique breathed heavily as the blood gushed from his thigh. A small puddle of blood formed on the floor beneath his feet, and he couldn't keep still. Face folded his very bloody Buddy and put it back in his pocket, wiping the blood on his hand on his pants leg. He then removed his shirt, wrapped it around his hand, and kicked Enrique in the chest, causing him to fall onto his back. He grabbed the hot work lamp and placed it close to Enrique's face. Enrique groaned from his wounds, moving his head from side to side, knowing that his torture was far from over.

"Aight, dammit. You've got one last chance to talk, or this is going to get really bad for you. I'm gonna ask you questions, and you're going to tell me everything I want to know. The more you tell me, the less I'll torture you, but if you decide to keep up this silent treatment, I'll take my time. Day by day, week by week, and maybe even month by month, depending on how long you can last just to make sure that you feel every bit of the hell that I'm gonna unleash on you. And if you think I'm playing, I dare you to try me," Face instructed.

The room was quiet for a moment. Nassar had finally caught his breath, but his eyes were full of trouble.

"What is Diaz planning, and why are you involved?" Face asked.

Enrique scrunched up his teary face and remained silent. Face looked at Hong, and Hong nodded back to him.

"So, you really wanna do this the hard way, huh?" Face shook his head.

Face grabbed Enrique's hair and yanked his head back. Enrique grunted as he saw his reflection in Face's shades with the burning light coming toward him.

"I like doing things the hard way, too," Face said.

Face pressed the hot lamp on Enrique's cheek, and he began to wail. The lamp instantly burned his skin, smoking as it cooked his face. His skin stuck to the lamp as Face slowly pulled it away. Enrique thrashed his head, trying to escape Face's grip.

"Now I'll ask you again. What does Diaz have planned and why are you involved?" Face asked calmly.

Nassar cleared his throat and got Face's attention.

"I feel as if this is partly my fault," Nassar interjected.

"What do you mean?" Hong asked.

Nassar slowly rose to his feet and took a step with his cane. He looked at the beaten Enrique and lowered his head.

"Many years ago, I found Enrique as I was coming back in town from a celebration with family. We hit something in the road, and it so happened that Enrique saw what happened and offered his services to us. At the time, he did not speak much English, but because he was so helpful, I recommended him to Diaz. For all I knew, Diaz gave him a job and helped him learn English. I had no idea he would have him turn against us like this. I have brought shame to our unity." Nassar sat down and dropped his head.

Face released Enrique and approached Nassar.

"This is not your fault. He had every bit of sense to decide to keep himself out of this situation, and he chose to go against us. You may have given him a chance at life, but he decided to do nothing with it, which has led us all to be here today. Hell, it's probably a good thing you did meet him in some way because you two may never have known of Diaz's motives," Face said, extending his hand.

Nassar took Face's hand and smiled.

"You are a man of great admiration," Nassar said. "I thank you. Have your way with this traitor!"

Face turned and approached Enrique. He stood over him with a whirlwind of evil thoughts running through his mind. He ran his hand across Enrique's chin, examining his badly burned cheek.

"You ready to talk now, traitor? Let's see how good your English is," Face said.

Enrique's body shook, his breath trembling. He opened his eyes and saw the reflection of his treachery in Face's shades. Nassar's voice echoed in his mind, and he instantly became overwhelmed with regret. He dropped his façade of anger, and the wells of his eyes began to fill, knowing this was the end for him.

"I...I was"–Enrique cleared his throat–"I was doing what I was told."

"That's not what I asked you." Face grabbed the lamp. "I asked you what Diaz has planned. Now tell me or I'll burn you again."

Enrique began to breathe faster.

"Okay, okay! I tell you! I tell you," Enrique cried. "Señor Diaz wants to control the city. He wants to kill the Nassar and Hong families."

"And how does he plan on getting rid of us?" Hong approached.

"He make plan to frame you; he wants you two to fight," Enrique replied.

"So he was going to try to make enemies out of us? What deceit!" Hong replied.

"He plan to destroy your business, he wants your familias gone," Enrique said.

Hong looked at Nassar, who shook his head and closed his eyes. Face grinned at Enrique and twiddled the lamp.

"So you're a little rogue agent, I see. What does Diaz want with me?" Face asked.

"He no wants anything with you, he want to kill your brother. He no like your brother, but he say he want you to work for him," Enrique replied.

"Work for him?" Face inquired.

"Si, he say he like you since your brother gone. He think your brother no good for business," Enrique replied.

Hong stepped back from Enrique and began to message his father again.

"I have to alert my father. That bastard has been watching all of us. We must take him out before he takes us out," Hong said.

Tears of shame dripped from Enrique's ears as he thought of the life he had wasted.

"I no understand why he no like your brother. He want me to kill him that day. I could not do it. I had a brother, and he die. I see you and your brother, and I did not want to see what been done to me. Señor Diaz, he kill me if I no kill him, so I do what I do to keep him alive. I no lie to you, I tell you truth," Enrique sobbed.

Face looked down at Enrique and released a deep sigh.

"You know, it's sad. It's sad that this is the world we live in," Face said, "but what's even   sadder is that you think I'm stupid."

Enrique's face lit up with fear.

"No! No! I no thi—"

Face slapped Enrique, spattering blood across the floor.

"Yeah you do, you think I'm stupid! Everyone knows damn well that Diaz has his goons all over the penitentiary my brother is at, and it won't be long until they get the message to kill him! You may have let him live that day, a clever move, but you aren't fooling me! You only let him live to draw attention away from Diaz's plot! That's why you hid!" Face yelled.

Face punched Enrique in the face and started to choke him as he lay defenseless. Enrique helplessly strained as tears burst from his eyes, his life slowly slipping away. Face squeezed with all his might, his strength rising from the painful thoughts of his brother.

"My brother is going to die no matter what I do, and it's your fault. All you had to do was leave." Face gritted his teeth. "You could have taken what you knew and gotten away, but no, you chose to get involved in something that had nothing to do with you. Did you think that you'd get away? You thought I couldn't find you?"

Face squeezed tighter and tighter as faint noises escaped from Enrique's mouth. His bloody saliva drenched Face's hand.

"Even more, you put your own people in danger. You should have told your family to leave," Face giggled. "Your son put up the best fight he could to protect your wife, and as for her, well, let's just say she's gonna make quite the mule for me. It's an eye for an eye in this game, and for the life of my brother, you gotta die!"

Face released Enrique and delivered a stifling stomp to his chest. Enrique gritted from the pain of his ribs cracking as he watched Face grab the lamp and kneel over his twitching body.

"I'll make sure Diaz visits you real soon," Face said.

With all his might, Face jammed the hot lamp into Enrique's eye socket. Enrique's body jumped as the bulb exploded, electrocuting him and shattering small shards of glass into his face. Blood leaked from his nose and mouth onto the cold concrete floor as Face forced the lamp into his socket until the lights surged and went out. His deep breaths echoed through the darkness as he inhaled the euphoric smell of cooked flesh. He pulled the lamp away as he rose to his feet, leaving his enemy massacred. Smoke from the burnt flesh faded up through the air as Enrique's soul departed from his body.

"Hit the switch," Face commanded his goon.

Face's guard used his cell phone to find the fuse box and turned the lights back on while his other guard opened the backdoor to air out the room. Face wiped Enrique's bloody saliva from his hand with his shirt as he turned to Hong and Nassar with haste in his voice.

"It looks like this is a bit more complicated than we thought, so we're going to have to work together on this," he said.

"I was thinking the same," Hong replied.

"Where do we begin?" Nassar asked.

Face paced back and forth as he quickly assembled the plan for the trio's next move.

"First things first, we gotta make sure we are all protected. Based on what he was saying, Diaz is only after you two. I assume he's been to your houses, right?" Face asked.

"Yes," Hong replied. "Several times over the years."

"The same with me," Nassar added.

The men all rubbed their chins, trying to think of what to do. Face was anxious to figure something out before the others did to prove himself a valuable asset to Nassar.

"Aight, uh, I'll make you guys an offer, a token of my appreciation for making me a part of your team, if you will. If you want a place to keep your families safe, by all means, they can stay here, at least until Diaz is taken care of. No one knows about this house, thanks to a few friends I made. Figured I would need to find something that I could keep off the grid, like a safe house for the safe house. I keep a few guys out here just in case, though. You're more than welcome," Face offered.

"I thank you for your generosity. I told you, Mr. Nassar, he's a great addition to the team." Hong grinned in admiration.

"It's no problem. We've got businesses to run, and we've gotta be alive to do it. They can bring anything they want with them to make it home until everything's taken care of, so long as they don't make anyone aware of this location. Let's go back upstairs." Face signaled his guards. "Clean this up."

The men proceeded upstairs without looking back at their betrayer. Face took them on a tour of the house and allowed them to select the rooms they would occupy. There were cameras all around the house that led to a surveillance room that Face monitored from his smartphone. Their guards remained on the ground floor as the three men walked about the house checking out the rooms.

"So that was the last room. Everyone can be on their own side of the house and have their own bathroom," Face said.

"This is very convenient, Face. I think I'll take you up on your offer and stay here until this mess with Diaz is resolved," Nassar said.

"No problem. Just let me know when you're coming, and I'll have my guys here to take care of everything for you," Face replied.

Hong checked his phone and was shocked by a message from his father's caretaker.

"It appears my father has agreed to stay here as well. I'll do some shopping for him and have him here later today, but I won't be staying. I refuse to allow that fool to force me into hiding."

"I understand." Face nodded. "The offer's always on the table if you decide you want to stay."

The men were suddenly interrupted by the sound of footsteps coming up the stairs. From the staircase appeared a tall, dark, brawny man dressed in black jeans with a black shirt and gold chain with an angry mug on his face holding a briefcase.

"Wassup," the man said with a deep, gritty voice.

"Wassup, bruh," Face greeted the man. "Mr. Nassar, this is Deuce. He and Hong have met before. Deuce is my right-hand man."

Deuce approached the men and handed over the briefcase to Face, then turned and shook Nassar's hand with his crippling grip. Refusing to appear intimidated, Nassar kept a straight face and looked Deuce in the eyes as he endured the painful handshake.

"Why do you look so angry, my friend?" Nassar questioned.

"He is a little standoffish to people he hasn't met, as we all have to be in our line of work," Hong assured him as he reached for Deuce's hand.

"Please don't be offended, Mr. Nassar. He's just doing his job," Face added. "He was actually the one that advised me to watch out for our friend in the basement."

"You are a good man." Nassar smiled.

"I feel like you are too," Deuce replied.

"So, to catch you up, Deuce, Diaz isn't trying to kill me. He was only going after De'Angelo, but he wants to kill Hong and Mr. Nassar, so now we've all teamed up to take him out, and then we're going to take over his territory," Face stated.

Deuce calmly raised his brow at Face as he processed the benefits behind the hostile takeover.

"That means you get to use your new toys." Face grinned.

Deuce's face slowly turned into a grin, and the two men began to laugh.

"I knew today was gonna be a good day," Deuce replied.

"Exactly, but let's not waste any time. We've got to put a plan together immediately," Face directed. "You gentlemen go ahead and get everything situated at home. I'll be here for the rest of the day, and once you are both settled, we will meet and figure everything out."

"Agreed," Hong said. "I'll be back with my father later this evening."

The men cleared out of the house and went back to their cars. They all shook hands one last time in solidarity of their alliance. The next meeting would be the start of a civil war to protect their territories. With thoughts of his next endeavor,

Face planned with Deuce on where to start with their master plan. There would be money, but most certainly there would be murder.

CHAPTER 3

FROM BAD TO WORSE

SUNDAY, AUGUST 9TH was the last night of freedom, as school would start tomorrow morning at 8:20. The magnificent rays of sunshine gleaming through the clouds presented a ray of hope, but the dreaded thoughts of isolation only placed Ryan deeper into his depression. He and Camille traveled down I-285 to their new apartment, every mile traveled making Ryan's anxiety stronger. The music on the radio turned to rubbish as Ryan soon found himself enraptured in the twisted romance of his depressing thoughts.

Memories of past school years reappeared in his mind. The mild bullying still felt like it had happened yesterday because of having to forcibly harbor anger-filled thoughts of being victimized with no restitution, the confusion from immature girls looking for someone to fight for their attention, and being best friends with someone at the beginning of the school year but sworn enemies by the end. The vicious cycle would continue, only this time he would be the new kid on the block, making him an easy target. Ryan rested his weary head on the headrest and sighed. Camille glanced over at him and acknowledged his expression with concern.

"You okay?" she asked.

This is your moment, tell her the truth, he thought to himself. Ryan inhaled deeply, ready to unleash his emotions, but he instead closed his eyes and turned his head.

"Yeah, I'm just tired," he lied.

Camille looked over at him again and smiled.

"It's gonna be alright, baby," she assured. "I know it seems fast, but trust me, I'd never put you in harm's way. Reginald and I have a—"

He closed his eyes and tuned out his mother's voice and recapped his most memorable thoughts of his summer with his Uncle Carey and cousin CJ. He remembered running around with the girls he and CJ met in the neighborhood and the countless hours they'd spent playing their favorite video games together, usually ending as the sun rose in the morning. He smiled, remembering the fast speeds they'd traveled as his uncle raced people on the highway when they cruised through the city. Of all his summer memories, he still felt the strain his uncle left in his muscles as he and CJ were pushed to their limits exercising three days a week. His uncle's voice echoed in his mind as he lay back on the weight bench.

"Remember, inhale up, exhale down," Carey instructed.

Ryan continued his set with fire in his arms.

"Gimme five more...three...two...gimme two more. C'mon, I got you. There you go. Good job, nephew," Carey coached.

He passed Ryan his water bottle, urging him to take a sip. "I want you boys to listen to me for a second."

CJ and Ryan wiped the sweat from their foreheads and listened attentively.

"I want you boys to know that I'm proud of the both of you. I remember back 16 years ago on that Wednesday in May, one of you born in the morning and the other at night. Who would have thought me and my sister would have our kids on the same day?"

They chuckled.

"It was a good day, even though it came at a cost."

A strong sentiment filled the room as Carey paused, thinking of his late wife.

"CJ, you would have loved your mother. I wish you would have been able to have her with you all these years. You were the only thing

she loved more than me," Carey sighed. "She was a goddess basking in the elegance of her own spirituality. You carry her essence, son. I want you to always remember that no matter what, you represent the greatness that once was your mother. I only helped it manifest."

The father and son shook hands and shared a long hug.

"I love you, son." Carey's voice cracked.

"I love you too, Pops," CJ replied.

Carey wiped his eyes and sighed.

"I swear, I'll never get over that woman." He grinned.

Carey focused his attention on Ryan and cleared his mind.

"Nephew"—he shook his head—"damn, boy, you've grown up on me."

They chuckled.

"I know your journey in life hasn't been the greatest, what with that bastard of a father you got—hell, you can barely even call him that—but anyway, you have come a long way in this world, farther than most. Believe it or not, you've defied the odds, statistically. Based on what those psychotherapists believe, you're not supposed to be doing as well as you are. You're smart, you're talented, boy, I still have the portrait you drew of your aunt framed in my room. Looks better than the actual picture. Needless to say, I'm proud of you, nephew."

The uncle shook the hand of his nephew.

"I know things in life are about to change in a major way for you, nephew. I can only hope that my sister is making the right decision with this guy, but you know you always have a place over here with us. I just want you to remember, you have the power to do great things, nephew. When times get rough, I want you to look deep inside yourself and harness that inner strength that gives you the power to go beyond your limits. When you look in the mirror, don't just see your reflection, see that hero that lives within you. Make your actions fierce, make your movements bold and your manifestation incredible."

He looked at both of the young men.

"You are the heroes of the next generation."

The memories created over the summer would not soon be forgotten. His uncle's lessons over the years were the only thing he had to keep his mind focused on graduating.

"—like the new apartment," Camille faded in. "The new complex is called Garden Crossing. Now, please don't get mad, but we'll only be here for a little while. Reggie and I are trying to get us a house to rent because his lease is almost up. They have a smaller swimming pool than where we were before, but the hills here are definitely smaller to walk up."

"I just hope everything is big enough," Ryan said.

"Well, don't get too settled in here, I'm hoping we can get out of here soon. It's farther away, but I think it's in the same district, so at least your school won't change," Camille replied.

"La-di-da." He made a face. "What's the name of my school now?"

"It's called Myser Bell High. I checked it out, and it seems pretty decent," Camille said.

Ryan sighed with a vague look on his face. Camille glanced at him as she switched lanes.

"What's wrong, baby?" she asked.

Ryan was again presented with an opportunity to make an honest statement but again refrained.

"Nothing," he continued to lie. "I just...I've hated school since fourth grade, and I guess I'm not looking forward to this change of school in the middle of everything. I just wanna get it all over with."

"Well, like I always say, you better learn it all now or else you'll wish you did later." Camille smiled.

"Yeah, I guess so." Ryan frowned. "I feel like it's all lies anyway."

They rode the rest of the way tuning out each other's silence with the music on the radio. Moments later, they reached their exit, and as they sat at the red light, Ryan looked around, hoping to find something that sparked his interest. The area was surrounded by cheap motels, old restaurants, and warehouses lined with 18 wheelers loading for their trips. Nothing that piqued his personal excitement. As they journeyed farther down the street, the surrounding area morphed into a residential neighborhood. On the left side of the street was a large community of houses and a church with young children running around on the playground, and to the right were rivaling gas stations adjusting their prices.

Camille turned on a road between the two gas stations, and they were soon surrounded by pine trees on each side. Hidden between the trees were several entrances to apartment complexes, all beginning with the name Garden. There were Garden Lane, Garden Springs, Garden Trails, Garden Grove, Garden Valley, and finally their complex, Garden Crossings. Camille stopped by the call box to type in her code, and shortly after, the gates opened, welcoming them home. As they entered the complex, Ryan observed the attractions hiding under the abundance of trees. Behind the leasing office was a large swimming pool paired with a small hot tub surrounded by a black gate. Farther up was a tennis court next to the first apartment building, and parked out front were all kinds of different models of cars: old, new, and broken down. Next was the trash dumpster that reeked of spoiled milk baking under the sun. They quickly rode up a steep hill to escape the nose-turning stench.

No one appeared to be outside despite how full the parking lot was. The neighborhood seemed calm and relaxed as the evening skies changed to a mixture of red, orange, yellow, and purple. The glamorous sight put Ryan at ease as he equated the tranquility with his days in Decatur running through the neighborhood with Byron. They rolled past two more buildings and finally reached theirs.

"This is our new apartment," Camille said.

The building was nothing too extravagant to look at but appeared to be a decent living space. It was gray with years of dirt covering the lower panels. The entrance to the breezeway was made of brick with a hanging sign that said *1000-1008*.

There were screened-in balconies in the front along with a patch of grass in the front and a few trees off to the side with a walkway. Ryan retrieved his suitcase from the backseat, and he and Camille headed toward the building. Ryan walked slowly in hopes that someone would appear, but there was not a soul in sight.

As they crossed through the breezeway, a cool chill blew away the evening heat. To the left were walkways leading to two different apartments with a small staircase in the middle leading to the other four apartments, and to the right was the staircase that led to the apartments at the top.

"We stay upstairs," Camille said as she took the first step.

"Finally, an upstairs apartment," Ryan said. "I was getting tired of people stomping on the floor all the time."

Ryan picked up his suitcase and carried it up the wooden staircase, his new strength apparent.

"Your uncle put y'all to work this summer, I see," Camille commented.

"I was already strong." Ryan grinned.

As they reached the top of the stairs, Camille turned left, leading Ryan to a large black door.

"We stay here, apartment 1005," she said.

The doors in the complex had been painted black a few days before to accent the gray panels as a cheap renovation for the complex. The amateur finish ended at the doorknob, which was still rusted with tiny specs of black paint on it. In the center of the door was the peephole, which had slightly been painted over.

"Damn people act like they can't paint a door," Camille fussed.

She scratched the paint off the peephole as she unlocked the door, and a loud click rang out. She opened it, and they both stepped inside the dark apartment. Camille turned on some lights and commenced a short tour.

"Let me show you around," she said.

Ryan followed his mother through the two-bedroom apartment. They had a nice-sized living room filled with Reginald's faux leather furniture. The kitchen was smaller than at their old apartment, but the screened-in balcony added a nice touch. They walked to the other side of the apartment and opened the closed bedroom door ahead.

"This is your room."

Camille turned on the light. Inside sat Camille's old bed and dresser with her TV on top. There was a big window on the wall facing the street absorbing the yellow glow of a streetlight and the shadow of a tree that was just outside the window. Ryan's art desk fit snugly in the corner of the room next to the dresser.

"I got rid of your old bed. It was time for that thing to go, so you've got my old mattress and dresser for now," Camille said.

"More space, won't argue with that," Ryan said. "What did you do with all my art supplies?"

Camille pointed over to the dresser and closet door, remembering how serious Ryan was about his art supplies.

"All of the small stuff should be in the top drawer of your dresser, and everything else should be in the closet. I tried to make sure I got everything. You had a lot of old drawing books. Go ahead and unpack, and I'll go cook something to eat," Camille said.

"Okay," Ryan said.

Camille stepped to Ryan and hugged him tightly.

"Welcome home, baby," she said.

She turned and walked out of the room as Ryan took a look around and compared his new space to the old one. It wasn't as big as the room he'd had at Evergreen Hills, but he felt that it was big enough for him. He looked inside of his closet and found his art supplies placed neatly upon a section of shelves that were piled to the top with two sides to hang his clothes on. He sighed, frustrated by the idea of having to reorganize his supplies again.

"I guess this is home now," he said to himself.

Time passed by slowly as the evening turned to night. As Ryan finished folding his clothes, the aroma of spaghetti brought his attention to the kitchen. The sauce bubbled like boiling lava over the beef, waiting to be devoured with noodles and a side of garlic bread baking in the oven.

"Dinner should be ready soon," Camille said.

"Okay," Ryan replied.

He began to walk back to his room, but before he could turn the corner, he heard a key go into the front door. He peeked at the lock as it turned to the left, the doorknob turned, and the door opened with a low-pitched squeak. From the doorway entered a dark-skinned man standing nearly six feet tall, carrying a lunch bag.

"What's up, Ryan?" Reginald stated with his northern accent.

"Hey, Reggie," Ryan replied.

There was no present tension between Ryan and his stepfather, Reginald Harrison, but there was also no fulfilling bond between the two. Reginald was a local truck driver for a major company delivering products to in-state businesses desperately trying to make his way into a management position.

"How was work?" Ryan asked.

"Work was work. I'm just glad it's over," Reginald replied.

The two shook hands, and Ryan quietly headed back to his room as Reginald proceeded to the kitchen.

"How are you, sweetie?" Camille asked as Reginald walked up to her for a gentle kiss.

"I'm good, baby." Reginald inhaled deeply. "M-m-m, somethin' sho' smells good!"

"It ain't nothin' but spaghetti, and you know that." Camille laughed.

Reginald set his lunch bag on the counter and proceeded to the bedroom.

"I'm about to take a shower," he stated.

"Okay, the food should be ready by the time you get out," Camille replied.

Back in his room, Ryan was texting his cousin CJ about the new apartment. He still had mixed feelings about the complex, but his heart was still somewhere on the eastside.

*It's aight, but it ain't the eastside...*he sent.

Did u c any girls? CJ replied with the looking eyes emoji.

*It's a desert out there but I ain't lookin' anyway...*Ryan replied with a cactus.

You a fool! CJ replied.

Ryan looked up from his phone and noticed a small silver jewelry box on his dresser. He walked over to it and read the tag hanging from it: *To: Ryan, From Granddad*. He picked up the box and shook it to get a feel for what it was, but before he could open it he heard a shout from his mother.

"Dinner's ready!" Camille screamed from the kitchen.

Ryan and Reginald came from their rooms and took their seats at the dinner table. Their plates were already made with a large helping of spaghetti and string beans, a piece of garlic bread, and a refreshing glass of sweet tea. Camille sat down, and they all bowed their heads to bless the food.

"Dear Lord, thank you for the food that we are about to receive for the nourishment of our bodies for Christ's sake. In Jesus' name we pray, Amen," Camille prayed.

"Amen," Ryan and Reginald said.

The three enjoyed the delicious meal, but Ryan quickly found himself full from his unsettled emotions about his mother's marriage. He hadn't spent much time with Reginald before this, leaving more to the mystery of his perception of Reginald's character. Forced into the current situation, he decided he would isolate himself from their relationship. He spun his fork around to capture a bite of the warm spaghetti when his subconscious thoughts began to emerge, flashing back to the last time he'd seen his biological father.

It had taken a long ride in the car to get to this place, but they'd finally arrived. Antonio Davidson got out of the car and waved to a large group of people standing by a grill with a sign that said Welcome Davidson Family. *Antonio opened the rear passenger door and very quickly, seven-year-old Ryan jumped out of the car. A few other children were running around but none he could remember as it had been four years since he had last seen this side of his family. The adults by the grill were tall, all different shapes and sizes. They all spoke kindly to Ryan as he smiled; however, Antonio's face maintained an angry mug.*

"He looks just like you," they all would say as Antonio grunted with disgust. Ryan walked away to play with the other children as Antonio sat down and watched him with an evil eye, drinking a beer in a brown bottle. The smile on Ryan's face grew bigger as the other kids played with him. Shortly thereafter, the adults took the kids to the pool in the park. Antonio stood behind the fence surrounding the pool drinking another beer and staring angrily at his son. A couple of hours went by, and all the food was done. As the kids were getting out of the pool and heading back to the picnic area with their parents, the sight of an open pool sent a heinous idea through Antonio's mind.

He grabbed one of the smaller girls before she could run off. By now all the adults and most of the other kids were far away from the pool, and Antonio put his plan into action. He took Ryan and the other child by the hand and walked them around to the 12-foot section of the pool.

"I'm gonna teach you how to swim in the 12 feet today, Ryan," Antonio grinned.

"But I just learned how to swim in the 5 feet," Ryan replied.

The other child stayed quiet.

"You'll be okay. Listen, this is what I'm gonna do. I'ma throw you and your cousin in at the same time, and you have to save her," Antonio advised.

"But I don't know how to swim in the 12 feet yet, Daddy," he said with fear.

"It don't matter, Ryan, cause I'm still gonna throw your cousin in. I'm not gonna save her, so you got to, you gotta save her from drowning. If you don't, she's gonna die. She's gonna drown in the pool and die. You don't want her to drown and die do you, Ryan?" Antonio threatened.

Tears fell from Ryan's eyes as his frightened face turned into confusion.

"No," he cried.

"Okay, well, come on so I can teach you," Antonio stated.

"Daddy, I don't wanna learn how to swim anymore!" Ryan pleaded.

He tried to pull away but was caught in Antonio's grip.

"Hey, you wanted to come and see me so bad, so now you're gonna learn how to swim in the 12 feet today!" Antonio bullied.

"Bu–"

"Shut up, Ryan! You're going to learn and you're going to learn now, so get ready," Antonio commanded.

Ryan tried as hard as he could to focus on saving his cousin as he wiped the tears from his eyes, but fear took over his bravery as Antonio's grip on his wrist grew tighter. He looked back for help, but unfortunately, there was no one there to save him.

"I'm counting to three and then I'm throwing you both in," Antonio stated.

Ryan sobbed as tears dripped from his chin. The other kid was still quiet.

"One," Antonio's voice grumbled as Ryan shrieked.

"Two," Antonio grumbled, increasing his grip on Ryan's wrist.

"Three!" Antonio shouted.

Like bait on a fishing line, Antonio cast Ryan into the air. Ryan hollered and flailed around, anticipating the cold crash into the middle of the deep water. What was only a matter of seconds felt like an eternity. Finally, his little body splashed into the cold water and bounced up for him to see that Antonio had never let the other kid go. He held onto the other kid. He spared the other kid. He turned and walked away with the other kid. That bastard left his son.

Kicking and screaming, and his arms and legs weakening, Ryan began to lose his 12-foot deep battle with the water. He immediately knew what his father was trying to do. He knew his father wanted him to die. It wasn't fun anymore. This wasn't what he wanted. He didn't want to save his cousin. He didn't want to learn how to swim. He didn't want his daddy to save him. He wanted his mother. He wanted his toys. He wanted his grandmother. He wanted his grandfather. He wanted his uncle. He wanted to live. He didn't want to drown. He didn't want to die.

He managed to release one last shout above water and reached his hand out one last time, but the only reply he received were the sounds of water splashing around him. Bubbles flowed from his mouth, and he sank deeper and deeper into the chilling water. He was panicking, but no one was coming to save him. He was kicking, but he wasn't getting closer to the top. He was drowning, thinking he was going to die. His eyes started to close. Everything was grim. His body got colder. Suddenly, someone grabbed his wrist, then his arm, and then his body. They went up and up and finally, Ryan's head was out of the water. He coughed a lot. He could breathe again. He felt life returning to his body. He wasn't drowning anymore.

They swam to the edge, and the mysterious hero pulled Ryan out of the pool. Ryan quickly calmed himself, wiping his fear-filled eyes of dread as he recognized his big cousin Darius. Darius had been in the bathroom and saw Ryan drowning when he came out.

"Hey, you're 'Tonio's son. How did this happen? I saw you get out when they said the food was ready," Darius inquired.

Ryan got to his feet and told Darius of his harrowing encounter with his father.

"My daddy said he was gonna teach me how to swim in the 12 feet, and he said he was gonna throw me and my other cousin in, but he only threw me in, and when I came up, I saw him walking away," he cried.

"He did what?" Darius exclaimed.

Darius took Ryan by the hand, and they quickly walked back over to the rest of the family members. The elders immediately inquired about what happened to the young child. Again, Ryan told them all of his harrowing encounter with the cold waters of the 12-foot pool. A wave of shock and malice filled the area as some people believed Ryan and some others did not. A seven-year-old child stood trial before his elders, and his only eyewitness could barely speak a full sentence. Finally, the elders began their search for Antonio. As they spread into the parking lot, Antonio was nowhere to be found, with only the discarded belongings of Ryan scattered in the parking spot he'd once occupied. No one else was around to see it. No one saw him toss Ryan in the pool. No one heard what he said to Ryan.

Darius took Ryan to his car to keep him safely away from the rest of the family. He called Antonio several times but never got an answer. Darius then gave the phone to Ryan to call his mother, and he told her what happened. A while later a white car sped to the scene. Darius went over to the car and pointed to where Ryan was. It was Camille and his Uncle Carey. They got out and got Ryan out of the back seat of Darius' car.

"Are you okay, baby?" she wept, squeezing him tightly.

More tears came from Ryan's eyes.

"Yes," he sniveled.

He felt safe. He was alive. He wasn't drowning. He didn't die. His mother put him in the car, and Darius sat with him. His mother and uncle walked toward the other elders looking for Antonio. She was too far away to be heard, but Uncle Carey had to hold her back from attacking Antonio's mother. Darius said something, but it was too fast for Ryan to understand. A few minutes passed, and Ryan's warrior walked back to her car. Darius got out, and Camille thanked him for saving Ryan, for believing Ryan, for not letting him drown, for not letting him die. Then it was time to go.

"See you later, lil cuz," Darius said with grief.

"Bye." Ryan waved.

The car turned, and they went away from the people. Away from Darius. Away from Antonio. Away from the 12 feet. Away from drowning. Away from death....

"Ryan. Ryan. Ryan!" Camille yelled.

"Huh?" Ryan shook his head.

"You've been playing with your food for the past few minutes. Is something on your mind, baby?" she asked with concern.

Ryan looked at the warm spaghetti and half-eaten garlic bread on his plate and realized that once again, his silence had not gone unnoticed.

"Oh, no, I'm just...tired, I guess," he lied.

"Well, we have some things we need to discuss with you. Reggie, you start it off," she said.

Reggie sipped his tea and cleared his throat.

"Me and your mom talked about it, and now that we live together, we came up with a few things that we thought would be good for you. First, we agreed that your curfew should be 10 o'clock, and I noticed a few things that I'm going to help change about you so that you can have the right mindset to become a man."

Ryan raised his brow and turned his head to his mother. The newly enforced rule of a curfew was preposterous. He had never had a curfew his entire life, and now at 17, his freedoms were being infringed upon.

"What he means, baby, is that we want what's best for you. With your father not being in your life, Reginald has some things in mind that he believes will lead you in the right direction," Camille said.

"What does Antonio not being in my life have to do with me having a curfew?" Ryan asked with a side-eye.

"First of all, you don't have a job, you don't do anything after school, and you need to be focusing on school so you can graduate. Besides, all you do is sit in your room and draw all the time anyway, so you need to be in the house by 10 during the week. End of story," Reginald said.

Ryan looked down at his plate and remained silent. Thoughts of his lost battle were quickly tuned out by the faint sound of music playing as a breaking news report flashed on the TV screen in the living room.

"Turn this up. I want to hear this," Reginald said.

Without arguing, Ryan walked over to the TV as a means of getting away from the table. The broadcast switched over to the news chopper hovering over a dark neighborhood in Atlanta showing police loading men into large vans. Several ambulances and police cars lit up the area with their red and blue flashing lights.

"Police are saying the shootout occurred because of an alleged fight that broke out between two local gangs around 6:30 p.m.," the reporter stated.

A woman tore her way through the crowd screaming her son's name. She crossed the police barricade and jolted through the area, looking for him and being tailed by two officers as she ran through the crime scene.

"Residents of the area were seen fleeing the scene and into their homes, under cars and even into dumpsters trying to avoid the waves of bullets flying through the air..."

She outran the officers, looking left and right for her son until she was stopped by the sight of another officer covering up his cold dead body. She shrieked in terror at the sight as she stumbled and fell at his feet. The officer motioned to keep her away, but he stopped and dropped his head in sorrow. The woman embraced her son's dead body, clenching him tightly to her chest. The officers following her caught up to her and quickly terminated their chase, allowing her to grieve.

"You see, that's the type of stuff I'm talking about right there. That's what we want to keep you away from. All this violence is nonsense," Camille said.

A detective walked up to the officers and demanded that the woman be immediately removed from the scene. The officers looked at each other and then at the woman, unsure how to approach the grieving mother. Hearing all of what was being said, she bid her son farewell and kissed his forehead. She slowly lay his body on the cold, hard ground and exhaled a long sigh followed by rows of tears. She stood over him, her clothes and hands covered in his blood. The two officers escorted the woman to one of the ambulances to get her cleaned up before they questioned her about her son.

"Judging from the things that have taken place here tonight, police are probably going to be here for quite a bit of time. It's just been truly tragic here tonight. I give my deepest condolences to every family who may have lost someone here. Back to you in the studio," the reporter closed.

"Man, that's messed up," Ryan said to himself.

"That's why I did everything I could when you were growing up to keep you away from stuff like that, because if I ever lost you, I don't know what I'd do," Camille said.

"I know, but we never really lived in a bad area like that," Ryan replied.

He walked back to his seat, and suddenly, his appetite was gone.

"You're right," Camille said, "but sometimes things just happen to people. I'll never forget this boy I went to high school with got shot after a basketball game at the park because he scored the winning shot on some guy. He didn't even do anything wrong, he just got shot because somebody decided to be stupid. In fact, the guy that shot him is still in prison today."

"I mean, people have died for less, but I get it," Ryan said.

"Just the game," Camille said. "Finish your meal."

"Oh, I'm not that hungry anymore. I'm kinda tired," Ryan said slowly.

"Okay, baby, just rake out your plate and put it in the sink—"

"Actually," Reginald interrupted, "wash it off in the sink and put it in the dishwasher. I can't stand dishes in the sink. That's one of the new rules we're gonna have around here."

"Um, okay," Ryan replied.

He followed Reginald's orders and raked the scraps of food into the trash can then rinsed the plate off in the sink and placed it in the dishwasher. Reginald grunted and darted toward Ryan.

"No, wait, you put it in the wrong way. This is where we're going to put the plates, and this is where we're going to put the bowls, and I'm sure you already know where the glasses go. Top rack. I don't want to see any glasses on the bottom rack. Matter of fact, sit down right quick. There are some other things I want to cover."

Ryan sat back down at the table, and Reginald turned the TV off. Camille quickly took her and Reginald's plates into the kitchen.

"You have some new responsibilities around here," Reginald explained. "I don't want you eating in your room. Second, these carpets are clean, and they are going to stay that way, so take your shoes off at the door, and also don't put your hands on the wall. Every Saturday morning you'll get up and clean your room and bathroom before you do anything. The tub, the toilet, and the sink need to be white, and the counters should be spotless, and the mirror better not have any streaks on it. You need to make sure your bed is made every day, and your room needs to be clean. Make sure you dust off your dresser and wipe it down with the wood polish. You know how to use that, don't you? You just spray it on and wipe it around in circles until it fades away."

Reginald went on explaining his expectations, seemingly without taking a breath. Ryan glanced at his mother, hoping she would interject, but she said nothing. He remained silent as well, observing the annoying character of a man that barely knew anything about him.

A few hours passed, and the night found Ryan in his room putting away his sketchbook for the evening as he prepared for the next day. Camille quickly knocked and entered his room nervously, ready to make another attempt at cultivating his emotions.

"Hey, just coming to check on you," she said.

"I'm good," he said, packing his book bag.

Camille looked around the room aimlessly and leaned against the dresser.

"So...do you think you're ready for school tomorrow?" Camille asked.

"I guess. I don't really have a choice now," Ryan replied.

"Well, it can't be that bad." She smiled. "You're a senior. It won't be too hard, and you don't have much time left. All you have to do at this point is show up."

"Yeah, but...I don't wanna go to school out here, though. As much as I hate school in general, I'd rather have stayed with Grandma and graduated where I was at, especially with this dictator that thinks I'm incompetent," he replied.

Camille sighed, unsure how to manage the pressure of being in the middle of the two.

"Look, I know Reginald's methods may seem a little... extra but—"

"What exactly does he think about me because clearly he doesn't realize I'm 17," Ryan interjected.

Camille looked around for an idea, knowing there was no justification for Reginald's ill-managed speech.

"I don't think that his reasoning for you having a curfew is so much about you being 17," she said.

Triggered by her passivity, Ryan looked at Camille with every bit of seriousness in his eyes.

"Ma, you know exactly what I'm talking about. Do not insult my intelligence," he charged.

"Okay, I know what you mean," she surrendered. "I wanted to stop him because he sounded crazy."

"He was talking to me like I'm eight! I'm 17, I know how to wash a freaking bowl! And so what if I don't do anything after school? At least I'm not out here like the rest of these fools breaking in houses and doing dumb stuff," Ryan defended.

Camille grabbed Ryan's hand in an effort to keep him calm. "Quiet down, I don't want him to hear," she hushed him.

"Sorry." Ryan pulled away and turned to the window.

Camille went to the bedroom door and peeked around it, listening for any sound of Reginald's presence. She quietly closed the door and continued her conversation.

"I know this is probably the biggest adjustment that we've ever encountered, but the fact is I don't have much room to argue. At the end of the day, Reginald is the man of the house, and you know how it goes: his house, his rules," she said.

Ryan scoffed and looked out of his window at the night sky. He palmed his chin then ran his hand through his hair to the back of his head. Camille leaned on the dresser with her head down, and there was a moment of silence. She raised her head and released a deep sigh.

"I'll make a deal with you," she said. "I know you didn't plan on it, nor do I know what your plan is after you graduate, but...I will talk to your uncle about you staying with him for the rest of the school year once we get the house, if you promise me that you'll go to college and at least get your bachelor's."

Shocked by the offer on the table, Ryan released the blinds, remembering the conversations he'd had with his uncle. He turned to his mother and exhaled deeply as he looked into her troubled eyes.

"I'm not going to leave your side," he declared.

Camille reached out for a hug, and they shared a long embrace. They broke apart, and she put her hand on the side of his face as he lowered his head.

"Just give it a chance," she pleaded. "I know it's going to take some getting used to, but please, just give it time. I'm sure everything will be alright, and you know that if you ever have a problem, you can always come to me, right?"

"Mmm-hmm." He turned his head.

Sensing his discomfort, Camille decided to end the conversation. She kissed Ryan on the forehead and rubbed his shoulder.

"I'll see you in the morning. Try to get some rest. Good night," she said.

"Good night," he replied.

The sound of Camille's footsteps echoed like drums as she walked back to her room. Ryan plugged his charger into his cell phone and linked it to his stereo. He played some '90s R&B and changed into his comfortable basketball shorts. He sat on his bed, removed his shirt, and threw it in his dirty clothes basket and lay back silently in the darkness. He surrendered his heart to the romantic tales of the music to ease his mind until he drifted off to sleep. The melodic flow brought dreams of a mystic fire that burned with a bright red flame above and below the horizon. Ryan floated aimlessly through the flaming abyss, his eyes closed and mouth shut, soothed by the warmth of the flames. The warmth ran up his spine and behind his ears, comforting him and bringing a grin to his face. He reached out and touched the flames, and the fire formed an aura around him, bringing peace to his spirit. He spread his arms out and absorbed the energy from the fire, releasing a soothing exhale.

Suddenly the flames began to fade away, and the temperature quickly began to drop. Ryan curled his body into the fetal position and went into a violent shiver. The air became thicker and made this once mystic abyss hard to breathe in. Giant mountains of ice began to form, entrapping Ryan within the sub-zero temperatures. A strange wind began to blow with the strength of a hurricane, tossing Ryan into a whirlwind. Suddenly, there was an ear-bursting thunderclap, and the icy mountains shattered into serrated blades of ice. Ryan screamed in agony as the ice sliced all over his body, the strong winds still slinging him around.

The alarm clock boomed Ryan's favorite song as the 7:00 a.m. alarm awoke him from his nightmare. He swiped away the notification, and a few seconds passed before he slowly began to move. He rolled over and took a deep breath and lay still for a few moments more. He eventually perched himself up and wiped the crust from his eyes and stretched his body, twisting himself until he heard his spine pop. Seconds later, he flung the covers off his body and got out of bed, the cold room giving him a slight chill as the heat from his warm comforter escaped his body. He grabbed a pair of socks from the drawer and proceeded to the bathroom to begin readying himself for the day. The scent of the minty toothpaste awakened his senses, allowing him to open his eyes a bit wider. As he rinsed the toothpaste from his mouth, he heard his mother's footsteps approaching the door.

"Good morning, sweetie," Camille mumbled.

"Morning," he spit.

He wiped his mouth on a towel and opened the door. Camille was in her robe with her hair wrapped, appearing to have not had her morning coffee. She reached out and hugged him, but Ryan quickly pulled away as her body felt cold against his skin. They stepped into his room, and he began to make up his bed.

"Do you have your clothes picked out for school?" she asked.

"Yeah, they're on the chair." He pointed.

"Okay, do you have everything that you are going to need?" she asked.

"I packed everything last night, Ma," he sighed.

"Okay. Still worried about school today?" she prodded.

Ryan turned and looked at his mother, still irritated from their conversation from the previous evening.

"It seems like you are more worried than me," Ryan said.

Camille lowered her head, and Ryan went back to making his bed. She looked up at him with concern about the mild anger he was projecting.

"It's just that, well, I know this is new for you—"

"And you really want it to work out for the both of us, and my nonchalant nature makes it hard for you to be optimistic. Ma, relax. I'll either adjust or I won't." Ryan tossed his pillow

"Don't say that," Camille whined. "You know I'm doing the best I can."

Playing coy with a grin, Ryan set the pillow down and calmly dismissed his mother.

"I know, but you also have to finish getting ready for work. I'll be fine, Ma. I promise."

Camille's face broke into a smile, unable to resist her son's wit.

"Well, go make yourself a bowl of cereal. I'm finna get ready for work. I'll take you to your bus stop when I finish getting ready." She smiled.

"Okay," he replied.

As Camille left his room, Ryan dropped his smile and started getting dressed. He walked back into the bathroom to fix his hair in the mirror, but as he studied himself, he noticed dark circles around his eyes, signs of another sleepless night. He shook his head and walked to the kitchen to make a bowl of cereal. He received a text from his uncle as he poured his almond milk.

Keep your head up nephew!! Have a good day at school! the text read.

Thx unc ... Ryan replied.

Moments later, Reginald emerged from his room, groggily dragging himself into the kitchen, not noticing Ryan sitting at the table.

"Morning," Ryan said.

Reginald looked over at Ryan as if he had done something wrong, but then nodded his head and walked into the kitchen. Looking at the time, Ryan quickly finished his bowl, rinsed it, and placed it in the sink. Just as he turned to exit the kitchen, Reginald grabbed his shoulder and forced him toward the sink, causing Ryan to quickly grab the counter to catch himself.

"When you get finished with a bowl or plate, put it in the dishwasher! This is your final warning!" Reginald groaned with authority.

Shocked by Reginald's gesture, Ryan refrained from making eye contact, unprepared for confrontation as his heart began to race.

"My bad," Ryan replied.

He looked down at the bowl and spoon, desperately trying to swallow his pride, and proceeded to place them in the dishwasher. Reginald watched over Ryan's shoulder, anxiously waiting for him to make a mistake.

"That's not where the bowls go! I showed you where they go last night! You forgot already?" Reginald attacked.

Camille overheard the commotion from her bedroom and rushed into the kitchen to end the altercation as she struggled to put her earring in.

"Reggie, calm down! He made a mistake. He just needs time to get used to doing that," she said.

Reginald stood over Ryan with his body swelled as he looked at Camille with a fierce rage in his eyes.

"Man, l just showed him last night, how he gon' forget that fast?" Reginald replied.

Camille kept her distance, clenching her knees as she spoke firmly to her morning nemesis.

"Because he's human, and he's going to make mistakes every once in a while. Let it go," she replied.

Unable to form a valid response, Reginald scoffed at Ryan and turned to walk back into his bedroom.

"Well, he need to hurry up and learn cause..."

His words became lost in a muffle as he closed the bedroom door. Ryan closed the dishwasher and dried his hands on a dishrag. As he rested the rag back on the sink, he tightly clenched the countertop and began to breathe heavily. His legs began to jolt with energy, and he gritted his teeth. Camille calmly walked over to him with caution, looking back to make sure Reginald wasn't watching. As she approached him, she reached out her hand and spoke to him calmly.

"Baby, it's okay. Calm down and just breathe with me for a moment," she begged.

Ryan's body began to shake as he gripped tighter on the countertop. Camille inched closer, quickly realizing the knife set was not far from his reach. She continued to say soothing things to him, moving more to his left side away from the knives. Keeping her arm extended, she softly rested her hand on his left shoulder. His shoulders quickly tensed up, and he sharply turned his head, looking over his left shoulder at her.

"It's me, baby, it's okay. Please relax, please let it go for me. Please?"

Ryan turned around and locked eyes with her, tightly clenching his fists, trying to control his rage.

"You've got to relax, baby. I know you're upset, I'll handle it. Let me handle this. You know I've got you," she reasoned.

Ryan's eyes flashed over to Reginald's bedroom door, infuriated and ready for conflict resolution. Camille placed her hand on his cheek and turned his head back to her.

"Look at me, Ryan. Look at me. Just breathe, relax, and let it go. You have something bigger ahead of you to accomplish. You are stronger than your emotions," she soothed.

Receptive to her words, Ryan pulled in his fist, and a fiendish grin appeared on his face. He tilted his head back and released a sinister laugh that rocked Camille's spirit as to what was inside of her baby boy. He took a deep breath and exhaled, lowering his head to open his eyes and look at Camille calmly.

"Now go get your bag and wait by the door and we'll leave in a second," Camille said.

"Okay," Ryan said.

Ryan exited the kitchen and walked back into his room as if nothing had occurred. Camille walked back into her bedroom and found Reginald sitting on the bed going through his cell phone. He looked up at her angrily and then looked back at his phone.

"There was no need for you to yell at Ryan like that over a damn bowl in the sink. He's been gone all summer, and I would appreciate it if you gave him some time to get used to living with you," she defended.

Reginald lay back on the bed and turned his head away from Camille. She scoffed at him and grabbed her purse and exited the room, leaving the door open.

"Close the door!" Reginald yelled.

"Get up and close it your damn self," Camille yelled back. "Let's go, Ryan."

Ryan hastily opened the door, and they headed out to the car. Camille uttered to herself in anger as she tried to forgive Reginald's ignorance. She put the keys in the ignition, and the roar of the engine shook the car. Camille placed her hand on her head and sighed.

"I'm sorry you had to see that. Reggie is kind of funny in the morning, especially when everything isn't perfect." She sighed again. "But don't worry about it. I'm going to talk to him, and we are going to fix this, okay?"

"Aight," Ryan said.

He flashed back to the excessive force Reginald had used when he grabbed his shoulder, feeling the sting of his nails. He peeked over at his mother as she pulled off and wondered if she had been grabbed by Reginald the same way. Instead of discussing the situation, he again decided to remain quiet. He looked at the apartment in the rearview mirror, and a cold feeling ran down his spine. Moments later, they arrived at his bus stop, where several other students were standing on the corner waiting for the bus to arrive.

"Do you want to stand outside, or do you want to stay in the car?" Camille asked.

Ryan looked over at the other children, and his standoffish emotions wrapped him in their warmth.

"I'll stay in the car."

While they waited, they listened to the Joe and Oneida morning radio show on V-107. The hosts were talking to callers about the violent shootout that had occurred the night before. Although there were arrests made, the callers and the host felt as if no real justice had been served.

"I mean, think about it, Oneida. We hear stories about this type of stuff all the time on the news, and at the end of the day, what is actually being done in these areas to prevent something like this from happening again?" Joe said.

"Exactly," Oneida said. "Half of these areas across the state are out of control with crime, and the local and state governments refuse to fully address these issues. They know when and where these crimes are happening, they know how to stop these crimes from occurring, but they are not taking the actions necessary to stop this nonsense from happening. It's crazy!"

"We're gonna take a couple of calls to get your opinion on this situation," Joe said. "Caller, you're on the air."

"Hi, this is Kelly from Stone Mountain," the caller said.

"Hi, Kelly, welcome to the show," Joe said.

"Thank you," Kelly replied. "I totally agree with you all when you say that these problems can be avoided because all that these police departments need to do is beef up the police patrol in these problem areas, but they don't want to do anything because they want us killing each other."

"That's right!" Oneida said.

"Yeah," Kelly continued, "and like for example, when I was growing up there was a crack house right down the street from my house. The entire neighborhood knew about it, the cops knew about it, and for years nothing ever happened to it until the land was bought by some company and they tore it down to build condos. It's things like that that not only make our cities look bad, but also make the people look bad, and because the government refuses to step in and help correct these issues, we continue to get a bad rap about everything."

"So true, so true," Joe replied. "It was the same type of thing where I grew up. I lived next door to a drug dealer, and every other day there would be something crazy going on at his house. There were a few shootings, a couple of bullets came through the walls in my room, and someone was murdered. Once that happened, he was out. The police finally came and got him. It was absolutely ridiculous!"

"Oh, you really had it bad," Oneida said. "It is truly a blessing nothing bad happened to you or your family."

"I know," Joe sighed. "Let's take another call. Caller, you're on the air."

"Hey, this is Troy from East Point," the caller said.

"Good morning, welcome to the show," Oneida said.

"You know, there's a lot of things that go on over here in the streets that I don't understand. It's like when I'm rollin' down the street, I see all kinds of craziness, like undercover prostitutes, dealers pushin' drugs on kids, sometimes as young as middle school, and it's like right there in the face of the public. The police and the government are in on all the stuff that's going on so what we really need to do is come together and stop allowing this stuff to go on," Troy stated.

"That's absolutely right," Joe said.

"But the problem with our communities is that we got people that are afraid to stand up and speak what they believe in. They choose to deal with that crap 24/7, and then you got those people who don't want to take the time to unify for a good cause, so we go around in that same circle. If we're gonna get all of these problems out of the ghetto, then first we need to get over ourselves and get on the issues," Troy added.

"Amen to that," Oneida replied. "Very well said."

"Like the man said, people, we have to get over ourselves, and on the issues," Joe said. "Okay, we're gonna take a quick commercial break and when we come back, we're gonna talk more about this. It's Joe and Oneida in the morning on V-107."

The students waiting at the bus stop began to gather their things, and seconds later the school bus pulled up. Ryan grabbed his book bag and stuffed his cell phone in this pocket.

"There's the bus. Okay, baby, remember, you ride bus 526," Camille said.

"Aight, see you later," Ryan replied.

Camille reached out for a hug but was left hanging as Ryan quickly exited the car and hurried to join the line of students boarding the bus. He looked back and waved to Camille, who sighed as she waved back before pulling off. As the students entered the bus, the driver greeted them by telling them where they needed to sit.

"Girls on the driver's side, boys on the passenger side of the bus."

The children filed down the aisle of the bus, looking for the nearest seat. Ryan luckily found an empty seat and plopped into it. He reached into his pocket and pulled out his headphones, scooting closer to the window to lean his head on it and allowing the music to carry him on the morning journey.

He observed some of the sights as they traveled across town to Myser Bell High School. Eighteen wheelers filled the turning lanes as they passed through the industrial area of the city. Horns sounded off as other drivers weaved through the traffic on their commute to work, and warehouse workers could be seen loading and unloading merchandise from trucks backed into docks. The morning sun peeked through the tops of the large pine trees as the bus turned into a large subdivision. There was a lake blanketed by the early morning fog with silhouettes of fishing poles off in the distance. Children were walking on the sidewalks headed to another year of academic torment carrying large backpacks full of books. They came to a stop at a red light just before the school, and Ryan noticed a gang of boys crowding outside of a closed building. The boys stood around taking puffs of weed and showing off their stolen weapons to each other, sometimes flashing them to people passing by.

The light turned green, and the bus began to roll on. The front of the school was hidden by school busses unloading students. By the road was the school's old rusted and forgotten sign, some of the letters from the name missing. The fiberglass cover was impossible to see through, and the school had placed a small sign near the old sign that read, *Welcome back Myser Bell High Students.* As a prank, someone had crossed out some of the letters and added a few to make the sign read *MisraBell*.

Ryan removed his headphones and gathered his things as the bus bounced over a few speed bumps. They came to a stop in front of the school's old mural, a blue and black horse with blood-red eyes posing with a vicious mug. Years of weathering had damaged the mural with watermarks, but it still managed to appear ferocious. Above the horse in big, bold letters read, *Home of the Thoroughbreds.*

"The Thoroughbreds," Ryan whispered to himself.

The sliding door opened, and the students began to file out. Ryan stared into the eyes of the horse as he passed by the mural. The vicious horse looked more like a beaten mule up close with chipped and fading paint. The students walked through the school's main entrance and were directed to follow signs leading to the school's cafeteria.

The entrails of the school were more desirable than the outside as the building had gone through renovations over the summer. The walls were freshly painted white with blue trim on the doors, and the freshly buffed floor tiles glistened in a blue and white checkerboard pattern. The main office was full of parents who were being redirected to the counselors' office to get their kids registered for school. Down the hall was the school resource officer's office, a small office with a desk and a window with a small view of the hallway. The SRO, a middle-aged, heavy-set Black man, stood in the doorway mugging at the students as they passed by. He stared at the boys with daggers in his eyes, daring any of them to look back, and he cocked his head to the side with a grin as he looked the girls up and down with lusty eyes. As Ryan passed by, the SRO quickly stepped in front of him, puffing his chest up and staring him down. Ryan looked up at the man, his eyes slightly squinted and calm.

"You," the SRO said with disgust. "What is your name?"

Quick on his toes, Ryan deployed his sarcasm to handle the developing situation.

"R-Richard," he lied.

"Your last name, boy!" the officer raised his voice.

"Sanders," he replied calmly.

The two locked eyes, and other students stopped their walk and began to watch while a few other students pulled out their cell phones to record the altercation. The officer tilted his head back and frowned with a large wrinkle over his brow.

"You gonna give me problems?" the officer bucked.

Ryan slowly raised his brow, still holding back his anger from this morning's altercation.

"You stopped me. I don't know what your problem is, sir," Ryan sarcastically stated.

The officer raised his brow as some of the other students created a stir at the new kid's bold statement. The officer looked around and noticed he had a crowd forming around him and suddenly he remembered the lecture he'd received the last time he'd instigated an altercation with a student. Ryan heard the snickering of the others around them giving him the confidence to stand his ground against his new foe. Refusing to be intimidated by Ryan's emotionless face, he crossed his arms and stepped toward Ryan in a desperate attempt to showcase his dominance.

"I better not have any trouble out of you this year," the officer grunted.

"Well, that depends, Officer. Are you going to watch and wait for me to do something, or are you going to go across the street and harass the obvious gang hanging out in front of that building?" Ryan grinned.

The crowd of students stirred louder with oohs and laughter at the officer's failure to intimidate. The officer's face scrunched up, and he made a hard turn back into his office, closing the door behind him. Ryan watched as he plopped into his seat and stared at him from the small office window. The officer put two fingers up to his eyes and pointed at Ryan, causing him to counter with a sarcastic grin. Some of the students began to crowd the officer's window, laughing at him and running away as he pointed at familiar faces. Ryan hurried off, following the signs to the school's cafeteria.

Inside the cafeteria were students eating breakfast and a check-in table for new students and repeating freshmen. The line for the new students had about five people standing and looking around at the cafeteria's upgraded interior, and the line for the repeating freshmen was long and full of students either trying to hide their shame or shouting out to all of their friends they noticed for attention. Two women were sitting at the table with papers manually going through all names of the students. They were frustrated by the morning rush, their coffee cups empty and stained with lipstick. They were efficient in moving the lines along, shushing the rambunctious students in line showing off.

"Good morning, last name?" the woman said.

"Scales," Ryan replied.

The woman went down the list to find his name and put a checkmark next to it. She gave a hard look at the last name and made a face, tapping her pen on the table.

"Scales...Scales...why does that sound so familiar?" she said to herself.

"No idea. I just moved out here." Ryan raised his brow.

"From where?" she inquired with a smile.

"Decatur," he answered.

"Decatur…Decatur…" The woman thought.

She gathered his paperwork detailing his class schedule and a map of the school. As she handed the papers to him, she caught a better glimpse of his face.

"Are you kin to Hank Scales?" She grinned.

"Yes. He's my granddad," Ryan replied.

The woman's eyes widened, and she rose and ran around the table to steal a hug, catching Ryan off guard. He nervously accepted the woman's hug, looking to the others in line for help.

"Oh, my goodness! You were the grandson he was raving about all those years ago!" she exclaimed.

"Yup, that's me, or possibly CJ," Ryan said, irked by the woman's excitement.

"I know you don't remember me, but Hank—we called him 'The Hankster' back then—he brought you by the office once when you were about knee-high, and we just fell in love with you," the woman went on.

Ryan played coy, keeping a slight grin on his face and hoping the woman would quickly end the conversation. He had already made one scene with the SRO, and now this woman was drawing more attention to him. The other students in line began to quietly mimic the woman's excitement.

"I tell you, that Hank was a handsome man." She grinned. "And he has a very handsome grandson. Tell me, how is that handsome man doing these days?"

The woman gave him an out, and he quickly thought of what to say to end the conversation with the certainty that no other question would be asked.

"I'm not too sure. After his retirement party, he left us all and moved up to Detroit and got remarried, so I don't see him much," he bluntly replied.

The woman gave Ryan a look of dismay, and he smiled in the back of his head. He waved the papers to the woman and turned away.

"I'll tell him you said hi if I talk to him."

He continued on his journey through the school's hallways, now trying to find his homeroom class. One side of the hall was blanketed with lockers while the other side read in bold, blood-red letters, *GO THOROUGHBREDS!!!* He passed by a few classroom doors and saw some students were already sitting, waiting for the day to begin. He recapped the incident with the SRO thinking of what he was going to do the next time he saw him knowing they would cross paths again. The thought sparked his creativity and gave him an idea for later.

The map led Ryan to the third floor of the school. This area of the school was not finished, with renovations expected to be completed by the end of December. He stepped into the classroom, where a few students had already found their seats. Sitting in the back-right corner of the room was Mr. Johnson, staring at his computer screen. He was a middle-aged White man, balding with red spots on his face from where he'd cut himself shaving his beard. He peeked over his screen and looked at Ryan.

"Morning," he said dully. "What's your name?"

Mr. Johnson picked up the roll call sheet and a pen.

"Ryan Scales," he replied.

He went down the list and found his name and put a checkmark next to it.

"Scales, Scales, Ryan X. Scales. Hmm." Mr. Johnson made a face. "You a Muslim or something?"

The ongoing joke with his name had followed him to his new school. Ryan simply shook his head and ignored the question.

"Nah, I'm just a guy," he replied.

"Oh, well, just take a seat over there"–Mr. Johnson pointed–"and keep it quiet. I'm trying to sort through this paperwork. I've got to find a damn good lawyer."

As he looked back at his laptop, the stress in his eyes was evident. Ryan turned and took a seat by the window that was clouded with dirt and dust from the renovations outside. He reached into his book bag and pulled out one of his sketch pads and a pencil and began to draw an image he'd thought about earlier. A few more minutes passed, and the bell rang, initiating the school day. A beeping noise came from the intercom followed by a woman's voice with subtle excitement.

"Good morning faculty, staff, and students! This is your principal, Mrs. Kirkpatrick, welcoming you to a brand-new school year here at Myser Bell High School!" she said.

"Yeah, another year of hell babysitting," Mr. Johnson said to himself.

"Let's start this year off as we always do with the Pledge of Allegiance!"

CHAPTER 4

TRY AGAIN

AN UNSETTLING NERVOUSNESS seized an unmasked Face as he slowly approached the prison gates. Every step toward the solid building brought back horrid memories of his experiences in juvenile hall. He looked over to the prison yard and remembered the countless battles that had occurred in and out of the cells when sudden flashbacks of a specific fight from his past entered his mind. He could see the sharp edge of the field toothbrush being aimed at his eyes. He could smell the odor of his cellmate as he tried to pin him down. He could feel the scrutiny of racism he'd encountered from the officers as they pulled them apart. He tasted the blood in his mouth from the blows to his jaw. He took a few deep breaths to keep himself calm, hoping not to alert the prison guards. The line reached a stopping point, and a prison officer stood before them and pointed toward a large sign posted on the wall.

"Ladies and gentlemen, please move over to your right. Please empty your pockets and remove all personal items such as jewelry, belts, hats, shoes, jackets, shades, anything made of metal. Put them in the tray and pass them along to Officer Sammons to be scanned. You will then walk toward me through the body scanner. If you beep, walk back through the gate and try again. If you have any of the prohibited items, mainly the ones that are posted on the sign, they will be confiscated, and you may be placed under arrest. Understood?"

No one spoke. The officer sighed.

"Alrighty, then, let's get this process started."

Face removed his jewelry, jacket, and belt and placed them in the tray and attempted to walk through the body scanner. The officer stopped him before he took a step forward.

"Seriously, guy?" the officer grunted. "We literally just went over this, no shades!"

Face looked over at the sign and looked back at the officer.

"We're waiting on you, sir! You wanna see your people or not?"

Face took a deep breath and lowered his head. He grabbed his shades with both hands and slowly pulled them off, feeling the stings from the filed toothbrush slashing deep into his ruined face. The room was struck with silence as the officers and visitors stared. Face placed his shades in the item tray and walked clear through the body scanner without a beep. He looked the screening officer directly in his eyes, who nervously looked away in shame.

"Uh, you can wear your shades if you want. I'll uh, I'll let you through," the officer offered.

Face stood motionless and stared at the officer in an attempt to force him to make eye contact, but the officer lowered his head, looking no higher than Face's chest.

"No, I won't do that because that's against the rules," Face replied with piercing eyes.

Face gave the other visitors a cold stare as he rejoined the line. The officer shook his head and collected himself from his embarrassment as he looked over to the other officer, who threw his hands up and shook his head. He walked to the front of the line and counted everyone off, catching the eye of Face.

"Everyone follow me. This way please, single file," the officer said.

The line made its way down a hall leading to the visiting area. The officer could feel Face's eyes burning through his skin with each step they took. They arrived at the visiting room that was stocked with several guards and one standing outside the door. They ushered in the visitors and guided them to their booths. The leading guard stepped over to the guard at the door after Face passed by and nodded his head at him.

"Keep an eye on the last one," he whispered.

The gate officer observed Face's walk, witnessing nothing more than a slight limp as he approached his booth. He signaled to the other guards in the room, advising them to watch him closely. Face grinned as he took his seat, sensing the trouble he was causing, but his amusement was short-lived as his anxiety crept upon him. He stared at his blank expression looking back at him in the booth's glass window. The scars around his eyes brought back memories of his older brother De'Angelo trying to console him, telling him everything was going to be alright. He heard the voices of the guards in his cell shouting at him when they finally came to break up the fight as everything turned red. He remembered his pitiful screams as his face was slashed repetitively and began to shudder. He closed his eyes and lowered his head, desperate for the voices to stop when suddenly there were three taps on the glass that made him jump. De'Angelo smirked at him as he took his seat and picked up the phone. Face sighed and picked up his phone, nervously tapping his foot.

"Still messes with you every time, you good?" De'Angelo asked.

"You know I hate coming to this place," Face replied nervously.

The guards witnessed Face's strange behavior and signaled around to continue watching him.

"So did he recognize you?" De'Angelo smirked.

The leading guard stood by the doorway, anxiously waiting for Face to do something wrong. Face looked up at De'Angelo with a grin, feeling the energy of the guard's eyes burning down his back.

"He made me take my shades off when I came in, and I made him look at me, so he definitely knows it's me." Face laughed. "How've you been?"

"Ah, you know, it's prison. People fightin' and stabbin', actin' hard, racist prison guards, everything you see on TV. What's good, tho'? What the streets lookin' like? You holdin' it down for me, right?" De'Angelo played.

Face looked around the room and spotted the guards quickly turning their heads away from him. He took a deep breath and leaned back in his seat and smiled.

"A very good friend of mine made me an offer as district manager." Face grinned.

De'Angelo eased back in his seat and raised his brow. His eyes widened, and he grinned back at Face, nodding his head.

"Oh snap, so you're getting a promotion?" De'Angelo replied.

"Yeah, looks that way. I even met the other district manager he was telling me about," Face said.

"You talkin' 'bout the old dude from out of town?" De'Angelo questioned.

"Yeah, that guy! Real cool guy. We all met up a little while ago, and they are helping me get set up with the board of directors," Face said.

They knew the guards were listening in on their conversation in hopes of finding something to charge them both with, but they contained their excitement and focused on the conversation as they eyeballed the guards on both sides of the glass.

"What about that one guy from down south? They say anything about him?" De'Angelo asked.

Face lowered his head and looked at the bottom of the glass.

"They brought him up on embezzlement and corruption charges, so he's getting fired, and I'm taking his position," Face said.

De'Angelo sat back in his seat and brought his fist to his mouth. He and Face stared at each other for a brief moment as they both processed the new developments.

"You think you're ready for a job like that? Takes a lot of work," De'Angelo said.

"It seems like a lot, but they're helping me," Face replied.

One guard began to pace around the booths trying to clue in on their conversation, but De'Angelo and Face kept their eyes sharp.

"Gotcha. So, when are y'all making these changes?" De'Angelo asked.

"Soon, real soon. Hopefully soon enough for me to work on getting you out here once I get started," Face said.

De'Angelo grinned and looked at the bottom of the glass.

"You don't have to worry about that, bruh," he said.

"What'chu mean by that?" Face raised his brow.

De'Angelo looked off into space, and his grin disappeared. Face sensed a change in his brother's energy watching De'Angelo's eyes find their way back to the bottom of the glass. De'Angelo looked up into his baby brother's eyes, taking the conversation to a new low.

"They aren't letting me out of here alive, bruh," De'Angelo said.

Face remained quiet and stared at his brother, struggling to keep it together. His anxiety began to rise, knowing this conversation would not end happily.

"He's not going to stop coming for me even though I'm in here, we already knew that. I've had plenty of people in here watching me, and I know it's gonna happen soon. It's over for me, man, it's all about you," De'Angelo said.

Face looked around the booth, struggling to keep a straight face as his eyes began to well up with tears. De'Angelo lowered his head in sorrow wishing there was something he could say to ease his brother's pain.

"When I think back to that day...I just remember you telling me how we didn't need to be out there. I should have listened to you. We should've sat our asses down somewhere," De'Angelo said.

There was a moment of silence between the two. Neither of them would look at each other as a means of keeping the compounding emotions down. The onlooking officers became more curious of their change in behavior and paid closer attention to them.

"I'm sorry I brought you into this, lil bruh." De'Angelo wiped his eyes. "But you know, you'll be great in your new position. You got people skills, and you know your work. I ain't wit' all dat. You gon' do just fine, I know it."

De'Angelo grinned as he looked at Face, who was crushed by his brother's statements. A tear escaped from his eye and was quickly wiped away before anyone else saw.

"Look, man, I know how much you hate coming to this place"–De'Angelo stared at his brother–"so don't come back."

The two looked at each other and scrunched up their faces to fight back their tears, which were anxiously trying to flow over. Feelings of isolation surrounded Face as he once again found himself thinking back to the conversation that he and his big brother had had many years ago in the living room of their house. De'Angelo had placed his hand on his shoulder and looked him in the eyes and told him it was gonna be alright, but it seemed his brother's words had proven to be false. With the thick glass pane between them, De'Angelo and Face stared at each other.

"I love you, bruh."

"I love you, too. It's gonna be alright."

The two brothers continued to talk, their hearts breaking as they reminisced on their days running the streets together as young teenagers, stressing out their mother, and smiling through their pain. Face had left home without his usual mask, but he hid his sorrow from his brother with a smile.

Clear skies over the prison's courtyard revealed a beautiful sight flying through the sky. A golden falcon soared high on the horizon, gleaming brightly like the early morning sun. The tower guards were struck with awe as they witnessed the beauty of the falcon flying over the prison. Flocks of birds went into a frenzy as they dashed to clear a path for the falcon, fearful of becoming its prey. The immaculate falcon flew over the hills and valleys of the state, displaying its divine beauty to those who were fortunate to catch a glimpse of it before it disappeared.

The falcon spread its large wings and began to descend from the sky, circling a building on the southside of Atlanta. As the falcon neared the building, onlookers stopped and pointed to the sky, starstruck by the rare sight. The falcon circled the building one last time and found a place it believed would be safe to land. Sitting by the window in his history class, Ryan carefully sketched a drawing from an idea he'd had for a while as he listened to another bitter lecture by Mr. Johnson. He looked carefully over the page, focusing on the curvature of the line he'd drawn. Suddenly, the room was shaken by the sound of the falcon shrieking as it prepared to land on the ledge of the window. Ryan jumped in his seat as the bird appeared to be coming straight for him. The falcon perched itself in the window and appeared to lock its eyes on Ryan, moving its head around to get a better view.

"What the hell was that?" Mr. Johnson walked toward the window.

Ryan looked at the falcon and instantly became mesmerized by its golden feathers glowing in the sunlight. As Mr. Johnson approached the window, the falcon puffed its chest and spread its wings, releasing another loud shriek. Desperate to get the falcon to fly away, Mr. Johnson tapped on the glass to try and intimidate it.

"Go away! Damn bird scared the hell out of me."

The effortless taps didn't make the falcon leave, but instead the falcon lowered his wings and quietly sat on the ledge with its eyes locked on Ryan. Realizing who the bird was looking at, Mr. Johnson turned his attention toward the young artist.

"Well, it seems to like you, Michelangelo, but it looks like it made you ruin your drawing. I guess that means you can pay attention to me for a change. It's all my ex-wife had to do," Mr. Johnson scoffed.

Ryan looked at his drawing and realized that his jump had caused him to cross right through his sketch. Rather than be upset about his drawing, he found himself more irritated by Mr. Johnson's slick remark, watching him as he walked back to his desk.

"Crazy bird. Anyway, back to what I was saying. So, in 2012, some guy thought that the Mayan calendar predicted the end of the world. It was crazy, like the idea of marriage. Even had it down to the world ending at 6 p.m. People were selling their homes, giving up all of their possessions, doing all kinds of dumb stuff. What I didn't understand is how is it that a 'new age' society of people allowed an ancient tribe, beings that had been dead for hundreds and hundreds of years, to suddenly bring relevance to their calendar. All these Bible thumpers were suddenly struck with grief because the Mayan calendar said the world was going to end, but just before that, literally no one cared about the Mayan calendar," Mr. Johnson explained.

Ryan directed his attention to the falcon, inspired by its arresting beauty. The falcon tilted its head, quietly staring back at him.

"Scales!" Mr. Johnson called out.

Ryan snapped his neck toward the irritated Mr. Johnson, who decided to present a challenge.

"Seeing as your newfound feathery friend has you distracted today along with your constant drawing, why don't you summarize your thoughts as to why the Mayan calendar was so important to American culture?" Mr. Johnson curled his lips.

Ryan looked around the class and noticed everyone was staring at him. Some students began to snicker, thinking he was embarrassed by being called out.

"We don't have all day, Ryan." Mr. Johnson tapped his foot.

Ryan raised his brow and locked eyes with his teacher. The falcon spread its wings and puffed up its chest.

"Given the geographical location of the Mayans and the half telling of their story that we learned today, I've concluded that the

Mayans, much like any tribes in the area at the time, didn't suddenly disappear but were wiped out by your great uncle Christopher Columbus and his goons. As they raped and pillaged through Central America, at some point they must have come upon someone making a calendar and killed them. Then, hundreds of years later, some would-be archeologist searching for something to steal to put in a foreign museum found it and lost his mind because he didn't understand it, which led to propaganda and the manipulation of the simple American mind," Ryan stated.

There was a moment of heat between the two as Mr. Johnson frowned at Ryan's sarcastic grin. The other students laughed at Ryan's slick jab at Mr. Johnson.

"Columbus was not my uncle, but I'm sure he was related to my ex-wife," Mr. Johnson replied.

The bell rang, and the students began to close their books and head to the door.

"All right, students, tomorrow we will start off on Chapter 6 with the Aztec empire," he rushed. "Scales, I need to talk to you for a minute!"

Ryan scoffed as the other students filed out of the classroom, laughing at him. As he gathered his things, the falcon in the window flew out of view, leaving one of its golden feathers behind. The final student exited the classroom, and Mr. Johnson took a seat at his desk and pulled out the papers from last week's essay. Ryan approached Mr. Johnson's desk and spotted a paper with 'Child Support Attorney' circled in red.

"All right, I've gotta call this damn attorney by 2:15, so I'm just going to be frank with you," Mr. Johnson said. "I've had some pretty slick students in here before, but I'm not a fool, not by a long shot. Absolutely nothing gets by me. In fact, the only person who has ever gotten by me is my ex, that bitch. Anyway, look at this."

Mr. Johnson pulled out Ryan's essay from the stack of papers and laid it on his desk. Ryan looked at his unmarked essay and noticed it hadn't been graded like the others.

"Now, if you are honest with me about it, I'll only count it as one zero instead of my policy of three. And I'm only doing that because other than your constant drawing, you don't disrupt my classroom."

"You think I cheated?" Ryan said.

"No, I don't think you cheated, I know you did," Mr. Johnson attacked.

Ryan looked at Mr. Johnson, confused by his accusation, and immediately went on the defensive to save his grade.

"How could I have possibly cheated on an in-class essay?" Ryan asked.

"Look, my patience is running thin with all the stuff I have going on. Just tell me the truth, and it'll only count as one zero," Mr. Johnson demanded.

"But I didn't cheat!" Ryan defended.

Mr. Johnson leaned back in his seat, stricken with laughter at Ryan's poor defense.

"Wow, you kids these days. Try to give you a way out, and you lie straight to my face."

Ryan took a deep breath, feeling his anger rising at the sound of Mr. Johnson's voice.

"Look, I said I didn't cheat, and if you think I did, prove it," Ryan demanded.

"You want me to prove it? Fine, no problem," Mr. Johnson chuckled. "Look at this and tell me what you see."

"No, you look at it and show me where I cheated since you're accusing me," Ryan asserted.

"All right, fine." Mr. Johnson pointed at the paper. "Look at the detail of the work. Look at how every paragraph has an established subject, gives more evidence than what the book offers, makes each point, and doesn't vary from the topic! There is no possible way that you could have written this. I don't believe it."

Ryan took a step back and pointed at his desk.

"I sat at that desk by the window and wrote this in front of you last week!" Ryan grunted.

"You may have written it, but the information had to have come from somewhere else, Ryan, and you know it! You and I both know the majority of the information in this paper isn't in this book!" Mr. Johnson crossed his arms.

Ryan flailed his arms in the air, and his neck began to stiffen. His eyes cut through Mr. Johnson as he looked at him, ready to attack.

"I know the information came from somewhere else because I studied for this assignment at home! If you read the paper, you'd know that all of the historical information I wrote about is true," Ryan proclaimed.

"And why should I believe that, huh?" Mr. Johnson asked. "I already know what the truth is. The truth is you come in here every day and you're quiet. I never hear as much as a peep from you because you're always drawing during my lectures. You're so quiet and detached from the rest of the class that you don't participate in any of the class discussions. Basically, this is an art class for you!"

Ryan closed his eyes and took a deep breath. His balled fists shook at his sides, ready to unleash the impending doom circulating within. He exhaled and opened his eyes, taking his time to breathe before looking at Mr. Johnson.

"I'll tell you what I do know," he said calmly. "Your lectures come from a place of trauma and bitterness toward your ex-wife because she seems to always come up in the class discussions, and despite the fact that you appear to hate her so much, you still married her all those years ago. The real truth in this situation is that you hate your job because this school district is one of the most underpaid in the metro area, which presents another problem for you because you know child support is fast approaching on the horizon. The other truth is that because this is one of the most underpaid districts, you don't expect much from your students, especially the seniors because after we graduate it's only a matter of time before we become statistics, and you've gotten used to that. So, go ahead, give me the three zeros—in fact, make it six if it makes you feel better!"

Ryan turned and walked toward the door, leaving Mr. Johnson speechless. Just as he was about to cut the corner, he stopped and looked back at Mr. Johnson with daggers in his eyes.

"Just know that taking your anger out on me isn't going to bring your wife back, but it will make things a lot harder for you in the classroom," he threatened.

Mr. Johnson sat in silence, defeated by Ryan's defense. He sighed as he leaned forward, placing his head into his palm.

"Dammit," he whispered.

He reluctantly reached for his red ink pen and angrily wrote the number 100 on Ryan's paper. He could hear his soon to be ex-wife's voice in his head taunting him as he began updating the grade book.

Ryan furiously walked through the hallways, turning the heads of the other students as he made his way to his final class. He mumbled to himself, cursing his teacher and hoping that no one else would take a chance at his rage that day. He kicked through the double doors leading to the music and arts building, sending a loud booming noise through the breezeway.

The soaring falcon overhead silently found a spot to land while it continued to observe Ryan's every step. The near vacant breezeway was also occupied by one other girl walking toward the music and arts building. She struggled to walk as she carried her full backpack and toted her hard-shell saxophone case. Quickly observing her struggle, the innate teachings of his uncle forced him to quickly calm down before he frightened her more than he believed the doors may have. He slowed his pace and hollered out to her to keep his distance.

"Hey, you need some help?" he asked.

The girl glanced over her shoulder but kept moving forward, dragging a part of the heavy case on the ground.

"Oh no. I got it. Thanks," she replied.

The girl trekked on, leaving Ryan dumbfounded as her struggle continued. The falcon shrieked loudly from the roof, spreading its wings and puffing its chest. Ryan looked up at it for a moment and was again drawn to its golden glow in the sun. He shook his head and saw that the girl had stopped to give her arm a chance to rest. He ran up to her and made an attempt at being social.

"Hey, I can carry this for you. It's no problem." He grabbed the case's handle. "I'm Ryan, by the way."

The girl looked up at him and shyly smiled as she massaged her wrist. She was a little short with long, natural red hair that reached the middle of her back. Her yellow skin complemented her hair along with her beautiful deep dark brown eyes. The tension in his forehead eased, and he began to settle back to his normal self, stricken by her beauty.

"Thank you, and I'm Kristine." She grinned.

Ryan felt the weight of the case as he picked it up and looked at Kristine in shock.

"You carry this to class every day? The hell's this thing made of?" he asked.

"Oh, it's my dad's old saxophone case," she giggled. "My old one broke at the hinges, so I'm using it until he gets me a new one."

"The sax... Oh, you're headed to the band room. I'm headed to the art room. I can walk you there," he offered.

She brushed her hair behind her ear, and a big grin appeared on her face. She turned her head and glanced at Ryan, trying not to blush.

"Well, aren't you kind?" she replied.

Playing coy to her obvious attraction, he kept a relaxed humor as he engaged.

"I mean, I'm just a guy," he replied.

They began to walk toward the building, and he rushed ahead of her and grabbed the door. Astonished by his chivalry, she brought a hand to her chin and looked at him sideways.

"Where are you from? Because you're definitely not from here," she asked.

"I'm from Decatur." His slick Southern accent emerged.

"Where it's greater?" She grinned.

She looked into his brown eyes as she walked into the building and covered the lower half of her face to hide her now red cheeks. He watched her as she entered, admiring the length and beauty of her hair. Kristine made minimal eye contact, fearing that he would make her cheeks turn red again. Caught up with carrying on the conversation, Ryan barely noticed his hand getting tired.

"...and sorry if I scared you earlier with the doors. One of my teachers kind of pissed me off," he apologized.

"That was you? I figured somebody was just late for class," she said.

They reached the band room, and Ryan returned her saxophone case. They nervously stood outside the door trying to figure out how to break away from each other. Kristine twisted her hair around her finger, and he looked at his watch as they awkwardly tried to resist looking at each other.

"Well, thank you for carrying this heavy thing. I appreciate your kindness." She grinned.

"Oh, nah, it's nothing, just being a gentleman, you know," he said. "Well, uh, I'm gonna go to art and try to...paint out my frustrations."

Why did I say that? He thought as he closed his eyes and shook his head. He knew he had lost her by the sound of her giggles.

"Maybe you can tell me about what upset you while you walk me to my bus." She blushed.

He opened his eyes and looked into hers. They smiled at each other, causing his dimple to show.

"Yeah. Yeah, I'll do that," he replied.

Kristine snatched up her heavy case and turned toward the room with her head down.

"You're going to have me walking in here blushing. I can't look at you." She grinned. "I'll see you after class."

She escaped his charm, quickly entering the classroom, leaving him in a slight daze until the warning bell rang a few seconds later. He snapped out of his hypnosis and darted to the art room with a newfound inspiration to paint.

Outside, the falcon was still perched up on the rooftop. It turned its head, taking note of its surroundings and then looked up at the sun. It spread its magnificent wings, and its feathers glistened in the sunlight.

Hours passed, and the hot sun scorched over a remote area along the Nile River. The land flourished with vegetation, hiding the many species of animals, an area that had been uninhabited by humans for ages. A lone lioness that had separated from its pride walked through the thick of the jungle in search of water. She had been walking for hours in the hot sun, panting loudly as her paws left their prints in the dirt.

She found her way to the river guided by a gentle breeze that cooled the air. The gentle lioness eased her way to the side of the river, looking around to ensure that she could safely lower her head to drink. With nothing but birds in sight, the lioness began to get her fill of the water. She raised her head to give herself a moment to let the water flow through her system, looking around again to reassure her safety. She looked back at the water and was frightened by the green eyes staring back at her. Her attempt at escaping was futile as Lamia quickly reached out from the water and dug her claws into the lioness's front legs. From the waters came her giant snake body that quickly wrapped around the lioness, squeezing out the last seconds of its life as she bit into its neck. Muffled cries for help were silenced as Lamia ensured that the lioness was no more. She grabbed it by its tail and dragged its lifeless body back into the wooded jungle.

Hidden deep within the jungle of twisted trees was a lost kingdom overtaken by the elements. Ancient stone carvings and hieroglyphics marked the entrance to the dark palace, telling the forgotten stories of the past. The surface of the kingdom had been destroyed over time, the stones resembling a tenement wrapped in vines. Lamia slithered her way inside with the dead lioness, her eyes glowing in the darkness. She made her way down a stairway lit by torches revealing dried blood stains and nail marks along the walls.

She entered a large room filled with riches undiscovered by mankind and piles of gold coins about the floor. She found her brothers in their natural forms wearing black and gold robes with arm bracers. She joined them, transforming into her natural state, revealing the likeness between their tanned honey brown skin tone. Mabaya's eyes shone a bright gray while Wivu's eyes changed with his mood. Their hair was thick with curls that coiled like a snake. As Lamia regressed to her natural form, the snakes of her hair coiled into long curls that puffed beyond her shoulders. Her eyes changed to a mystic green that revealed her truly wicked nature. Her tail molded into her body, and from it, her legs and feet formed. She was dressed in a sheer cloth robe with golden armlets about her right and left bicep with two small snakes coiled around her wrist. Keeping her precious elements covered was her favorite Burmese albino python.

She dragged the dead lioness in front of her brothers and dropped it to the floor. They looked at her angrily, disappointed with the meal she'd set at their feet.

"The hind legs are mine, you two can fight over the rest," she said.

"Why did you drag it through the dirt, you fool?" Wivu charged.

"Because I killed it and carried it on my own!" she hissed.

The two walked up to each other, hissing and growling, engaging in a faceoff. The battle was quickly interrupted by Mabaya pushing them apart, knocking Lamia down.

"Now's not the time for your buffoonery," he roared. "We have more pressing matters at hand."

Lamia rose to her feet and crossed her arms, flashing Wivu a death stare. He looked back and smirked at her embarrassment. Mabaya turned and crossed his arms behind his back, looking into a dark pool of water.

"It appears that our cousins have surpassed the ages of the longest living elders," Mabaya said, "but according to my research, they should have died some time ago."

"They'd be dead already if Lamia would stop getting caught every time she tries to devour a soul," Wivu snapped.

"They'd be dead if I didn't have to save you every time they start to pick you apart," she hissed.

"Quiet!" Mabaya roared. "Are you even listening to what I'm saying, Lamia?"

She looked at Mabaya, then began to walk toward a luxurious chair she often lay across.

"So what if they haven't died? They can't even escape," she said.

The snake around her waist slithered up to her chest and made its way around to her arm and then her hand. She kissed it lovingly and looked over at Mabaya, who stared at her angrily.

"When was the last time you really took a look at them, sister? Have you ever once wondered why they've always been so strong in battle?" Mabaya asked.

Lamia propped up her feet and rested the tail of her snake on her torso. Wivu ignored them as he grabbed the deceased lioness and cut her open with a large knife.

"They're gods," she said. "All of the gods we faced were strong. These two are just incredibly hard to kill."

"You are not understanding. With age comes some form of weakness, whether it be in speed or strength. They have not changed at all from the time we began attacking them," Mabaya said.

"You're losing yourself." Wivu hacked into the lion's flesh. "We've had them beneath us too long for it to matter anyway."

Wivu stretched the lioness open and pulled its guts out onto the floor. He licked its blood from his fingers and continued cutting.

"No, Wivu, it does matter. It makes no sense why they haven't died! The ancient gods only lived around three and a half millennia, and they lived even longer before they fell upon Earth. Heru and Anpu were born well after life on this planet was tamed. They should have died by now. They may be full-blooded gods, but they aren't immortal," Mabaya stated.

He crossed his arms behind his back and began to pace back and forth while Lamia laughed at his quarrel, stretching her long body.

"Goodness, Mabaya, you sound like a troubled mortal," she giggled.

"We are the ones in trouble, Lamia," Mabaya insisted. "They aren't aging. They've lived longer than us, but we look older than them! They aren't cracking, and I don't understand it!"

Wivu laughed as he ripped away parts of the lioness, separating them by preference of meal.

"I think Heru hit you pretty hard last time, brother. They might not be aging, but they're trapped in a place we control. There's no need for you to fear their existence," Wivu declared.

Mabaya's eyes widened as a solution to their problem developed in his mind.

"That might be it," he said.

He motioned with his hands, and a golden aura formed before him. Images of a stone formation appeared with four stone pillars centered on a large square. Mabaya carefully observed it for a moment and suddenly had an epiphany. He swiped his hand across the image, and it disappeared into dust.

"The Gateway Stones, that has to be it," Mabaya said.

Lamia rose from her chair, leaving behind her precious python, and made her way to the dark pool, disrobing as she entered. A steamy mist appeared above the water as she submerged herself in the warm waters.

"What about them?" she asked, sinking into the dark water.

"We moved the stones so that only we could control access between two of the realms, but Duat is timeless, and the properties of its makeup differ from those of the Life Realm," Mabaya stated.

Lamia relaxed her head on top of the calm waters, joined by a large anaconda that emerged from the dark pool.

"What does all that mean?" Lamia asked.

"As long as Heru and Anpu remain in Duat with the gateway locked, they will be virtually immortal," Mabaya said.

"I don't care," Lamia replied. "Let them stay in Duat forever. They can't do anything from there."

In a fit of rage, Mabaya swiped his hand across the pool and sent water flying into the air with Lamia. She crashed onto the hard ground but was quickly swept up by her hissing python as Mabaya fearlessly approached.

"You careless fool, don't you know that you will encounter them once you die?" he yelled.

He balled his fist and turned away from Lamia, pondering what to do about the situation. He had a few incomplete solutions but none that would come without some form of conflict. He grunted with frustration, wishing for a better way.

"We may have to reopen the portal," Mabaya said.

Shocked, Wivu quickly rose to his feet and approached Mabaya, believing his brother was going insane.

"Do you hear yourself, brother? Are you suggesting we reset the Gateway Stones and reopen the portal, giving Heru and Anpu access to the Life Realm, based on your belief that they haven't aged from the time we trapped them in there? I don't know if your mind is functioning properly, but we have yet to kill them over the last few millennia, and if they are freed, it will be hard to find a place where we can't be easily found," Wivu stated.

"Do you have an idea of what to do then, brother?" Mabaya asked.

"Don't be foolish, Mabaya. We possess the upper hand, and we should keep things the way they are until we defeat them. There is more to this than what you are revealing. What is bothering you?"

Mabaya sighed and scrunched his face with anxiety, looking away from Wivu. He crossed his arms and shook his head, afraid to speak his next sentence.

"I fear that death is upon us," Mabaya said.

Wivu stood quietly, shaken by his brother's words. The once fearless Mabaya had been stifled by the belief that their fiendish reign of terror was challenged by the inescapable threat of death.

"We've held them at bay for thousands of years, but I feel as if there is something that they are up to. Something that might help them succeed in defeating us."

Wivu tossed his head back and laughed at his brother's paranoia with a false sense of confidence.

"Goodness, Mabaya, you're scaring yourself. You think if they were really up to something that they'd wait until now to finally take action? We would have encountered this situation eons ago."

Mabaya turned to Wivu with sincerity and looked him in the eyes, causing Wivu's laughter to fade as he witnessed the fear in his brother's eyes.

"You may be right, but what if now is the time? What if now they have what they need to defeat us? Something does not feel right, Wivu. I just don't know what it is," Mabaya said.

"Look, I understand your worries, but I refuse to reopen the portal! We don't know what kind of danger we may be inviting into our lives once they get out. Now I'll help you think of something to do to stop them, but we cannot open up that portal," Wivu said.

Mabaya sighed and released the tension in his shoulders.

"Agreed," he said.

"Good. Remember, brother, we are the living gods of these realms. There are none that will defeat us," Wivu said.

Mabaya shook his head, reassured by the words of his brother. He placed his fears in the shadows at the back of his mind, battling logic with emotions formed from his ego.

"Where's Lamia?" Wivu asked.

They looked around the area for her, but she and her snakes had disappeared without a trace.

"She must have gone out again. I refuse to wait for her to return to eat. Her food is mine," Mabaya said.

The brothers laughed, and Wivu continued dividing the parts of the lion. Back above ground, nightfall cloaked the kingdom, displaying millions of stars and a full moon that glared brightly in the night. A bluish-white hue covered the ruins of the kingdom, creating a silhouette of Lamia, who hid within the vines alone. Her green eyes were filled with tears as she cried to herself, coiled up with her beloved python. She stayed there for hours, wiping her tears away until she fell asleep calmed by the distant sounds of the Nile.

CHAPTER 5

EYES OF A KILLER

L ATE AT NIGHT sneaking under the cover of darkness, a shipment of drugs was being transported by cartels using motorized rafts. They narrowly slid by the watchful eye of the Coast Guard as they made their way to a specific location on the Gulf Coast. They finally arrived at an area where several vans were waiting with men ready to load. The lookout stood near the road hidden behind bushes and gave them the signal to begin the exchange. The men quickly loaded up the vans, and they broke out in different directions with destinations around the country.

A non-stop six-hour drive brought the traffickers to a large private residence far beyond the outskirts of the Atlanta city limits. There was a black gate that surrounded the property along with a call box the drivers used to gain entry. Once inside, they pulled around the long driveway to the backside of the property where a crew of migrant workers was ready to unload the merchandise. Observing the intake from his balcony, the notorious drug lord continued his meeting with his new protégé.

"It took a while to get to this point in life, young man," his deep scratchy voice said.

He relaxed in his lounge chair, lighting his Cuban cigar with a match. He then shook out the flame as he puffed, playing with the smoke sifting through his thick mustache.

"I've seen terrible things and have had to do even worse just to survive," he said with a thick Latin accent. "There comes a point in life where certain things become necessary, and everything you once thought was impossible becomes an option."

He took another puff of his cigar, and his eyes dimmed as the smoke filled his lungs. The exhaled smoke drifted around his shades and above his head, forming horns in his peppered hair.

"Torture was one of my favorite tactics when it came to getting what I wanted."

Flashbacks of his younger years revealed the heinous nature of his past. Vivid images of murder and torture told the story of victims who were caught in the crossfire of his wrath.

"They speak of a code of honor, only to kill a man, but what people don't understand is that man can plant a seed that can grow to come back and get you when you least expect it. You must defy honor and only think of your survival because your future depends on it."

Rising from his seat was an older, portly gentleman that appeared to be nothing like what he used to be.

"Obviously, you understand the risk of this business because you've come this far, eh. What did you say your name was again?"

"Face," he replied.

"Ah yes, Face." He grinned. "I'm assuming because of the paint, of course. Good tactic. No one truly knows what you look like."

"You and I aren't so different, Mr. Diaz. I understand the importance of making sure I have the upper hand over my enemies as well as in any other situation. It's not a matter of trust, it's just business," Face said.

Diaz smiled at Face and laughed an old, sinister laugh. "Fortunately, we are friends in this matter. Come, join me inside."

They entered Diaz's office filled with marvelous decorations from all around the world. On his wall was a mural of him and his family, a painting Face made sure to get a good look at.

"I like you, hijo. You remind me of myself when I was your age, so young and full of ambition," Diaz said.

Diaz took a puff of his cigar and passed another one to Face. Face put the cigar in his mouth and leaned in toward Diaz to light it for him. He inhaled the smoke and curiously looked at the cigar as it was his first time smoking a real Cuban.

"Thank you." He exhaled the smoke.

Diaz turned and walked back to his office chair that looked like a corporate throne. He removed his shades, revealing his tired brown eyes.

"It's a risky business. I have a wife and two children now. I wouldn't do anything to put their lives at risk, but in the back of my mind, I know that someone, one day, just might. By the way, I'm sorry about your brother. It is a shame what has happened to him," Diaz stated.

Face raised his brow, quickly remembering to play coy about De'Angelo. He wanted to attack Diaz, but the time wasn't right. He glanced at the mural of Diaz's family on the wall and took another puff of his cigar. He slowly exhaled the calming smoke as he looked into Diaz's eyes behind his shades.

"My brother was always headstrong, often putting his actions before his thoughts, but with any hope, he'll survive while he's in there," Face replied.

"I certainly hope so. I hear these American prisons are dangerous, full of egos and gang activity," Diaz said. "You can't be like your brother in this business. You won't survive long."

Diaz looked into Face's shades and nodded his head at his reflection. He found himself intrigued by Face's disguise, and a slick grin appeared across his face.

"They say no man should ever question another man's methods," Diaz said, "and I'm sure you've been asked this thousands of times, but I–"

"The paint?" Face interrupted.

"Yes, it's different. Very interesting to me," Diaz complimented him.

"Some of my greatest work." Face grinned. "It started when I was a teenager. Mind if I look around?"

Diaz nodded, and Face began to walk around the room, observing the priceless possessions. He walked over to a table that had a mystical looking sword on a stand. Its sheath was black with a golden dragon head on the ends, and the handle had a dragon carved into it. He ran his finger along the dragon, anxious to see the blade.

"At first it was just a complex from a situation that happened some years ago, but over time it became reality. I used to ask myself what gives the White man the right and privilege to take what they want with no regard for who or what they destroy in the process? What is the 'Divine Right' that the monarchies of Europe built their kingdoms upon? Who told them they were gods?"

Face stopped in front of a mirror, pretending to be awed by his philosophical words and artistic appearance.

"And then one day, I realized that I was a trickle-down victim. Shortly after, I identified myself as a direct victim, and on that day, it all made sense. They take what they want with no regard—it's just as simple as that. So I decided to do the same. As far as the white paint, I wear it so when they see me, they see themselves, the Face of fear."

Diaz leaned back in his chair, thrown by Face's intelligence.

"Ah, I see. Hmm, makes perfect sense. I like the way you think, hijo, very artistic," Diaz said.

"Gracias." Face grinned. "Like I said, some of my best work."

The two killers stood before each other confidently. Diaz, impressed with Face, felt as if his next plan could flow perfectly with De'Angelo out of the way. With his true intentions hidden, Face continued to play along with Diaz's game to secure the next move.

"Your methods are quite impressive, hijo, but let us not get carried away so quickly. I need to lay ground rules," Diaz said.

"I'm listening," Face responded.

Diaz rose from his desk, leaving his cigar in the ashtray. He walked over to the bar and pulled out a crystal decanter filled with his favorite brown liquor and poured two drinks. He approached Face and handed off the glass to him. They both sipped the drink without flinching at the bitter taste.

"A young man of your potential has the ability to go very far without detection in this business. I trust no one, therefore, all deals no matter how big or small will be handled directly with me," Diaz said.

Diaz looked directly into Face's shades and straightened his wrinkled face.

"This means if I'm out of town, or just not here, you're shit out of luck. I have had dealers killed for trying to conduct side deals with my workers."

Diaz walked over to the sword Face admired and picked it up. He unsheathed the blade and playfully swung it around.

"Segundo, do not ever come here unannounced. If you can't reach me by phone, there is a reason. Again, I have had people killed for disobeying my rules. Third, do not come here with anyone without my approval, and make sure you are not being followed. I don't know your friends, I know you."

"I assume you've had people killed for this as well," Face joked.

Diaz grinned and waved the sword at Face. He then sheathed it and placed it back where it belonged.

"You're catching on, hijo. Fourth, you know my district is in the midst of expansion with my night clubs and other things, so make sure you make a contribution by showing up every now and then."

Face finished his drink and handed the crystal glass back to Diaz.

"You finished that pretty quickly. You're supposed to take your time with this," Diaz said.

"I was thirsty," Face said. "I've never really been the kind to savor a drink. I like to get it done and over with."

Diaz looked at Face and raised his brow. "Interesting perspective."

He took the empty glass from Face and walked it over to the bar where he would later hand wash it.

"One final rule, which is the most important rule, and one many can't seem to follow. Don't ever cross me or my family because if you do, I will not stop until I have not only killed you but your family, friends, even so much as your church members. And that, hijo, is no joke. Understood?"

Face felt the intensity in Diaz's voice and thought of his brother. Revenge pulsed through his veins with thoughts of De'Angelo on the other side of the glass. He wanted to take the blade and shove it into Diaz's mouth and watch as the blood gushed from the back of his head, but his better judgment prevailed, reminding him that he was already in the process of laying the foundation for Diaz's assassination.

"You have my word, Mr. Diaz, or else you will have my head," Face replied.

Diaz smiled and extended his hand with a crooked smile. "To new business endeavors," he said.

Face firmly gripped Diaz's hand, overpowering Diaz's grip as he shook.

"To the best business endeavor."

The crushing power in Face's grip shook Diaz to his soul, but he maintained a straight face through the handshake. He turned away as they released and walked back to his desk, nursing his hand as he went. He plopped back into his seat and cleared his throat, wiping away beads of sweat forming on his forehead, and suddenly began to get nervous.

"I—I don't know what it is about you, but I see so much of myself in you. I can only assume that I am slightly overwhelmed."

Face grinned at him, hoping he had broken the old man's hand.

"No need to feel nervous. I consider it an honor. However, I know your time is precious, so if there is nothing more to discuss, I say we move forward with the deal."

They both headed to the garage where Face's utility van was being loaded with supplies. Face shook hands with Diaz again, this time giving mercy with his handshake.

"It's best to take the street route until you get into the next city. The highway patrol is everywhere on this end," Diaz instructed.

"Thanks for the heads up," Face replied.

"Call me when you're ready for more," Diaz said.

"No worries, I got you."

Diaz signaled for his men to escort Face off the property. His nerves seemed to calm the farther away Face got from him. He pulled out a cigar from his jacket, struck a match, and fired up. Despite how nervous Face made him feel, his years of being the villain comforted his pride and calmed him down. He exited the garage and exhaled the smoke from his cigar with a malicious grin forming across his face.

"I warned you not to cross me, De'Angelo. Your brother is mine," he laughed.

Face made his way through the city, closely watching his surroundings and noticing that Diaz's property was a few miles away from the nearest house. There weren't many people that lived in the area, making Diaz's operation easy to monitor. He pulled out his cell phone and called Hong to initiate their next move.

"How'd it go?" Hong inquired.

"The deal is done. I'm headed back to the spot now, so have your and Nassar's guys ready," Face said.

"How did he seem? He say anything about us?"

"He was a little too confident. The bastard even brought up De'Angelo. I wanted to break his face," he grunted. "He didn't bring you guys up. He's crazy, not stupid, but he's not on to me. He probably thinks this is all about drugs."

"Don't be fooled, my friend," Hong warned. "You and I both know he has a hidden agenda. We have to be more careful than we've ever been if we are going to pull this off."

Face made his way toward the highway and pulled into a gas station just before the highway's on-ramp.

"Trust me. I know not to go into this blindly, but we have to move quick. I gotta do something before something happens to my brother in there," Face said.

"I understand. We'll move as quickly as we can, but we have to be cautious. We still have to keep the attention off of us long enough for us to coordinate this move. I will speak to Nassar and have his men and my men meet you at my warehouse at the Industrial Grounds."

Face got out of his vehicle to pump gas, looking around to make sure he hadn't been followed.

"Aight, I got you. I should be there within the next hour."

Face's line beeped, and he saw that Porter was calling him.

"Hey, I got a call coming in. I'll see your boys there." He clicked over. "What's going on?"

"We got a problem," Porter said with urgency.

Nervous, Face clenched his gun and frantically looked around.

"What the hell happened?" Face grunted.

"One of your boys got caught on a delivery a couple days ago, but we're just now finding out."

Face removed the gas pump from his vehicle and shoved it back into its place.

"The hell you mean you're just now finding out? How'd you even let this get by? They are supposed to call you or Simmons if something happens!"

Face angrily started the van and jetted toward the highway, fussing at Porter.

"Look, I'm not sure just yet of all the details. Simmons is getting more information as we speak, but the problem is he's already out," Porter said.

"So we got a snitch on our hands?" Face sighed.

"Potentially. We haven't been able to get our hands on any information thus far, but if he told them anything about Illegit, this could turn into something huge."

Face switched lanes, cutting off a truck as he passed.

"Get out of the damn way then," he shouted at the honking driver. "Sorry, I'm coming back from the deal with Diaz. Who is this guy?"

Porter looked at the computer with Simmons and glanced at the name on the screen.

"Carey Scales. Stays on the southside of Decatur. Doesn't have a long rap sheet. Sound familiar?" Porter asked.

Face let his foot off the gas and began coasting after noticing a state trooper up ahead. He sat back in his seat and relaxed as he passed by, hoping he hadn't drawn attention to himself.

"Nah, most of my guys go by nicknames. I can't say I keep a file on everybody, but I try to keep an eye on them."

"You need to lay low until we can get more information. Where are you going after you make your drop?" Porter asked.

Face looked at his watch. It was 1:15 p.m.

"Meet me at my spot outside of the city and bring me the file so we can figure out what to do about this guy. We gotta make a plan immediately," Face said.

"Gotcha. We'll be in touch."

They ended the call, and Face continued to his drop. He banged his fist on the steering wheel in frustration and threw his hat into the other seat.

"Dammit, I don't need this right now!" he shouted.

The lunch bell rang, and the hallways quickly filled with hungry students. Ryan dipped through the hallways to meet up with his beauty, Kristine. It had been a calm day as he spent most of his time in class working on new sketches, grinning with satisfaction over his brilliant work. His excitement readied him to kiss the soft lips of his new flame before he had his meal. He walked into the cafeteria and looked around for his girl, finding her at a table with a group of her friends and their boyfriends, but rather than laughing and smiling as they normally did, they appeared to be trying to calm her down.

Seeing him on the approach, one of Kristine's friends tapped her shoulder and pointed at Ryan. Kristine turned to him, trying to hold her anger inside as he took a seat beside her at the table. His grin vanished, and his face scrunched with a warrior's concern as he softly rested his hand on her shoulder.

"What's wrong?" he asked.

She looked into his eyes, and a frustrated tear ran down her cheek. She wrapped her arms tightly around him as he and her friends rubbed her back to console her.

"It's okay, girl."

"Your man is here now, tell him what happened."

Adrenaline fused with Ryan's blood, and his senses tingled with the call to action. He struggled to keep his composure for Kristine's sake as he anxiously waited to hear what happened. She lifted her head and dried her eyes on her sleeve, wishing she could have better contained her emotions. She looked away from him, hoping her silence would get him to abandon the conversation.

"Baby, what happened?" he said calmly. He placed his hand softly on her cheek and pushed her face in his direction. "Look at me, baby. What happened?" He carefully wiped another tear away.

Her friends crowded around them to prevent others from witnessing her tears. She looked at her friends and back at Ryan, allowing another tear to roll down her cheek.

"One of these stupid ass boys tried her," one friend said.

Ryan's forehead scrunched up, and his eyes sharpened. He felt the rush of anger pulsating through his muscles. The calm in his voice declined, and anger reshaped his face.

"What did he do?" his gritty voice asked.

She looked into his eyes and saw his fury awaiting an answer and lowered her eyes.

"You have to tell me what happened, Kristine. What did he do?" he asked again.

Her friends continued to rub her back and encouraged her to speak. She took a deep breath to calm down and crossed her arms.

"DeMarcus kissed me," she said.

Ryan's face twitched, and his eyes opened wider, revealing the calm of his villainous rage. There was a tingling in his calves, and his hands began to shake.

"He did what? How?" He exhaled heavily.

Kristine's friends surrounded Ryan as his rage grew, fearing that his rage would get the best of him as Kristine told her story.

"He grabbed me in the hallway after class. I pushed him off of me, but he grabbed me again and forced me in the little space between the lockers on the second floor and kissed me. Then he ran off laughing while I was trying to slap him," Kristine said.

Ryan quickly rose from his seat enraged, frightening everyone at the table. The veins in his neck popped as his brain formed a picture of the scene she'd described. Kristine stood up and grabbed his hands, along with her friends' boyfriends in hopes of keeping him calm.

"C'mon, bro, be cool. You don't wanna draw attention to yourself," one guy said.

Ryan looked at Kristine and noticed a bit of confusion on her face. He regained control of his fury as his calves shook from the adrenaline rush.

"Why were you afraid to tell me?" He raised his brow.

"Because I..."

She looked at him with tears in the wells of her eyes, and her voice cracked. "I didn't think you were going to believe me. No one ever believes me, and I...I love you, and I don't ever want you to think that I'd do something to you like that," she cried.

Touched by her statement, Ryan's shoulders dropped, and he released the tension in his forehead. He exhaled a heavy sigh and embraced Kristine as she wrapped her arms around his neck. They held each other for a moment, and he released her, gently placing his hands on her cheeks and looking deeply into her eyes.

"Why'd you think I wouldn't believe you? I wouldn't have asked to be with you if I wasn't going to believe you. I love you," Ryan said.

Her friends stood along in awe, pressing their hands to their hearts and smiling at their boyfriends.

"You're my girl, and because you're mine, nobody can touch what's mine." His face shifted. "So where is he?"

Ryan's furious gaze immediately returned, and his eyes scoped every face around him as he stepped away from the table. Kristine's friends quickly went after him, hoping to prevent an incident.

"Babe, calm down, please," Kristine pleaded.

"Bruh, he ain't worth your time, at least not here," another guy commented.

"Nobody handles my girl and thinks I'm supposed to be cool about the shit!" Ryan powered forward.

Other students in the cafeteria began to look up from their lunches, watching Ryan charge for the door. Kristine jumped in front of him and placed her hands on his shoulders.

"Baby, please calm down. You haven't eaten yet. Can you please just come eat with me? I just want to have lunch with my man," she begged.

He stopped to look into his girl's eyes and saw her desperation. Suddenly, he could feel the eyes of the other students staring at him. The unwanted attention forced him to calm down, and he played off the situation with a smile, breaking into his infamous laugh.

"Aight, baby. C'mon, let's eat," he chuckled.

They all joined the lunch line, Kristine clenching Ryan's arm like a leash on a vicious dog. Shortly after they joined the line, the bit of attention they'd received dwindled, and things began to go on as if the incident had never happened. Kristine enjoyed her lunch with her man and their friends, engaging in laughter and stories about teachers from other classes and adventures from the night before. The bell rang, signaling the end of lunch and preparation for fifth period, and they all quickly gathered their things and exited the cafeteria.

The group made their way through the hallway, the girls giggling as they held the strong hands of their boyfriends. Suddenly, they all stopped abruptly in the middle of the hallway with Ryan's and Kristine's eyes locked on a specific person. There he was, DeMarcus, standing alone at his locker. Ryan grunted like a bear frightening its prey. Kristine clenched his arm as she and her friends failed to discreetly hold him back, Ryan swiftly marching toward the foolish boy.

"Baby, please. Come on, let's just go to class. We don't have to deal with this today. Please, let's just go," Kristine pleaded.

Ryan stopped, gently pulling his arm away from her, and looked into her eyes.

"Relax, baby. I just want to talk to him," he replied calmly.

Ryan continued his expressionless march with Kristine and her friends close in tow. He slowly approached DeMarcus at his locker, keeping a short distance between them.

"DeMarcus, I need to talk to you," Ryan grunted.

DeMarcus Grant wasn't the biggest of the boys at school, but his cocky demeanor dared anyone to correct him. Standing about 5'8 and around140 pounds, he didn't appear to be much of a threat, but it was that cocky grin that always seemed to spark trouble wherever he went. He turned around and was shocked to see Ryan's emotionless face along with Kristine and her group of friends standing behind him. Refusing to allow his fear to show, he tilted his head to the side and grinned.

"Wassup?" he chuckled.

Keeping his emotions under control, Ryan cleared his throat and placed his hands at his sides. He took a breath and calmly spoke to DeMarcus.

"Kristine tells me that you kissed her. Is that true?" he asked.

DeMarcus looked at Kristine, who along with her friends stared back at him with fury in their eyes. He crossed his arms and grinned as he looked back at Ryan with a pompous expression.

"Yeah, I did. What are you gonna do about it?" DeMarcus brazenly answered.

Time slowed almost to a stop, and sound became a silent whisper in Ryan's ears. He looked at DeMarcus standing confidently with his arms folded and grinning without a care in the world as his eyelids slowly closed on the image. There was a loud banging noise that echoed through Ryan's mind in the darkness. His eyes reopened and revealed his left arm fully extended with his hand tightly gripping DeMarcus' neck. DeMarcus' back was forced against the lockers, and his arms were no longer confidently folded as they held onto Ryan's arm, desperately trying to break free. The cocky smile he'd once worn had transformed into frantic gasps for air.

Unaware of what had happened, Ryan felt something pulling on his right arm. He blinked and turned his head, awed by the sight of his fist tightly balled and ready to strike with several different hands struggling to pull his arm back. Slurred voices echoed in his head, but he was unable to fully make out what they were saying. *Eeh-em-go* was all he could hear in slow motion. He blinked and looked back at his left arm and noticed it had lowered with DeMarcus now on his knees. Another pair of hands grabbed his arm and forcibly removed his grip from DeMarcus' neck, and suddenly he was lifted from his feet. He continued to blink, his eyes going further away from DeMarcus with each blink.

The guys carried Ryan outside to the courtyard and set him down next to a table. He appeared to be in a daze as Kristine placed her hands on his cheeks and looked into his fuzzy eyes. They all circled around him, bickering about what had happened as Kristine began to shake him to get his attention. Her words were muffled as he looked at her with an emotionless gaze. He continued blinking, and her words began to be clearer as he felt her hands gripping his shoulders. He placed his hands on her wrist and blinked again, this time responding to his name.

"Ryan!" she said.

He gripped her wrist a little tighter and began to shake his head. Everything around him became normal.

"Huh? What?"

He looked around in dismay, backing away from Kristine and falling onto the bench seat connected to the table. Kristine's friends simultaneously began to question him about his actions with the concern of what was to come.

"Why did you do that?"

"You didn't have to take it that far!"

"You shouldn't have done that."

"He gon' call his brother."

Confused by their comments, Ryan stopped everyone to try and figure things out.

"Wait, wait, wait. How the hell did we get outside?" he asked.

The group looked at him, dumbfounded by his question.

"What do you mean, how did we get outside?" one of the guys asked.

As the bickering continued, Kristine thought back to a phone conversation they'd had a few weeks before. She placed her hand on his chin and looked into his glossy eyes and quickly realized his question wasn't a joke.

"You really don't remember what happened, do you, baby?" she asked.

"Nah, I don't." He looked into her eyes. "What did I do?"

The group became silent as they looked at their confused friend. Ryan's eyes widened with anxiety as he sat and listened to his friends give vivid details to his blinded actions. The tale of his violent actions gave light to the uncontrollable darkness he believed lived within him.

"...and then we were like, 'Let him go, let him go,' but you had, like, this death grip on his neck, and he was on his knees, and I had to rip your hand off of him. You probably left a few scratches in his neck."

"Yeah, and then we picked you up and carried you outside. That shit was crazy!"

Ryan lowered his head as Kristine sat next to him and rubbed his back.

"I didn't try to hurt any of you, did I?" he asked.

"Nah, you were cool when we tried to grab you, but we were trying to stop you before you even got to him," one of the guys said.

"Were there any teachers around?"

"They'd be on us by now if there were, but forget the teachers, bruh. It's you we're worried about. Of all people, why'd you have to go off on that fool?" another guy asked.

"What's so special about him?" Ryan asked.

The group fell into shock at Ryan's confusion.

"You don't know who that is?"

"Kristine, you ain't been on your job."

"You really ain't from around here."

The group gave Ryan the grim details of his new nemesis with tragic stories of yesteryear uncovering an unsettling fear from the backs of their minds.

"He's got a brother named Paul, but he goes by Punch. He used to go here back when we were freshmen, and he and his friends kinda formed a gang. They used to go around terrorizing people and shit."

"They even used to mess with the teachers."

"I don't know if they actually graduated, but they're too old to be here. Anyway, when DeMarcus started here, they'd show up from time to time beatin' up anybody that he told them was giving him problems."

"They put somebody in the hospital last year. Slammed a huge rock on the guy's head. It was sad."

"Now that this has happened, he might call them on you."

Ryan leaned back on the table and sighed. "You know, this would have been nice to know a lot sooner, like when we were all at the lunch table, but it is what it is," he said.

"Baby, that's my fault," Kristine said. "I'm sorry I didn't say anything about him before. It's just, well he was a non-factor. I didn't think this would ever happen. You guys go ahead and go to class. I'm gonna walk with him. We'll talk later."

The group agreed and dispersed, and Kristine scooted closer to Ryan to hold his hand as they sat. They both looked off at the swaying trees in the distance with birds flying over top.

"This is what you were talking about? The blackouts?" she asked.

"Yeah." He nodded. "They never end well. It's been so long. I was doing so good."

Ryan lowered his head and sighed, contemplating whether he should reveal the mishap to his mother. Kristine wrapped her arms around him and kissed his cheek.

"And you're still doing good. You had every right to do what you did, and I'm not mad at you for defending my honor."

Ryan gently pushed Kristine away and ran his hands to the back of his head.

"It's not about defending your honor, it's...it's much more than that. I can't allow myself to lose it like that. I mean, if all of you weren't there, there's no telling what I would have done."

Ryan rose from the table and took Kristine by the hand.

"Look, I can't keep you out of class because of me. We can talk about this later. I've got some thinking to do," he said.

Kristine nodded her head in agreement and stood up from the bench. As Ryan began to step away, she pulled on his arm, urging him to stop and look at her. She stood before him, her puffy eyes and troubled face bringing a tenderness to the situation. Ryan again released the tension in his shoulders as they embraced, Kristine placing her head on his chest.

"I love you," she sniffled.

"I love you, too," he sighed.

UNDER WATCH

NIGHTFALL REVEALED THE majestic city lights far in the distance as crickets surrounding Face's residence chirped in the cool air. The property was secured by armed guards from the allied districts as Hong and Nassar adjusted to their temporary circumstances. Face nervously tapped his fingers on his office desk as he reviewed the file of Carey Scales with Porter and Simmons. He poured himself a drink and rubbed his forehead, thinking of all that he had at stake.

"So this is all you can get? You can't confirm if he said anything or not?" Face asked.

"We can't get that information from anyone in the department without raising an eyebrow, but by the way the situation looks, I say he has," Porter said.

Simmons looked up from his laptop and removed his glasses, hoping to bring some thread of peace to the situation. He had been searching for hours for some way to cover up their operation in case things had gotten exposed, but with no other plausible course of action, he recommended the most simplistic option they had.

"Look, there's not much we can do as far as the department goes, so it's nothing to stress over. We've just gotta be faster than them. We know who he is, we know where he is, we just need to go get him," Simmons said.

Face looked at Simmons with piercing eyes as he pointed at Carey's mugshot on the page.

"Nothing to stress over? I'm plotting to take out one of the main players of the districts, and this ass could be the one person to shut it all down for me, and you think there's nothing to stress about? Do you know who's in the other rooms of this house?" Face attacked.

Simmons replaced his glasses and dove back into his computer screen while Porter paced back and forth along the pattern of the rug. Face picked up the hard copy mugshot and looked over it, hoping for an idea to pop into his mind.

"I say we just go get his ass now. We know where he's at," Face said.

"No, we can't do that just yet. It'll look too suspicious," Porter replied.

"How so?" Face asked.

"First of all, the arrest was made only a few days ago, so he's definitely being watched. Second, even though it wasn't marked, he was caught with your stuff. Even if we send someone else to do it, if they leave so much as a trace of evidence, it could find its way back to you. We gotta be strategic in our approach to this," Porter explained.

Face tossed the mugshot back on the desk, and Porter continued pacing along the rug. Simmons pulled up a map of the area their suspect lived in and found that was located in a mid-sized community of homes several miles away from major intersections and shopping facilities.

"We've got to be smart about this one," Simmons said. "Looks like there's two ways in and out of the main area. Mostly local traffic but there's still the factor of going unnoticed in and out of the neighborhood, and there's a lot of ground to cover leaving the place and getting back to a more populated area."

The men remained in deep thought. The ticking of the large clock in the corner echoed through the room as Face's mind spun from stress. He tapped his fingers on his desk and groaned as his nervousness set in.

"Wait! I might have something," Porter said.

"What?" Face asked.

"Lemme think."

Porter looked off into space, waving his fingers and biting his lip as he arranged his thoughts.

"All right, so whatever we do, it's gotta be quick and quiet, so we have to set him up. They've got eyes on him enough to know when he's on the move, so we've gotta get him before he makes any kind of move. Do you know anyone that might know him?" Porter asked.

"Maybe." Face thought. "Usually, my guys run with an extra person in case anything goes wrong, which makes me wonder what he was doing alone that day."

"Perfect! If we can find out who he runs with, we might be able to get him to let us know what's going on and use him to make everything look like an ambush. Now if he's an informant, they're going to expect him to be in a specific place by a certain time, and if he doesn't show they'll look for him," Porter advised.

Face nodded his head as he processed Porter's plan, pulling out his cell phone as he thought of who to call to get the information he was after.

"Well, if they're already watching, I can arrange something, a place for him to be. That way we can take care of him on the way there or at his house. What you think?" Face suggested.

Porter rubbed his chin and nodded his head, processing the plan in his mind.

"It could work, it could definitely work. Just give me a day or two to get it all together."

Suddenly, there was a knock at the door. The detectives looked up as Face advised the visitors to enter. In walked Nassar, limping with his cane, accompanied by Hong ending a call on his cell phone as he played with his hair.

"Evening, gentlemen, so sorry to interrupt your meeting," Nassar said.

"It's no problem, we just finished," Face replied. "You two get that plan together, and I'll figure out who he knows. Call me if anything comes up."

"Gotcha," Porter confirmed.

Simmons quickly closed his laptop, and he and Porter exited the room. Nassar gave Simmons a dirty look, watching him closely as he passed by, making his way to the love seat. The old man rubbed his tired knees as he sat.

"I just got off the phone with my guys. Everything has been secured. Thank you," Hong said.

"No problem," Face replied.

"Everything alright with you? You seem a little stressed," Hong inquired.

Face gathered the papers on his desk into a neat stack and placed them in the drawer.

"It's nothing, just gotta take care of a stool pigeon," Face grunted.

Face reached for his drink, now watered down by the melting ice in the glass. He swooshed the bitter liquid around in his mouth and gulped it down.

"I gotta eat something," Face said.

"You've got to relax, my friend," Nassar said.

Face grinned and leaned back in his seat, taking the advice of the aged professional.

"I'm trying, I'm trying."

Hong looked out of the window at the distant city lights, remembering the lesson of his father's optimism.

"Worry not, Face. I know it seems impossible right now, but in essence, the sands are moving in our favor. We are now aware of what Diaz is doing, and now we can do what we must to stop him. There is no more confusion," Hong said.

"So what's the next step?" Face asked.

"You must do one more deal with him before we can make our move," Nassar said.

Face groaned with anxiety and placed his head in his palms. The stress of another loaded drive was too much for him to bear with the potentially dangerous matter developing. Even more, he feared making Hong and Nassar privy to his situation for fear they might abandon their ideas of partnership with him.

"Another one? Shouldn't this have been enough?" he asked.

"You have to build your trust with him. It will not take too much longer," Nassar advised.

"Yeah, but, my brother. He's..."

Hong walked over to Face and quickly placed his hand on his shoulder.

"I know you worry about your brother just as I worry about my father, but we can't do much for him while he's in there. If we act now, you'll be killed, and everything we have worked for will be in jeopardy," Hong advised.

Nassar grinned at Face and slowly rose from the couch, using his cane to gain balance.

"I can say that I admire your apprehension, Face, but you must be just a little patient. The opportunity you're waiting for is just around the corner."

"What do you mean?" Face asked.

"Every year around this time, Diaz goes back to his home country to see his family. He'll take his wife and children, and they are usually gone for a week. During this time, his home has minimal security as he releases most of his men for their own personal vacations before he leaves, but there's one thing the greedy bastard will never turn away," Nassar explained.

"Money," Hong said.

"The deal is strictly about engaging with him to build his trust with you," Nassar advised.

"Diaz oversees all of his deals. The hope is that if you are well established with him, he may be willing to do one last deal with you just before he leaves, and that's when we get him," Hong said.

Face hopelessly looked at his cell phone as he searched for Diaz's number. He started to believe that his brother might have been right to advise him to forget about his well-being, for the plan to stop Diaz seemed to be taking longer than expected.

"How long before he leaves?" Face asked.

"I believe he will leave town at the beginning of next month, giving us three weeks to coordinate," Nassar said. "You must make the next deal as soon as possible, giving us a chance to make another deal before he leaves."

Face looked at Diaz's number on his contacts screen, unable to escape the thoughts of his brother dying in a prison cell. De'Angelo's words on the last visit echoed in his mind, making it hard to relax in his seat. If losing his brother was the cost, he would be sure to make Diaz pay in full for his offense.

A few days had passed since the incident with DeMarcus had occurred, but the matter had yet to be forgotten. Kristine had spent the last few days paranoid that her beloved would be the victim of a vicious attack, jumping at instances of loud noises and people shouting. She was upset with Ryan for his disregard of her emotions over the last few days as he showed no sign of caring about the situation, but in reality, his mind was occupied with concerns about his blind actions. He had spent the past few days wishing it hadn't happened, keeping it a secret from his mother. Faulty cameras around the school building aided in hiding the incident from the school's administrators, leaving any mention of the situation to be considered hearsay.

The school day had come to an end, marking the beginning of the weekend. Teachers and students rushed from the building eager to get an early start on their festivities, for the two-day break was much needed. The sounds of two boys arguing made Kristine clutch tightly to Ryan's arm, nearly causing him to trip.

"Whoa, babe. Relax, they're on the other hall," Ryan said.

"Sorry babe, I'm just—"

"I know you're scared of something happening. Just relax, we already talked about that," he interrupted.

They cut the corner of the hallway that led outside to the school buses. Students were everywhere discussing their weekend plans or running to their buses to get a good seat. The students with cars blasted their music in the parking lot, competing for attention among their friends.

"I know we talked about it, but that doesn't change the fact that I worry about you," Kristine snapped.

"Babe, there's nothing to worry about. You're scaring yourself," Ryan replied.

They made their way through the crowd and down the rows of buses debating Kristine's smothering concern.

"You're so...UGH! I wish you'd just listen to me!"

"I have been listening to you, I just don't care about that shit, and you shouldn't either. Look, if something happens, it happens. I'm not about to be like you over here living in fear over nothing. I ain't scared to die. Hell, I kinda welcome the thought," Ryan said.

Kristine stopped in her tracks, hurt by Ryan's selfish comment, and ripped her hand away from his. Ryan turned and looked back at her, unmoved by her wrinkled frown.

"How could you say something like that?" she asked.

She charged past him toward her bus, and Ryan pursued her with grief hoping to soothe her before they departed.

"Babe, wait!"

He caught up and walked alongside her, hoping she would stop and listen, but Kristine focused forward, ignoring him as her eyes began to well up with tears.

"Babe, listen, I didn't mean it like that. Don't cry, at least not in front of all of these people," he begged.

Kristine walked faster, trying to lose Ryan in the crowd. He rushed up to her as they approached the entrance to her bus and managed to grab her hand just as she had made it to the steps.

"Babe, just listen to me for a sec. Please."

Kristine stopped and slowly turned to look at him. Her eyebrows were scrunched up in anger, but her eyes told a story of worry and concern as a tear rolled down her cheek. Ryan attempted to pull her in for a calming embrace but was rejected by the push of her hand.

"What do you have to say, Ryan? And before you speak, I want you to know that I have had nightmares about you every day this week. I'm sorry if my care is too much for you, but this is what I feel for someone that I love, so what do you have to say?"

The brave fool had struck a nerve with his woman, and not wanting to contribute more to her hurt, he felt it was best to let her go.

"Nothing, I'll...I'll call you later. I love you."

Kristine angrily shook her head and pushed Ryan by his shoulder.

"You're such an asshole," she shouted.

She hurried onto the bus, leaving Ryan alone in his arrogant misery. There was no hug nor loving good-bye kiss, and others around him began to laugh at his embarrassment. He blew into the air and looked into the tinted windows of the bus, refusing to allow her to have the last word.

"No babe, I'm a dick! I'm a dick," he snarked.

He hurried along to his bus, catching it just as the driver was about to pull off. He quickly joined another student in a seat and pulled out his cell phone. He typed a text to Kristine, feeling sorry about her tears, but changed his mind before he sent it. His mind was again overwhelmed by the loss of control he experienced, drawing comparisons to the other times he'd allowed himself to slip. After making several stops, the near-empty bus finally made its way around to his stop. Ryan exited the bus and quickly realized that he was the only student getting off today.

"Have a safe weekend," the driver hollered as she closed the doors.

The bus pulled off, and he began walking toward the entrance of his apartment complex. Images of the awesome destruction from his previous mishaps appeared in his mind when suddenly he was startled by the sound of screeching tires behind him. Two black cars were speeding toward him on the narrow street, leaving barely any room for Ryan to avoid being hit. He stood motionless like a deer in headlights as the cars quickly approached him, their engines roaring like demons. The drivers slammed on the brakes, stopping only a few feet away from Ryan. His heart pounded as his eyes quickly scanned the dark tinted windows until he recognized a familiar face in the passenger seat.

"DeMarcus," he whispered.

The doors opened, and five people exited each vehicle with their eyes locked on the lonely fool before them, but these weren't the students he attended school with.

"I know you didn't think it was over, bruh." DeMarcus jerked his head. "I know ya girl told ya 'bout me."

DeMarcus' infamous grin returned with the insured protection of his brother Punch and their janky friends. They slowly walked toward Ryan, cracking their knuckles and uttering threats of harm. Ryan's calves jumped as adrenaline flowed through him, but the brave boy couldn't decide whether to run or fight. He could hear Kristine's voice in his head crying her concern for his safety as the moment unfolded.

"You thought that shit was smooth the other day, didn't cha?" DeMarcus chuckled. "You done messed up now, homeboy."

Ten was nine too many for Ryan to take on, and his apartment was too far for him to run. There was a wooded area across the street where he thought he might be able to lose them, but he would first have to get by them. DeMarcus confidently stepped closer to Ryan with his crew close behind him. Ryan grabbed the hanging straps of his backpack and pulled them to secure the small load. DeMarcus closed in, leaving less than a foot of space between them. His eyes were relaxed and his smile confident, prepared to make light work of his trapped victim, but Ryan fearlessly stared back, his eyes sharpened and his mouth scrunched with anticipation. While the others crowded behind DeMarcus, Ryan noticed a small escape route to his left in his peripheral. He would have to be quick, for failure to elude the men would lead to an unfortunate violent outcome. He concentrated on his breathing and repositioned his stance to disguise his shaky legs, hiding a balled fist behind his thigh. The gang stood before Ryan, ready and waiting for DeMarcus' word to attack. Feeling cocky, DeMarcus stood before Ryan with his guard down, egging him on to fight.

"Oh, so you ain't gon' run, huh? You think you Bruce Lee or something?" DeMarcus laughed.

A mysterious golden falcon appeared above, circling the altercation with its eyes glued on the two opposing forces. It gradually flew lower, remaining unnoticed by any of the men.

"You know what? What you did was bold. Stupid, but bold. So I'ma be nice, I'ma give you a chance to get a hit in before me and my boys stomp the black off of ya." DeMarcus grinned.

DeMarcus raised his arms out to his sides, inviting Ryan's hand to hit his unguarded face as his followers readied themselves to attack. Suddenly, the low-flying falcon released a frightening screech that caught all of the men's attention. The curious attackers reluctantly looked up, taking their eyes off of their target. Ryan seized the moment and swung his right fist with all of his might, striking DeMarcus on his jaw, and immediately broke off at full speed to his left, darting away from the distracted men. The punch knocked DeMarcus into a daze, his legs locked up, and his arms dropped to his side as he fell face-first to the ground.

The men broke from their distraction and noticed DeMarcus lying on the ground as Ryan zoomed by them toward the intersection. His muscles surged with adrenaline as he ran for his life, pushing his body to its physical limits. Just before he could dash through the intersection, he spotted the running lights of a speeding pick-up truck in his peripheral vision. The driver blared his horn, the engine roaring as he sped down the empty street. Ryan stomped his foot and pivoted into a spin, the truck missing him by mere inches. He felt the rush of air from the truck passing, and panic filled his face as he gasped for a breath. Blinded by the near-miss, he had completely forgotten about the men giving chase behind him and was quickly pummeled to the ground.

The rough pavement scratched his arm and face as he was tackled hard into a short slide. His blurred vision gave shape to a dark fist falling from the sky. He was struck hard in the face several times, and everything seemed to go black. He was met with a barrage of blows to his body, each hit causing him to slip further and further from consciousness. The beating continued for what seemed to be an eternity on the empty streets, his blood staining the unkempt pavement. They stomped his hands and kicked him until he appeared to be unconscious.

Punch had aided DeMarcus to his feet using his shirt to wipe away the blood spilling from his brother's mouth. DeMarcus massaged his jaw, flinching as sweat rolled over the scratches caused by his face hitting the ground. The pair stumbled over to the beating, watching kicks and haymakers get thrown around. As they approached, DeMarcus jumped at the sound of Punch's switchblade. He turned and saw the knife in his brother's hand, the sharp blade still stained with dried blood.

"Cut him," Punch ordered DeMarcus as he handed him the knife.

DeMarcus trembled as he grabbed the knife, losing the boastful confidence he'd once carried. He had rejected the past warnings of his brother, who had grown tired of handling his vengeful endeavors. He would be forced to commence the gang's ritual of marking their victim with an elaborate cut.

"Get ya hands dirty. Put that shit on his head where he can't hide it," Punch commanded.

Punch balled up his fist, threatening to beat up his little brother. The scared DeMarcus trembled over to the motionless Ryan, looking down at his beaten body. His face was bloody, the thick red liquid dripping from his nose and mouth creating a small pool before him. DeMarcus reluctantly grabbed Ryan by the bottom of his shirt and crumpled it up to his neck to pull him up. Ryan's limp head dropped to the side, bloody saliva spilling from his mouth. DeMarcus observed his bloody face, trying to keep his cool in front of the other guys, but secretly, he didn't have the stomach for blood and gore.

"Hurry up!" Punch shouted.

The men crowded around them to hide their heinous actions. Fear coursed through his veins as DeMarcus clenched the knife in his hand. He hadn't thought it was going to go this far, but what he feared more was what his brother would do to him if he didn't commit to the act. He struggled to hide his nervousness as he prepared himself for what he was about to do. He placed the tip of the blade in the left corner of Ryan's hairline and cut through his thick hair toward the back of his head, the first move of their signature mark. DeMarcus' heart beat like a drum as blood spilled from the open cut. His stomach turned, and he struggled to maintain a straight face. Just as he was about to finish the mark, the sound of a police siren blared in the distance.

"Oh shit, run!" Punch hollered.

The crew looked up and went into a frenzy getting back to the cars. DeMarcus frantically released Ryan and took off in the scramble, causing his head to drop hard to the ground. The cars quickly peeled out as a lone cop car's tires screeched to a halt in front of Ryan's motionless body in the intersection. The officer, who was actually in pursuit of the truck that had zoomed by, jumped from his vehicle, ignoring the sound of the screeching tires of the fleeing cars, and ran over to Ryan.

He leaned over the bloody boy, looking for signs of life as he radioed in to dispatch.

"Dispatch, this is Officer Smith! I've got a 10-54 on Garden Walk right out front of Garden Crossing Apartments."

The golden falcon took off from the trees and circled through the air around Ryan, releasing its shrieking caw. Ryan's body shook as if a jolt of energy had entered it, and he slowly cracked open his bruised eyes. He released a painful groan as he tried to turn his head. He saw the blurred image of the officer leaning over him and the falcon circling above. He struggled to breathe, slowly reaching his hand out to the officer, who knelt down and grabbed his hand, shocked that the young man was still alive.

"Cancel that dispatch, I have a 10-53! Victim appears to be a minor! Send an ambulance ASAP!"

He gently squeezed Ryan's hand and placed his other hand on Ryan's chest.

"Stay with me, son, you're going to make it. Just stay with me," the officer pleaded.

The golden falcon landed a short distance away from them, turning its head and looking at Ryan as he lay on the hard ground. Relieved that help had come to Ryan's aid, the falcon shrieked and flew back into the air. One of its golden feathers drifted from above and fell next to Ryan's head as it began circling them again. Time began to slow down, and the officer's voice became a grumble in Ryan's ears. His grip on the officer's hand began to weaken, and everything faded to black.

Ryan awoke in the back of an ambulance, the loud siren blaring through the city streets. He found himself unable to move as he had been strapped down to the gurney. He moved his left hand and felt the pinch of an I.V. and slowly laid it back down. His groans alerted the EMT, who rushed over to his head.

"Can you hear me? He's waking up! Can you hear me, kid?" the EMT said.

She looked into his eyes with a flashlight pen, and he squinted, groaning as he attempted to turn his head. He mumbled something, but the EMT couldn't understand him.

"Mmma-hmmm," he mumbled.

"Mahim? I can't understand you, kid. Listen, the officer said you got hit by a truck, but it looks more like you just got in a really bad fight."

Ryan slowly moved his right hand and began to pat his thigh. The EMT looked and touched his thigh.

"You've got pain in your thigh?"

"Maaa-huuumm," Ryan mumbled.

Ryan attempted to reach into his pocket but because of the straps, he was unable to bend his arm enough to get in. The EMT quickly realized what he was doing and offered to help.

"You've got something in your pocket?"

"Mmm-hmm. Mah-mah," Ryan groaned.

The EMT reached into his pocket and pulled out his cell phone. Ryan reached his hand up as far as he could, tried to pull down the neck brace, and cleared his throat.

"Mama. Call my mama," he mumbled.

He groaned as he scrunched up his face and closed his eyes, trying to focus on breathing through the jolts of pain that plagued him. He could hear his mother screaming through the phone as the EMT informed her of the near-fatal accident.

A few hours passed, and Camille sat distraught in a cold hospital room with her beaten son. His face was badly scratched and swollen, bandages all over to cover up the cuts. The wounds left the doctors no choice but to cut down his hair in order to put in the stitches along the side of his head. His left arm was in a sling with a finger brace, and his right hand had several bandages on the fingers. His mouth was puckered and swollen, making it painful for him to speak.

"I still don't understand how this truck hit you. Why were you even that close to the street? Did you not hear the truck coming? I hope they find the bastard that hit you," Camille rambled.

Ryan simply groaned and nodded his head quietly. He thought back to when he'd walked with Kristine to her bus and remembered her calling him an asshole for underappreciating her concern. He wanted so badly to call her and apologize, but he couldn't bring himself to face the music of her alto sax. He wanted to tell his mother what had really happened to him, but he feared that they might be met with retaliation from the gang if he went to the police. There was a knock on the door, and a doctor entered, reviewing notes on his laptop.

"All right, Scales, it is, right?" the doctor asked.

"Correct," Camille answered.

The doctor examined Ryan's injuries and looked over his notes. Puzzled, he reviewed the X-rays on file, looking closely at the images of Ryan's skull. He peeked over at Ryan again and began to scratch his head.

"This is strange," the doctor said.

"What?" Camille inquired.

"It doesn't make sense. These notes are saying you were hit by a truck, but according to your injuries"–he looked at Ryan–"you look like you got, well, jumped."

Camille looked at the doctor in disbelief and then at Ryan, whose eyes were scanning the floor.

"I don't understand, h-he looks mangled! I mean, even the cop even said he got hit by a truck," Camille said.

"Well, this truck didn't mess him up as bad as I would think it should've. There's no trauma to his skull or brain, although his face is pretty beat up. There are no major breaks other than his finger, but nothing that he won't recover from in time. He definitely hit the ground hard, what with the stitches, and that raises an eyebrow too, but according to the report, this truck was speeding when it hit him, and with the majority of his injuries to his upper body, I just...well, he's here, and he's not as hurt as he could be, so that's good news. You're a lucky young man," the doctor confirmed.

Camille released a sigh of relief and placed her hand on Ryan's shoulder. Ryan quietly flinched in pain, hoping the doctor would hurry and finish with his briefing.

"I'm going to write you a prescription for him, Mom, and this'll make it a little easier to deal with the pain. You're definitely going to want to take it easy on the left side where the stitches are. Don't get them wet and get yourself some ointment to dress the stitches and the scratches on your face. I'll give you some stuff to wrap your wounds in. Other than that, just stay home and get some rest, and if you have any problems, don't hesitate to come back to the ER," the doctor advised.

After signing a few forms and stopping at a 24-hour pharmacy, Camille and Ryan headed home. Ryan had not uttered a word since leaving the hospital, but Camille had been on the phone calling everyone to let them know he was okay. He reclined the seat, looking at the stars above through the sunroof as they made their way to the apartment. A dark shadow flashed overhead, blacking out the stars for a split second, but it was too dark for Ryan to figure out what the shadow belonged to. Camille peeked over at him as she prepared to end her conversation. She hadn't spoken to Reginald yet and hoped that this wouldn't bring another issue to her already frustrating day.

"Just come by tomorrow and see him, he's trying to rest now, Ma...I'll tell him... All right, bye," she sighed. "That was your grandmother, she's coming by to see you tomorrow. Babe, you've gotta be more careful out here. I'm already going through enough. If I lose you, I don't think anyone will be able to console me."

"I know," Ryan uttered.

"How are you feeling?"

Ryan sighed and closed his eyes, thinking about the attack. "Like I got hit by a truck," he said.

They made it to their apartment, and Camille ushered Ryan to the door. Inside was a drunken Reginald who had been drinking since he'd arrived home a few hours before. They walked through the door and went directly to Ryan's room to put his stuff down.

"Camille!" Reginald hollered. "Where the hell you been?"

"I'll be in there in a sec," Camille replied.

Reginald continued to holler in a drunken muffle, making his words sound like mush. His drunken aggressive behavior had become the norm over the past few months, but rather than discuss Reginald's obscene actions, Camille sighed and rolled her eyes at his voice to keep the peace.

"Just put your stuff down, and I'll make you a smoothie," Camille said.

She hurried into the living room to calm Reginald down. Ryan checked his cell phone, swiping through notifications, and realized he had no missed calls or texts from Kristine. He began to worry if he even still had a girlfriend. He carefully placed his phone on the charger, flinching at the throbbing pain in his arm.

He walked into the kitchen, listening to Reginald arguing with Camille over her whereabouts. He peeked around the corner and saw one of Reginald's arms flailing around, spilling drops of beer from the bottle, and his mother standing still, trying to hold herself together. With every word from Reginald's mouth, he could see her growing more and more frustrated. He came from around the corner into Camille's view, and she directed Reginald's attention toward him.

"Here he is, look at him," Camille said.

Reginald turned and looked at Ryan, his eyes droopy from the alcohol. He studied Ryan hard, the hurt boy trying not to breathe in the alcoholic stench coming from his mouth. Reginald stood up straight and crossed his arms and laughed at Ryan. Offended, Camille snapped at Reginald for his lack of compassion.

"Don't laugh at him, he's in pain," she yelled.

"What, he ain't hurt. That boy ain't got hit by no truck." He sipped his beer. "He looks like he got his ass whooped."

"Go in the room, now," Camille commanded.

Reginald staggered to the room, looking back and laughing at Ryan as he bumped into furniture. Ryan watched the drunken fool stumble into the dark shadows of his bedroom, angered by his words but more upset for his mother. He calmed himself down, knowing that he was not in the condition for any kind of fight. As reality set in, he began to wonder what trouble awaited him once he went back to school. Before he could send himself into oblivion with his thoughts, Camille rushed over to comfort him from Reginald's unkind words.

"Don't worry about him, baby. I'll handle that. Just take your pills, and I'll have your smoothie ready in a minute," Camille said.

She proceeded to her room with her frustrations heavy on her shoulders. She opened the door and began shaking her head when she saw Reginald passed out on the bed. She sighed, and the door slowly closed behind her. Ryan proceeded to the bathroom, quickly discovering the joy of taking off his shirt with a severely sprained elbow. He stood in the shower and watched the dried blood spiral down the drain. He remembered to stay back from the showerhead, careful not to let the hot water get into his wounds. He gently dabbed his face with the rag and wiped the dried blood from around his mouth.

After his shower, he dried off and wiped away the fog from the mirror. He looked at his swollen lips and eyes and tried to look at his stitches. His hair was completely jacked up, and he began to feel a deep sense of sorrow as Kristine's words echoed in his head again. He dressed his wounds and wrapped his stitches, neglecting his sling for the night. He looked at his toothbrush and knew the pain would be too much for him to bear. He settled for using mouthwash, which seemed to hurt more.

He went into his room and struggled to put on his boxers and basketball shorts. The sounds of appliances running and cars outside irritated him, and he found it painful to sit still as he sat on his bed. He hopped off the bed and nervously looked around his room, but there was nothing there. He walked toward the living room and peeked around the corner, noticing the lights were off and the master bedroom door was closed. The kitchen was dark, and again there was nothing there. Camille had forgotten to make his smoothie, but the pain in his mouth made him forget about his hunger.

He nervously checked the front door to find that both deadbolts were locked. Lastly, he stepped to his window and peeked through the blinds, determined to find something, but saw nothing but parked cars under the streetlight. He sighed, looking around his room again before giving up. He didn't know if he was paranoid from the fight or if this was a side effect of his pills, but he felt like someone was watching him.

He strained as he got into bed, careful not to disturb his sprained elbow. He looked at his phone again, and it was now after 10 p.m. Not a call or text had been received from Kristine, and he knew her silence wouldn't end until he said something first. The phone rang four times, and he assumed she wasn't going to answer, but just before he could end the call, she picked up.

"Oh, now you want to call?" Kristine grunted.

"Hi, baby, I'm sorry, I missed you, too. Been busy these last few hours," Ryan replied.

"Busy? So busy you couldn't even send a text? See, that's what I'm talking about. Just because we argued doesn't mean that you need to ignore me!"

"I wasn't ignoring you."

"You really just...wait. Why do you sound like that?" she questioned.

Ryan sighed and remained silent.

"Hello? I asked you a question," Kristine said.

He closed his eyes and exhaled deeply, knowing the conversation was about to get much worse.

"I was at the hospital earlier. I'm gonna be looking a little strange for a while," he replied.

"The hospital?" she gasped. "What hap...oh no, please don't tell me that..."

Ryan heard a beep on his phone and prepared himself for Kristine's tongue lashing. He looked at his phone screen and saw Kristine's distressed face. He shook his head, hoping she would let him off the hook. He wished he'd just sent a text.

"Turn your camera on! I need to see your face!" Kristine demanded.

"Babe, no, just wait until tomorrow. You don't need to see me right now," he said.

"Turn on your camera, Ryan! I'm serious!" she shouted.

"Isn't your mom home? She's gonna get suspicious with you screaming like that," he deviated.

"Ryan, ooh...stop playing with me. Turn your camera on or I'm breaking up with you," she threatened.

Kristine made it clear that she wasn't going to allow him to get her off subject, and with each passing second, he veered closer to being single. Cornered, Ryan groaned as he sat up in his bed. He accepted the notification and held the camera near his chest.

"That's not your face, Ryan. You are really trying me right now," she said.

Ryan looked down at his phone and slowly raised it toward his face. Kristine immediately burst into tears, dropping her phone as she cried.

"Babe, c'mon, calm down. I'm okay. I'm okay," he lied.

Kristine went into a panic as she struggled to find her phone on the floor. She wiped her eyes and looked at her screen, and more tears began to fall.

"No, look at your face! You're not okay! Oh my God!"

"Babe, you gotta calm down. I don't want your mom to hear you crying," he instructed. "Breathe. Talk to me."

"Okay," she cried.

Kristine breathed heavily as she struggled to calm herself. She tried to prop her phone up on her nightstand, but her shaky hands caused it to continuously fall.

"Babe, lie down and use your pillow to prop up your phone."

She followed his instruction and cuddled up next to her phone, wiping her eyes as she looked at his beaten face.

"What happened?" she whined.

"First, let me apologize. I'm sorry for being an asshole and not being considerate of how you felt. I really should have listened to you."

"DeMarcus did this to you." Kristine angrily sat up. "That bastard! This is all my fault. I just shouldn't have told you."

"Kristine, calm down. You didn't do anything wrong, and this is not your fault. I would have been even more mad if you hadn't told me. This didn't happen because you told me, this happened because I lost it. That's a whole different set of circumstances. Okay?"

The crying girl quietly succumbed to her man's understanding, secretly still blaming herself for the harm that had been brought to him.

"Okay," she coughed.

"Now go to the bathroom and clean your face up, baby. You're too pretty to be crying over some dude." He grinned painfully.

Kristine smiled at his joke and started to cry again, more in control of herself. She rose from her bed and snuck to the bathroom to wash her face.

"Can you, um, tell me how everything happened? Like how did they even find you?" she asked.

She entered the bathroom, locking the door behind her and propped her phone up next to the sink. She grabbed a face rag and began running warm water.

"It was crazy," he sighed. "I had just got off the bus and started walking home. Next thing I know I heard tires screeching behind me. They must've already been at the school before I left."

"No wonder I was so nervous today. Something just didn't feel right," she said, wiping her eyes.

"It's kinda funny, though. Him and I guess his brother. It was like 10 of 'em."

"Ten?" she zoomed into the phone.

"Yup, all for lil ol' me," he laughed. "Anyway, they roll up in two cars and stop in front of me. Ol' boy gets out trying to talk hard in front of his brother. He gets all in my face, talkin' 'bout, 'I'ma let you hit me.'"

"Why didn't you just run?" she asked.

"Run? First of all, my granddad taught me how to fight, he didn't teach me how to run. Second, I didn't even make it into the complex before they rolled up on me. It was way too far to run, and too many of them to outrun." He scrunched his face.

"My bad, I forget how much of a warrior you are," Kristine giggled.

"So, he's all in my face, right, and I had like one chance to make a run for it, but something happened, like a loud noise or something, I don't know what it was, but I didn't move. DeMarcus raised his head up, and I busted him right in the jaw and took off." He smiled.

"Oh my God, you hit him? In front of all his boys?"

"Hell yeah, I hit 'em! What you think I did, gave 'em a hug?" he scoffed. "Anyway, I took off toward the intersection. I was tryin' to dip off into the woods, but before I could even cross the street, a big ass truck zooms by, and it almost hit me, like I was inches away. I could feel the wind as it passed by," he said.

"I almost wish you would have gotten hit by the truck," Kristine said.

She walked back into her room and cuddled up next to her phone on the bed. Ryan sighed and shook his head, thinking back to the truck.

"Yeah, but I don't think I would have made it if I did get hit. This truck didn't seem like it wanted to stop," he said.

He went on telling her the gruesome details that he could remember from the evening, even showing her the full extent of his injuries. A few more tears fell from Kristine's eyes, but her spirit was calmed by Ryan's charm.

"So your mom thinks you were hit by a truck?" she asked.

"Yeah, and that's how I gotta keep it. She's going through too much right now, and the last thing I need is her worrying about me," he replied.

"I understand. Well, I can see if my mom will let me borrow the car and come see you tomorrow," she said.

"No, babe, just wait 'til Monday. I'd let you come, but my mom's husband is...stupid. I don't want to have you around that. Hell, I don't even want to be here, but I'm afraid to leave her by herself."

"Okay. Are you sure, though? I could meet you at the front of your complex, just for a little while." She smiled.

Ryan smiled back, looking into her eyes. He moved the phone toward his face and kissed the screen.

"Girl, you better stop being so sweet to me," he flirted.

"Yeah, I know," she replied. "You know I love you, boy."

"I know, and I love you, too, girl."

Kristine smiled and kissed her screen. She looked into the corner of the phone at the time and sighed.

"I gotta get ready for bed, babe. My dad's coming to get me tomorrow morning around 6:30 for volunteer work at the women's shelter. I gotta get those hours in to look good on my college applications. Please get some rest though, baby, and think about letting me come see you."

"I'll think about it, babe. I shouldn't have any trouble sleeping. The day was exhausting enough."

They brought their phones to their faces and kissed the screens again.

"Goodnight, sweetheart." He smiled painfully.

"Goodnight, baby." She smiled.

Kristine ended the call, and Ryan tossed his phone aside for a moment. He sat in his bed, looking at the pattern on the comforter as he listened to the rain tapping at his window. The low thunderclaps soothed his mind, and he finally stopped thinking about his mother. He grabbed his TV remote and streamed his favorite cartoon, *Dragon of Darkness*, and began watching an episode. He turned off the lights and wrapped himself as snugly as he could in his comforter. His pain medication kicked in, and the druggy side effects made everything hazy. His eyes struggled to stay open, and the words of the cartoon characters began to slur in his mind. Finally, the beaten boy closed his eyes and drifted off to sleep.

"I will avenge my tribe and put an end to the torment of my people!" the TV roared.

Lurking in the woods across the street from the building was the golden falcon staring closely at his window. It had been watching him, sensing his conscious energy and waiting for its moment to move in closer. It flew across the street into a tree just outside of the window, silently arranging itself on the branches. The falcon looked around to ensure that it was alone in the wet darkness. It spread its wings and suddenly began to glow gold, transforming into a golden aura. It drifted through the window and made its way into Ryan's room.

The aura sank to the floor, listening closely as the sleeping boy turned in his bed. The aura silently rose from the foot of the bed and blanketed Ryan, taking the shape of his body as it moved up to his chest and began to glow brighter, slowly advancing toward his head. It entered his body through the orifices of his face without waking him and disappeared without a trace.

A powerful lightning bolt crashed into the ground before him, and Ryan found himself running scared through a dark hilly terrace. The sky was completely black with ear-shattering thunder and lightning bolts striking the hills every few seconds. The lush, green, grassy hills blew violently in the wind as if a horrendous storm were about to destroy the lands. Ryan continued running to the tops of the hills when he was suddenly stricken with fear at the monstrous call of his name.

"RRRYYYY-AAAAANNNN!!" the voice roared from above.

He looked up into the dark sky and panicked as the lightning revealed the underbody of what he thought was a giant snake. His heart raced as he sprinted down the hill and up another, thinking the snake was chasing him. Flashes of lightning revealed images of the twisted body hidden within the clouds as it angrily groaned Ryan's name louder and louder.

"RRRRRYYYY-AAAAAAAAANNNNNNNNN!!" the beast roared.

Ryan ran as fast as he could but saw no end to the hills. He ran to the top of another hill but was blown back by a wave of fire that blazed down from the sky. He barely dodged the blaze without a chance to catch himself as several more lightning bolts struck the ground around him and trapped him in a small space just before the firewall. The fire took shape and wrapped itself around the hill, surrounding Ryan and leaving nowhere for him to run. Ryan frantically looked around at the frightening flames when suddenly they began to form into the scales that he'd seen in the sky moments before. His eyes followed the transforming scales to the flaming wall in front of him and watched as they synced into the head of a giant dragon.

Its head pointed straight toward the sky, and a bolt of lightning struck the tip of its long snout, giving it life. The dragon roared, spitting fire from its mouth into the air as Ryan stood in awe at the beast's breathtaking power. The giant red dragon constricted on the hill and lowered its enormous head from the clouds, towering high above Ryan as he stared at it. Its scales turned blood red with large black spikes that traveled down its back to the tip of its tail. It had two large horns that pointed outward from its head with long whiskers that wildly blew in the wind. There were rows and rows of teeth in its mouth that disappeared behind the black smoke emitting from its throat. Lastly was the menacing red glow of its angry eyes staring deeply into Ryan's frightened soul.

Ryan anxiously looked up at the enormous red beast before him, calmed by the warmth of its body. He dropped his hands and stood as still as he could in the violent winds, listening to the thunderous breaths of the dragon. He regained his composure and stood fearlessly before the beast, awaiting its words.

"What do you desire most?" the menacing dragon asked.

Ryan immediately thought of the painful past, his mind reliving the instances where the mental battle scars were created while dark and shadowy images of his past appeared above him in the sky. His cold, dark feelings beckoned for the one thing he had always wanted, a desire he was never able to satisfy, a wish he was taught to never fulfill. He scrunched his face and gritted his teeth and angrily shouted his answer.

"Revenge!" His desire echoed.

Smoke drifted from the dragon's mouth, and it began to grumble again.

"So be it," the red dragon replied.

The dragon's eyes glowed brighter, and its body began to turn back into fire. The blazing dragon unraveled itself and flew up into the sky, disappearing into the black clouds. The violent winds grew stronger and stronger, leaving Ryan immersed in total darkness atop the lush hill. Just as he thought the ordeal was over, Ryan was struck by a massive bolt of lightning, and his body was cast into the air. He opened his eyes and witnessed the menacing red dragon emerging from the clouds, flying toward him with flames blazing in its mouth. The dragon roared, ripping open a gateway on Ryan's chest. They zoomed closer and closer toward each other, and the dragon dashed into the gateway, engulfing Ryan as it dissipated into a long stream of fire. He screamed in agony as the power of the red dragon burned through his body, releasing its power into him. The pitch of his scream deepened to the grit of a battle cry, and his eyes began to glow red. His veins bulged all over his body as the overwhelming power flooded his senses. Lightning struck all around him as he unleashed a hellish roar, shattering the hills like glass beneath him.

CHAPTER 7:
WE ARE ONE

RYAN SHRIEKED, IMMEDIATELY sitting up in his bed as he awoke from his hellish nightmare. He was shaking and sweating, his arms locked and his hands tightly gripping his sheets as the morning sun gleamed through his window. He caught his breath and slowly eased himself back down on the mattress, listening to the birds chirp outside. Images of his dream took shape on the ceiling as he recalled everything he'd seen. The pain of hunger reminded him that he hadn't eaten since lunch at school the day before, so he associated the misunderstanding of his dream to his appetite. He got out of bed and proceeded to the bathroom to brush his teeth.

He entered the bathroom and reached for his toothbrush, not paying attention to himself as he applied the toothpaste. He raised the toothbrush to his mouth as he looked into the mirror and immediately froze with his mouth wide open. His eyes were filled with disbelief as he stared at this normal-looking image in the mirror. He set his toothbrush on the counter and continued to observe himself. He touched his face, and it didn't hurt. He opened and closed his mouth several times, and there was no pain. His face and eyes reduced themselves to their natural state, and his skin was all one color again. He inhaled deeply and shook his left arm, shocked to find that the pain in his ribs and arm was gone. He removed the finger splint from his left hand and flexed, discovering that his hand was more powerful than before.

Anxious to see his true self, he began removing the bandages from his head. His skin was flawless, his lips were plump and healthy, his nose was shining, and his nostrils were wide open. His stitches had fallen from the healed skin, and the shaved hair showed signs of regrowth. He stood in the bathroom happy, scared, and confused, smacking his face to make sure he was awake. When all else stopped making sense, he did the only thing he could think to do.

"MAMA!"

Camille frantically paced back and forth as she spoke with the nurse's hotline. She could barely keep still, confused about her son's progressive condition and angry because the nurses couldn't tell her anything. She touched his face and turned his head, searching for a flaw, but could find nothing.

"I-I just don't understand. We were literally at the hospital last night. It hasn't even been 24 hours!"

She walked over to him and ran her hand across the side of his head, feeling how smooth it was against her fingertips. She looked at her hand, hoping for a trace of some kind of injury, but again she found nothing. She scoffed at the nurse on the phone and walked over to the counter to grab his medication.

"I can't pronounce the name of this but it's 800 mg. *Take one pill every 6 hours for pain relief.* Ryan, how many of these did you take last night?"

"One," he replied.

"Okay, he said he only took one, but it doesn't make any sense... You've got his file right there in front of you. He got hit by a freaking truck, and now he looks like he could run a marathon," Camille fussed.

She circled around, nervously running her fingers through her hair as she tried to get answers from the woman. Ryan looked at his hands, feeling something different about himself, but he was unsure as to what it could be.

"Lady, you've got to understand, he had stitches! Have you ever heard of stitches? They had to cut off some of his hair to put them in! The hair even grew back, like, you can't even tell he was ever hurt...Well of course I'm happy he's doing better, but I would like to know more about what the doctor gave him to make this happen so quickly!"

Camille was losing her mind. Ryan stood up from his seat and flexed his arms, surprised by the strength he felt in them. He touched the side of his head and then ran his hand through his thick hair.

"I want to get a haircut," he said.

"Bring him in for more tests, but...I'll—I'll call you back," Camille scoffed as she ended the call.

Camille turned to Ryan, filled with a worried happiness and hugged him tightly.

"My baby boy. They say they want to run more tests on you, so give me a minute to get dressed and I'll—"

"No, Ma, relax," Ryan interrupted. "I feel fine. I just want to get a haircut."

"A haircut?" Her eyes bulged from her head. "You just got hit by a truck, and you want a haircut? Are you serious? You really do need to go to the hospital."

"No, Ma, I'm fine, really. I've never lied to you about being hurt, and I wouldn't fake feeling better. You were there yesterday just like I was. I'm just as shocked as you, if not more. It's not a dream, it's not a prank, this is reality—trust me, I made sure. I don't know how to diagnose this one, but let's just say it's a miracle and call it a day."

He placed his gentle hands on his mother's shoulders and gave her a look of reassurance. Camille caved and nodded her head, accepting her son's words.

"Okay. I'll try to put this behind us, but what about everyone else? Your grandma, your uncle, they want to see you. Your grandma is coming by today. Your granddad, he called—"

He grabbed her hands and calmed her. "Then I need to get myself looking good before she gets here. Just give me the keys, and I'll be back."

Camille was immediately concerned about his mental state, fearful of the perfect smile that stretched across his face. She opened the door to her room and grabbed her keys from the dresser, reluctant to hand them over. She looked into his eyes as he reached out his hand to her.

"You better not get hit by another truck," she joked.

"I won't," Ryan laughed.

He grabbed the keys and gently pulled them from his mother's protective grip and hurried back to his bathroom to take a quick shower. Camille sat on the couch and sighed as she tried to gather her thoughts. She began to question herself, wondering if she had imagined the whole ordeal.

In the shower, Ryan flexed and stretched his muscles, astonished by the keen presence he felt within himself. He felt more able than he had ever felt enjoying the sudden clean bill of health. He washed his hair, profusely scrubbing the left side as he thought back on the attack, wondering if he too had imagined the whole thing. Had he been attacked by a rowdy pack of overaged gangsters protecting a stubborn fool that deserved more than a punch in the face, was he actually hit by a truck, or was the day before just a long dream?

He got dressed and drove across town to the barbershop he'd frequented over the years in hopes that the familiar faces inside would give him a haircut without making noise about the left side of his head. He parked the car and looked at himself in the sun visor's mirror. The abnormal goodness he felt began to fester in his mind, but he ignored his feelings and headed into the shop, believing that getting his appearance together would fix everything. Ryan exhaled a deep breath and proceeded to the door of the shop. He looked through the large glass windows and noticed that the shop was virtually empty, a rare sight for an early Saturday.

The men inside traded stories about their evenings and their days of yesteryear chasing women and getting caught up with things in the streets. There were three barbers by the names of Smitty, Jackson, and Hill, older gentlemen that had opened up the shop a few decades ago. Along with them was Phil, also older and portly, who spent his retirement hanging out with his old war buddies at the barbershop. Smitty sat in his chair, enthusiastically telling the men about his encounter from the evening before.

"And then I hit her with the ol' Barry White voice, I said, 'Baby, I don't care if it takes forever, I'll sit here and I'll...I'll wait on you forever if I've got to.' Boom, got'er!" Smitty exploded with laughter.

The men fell over with laughter as they always did with each story told. Sometimes it was like a competition to see whose story was better or worse than the other. There were plenty of half-truths and lies told to make the stories more interesting, especially when the sorties involved women. Ultimately, the gentlemen always retained a high level of respect for each other, except for when it came to sports.

"Heh! I remember talking like that to my sweet Petunia back in the day, rest her beautiful soul." Phil removed his hat. "I would buy her a flower every day and massage her feet every night."

Phil looked lovingly at the ceiling above, reminiscing about his late beauty. The barbers looked at him sarcastically, tired of his old stories of the woman that had passed a decade ago.

"Phil, that woman been gone ten years. She obviously had you whipped," Hill laughed.

"She might be gone, but that whippin' ain't been forgotten," Jackson added.

"Whipped doesn't begin to describe how that woman had me," Phil said.

The men burst into laughter, continuing to clown over their stories as Ryan walked up to the entrance. The bell rang as he opened the door, and the men looked up at the lone teenager and greeted him with excitement. Smitty rose from his seat with a giant grin on his face, happy to see his favorite client.

"There he is, Brother Scales! How you been, son? What the hell happened to your head?" Smitty raised his brow.

Ryan immediately lowered his eyes as the others gawked at the missing hair.

"I'm good, had a little mishap with the edger at home," he lied.

"That ain't no mishap there, boy, you done f'd yourself up!" Hill hollered.

"Nah, it was late at night, and I was tired."

"Tired? Boy, you too young to be tired! Back in the day, we never slept. Ain't that right, Phil?" Hill pointed.

"Damn right!" Phil shouted.

The men burst into laughter as Ryan came around to greet them individually. He first approached Jackson, who was sweeping loose hair off the floor.

"Hey, how's that fine mama of yours?" Jackson smiled.

"I done told you, Mr. Jackson, don't be talkin' 'bout my mama now. I'll beat you up," Ryan laughed.

"You should beat yourself up for that horrendous hairdo you left on your head!" Hill shouted.

The men broke into laughter as Ryan faked a grin to keep his story going. He next approached Hill, who fist-bumped him as he ate his lunch.

"You know, son, you were growing into a fine young man until you messed up that head of yours," Hill laughed.

"Thank you, Mr. Hill. I appreciate that." Ryan smiled.

"All right, y'all, lay off of him. He's gettin' ready to graduate this year, so he was probably practicing for when he's out of town, right, son?" Smitty diverted.

"You goin' to the military, son?" Phil asked as he shook his hand.

"Nah." Ryan shook his head. "I've seen how the government treats the veterans. You shouldn't have to beg for food and medical treatment after you've fought for your country."

"Teh, no argument there," Jackson agreed.

Smitty dusted off his seat as Ryan took his place in the chair and tossed the apron around his neck. He picked at thick parts of Ryan's afro, trying to figure out how to fix the monstrosity. The indifference Ryan felt inside appeared on his face as Smitty turned the chair toward the mirror.

"Well, no matter what you do, I'm proud of you, son," Smitty said. "Now, what are we gonna do with this?"

Ryan gazed at his incomplete afro, and the idea of long hair didn't appeal to him anymore. He no longer saw himself, but only the image of what he had become overnight.

"I want something different, a fade," he replied.

"Skin fade?"

"Yeah. Fade the sides and leave a couple inches at the top."

"All right, I got just the look for you."

Ryan sat still in the chair watching his hair fall into his lap. He remained quiet, not engaging in the conversations the men were having, an unusual behavior, Smitty observed. He didn't check his cell phone, he just sat there, thinking, wondering, trying to figure out what happened to him. What could have brought this sudden healing? Was there some sort of miracle that happened to fall upon him?

Time passed, and Smitty dusted off the loose hairs on Ryan's face. He turned him toward the mirror, and they observed the cut.

"What do you think?" Smitty asked.

"It looks good, but it needs something," Ryan replied.

"Hold tight, I got something the young boys showed me the other day."

Smitty reached into his drawer and pulled out a tool that resembled a small tennis racket. He placed it on the top of

Ryan's head and began making circles until the hair twisted upward into tiny spikes.

"There you go. Never did a style like this before. I think it looks pretty good," Smitty said.

He turned the chair toward the mirror, allowing Ryan to observe the expert barbering. He examined each part of his head, satisfied with Smitty's handiwork.

"Yeah. Yeah, this is it right here. I like this. Excellent work, Mr. Smitty," Ryan said.

"That's what I do, Brother Scales." Smitty grinned.

Smitty wiped the faded areas of Ryan's head with alcohol and sprayed sheen around his head as he lowered the chair. He removed the apron, and Ryan rose from the chair looking like a brand-new person.

"Lookin' real sharp there, son," Hill said.

"He's gonna get them young girls with that cut," Jackson smiled.

"You know, I had a cut like that once. My wife was so upset, she accused me of being up to something until my hair grew back," Phil laughed.

The men laughed at Phil for telling yet another story about his wife, but Ryan couldn't bring himself to laugh at the joke. Still feeling the abnormal good within him, Ryan decided it was best to leave the shop rather than stick around as he normally did. He reached into his pocket and pulled out his wallet to pay but was swatted away by the kind Smitty.

"No, son, this one is on the house, and take this with you for your hair. I'll get another one." Smitty handed over the styling tool.

"Oh, thank you, Mr. Smitty." Ryan nervously grinned.

They gave each other a firm handshake, and Ryan gave his good-byes before he headed out the door.

"Be safe, young brother," Hill hollered. "And don't go messing with that big head of yours. Leave it to the professionals!"

Ryan got to the car and opened the door, removing his jacket as the weather had warmed up over the last hour. He heard the bell of the barbershop door ding and turned to see Smitty walking over to him.

"Hey, you got a second? I wanted to ask you something."

Ryan battled his anxiety, not wanting to talk about anything with anyone. He nervously looked back at Smitty and knew the conversation would have something to do with his demeanor in the shop. He kept the car door open, providing a little bit of space between them.

"Yes, sir. W-what's going on?"

Smitty looked at Ryan with sincerity, cupping his hands at his torso.

"You know, you've been a client of mine for over 10 years now—hell, I look at you like a son. I've seen you grow over the years. I've seen your mannerisms change as you matured, but I've never seen you come into the shop and be completely quiet the entire time," Smitty said.

Ryan's throat began to feel dry. His dysfunction hadn't gone unnoticed, and he hated the thought of others being able to see him in the midst of it. He quickly painted on a smile, rejecting eye contact as he spoke.

"Oh, I'm good. Like I said before, I'm just tired. That's all," he lied.

"You sure?" the elder inquired. "You don't look tired to me, you look worried. Now, I know your mom got married a few months ago, that's a big change, and you know our friendship goes beyond the walls of this barbershop. You can talk to me about anything. You know that, right?"

Ryan looked back at Smitty, trying to decide what to tell him. He could talk about Reginald's present alcoholism and how he didn't like leaving his mother alone with him. He could also tell him about the beating he'd taken from the gang yesterday, or the possible hit and run that he was unsure of.

"Yes, sir, you know I know that. That's why I like to come here, but trust me, I'm okay. I really had a long night, drawing and such, you know," he continued to lie.

Smitty raised his brow, looking at Ryan's obvious nervous demeanor. He accepted that his help was unwanted and nodded his head.

"All right, son. I'm here if you need me," Smitty said.

"Gotcha," Ryan replied.

"Be safe gettin' home," Smitty said as he tightly shook Ryan's hand.

"I will."

Smitty turned to go back into the barbershop while Ryan entered the car. He put on his shades and pulled off with his new look, playing music to try and space out on the ride home. Just as he got on the highway, a call came in from his grandfather up in Detroit. His strong voice came powerfully through the radio.

"Ryan!" Hank said.

"'Sup, Granddad."

"What's this I hear about you getting hit by a truck? You don't know how to cross the street?"

Ryan banged his fist on the steering wheel, forgetting his mother had called and told people about what happened.

"Uh, yeah. I don't really remember it, but according to the cop that found me, I got hit by a truck he was chasing," Ryan said.

"What in the world is going on down there?" the old man sighed. "Well, I'm glad you're okay. Camille called me this morning, but I missed her call. You sound like you're driving."

Ryan looked in his side-view mirror, watching out for the speeding cars as he switched lanes to get on the entry ramp for I-285.

"Yeah, I am. It's strange, Granddad. I woke up completely healed, like, everything went away."

There was some shuffling through the speakers, and then everything went silent for a moment. Hank came back to the line and coughed.

"Sorry, grandson, I dropped my phone. Can't get the darn thing to work half the time. I'll tell you what, I'll just call you when I get home. Is that okay?"

"All right." Ryan became irritated. "I'll talk to you later."

The music came back on, and he turned it up louder as he cruised the highway back to his apartment. As he pulled up to his building, he noticed a familiar car in the parking lot. He'd forgotten that his grandmother was coming by to see him and noticed that Reginald's car was gone. He parked and rested his head on the steering wheel, trying to keep himself calm. The unanswered questions of his health made him wish he had chosen to go back to the hospital. He looked at his apartment window and shook his head.

"Here we go."

Inside the apartment, Camille and Alpharetta were sitting on the couch discussing the conditions of the area and Ryan's safety. The discussion sounded more like an argument with Alpharetta raising her voice and snapping with her tone.

"I don't care if it was a bicycle, I can't depend on this area being safe enough for my grandson to be out here," Alpharetta hollered.

"It was a high-speed chase, Mama—"

"I don't care what it was! You got a lot of fools out here getting into stuff for no reason. Why were they running? The truck was probably stolen," she added.

Camille dropped her face into her hand, struggling to hold her own against her mother.

"That could have happened to him anywhere," Camille said.

Alpharetta angrily leaned in toward Camille, feeling sassed by her statement.

"I don't give a damn where it happened, Camille, the fact is that it happened! Why is it so hard for you to understand that? And then you let him go out to get a haircut by himself in his condition. What if something happens to him?"

The sound of the front door unlocking echoed through the apartment, giving Camille an out from the argument. The women jolted from the living room and ran toward the door, watching as it slowly creaked open. Surprised, Ryan stared back nervously at the brown eyes staring at him. Shocked by his refined appearance, his grandmother snatched him into the apartment and wrapped him in her arms.

"Oh, come here, my sweet grandbaby!" She squeezed him. "Oh goodness, are you hurt? Show me your stitches."

She twisted and turned Ryan, looking for an injury, but found nothing. She grabbed his chin and pulled his head down, observing the slightly spiky fade.

"Where are the stitches at? I thought you said there was a cut on his head, Camille," Alpharetta pondered.

Camille crossed her arms, staring at her mother, irritated by the sudden delightful change in her attitude.

"That's what I was trying to tell you. He completely healed up overnight, which makes no sense, but he looks better than ever." She observed his head and smiled. "I like your haircut. You look just as handsome as your granddad in his prime."

"Thanks, just something I came up with. I might keep it for a while," Ryan said nervously.

He could feel his grandmother's eyes scanning his body like the CT scans from the night before. Her worrisome ways never fared well when it involved him.

"Well, how do you feel? Is your head still hurting? Can you use the bathroom easily?" Alpharetta asked.

Her annoying questions echoed through his head with no plausible answers in sight. Unsure of what his body was telling him, he mustered up a fake grin and prepared his escape to the bathroom.

"I feel great, Grandma." He motioned toward the bathroom door. "I don't have any pain at all. I actually feel better than I did before the accident, but now that you mention it, I do have to use the bathroom and wash this hair off of me."

He locked the bathroom door behind him and released a sigh of relief. No sooner had he left the women than he could hear them continuing their argument through the door and shook his head. He looked into the mirror at his unfamiliar face, astonished at how the haircut completely changed the way he looked. He ran his fingers along the side of his head remembering the cut DeMarcus had made, anxious for Monday to come. The hot water soothed him as it ran down to the roots of his scalp, for it had been a while since his hair was short enough to feel the waters.

He went back into his room and put on his sweatpants and a T-shirt, rubbing the smooth area on the back of his head as he looked at his phone. A text had come through from Kristine while he was in the shower.

Hey babe, hru feeling? I love U. Still with my dad. Thinkin' of U. Hope ur OK. I miss U.

He wanted so badly to call her for clarity, but instead set his emotions aside and gave a simple reply.

Good afternoon My Cutie. I'm ok. I got a haircut. Tell ur dad I said hi. Me love you.

For hours he quarreled with the foreign feeling in his body. The restless boy paced around his room, stopping to sit on his bed or on his floor. He was unable to muster up the desire to create art from his frustrations as he normally would, nor could he find the words to communicate his emotions with his mother. He wanted so badly to talk to someone but didn't want to be bothered by their annoying concerns. The room orbited around him, and his mind continued to twist with worry. The sun eventually fell behind the trees, and Ryan sat still on the floor in the darkness. He had not eaten or left his room, nor had anyone come to check on him. The apartment was quiet with the faint sound of cars and his mother's TV echoing in the air around him. His cell phone lit up and vibrated on the bed. Slowly, he crawled onto his bed to answer the video call from Kristine, who had just gotten back to her father's house exhausted from the day.

"Hey, babe!" Kristine smiled. "Why is it so dark over there?"

"I'm sitting in the dark," Ryan replied.

"Well, I want to see your face. I don't care how ugly you think you are. Show me your haircut, I've been waiting to see it all day!"

Ryan sighed, still uneasy about his early morning discovery. He didn't feel confident that Kristine was the right person to talk to, but she was the only person that he knew would listen.

"Babe, there's something I want to talk to you about first."

She gasped, "Oh wow, you sound so much better! What's on your mind, babe?"

Kristine zeroed in on her screen, looking for clues to their talk. Ryan clenched the phone tighter, anxiety filling his mouth with confusing sentences and answerless questions.

"Yeah, so"–he hesitated–"remember last night when we talked…and you saw my face and everything?"

"Yes."

"Aight…something happened last night, and I–"

"Did you cheat on me?" Her big eyes widened with suspense.

"What? Babe, no. C'mon, seriously?" Ryan grunted.

"I know, I know, sorry. You know we watch the Jabari Show every day, I just, sorry, continue."

Kristine sat quietly watching the dark screen, the glare of Ryan's eyes barely showing.

"I had a really weird dream last night. More of a nightmare, if anything. I was running, fast, like, gone. It was a bad storm but no rain, just loud thunder and lightning. The sky was completely black, and I was running on hills, like really lush green grassy hills. I look up and there's this giant red dragon in the sky. I think he was made of fire or somethin'. So I keep running, I run 'till I can't run anymore, and then it traps me in its tail and lightning strikes around me."

"Did it eat you?" Kristine asked.

"Nah, but I kinda wish it did. He asked me a question. He asked me what I desired most. I thought about it for a second and told him revenge, and that's when it got crazy. He said something and then flew into the clouds. I got struck by lightning, and my body got thrown all through the air. I opened my eyes and saw the dragon turn into fire and fly into my chest, but I could feel it! I felt all of it, and I've been feeling weird all day, but that's not even the worst of it."

"Relax, honey, it's okay," Kristine tried to comfort him. "You had a traumatic experience, so it's probably just your subconscious thoughts going crazy."

Ryan looked at Kristine's innocent face on the screen, knowing there was only one way he could make her understand.

"Look, babe, I...I can show you better than I can tell you. Prepare yourself for this," he said.

Ryan reached over the side of the bed and flipped up the light switch, illuminating the room. Kristine watched her screen closely, waiting for Ryan's reveal as he adjusted the phone in his hand to show his full face.

"How can my subconscious explain this?" he stared into the screen.

Kristine's jaw dropped at the sight of her man with his flawless face uncovered. There were no bloody bandages or swollen cheeks on her screen, but instead was the face of a handsome young man with a stylish haircut. Kristine nearly dropped her phone, joining him in his confusion.

"Oh my God! Your face, it's—"

"I know! Look"—he turned his head—"even the hair grew back. I just got a haircut to make it even, but do you see? This has been my day, and I don't understand it!"

Kristine stared at him for a moment as he looked away from the screen, observing his appearance. She watched his eyes and his lips, looking for an answer.

"This may be the wrong question to ask, but I have to know," she stated.

"What?"

She blushed a little, taken by his new handsome look.

"First I wanna say you look sexy with that cut."

"Thank you." Ryan nodded.

"But did you fake your injuries yesterday for sympathy because you knew I was mad at you, or was it because you wanted to build up anticipation for your haircut?"

Ryan scrunched up his brow, insulted. He started to hang up but chose to engage with her questions out of fear of being alone.

"Look, I can show you the paperwork from the hospital and the pain pills they gave me. I don't have to lie to you about any of this. My damn hair grew back. I can't fake hair loss!"

His eyes pierced the screen with frustration as he tried his best to refrain from throwing the phone across the room. Sensing the tension in his voice, Kristine quickly tried to defend her case.

"Babe, wait, just hear me out for a second," she said.

"Why should I? First, you think I'm cheating on you, now you're asking me if I lied about getting my ass kicked because I wanted to show off my haircut. You think seeing you cry last night was fun for me? You think the shame of telling you that you were right in the worst possible way is a joke to me? I'm losing my damn mind over here," he grunted.

"Babe, I'm sorry, I just–"

"You know what, I'm, I'm just gonna talk to you tomorrow. I need to be alone right now. Goodnight. I love you."

Ryan hastily ended the call and tossed his phone to the other side of the bed. He went to brush his teeth and angrily eyed different parts of his face as he brushed. He wiped his mouth with a face rag, wanting to feel the pain he'd endured just to feel a sense of normality, but he felt nothing but imbalance. He walked back into his room, slamming the light switch down, reentering his lair of darkness, and continued pacing back and forth again, this time talking to himself out loud.

"What the hell is wrong with me? Who the hell am I in this body? What's wrong with me?" he grunted.

He balled his fist and gritted his teeth, roughly rubbing his head in frustration until his mind grew too tired to think. He crawled into bed and lay still with his eyes wide open until everything suddenly began to change colors. There was a clear blue sky in the middle of the Sahara Desert. Ryan was again running as fast as he could, creating a sandstorm behind him. Before him was a bright light that he appeared to be getting closer and closer to with each step. His eyes were fixed on the light, pushing his body beyond human limits to catch the bright ball. He reached out to touch the light with his eyes wide open and full of desire.

Suddenly, he heard a familiar sound that nearly burst his eardrums. He looked into the sky and saw a giant golden falcon, the same falcon that he had seen when he was attacked. The falcon continued screeching as it descended from the sky. It swooped closely over Ryan's head, and the force of its movement ruffled the sands and sent Ryan through the air into a hard crash. Before he could get back to his feet, the falcon landed in front of him, slowly tucking its wings, and lowered its head toward Ryan. Terrified, Ryan crab-crawled backward through the sands, unable to breathe as he stared at the behemoth of a bird before him. The bird didn't seem so big in the air, but it towered over him like a golden statue. Before long, the light he was chasing disappeared in the distance, and the sky began to go dark.

The falcon spread its wings, and a golden aura began to form around it. Its large, piercing eyes stared at Ryan, looking for the purity in his soul. Ryan lay still in the sand, afraid to move yet awed by the bird's magnificent presence. The bird puffed up its huge chest as it slowly approached Ryan, stopping right before his feet.

"Ojore," the magnificent bird said.

Ryan dug his fingers into the sand, hoping to feel a weapon to grab hold of.

"Ojore." The bird spoke again.

"Get away from me!" Ryan screamed.

"Fear not, Ojore! Join me and I will teach you, brave warrior! Trust me, I will help you achieve your revenge, Ojore."

Ryan immediately remembered his dream with the red dragon and assumed this was a frightening continuation. He reduced his fear and took control of his breathing, rising to his feet before the bird. He kept his guard low, his eyes locked on the giant falcon. The falcon took a few steps back, giving space between them as they stared into each other's eyes.

"I've seen you before. You're the bird that I saw at my school, and I think you were there when I got jumped. Who are you, a-and why should I trust you?" Ryan sputtered.

The bird grunted and squinted its eyes. It extended its glowing wing out toward Ryan, who reluctantly took a step back.

"Take my wing, Ojore, and I will show you who you truly are," the bird replied.

Ryan looked at the tip of the bird's massive feather, contemplating his next move. Fear and anxiety rumbled in his gut, suppressed by a rising thirst for knowledge. Could this bird be the answer to his healing and the imbalance he had felt all day, or was this another nightmare about to commence? They were soon surrounded by darkness atop the sands, the only light being the aura of the falcon. Seeing no other option, Ryan slowly extended his arm and grabbed the feather.

The falcon's aura began to flow wildly around them, sending the sands into a frenzy. The falcon screeched, and the aura burst into a golden ball of energy surrounding them in its light. Suddenly, Ryan felt the familiar feeling of a power rising within him. He groaned as the power grew stronger and stronger until it could no longer be contained. He released a hellish battle cry as his skin turned bright red and embers fell from his body. He burst into a giant fireball, shaping into the giant red dragon that had haunted him in his previous dream. The dragon roared menacingly as it flew high into the dark sky. The falcon screeched and flew into the air after the dragon, engulfed by its flaming aura. The two began to rapidly spiral around each other until they blended into one blinding white light with the silhouette of a god taking formation.

"Wake up," we said to our consciousness.

Our eyes opened as if we had been startled, but we quickly calmed down, realizing that we were in our room. It was bright, and we could hear footsteps approaching from the hallway. We sat up in the bed and stretched as the door opened.

"Good morning, baby," Camille said. "How'd you sleep?"

We wiped the sleep sand from our eyes and popped our neck, refraining from talking about the dream we'd had the night before.

"I slept good; I went to bed pretty early," we replied.

She rested her hand on our shoulder and leaned in to give us a forehead kiss.

"Well, go ahead and get up, we're going to church today. You gotta give thanks to God for keeping you alive and for healing you so quickly," she said.

Ryan's face turned to a frown, and he released an annoyed groan.

"Don't be like that, you'll lose your blessings that way," Camille sniped.

"All right, all right, I'm getting up," Ryan agreed.

Camille left the room, and we stretched again, flexing all the muscles in our body. Somehow everything seemed to feel better. There was a calmness that seemed to surround us as we walked to the bathroom. We applied the toothpaste to the toothbrush as we always did and looked into the mirror to correct our aim, and suddenly it was yesterday all over again.

Ryan stared into the mirror, terrified of the beast staring back at him. He dropped his toothbrush on the countertop and slowly backed away from the mirror, nearly falling into the shower.

"Hello, Ojore," the dragon-headed god said.

He was terrified. Ryan quickly picked himself up and thought he was still waking up. He reached for his rag and wet it with warm water, refraining from looking into the mirror before he washed his face. He slowly wiped the rag down from his forehead, cautiously opening his eyes. He appeared normal again and commenced rinsing his toothbrush and adding more toothpaste. After he brushed his teeth, he spat and rinsed his mouth, rewetting the rag to wipe his face again.

"I've shown you your true self."

Ryan's gut dropped to the floor, panicking as he stared back into the mirror. He recognized the voice he heard and frantically looked around the bathroom. He slowly opened the bathroom door and peeked his head out, looking for someone to be standing around but saw no one. He crept back into his room and looked at his cell phone. There was a text from Kristine from the night before that he hadn't read.

"I will bring you to the truth, Ojore."

He tossed his phone and backed into a wall as he looked around the room.

"Who said that?" he quietly uttered.

"I did," the voice replied. "I've given you my essence. We are now one."

Ryan shrieked and dropped to the floor, trying to hide on the side of his bed. He looked around his room, unable to find the source of the voice when he suddenly remembered the dream he'd had the night before. Images of the golden falcon appeared in his mind.

"I have shown you your true self, and now I will bring you to the truth."

Ryan crawled into his dark closet, leaving the door slightly ajar to peek back into his room but still saw nothing.

"It's too early for pranks, Mom," he grunted.

"Do not fear me, Ojore. I am not here to hurt you."

Ryan quickly closed the closet door, trapping himself in the darkness.

"This is it. This is what I was feeling. I'm losing my mind! These dreams just don't stop, I gotta wake up," he said to himself.

He curled into a ball and covered his head, believing he was experiencing a schizophrenic breakdown. His breaths echoed in his head, the quiet sounds of his room blasting in his ears like a concert of confusion.

"You are not losing anything, and this is not a dream, Ojore. Rise to your feet, young god, and I will bring you to the truth."

Ryan looked up to the ceiling, clutching his hand to his chest as his heart banged on his sternum.

"God?" Ryan cowered in fear.

"I am not the god you were taught to believe in, nor am I the evil you were taught to fear. I am Heru, God of the Sky, and your ancient ancestor."

"My ancient ancestor? But—"

Camille's footsteps alerted Ryan from the hallway. He quickly jumped to his feet, scrambling to grab clothing in the dark. She entered his room and heard him shuffling in the closet. Her watchful eye noticed the closet light was off and knocked to uncover what he was up to.

"Ryan, what are you doing?" Camille asked.

"Nothing, I'm getting dressed," we replied.

"In the dark?" Her face turned.

"Yeah, I'll be ready in a minute. Putting on my shirt."

Skeptical of his actions, Camille quickly flicked the light switch and opened the closet door to find her son dressed and buttoning up his shirt.

"I told you I was putting on my shirt." We grinned.

Camille looked us up and down, finding nothing out of place but our upbeat demeanor. Fortunately, seeing us happy was something that she had been hoping for, so she didn't get too suspicious.

"All right. I'm gonna go get dressed. I'll be ready in 10 minutes," she said.

She left the room, her curiosity following close behind her. We listened for her footsteps to position her back in her room. The sound of her door closing put us at ease for the moment.

"What just happened? How did I get dressed that fast? She was in the hallway," Ryan pondered.

"There are many things that you are capable of. I promise to reveal all things in time. I can't discuss everything with you now because there are too many disturbances. I will be with you as I have combined our essences. It is time for you to unlearn and relearn your history, Ojore," Heru advised.

"Ojore? What's that?" Ryan asked.

"O-jo-reh. It is your name. It means man of war. I refuse to call you by the name given by your mother. You are a god, and I will prepare you as such," Heru said.

"I'm a god? Wait, hold up, this is going too far."

Heru released a mighty grunt that loudly echoed in Ryan's head, bringing him to his knees as the blinding noise rocked his eardrums. He groaned as he covered his ears and pushed his head against the rough carpet.

"Listen closely, Ojore. I guarantee you I am as real as the bloodshed of your ancestors all over this world. Listen closely, and I shall give you your first lesson," Heru asserted.

The echoes stopped, and the frightened boy turned on his back, grunting as the pain subsided.

"I'm listening," Ryan strained out.

"Good. Now, you were taught that there was only one god in this universe, correct?"

"Yes," Ryan agreed.

"Now, I know they've taught you about the mythological Greek gods, so what is the offspring of a god and a mortal referred to as?"

"Um, a demigod?"

"You're catching on quickly."

Ryan sat up from the floor, skeptical of Heru's questioning.

"They've taught you for centuries that you are a child of this god, and that it is blasphemy to speak of yourself in a higher light. Do you believe this ideology makes sense?"

Ryan's face scrunched up, taken by the question. He struggled with his answer, afraid of what might happen if he answered incorrectly.

"Where are you going with this?" he asked.

Heru calmed his voice, taking his time to carefully ask his final question.

"If this god is your father, and you are the mortal offspring of this god, then what does that make you?"

Ryan froze, his brain battling conviction with curiosity. The room began to spin as the question echoed in his head a thousand times more. The events of the days prior suddenly weren't so vague and unexplainable.

"I've watched you long enough to know that your soul is not lost, Ojore. You are plentiful in what others refer to as common sense. I've listened to your conversations, and I know you have questions about life that you don't understand, the biggest being about your ancestors and their beliefs before the barbarous story of slavery and indoctrination of what you think you believe now."

Nervous from Heru's statement, Ryan scrambled for a rebuttal with his brain running around in circles.

"Yeah, b-but—"

"The law of attraction states that you put your desires out into the universe, and they will come to you, but you can't be afraid when the universe answers you back."

Voices of his past conversations began to echo through his mind. He could feel the unfamiliar essence of his energy aligned with Heru and struggled to find the words to make sense of the situation.

"Don't be afraid of what I'm saying to you, for your fear is tied to what you do not know. You have the divine ability to comprehend things on a higher level, and with a firm affirmation, I declare that I will reveal all that you desire to know and more in time. Now, rise to your feet, Ojore. From this day forward, you are no longer a man, you are the God of War!" Heru proclaimed.

We rose to our feet, clean slated with the knowledge of the world in hieroglyphics. We breathed differently, our senses tingled with curiosity and unfamiliar sensations. Our thirst for understanding became quenched by something we could feel, though the cup was only half full. There were so many questions waiting to be answered—and then Camille came out of her room.

"Let's go, Ryan," she hollered.

We quickly put on our shoes and grabbed our cell phone as we hurried to the door. The world outside looked and felt familiarly unfamiliar as we traveled across town to the church. Though we knew what things were, the reality of their existence was vague. We could hear things we hadn't heard before. The people on the street seemed different, having a keen essence in their presence that had not been discovered before. Shapes and angles weren't elementary fundamentals that we learned in art class. There was more to this day to be learned, things that we would learn over time.

We arrived at the church just before service began. Camille had an interest in singing in the choir. It was her way of releasing her stress as she usually swallowed her depression with bad television.

"Make sure you get a good seat. I'll be coming down to get you when it's time," Camille said.

She quickly grabbed her choir robe and ran into the church to prepare for the morning service. We walked through the parking lot to the front doors of the sanctuary, keeping our head low as we snuck between the cars.

"You shouldn't come here. I saw how they kidnapped and taught our people this religion to make them subservient," Heru said.

"Look, if I wasn't forced to come here my entire life, I never would have. A lot of the stuff I've learned doesn't make sense, but if you're really who you say you are and I'm not having a schizophrenic breakdown, then I'll happily stop coming," Ryan replied.

"I'm happy that you are open to learning and understanding."

We found a seat in the middle row at the back of the sanctuary. We watched the pews fill as the church conducted service. We traced the giant cross that hung above the choir with our eyes—something about it didn't look right anymore. The choir sang songs that sent a few of the church members into an emotional frenzy. The collection plate was passed down the pew toward us, and we quickly handed it off to the next person without giving it a second look. The pastor delivered his sermon with his usual message of giving generously so that God will bless you, a message that we never received.

"See here, the Bible says you supposed to give to the chuch! Ha, see, some of y'all out there, ya got tiiiime for the job. Uh-huh, you got tiiiime for the boys, ya got tiiiiiime to go to the club every Saturday night and spend money on ya drugs and alcohol...but you ain't got tiiiiime to come to chuch and give that money....to the Lawd! And you call yourselves Christians!" the pastor preached.

Several people in the congregation hollered out to the preacher, as others cried in their shame. There was a greater disconnection from the social narrative as we observed the behaviors of the people. The message felt like more of a lie to us, a lie to keep us following blindly.

"It hurts me that there are so many that don't know anything about their culture. There's an entire world out there, and most of these souls have never been farther than down the street," Heru said.

"What's crazier is that we aren't allowed to question certain things we don't understand, and they call it blasphemy if we do. They teach us not to lean on our own understanding and to just give it all to God. To me, it's always sounded like a cult," Ryan said.

Suddenly we were shushed by an older woman sitting in front of us. We forgot that Heru was only a voice in our head. Our eyes wandered, looking at the fixtures hanging from the walls and the ceilings. A painting displaying the 10 Commandments hung from the wall, setting off anger in Heru's spirit.

"They stole this from us!" Heru roared.

We sank down in the pew and covered our mouth with our hand, looking around first to see if anyone was watching us.

"Stole what?" Ryan whispered.

"These 10 Commandments! This is from our culture."

"What part did they steal?"

"This is incomplete. This is only 10 of the 42 Divine Principles of Ma'at."

"Ma'at, what's that?"

The woman in front of us turned and shushed us again. We gave her an awkward look and sunk lower in the pew.

"Ma'at was the Goddess of Truth, Justice, and the Cosmic Order of Egypt. Her legacy was highly revered by the gods and the people. Ugh, it sickens me to see her legacy depleted like this," Heru groaned.

"Well, I guess that should be lesson one," Ryan whispered.

The preacher's sermon neared its end, and the choir rose from their seats and began to sing their closing song. Our eyes looked through the choir members and noticed Camille pointing toward the pastor, signaling us to go up to the altar.

"There may be some of you looking for the truth. Some of you may be looking for a new chu'ch home. Little girls and little boys looking for understanding. Come on down to the altar and let the pastor lay hands on ya. I'll show you who God is," the preacher said.

We could feel Camille's energy, her eyes demanding we leave the pew and stand before the congregation. We ducked our head as the people rose to their feet and sang along with the choir.

"She's watching us," Heru said.

"I know. She's gonna be so mad if I don't go up there. I should probably go just to keep things quiet," Ryan scoffed.

"That isn't what you desire, so why do it?" Heru questioned.

We observed the children happily standing alongside their mothers and fathers knowing that the service was coming to an end. We glanced back at the choir and noticed that Camille was stepping down from the choir loft and approaching the altar. We sighed and shook our head, knowing what would happen if we didn't move.

"I have to go down there," Ryan said.

We made our way to the end of the pew, careful not to step on anyone's feet. The woman that shushed us gave a very dismissive look as we passed by her pew. There was a short round of applause as people noticed us walking toward the altar, which only added to the embarrassment of the situation.

"What are you going to say to them?" Heru asked.

"I don't know, nothing that's going to sacrifice our little arrangement. I really don't want to do this. Today has already been crazy enough. If this is a bad dream, please wake me up now," Ryan replied.

"Tell them the truth they so badly need to hear," Heru suggested.

"You and I both know they ain't ready for that. I don't know if you've seen our people defend this religion, but it ain't pretty if you ain't a part of it. I'll tell them something they'll believe."

Once we reached the mile-long trek to the altar, we were greeted by Camille with a strong hug. We struggled to hide our anxiety as we stood before the people, hoping that a few others would come up to the altar to take the unwanted attention away from us, but everyone decided to get saved another day.

"We have here two familiar faces," the pastor said.

He looked Camille up and down, lusting over the beauty of her face.

"Sister Camille Scales, mmm, you've grown to be a very fiiiiine young lady, my dear."

She smiled at his tired perversion and then he turned to us.

"We also have her son, young brother Ryan Scales. Young man, I understand you're here to testify."

We said nothing. The congregation began to clap and cheer us on.

"Well, it's not often we get to hear from the youth, so I'm gonna pass the mic on over to you and let you give your testimony to the people."

The preacher handed the mic over to us and took a step back. We looked at Camille, smiling back at us with tears in the wells of her eyes. We turned our head toward the congregation, their eyes beaming at us, some of them still cheering us on. We didn't know what to say. We didn't know how to tell them everything they had been taught was a lie, nor could we walk away from the situation as if it never happened. We just wanted to end the moment so the men could get to their football games. We flailed our arm and brought the mic to our mouth.

"I got hit by a truck."

And the crowd went wild. We stood there and delivered a humiliating story of the truck that nearly killed us on the side of the road. Everyone shouted with great jubilation as we gave the detailed story of how an innocent boy battled with death and his determination to live, but at this moment, his death would have been a more reasonable plot.

Church service ended, and we kept our head low sneaking through the parking lot to the car. We had enough social anxiety for the day. Once we reached the car, we looked back and found Camille standing by the church doors cackling with some of the other members about us.

"Oh my God, woman, come on," Ryan groaned.

We checked our cell phone, still notifying us of the missed text from Kristine. We had no idea how to explain this to her.

Babe, I'm sorry. I shouldn't have accused you of anything. It's just been crazy this last week. Can I please come by later so we can make up?

She had sent the text at 8:03 this morning. We hoped she didn't think we were still mad at her.

Hey babe, sry 4 the late response, mom dragged me to church. I'm not mad at you. I understand what it looked like...Today isn't the best day though. I'll find u tomorrow morning as soon as I get to school...I miss u...

"She's coming now," Heru said.

We heard the sounds of the doors unlocking and quickly ducked into the car. The humiliation may have been over, but the torment hadn't yet come to an end. Camille got into the car and immediately began telling us how everything had gone during the service as if we weren't there for it.

"We're going to stop by your uncle's house for a minute. He wants to see you," Camille said.

"Great." We rolled our eyes.

We were anxious to get home to learn about the mysteries of the weekend, but it seemed Camille wanted to make a spectacle out of us for her own comfort. We rode through Decatur, taking the backroads to Stone Mountain, gazing at the farmland across from the train tracks.

"Your ancestors were here long before they were forced into slavery. This was their land. Our culture has covered the entire world. We even built pyramids in Antarctica and other planets. They've tried to erase us everywhere they go," Heru said.

We pulled into Carey's driveway, catching him and his friend Kenny in the garage loading something into his van. Kenny quickly closed the back door to his van before we got out of the car with a suspicious look on his face. Suddenly things began to feel different. Carey's energy felt off, and we could sense nervousness behind his smile. Something wasn't right, but there was nothing clear enough to bring up.

"Nephew!" Carey shouted.

"Wassup, Unc," we muttered.

He yanked us in with a strong handshake that turned into a hug.

"Let me look at ya," he said, playfully moving our arms and our head.

"Well, you don't look like you got hit by a truck. What the hell kinda truck was it, a toy truck?" Kenny joked.

We all laughed. We still couldn't understand Carey's vibe. We strayed away from the topic in hopes that it would later reveal itself.

"I like the fresh cut, nephew. It's on point," Carey said.

"Kinda woke up and wanted something new, and I think it was a red pick-up truck that hit me."

The door to the house opened, and out came CJ, staring at us as if he had seen a ghost.

"Oh snap, back from the dead! The Revenant Ryan. Nice cut, cuzo," CJ said.

"Thanks," we replied.

We shook hands with him. Strangely, everything about him felt normal. Kenny looked at his cell phone.

"Aight, I'ma head out. I gotta get this across town by 3. I'm glad you doin' good, Ry, it could have been a lot worse," Kenny said.

"Definitely. Be safe on the road," we replied.

Kenny hugged Camille and shook hands with Carey.

"I'll call you," he said as he made his way to the driver's seat.

Kenny's energy felt as it had always felt over the last decade: distant. We could never tell what his intentions were; we just knew not to question the alleged friendship he had with Carey. Feeling these energies was so bizarre. We could hear their heartbeats and sense their moods. We felt stronger than all of them.

CJ and we cut out and went to his room to continue our vendetta in video games while Camille and Carey migrated to the living room, conversing about the weekend. After being there for hours, we realized that Camille had come not to show off the resurrected God of War, but to talk to her brother about us coming to stay with him. All we had to do was pick a college.

We didn't even have to get accepted. After a while, it was finally time for us to go. We proceeded to the car with haste but quickly slowed down, remembering it was best for us to act like everything was normal. Carey's energy was still giving off strange waves as we all walked to the car.

"Well, y'all be safe gettin' home. Nephew, I'm happy you're doing good, but please be careful when you're walking to your apartment," Carey joked.

"Aight, Unc," we laughed.

"I'll call you on Tuesday, Camille."

"Okay, I get off at five," she replied.

We all gave our good-byes and got into the car. Camille was silent for a while, playing the radio until we got to the highway. She looked over at us for a moment, we felt her eyes examining our head, tracing the area where our missing hair once was. She turned down to the radio and cleared her throat. We'd been anticipating this conversation for months now.

"So I was talking to your uncle. With everything going on this weekend, I completely forgot to tell you the good news," she said.

"What good news?" we inquired.

"Well, on Friday, Reginald went to see the people at the housing authority, and after reviewing everything, they approved him for the house."

"That's great." We grinned, still awaiting the good news.

"Yeah, but the process is going a lot faster than I had anticipated. We move next weekend, and the house isn't in the same district as your school."

"Oh."

We continued playing coy, waiting for her to get to the meat of her conversation with Carey. We could sense her uneasy emotions as she danced around the topic of what that move meant for us.

"Now I remember the conversation we had a few months ago—"

"Which one? There are so many," we joked.

Camille cleared her throat, pretending to focus on the road. The conversation seemed to get tougher for her.

"I brought you to your uncle's house to talk to him about what we agreed on. Have you found a college yet?" she asked.

We relaxed in the seat, gazing at the trees in the window. There had been minimal research done as far as colleges went, and not a single application had been sent.

"I looked at a few schools that have major art programs within the state. I was thinking I may even have to travel out of state on a scholarship to get into a good art school. Maybe even overseas in Europe. They really like art there," we lied.

Camille sighed, her head heavy with concern and worry. We felt a sadness rising within her.

"Well, I talked to Carey about you coming to stay with him, and...he agreed, so long as you have a plan after graduation, and seeing as you seem to, you'd be moving into his guest bedroom next weekend."

Her sadness cried out from within. It felt terrible. We couldn't be happy knowing she carried this emotion with her. Something was wrong inside. These energies felt so destructive.

"Okay, that's cool. Uh, I guess I'll start packing after school tomorrow," we replied.

"Speaking of school, I'm gonna withdraw you from your school sometime this week, possibly before Friday so we can get everything packed and in motion."

"Say something to her. I know you feel it," Heru urged.

We scoffed internally. We looked at her face, her glossy eyes shining from the side. Did she not want her baby boy to go, or was she afraid of being alone without us?

"Ma, you know if you don't want me to go, I'll stay."

"No, baby, it's not that. It's just...you're all grown up now, and soon you'll be leaving me for good. It's been seventeen years. You're not my little boy anymore. This is more than just a move for me, it's a move for us."

She lied straight to our face. We could feel the pain in her gut. She was thinking about it, imagining what it would be like without us being there. She didn't like it.

"I'll kill him if I have to," we whispered.

"Huh?"

"I said don't sweat it. I love you, too."

CHAPTER 8

THE CALL OF HEROISM

THE SUNSET OVER the horizon prompted the illumination of the city in the distance. Face sat in his office with Porter and Simmons going over information concerning the task of the week. Face, still battling with anxiety over his brother's situation, felt a strong determination to beat Diaz to the punch. Time was wearing down, and a move had to be made soon.

"I've got a whole fleet of guys ready to jump," Face said. "Even though he's in the woods, we still have to think about crowd suppression. I'm surprised he's lasted as long as he has in that area."

"For the most part we'll have to keep a low profile coming in and out of the area. This is the kind of town where things out of the ordinary don't go unnoticed," Porter said.

Simmons sipped his beer as he closely observed a map of the area around Diaz's house. He rubbed his shaved chin while formulating his opinion of the job.

"His property sits on a single laned road, not too many nearby neighbors, and the opposite of the road takes you further into the county. I have a guy out there that's up in the ranks that owes me a favor. You can have your guys ransack the place and search for anything extra that might be on the property, and I'll get my guy to buy us a little time to get in and get out," Simmons advised.

"That's perfect." Face nodded.

Face looked over a list of Diaz's fronts provided to him by Hong. There were several titles ranging from lounges, nightclubs, and restaurants that spanned over the metro area throughout his district. Face released a loud grunt and rose from his desk to look at the city in the window.

"You good, brother?" Porter asked.

"Yeah, I'm just...frustrated. I'm aight," Face responded.

Porter and Simmons looked at each other and collectively chose to ignore Face's outburst. They continued looking over the documents silently when suddenly, Face's cell phone began to vibrate on his desk. Porter tossed him the phone, and he and Simmons quietly eavesdropped while Face took the call.

"Yeah, waddup, Deuce? You found him? You brought him here? Aight, I'll meet you in the garage." Face ended the call. "Let's walk, y'all."

Face grabbed his jacket and exited the office, Porter and Simmons\ curiously following close behind as they made their way downstairs.

"What's going on?" Porter asked.

"Deuce found something that's going to alleviate some of my frustration. He's waiting for us in the garage."

The men entered the garage, where a dark van was backing in. The passenger door swung open, and Deuce exited the vehicle, directing a couple of henchmen to begin unloading the van. He walked over to Face, and they shook hands as he delivered the good news.

"He's the driver. Said he was over there with him today. Told him you wanted to talk to him," Deuce said.

Face glanced over at the van and signaled at the driver's window. The van shut off, and the driver door swung open. The driver exited and walked up to join the group of men waiting to meet him. He stopped beside Deuce, calmly looking into Face's shades.

"You wanted to see me?" the man asked.

Face took a step toward the man, briefly analyzing his face. He crossed his arms, exhaling his frustration.

"I understand you have some information that is detrimental to my business," Face said.

"Yes, I do." The man grinned.

"Good, follow me to my office. I'd like to hear everything you've got, uh, what did you say your name was again?"

Face extended his hand to the man, who smiled and firmly shook it.

"They call me Kenny."

The men retreated to Face's office and listened as Kenny gave them the details of Carey's arrest. He gave them everything dating back to when they started working together up to where he currently worked and even gave them information about CJ. He advised them of the tracker that was given to Carey to wear while he was out on runs, making him an easy target to find if he ever went off course. He told them everything there was to know about his alleged best friend.

"He was tellin' me about when he got pulled over, and all I could do was be silent. He sounded like he was gon' snitch, but I wasn't sure cuz I figured y'all would be on it once the word got out that one of your boys got stopped," Kenny advised.

"How long have you known him?" Porter asked.

"'Bout a decade. We started about the same time, and they paired us up. I started makin' runs on my own cuz he kinda started getting sloppy when his son got older. I can't have nobody messin' up my money, so when Deuce hit me up, I let him know everything."

Face leaned back in his chair, rubbing his chin and trying to hold in his frustration.

"I think I've heard enough. It's time to make a plan, and you're going to be a part of it," Face said.

"What you need me to do?" Kenny asked.

"Good question." Face turned to Simmons. "Sims, how should we approach this one?"

Simmons folded his arms and blew up into the air. Porter tapped his fingers on the desk, trying to help him conjure up a good idea.

"Well, the thing is, he's being tracked, so whatever we do, we gotta catch him right before he makes his move," Simmons advised.

"Right," Porter added. "And wherever he's supposed to go, they'll be there waiting for him."

The men briefly brainstormed while Simmons and Porter attempted to research files to find out what officers were tied to Carey's case. Deuce snapped his fingers, and a slick grin appeared on his face.

"What if we get him while he's at home? That should make it easier on us," Deuce suggested.

"That could work." Simmons nodded. "We'd just have to get to him before he activates the tracker."

"And that's where you come into play, Kenny." Face grinned. "I want you to take us right to him."

Kenny raised his brow, his eyes glued to Face's shades as he approached him. He stared at his reflection, knowing that he had bitten off more than he could chew. He could not refuse his presence at the scene of the crime, for it would only create another crime scene.

"Yeah, I want you there. That way we can get the drop on him before he activates that thing."

"I-I can do that." Kenny nervously nodded.

Simmons scrolled through the file and noticed that updates had been made.

"Perfect, I got the names of the officers on his case. We can handle them this week, cool the tail on 'em to get this done," Simmons said.

"Great. I can set up a fake run for him to make, so you gotta get to his house early, Kenny."

The men continued to piece together their plan to take down the threat. Porter and Simmons left shortly after to start handling the officers on Carey's case. Face sensed Kenny's uneasiness as he and Deuce escorted him back to the garage. Kenny could hear Carey's voice in his head and see images of CJ in his mind, making it impossible to go through the night unbothered. Kenny nervously walked toward his van, tightly clenching his keys while Deuce grabbed a set of keys hanging from the wall and made his way to one of the cars.

"I gotta make a run to the spot. I'll hit you if anything comes up," Deuce hollered to Face.

"Aight, I'll see you later," Face replied. "Hold up, Kenny. I got one more thing."

Kenny's heart began to race, afraid that Face was going to kill him once Deuce pulled off. He slowly turned around, trying to hold his composure in front of his boss. Face observed Kenny's body language and grinned at him.

"Relax, I'm not going to kill you," Face said.

Kenny raised his head, nervously laughing away his discomfort.

"I can tell you have something on your mind. I understand you've known this guy for a while, but he's a part of something that could destroy all of us. He might be your friend, but eventually, he was going to sell you out. They'd come after you once they got what they wanted from him. You did the right thing comin' to us, so to ease your pain a bit, I have something for you."

Kenny closely watched Face's hand as he reached into his jacket and pulled out a stack of cash.

"Take this and lay low until I call you. I don't want you on runs anymore. If this goes the way I want it to, I'll have you managing one of the houses."

Kenny nervously looked up at Face and back at the money. The situation was simply logistical, despite his betraying emotions. It wasn't about the money, it was the principle, but the money made it all right. It was only a decade, and they weren't real brothers. CJ wasn't his real nephew. Logistically, his life would go on unbothered. He felt his soul transfer over to Face as he reached out his hand and took the money.

"Now get out of here. We haven't seen each other all day, got it?"

"Yes, sir."

Kenny quickly hopped into his van and pulled off, anxious to get away from the emotions he'd abandoned. Face pulled out his cell phone and called Hong as he let down the garage.

"We need to move this week."

Later that evening, we sat quietly on the corner of the bed by the wall. The dim light from the streetlight outside the window lit the room as we survived another evening of small arguments from Camille and Reginald. They retreated to their bedroom, this time without the neighbors downstairs banging on their ceiling. As much as we didn't want to leave Camille alone to fight with him, their energy readied us even more for the move to Carey's. Our cell phone vibrated, breaking the silence in the room with a text from Kristine.

I'm sorry I said what I said yesterday. Plz forgive me. I miss you.

We'd completely forgotten to text her earlier but weren't in the mood to talk right now. *Hey babe, I'm not mad at u. I just haven't really been feeling good today. Let's just see each other in the morning. I luv u.*

We couldn't talk right now. She wouldn't understand us. We didn't think we could ever tell her. Maybe it was best that we were moving, but that was something else we had to figure out… how to tell her.

"Are you ready for your next lesson?" Heru asked.

We weren't sure how to answer yet. So much had happened throughout the day. The various energies felt by everything had drained our mind, but we couldn't say no. The life of uncertainty we'd lived not even three days ago had fueled our quest for knowledge. We wanted to know everything. We still couldn't understand how we had not lost our minds yet.

"Yes," Ryan replied.

"Lie down. It will be safer to teach you in your sleep," Heru advised.

We kicked off our socks and got underneath the comforter with our eyes wide open, waiting for something to happen.

"Close your eyes, Ojore. I will bring you to the Spirit Realm and reveal myself to you," Heru instructed.

Our eyes closed, and almost immediately Ryan felt himself travel across the cosmos. There were millions of different galaxies and billions of stars that zoomed by him as he traveled at light speed. He was amazed by the flashing lights and shooting stars, reaching out his arms and trying to touch new worlds. The lights began to disappear, and suddenly everything went black. He looked down and realized he was slowly descending upon an endless plane of sand. There was a calmness in the air that covered him. His eyes closed, he listened to the soothing sounds of the wind softly blowing around him, and a grin appeared on his face.

"And now I shall reveal myself to you."

Ryan's eyes flashed open, and he dropped his arms to his side, noticing a golden glow circling above him. The glow released a loud shriek and suddenly transformed into a giant golden falcon. Ryan watched the bird continue its descent toward him, awed by its grand aura. The giant bird landed before Ryan, spreading its wings and puffing out its large chest. The falcon stood still as if it were striking a pose and began to absorb its flowing aura. Its beak caved in and took the shape of a man's face while its feathers began to smooth out. Its wings shortened and took the shape of strong arms. Its talons receded, shaping themselves into feet. Its legs grew longer into those of a human, still towering over Ryan.

Ryan watched the aura take its formation, recognizing a similar power within him. The aura completed its shape, and its golden glow disappeared. Before Ryan stood the ancient God of the Sky in his natural state. His jewelry glowed as if sunlight were shining directly on it from above. His dark skin glistened with a smooth sheen. His sharp eyes were golden as he and Ryan looked at each other, face to face for the first time.

"Hello, Ojore. I am Heru, God of the Sky, and your elder ancestor."

Heru extended his large hand, and the two grabbed each other by the wrist, commencing an exchange of power between them as they looked into each other's eyes. The air around them warmed up, sending small waves of air over the sands. They released, leaving an honorable smile on Heru's face. Ryan stared back in confusion, unsure if this was all another dream.

"It's nice to finally meet you. I am sure that you have many questions, all of which will be answered in due time. Look with me into the sky, and the histories of the world's past will be revealed to you."

The two looked toward the sky, and the stars reappeared, forming constellations that created images of the past from Heru's thoughts.

Thousands of years ago, I fought my uncle Set to avenge my father's death and reclaim my kingdom. Though I was successful in avenging my father, I was negligent to investigate all that had transpired with Set. He betrayed us, dealing with invaders from the north. He went to them and made a deal that essentially doomed us. Our land for their women. They gave him women by the thousands until one was capable of conception. She gave birth to three demi-gods, Mabaya, Wivu, and Lamia, and they were just as evil as their father. I killed Set when they were still young, but he had given the invaders instructions as to how to raise them.

Years had gone by, and there was peace among the lands of ancient Kemet. I ruled my kingdom fairly with the other gods by my side. Happiness was abundant about the lands as I made it my mission to teach and care about the people of the kingdom, but one day, that all changed. The spawns of Set invaded the lands, mercilessly killing off the gods and the people of the land. I held each one of them in my arms as they took their last breath, vowing vengeance for their souls. We fought as hard as we could, but they had a ruthless ally that we did not suspect. The invaders of the North fought alongside them, pillaging the lands and murdering the people of my kingdom. It broke my heart to see my people fall.

There came a time where I advised the people of my kingdom to leave, as it had become too dangerous to occupy the lands. We were attacked as they began their migration. I fled to the Gateway Stones near my kingdom. These stones allowed the gods and me to travel between life and death to a place called Duat where my brother, Anpu, reigns. He bore witness to leading all of the fallen gods on their spiritual journey to the afterlife, an unsettling hurt. I opened a portal and hid from their sight in Duat, hoping that it would give me time to build myself up to destroy them, but they were smarter than I anticipated. They knew of the stones and moved them, disabling our powers to travel through the realms of life and death and trapping us inside of Duat. In doing this, they also blocked the process of reincarnation. So many souls have not been able to fulfill their journey of spiritual manifestation. Sadly, this did not protect us from the wrath of the evil three.

They would periodically come to Duat and pillage, as usual, feeding on the energy of the souls to keep their strength. They made deals with the souls, promising them life in exchange for their loyalty. Anpu and I have viciously fought them for eras, unsuccessful in bringing them to defeat. I found that if I transformed into my spiritual animal, I was able to leave Duat and travel here to the Spirit Realm, and also into the world in search of a new savior. What I saw broke me, for over time our people were decimated and their societies destroyed. I reached out one last time, and the universe led me to you, Ojore.

I have found it in my will to bring you to the light and teach you the way of the ancient gods. You are Ojore, man of war. As a god, your role is God of War. The original God of War was Montu, a brave and invaluable warrior. He served the kingdom with distinction and poise. Night fell upon the lands as he patrolled, and he was ambushed by the evil three. He gave his all, trying his best to hold them off until help arrived, but unfortunately, he was brought to his death by a stab through his heart with his own dagger. I found him just before he took his final breaths. He died leaving behind the legacy that I now bestow upon you, Ojore. Through you, the lives of the gods and our people shall be avenged and their deaths no longer in vain. We are counting on you, Ojore.

The stars formed into the souls that dwelled within Duat. They surrounded Ryan, reaching out for a single touch, begging for vengeance and freedom. The sight frightened him as they closed in on him, his enlightened senses feeling their distressed energies and screams. They pulled at his soul and brought him to his knees as they transferred their sadness and frustration. Their crippling power strained his energy as it settled deep within.

"The misfortunes you have endured are truly no fault of your own," Heru reassured. "It is not the ability that you lack; you only lack the knowledge. Your energy centre is unaligned, making it impossible for you to progress in your spiritual growth."

"Energy centre?" Ryan raised his brow.

"You may understand better if I were to say chakras."

"Chakras? I thought that was just some cartoon stuff?" Ryan questioned.

"No, Ojore, your chakras are very real, and yours are blocked. It seems you've heard of them before, but your primary chakras are important to your spiritual growth," Heru said.

Ryan rose to his feet and watched Heru raise his hand. The stars began to travel across the sky and formed into several enormous star clusters. They changed colors as the cluster's vertically aligned in the dark sky representing the divine alignment of the chakras.

"The chakras serve as our connection to the universe and our physical being. When they aren't in proper alignment, we lose the ability to control ourselves and our powers," Heru explained.

"Powers? You mean like what you made me do at school?" Ryan asked.

"Exactly, Ojore. You have the ability to do great things when your chakra energy is aligned. Anything I can do, you can do. You are only limited to the limits you set for yourself."

The young boy's interest rose with questions as he glared at the mystic colors in the sky.

"Do all the different colors have a meaning or something?" Ryan asked. "The show I used to watch never really explained them, they just had a guy meditating, and something like this would form in front of him as his body glowed."

"Yes, they do all have a meaning, and they also serve specific purposes, but together they all promote the harmonious relationship between man and spirituality."

Heru swayed his hand across the sky again, this time forming the starry outline of a human body. It found its place in the sky, aligning perfectly around the glowing chakras.

"What you see before you represents the perfect chakra alignment and their placement along the human body. I will explain the main seven you've seen before; the rest you will learn about over time. The red chakra at the base of the body is the root chakra. It is what gives us stability and it is where the confidence of our ability lies. The power of this energy regulates the others, so if it is blocked, the others will also lack their ability to perform.

Traveling upward is the sacral chakra. I sometimes feel that this chakra is the most important because its attributes pertain to how we relate to the emotions of others and ourselves, along with our creative and sexual energy. With our essences aligned, I feel that this chakra is not as free as it should be, understandably. Still, the dysfunction of this chakra in you goes deeper."

"Sounds like you can feel my depression," Ryan joked.

"You are not so much depressed as you are angry, Ojore. You act on your emotions only to be calmed by an outer influence. If you were depressed, I don't believe you would be able to handle what I have shown you. Your anger is not your problem; it is your lack of control. Getting this chakra in alignment will allow you to master your abilities," Heru advised.

Ryan looked up at Heru in an amazed gaze, "Oh."

"Continuing, we have the yellow chakra, which is the solar plexus. This chakra is like a combination of the root and sacral chakra, as it caters to your ability to be confident in yourself and in control of the life you choose to live. This chakra is in dire need of development in you, but do not be alarmed, Ojore, for this is not a bad thing. The world you live in prevails by your failure; therefore the odds have never been in your favor. As I've heard the term, you are a product of your environment, but somehow your energy has still managed to defy the odds."

"But I –," Ryan scratched his head, "– I haven't done anything... well, at least nothing major."

Heru turned to Ryan with his eyes wide and slightly glowing. Ryan's heartbeat echoed into deep space as he glared back at Heru, thinking he had said something wrong.

"The downfall of this chakra is that when it is out of alignment, you will experience overwhelming shame and self-doubt."

Heru's words resonated deep into the darkness of Ryan's mind allowing the young student to hear himself. The years of downplaying his abilities and blaming himself for the actions of others wrapped his mind in its toxic darkness, reminding him that he still was not the person he wanted to be. His eyes fell to the Dark Sands as anxiety attempted to set in.

"Head up, Ojrore, we still have more to discuss," Heru said sternly.

Ryan's anxiety suddenly whipped away as he snapped back to the solitude of the Spirit Realm. Even the darkest of his thoughts were inescapable from the other side of the universe. Heru brought their focus back to the aligned chakras, trying to ignore the darkness of his own mind plagued by captivity.

"Next is the heart chakra. As the name suggests, you can likely guess that this chakra has influence over your ability to give and receive love; this includes self-love. It makes me proud to say that you are not suffering here, Ojore," Heru said.

"I'm not?" Ryan looked on in confusion.

"You may not love yourself the best as you could, but you do not subject yourself to damaging things that could make you worse. You care deeply about the ones in life close to you, and you have a genuine kindness to strangers that you aren't wary of. More importantly, despite how things have gone between you two, you're ready to give your life for your mother. Your heart is what got you this far."

Ryan turned to Heru with a concerning side-eye.

"I don't know if I like how much you know about me."

"Who else are you going to trust?" Heru snarked.

The two locked eyes, Heru confidently grinning at Ryan. There was no one else, at least not on Earth.

"Continue," Ryan conceded.

"I thought you might say that," Heru laughed.

As they turned their attention to the light blue chakra in the sky, Ryan exhaled a deep breath, trying to calm his defenses. His untimely teacher had nearly driven him insane with his sudden appearance. Still, in their short time together, he could not conjure up a reason not to trust him. Acting on his mortal instinct, he decided to be quiet and withhold any more information until he was sure that Heru truly knew him.

"The throat chakra is what gives our hearts a voice. Your ability to communicate is a power within itself. Think of your freedom of expression as a power and not a privilege. The universal law of attraction can will you anything that you want. Right now, you are looking for understanding, but you will not gain that knowledge if you do not put your trust in me," Heru advised.

"How did you—"

"Remember, Ojore, our essences are aligned. I can hear your thoughts and feel your emotions, though I try not to pry into the dark spots of your mind. My understanding of you is based on what your life experiences have taught you. I want to elevate the way you think, but you have to trust that I'm here to help you. You and I both know that fighting ten men is an impossible feat for you as a mortal, but nothing is impossible for a god."

Ryan lowered his head as the moment grew to be almost overwhelming.

"I'm sorry, I just—"

"I know. It's a lot for me too, Ojore."

The two glared back into the sky, bringing their attention to a bluish-purple chakra.

"This one is what I consider to be the most important on a spiritual level. The eye of the soul or the third eye chakra grants us an understanding of things beyond what we see on the surface. It may grant you visions and also enhance your intuition, better preparing you for the task ahead. When this chakra starts to come into alignment, it will bring you closer with the divine or your spiritual connection to your powers and the universe. It is essential that your third eye be strong, for it is what you will need to unlock your final chakra when the time comes.

The violet chakra is the crown chakra, and it is your most high chakra. It is the power that connects you to your spirituality. It is what gives you access to your higher levels of consciousness and ultimately unlocks your complete transformations."

"Transformations?" Ryan questioned.

"As I've said before, Ojore, you have the power to do great things. You are only limited to the limits you set for yourself. It's all about how far you are willing to go."

The idea of transforming into a divine being intrigued the young warrior as he thought of the sleeping abilities his ancestors blessed him with. There was more he wanted to learn to do, but he had his heart set on revenge for now. Heru swayed his hands again, and the chakras shrank, allowing a bright white light to form above and a blackened light to develop below.

"What are these last two?" Ryan asked.

"The dark energy is your Earth chakra, and the lighter one is your star chakra. Like the others, they are both spiritual energies, but their powers are more divine. The Earth chakra connects you with the energy of the Earth, allowing you to be one with nature. It is your spiritual grounding, and when in alignment with this chakra, it will grant you the energy from Earth's life force. It will also cater to your healing abilities.

The light chakra is the chakra that governs us all, as it is linked to your soul purpose. This is the chakra that keeps us and guides us on our spiritual journey. If we were ever to lose ourselves, it is the energy that will bring us back into alignment with the divine powers of the universe. It is the deliverance to your highest destiny, but it is detrimental that you are aligned with your crown chakra to achieve the optimal greatness behind its power. That is all I will tell you for now. I will teach you of your secondary energy centre once we have found the alignment of your primary chakra energy."

"You mean there's more?" Ryan shrugged in bewilderment.

"There are many more things to learn, Ojore. Understanding your abilities and having the knowledge to use them is the most powerful weapon in your arsenal. For now, all you need to remember is that your heart chakra is like a bridge that connects you to the universe. Protect your heart at all cost," Heru instructed.

"I have given you the knowledge, and you possess the power, but now you must learn to control it. You are the God of War."

The might of Heru's words awakened a sleeping energy within Ryan. He breathed heavily like a beast fending off a threat, and a sinister grin gleamed across his face. His body began to shake, and the souls surrounding him turned into fire. The fire empowered him as his grin turned into a mug of malice. The burning fury powered through his soul, and he started to growl as the fire around him rose higher and higher. He bent his knees and clenched his fist, unconsciously concentrating his uncontrollable rage on the rising power. He growled louder and louder, craving the lustful joy of revenge on his hands. Heru stood before him, daunted by his hopeful's supreme power. The times were kind to the spiritual energies, as Heru felt the untapped power prove to be stronger than ever before. He summoned his staff and confidently lifted it toward the sky and called out to the ancients.

"Ancestors, your calls for vengeance have been answered. The God of War is chosen. I beckon your protection, I beckon your direction, give him all that is needed for his manifestation!"

A red essence arose from the fire and flowed into the sky, forming a red dragon. It coiled above like a snake forming a long tail from the fires on the ground.

"The dragon. The chaotic power, an untamable force by any god. A power bestowed among only the worthiest of gods, symbolizing hidden knowledge and strength. Courageous and full of mystery. In time, you will discover everything your powers are capable of. Red, the color of blood and fire. Your power stems not only from your own emotion but the wrath and malice of all that dwells throughout the universe. Your dark powers will be the fury of the gods flowing through you. Fear not these powers, for their thirst for vengeance will drive your hunger."

Red sparks of light popped at the top of Heru's staff, forming into a red ball of energy. Heru grinned as the energy manifested into a bright red glow.

"The ancients have found favor and deemed you worthy of their blessing. They bestow their wraths upon you in the hopes that you discover and trust your own."

Heru powered up, his golden aura encircling him above the fire. He charged his energy into his staff with his eyes piercing through Ryan's chest.

"Ojore! I charge you with the divine duty to fight for the will of peace by shedding the blood of the illegitimate evil that has fallen upon the Earth. You will lead, justified by the principles of Ma'at, and you shall rule with an iron fist. This be the blessing of the gods before and after, on this Earth and in Space, in this time and before time. I give you my humbled guidance to train and build you. The prophecy has been revealed. You are the unstoppable will of vengeance!"

The charged energies rippled through the universe as they stood upon the sands of time. Ryan strained as he struggled to contain the diabolical power aching to be released.

"By the power of fire and the wrath of the ancient Gods of Kemet, unleash the power of the Menacing Red Dragon!"

The red energy ball darted toward Ryan, piercing him through his back and rapidly consuming his soul.

"Feel the fury!" Heru roared.

Ryan's growls transformed into a great and powerful roar that called for the blood of his enemies, inducing a brief transformation. His eye color turned a deep, bloody, and furious red. His canine teeth sprouted into long, sharp fangs, spilling saliva from his mouth onto his chin. His nails grew into short, flesh-ripping claws that complemented his ferocious fangs. His hair spiked up into jet black coils teeming with energy as his fiery aura flooded the lands and propelled him into the sky, roaring for revenge. The essence of the dragon scattered across the sky, reforming the stars of the universe. Ryan's fiery aura shaped into the dragon from his dream and carried him back across the universe, emitting light energy as he passed by millions of galaxies with the cries of the fallen resonating in his head like an ear-shattering roar.

We woke up, slowly opening our eyes to the sound of our cell phone's alarm going off. The room was warm, as if the fires from our dream weren't far away. We got out of bed and started our day. Everyone from our bus stop rode the school bus that day.

We felt all the energies of the students on the bus. They were all in distress. So many feelings of suicide were in the air. This feeling was disturbing. We closed our eyes and tried to drown out the energies, and it seemed to make us feel more of them around us. We felt the woman in the car on our left; she was deep into her depression. This felt so strange. Why did we feel it if we didn't care about it? We must learn to ignore it. We couldn't live every day like this.

The energies seemed to get worse as we approached the school. So much negativity. Their energies screamed for freedom, as if graduation wouldn't be relief enough. Suddenly, we felt a familiar energy. It didn't feel good. It was threatening. The energy drew us toward the window, but there was nothing we would deem a threat in our view.

"What is it?" Ryan whispered.

"You will see. Tell me what you feel," Heru responded.

Our chest tightened, and the fiery blood within us charged through our veins. The other energies seemed to fade away as this energy engaged our senses and aggravated our rage. The heavy breathing started again as our heart pounded like a bass drum. This was unreal.

"I feel it. I feel my power," Ryan grunted.

We licked our lips to prevent saliva from dripping from our mouth as the taste for revenge flooded our senses. The bloodlust for destruction continued to rise.

"Control it, Ojore! Your desires are strong but only as strong as the being in control," Heru advised.

We took a few deep breaths, and after a few moments, we found the medium of our rage and settled our face. The bus finally parked, and the students exited as if it were a walk of shame. We waited for everyone to go in front of us before we rose from our seat. As we approached the driver, we looked into his rearview mirror. There it was. Our face. Those stressed, piercing eyes, the wrinkled forehead, the sharp brow. The change in our hair only added to the visual effect. Not only were we dangerous, but we looked like it, too.

We stepped off the bus and were immediately hit with another wave from the disturbing energy. We inhaled the air like a drug, feeling an infuriating sensation shiver down our spine. We grunted and gritted our teeth.

"Control it, Ojore," Heru warned.

We shook our head and exhaled deeply, walking toward the school's main entrance, the same direction the strange energy was located. We felt like a wild beast trapped inside of a cage as we struggled to keep a straight face. The fury was unlike any emotion we had ever experienced, making it so hard to hide. Our chest out and fists balled, we pressed on, ready to dismantle the threat ahead. Suddenly, everything flashed red.

"Keep walking! Do not stop," Heru ordered.

There he was, DeMarcus, with that slick smile on his face. The fury pounded through our hands like the rigorous talons of a falcon ready to rip out his trachea. We felt so much rage that we grunted loud enough for him to hear as we came upon where he was standing. He looked at us, and his pathetic smile quickly turned to a look of dismay. He stood motionless as we passed by, his eyes locked into ours.

"Control yourself, Ojore. Say nothing. We'll deal with him when the time is right."

The rage was written all over our face. His jaw dropped as we got closer. It was as if he saw a dead man walking on water. There was no blood, there were no scars, there were no bruises, just a fresh haircut and an angry face. We moved closer to him, and time seemed to slow down. Our stride carried an unmistakable confidence as we turned our head, watching him fearfully watch us walk by. We could feel our fury lunging from our body trying to rip at his soul, but we continued our stride silently, swallowing our words as instructed. We could hear his heart trembling with the smell of adrenaline in his blood. Our sinister grin curled to the left as we turned our head straight after walking past him.

"He's afraid," Ryan whispered.

"Definitely," Heru agreed.

"That rush, it was so strong. It felt bad, yet so good."

Our eyes widened as our nerves settled from the infuriating sensation. The tension in our muscles relaxed, and we began breathing normally again.

"As the God of War, you must learn to control your powers before they take control of you. There is still much for you to learn," Heru advised.

We walked to the crowded cafeteria looking for Kristine. There were so many different energies filling the air, worse than what we'd felt on the bus. We pulled out our cell phone to send a text.

"No. Try to find her," Heru instructed. "Try to sense her energy."

We stepped aside and put our back against the wall. Our eyes peeked around the cafeteria, looking for a sign of her location.

"Not with your eyes, Ojore. From your spirit. Every being in this universe has an energy that cannot be created or destroyed. You must feel for her energy. It should be easier for you to find her because your spirits are intertwined. Feel for her."

We exhaled slowly and closed our eyes. The voices of the surrounding students at tables meshed together, creating blue waves of energy that created a trail from their origins. With each breath we took, we began to see clearer images of energies around us. Our head turned slightly left, and a red beam of energy appeared before us. We opened our eyes and walked in the direction our head turned.

"That's good, Ojore. You're learning quickly," Heru said.

We shuffled through the crowd and found Kristine sitting at a table with a group of her friends. We didn't like what we felt. She was worried. What could have happened this early in the morning? One of her friends saw us approaching and directed her attention toward us.

"Hey, baby," we said.

Kristine quickly rose from her seat and wrapped us in her loving arms, but we couldn't help but feel disconnected from her. We could feel her friends staring at us. Their energies were startling as if they weren't the same people from last week. We didn't like this feeling, but we had to pretend as if everything was all right. We put our arms around her and gave her enough of a squeeze to let her know that we were alive.

"Are you feeling better today?" she asked.

We didn't want to answer. She ran her hand along the side of our head, tracing her fingers along the shaven part of our head.

"I feel strange," we replied.

"He damn sure doesn't look like he got his ass beat Friday," one girl said.

We looked at her friends, our eyes full of uncertainty. We looked at Kristine, still carrying her worried energy. She offered us her seat and began to rub our shoulders.

"What all happened to you this weekend? Start from Friday," Kristine requested.

Outside of the school, DeMarcus nervously made his way around to the vocational building. His hands trembled as he struggled to dial his brother's phone number in the crisp morning air. He shook as if he were standing in below-freezing temperatures as he held the phone to his ear.

"Bruh, I n-n-need you...It's the s-s-same guy. He's here...and-nd-nd he doesn't l-l-look hurt," he stuttered.

The frightened boy paced back and forth, piecing together what he'd seen to his brother. His calves buckled from the fight or flight syndrome setting in. He had never been more terrified in his life.

"H-h-he's untouched! Like-like- like Friday didn'een happen! He looked at me, like, bruh I just, I just...y'all need to come and get this dude."

DeMarcus slowed his pace and calmed his nerves as he carefully listened to the instructions of his brother. His taunting grin reappeared on his face, confirming he had once again gotten his way.

"Lunchtime? Heh, no problem," he chuckled as he ended the call.

He took a deep breath and exhaled a sigh of relief and laughed. Feeling safe again, he walked back to the front of the school with a newfound confidence.

"And that's what happened. I just woke up like this," we explained to the group. "I only took the medication from that night."

They looked at us, turned by the facts of the story. Our blank expression gave them no reason to deny anything we said.

"So why did you get a haircut?" one girl asked.

"I don't know, I just...I felt like I needed a change. Suddenly I didn't want all my hair anymore. The twists were just something my barber added to the cut," we replied.

Kristine looked at us and kissed our forehead.

"You still look like you have a lot on your mind," she said.

The warning bell rang, signaling that it was time to get to first period.

"I do, we'll talk about it later. C'mon, I'll walk you to class. We'll see you guys later."

We took Kristine by the hand and exited the cafeteria. Her hand was cold, almost freezing compared to ours. It didn't fit within the laces of our fingers as it did before. She didn't feel the same to us, but we couldn't tell why. The energy between us was so different, but we didn't feel compelled to fix it. We reached her class, and like always, we kissed each other good-bye before she entered the classroom, but we didn't feel the affection as we had before. Why was her energy so different all of a sudden, and why didn't we care? Going through class was no different. The bland and depressing energies around us begging for the final hour of the day haunted our brain like a migraine. By the time we reached 4th period, we were mentally drained.

"Why can't I stop feeling everyone's energy?" Ryan whispered.

"Your mind is conscious of all of the energies around you as if you were a newborn baby. You are emitting a centrifugal force from your mind, and as it feels for these energy waves, you feel everything it reaches for. It is beneficial, for you'll always be aware of what's around you, and once you learn to concentrate your energy, you'll be able to control what it is you feel," Heru explained.

We sighed and rested our head on the desk, trying to tune the world out. The lunch bell rang, and with dread, we walked to the cafeteria. We didn't want to feel Kristine's energy, we didn't want to feel the mixed feelings of her friends, and we definitely didn't want to have to subdue ourselves if anything popped off at the sight of DeMarcus. We entered the cafeteria, this time locating Kristine more easily by her energy waves. As we approached her table, a strain of anger tapped our cerebellum.

"Sit down," Heru ordered.

We closed our eyes and swallowed, carefully taking our steps so as not to change course.

"I know you feel that," Ryan said.

"I said sit down," Heru bucked.

We joined Kristine and her friends sitting in the open seat she'd saved for us. The irritation was etched into our face, us feeling the fury reawakening inside.

"Uh, what's wrong, baby? Why do you look so mad?" Kristine asked.

We looked up and noticed all of them staring at us. Dammit, this was driving us crazy. Our muscles were tightening. We couldn't stand this feeling. We could feel people looking at us, and they weren't just at this table. We were breathing heavily again. We palmed our face.

"I'm leaving this week to go live with my uncle. My last day is someday this week. Probably today."

We angrily looked into her shocked eyes, and quickly the energy at the table shifted from bad to worse. The rage within us continued to grow, this time even stronger than it had been this morning. We couldn't sit still with this. We kept roughly running our hand around our head, the heavy sighs getting louder with each awkward moment.

"You're moving?" Kristine cried.

We started to shake. We palmed our face with both hands.

"I don't think I can do this," Ryan whispered.

"You can do anything," Heru said.

"I can't deal with this rage," we quickly uttered.

Kristine's friends looked on with sadness and worry as tears began to well up in her eyes. We were about to break her heart, but we couldn't stop it.

"Listen. A lot of strange shit happened this weekend that I can't talk about because I don't even understand it myself."

There was a rise of fury that pulsed through us. We roughly rubbed our head and exhaled, trying to control the unstoppable force.

"My mom told me yesterday they got the house, and she's gonna let me stay with my uncle, and that's the best thing for me at this point."

We nervously tapped our fingers on the table. We could feel so much happening behind us. We palmed our face again and lowered our head. We were starting to sweat.

"Why should I trust you? How do I know you can do what you say you can do?" Ryan angrily whispered.

"Hmph. Fine, I'll show you a fraction of what you're capable of," Heru said.

Before Kristine could speak, we dropped our fist on the table, leaving everyone with their eyes wide open. We leaned toward our former beloved and kissed her one last time. We felt the doors of our rage open and release a flood of energy through our body.

"I love you. I have to go now."

We rose from the table and quickly turned away. Suddenly, everything changed in a blink of an eye. Our eyes turned red, sharpening our vision and tracing the opposing energies we felt around us. Our canines sprouted into long, sharp fangs peeking out beneath our upper lip. Our fingernails grew into short claws prepared to shed the blood of anyone that got in our way. The heavy breathing became deep grunts of a rage ready to be unleashed. We heard Kristine's sobs urging us to come back fade into silence as we walked to the other side of the cafeteria, feeling out the negative energies around us.

"There's ten of 'em," Ryan grunted. "The same ten from Friday!"

"Watch closely what we do," Heru advised.

We marched over to where DeMarcus was sitting. He had been watching us the entire time, rising from the table as we approached. We felt four energies following us from behind, and another five jumped up from the table with DeMarcus. The moment presented itself. They were all here. This was why we'd waited.

DeMarcus backed away from us with his signature grin on his face. We were ready to wipe it off with our fist. Our eyes locked on him.

"You should have stayed home today, fool." DeMarcus smiled.

We sensed movement coming toward us, a punch closing in over our right shoulder. We tilted our head to the left, and our left hand reached over our shoulder and snatched the closed fist toward the front of us. Our right arm quickly extended forward and struck backward with a vicious elbow into the torso of the man that had been the first to kick us in the face, breaking his ribs and sending him to the ground gasping for air. Nine more to go. We could hear the uproar of the other students, anxious to see a brawl. The fury was now concentrated into our arms and legs. There were three more behind us, and the rest were fast approaching from the front. We saw DeMarcus cowering behind the group in front of us, hoping that the event would play out in his favor.

We stretched our right arm from our body and went into a spin, our claws scratch-slapping the face of the guy who'd stomped our hand, sending him bleeding into bystanders, watching us make short work of the men. Eight more to go.

Our left hand followed, reaching out and grabbing the throat of the guy that had tackled us just after the truck missed us. We sank our claws into his neck, piercing his trachea. Our right hand charged and rushed back to his face, knocking him dangerously across the jaw. His head rattled as we drew back our arm, quickly raising our foot into the air and kicking the guy who'd punched us in the face back when we had been trying to get off the ground. He quickly fell to the floor, a few of his teeth popping from his mouth as he hit. We released the guy in our left hand, and he quickly dropped to the ground. Six more to go.

We slowly turned around, and there were four men in front of us ready to fight but afraid to strike. One of them was DeMarcus' brother.

"The one that gave him the knife," we said.

The guy that kicked me in the back rushed at us, swinging. We dodged a couple of his punches, observing his movements as his arms passed our face. They were all too slow. We dipped low and pounded his gut with our fist, the force of our punch damaging his kidney. We felt his energy fade as his breath left his body. He dropped to his knees just in time for us to deliver a devastating backhand to his face that sent him to the floor. Five more to go.

We stepped toward the frightened men, noticing the smile had faded from DeMarcus' mouth. We hoped it would come back, either that or we'd settle for breaking his jaw. The two men that had engaged in stomping us rushed at us with intensity. Suddenly, something flashed in our head. The guy we'd slapped across the face had risen to his feet and was about to deliver a chair to our head. We dipped into a spin, narrowly missing the attack, and grabbed him by his arm and leg, tossing him into the other two approaching men. He flew face-first into one guy, instantly breaking his nose and knocking him out. Four more to go.

The other guy was knocked to the ground by the force of the man thrown at him. He moved slowly as he struggled to get up, an error that would cost him dearly. We launched into the air and curled into a ball, our red eyes zeroing in on his leg. We could hear ourselves charging our rage as gravity brought our energy downward. We drove our legs out with precision, aiming and landing directly on his right knee, shattering his bones into pieces upon impact. He hollered in agony, unable to remain still and yelling louder every time he tried to move. Three more to go.

DeMarcus continued to back away from the action, watching us as we ran through his obsolete team of fools. We could taste his fear on the tip of our tongue, revisiting the fight or flight reaction from this morning. The guy that had twisted our arm ran at us with everything he had, which wasn't much for his defense. We jumped into the air and wiped him out with a spinning back kick to the face. His lip split from the friction of our shoe, and he hit the ground with blood gushing from his mouth. Two more to go.

Anxious to get to DeMarcus, we decided to go on the offensive with Punch. He stood there, his guard up with fear in his eyes, looking as if he wanted to reach for something. We refused to give him another opportunity to hurt anyone else. We jolted toward him, growling like the dragon from our dreams, our blood-red eyes locked on his face. He ran at us with all of his might charging through his legs, but his speed and strength were no comparison to ours. Our feet left the ground as we lunged ourselves at him. Our fingers cut through the air with our arms open, ready to wrap him up for the takedown. We tackled him to the ground, sliding back across the floor from where he came.

We mounted him like an enraged cage fighter and quickly grabbed him by the throat, zooming in toward his face. We saw fast feet moving in our peripheral vision, but we'd get to that later. He slowly opened his eyes, dazed by the hit. We squeezed his neck tighter to get his attention. His eyes opened wide as he witnessed the infuriation of our red eyes.

"You gave him the knife," we grunted.

We placed our right and middle fingers on the side of his head and pushed our claws into his skin.

"Now we'll cut you."

We dug our claw from one side of his head to the other, ensuring that the damage would forever be noticeable even after it healed. He screamed in agony from the slash, and we shut him up with a hammer punch, putting him to sleep. Last one.

DeMarcus had abandoned his broken team and tried to make a run for it. We turned our head and saw him making his way toward the side exit of the cafeteria. The crowd quickly jumped back as he rushed toward the door. We jumped from Punch's unconscious body and zoomed across the floor toward DeMarcus, our rage pounding through our hands. We reached out with our left hand and caught him by his collar. He shrieked in fear as we yanked him into a spin. He tripped over his foot and slammed backward into the wall.

His relief was cut short as he was quickly met with our left hand slamming into his neck and taking a powerful grip of his throat. The sounds of his strained breaths excited our rage as we charged our right fist. His attempts at breaking free were futile. He wasn't smiling anymore. We wanted to make sure he didn't smile again for a long time. We punched him across the jaw repeatedly, his head rattling around like a reflex bag. Blood flew from his mouth and spattered on the wall with each punch. We released fits of rage upon every hit. Each hit was like vengeance for everyone he had used his cowardly powers against, and it felt so relieving to bring him to defeat. We charged our fist for one last punch, releasing him from our deadly grip. Before his knees could bend to fall to the ground, we rocked him with a sucker punch, sending him flying into a crowd of people. With his jaw broken, we completed our mission of wiping his smile from his face.

The crowd raved at the sight of the beaten fools. We suddenly felt more disturbing energies from the front of the cafeteria. The SRO and other administrators were rushing in to stop the altercation. We dashed out of the cafeteria's side exit and hurried off campus, our breaths sounding like a wild beast chasing its prey. We ran into the woods to escape sight, juking around the trees until we found an open back yard. We made our way through the streets, running at top speed through the industrial city heading back across town to our apartment. We jumped over and across cars in traffic, narrowly escaping being hit by a semi-truck. We were running fast, but we weren't showing any signs of being winded at all. We flew by cars driving down the busy streets, sensing the energies of people that happened to notice us.

After a few moments, we reached the gates of our apartment complex. We flipped over the fence and continued running through the complex to our building. We felt free. We were unstoppable. We were invincible. We had never run this much in our life, and we literally had just run across an entire city in a matter of minutes. Finally, we reached our building and jumped up the stairs, stopping right in front of our door. Our heavy breathing began to calm. We looked at the dried blood on our hands in disbelief, shocked by the pointy claws on our fingers. We had seen it all with our own eyes, yet it was still inconceivable.

"Did we just, did I—? That power...so much rage. I...I felt it. I felt it all," Ryan said.

"Enter your place and look into the mirror," Heru said.

We reached into our pocket and got our keys to open the door. We rushed inside and ran to the bathroom and were struck with amazement as we gazed at the god standing in the mirror. Our blood-red eyes shone like an open cut. Our fangs were long and glorious as we had always wished for. We admired the grittiness of our face, the true embodiment of what our anger looked like. The haircut made us look even more sinister. It was the best and worst we had ever looked.

"As I told you before, Ojore, I will show you what you are capable of. Trust in me, and I will teach you everything there is to know about your power," Heru said.

"But that power, I just, I just...I broke them. I broke them without even trying! I was jumping through the air, and... I have claws. I have claws! And fangs! I've never hit someone so hard in my life. I...we...we literally just ran across town," Ryan shouted.

"You are the God of War. I've only given you a mere taste of your own power. Imagine what you could do once you're in control."

We looked into the mirror once more, knowing that we'd never go back to the way we once were. The pain we once felt withered away and along with it sorrow. After all these years, we had been awakened. The fate of the gods rested in our hands. We were the last hope.

CHAPTER 9

CALL TO ACTION

DE'ANGELO QUIETLY SAT in his cell reading literature promoted by one of his favorite rappers. The prison kept the air conditioning on full blast throughout the season, but the clever criminal had learned a few tricks from other inmates that allowed him relief in his cell. He'd taken a few wet paper towels and stuck them to the air vent, creating a paper coating over the vent to keep the cold out as he battled the fall evenings. The prison was booming with activity with the cell doors open, allowing the prisoners to walk around and visit other cells. It had been a while since an incident had taken place between the cell walls, something that could change in a matter of mere seconds.

A middle-aged Latino male walked purposefully through the prison with a mean mug on his face complementing the facial tattoos he had gotten in his time there. Across the back of his head was the word *DIABLO,* the name given to him by his boss before he began to serve his time. His fist was tightly balled, and the other prisoners smoothly eased to the side to stay out of his way. He reached the center of the housing area on the bottom floor, passing by another one of his goons, and quickly passed off something under the watchful eye of the guards.

The goon carefully watched his back as he eased his way through the crowd toward the U-shaped stairs. The look of deceit was written in the scars on his face. He took his time going up the first flight of stairs, making sure the guards hadn't caught on to him. He glanced at Diablo, who nodded at him and walked off, signaling to go forward with the plan. The goon reached the top of the stairs, where he spotted a young prisoner standing by the wall. He straightened his face and nodded his head, and the goon crossed paths with a younger gangster, a quick pat on the back disguising the handoff just beneath the rails of the walkway.

The young man traveled down the walkway, his eyes filled with apprehension as he clenched the object in his hand. He focused on the 7th cell down, his breaths becoming more elongated with every step. Coming from the opposite direction was an older Latino male carrying the same demeanor. The two glanced at each other and nodded as they approached the opening of the cell. They came to a pause, inconspicuously observing the area around them for guards or prison snitches. With no threats in sight, they again looked at each other and nodded.

De'Angelo skimmed through the last paragraph of his book, his interest lost in the action of the pages. He tossed the book to the end of his bed and stood up to look out of his window. He observed the guards in the watchtowers, seeing nothing but their silhouettes and the long barrel of their rifles. His back turned to the door, the gangsters made their move. The young gangster rushed into his cell, revealing a shank as he raised his hand to stab him. The man's pounding footsteps alerted De'Angelo, causing him to quickly turn and swing.

The young gangster slashed at De'Angelo but was quickly met with conflict as De'Angelo grabbed his wrist with both hands, desperately trying to keep the sharp end of the shank away from himself. The two men grunted through an intense power struggle, their eyes both locked on the shank. Killer instinct filled the gangsters' faces as they swayed back and forth. De'Angelo shifted his weight and forced his attacker's hands to his right, following up with a damaging right cross to his jaw. The punch sent the would-be attacker into the wall, and the shank dropped to the floor, but the angry De'Angelo refused to give him mercy. He punched and punched, cursing at the unconscious fool as he continued to beat him.

De'Angelo quickly rose to his feet and stomped the goon before thinking to alert the guards of the incident. He kept his eyes on the motionless man as he slowly backed out of his cell, hyped with adrenaline. Just before he reached the door, the older gangster keeping watch rushed behind him and shanked him in the back. The silent killer quickly placed his dirty hand over De'Angleo's mouth before anyone could hear him scream. De'Angelo's eyes opened wide with pain as the goon forced the shank deeper and deeper into his back, lifting him slightly off his feet as blood dripped to the floor. De'Angelo's knees weakened, and he began to lose strength as he succumbed to the bite of the shank. His hands sank down to his sides as his life faded, the world around him turning cold. The gangster slowly lowered him to his knees and grabbed him by his hair.

"Sr. Diaz le envía saludos."

The goon broke the shank and pushed De'Angelo face-first to the floor. He rushed out of the cell with his bloodstained hands, leaving behind his unconscious partner and a fragment of the bloody murder weapon. De'Angelo desperately tried to crawl toward the door to get help as he bled out onto the floor. His strained calls for help went unheard as the fatal wound worked to shut his body down. He reached out his hand for one last desperate effort for help, but his head slowly sank to the cold, hard floor. The former gangster lay there dead in a pool of his own blood.

The next day, Face paced back and forth in his office while he was on the phone with the prison lieutenant. Deuce silently watched as his dear friend struggled to hide his grievance. The hurt could be heard in his voice as he responded to the agonizing details of his brother's death.

"And you said he was just sitting in his cell reading a book?" Face cleared his throat.

Aware of his partner's nature, Deuce quickly sent a text to Kenny in an effort to keep things under control.

Get ready. We need 2 make a move ASAP.

"And where were the guards when all this happened?" Face asked.

There was a knock at the door, and Deuce quickly rushed over to answer. He peeked out and saw that it was Hong and Nassar and signaled them to be silent as they entered the office.

"No. No, just...just bury him in the prison's cemetery. I've got to go. Thank you for calling." Face ended the call.

He walked around to his chair and flopped into his seat, tossing his cell on the desk. He looked up at the ceiling and took a deep breath.

"Is everything all right?" Hong fluffed his hair.

Deuce walked over to Face and placed his hand on his shoulder. Face exhaled and lowered his head as he removed his shades to dry his eyes.

"De'Angelo's dead. A couple of Diaz's boys got to him."

The men were immediately struck with shock. Hong tugged on his hair as he looked at Face with unhappiness.

"I give you my deepest condolences, my friend," Nassar said.

"My brother, I am sorry," Hong said.

Face shrugged Deuce's hand from his shoulder and reached into the drawer of his desk, pulling out his guns. He rose from his desk furious and ready to kill.

"I want him dead! I want him dead today!"

He moved by Hong and Nassar toward the door, leaving his shades on the desk. Deuce quickly moved toward him, urging him to wait.

"Wait, bruh, wait! We can't make that move just yet, but we can make it this week."

"I don't care anymore!" Face turned to Deuce. "I want that bastard dead today!"

"We gotta care!"

Deuce grabbed Face's shoulders and looked into his stressed eyes. It was not the first time Deuce had played the voice of reason, and in this case, he saw himself as the antagonist.

"Look, I know you're hurt, but it'll do us no good going after him now if we don't resolve our other issue first."

Face grunted as he clenched his pistol tighter.

"Where's Kenny?" Face asked.

Deuce's cell vibrated with a new text from Kenny. He looked at his phone and grinned a sigh of relief.

"Ah, this is him, see?" He shared the screen. "I texted him while you were on the phone because I knew you'd be ready for action."

Deuce quickly read the text, hoping that the response would be good enough to calm Face down in order to carry out their plot.

"He said everything's ready to go. We can take out ol' boy tonight, or whenever, so it's on you now. Let's do this first, and then we go after Diaz," Deuce pleaded.

Face took a moment to breathe and slowly walked back to his desk to sit down. Deuce looked over at Hong, both of them relieved that the crisis had been averted. Face placed his guns on the desk and dropped his head into his hand.

"We can move on Diaz as soon as Thursday. Mr. Nassar and I have our things in order with our people who'll be assisting you with the takedown," Hong advised.

"Then we'll catch him Friday morning, right before he leaves," Face advised. "I'll call him to make the deal later, I gotta...I gotta get myself together first."

"Understood. We will leave you to handle your business," Nassar said.

The men turned to exit the room. Hong stopped at the door and turned to look at Face.

"His family deserves no more mercy than he does."

He exited the office and quietly closed the door. Face tapped his fingers on the desk, knowing he couldn't waste time grieving. He put on his shades to hide his eyes and reached into his drawer and pulled out his shoulder holsters. He placed his guns in their respective slots and checked to make sure the extra magazines were secured.

"Deuce, call up the boys. We gotta ride tonight."

He flung his jacket over his shoulder and exited the office, leaving his scattered emotions behind.

For a good minute, we felt like everything was about to go down the drain for us. Camille took us to school a few hours after school started because she'd gotten a phone call about what happened yesterday. She was mad but not at us. We'd told her what happened, at least what we felt we could tell her. We had never seen her so frustrated. Reginald didn't seem to care, but we really didn't care if he did or didn't.

She was ready to raise hell before we even got to the school, vowing to tell off the principal, staff, and anyone that dared to try to make us out to be the culprit. The expectation was a bit rowdier than what actually happened. We got to the school, and we tried to keep our head low because we didn't want to be seen by anyone. Kristine was on the phone with us all night trying to figure things out. We seemed to get nowhere with the conversation because she refused to accept us breaking up. She wasn't going for that "friends" shit. We got to the front office, and they immediately sent us to the principal's office, who had the SRO conveniently standing by him waiting with handcuffs in hand.

"Ms. Scales?" Principal Kirkpatrick extended her hand.

"Mrs. Harrison," Camille corrected. "And what is this officer doing here?"

The principal lowered her hand and straightened her face to take her seat. The SRO looked at Camille as if she were just another bad parent. We could feel the dark energy coming from the pair. They wanted nothing more than to send us away.

"Well, let's just get down to business then, Mrs. Harrison. Yesterday your son was involved in a fight with another student and a group of individuals. According to the school's zero-tolerance policy, any student that fights is to be arrested and sent to juvenile hall; however, that didn't happen with your son yesterday," Kirkpatrick stated.

The principal turned her computer screen around so that we could see the different angles of the cafeteria's cameras and played the video. We watched in awe as we saw a full replay of everything we did, almost reacting to some of the punches and kicks we threw. She pointed at the screen and looked up at us.

"That you, Ryan?"

"Yes, ma'am, that is certainly me," we confidently replied.

We could feel Camille's energy. She was definitely angry, but we welcomed the conflict. We were either going to go to jail to fight DeMarcus again, or we were going to let the officer take us and escape just because we could. It all depended on how Camille responded. The principal leaned back in her seat, appalled by our confidence. She waited to see the smile appear across our face, but we held our ground. The mixed energies in the room were confusing us because Camille hadn't said a word. She was actually watching the video although we had already told her what happened. She sat there observing the screen as if it were damning evidence against me. The SRO began to grin. He'd been waiting for this moment since our first encounter.

"Well, Ryan, let me advise you and your mother of some of the damage you caused yesterday. DeMarcus Graham has a broken jaw, quite possibly from when you grabbed him by his shirt, flung him around, and beat his face several times before throwing him into a crowd of people. On top of that, there were other injuries, including deep cuts and scratches, which leads us to believe that you were in possession of a weapon, which also explains why you fled the school immediately after you brutalized Mr. Graham by the exit door. I believe that you targeted Mr. Graham, and that kind of violent behavior will not be tolerated by anyone at this school."

The SRO stepped from beside the principal and approached us, cycling his handcuffs.

"Stand up and put your hands behind your back, kid."

Suddenly, it got real, and even faster, it got relaxed. Camille seemed to snap out of her entranced state, and the anger she was holding inside came out. She extended her arm across us and pointed her finger at the officer. Her head snapped in his direction, and her eyes were the fiercest we had ever seen them.

"Don't touch my son," Camille said.

The officer froze in place. It was like she had superpowers or something. She turned her head back to the principal, who was not prepared for verbal combat.

"I sat here and watched this entire video, and quite frankly, I don't give a damn what my son did to those boys, or should I say men?"

The energy in the room shifted. We could smell fear developing from the principal. Her eyes got a little wider once she heard the word *men*. She knew where this was going before it left.

"Ryan told me all about these men that were in the video, how they used to be students here years ago, and are apparently caught up in the nostalgia of their glory days. I would think they enjoy nothing more than gang banging and preying on the young girls here, which I'm sure you're aware of."

The principal raised her hand in defense, trying to get a word, but this lady wasn't having it.

"Now, Mrs. Harrison–"

"Don't 'Mrs. Harrison' me! This ain't about me. Yesterday my son was caught up in a fight, jumped rather, by nine individuals who do not go to this school and haven't been students here in years. What the hell were they doing here, and where was your beloved SRO when they showed up? And you have the audacity to make my son out to be the bad guy in all of this?"

The principal stuttered, trying to give a quick response, but couldn't say anything. The SRO took a step back and lowered his hands. Who was this woman sitting next to us? Had she been visited by an ancient goddess in her dreams, or were our powers rubbing off on her? We had never seen Camille this infuriated before. We would expect this kind of assertiveness from our grandmother, but not from her. This was new. We liked this.

"I figured you wouldn't have much to say, much like I don't have the time to deal with this shit all day, so let's get to the point. By showing me this video, all you did was confirm what my son said is correct. That he alone beat the asses of nine men and one student that attempted to jump him in the cafeteria at lunch yesterday, and by the looks of it, there are about a hundred other students that would say the same thing if this particular case went to court."

We sat still looking into the principal's eyes like that bad kid that can't be stopped by anyone. We kept a blank face as the irrefutable facts were written all over her troubled face. From this, we could tell she hadn't expected Camille to love us this much.

"I came here today to withdraw my son from this wretched school because we're moving later this week. It seems that you have no form of morality or compassion for any of the students that go to this school, if that's what you choose to call it, so it looks like I'm going to handle you the hard way. Either you surrender my son's transcripts and let me withdraw him from this school now—"

Camille raised her left hand, revealing her ace in the hole. She had her cell phone. She had the voice recorder on. She had been recording the entire time. We didn't even notice she had her phone out.

"—or I'll contact Channel 2, 5, 11, and 46 news and tell them everything we've discussed today."

Camille, if you didn't know it already, we love you.

We walked out of the office with transcripts in hand. We felt like a fighter after winning a championship match. A small grin appeared on our face as we approached the exit doors.

"Ryan!"

Somehow her energy went unnoticed. Camille and I turned to find Kristine standing in the middle of the foyer with pity masking her face. Camille looked at me briefly and shook off the tension she carried from the office.

"I'll wait for you in the car."

Camille walked out of the building leaving us with our final moment together. We walked up to her, and her eyes got very glossy. This wasn't the first time she had cried today, and we knew this moment wasn't going to make it any better. She didn't have the distraction we had to keep our minds off of it. We were face to face looking into each other's eyes, no idea what to say, and not wanting the help of an ancient god to help softly let down this girl's heart. We sighed and looked down at her shirt. Her eyes were too much for the moment.

"Hey, baby," we lowly uttered.

"Hi," Kristine replied.

Her face scrunched up, and a tear fell from her eye. Just as she wiped the tear away, we grabbed both of her hands and held them. She squeezed our hands tight. We could feel her energy. There was so much love and confusion. Kristine really loved us, more than we imagined she would. It had only been a few months, and honestly, we didn't expect this much love from her. It was all in her eyes.

"I know this hasn't been the best day for you," we said.

"No, it hasn't," Kristine replied.

We looked through the office glass to make sure no one was watching, and Kristine began quietly sobbing. We had to be honest with her—we loved her. We loved her more than any girl at this point in our lives. We owed her that much for essentially breaking her heart. We took a deep breath and exhaled our emotions in the air. This was hurting us more than we could show.

"I said a lot of things last night that didn't even make sense to me. The truth is, I don't want to leave you. You were the only reason I used to come to school, just to see your face and that smile. This whole thing is crazy, you know. I didn't know what love could be like before I met you, but I'm happy that I can say I experienced how sweet it is to be loved by you."

We felt our chest getting heavy. The tension in our head built up, and our eyes got misty. This was it. This is what she had been trying to give me. This love feeling.

"I don't want to leave you, Kristine. I really don't, but there's a lot going on with me right now. I know you love me enough to want to go through it with me, but I love you enough not to let you put that stress and strain on your head."

Kristine raised her head and looked into our misty eyes. Her cheeks were wet with tears from our pain.

"But I'm your girlfriend, that's what I'm supposed to do. I'm supposed to be here for you, Ryan," she whined.

We closed our eyes. She was hitting us right in the heart, and we couldn't take it. Our emotions were feeling the extremes of love, and we were struggling to control it.

"I know, baby, but I can't do this to you. My heart won't let me hurt you more than I am now. I'm moving, and then we're going to graduate and there's no telling where our lives will take us from that point. But it's not a distance thing, baby. I've got problems, real problems, and I need help, the kind of help that you won't be able to give me. I don't want to do that to you. You've got so much going on in your own life that at a distance, I'd only be more of a problem for you. I don't want that. You don't deserve that, and I'd never want to do that to you."

We sighed. We hadn't even been that honest with ourselves before. We placed our hand on her chin and lifted her face. She looked into our eyes, and for the first time, we saw Kristine like we had never seen her before. We were gonna miss our girl.

"You are the best girlfriend I've ever had, the greatest love I've ever felt, and I don't know if you understand what that means to me. You have a love unlike any other woman, a love that is superior to anything I may ever experience. I love you, Kristine, and I mean that. No matter where I go in life, no matter how dark my days get, I want you to know that no matter what happens, I will always love you. I'm gonna miss you, baby. I'm gonna miss you every single day."

One of our tears managed to escape the threshold of our eyelids, but we didn't care who saw us at this point. We had a beautiful girl, our first love, sharing a moment of her love for us, with us.

"I'm gonna miss looking into those beautiful eyes and getting lost in them every morning. I'm gonna miss kissing those soft lips, easing my mind and depleting my frustration. You are a gift from the ancient gods, and I'm so glad I got to love you first."

Where were these words coming from? We drew, we didn't write. Was this love, too?

"I'm going to miss you, too," Kristine said. "I'm gonna miss seeing your big head every day coming at me with those big, soft lips. I'm gonna miss your strong arms wrapping around me and holding me tight on my bad days. Most of all, I'm just gonna miss your presence. You were the only thing that kept me at peace. I love you, Ryan Scales, and I want you to know that no matter what happens, no matter how much time goes by, there won't be a moment when I won't think about you, and you can always come back. I'll greet you with open arms then, just as I do now."

We lovingly embraced, and suddenly our energies went wild. It felt like a strong transfer going back and forth. Tears dropped from our eyes as she hugged us tightly around our neck and cried into our chest. We squeezed her tighter, trying to handle what love was doing to us. We didn't want to let her go, not ever.

"I love you," Kristine sobbed.

"I love you, too."

We slowly released Kristine and suddenly felt a coldness between us, as if something had gotten disconnected. The energy transfer was complete. We would always have a piece of her and she a piece of us. We tried to quickly wipe our eyes, but she caught us as she dried hers.

"Aww, you really do love me," Kristine joked.

We smiled at her, and we both began to giggle. It was the first time she had smiled since Monday.

"You know I do, baby. Don't ever let anyone tell you I don't," we said.

We took off our jacket and put it around her. She loved seeing us in this jacket.

"I want you to keep my jacket. May it warm your heart, as it did when you first saw me in it."

We laughed again, and we helped her put her arms through the sleeves. She wrapped herself in it and smelled it with a warm sigh.

"Ah, it still smells like you." She grinned. "Well, I know you gotta go, so..."

Our hearts full of hope, she looked into our eyes.

"I'll call you later, baby, once everything is situated." We grinned.

Her smile lit up. We were gonna miss that smile. We embraced once more, and that warmness returned. We kissed each other with all the passion and fire that we could muster, the best kiss we'd ever had. We released once more, locked into the spots we stood in.

"Well, one of us has to walk away first," she said.

"That ain't exactly the easiest thing to do right now," we replied.

"Well, your mom's outside waiting for you."

We had completely forgotten about Camille. She was giving us a moment, not a day, and she was already heated.

"Yeah, yeah, you're right. I'd better get out of here. I'll call you later, babe."

"Okay." Kristine smiled.

We slowly turned to walk away, leaving behind the first woman that ever loved us enough to make us want to love her back. It was the best-worst feeling in the world, and we were happy-sad about it. Every step we took felt like our knees were going to break.

"Hey!" Kristine called out.

We turned around and looked back at her as she stood with a faint grin.

"It might be over now, but it's not the end," she said.

We smiled at each other, hoping we'd be able to smile like this again one day.

"It ain't over till the fat lady sings, so don't get fat," we joked.

We both laughed. We'd made her smile again. Our knees felt a little better now. The joke served as a mere distraction from the fact that we were saying a long good-bye to each other.

"I'll call you tonight, baby." We eased our way out of the door.

"I'll be waiting."

We walked to the car, our eyes glossy and puffed from the tears. We tried to put on a fake smile, but we couldn't fake this new feeling we felt. Her essence embraced us as we got into the car. Camille took one look at us and knew what happened. She gently rubbed my shoulder, and her motherly concern kicked in. We needed it, we really needed it.

"You okay, baby?"

"I will be," we sighed.

Camille could never bear to see Ryan hurt, which is why we'd started hiding it in the first place, but we couldn't hide this. This was a different kind of pain. She leaned over her seat and kissed us on the cheek.

"Wanna talk about it?" she asked.

We looked down at the floor, our head slowly sinking to our chest. For us to be a god, love handled us as if we were mere mortals.

"Yeah."

The sun had just set over the horizon while Carey and Kenny relaxed in Carey's living room. They were sitting on the couch having a couple of beers and telling of their struggles of the day as they usually did before they went out on their drops. The two were playing each other well, hiding their true emotions with their inebriated lies. They were both eyeing the clock in preparation for their separate evening events.

"...and I basically told them that I know I'm the best candidate for the position, you know. I got the routes down. I know the vehicles inside and out, so hopefully I can get this CDL training taken care of and be done with this shit for a while, or at least be able to expand a bit," Carey said.

"It'll work out, bruh, you just gotta trust the process," Kenny replied.

Carey peeked at his cell phone to check the time then unlocked his phone and began scrolling through his apps, fearing that Kenny might have become suspicious of his actions. Kenny observed Carey in his peripheral, stretching his arms to drive the attention away from himself as he checked the time on his phone. Carey struggled to keep his nerves at bay as he waited for Kenny to leave to retrieve his load for the drop. The two friends had essentially gone rogue on each other, leaving no room for trust.

CJ came downstairs from his room with his laptop and plopped on the love seat adjacent to the couch. He didn't say a word, but the clicking sounds from his laptop could be heard throughout the room. The sound disturbed Carey's troubled mind, aggravating his paranoia.

"W-w- what you workin' on, son?" Carey asked.

The keys clicked a few seconds more and then came to a stop. CJ looked up from the screen, rubbing his head.

"It's a paper for an English class discussion. I gotta write something about how the art of war correlates to betrayal and deception, kinda like the war in Iraq when the president lied and said they had WMDs so they could infiltrate the country, and then the war in Afghanistan when they killed their former business partner and used the military to protect their valuable assets. Those are just some of the examples I pulled from."

"All right then." Carey nodded his head with pride.

"You got into any colleges yet?" Kenny asked. "You smart as hell, yo."

"I got it all from watching you two talk about stuff over the years, and I've submitted a few applications, I'm just waiting on a response." CJ confidently grinned.

"Like father, like son," Kenny said.

Carey grinned, looking off into space as the moment bought him a little time to clear his head, but Kenny was on to him. He was unsure as to what Carey was hiding but refused to wait any longer to figure things out. Kenny checked his phone one last time and decided it was time for him to take his leave.

"Aight, bruh, I'm 'bout to dip. Come lock me out," Kenny announced.

Relief appeared on Carey's face behind Kenny's back as they walked to the door. Kenny irritated Carey as he purposely walked slowly in hopes that something would happen. Kenny patted himself down at the door to ensure that he had all of his belongings before he left. Just as he was about to step out of the door, Carey's phone rang. Kenny quickly turned around, catching Carey as he frantically pressed the volume button to mute the ringer. Carey put the phone in his pocket and faced Kenny at the door.

"You ain't gon' answer that?" Kenny asked.

Kenny looked at Carey with piercing eyes. Carey, close to losing his cool, grinned and played off the phone call as if it were nothing.

"Nah, it's this lil' chick from my job, I think I told you 'bout her. I'll call her back after we get finished with everything tonight."

The two gave each other an awkward side-eye, recognizing the rising tension between them. Kenny fought his urge to further investigate, seeing that his suspicious foe stood firm on his answer.

"Aight, I'll be back right around 11 to pick you up, so be ready when I get here," Kenny said.

"Gotcha," Carey replied.

Kenny turned to walk to his van, and Carey quietly closed the door behind him. He pulled out his cell phone to quickly check the missed call as he rushed upstairs to return it.

"Hey, it's me...Yeah, yeah, we're on for tonight. We should be there around midnight...It's gonna be me and one other guy."

A few hours passed, and the dark of night coated the neighborhood. The subdivision was a little older with a few streetlights that had been out for years after the HOA had been dismantled. CJ had come downstairs to grab something to drink before he settled in for the evening. His eyes were tired from staring at his computer screen, writing his paper. With only a few more paragraphs to go, he was confident that this would be the assignment that got him recognition from his teachers.

He poured himself a cup of orange juice and proceeded back to his room. He took a sip from his cup as he walked through the hallway and heard a knock at the door. He looked at the clock hanging on the wall; it was 10:23. Carey had advised him that Kenny would be there around 11 p.m., but he assumed that Kenny had decided to come back early. He peeked out of the living room window and saw what looked like Kenny's van parked on the street, which was strange because he had always known Kenny to back into the driveway. Reluctant to alert his father, CJ opened the front door. What he witnessed sent his cup falling to the floor, spilling his juice on his feet. He was quickly snatched by the collar of his T-shirt with the Buddy pressed gently under his chin.

"Shhh," Face shushed him with a grin.

Before CJ was Face, calmly holding his cleaver pocket knife to his neck along with several of his goons with their guns drawn. Among the dangerous men was Kenny with a guilty expression. Face backed CJ into the house slowly with several of his goons quietly in pursuit. They closed the front door and reassembled in the living room. Face turned CJ around, placing his hand on CJ's shoulder as he continued to hold the knife to his neck. CJ stood motionless, stricken with fear as the men took their positions in the space. Tears rolled down his face as he looked at Kenny, whimpering the question, *Why?* Kenny ignored him, doing his best to keep himself straight in front of Face.

"Go get him," Face whispered.

Kenny nodded and closed his eyes as he turned to the stairs, reopening them with a deceitful purpose. He called for Carey as he made his way up.

"Bruh, it's me!" Kenny hollered.

"Come on up, bruh. I'm just looking for my jacket," Carey answered.

Kenny proceeded up to Carey's room, tucking his gun into his pants. CJ feared the worst as he saw Kenny disappear upstairs. His fear began to wear him down, and he exhaled a few whimpers as he breathed, catching the attention of Face. Face leaned down toward CJ to give him a suggestion for his survival.

"Make a single sound, and I'll shove my knife through the bottom of your chin and pull your brains out through your mouth."

Kenny stood in the doorway of Carey's room and caught him exiting his closet with his jacket. He stared at Carey, struggling to hide his shame behind his piercing eyes.

"Wassup, bruh. You early, ain'tcha?" Carey put on his jacket.

"I figured we'd get somethin' to eat. It's gonna be a long night," Kenny replied. "You seem to be ready anyway."

Carey grabbed his skull cap from the bed and walked back to the dresser to grab his gun. He tucked it into his pants and pulled his shirt down over it.

"Just wanted to be ready when you got here."

Carey walked past Kenny and exited the room and made his way toward the stairs. Kenny followed him close behind, quietly drawing his gun and hiding it behind his leg as they proceeded downstairs.

"Where you wanna ea...the f—"

Carey stopped in the middle of the stairs, catching a full view of the men in his house with Face in the center holding his terrified son captive. He felt his fear bomb into his gut, petrified at the sight.

"Dad!" CJ shouted.

Carey's eyes widened, and his mouth fell open in shock. The horror stories he had heard in the past about Face began to flash in his head as he stared into the glare of his chrome shades. He saw the Buddy at his son's throat and could feel it pressing against his own neck. He immediately knew this wasn't going to end well for him. He had been found out. A shudder ran down his body as he heard the hammer of a gun being pulled down beside his head.

"Walk," Kenny commanded.

Carey's breath seemingly left his body as he slowly turned his head toward Kenny and instead found his pistol aiming at him from point-blank range. Carey's shoulders tensed up, tucking his neck in fear.

"Kenny, what are you—"

Kenny angrily forced the pistol closer to Carey's face, reminding him this was not a drill.

"I said down the fucking stairs!" Kenny thrust the gun closer to Carey's face.

Carey threw his hands up in submission as the terror he felt stole the power from his body. His knees buckled, feeling the presence of the cold steel close behind his head. Carey struggled to keep his composure in front of his crying son, reluctant to look into the shades of his captor dimly lit by the lamp on the side table. The sounds of his son's whimpers sparked a useless fury in him, knowing his retaliation would cost them both their lives. Kenny forced him to stand in front of the men directly across from where CJ was being held and quickly snatched the gun from his waist. He backed away, lowering his gun and shamelessly staring at Carey in anger. Carey stood defenseless and appalled by his former friend's betrayal. He kept his eyes on his son, watching his tears fall.

"It's okay, son, it's okay," Carey lied. "Please, let him go. He doesn't have anything to do with this."

"Oh, but he does," Face said. "This is an Illegit Family discussion, much like the one you had with the police when you got caught a while ago."

Carey felt a bowel-shifting pain in the pit of his stomach. His mind was riddled with questions trying to figure out how Face had found him out.

"You were about to have us, your Illegit family, caught up in a sting operation all because you were negligent and didn't want to do your time. How dare you?" Face said.

Face taunted Carey, slowly dragging the dull side of his Buddy around CJ's head.

"We took care of you. We gave you a job, we gave you money, and this, Carey, this is how you repay us?"

Face lightly pressed the blade under CJ's eye, catching a falling tear. CJ's eyes locked on to the knife as his knees began to tremble.

"Just look at me, son, focus on me. I'm right here," Carey instructed.

CJ hesitantly focused his eyes on his father as another tear fell.

"That's it, son, just focus on me. It's going to be okay. C'mon guys, please, just let my son go."

Face's sinister grin broke across his face. His evil laughter brought the room to silence. He closed the knife and put it in his lower jacket pocket and placed his hands on CJ's shoulders. He leaned toward CJ's ear again, peeking over his shoulder at Carey.

"Yes, son, focus on your daddy over there. See how weak and defenseless he is? He's just puttin' on in front to keep you from crying, but he's scared. Did you notice he hasn't even responded to my statements yet? Why you runnin' from the subject, Carey? Huh?"

Kenny looked on at Carey, still masking his shame with an angry mug. His eyes never turned to CJ, hoping not to damage his memory too badly with this situation.

"Still nothing? Not even an apology? You're pathetic. Guys, put your guns away."

The men tucked their guns into their pants and holsters and began popping their knuckles. Carey looked around the room, terrified by the echoes of the cracking sounds. Kenny took a couple of steps back, watching everyone closely, still clenching his gun tight.

"I like that sound," Face chuckled. "Tell me, sonny, have you ever seen your daddy get his ass kicked?"

CJ remained silent, his words trapped by the mucus building in his throat.

"Well, he's definitely your son," Face chuckled. "Beat his ass!"

The men attacked Carey like a pack of wild dogs, rushing him with their balled fists, refusing Carey a moment to brace himself. CJ pleaded with the men to stop the beating as he defenselessly watched his father get struck with staggering blows. Face wrapped his arms around CJ and grabbed his jaw, preventing him from turning his head away as his father was kicked and stomped to the floor.

"Keep your eyes on your father, sonny! Focus on his face! I want you to remember this beating!"

Kenny stood back from the pile-up watching his friend get broken down. His guilt weighed heavy on his heart, wanting to save his friend and break up the fight; however, he knew he wouldn't survive the consequences. He was just as defenseless as Carey, a puppet to Face's game. The beating went on a few more moments, and finally, Face decided to call the men off as he grew tired of CJ's pitiful cries.

"Aight, aight, that's enough, I want him to know what's going on. Get up, Carey! Your son's still watching in terror," Face laughed.

Two of the men forced Carey up on his knees and released him. He quickly caught himself, dropping his hands to the floor to prop himself up as blood spilled from his nose and mouth. He coughed and hacked, trying to catch his breath as Face and his goons laughed at him. Kenny looked down at him, riding the fence of his emotions. A swift kick in the face dazed him, and he slowly began to droop back to the floor. Face pushed CJ toward his beaten father, tripping him up for a laugh.

"Go help ya daddy, kid. C'mon, get up. I swear you're just like your daddy. Are you a snitch, too? Asking for a friend."

The men laughed at CJ as he groveled over to his bleeding father and held him up with his face full of tears. Carey clenched his cracked ribs, wheezing hard as he tried to catch his breath. He moved CJ's arms away from him and wiped his blood on his sleeve as he looked up at Face.

"You know how things go down with this family. What the hell were you thinking? You've got two detectives waiting on you to get to the drop point right now. Do you have any idea of what you would have destroyed? Speak up, dammit!" Face roared.

Carey inched forward on his knees, pushing CJ behind him as he looked up into Face's shades from across the room.

"I'm sorry, I-I was just looking for—for a way out," Carey said.

"A way out?" Face yelled. "You put your family in jeopardy because you wanted a way out?"

Face angrily approached Carey at a grim pace, his anger shaking through his fist.

"The Illegit Family is not a stupid gang that turns on you for wanting to get out. We are a family, the Illegit Family! If you wanted a way out for your son, I would have let you go!"

He stopped a few steps before Carey, looking down at the small pool of blood that leaked from his face.

"You chose not to protect your brothers because of your own selfish needs, even worse, we don't even know what they might know. You better thank ya boy Kenny here for letting us know what was going on before things got worse."

Kenny's eyes flashed across the room at the open floor, avoiding the staring eyes of his traumatized friend. He tried to remain quiet, but his guilt would not allow him to act without an explanation. His face scrunched up in frustration, and he banged his hand on the banister.

"You were going to get us all jammed up, bruh. You were about to get me jammed up tonight! Like, you didn't even tell me to chill out tonight, you didn't care anymore. I was your boy, and you were gonna turn me in and snitch on all of us. Once you told me what you did, I knew it was only a matter of time before you got me, so I had to get you first," Kenny explained.

Tears of betrayal fell from Carey's eyes as he listened to Kenny vent. Their bond, once cemented by their hunger for making their lives better, was destroyed by the same appetite. Carey looked up at Kenny with his swollen eyes in sorrow for what he had done, though he still yearned for justification.

"Why, why like this, Kenny? You didn't have to bring CJ into this. What about him?" Carey cried.

Face raised his brow and focused his shades on Kenny, tilting his head to the side in curiosity.

"Yeah, Kenny, what about him?"

Face brought his hand up to his chin and made a finger gun, a motion seen by everyone in the room. Kenny looked down at his right hand, still wielding his pistol. He then looked up at Face, who had crossed his arms, the other goons brandishing their weapons. He turned his head and slowly raised his pistol from his side.

"Ken, no, please don't do it! Not you, bruh!"

Tears filled the wells of all of their eyes as the barrel of the gun found its mark.

"C'mon, bruh, listen to me! Please don't!"

He gritted his teeth as the emotional waves between them became too much to bear. He slid the hammer back with his shaking hand. Innocent pleading became jumbled words inaudible to the ear.

"I'm begging you, please! Don't shoot! No!"

Fear petrified the victim who watched as he met his demise.

"All you had to do was shut up."

The gun's blast echoed through the house as the .45 caliber bullet made its short travel to its target. The wide-eyed teenager watched the gun flash before his eyes. His head whipped backward as the bullet struck his forehead, breaking his skin and cracking through his skull to the frontal lobe. It made a quick passage through his brain, making his eyes cross as it ripped through his cerebrum, exploding out the back of his skull, spewing brain matter and blood all over the floor and wall behind him. He dropped to the ground, his eyes still open as a puddle of blood quickly formed from his leaking brain and mouth.

Carey released a hysterical cry as he turned and witnessed his dead son lying on the floor behind him. He reached out his hands but was too afraid to touch CJ, knowing that his death had come as a result of his negligent actions. There was nothing he could do to revive him, and he was now alone with the initial threat. Kenny lowered his gun, turning away as his tears ran down his cheeks. He walked toward the front door and waited with his gun in hand, stealing his moment to grieve over his beloved friend.

"Well, I guess that answers my question, gentlemen." Face grinned.

Face reached inside of his jacket and pulled his pistol from the holster. He looked down at Carey, still staring at his son's lifeless body with a broken heart. Face gave him no sympathy, continuing on with the surprise visit.

"You said you wanted a way out. It looks like you got what you asked for."

He aimed the pistol at Carey's head from point-blank range.

"Tell my brother I send my love."

Kenny stood alone by the front door with his belabored face dried of its tears. His eyes closed at the sound of Face's gun blasting Carey's brains all over the body of his fallen son. He lowered his head and rubbed his forehead to keep his tears from falling. Face blew the smoke from his pistol and grinned at his victim, his goons laughing along with him at the sight.

"Aight, party's over. We need to get out of here," Face said. "Kenny? Kenny?"

Kenny was still standing by the door in a daze, unaware of Face calling his name. Face walked up behind him and reached out to touch his shoulder.

"Kenny."

Kenny shook and turned with a startled look on his face, his hands shaking as he looked Face up and down.

"Whoa, relax, bruh. We got the man we're after. It's time to roll," Face instructed.

Face quickly examined Kenny and determined that he wasn't fit to drive.

"Ehh, let me get them keys."

The men quickly filed out of the house and down the stoop with Face in the middle of the pack, leaving the last goon to lock the bottom lock on the front door and wipe the fingerprints from the door handle. Face struggled to holster his pistol as they hastily made their way to the van. He didn't feel the weight of his Buddy fall from his lower jacket pocket, nor did he hear it land in the shrubs alongside the stoop over the rumble of the men's steps. Kenny looked back at the house through the tinted rear window. As they disappeared into the darkness, so did the house with all the memories he'd once had there.

The detectives grew impatient waiting for Carey's arrival to the drop spot. After several unanswered phone calls and text messages, they became suspicious of his unresponsive behavior. The bright lights of a van never found their way to the abandoned area.

"Where the hell is he?"

"Forget it, we're going to his house. We're not taking any chances on this bust."

The detectives radioed in and alerted their stand-by team to make their way to Carey's house, unaware of the tragedy they would soon discover. Three cars emerged from their hidden locations and quickly pulled back onto the main roads, passing by a dark car sitting on the side of the road. As the cars sped down the quiet street, a light from a cell phone shone over the eyes of two rogue detectives. They watched as the red brake lights faded into darkness down the street. The detective in the passenger's seat swiped right on his cell phone and placed it to his ear.

"They're leaving," Simmons said.

"Aight, y'all get back to the house. We'll talk when you get here." Deuce ended the call.

"Another soldier in the game," Porter said as he started the car.

BLAZING FIRE AND CURIOUS ENERGIES

THERE WAS A time when we thought that love would be the only thing in this world that couldn't hurt us, but we couldn't seem to forgive ourselves for being so foolish, even though we didn't do anything to make it happen. It was still our fault for not being ready, for not knowing what we now knew sooner. We'd failed, failed before we could even get started, and there was nothing we could do about it. We might have possessed the wrath of the gods, but we couldn't control the sands of time. Carey was dead. Our favorite uncle. Our only uncle. The man we wished was our father so badly, father to the son we called our cousin who was never anything less than our brother. Our only brother. Slain by a bullet through the skull at point-blank range and left lifeless on the floor. Both of them. Dead.

We might never forget that day, Camille's tears. An image we hoped not to live long enough to see again. A heart broken in a place beyond repair, and yet we wondered what the reaction would have been if it was us lying there on the floor with our names spelled in cursive with brain and blood on the wall. We held her until our shirt was soaked with all of our tears. *They were murdered, was* what she told us. *Shot in the head* was what she said. They weren't hurt, they weren't in critical condition, they weren't alive—they were dead. Dead and not coming back to this world again until we brought them back.

It was funny, we were two souls conjoined to fight one cause, but we couldn't help but feel that a piece of us was missing now. Something that we hadn't lost but was stolen from us unjustly. Where we thought we'd have the most rage, we found ourselves feeling the one emotion that we'd ignored the most: sadness. We cried more over this than we'd cried our entire lives. We cried in our room, we cried in the car, we cried at the funeral home, we cried at Alpharetta's house. We cried so much that Camille hadn't bothered with registering us for school yet, at least until this was finalized. We needed it. They say that pain is weakness leaving the body, so our only hope was that this crying was some kind of foreshadowing for the unholy hell we were going to unleash once the wells of our eyes dried up.

We visited Duat and met Anpu, who took the time to teach us a great deal about our fallen bloodline. We were happy people, educated, skillful, warriors without an enemy. And then one day, it all changed. Beaten and enslaved, trapped and thrown in cages. We heard the stories and felt the heartbreak of the God of Death. We learned how the culture was stolen and copied from the writing on the walls, weaponized against the people as a form of control, and kept the rich and powerful in place for generations, a vicious cycle that we were destined to end by freeing the souls. We saw them, we witnessed Carey's fear, something we never thought we'd see from the man who taught us to be fearless. CJ was so scared and confused. We stood on the dark sands with them, Anpu at my side to help me understand them.

"The most unfortunate aspect of life is the death of the ones we are close in souls with. Though they dwell here in the shadows of Duat, their energies still reflect upon you, Ojore. You are their only hope for vengeance," Anpu stated.

We stepped toward them, and all of our eyes were instantly filled with sadness. The confusion made us afraid to touch each other. We frantically looked each other up and down, hoping the situation could explain itself.

"What happened?" we asked.

Carey looked into our eyes and lowered his head in shame. He wasn't proud of whatever had caused this.

"They can't speak to you," Anpu said. "The souls of the spirit realm do not have a voice, only the thoughts of their actions from when they were among the living."

We sighed as we looked down at our feet upon the dark sands. We'd lost our favorite people, and we couldn't even figure out why it happened. The pain angered us as we balled our fists at our sides, wanting someone to transfer the pain to. We felt someone place a hand on our shoulder and looked up to find CJ with tears in his eyes. He'd had everything going for him, literally everything. It was only a matter of time before the world would be worshiping him for his great works, but instead, we grieved for his young soul. We stepped closer to them, and the three of us joined in an emotion-filled hug. We squeezed them as tightly as we could and left them with a vow that would assure them that they would not be forgotten.

"I will avenge you."

We couldn't stay long. The sight of so much unhappiness was too much for us to bear. Sadly, their deaths did something more that we'd hoped would never happen, something that didn't need to happen for so many reasons, but just one in particular. It brought us back together, the family, the immediate family. We didn't want to see anyone. The family unit was so small that the sight of the rest of them reminded us of how insignificant we were to them—at least that's how we felt. Our grandfather, Hank, decided it would be best to descend from his domicile in the northern region of the states to see off his only forgotten son who he didn't believe in, and he shivered. We didn't know what kind of father the retired lieutenant was, but he was all right as a grandfather. He had divorced Alpharetta before we had learned to make complete sentences, showing up periodically at different times of each year with toys, fishing trips, and sometimes bowling. He claimed that we were his favorite, but we later learned that we were all his favorites. We had some good vivid memories of crawling to him and riding in the stinkin' Lincoln, but it all went to shit very fast. We didn't remember when he left, we just remembered not seeing him for a long time, asking about him, and not recognizing him the next time we saw him. He left Carey with Alpharetta, Camille, and LaKwan for a life in Detroit. We don't want to sound bitter about making a choice for the betterment of his life, but who the hell retires and moves north?

There was also our auntie, LaKwan, or Fi-Fi, as we heard her correct Camille. Fi-Fi made us feel like we came out of thin air. She'd abandoned us, too. Not like Hank but probably worse. The middle child of the three, she gave Alpharetta hell in her youth, which didn't add up to how intelligent she was. When she was barely out of her teens, she gave Alpharetta the slip and ran off to California with some White man, Chuck. She'd met him when she was at work some years back. He was rich, he was married, and somehow, she changed that situation to them being rich and married. She had everything that she could ever want at her fingertips, and yet there was no trickle-down effect. It had been years since the last time we had seen her, but even after spending a few years with us in our youth, she never remembered our name. She called us everything but Ryan, a fairly easy name, only four letters in length, but no. There was no connection between her and us, but she gave us what little conversation she could. Not because she cared, but because she wanted so badly to antagonize Alpharetta and Camille. She had a hatred the God of War couldn't understand.

We didn't want to go home because home was now a new house with Reginald and Camille. Reginald barely seemed to care as it was. We felt that he was angry that we'd be around a little longer, but we needed to watch him anyway. Camille sent us to stay with Alpharetta while they moved everything into the new house. She'd convinced Reginald that we were too emotional to be lifting heavy furniture, and strangely he went for it. All this pain, all this hurt that we all silently held in as we sat on the front pew of the church, overcome with grief at the sight of closed caskets because the damage was too much to fix. We were all together again, yet we felt more disconnected than ever. Today was our first time seeing everyone since they got in town, and we wanted them to leave as badly as we felt they wanted to go.

Alpharetta and Hank sat on opposite sides of the pew. LaKwan and Chuck sat next to us on our left, and Reginald and Camille were on our right. We held Camille's hand as her tears stained her dress. We wanted to sit next to Alpharetta. We could feel her hurting badly, and yet she didn't show it, a message to Hank that he appeared not to miss. Reginald kept looking at his watch as if he had something better to do, not even putting his arm around Camille. Our eyes were red and puffy, and we wished it was because we had just powered up. A few of his friends spoke about him, even his friend Kenny. We had all shared great times over the years. Kenny appeared to be very troubled as he spoke. He could barely make eye contact with any of us.

The pastor came up to the podium to give his sermon, and all we could do was feel like we were being lied to as he told the story of a man who was nailed to a piece of wood in the name of our salvation. It seemed as if his death was in vain, and he wasn't coming back to redeem us. We wanted to walk out, but we didn't want to be followed, so we placed our face into our palm.

"You understand why I say that your mission is an important one?" Heru asked.

"I thought I did," Ryan whispered. "I don't think I thought it all the way through."

The pastor went on in his sermon, preaching about forgiveness and loving one another, but we didn't want to forgive whoever had taken our family from us. Forgiveness was a lesson we'd missed growing up, reinforced by tactics of eye for an eye to make things even, but we hoped the message of forgiveness would be received by Alpharetta and Hank in hopes that they would learn to let go of the past.

"Don't listen to the words of this man. His methods of forgiveness will only bring more sorrow to you," Heru said.

"I think you know I know that," Ryan whispered.

"The time we have is wearing thin, Ojore. Though I understand these are unusual circumstances for you, we must commence your training as soon as possible."

"Ya think?"

We thought we were heard because Camille squeezed our hand, but when we looked at her, she was still crying. We lowered our head and palmed our face again.

"I know that there is much I have to teach you, but I've been thinking, and it is my firm belief that this situation may be the best thing for you," Heru said.

We raised our brow to a strong point powered by anger and confusion.

"And how exactly do you plan to clean that statement up?" Ryan asked.

"What has happened to your family was a tragedy, a miscarriage of morality; however, you are the God of War, and I must get you ready for war. We will use this situation to help you learn to use and control your powers."

"How?"

"Your powers are fueled by the wrath of the ancient gods, an unstoppable force in the universe with a thirst that is only quenchable by revenge. If you promise to commit to your training and purpose, on the souls of the fallen ancestors, I will help you find and destroy those responsible for the murders of your family. This is my promise," Heru said.

Suddenly we were hit with a warm feeling. Not the kind of feeling that makes you feel cozy and safe, but the kind of warm feeling you get when you're preparing to wage war against the axis of evil. The dampness around our eyes dried up, and the puffiness withered away. We felt the rise and fall of our chest and a greater power within our palms. We wanted nothing more than to find and destroy them because forgiveness would never be as satisfying.

"I promise," Ryan said.

We had cried our last tear. Our face transformed from sadness to a dulled fury hidden by the shades we had in our coat pocket. It was time. We traveled to the burial ground, remembering past visits for distant family members. This ground was sacred, where many extensions of our bloodline had been buried long before. There was so much history six feet beneath our feet. We laid our roses on the caskets, purposely pricking our fingers on the thorns to affirm our promise in blood. We would avenge our fallen, all of them. We broke away from the family, leaving them to sob over the caskets as they prepared to lower them into the ground. We jumped back in the limousine with our minds set on starting our mission.

A while later, we all gathered at the church for the repast. We were glad we'd brought our shades because our facial expressions were too much at the time to be seen. We got tired of hugging people we barely knew. Somebody got makeup on our lapel, and we were just ready to go. It was all going to hell until the majority of us had finished eating, and the conversations started, the ones that confirmed our feelings after all this time.

"Nephew, nephew, come here, my dear. Auntie Fi-Fi wants to see you. My, have you grown!" Fi-Fi said with her beloved Chuck standing close by.

We didn't care too much that she called us nephew, but we knew the vindictive shrew didn't know our name. We looked over our shoulder and saw Alpharetta watching. She gave us the fakest hug we had ever received, like when a racist gives good customer service to someone they'd never speak to on a normal basis.

"So how've you been, Ricky?" Fi-Fi asked.

She was doing it on purpose.

"Well, Ryan has been taking care of business, trying to graduate with straight As."

"Oh, that's excellent, Ronny. I'm so happy for you. I bet your mom and grandma are really proud of you," she snarked, looking over at Alpharetta.

She was speaking loud enough to be heard. We could have sworn the only beverages here were water, lemonade, and tea, but her breath had the distinct scent of red wine. Fortunately for her, we were curious as to when she'd be leaving.

"So how are things with you and Chuck?" we asked.

"Oh, you know, vacations, expensive dinners, the usual," she laughed. "Actually, Chuck and I need to be getting out of here. We have a plane to catch to the Maldives that leaves in four hours. Listen, if you ever want to come to California and get away from your mother for a while, just give your aunt a call, and I'll fatten your pockets."

She didn't even care. She just came to pour salt in Alpharetta's wounds. She was beyond help. Fi-Fi went around fake hugging everyone as she prepared to leave, saving Alpharetta for last. The two exchanged words, and Fi-Fi appeared infuriated by what Alpharetta said, calling over to Chuck as she stormed toward the door. Chuck had been kind, shaking hands with everyone and offering his condolences to the family. He was an alright guy...blind, but all right nonetheless. He walked over to us and shook our hand.

"Ryan, I just want to offer my condolences, I know this is an extremely hard time for you and the family, and I want you to know that your aunt's offer will always stand on the table whenever you're ready," Chuck said.

"Let's go, Chuck!" Fi-Fi hollered.

Chuck heard the whip crack and released our hand, looking back and waving at the family as he and Fi-Fi made their exit. He'd remembered our name, and he was kind. An alright guy in our book.

We walked over to the table where Alpharetta was sitting along with Camille and Hank. We didn't know where Reginald went, and we didn't care. It appeared Hank was saying something to them that might be valuable to our ears.

"I just want to apologize for everything." Hank's voice cracked. "My son is dead, and I...I just want to make things right, not just to honor him, but to right the unchangeable wrongs I've done to this family."

Camille passed him a napkin to dry his eyes—she always was a Daddy's girl. He wiped his eyes, catching a blurred image of us walking up to the table.

"Ryan, grandson!"

He walked over to us and gave us the hug of a man who knew he had done wrong. We felt his sorrow. We just knew that he'd done the best that he could, which turned out to be the worst that he could, and with his eldest grandson standing at the brink of manhood, we assumed he felt like he had to raise us right before the streets got to us.

"I want you to hear this, I want all of you to know actually. I'm here to stay this time. I sold my house in Michigan, and uh, in a few days my things will be here, and I'll be living over in the Rockbridge Road area, not too far from where we used to live in Stone Mountain."

We wanted to be happy about this news. We wanted to embrace him and be happy about it. He placed his hand on our shoulder and looked into our shades.

"And you and me are gonna go fishing at Lake Point, just like we used to when you were younger," Hank said.

We wanted that to mean something to us. Maybe age had desensitized us, or possibly it was the funeral, but we didn't care about any of that anymore. We felt like we'd forever be seven in his eyes, the age we had been when he left.

The repast ended, and everyone went their separate ways. Alpharetta still wasn't saying much, but she insisted that we go home with Camille. She was finally going to cry tonight.

"Please be safe out there, Ryan. Look after your mother," she said with sorrow.

We nodded, saving our words to save her tears. We got in the backseat of the car and waved good-bye as we rode off. The ride home was silent. Surprisingly, Reginald had nothing to say to us. We quickly remembered there was a mission we were on and deployed our methods of teenage angst against our mother in her vulnerable state.

"Ma, when we get home, you mind if I take the car out? I just need to...get away for a minute. Maybe meet up with Kristine at the mall or something."

We hadn't talked to Kristine since last week. We'd been ignoring her calls and texts because we didn't want our favorite Cancer getting overly emotional about what was happening. We'd already cried enough. We'd probably call her later.

"That's fine, sweetheart, just please be careful. I can't take another loss anytime soon," she sighed.

Camille looked aimlessly out of the window. We had seen her hurt before, but this was worse. She was broken. If there was anything that she loved besides us and Reginald's drunken rants, it was her baby brother. Her nephew only sweetened the deal. We got to the new house, and we were a little impressed. It was big, with five bedrooms and three full bathrooms, a split level with a garage and a decent-sized yard. As we pulled into the two-car garage, Camille released a deep sigh.

"I gotta piss," Reginald uttered as he hurried out of the car and into the house.

We grabbed our backpack and helped Camille out of the car. It was like escorting a widow home after her loving husband died and she didn't care about the insurance money.

"You can give me a tour of the house later. I know you probably want to lie down right now," we said.

"Yeah, I do," she replied.

The downstairs was kind of dope, equipped with sufficient space for a family gathering that we would never have. We walked upstairs, and she pointed in the direction of our room.

"Your room is the one to the left. I tried to convince Reginald to give you the room downstairs so you could have your privacy, but he kept arguing that you might try to sneak out at night," Camille said.

"And go where?" we replied.

"That's what I said. You don't even do stuff like that, but that's what he used to do when he was your age. You'll be off to college by this time next year anyway, so it won't even matter soon, but all of your art stuff is in the closet. I didn't have time to organize it yet."

It probably would have made her cry if we told her that we hadn't looked at any colleges at all since we'd last talked about it. Most of the colleges had already passed their application deadline for next year's fall semester, and we didn't plan on spending money on application fees. The deal was we'd look into it, not that we would go. Plus, Carey had died, so the deal was null and void.

"Don't worry about it. I'll get to it at some point. Go lie down, I'll be back in a little while," we said.

Camille reached in her purse and turned over her keys to us. She reached in and hugged us tightly, releasing a deep sigh coated in sadness and worry.

"Please be careful. I don't think anyone would ever be able to console me if I lost you," Camille sobbed.

It felt like time stopped when that registered.

"I will. I'll be back before 11."

Camille kissed us on the cheek and slowly walked to her room and closed the door. This was a different kind of hurt she was experiencing. What would she look like as an inconsolable wreck? We went to our room and snatched clothes out of our bookbag that we hadn't worn yet. Black tennis shoes, black sweats, black hoodie, nothing incriminating. We stepped into our bathroom for a quick look in the mirror.

"Are you ready to start your training?" Heru asked.

"I was born ready," Ryan affirmed.

We got in the car and took a ride across town to the one place we were adamant about avoiding. Fortunately, the change in time made it easier for us to work with the cover of darkness. The evening sun had already made its descent behind the tree line, guaranteeing darkness by the time we got there. The highways were dying down with evening traffic because Wednesday afternoon is always a good day for a funeral. At least it wasn't raining.

"The most important part of your training is going to be your mindset. You must understand the prestigious honor it is to be the God of War. Carry yourself as such, and the respect that is due to you will be admirable. With the world in the shape it's in, there is truly no telling what else is out there," Heru advised.

"I feel like I've been walking around with an angry mug since I got these powers," Ryan said.

"It's your resting wrath. When you learn to control your powers, they'll always be at your fingertips. You don't ever need to be angry to use them."

"So what all can I do?"

"Heh, once you master your energy, all you'll have to do is use your imagination."

The sun set as we got off the interstate and made our way down the busy highway. Thoughts of Alpharetta at the funeral flashed through our mind. Never in life had we ever witnessed that look on her face. She was always something specific–happy, angry, disappointed—but today, she had been just a shell. She deserved justice, an answer to her never-ending questions, and we were going to get it.

We traveled down the quiet residential streets, observing cars pulling into their driveways. The closer we got to our destination, the more a strange anxiety grew upon us. We couldn't allow the feeling to overtake our initiative because there was too much on the line for us. We had to quickly learn to limit our emotions as we didn't need to feel anything that would further delay our process. The top were happiness and anger, happiness because we had to find our moments, and anger because anything that made us feel anything other than happiness must correlate to anger. We couldn't feel sadness; we could only feel anger.

We made the left turn into a neighborhood, and everything got quiet. We couldn't even hear the engine anymore. The energies in the area were dull with no kind of excitement detected. We slowed the car to a cruising speed, taking time to prepare ourselves for what we might see.

"You are ready. Fear nothing, Ojore. I am with you," Heru reassured.

As we came down the street, we immediately noticed something that had changed since the last time we were there.

"They got a new streetlight out here."

The former broken and outdated streetlight had been replaced with a new LED light pole that illuminated the area better than the porch lights on the houses. And then, there it was, Carey's house. We sat in the car and stared at it for a moment. The sight of it sent a cold chill down our spine. The house was dark, and there was still police tape on the stoop and front door.

"This is it," Ryan sighed. "I had so many memories in this house."

"We must get in there and search for anything that may be useful," Heru advised.

"But we can't just walk through the door. It's not as dark as it normally is with this new light, and people are still coming home from work. I don't want anyone to drive by and see me."

"Lesson one, Ojore. Until you master your abilities, you must use your first basic skill of stealth. You know this area well. Figure out how to get inside."

"Can't you make me fly over the house to get to the back of it, or just magically open the door or something?"

"If only I could. My abilities are limited through you," Heru said.

We took a few moments casing the house from the car. The house to the right was well lit, lights on inside and out. There were windows on the side of the house, so going in between them was out of the question. The light pole caused the house on the left to cast a shadow on the other side of the house, leaving enough light to still be seen but not as clearly. We scoffed. We were going to have to be smart about this because we'd probably already been seen just sitting here in the car. We pulled the car down the street and doubled back, stopping a few houses down, and parked to think for a second.

"I'll run for the shadows," Ryan said. "If I remember correctly, there should be a spare key to the back door inside the top of the grill back there—that's if it's still there."

"Let us begin," Heru said.

We looked around the area to make sure there was no one standing outside. We slipped on our hood and got out of the car, carefully closing the door to avoid alerting anyone. We quickly walked toward the house, trying to be inconspicuous as possible, but the glare of car lights shined on the houses in the distance. We took off and made it before the car cut the corner without catching us in the yard. The car passed by, barely missing us with our back against the wall of the house. We crept to the fenced-in backyard, hopping the gate with a high leap. We peeked around the corner to the back porch, where the grill sat in plain view. The neighbors on the right of the house had their porch light on, and there was someone sitting by the window in the back of the house. We had to be quick.

We crept to the grill facing the neighbor's house, staying low to avoid detection. We slowly lifted the grill. The rusted steel hinges made a little noise but not enough to be heard from far away. We felt under the grill for the key and slowly set the top down. We put the key in the door, anxious to make our way inside and discover something.

"Wait, Ojore! No one must find out you were here," Heru advised.

"Crap, I almost forgot," Ryan said.

We quietly took off our shoes and set them at the door. We checked the cargo pocket of our sweats and pulled out our work-out gloves, a take-home gift from our late uncle. He'd gotten CJ a matching pair, too. After putting them on, we quietly made our way into the house. Everything was off, and the house was cold and lifeless. Though there were no present energies, we felt hints of energy from everyone who had been in the house recently. The past energies were unidentifiable, and there were more than 40, possibly from the investigation. We stepped through the kitchen and into the living room, and our anger intensified.

"This is where it happened," Ryan grunted.

The dried blood spatters were not a decorative piece to complement the dried blood pools on the floor. We closed our eyes, and suddenly we could see ghostly reenactments of their deaths over by the stairs through our mind. We couldn't see the faces of their murderers, but we watched them take their time beating Carey and murdering both of them. It felt like it had happened right before our eyes. We dropped to our knees, overwhelmed by the visions.

"No, this can't be how it happened! It can't be! Why would anyone do this to them?" Ryan hollered.

"Pull yourself together, Ojore! Control your emotions like you would your powers," Heru instructed.

We opened our eyes with our rising fury contained under a thin layer of skin. The anger compelled us to keep looking around the crime scene for something the police might have missed. We were careful to avoid sabotaging evidence as we looked in, on, and around everything in the living room. We checked upstairs but found nothing that was out of the ordinary. There was no sign of foul play in the garage either. It appeared that this wasn't a robbery at all.

"This was a hit."

After searching for a good hour, we felt as if we had exhausted our efforts. We had checked every inch of the interior of the house, but there was nothing that stood out, nothing that gave even a smidgeon of suspicion. A well-executed murder. We wallowed in confusion to the back door, our hopes fading away like the energies that faded from the living room. The silence mocked us as we looked back at the dark room from the back door.

"There has to be something around here somewhere," Ryan said.

We pocketed the spare key and snuck out of the house. How could we avenge the deaths of our loved ones without a clue to give us a place to begin looking? Why would an execution of this caliber be brought upon our family?

"Ojore, pay attention! We still can't be seen!" Heru warned.

We quickly glued ourselves to the wall as a car passed by. We had to get it together, or our emotions were going to get us caught up. We crept closer to the front corner of the house, hearing the sound of cars in the distance. We peeked from behind the wall to see if any cars were coming and noticed something glowing through the shrubs by the stoop, which was strange because this side of the stoop cast a shadow over the shrubs from the streetlight. There was something over there.

"What is that?" Ryan curiously asked.

"You're seeing with your third eye," Heru said. "You've made a discovery."

The concept of stealth was quickly forgotten as we ran over to the glowing light. We dug through the shrubs and pulled out a cold steel object and held it up to the light. Suddenly, we were struck with a wave of energy that snapped our head back. Our eyes rolled back, and we were surrounded by darkness. There were hundreds of agonizing screams telling the tale of brutal murders from years ago until now. The cries of men and women begging for their lives, the screams of people being sliced and stabbed, their blood dripping from the blade onto the cold, hard ground. They yearned for vengeance. The images of their deaths crowded our mind like a compilation of heinous murders. We could feel our body trembling as the souls of the fallen whirled around us.

Suddenly, they all whirled off in one direction, and from the darkness emerged several energies—the same fading energies that we'd felt inside the house, only this time they had more of a presence. There was one in particular that caught our eye. This energy was more complete than the others. It had a detailed shape and color. It had on clothes. It had a face, a face we had never seen before. The energy appeared to reach into its pocket and pulled out a knife similar to the one we were holding. It was him, this was the owner of the knife, this man with this...face. There was one more energy that we could feel. This one was almost like the other, but it had a shadow over its face, though it felt familiar, as if we knew him from somewhere before. The others had fading shapes, and all we could make out were their hands and feet.

We turned back to the energy with the face, and the others disappeared. The energy stood confident with a smile. It wiped its hand over its eyes, and they turned into pools of darkness, looking as if it were wearing shades. It tilted its head and appeared to be smiling at us. We looked at the knife and flicked it open, the dark energy following suit. We stared each other down, circling around and creating a ball of rage between us. We heard our uncle scream, and suddenly we shook ourselves back to reality. We were still standing in the yard holding the knife up to the light like we had just found it. We flicked out the blade to make a quick observation of it.

"Buddy," Ryan read on the blade.

"Check the other side," Heru advised.

"ILLEGIT. I've heard this name before. They're some kind of gang—at least that's what they say about them on TV."

"Let us leave this place. We have found what we were looking for."

"Right."

We closed the knife and stuffed it into our pocket. It belonged to us now. We hurried back to the car and drove away, hoping no one had seen a suspicious man standing in the yard of a crime scene. As we exited the neighborhood, a patrol car entered and drove slowly past us. We stared at our rearview mirror until the car disappeared around the corner. We drove back to our new dungeon, feeling the energies of the images we'd felt while holding the knife. A couple of the energies gave off strong forces, while the others seemed normal—like the people we'd pass by on the way to school, but they weren't irrelevant. Some felt scattered over the city while others were together.

"As much as I would like to go after all of them now, I believe it would be best if we made a plan of action to terminate them thoroughly," Heru said.

"I agree, but we can't take too long. I don't want them to get away," Ryan said.

"Then we must start your training. We have to get you in tune with your spirituality. It will be what guides you when you're on your own. Right now, you're feeling what I sense, but you must be able to sense these things on your own. Once you master your third eye, you will be unstoppable," Heru affirmed.

We pulled up to the house, noticing only the glare of the TV coming from Camille's room. Reginald's car was gone, nothing unusual. We didn't need him to be here right now anyway. We went upstairs and knocked on Camille's door.

"Come in," she said, her voice muffled.

She was lying under her comforter, a roll of tissue sitting on her bedside table. She had cried herself to sleep while we were gone.

"Just wanted to give you your keys."

"Oh, okay," Camille sniffled. "How was Kristine?"

"Huh, oh she was okay. She was just concerned about me, you know. She said she gives her condolences," we lied.

"Tell her I said thank you."

"I will."

We reached over and hugged her, leaving behind a goodnight kiss on her forehead. We quietly exited the room and headed to take a shower. The warm water soothed our minds, giving us a chance to release the stresses of the day and allow the newly found information to process. We dried off and looked at ourselves in the mirror. Our face was changing. We'd never had the innocent glow of a child, but the fury that dwelled beneath our eyes gave us the appearance of a hardened warrior. Our days of laughter had not come and were already seemingly over. There was no more time to play... we were at war.

We put on our usual basketball shorts and put our phone on the charger and sat on the bed with the knife in our hand. We observed it, paying close attention to the sharpness of the blade. We could see all the blood that had been washed off of it over the years. The owner had to know it was missing. A knife of this quality doesn't just get lost.

"I will let you rest this evening. Starting tomorrow, we will go headfirst into your training," Heru advised.

"How will we start?" Ryan asked.

"Your training will be spiritual. Your concentration will be detrimental to everything we do. I will first teach you to meditate. From there I will teach you of your abilities one by one."

"How long do you think it will take until I'm on your level?"

"You're already there, Ojore, but you must trust in yourself and believe in your ability. You used your third eye tonight; now you must learn to control it."

"What does that mean?"

"You'll find out in time. Now rest, young god. Your vengeance begins tomorrow. The world will feel your wrath as the God of War!"

We turned out the lights and lay down, staring at the ceiling, still clenching the knife to our chest. We were ready to learn. We were ready to fight. We desired the blood of the guilty on our hands.

"I will have my revenge."

Ryan drove through the city in a stripped car with a mysterious woman. The car had no lights with dark tinted windows. They pulled up to a skyscraper, their eyes focused on the top of the building. They nodded at each other and exited the car, casually walking into the building dressed in black pants and shirts with long overcoats. As they entered the building, they walked over to the receptionist desk, the mysterious woman remaining silent. Ryan began flirting with the woman at the desk, his mysterious woman casing the lobby before they made their move. Ryan continued to smile at the receptionist, her red cheeks blushing from flattery. She was distracted long enough for Ryan to slyly raise his sleeve to his mouth and give the signal through his dark watch.

The mysterious woman reached into her coat and whipped out a large revolver and shoved it in the receptionist's face, demanding the whereabouts of the company's CEO. The frightened woman was too afraid to cooperate, and the mysterious woman pistol-whipped her to the floor, accidentally causing the receptionist to trigger the alarm warning the CEO that they were under attack. The doors were suddenly stormed with several men and women that quickly took the employees hostage, forcing them to give up the location of their boss hiding high up on the hundredth floor. Ryan stood on top of the reception desk and put his face directly in front of the surveillance camera. He grinned at the lens and warned the CEO that his death was imminent. Suddenly, steel gates fell over the windows of the lobby, but the gates designed for the lobby doors were unsuccessful in deploying as they were strategically blocked by Ryan's squad of assassins. The mysterious woman handcuffed the receptionist and dragged her into a dark room, which neither of them would ever emerge from again.

The lights of the building shut off, leaving nothing but the light from the doorways to fill the lobby. Ryan's squad quickly equipped their night vision goggles and began forcing the hostages down the dark hallways, while the others began storming the lower floors and working their way up. Ryan jolted out to the car, speaking to someone on his dark watch as he ran down the building's stoop. On the receiving end was the Red Dragon, high in the sky being flown toward the building in a helicopter. He covered his glowing red eyes with a pair of dark shades as he stared at the CEO's office. He fastened on his muzzle made of dragon scales with sharp spikes in the corners. The helicopter turned sideways to allow him to swing toward the building. He adjusted his cadet cap and grabbed a rope fastened to the rails inside the helicopter and swung out from the opposite side. With a propelled flying side kick, the Red Dragon broke through the glass of the hundredth floor and instantly began his rampage.

He attacked the CEO, snatching him from his chair and throwing him onto his desk. The CEO proved to be a decoy, an outmatched henchman who stood no chance against the Red Dragon alone. The furious assassin made short work of him with an elaborate combo of kicks and punches that led his enemy toward the open window. The Red Dragon delivered a stifling spinning back kick that sent the foolish henchman flying out of the window and plummeting to his death.

The Red Dragon turned to find the CEO's secretary standing in strike formation. He dropped his guard, warning her to shy away from the fight, but the brazen secretary unsheathed a large combat knife and attacked him. He calmly dodged her advances, quickly turning the tables by delivering punch after punch to her face and body, breaking her down easily as he forced her into the office's open doorway. He grabbed her wrist and twisted her arm, turning the knife toward her chest. The secretary struggled to hold him off as the force of his might inched the blade closer and closer. He summoned his strength and forced the knife deep into her chest, piercing her heart. The once brazen secretary slowly slid down the door to the floor with her head drooping as the Red Dragon walked past her into the hallway.

The assassin turned to his right to find several agents dressed in tactical gear standing before him ready to defend the tower against his intrusion. The Red Dragon reached behind his back, pulled out a sword, and took his striking position, daring the team to move on him. They rushed toward him but quickly found that they were no match for the Red Dragon's incredible swordsmanship. He tore through them, swinging his blade with precision, leaving the hallway drenched with their blood. The assassin forced his blade through the backs of their necks as they each fell to the ground one by one. He heard the groans of one agent crawling toward the stairway in a desperate attempt to get away from the impending doom. The deadly assassin dragged his blade across the carpet flooring as he walked upon the hapless agent and stomped on his spine to keep him in place. The agent extended his arm, reaching for a hope that was not there. The Red Dragon raised his blade and aimed the sharp tip at the back of the agent's neck. He brought the sword down with an incredible force, the blade breaching through the agent's mouth. He yanked the sword left and right, instantly decapitating the cursed agent, his head spewing out blood as it bounced down the stairs.

The Red Dragon's dark watch began to go off, signaling him to immediately get down to the car. He turned and ran back into the CEO's office, strapping a tactical pack to his back. Without hesitation, he dove out of the window and charged down to the ground. Ryan sped off in the car, giving chase to the CEO escaping in a large black car. The Red Dragon pushed a button on the straps of his pack, and wings emerged, forcing him back up into the air. He glided through the air, making his descent toward the roof of Ryan's car as his watchful eye spied on the escaping vehicle. He grabbed the car's open window, and with a push of a button, the pack blew off of his back and disappeared in the distance. He slipped through the window and instantly removed his hat, shades, and muzzle and reached under the seat to unveil his mystic assault rifle.

The two cars swerved through the hot city streets, narrowly missing pedestrians and oncoming traffic. The CEO's dark car had fire projecting from its exhaust, giving it enough power to escape the assassins if he were able to reach a straightaway. Ryan remained hot on his tail, skillfully handling every swerve and curve they encountered. The Red Dragon readied his assault rifle and leaned out of the window, his sights set on the back windshield of the dark car. Single shots rang out, the bullets blazing dragon heads, hissing and ready to bite through their intended target. The bullets fizzed past the car and blasted through the back windshield, narrowly missing the driver's seat. The Red Dragon continued to fire, his red eyes glowing as he grunted with each missed shot.

Still blazing through the streets at high speeds, the cars came upon an intersection that seemed to be clear of traffic. The CEO sped through the red light, stomping on the gas as traffic appeared to clear up. Ryan desperately floored the gas, trying to keep up with their target, but just as they approached the intersection, two armored trucks emerged from opposite sides of the intersection, forcing them to slam on the brakes. The trucks slowed the pace of the chase, allowing the CEO to gain a great bit of distance from his attackers. The Red Dragon fired at the trucks but to no avail. Suddenly, the back doors of the trucks flew open, exposing several men armed with assault rifles.

They fired back at the car, narrowly causing the Red Dragon to drop his gun. The two ducked down and dodged the bullets, pulling back to avoid injury. Fearing their target might escape, the Red Dragon pushed the big red button on the dash, and his seat tilted backward into darkness.

Ryan hit the gas, confidently charging toward the armored trucks as the armed agents readied their guns for the next wave of bullets. The roof of Ryan's car began to fold backward, and from the middle of the car emerged a giant machine gun, the Red Dragon strapped into a seat on the back of it. The gun had large, revolving barrels, capable of shooting 10,000 bullets per second. A red light along the side of the cannon gave the Red Dragon precision aim at the targets ahead. He firmly grabbed the two handles and unleashed a hellish cannonade of bullets at the trucks. The hissing dragons bit into the armored trucks, causing massive explosions on the city streets. The trucks tumbled to opposite sides, crashing into buildings on the sidewalk and leaving the CEO's car exposed.

The chase escaped the city and continued down an open desert road. The CEO smashed the gas and zoomed further ahead of the two assassins, thinking he would easily escape. The Red Dragon fired at the car, striking the trunk, rear wheels, and gas tank, grinning at his successful hits. The CEO's gas tank exploded, propelling the rear of the car into the air. The car came crashing down on its side and toppled over several times, ejecting the CEO and sending him flying into the hot desert dirt. Ryan's tires screeched as he swerved to a stop at the crash site, he and the Red Dragon quickly jumping from their vehicle to apprehend their target.

The CEO crawled slowly on the hot desert sand, his body severely damaged in the crash. The Red Dragon approached the CEO from the side and grabbed him by the back of his collar. He yanked him up and forcibly held his arms behind his back. The CEO dropped his head in fear of facing his defeat. The Red

Dragon looked over to Ryan, inviting him to own the kill they had so long desired to achieve. As Ryan approached them, the CEO raised his head, revealing a shocking discovery. It was the spirit with the white face and shades Ryan had seen when he grabbed the knife. Ryan was instantly consumed with anger, the screams and cries of the fallen ringing through his head. He closed his eyes and covered his face, shaking from the unruly rage that was growing inside of him. His feelings of forgiveness battled with his intentions of death and destruction. His yearning for the CEO's blood overwhelmed his senses, and he snapped, roaring at the sky as his feelings for revenge consumed him.

Ryan looked at the CEO with his blazing red eyes. He roared once more, black smoke sifting through his fangs. He attacked, delivering crushing blows to the CEO, breaking his body even more with each punch. The rage proved to be too much for Ryan as he stepped back and flung his sword around from his back. The Red Dragon disappeared, leaving the CEO open for each slice of Ryan's blade. Ryan cut and sliced at his victim, spewing blood all over his own hands, face, and clothes, his mind deranged with words of pain, fury, and hatred. He swung his sword until his victim was a bloody pool that soaked into the desert sand. He struck a pose, leaning in toward the ground and flinging the sword backward. He aimed his open hand at the dirt and unleashed a giant red ki blast.

With the flash of the giant red light, the two were back in their car. They looked on at the road ahead with their sadistic mugs, ready to hunt down their next target. The Red Dragon's eyes began to glow again, and his body disappeared into red light. The blood-soaked Ryan continued to drive alone, his eyes projecting the fiendish red glow of the Red Dragon, his desire to leave no rock unturned as he exacted his revenge.

Face drove up the elongated driveway on Diaz's property in a work van, observing the drop-in activity. There weren't as many guards on duty at the front of the house, but there were several guards strapped with guns and enough ammunition to take on a small militia. Diaz awaited Face's arrival standing in front of his parked SUV packed with a driver, his wife, and young children. He anxiously checked his watch, ready to get the deal over with in time to comfortably travel and catch his flight.

Face pulled up to the palace, keeping a good distance from Diaz, who appeared curious about his parking job. Diaz looked back at his van but noticed nothing different from any other time Face had come, but he was on edge because of the unusual timing of the request. He took a few steps towards Face's van, watching him as he emerged from his vehicle. Face set his feet on the ground and closed his door, giving Diaz his one-of-a-kind appealing smile behind his dark shades and his freshly painted white face.

"Mr. Diaz, how are you?" Face grinned.

"Eh, I am pretty good, just a little, how you say, edgy. I may have not said before that I usually don't do deals on short notice when I'm leaving town." Diaz nervously looked back at his SUV.

"Ah, yes, my apologies for the short notice. I honestly have a large demand around this time, and I wanted to make sure I had it all," Face responded.

The woods surrounding the property were busy with men from Face's, Hong's, and Nassar's gangs. The allied troops snuck through the heavily wooded area armed from head to toe with weaponry ready to destroy Diaz's easily outnumbered team of assassins. They quietly crept as close as they could without triggering Diaz's security system, awaiting the word that it was safe to move. They held their positions, snipers getting their aim set on what would have been difficult threats. Face listened closely to the hidden earpiece in his ear as he stepped forward to shake Diaz's hand to further distract him.

Simmons typed quickly on his laptop, hacking into Diaz's security system. The detective focused closely on the screen, knowing that one wrongly typed key could trigger an alert.

"Almost in. Hong and Nassar's men are in position. I just need a few more seconds, and I'll be able to cut the power," Simmons advised.

Face shook hands with Diaz, giving him a firm, professional grip as he had when they'd met. The two looked at each other, and Face could see a bit of frustration in Diaz's body language. Face tried to pull his hand away from the shake, but Diaz squeezed a little tighter, looking into Face's shades with seriousness in his eyes.

"I must ask, to keep future business between us on good terms, that you make your deals early. I am only making this deal with you because I know that I did not advise you of my departure, but do not make this mistake again. Do you understand?" Diaz instructed.

Simmons entered a few more characters on the screen and bit his lip, waiting for the approval message. *Access Granted,* he read with a smile.

"I'm in! The front gate's opening and the power to the house is going out in seven seconds. Everybody, move in now!" Simmons shouted.

Face squeezed Diaz's hand tighter and snatched him closer, his evil grin quickly forming.

"I don't think you'll be around to make another deal."

The sounds of distant gunfire rang out, followed by the dramatic falsetto of Diaz's men being shot to death. Diaz yanked his hand away from Face, hoping to make a run for it after witnessing two of his men get their heads blown off. Nassar's ground team, who had already murdered the guards at the front gates, quickly drove up the driveway, stopping once they had an open view of Diaz running toward his vehicle. The assassin on the back of the pickup truck emerged wielding a rocket launcher and took aim at the SUV.

"ROCKET!"

Face ran and ducked behind his van as Diaz made a run for his SUV, but his old age and smoking habit had proven to work against him. The rocket fired with its sights set on Diaz's SUV, quickly passing over the yard of Diaz's dead soldiers. It flew by Face's van and dashed by a frightened Diaz, causing him to lose his footing. Diaz's defenseless family could only watch as their panicked father ran toward them, unable to defend them from the military-grade weapon. The rocket crashed into the SUV with an ear-shattering boom that sent the vehicle flying up into the air. Glass and shrapnel flew through the air, breaking off the doors of the vehicle and destroying parts of the house. The shockwave from the explosion twisted Diaz through the air and slammed him hard on the ground. The destroyed SUV crashed to the ground in a blazing fireball, taking the souls of Diaz's family in the wake of its destruction.

Diaz rolled on the ground groaning in pain as he struggled to pick himself up. He had severely sprained his ankle in the fall, and his nose was bleeding badly. He was slightly disoriented as he opened his swollen eyes to the blazing fire before him. The wicked boss's family was no more, and he knew he would soon join them on the other side. Face emerged from behind his van with his sinister grin, watching Diaz gape at the fire like a terrified child. He walked up to Diaz with his mindset on executioner.

"You know the phrase, Diaz, *Eye for an eye, tooth for a tooth,*" Face laughed.

Diaz plopped his hands on the ground, struggling to catch his breath as the sound of Face's voice riddled his spirit with fear. He attempted to crawl but only had the strength to move a few feet. Face walked up to him and stared Diaz down without pity.

"What do you think a shank in the back feels like? Does it feel like a kick to the ribs?"

Face kicked Diaz hard in his side, sending him tumbling over. Diaz groaned as he rolled over on his back, clenching his cracked ribs. Face looked at the blazing fire and smiled, finding comfort from the heat. He turned his head back to Diaz, who was still struggling to get away. He slowly crept up on him, taking his shades off and hanging them from his chain.

"You were much better off trying to kill Hong and Nassar. You might've lived a little longer."

Diaz tried his best to back away from the slowly approaching Face as blood rushed down his face, staining his clothes.

"No! NO!" Diaz shouted, throwing his hand up.

Face stood over Diaz with the blazing fire burning behind him. Diaz looked at Face, believing that he had already died, and Face was Satan greeting him at the gates of hell.

"No, Satan, perdóname! Perdóname," Diaz pleaded.

Face jerked up the delusional senior by his collar and delivered a powerful blow to his jaw.

"Look at me," Face said, violently shaking Diaz.

Diaz opened his swollen eyes while the faint smell of liquor and blood leaked from the side of his mouth. As he looked into Face's eyes, he could hear the distressed voices of his family over the crackling fire. Images of his crying children being swept away in the fire appeared above Face's head. The white-faced devil looked into the soul of his victim fueled with a desire for revenge.

"You clearly learned nothing from the old school. If you mess with one brother, you mess with all of them," Face scolded.

He turned to the blazing fire and began to grin again. He yanked Diaz up by his collar, forcing him to stand up straight, and staggered him over to the inflamed wreckage. Diaz stood limp, cradling his side and watching in fear as Face unholstered one of his .45s from his shoulder. The killer took aim, placing the red dot in the center of Diaz's forehead. The beaten victim had silenced his pleas, desperate to relieve his ribs of the pain of breathing.

"Enjoy your family vacation. I'll see you when I get there. By the way, tell my brother I said hi," Face snarked.

He pulled the trigger, delivering a bullet through Diaz's skull. The force of the gunshot whipped Diaz's head back and sent him falling into the driver's seat where the door had blown off of the vehicle, instantly setting him ablaze in his cashmere sweater. The legendary drug lord known as A.D. had finally met his death under the same circumstances he had formerly brought to others.

The teams of men stormed Diaz's compound from all possible sides, executing all of his men on the property without mercy. Several trucks traveled up the elongated driveway prepared to load up as much product and property they could hold. They tore down doors and windows, breaking into every possible room on the property, leaving nothing to be discovered by law enforcement, as they would possibly raid the property upon their departure. While the men pillaged, Face made his way to Diaz's former office, his eyes set on the sword sitting below the mirror. He walked up to the cold steel, unsheathing the sword, examining the blade, and striking poses with it in the mirror. He stood still for one final pose, this time deciding to take a selfie with his phone. As the camera flashed, a few members from his gang peeked in the doorway.

"What else do you want us to grab?"

Face rested the blade on his shoulder like a soldier's rifle and looked around the room.

"Everything in here is mine," he declared.

His family members raided the room, grabbing as many items as they could to load into the trucks. He continued to look at himself in the mirror. *Face, the conqueror*, he thought, dawning a new age of nemesis to the city.

CHAPTER 11:
THINGS CHANGED

THE ILLEGIT FAMILY takeover happened virtually overnight. Face, Hong, and Nassar worked diligently to put together a plan to infiltrate and remove the less relevant leaders in Diaz's organization in an effort to gain control before the word of his death got out. They started by evening out the resources once seized by Diaz to restore order to their districts. Face declared that the Illegit Family was strong enough to destroy Diaz's empire, a declaration he was not the least bit wrong about.

There was a nightclub just northeast of the city that Diaz had established as a front that had done quite well over the years. Diaz's distrust for cops directed him to establish his own private security for the club, which was operated by a man that district leaders only knew as Santos. Santos was never far away from the club, living a few blocks down the street from it in a quaint subdivision. Unaware of the events that had passed, Santos continued his evening as he usually did, leaving his house and rolling up to the club in his luxury car to sit in his office and watch the events of the night take place. There was a black SUV sitting at the corner of his street packed with an Illegit taskforce.

"He just left. Let us know when he gets there," the gangster said.

"Aight, got it," the lookout replied.

It was now a game of hurry up and wait for their moment to strike. Santos casually drove down the street, taking his time texting his mistress as cars flew by him, honking their horns. Moments later, he pulled into the club's parking lot packed with partygoers and half-dressed freaks ready to tear up the night. Across the street from the club in another SUV was the Illegit lookout watching the crowd.

"Yo, he's here! He's pulling his car around the back now," he hollered into his phone.

"On the way," the gangster replied.

The parked SUV fired up and repositioned adjacent to Santos' house. The driver turned off the lights and quickly briefed the crew.

"Aight, look, nobody important should be in there but his wife and whoever else, so get in, take everybody out, and we rollin'. Don't try to grab shit, this ain't no robbery. We gotta move! Now go!"

The other Illegit gangsters in the SUV filed out into the darkness, quietly making their way through the grass. Meanwhile, Santos parked his car around the back of the club where his private security guard awaited his arrival.

"Buenas noches, senior." The guard opened the backdoor.

"Buenas noches, terminemos esta noche con," Santos replied.

Santos carelessly walked up the stairs to his office overlooking the club. He commenced his usual activity, making himself a drink and lighting up a cigar he would get on his weekly visits with Diaz. He sent another text to his mistress wondering when she'd be arriving for his evening entertainment, not knowing that his entertainment was already on the way. Three SUVs zoomed down the busy street in formation. Inside were several members of the Illegit Family and their beloved leaders, Face and Deuce. Being that this was one of many hits to come, Face felt it necessary to make a personal appearance.

The team of gangsters at Santos' house snuck their way to the backdoor, carefully avoiding the shoddy surveillance system. A cocky man, Santos believed he was untouchable in his position and chose not to keep stronger security around his home. Santos angrily read a text from his mistress advising him that she wouldn't be able to make it with no real details as to why. He leaned back in his seat and sipped his drink thinking of who else he might be able to call. The Illegit convoy pulled into the parking lot of the club, Face's vehicle making its way to the back. Down the street, the other Illegit gangsters forced their way into Santos' house and bum-rushed his family, following their orders as instructed.

The convoy reached the backside of the club, gaining the suspicion of the standing guard. They filed out of their vehicles and approached the guard, who noticed that they weren't the club's usual patrons.

"Eh, can I help you?" the guard asked.

"We're here to see your boss," Deuce said.

"He's not expecting us," Face added.

Shots rang out from the front of the club as the Illegits in the other SUVs stormed the front door. The crowd went into a frenzy, stomping over others in their desperation to get away. The club bouncers were easily taken down, including any club-goer that happened to get caught in the crossfire. Alerted by the sound of gunfire, Santos checked the surveillance system and was startled to see that the club was under siege. He immediately grabbed his things and tried to rush out of his office. He pounded his phone's screen, desperately trying to call his wife as he ran downstairs. The phone was answered just before he could reach the back door.

"Que pasa?" the Illegit gangster laughed.

Santos was stopped in his tracks at the sounds of his wife crying in the background. He heard a gunshot just outside the backdoor and looked up in fear.

"No, no! Por favor no me mates! Por favor," his wife screamed.

The back door slowly creaked open, and Santos' stomach turned at the sight of Face and his minions looking back at him. A gunshot went off over the phone, and the screaming stopped. The call immediately ended with Santos dropping his phone to the concrete floor. He took off running with his only plausible escape being the front door, which he knew would not pan out well for him. The club had mostly cleared out, still infested with the Illegit squad. Santos made his way through the VIP section, getting down the stairs as quickly as he could, but unfortunately, he ran into a pack of Face's men, heavily armed and teasing him with their aimed weapons. Santos ran back in the opposite direction thinking he might have shaken Face and his goons but ended up running back into them, the back door no longer an option. He turned to run again but was clipped down by a bullet to the back of his leg from Deuce.

"Quit running. I ain't got all night," Face said.

Santos strained as his warm blood leaked onto the floor. The horrified man regretted his years of excessive alcohol abuse as he crawled. He looked back in terror as the man with the white face slowly approached him.

"The deed is transferred over," Face said.

He opened fire on Santos, shooting him several times in the head and back.

"Search the office, grab anything that looks important. Porter and Simmons will be here in a minute. Deuce, tell the other guys to get out of here. I'll be outside," Face instructed.

"Gotcha," Deuce replied.

The Illegit squad fled from Santos' house and jumped in the SUV. The tires screeched as they took off into the night without a trace. Face pulled out his phone to call Hong to advise him of the new developments. Deuce stepped out onto the dancefloor and advised his men to immediately head out. Several of the gangsters raided the office, flipping the desk and tossing pictures from the wall. They found money, a safe, and a ledger that would ensure devastation for any of the unlucky individuals that were listed in the book. Deuce held the door open for his Illegit squad as they headed to the SUV with the stolen items. They loaded them into the SUV just as Porter and Simmons conveniently arrived at the scene. They saw Face standing outside of his SUV and pulled up to him.

"It was tragic, you know, like watching a cornered mouse run from a pack of stray cats," Face said.

"How's it look in there?" Simmons asked.

"Bunch of bullet casings, probably some dead guards, there's one over there, oh, and he's in the hall," Face replied.

"The media is gonna have a field day with this," Porter sighed.

"Well as you can see, whatever is in that safe should make it all worth it. By the way, Simmons, you might wanna get in the office before everyone else does to get on the surveillance system," Face said.

"Gotcha," Simmons replied.

Deuce received a phone call from the other Illegit squad and alerted Face of their success.

"Yo, they said everything went good."

"Cool, aight, we need to get out of here," Face said. "You guys call me when this shit gets wrapped up."

Face and his Illegit minions loaded up and rolled out of the club parking lot and headed back to their suburban safe house as Porter and Simmons put on latex gloves and headed through the backdoor of the club. Porter searched the club for casualties, stealing Santos' wallet after marking his body. Simmons headed to the ransacked office and found the hard drive for the surveillance system and began deleting recordings from the evening. Moments later, several more police cars arrived at the scene, where they were instructed by Porter to start blocking off the crime scene, buying more time for Simmons to finish his illegal process. The cops guided panicked patrons to their cars and blocked off the entrance to the club's parking lot. News vans flooded the scene, interviewing terrified patrons to get the story of the evening. As they traveled down the highway, Face felt his pocket and remembered that something was missing from his person—something he always had a knack for carrying.

"Hey Deuce, you seen my Buddy? I feel like I haven't had it since Diaz's place."

"Nah, bruh, last time I saw it was the other day, I think," Deuce replied.

"It's probably in the other car," Face assumed.

The mayhem caused that evening fueled Face's anger in his war against the others in Diaz's organization. He went on a rampage, destroying everything Diaz had established. They burned down his restaurants and shot up small warehouses, taking out anyone that dared to stand in their way. His men carved Illegit into the brains of their targets and their families, leaving them destitute and defenseless. By the time word had gotten around that Diaz was no more, the Illegit family had already reduced the district's power to rubbish. Face, Hong, and Nassar quickly got to work putting the broken district back together.

Heru and Ryan sat deep in meditation upon the Spirit Realm's foggy horizon. The soothing sounds of deep water vibrated through the air, but there was no waterfall in sight. Heru's golden aura seeped from his skin and spread out around him, raising him above the low-lying fog.

"Breathe, Ojore. Allow the purity of the air to blend your senses. Control what it is that you feel. You are the wrath of our ancestors. You possess a power which only you can control, a power that surpasses those that stand against you. What is your desire? You have dominion to be great, just as you have the will to be terrible. The lighted path to excellence is paved with darkness that compels the forces of evil to recruit you. Fight the resistance in your mind. Empty yourself of all negativity and weakness, for only the strong will achieve the goal you must reach."

The room cleared of the fog, exposing Ryan sitting on the rough sands with his eyes closed. Heru hovered above him, his aura taking the shape of his wings. In the distance appeared the millions of their ancestors that had perished over the millennia against their will. There were the moans and groans of those plagued by betrayal, there were those defeated by pillaging, there were those victimized and enslaved, and many more that had fallen victim to a devastating demise.

"Hear their cries, Ojore. Let it ignite the fury that enchants the God of War to avenge. You have been chosen by the Divine Creator to rise and give fire to your aspirations. The ancestral gods spoke and chose you and only you. You are the ultimate conception, the genesis of supreme...you are the chosen one."

Ryan's aura seeped from his skin and spread around him, raising him from the ground. It formed horns above his head and dragon-like wings across his back. He began to breathe heavily as the power flooded his senses. His muscles gyrated, and his face twitched as he struggled to hold in the ravenous rage.

"Open your eyes and look at me, Ojore."

The two stared at each other, Heru as calm as a moonlit night, Ryan as furious as hurricane winds. The souls of their ancestors gathered beneath Ryan, reaching up to him.

"Fear not what your powers can do, for you have no power with fear. Embrace it. Let it fuel you, and use it to do your will."

Ryan's aura continued to grow, expanding further around him. The ancestors faded away as the aura spread beneath him and turned into fire. Heru raised his head, and their auras once again intertwined in a whirlwind of battle cries and flames. Their great powers rattled the realm.

"You are the chosen one!"

We woke up, inhaling deeply through our nose with our muscles tight and digging our fingers into the sheets. That ruthless energy settling in our chest scared us a little. The feeling of ultimate power appeared to be more than we'd thought it would be.

It sounded nice in theory, but now possessing it, we didn't know if we can handle it or what we are capable of. We couldn't fear this feeling, though. It was a feeling we must master in order to bring that feeling to our oppressors.

"You're doing well, Ojore, but we must try and speed up your progression," Heru said.

"Thank you. I'm trying, I just...well you know. It's a lot to handle," Ryan replied.

"I understand your emotion, but you must look past it and see your purpose. Only then will you achieve your goal."

We got out of bed and gave a start to our day as this would be our first day going back to school since the move. We'd gotten our room together but hadn't really taken time to explore the area. Our concern for Camille was ever-present, but more important was our training. Each night, we would journey to the Spirit Realm and focus on concentrating our energy. We never thought concentration required so much. Our power made us feel like destroying the entire world and then pillaging other planets scattered throughout the universe. It wasn't easy, but it was something we knew we had to do.

Camille drove us to school because we lived too close for us to ride the bus, but far enough away that it would be a walk. She still hadn't found a place of emotional stability, and Reginald wasn't doing anything to make it better. She was going back to work today, too. She couldn't hide her facial expression. She just looked empty. There were times when we wanted to tell her what we knew, but telling her would only complicate things for us at the moment.

The area was kind of country for what we were used to. There were lots of small businesses and gas stations on every corner, but nothing for anyone to really get into. Not that we cared; it wasn't like we'd be hanging out anyway. We just found it funny ol' Reginald thought we'd be sneaking out. We pulled up to the school and walked into the vocational building for the attendance office. We hadn't been there for more than five minutes, and already we knew this place was much different. Things seemed to be more organized, there was no weird smell, and there were all kinds of people of every ethnicity. We felt a bit of culture shock for a moment, which heightened our defenses. They were all putting on an act; they had to be. A female student was working up front, and she helped us get our paperwork together. Her energy seemed friendly, but we remained apprehensive.

"All right, ma'am, it looks like everything has been taken care of as far as paperwork, so you're good to go. I've printed out your schedule, and your first class is actually in this building. It's down the hall and to the left. Would you like me to walk you there?" the girl asked.

"Uh, no thanks. I'll find it," we said.

"Well, you all enjoy your day, and welcome to Monroe High." The girl smiled.

"Thanks."

We walked out of the office and stood in the foyer for a moment. Camille's face remained expressionless, still detailing all of her pain. If we had learned anything about her, we knew that she was a trooper. There were plenty of things that might have set her back from time to time, but nothing ever got her down.

"Well, I gotta get on to work, so I'll see you later," Camille said.

"I'll text you when I get home," we replied.

We hugged each other, and it nearly killed us to feel how broken she was. We had grown accustomed to her excitement about us going to a new school. She had never refused an opportunity to walk us to class, but given these circumstances, we understood that her joy wouldn't be around for a while. We missed them, too. She walked out of the building without looking back, and after watching her get in her car, we walked to class. The energies in the classrooms we passed seemed calm, at least for what could be felt from a bunch of high school kids.

We got to the classroom and listened to the commotion on the other side of the door. We looked at our schedule—AP Economics. Hopefully, the discussion of supply and demand wouldn't be too much for us today. All we had to do was be quiet, sit back, and observe. We knocked on the door, and after a few seconds, the teacher opened it. She was a middle-aged Black woman with glasses and a couple gray hairs here and there. By looking at her, we could tell this woman was highly educated.

"Good morning. How can I help you?" she enunciated.

Even though her spirit was warm and inviting, we still weren't ready for the amount of energy she had this early in the day. It threw us off.

"Um—" We looked at our schedule. "I'm new. I think this is my first class."

Her face lit up, and it scared us for a second. At some point in our life, we had become wary of seemingly friendly people until we became more acquainted. We were very, very stand-offish.

"You must be Ryan! Welcome, I've heard such good things about you." She shook our hand. "I'm Dr. Stegall. Class, this is our new student, Ryan..."

"Scales."

"Ah, yes! You can take a seat over by my desk there. We were just discussing generational wealth and some of the wealthiest people in history who amassed great fortunes. We've got a few names on the board here. Is there anyone that you would like to enlighten us with?"

Dammit, not even in the room for a minute and already we were in the spotlight. So much for our plan, and what good could this lady have possibly heard about us? That we could draw? That's literally all we were good for. Too bad our ancestors couldn't save us from this—or could they?

"Uh, I guess, well..."

We looked at the board and recognized the names of people who had recently lived, and all the easy ones had been taken. We had to dig deeper for our answer.

"He's not really from this time, but I guess you could add Mansa Musa. Um, he was the richest man in history. I think his net worth was over $400 billion during his time ruling over West Africa. He had control over the price of gold at one point and gave away so much of it that he accidentally made the price of gold fall and it kinda messed up the economy for a little over 20 years."

As much as we hated attention, everyone was looking at us. We could feel the intrigue and the envy in the room; it was time for us to shut up now. Dr. Stegall put her hands on her hips and smiled at us. We felt the words *Teacher's Pet* brand themselves into our forehead. The day was already going left.

"That's exactly who our lesson is about today! Thank you, Ryan. Now, students, you'll notice that Mansa Musa is not discussed in your textbooks, and you probably haven't heard of him before either. So get ready to take notes because your next test will have questions about him," Dr. Stegall said.

We reached into our bag and pulled out our notebook. We started to think for a moment that this could be a new start for us. We could truly use this as a chance to try. We only had a few months here, so it wouldn't hurt to get more involved in our academic achievement. It would make Camille proud.

"Don't stand against this one, Ojore. This one is not like the others. She may be a valuable asset to us in our time here," Heru said.

And then we remembered we were on a mission—cancel that. The day went on pretty well. Second period was AP Lit, something we really could have gone without considering how much we hated reading. It's like, we'd read and the words would create images, and then our imagination would kick in, and the next thing we knew, 20 minutes had passed and we were still on page one. The teacher was cool, though. His name was Mr. Stevens. He had a young face, but he was much older and all gray on top and on his face. We could tell he was very wise and extremely animated about his work, and he really tried to encourage everyone to think.

"Now, in the third paragraph, Carver states that he hungered. What do you think he was trying to convey to the audience here? What exactly did he hunger for? Ryan?"

Why do these teachers keep calling on us? Can't we be left alone today? We're still grieving!

"I think he just wanted love," we answered.

"Ah, yesssss, the one thing that can create or destroy a man in the blink of an eye! L-O-V-E, LOVE!" He wrote on the board.

Then we got to third period, my haven. The art teacher was friendly, as they usually are. He was a middle-aged White man with an afro and a short beard. Though the afro was hilarious, it matched his personality quite well. He had paintings on his wall from previous students of him with different hairstyles and accessories. They were pretty good.

"Ryan, we welcome you to our art class. I'm Mr. Bill Rose. Now as I've advised all of my students, I'm not an art teacher, I'm an influencer! Art is all about freedom of expression. This is not a classroom, this is a sacred place, and in this sacred place, we are free to be creators. Now, of course, I will give you an idea of the techniques we will be using, but ultimately, you, the creator, will design what it is that you want to express on your canvas. Everyone, pick up your paint brushes."

Where was this guy when we started drawing? If Camille had said that to us when we started drawing, we'd probably be showcasing at art galleries by now. This guy had the appreciation for artists that we all needed to have. We were starting to like it here, especially when we got to fourth period. This was a math class, but we swear this guy should have been a motivational speaker at colleges. His name was Mr. Tukes, a tall, middle-aged man who reminded us of a young Mr. T when you saw him on talk shows. He was full of strength and encouragement, and his personality and delivery made sure that everyone got the message.

"All right, class, in geometry you learned opposite angle over adjacent, but in life, you'll learn that the people you bring into your life need to parallel who you are and what you stand for. You see, the common thing we are taught is that opposites attract, but the lesson, class, the lesson here that we learn in this life, is that you need to be EQUALLY yoked! You girls meet these boys and vice versa, and you start having sex and you think, 'Oh, I'm in love, and we love each other,' and then, BOOM...might have AIDS."

We had fourth lunch so after our math class, we headed to the cafeteria. Of course, the lunch was still the same stuff, but for some reason, it tasted a little better. They had an outdoor courtyard for the students to hang out during lunch, so we went there and found a spot in the corner away from everyone. We ate and then we pulled out our sketch pad, flipping to a new page. We wanted to draw something new, something we hadn't drawn before. We took our pencil and started to draw lines, but we were interrupted by a disturbance across from us.

"Come on, Terrell, give me your lunch, man! Your mom still cooks for you," the boy laughed.

"I bet she put a little love in every corner when she made it," another boy laughed.

"Come on, guys, I just want to eat my lunch today," Terrell said.

"Well, I wanna eat Ms. James' lunch, too, so what are we gonna do about that?"

A typical group of jocks picking on one student, classic high school shit. We hated to see stuff like this, but we weren't playing hero today. We were just going to sit here and draw this picture until it was time to go.

"C'mon, Terry, leave that boy alone and let him eat," a girl said.

We looked up again trying to identify the girl, but someone was standing in front of her. We went back to drawing our picture, trying to get an idea of what to draw and how to draw it. The bell rang, and it was time for 5th period, Drama. We weren't much of a thespian, but we loved the arts, and we couldn't pick art twice as an elective. Somehow, we were the last to get to the classroom. It had a built-in stage, equipped with lights and curtains–apparently, the school board cared enough to give them what they needed. The teacher was the young and beautiful Mrs. Cowart, recently married, as she made sure to show off her ring with every hand motion. We found an open seat and tried to quickly sit down before we were noticed, but nothing got past this lady.

"You there, in the corner."

We froze in place.

"Are you Ryan?" She read from the updated class role.

"Yes," we replied.

"Okay, well, welcome to our class. I'm Mrs. Cowart, the director. I understand you're new to Monroe High, and we do things a little differently here. Put down your things and step on the stage and tell us a little about yourself."

This on-the-spot stuff had to stop. It felt like they were doing this on purpose. Was this in the school's curriculum to put new students on the spot? We put our bag in the seat, and our brain tussled over what to say. Finally, we decided to tell everyone the sarcastic truth.

"Uh, My name is Ryan X. Scales, because I have the 'X-Factor.'" We gestured. "I'm from Decatur...where it's greater, and I'm a senior."

"Great, the 'X-Factor,' that's mysterious. Tell us something unique about you," Mrs. Cowart continued to prod.

We shrugged our shoulders and let the words flow.

"Uh, I'm currently spiritually tied to Heru, the Egyptian God of the Sky, and he has reached down through his bloodline in search of me, because he and Anpu, the God of the Dead, are training me to become the new God of War, and my mission is to avenge the deaths of my fallen ancestors and protect the peace on Earth from all threats, internal and extraterrestrial."

And once again, everyone was looking at us. We knew we should have just said we liked to draw.

"That was amazing!" Her face lit up. "You gave us a whole new character. Does this character have a name?"

"Red Dragon."

"Ooh, I like that name, sounds dangerous!" Mrs. Cowart grinned. "I look forward to seeing how you develop this character over time. You may take your seat now."

We walked back to our desk as she began to introduce the lesson for the day. We pulled out our notebook wishing we could get back to our sketch. We hadn't drawn in a while, which wasn't normal for us, but whatever we were trying to draw was going to be a masterpiece.

"Class, we're going to do something a little different today. I want you all to write your own monologues. You can talk about whatever you want to talk about, and you can be you if you want, though I'd prefer if you created a character so you can work on your character development. We'll work on these today and present them tomorrow. Take your time. You can talk to each other, but keep it down," Mrs. Cowart instructed.

An easy assignment it was, but for some reason, we were stifled. We didn't want to write about the Red Dragon; after all, it was supposed to be a secret. We preferred to draw, but clearly, that wasn't going to be an option here. Our overactive imagination suddenly became a deserted town with rusted cars and tumbleweeds. We sat and tried to concentrate on an idea of what to write, but the blank pages in front of us were uninspiring.

"Hey, uh, I just wanna say, I think your character's pretty cool."

We turned our head to the right as we recognized the familiar voice.

"I'm Terrell." He extended his hand.

It was the passive kid from lunch. We wouldn't have taken him to be a thespian—we could feel that he was very shy, but only because his kindness was taken advantage of. He looked pretty normal, about my complexion and height, and his hair was curly. Nothing seemed to be too off with this guy, aside from his apparent shyness. We weren't in the market for making friends, but based on what we'd seen earlier, we could tell this guy needed one.

"Thanks." We shook his hand.

"I'm trying to work on my character development, but I'm nowhere near as far as you seem to be," Terrell said.

"Uh, it's nothing really, you just have to use your imagination, that's all I did."

"Yeah." Terrell looked down. "I've been told I don't have the best imagination."

"What's wrong with it?" We raised our brow.

"Well, they say the characters I portray are too 'real,' like I don't have any theatrical spirit. They don't have any kind of fantastical nature to them."

"But isn't that what theatre is about, portraying a character? I mean, it's your character; he doesn't have to be like everybody else. What is your character?"

"Oh, well, I...the one I had in mind is a guy. He's strong, courageous, confident, and he isn't scared of anyone, and he's a hit with the ladies, but he only has his eyes set on one, and her name's Adrianna."

"So your character is a man?"

"Yeah."

"In love with a woman?"

"Yeah."

It began to occur to us that there was an untapped potential in this guy that was dying to be set free. For the first time in ages, we decided to be friendly.

"Sounds like you've already got a plot to me. Why don't you write about this man as the man you really want to be and talk about your love for this girl? Should be pretty easy," we suggested.

"Nah, man, I—I can't do that. The other girls would snitch on me," he whispered.

"What do you mean?"

He ducked his head lower and leaned closer to us.

"Adrianna's a real girl. She's not in this class, but she goes here."

"Ah. So you have a crush on her? Well, just change her name."

"Nah, it's not that simple, man. You wouldn't understand."

And we weren't going to try to, but this guy needed a friend, a real friend. We continued to help him with his assignment until the bell rang. We can tell he appreciated the help, graciously shaking our hand after class. One more period to go. We were only required to have three sciences to graduate, but we'd chosen to take anatomy. We got to class pretty early and introduced ourselves to the teacher, Mr. Colbert. Right off the bat, we knew who this guy was. He was a young Black man, flexing his muscles every chance he got. He wasn't after the students, but that didn't stop some of them from going after him. He even had some of the teachers going after him in the parking lot. He seemed cool, though.

"Aight, man. I do things on a last-name basis, so I'm just gonna call you Scales. You can call me Colbert, or Colb for short, something my old students started. Now, you're a senior, so why are you taking anatomy?" Colb asked.

"Honestly, there was nothing else that interested me, but no worries, I'm a good student," we assured him.

"Oh nah, it's nothing like that. I can tell you're one of the good ones. I pass all the seniors that take the course as long as they show up to class a majority of the time, so just be cool. There are a few other seniors in here, but mostly juniors, but there's one in particular senior I think you might like, so I'ma hook you up," Colb said.

He looked around the classroom and pointed to a seat by the window near the back. "Go sit in that seat on the fourth row. You'll see who I'm talkin' bout when they come in, and you can thank me later."

"Thanks." We grinned.

That was probably the most relaxed smile we had shown all day. We took our seat and immediately pulled out our sketch pad. We were so anxious to break ground on this new drawing. All we had were a few squiggly lines so far, but we knew it would turn out to be something great at some point. We buried our face in our drawing and tuned out the world. We drew a few more lines, and finally we had a shape! Just as we were making progress, we heard something that got our attention.

"Hi, are you new?"

"Yeah," we uttered as we slowly looked up from our artwork.

We turned our head, and immediately everything around us went black as if we had traveled to the Spirit Realm. Before us stood the most beautiful woman we had ever seen. Her skin was deep and dark like the true color of vanilla bean with a soft and silky shine like moonlight in the night sky. Her big, beautiful, round brown eyes told us the story of her pure heart, gleaming like golden spears in the sunlight. They were angled just right on her face, enchanting, yet fierce like cat eyes. Her lips were big, lush, and full – the kind of lips that feel like nimbus clouds when you kiss them, and they were freshly covered in the finest of lip gloss. Her nose was the cutest thing we ever did see, a button nose as they call it. Her most wondrous feature was beyond the ranks of her undeniable beauty. Her long, thick, and full hair flowed from the top of her head and fanned out, passing her shoulders and going down her back. There was a golden aura that appeared around her that formed a crown on her head. She was the most beautiful girl in the world.

We definitely got caught looking for a moment, something we had not ever done. No girl had ever been so beautiful that we stared for a brief moment. Colb stood at the front of the class smiling at us, he wasn't playing about that hookup. He was purposely holding up class to give us our moment. We shook our head to break out of the trance this goddess of a woman had entrapped us in.

"Oh, uh, sorry, I uh…" we scratched our head. "I was- I was drawing."

"Oh, you're good, I was just saying hello. I'm Aaliyah." She extended her hand.

Her voice sounded like the breakdown part of a love song where the artist hits the high note proclaiming their love for their mate. We could feel our heart racing as we failed at keeping our cool. We looked into her eyes and read every detail about her energy. We could feel our defenses crumbling before us. We reached out to shake her hand hoping it would confirm everything that we assumed. Her touch was so warm and inviting, we felt it in our heart. For the first time in our lives, we felt at peace. We felt a deeper connection, more than what was on the surface.

"Nice to meet you." She smiled.

We could hear the melodic tone of Angela Winbush singing the hook of *Your Smile.* We had to concentrate on controlling our smile fearing that we would smile too hard. She had the kind of smile that could make a man surrender everything he had. Men would die to protect and preserve it. The kind of smile that you'd be willing to do absolutely anything just to see. Her smile was perfect.

"Oh, uh, it's…shit."

Enthralled by the vivacious beauty before us, we accidentally drew a thick black line right through our drawing. Damn, she's fine.

"Well, I gotta start over now." We grinned. "I'm not sure, uh, what I wanna draw yet."

"That's cool, I'm sure it'll come to you. Where'd you come from?" she asked.

"I'm from Decatur." Our accent emerged. "I just moved out here last week."

She was making conversation with us, making it a real challenge to not dote over her like a hopeless romantic. This must be the way Terrell felt about Adrianna.

"Oh, cool, I used to live in Decatur when I was a little girl. My dad and I moved out here years ago, but I miss living on the eastside," Aaliyah said.

This was a setup. It had to be a setup. Everything was perfect about this girl. Nobody is that perfect, but we couldn't sense any negativity coming from her. She was as legit as they come.

"Aight class, we have a new student, Scales, he's over in the back corner. Scales, did they give you a textbook because it appears that I'm out of them," Colb asked, putting books under his desk.

"Uh, no, they didn't," we replied.

"He can share with me, it's cool," Aaliyah said.

"Aight, cool, 'preciate your hospitality, Ms. Latrell. We'll continue from where we left off yesterday about the anatomy of the brain."

We scooted our stool a little closer to her and were instantly captivated by the pheromone-like fragrance she wore. We were losing it and couldn't understand why. We'd been around pretty girls before, but she had us mesmerized, and all she did was say hi. We focused on the pages in the book, and the words began to form her name. What was going on with this girl?

"It's her, Ojore! It's truly her!" Heru exclaimed.

We dropped our head and cleared our throat to play it off. "Who?"

"My lover, the Goddess of Love, Hathor. The resemblance between the two is uncanny. Everything about her exudes my long, lost love," Heru doted.

We felt a great sadness of millennial proportions fall over us. This meant more to us than anything.

"Ojore, you must court this one. I'll tell you more about her later, but she betokens everything essential to our existence. You must have her by your side."

We raised our brow and looked away from the book. We didn't even know this girl and already we were hoping for wedding bells. We took a breath and slowed down trying to focus on the lesson being given, but with every breath, we inhaled more of Aaliyah's magic. We just sat there trying to fix our face to hide our secret the entire time, taking a glance at her each time we thought she wasn't looking.

The final bell rang, and the school day was finally over. The students began to rush out of the classroom anxious to escape the walls of this building for the walls of their own home.

"Well, it was nice meeting you, Ryan. Maybe you can draw something for me one day," Aaliyah said.

We looked at her, and once again her smile melted our heart into a golden bubbling pool.

"Yeah, yeah, I can do that for you. One day," we replied.

Her face lit up and she turned to walk away.

"See you tomorrow." She waved.

We stood and watched her walk out of the classroom, saying good-bye to Colb as she cut the corner. That girl left and took a piece of us with her. We had to shake this feeling. Hopefully, the walk home would be enough. We walked to the front of the class and stopped by Colb's desk.

"What I tell ya? Hooked you up, right? Ha-Ha!" Colb grinned.

"I can admit, she's quite, uh, yeah." We grinned looking back at the door.

"You want this, man?" Colb held up an extra textbook.

Somehow, we knew this wasn't all a coincidence. Colb's sly grin turned into a laugh as he saw our smile form across our face.

"Nah, you can gon' and keep that," we laughed.

"Look man, I've read your file. Your grades are impeccable, I just wanna get you out of here. As long as you come to class, you straight with me, and if you don't come to class, she better be with you, you know what I'm sayin'?" Colb laughed.

"I gotcha, Colb, no worries," we replied.

"Aight, man, see you tomorrow."

"Have a good day, sir."

We walked out of the classroom grinning, something we had never done before. At least not since elementary. Today was a good day, a needed day from all the turmoil. We were now anxious to get home so we could get back to our training. We walked out of the front doors of the school, passing all of the busses, and walked toward the student parking lot. We wanted a car, but we didn't see the point anymore seeing that we could run as fast as them. As we walked toward the street, we felt a familiar energy close by and turned our head. It was Aaliyah, and she was all hugged up on the jock that was messing with Terrell.

"Him? Aw come the hell on, you gotta be kiddin' me!"

We knew there was something wrong with her, she was beautiful and smart and in love with an idiot. Dammit! It's always the pretty ones.

"Do not be fooled, Ojore, her love for him is not real," Heru said.

"What do you mean it's not real? No girl just hugs up on a guy like that, especially in high school, if she doesn't like him. Ain't like he got money," Ryan said.

"Go home, we must start our training. In time, the answer will reveal itself," Heru said.

We continued walking, trying not to look back at the tragedy, but out of the corner of our eye, we saw Terrell sitting alone in his car. He looked pitiful as if life itself weren't worth living anymore.

"That kid needs help," Ryan said.

"You can help him at school tomorrow, we've got work to do. Let's move," Heru ordered.

We began the walk home wishing we had a pair of shades because the sun was out, but thankfully it wasn't raining because we didn't have an umbrella. There were children walking home from school with their parents and loud music booming from the students that had cars. We were still thinking about Aaliyah, her beauty was sure to never escape our mind. We hoped that we would soon figure out the mystery behind her.

Back at the student parking lot, Aaliyah and the jocks were still standing around killing time. Aaliyah seemed desperate as she tried to hold Terry's arm, but he seemed to not want her touching him, moving his arms with everything he said.

"Aight, y'all we need to get to practice. Coach was on my ass about that shit last time," Terry said.

"You know coach, always tryin' to make better men out of us. Ol' livin' vicariously through you head ass," Leo added.

The other jocks laughed along with them, Aaliyah faking a grin. They gathered their things and put them in Terry's car and Aaliyah grabbed her backpack and put it back on. The jocks began to walk away, including Terry who didn't take the time to give Aaliyah a proper good-bye.

"Have fun at practice, babe," Aaliyah said.

Terry waved his hand in the air without looking back. Aaliyah took a deep breath and turned toward the street trying her best to keep her head up high. She began her walk home in the same direction Ryan went, popping in her headphones and blasting the music into her ears. After a moment, her smile returned and she seemed completely unbothered, even dancing a bit as she strolled down the sidewalk. A little while later, she reached her house and noticed there was an extra car parked in the driveway. She immediately began to worry, taking out her headphones as she walked up the stoop.

She crept up to the front door and heard voices inside. Two men were talking along with her father, and the conversation didn't sound like a pleasant one. She quietly opened the front door, gaining the attention of the men as they harassed her father in the kitchen.

"We're tired of your excuses, Omar. You need to get us our money, and we need it soon. It's been almost a year already," Sid said, noticing Aaliyah from the corner of his eye.

"You wouldn't want anything to happen to your beautiful daughter here, would ya?"

Aaliyah's eyes widened and she was stricken with fear.

"Sid, no. That's not even cool. She's a child," Murry said. "Head upstairs, young lady, the men are talking."

Aaliyah hurried up the stairs, sitting close by to eavesdrop on the conversation.

"The hell is wrong with you, Sid? You some kind of child rapist or somethin'? Your daughters are barely older than her!"

"Sorry, sorry,"." Sid lowered his head. "Just tryin' to, you know--"

"Don't say that shit again, or I'll kick your ass myself!" Murry threatened. "Now Omar, seriously, we need our money. You say you don't wanna work for us, you say you don't wanna give up your house, and I get that you fell on hard times, and it's gonna get harder if your daughter decides to go to college, but you owe us a debt and your past due."

"I know, and I apologize." Omar palmed his face. "Things are just falling apart and I'm trying to hold it all together."

Murry looked at his watch and scoffed.

"Look, we gotta get out of here shortly. I'm a reasonable man, Omar, very understanding, so, I'll tell ya what. I'll give you 'till the first day of spring to get the money, all of it, and we'll call it even. That work for you?" Murry offered.

"Yes, yes. That's more than enough time. I can...will have the money to you by then!" Omar swore.

The men shook hands and solidified the new deal. Omar smiled, his eyes warped with stress.

"Alright, but this is the last time, Omar. It's not gonna be pretty if we gotta come looking for you, got it?"

Omar nodded his head, looking nervously away from Murry and Sid.

"Let's get out of here, Sid."

The men exited the house and quietly closed the door behind them. Aaliyah crept down the stairs and locked the door, peeking through the blinds to make sure the men had left. She slowly walked toward the kitchen, catching a silent tear roll down her father's cheek. Omar struggled to keep his composure, the build-up of his depression spilling from his eyes.

"Are you okay, Daddy?" Aaliyah asked.

"Yeah, yeah, sweetheart, I'm okay," Omar lied, sniffing and wiping his eyes with this hand.

Aaliyah walked over to the sink and got a napkin for her father. He accepted it and wiped his eyes.

"It's just crazy, you know. I – I--" he sighed, "It's like ever since your mom died, I can't seem to get a break, and it's been years. So many years."

"Daddy, it's okay, I can help you. I can get a job and help us out of this," Aaliyah said.

"No, no, Aaliyah. It's out of the question. You just need to go to school like a normal girl. Get a scholarship and go to college, it's what your mom wanted."

"College can wait, they threatened to ki–"

"I said no, Aaliyah!" Omar shouted.

Aaliyah looked down at the table and sank into her seat. Omar turned his face away from her and lowered his head. They both began to sob, reaching out to hold one another after a moment. Aaliyah's fear of losing her father resurfaced, something he once promised her she would never have to face again. Omar was clueless as to what to do for the owed funds, but he was determined to figure it out by any means necessary.

CHAPTER 12

THE CONSTANT STING

NIGHTFALL DESCENDED ON the quiet suburban neighborhood. Homes in the area were dark as their occupants had prepared themselves to rest for the evening, but there was a light on in one of the rooms of the Latrell house. Inside of his bedroom knelt a troubled Omar before his bed. He was dressed in all black with a black jacket lying beside him. He bowed his head and closed his eyes and began to pray, struggling to hold in his sobs.

"Lord, I know I'm wrong for the things I've done out here in these streets, and I hope, I pray that you will forgive me for the things that I'm about to do. I just...I just don't know any other way."

He broke down for a brief moment, resting his forehead on his mattress. He dried his eyes and continued with his prayer.

"Protect my daughter, Lord. She's growing up too fast. Don't ever let her love a fool like me. Make her smarter than her mother. And to you, Alicia...I'm sorry. I'm so sorry baby. I miss you so much."

He caught himself in his moment and quickly fixed his face.

"Keep me safe out here, Lord. Bring me back to my baby. Amen."

Thirteen years ago, Omar Latrell was riding through the city. A hot boy in his prime, he was well known for always having something for the fiends. His seemingly lavish lifestyle gained him the attraction of the beautiful Alicia, a young girl he had met at the local college. The two found love with each other, and he sported her lifestyle, keeping her draped in the latest fashions. In exchange, she discreetly helped him supply drugs to the students around campus. The two would celebrate after big deals were made, sharing a night of wining and dining, capping off the evenings with lovemaking, from which their love child Aaliyah was conceived.

Overtime, Omar's reputation had gained him negative attention from others envious of his gains, but he blindly ignored their hatred believing that he could not be knocked off as others had been before. His arrogance was not shared by his significant other, as her excitement had turned to worry over the years.

A younger Omar sat on the couch in the living room packing baggies of marijuana on the coffee table. Alicia sat on the love seat on the other side of the room doing Aaliyah's hair as she sat in her plush princess chair. Alicia looked over at Omar, fearful that he might ignore the subject she was going to attempt to bring to him.

"Baby?" she said.

"Waddup, sweets?" Omar replied.

"I want to talk to you about something."

"I'm listening," he placed the baggie on the scale.

Alicia cleared her throat and repositioned herself and Aaliyah's head. She nervously sipped her drink and set it back down.

"I've been thinking lately–"

"You been thinkin' lately? 'Bout what?" Omar interrupted.

Alicia took a breath, letting go of Aliyah's hair and setting the comb down.

"Omar...how much longer are we gonna keep living like this?" she asked.

"What you mean?" Omar looked up.

"Baby, this...this life. The drugs, the fiends, it's not like it was back when I was in college. It's getting' crazy out here and it's making me paranoid. Like, every time I go out, I feel like I got a bunch of people looking at me, and not because I'm pretty, but because I'm your girl. You got real haters out here, bae, and I don't know what the hell they be thinkin', like that time them fools came knockin' at the door at 2:00 a.m. Aaliyah's growing up, and I don't want to raise her in this shit, not like this."

Omar looked into his woman's eyes and saw her sincere concern. He looked down at the baggies on the coffee table and then looked at Aaliyah as she innocently sat watching cartoons. He leaned back on the couch and sighed.

"C'mere, sweets," he said deeply.

Alicia walked over and sat next to him. He placed his arm around her and she rested her head on his chest. She closed her eyes and listened to his calm heartbeat.

"Look, I know things seem a little out of hand lately, but I got this. First things first, I ain't ever lettin' anybody get close to you or baby girl, aight? Yeen een gotta worry about dat at all. Y'all are my first priority. These fools might look, but they ain't gon' move. They know better than to mess wit' me, cuz they definitely don't wanna see my boys comin' through their hood, so scratch that thought."

"Okay, baby," Alicia sighed.

"Now, look, I hear you. I care about baby girl's future, too, that's why I'm tryin' to stack this paper. We can move in a few months. Set up shop in a safer place, that I'll promise you, aight?"

Alicia reluctantly agreed with Omar, nodding her head and kissing him on the lips. She walked back over to Aaliyah and continued doing her hair as Omar continued weighing his baggies on the scale. Time went on and Omar continued making his deals until the day came that he fulfilled his promise to Alicia. He had bought a house on the eastside of town, far away from the areas that plagued Alicia's mind. In a few months, Aaliyah would be starting elementary school, and Alicia would soon be starting a new job in the area.

They secured the last load of things in his car, mostly stuff from Aaliyah's room. Omar and Alicia took one last look at the place, happy to be leaving the risky past behind them. They secured Aaliyah in her car seat and headed to their new home. Blinded by their happiness, they were too far away to notice the thugs sitting in the car up the street from them, too distracted to realize that two men were inside watching them. Omar was too negligent to realize his haters wanted to make a move.

"There he go."

"Let's get his ass."

Omar pulled onto the freeway heading east on I-20. There was light traffic and only a few clouds in the sky. Omar cruised in the second lane at about 65 MPH as they listened to some smooth slow jams while Aaliyah sat in the back looking at clouds in the sky. Omar and Alicia sang the lyrics of the song to each other. She lovingly looked over to him, preparing herself to sing the next part. She placed her hand on his knee and cleared her throat, closing her eyes to take in a breath. Omar readied his ears to hear her beautiful voice, but when she opened her eyes, she screamed something that didn't match the lyrics of the song.

"Baby, look out!"

The scheming thugs had caught up to them, and one of them opened fire on the car with an automatic weapon. Alicia shoved her hand toward Omar's chest, trying to push him out of their view. Several shots pierced the cabin, sending everyone inside into sheer terror. Struck in his side, Omar swerved into the opposer's car and ricocheted back to the other side of the highway. The attackers hauled off, and Omar swerved to the very next exit less than a quarter of a mile ahead. Aaliyah's hysteria rattled his already shocked brain as he struggled to keep the car on the road. He pulled onto the exit ramp and couldn't go any further. To his benefit, an ambulance driver witnessed his swerving and followed behind him. He opened his door desperately trying to get to his daughter, but he succumbed to his injuries, passing out and falling to the ground.

Siren's blared in his ears as they rushed him to the hospital, his thoughts hazy as the hospital lights passed over his head. Everything seemed to go black after a while until the sound of beeps became irritating. Omar opened his eyes, waking up in an empty hospital room. He groaned from the pain from his wounds. A nurse walked in almost on cue, preparing to check his vitals.

"Mr. Latrell, you're awake. How are you feeling?" the nurse asked.

"Argh, shit, where... what happened?" he strained.

The nurse straightened her face and called for a doctor to come to the room. She stepped out before the doctor entered and whispered something into her ear. The doctor nodded and said something back to her. The women entered the room and closed the door.

"Good afternoon, Mr. Latrell. I'm Dr. Barker, and this is Nurse Baggs. I am the doctor that performed your surgery. I'm here to ans–"

"Surgery? What?" Omar interrupted.

"Yes, sir. You had multiple gunshot wounds on your left side and in your left arm. Are you aware of anything that has happened over the last couple days?" Dr. Barker asked.

Omar began to breathe heavily, turning his head as he struggled to remember what happened to him.

"I-I, we...where's my daughter? I want my daughter!" Omar demanded.

"She's safe, sir, Child Protective Services has her," Nurse Baggs said.

Omar tried to sit up, but the ache in his side forced him to stay on the bed.

"CPS? What the hell do they have her for? Why isn't she with her mother?" Omar questioned.

"The other young lady in the car, Alicia?" Dr. Barker asked.

"Yes, my wife, Alicia Latrell, why isn't she with her mother?" Omar hollered.

He lifted his head from the bed and looked at the women who were looking away from him.

"Mr. Latrell, I don't know how to tell you this. Mrs. Latrell didn't make it."

Omar froze. A chilling sensation ran down his spine and plopped to the bottom of his gut.

"Alicia? W-w-what happened?"

"According to the EMTs, one of the bullets...hit her in the head. She was pronounced dead at the scene."

Omar's eyes poured with tears and he flailed his arms through the air.

"Alica! No! ALICIA!!"

Because the firearm in his vehicle was registered to Alicia, Omar managed to escape jail time, but because of his record and reputation, CPS made it difficult to get Aaliyah back, releasing custody of her to Alicia's mother. Omar swore for the sake of Aaliyah that he would never get involved with drugs again, and after several months, a new job, and a legitimation process, Omar and Aaliyah finally settled into their quiet home in Decatur. Sadly, Omar and Alicia both came from small families, and the natural causes of death soon set them in the midst of loneliness together, bringing about new struggles as time went on. Occasionally, they would visit Alicia's grave and place flowers by her tombstone, but nothing ever filled the void of losing Alicia as a wife and mother.

Things appeared to be normal with Aaliyah in her youth. She was bright with dreams of being a doctor, hoping to one day save someone that experienced what her mother and father went through, but the shadows of fault followed close behind her as she reached puberty. She sought security after witnessing too many of her father's close calls. Though her essence was pure-hearted, her logic was damaged, mistakenly giving her love to the wrong people and taking their word on her protection. She was silent about her mistakes, fearing Omar's retaliation, and in time she learned to effectively smile through her pain.

Omar softly grabbed the doorknob to Aaliyah's room and peeked through the crack of the door. She was sound asleep, her clothes sitting at the foot of the bed in preparation for school the next day.

"I'll be back," he whispered.

He exhaled a deep sigh and closed the door carefully heading down the stairs. He left the house and disappeared into the night on a mission to figure out how to make the money he needed to pay his debt and ensure Aaliyah's protection.

The two gods descended into the Spirit Realm, traveling through the mystic mist that hung above the rough sands. They faced each other, bringing their right fists to their chests followed by a short bow of the head. Once at ease, Ryan sat upon the rough sands and closed his eyes to prepare for his meditation. Heru looked at him, remembering the war of his emotions in his battle against Set thousands of years ago, a war that had seemingly never ended. He formed a line in the sand in front of him, and the realm grew darker and colder, bringing Ryan to a shiver. Heru released a deep exhale, the cloud from his mouth forming the image of Hathor.

"The air had a slight breeze to it that night, a chill so unfamiliar. The memory of it hasn't left me," Heru said.

Heru and Hathor were flying through the night sky, their senses on high alert as they had recently mourned the loss of Montu.

"I didn't want her with me, but I also feared her being alone. She was always there at my side. A true and faithful love she was. After his death, she accompanied me to visit Montu as he transitioned over. His honorable death allowed him freedom to live among the ancestral gods, and in the wake of his death, we discovered that she was pregnant."

Heru wrapped his arms around his beloved, emotions of fear and happiness spiraling between them. Hathor placed her finger on his lips and kissed him to reassure him that everything would be all right.

"Everything was strange about that night. I shouldn't have left her alone, not for a moment."

The two landed on the grounds of their kingdom and walked up the large stairs. Hathor placed her hand on her belly, stopping at the top of the stairs, denying the care of the concerned Heru.

"Hathor began to feel sick as we scoured the area, and we flew back to the kingdom so that she could rest. She had a pain in her torso. I tried to assist her, but she refused and told me to go and secure the kingdom."

Heru flew low to the ground for a while, finding nothing that seemed out of the ordinary. He traveled back toward his quarters, anxious to get back to his lover. His travels were interrupted by the sight of two unusual figures walking the empty streets of the kingdom.

"I flew around for a while longer, but after seeing nothing, headed back to Hathor. That's when I saw them."

Heru took to the ground, ready to defend his kingdom against the threat. He summoned his spear and attacked, alerting the kingdom to the intruders.

"I was too caught up in my own emotions. I was so blinded in my rage to avenge Montu that I didn't recognize one fatal detail that could have made a difference. There were only two of them."

Heru violently swung his spear, knocking around Mabaya and Wivu until his ears rattled at the sound of his beloved crying out in agony.

"I heard her scream for me. I usually smile when she says my name, but it was the most terrifying thing I had ever heard."

Heru jolted from the fight, desperate to save his lover.

"When I got there, I was instantly broken. I knew she wasn't going to make it."

Hathor lay sprawled out on the floor with several deep stabs to her torso in a pool of her own golden blood.

"I held her tightly in my arms. Tears fell from both our eyes. I begged her to stay. I didn't want her to leave me; I was ready to trade my own life for hers. I kissed her one last time, even as her blood leaked from the side of her mouth. She placed her hand on my face until that final moment."

The roar of Heru's wrath shook the kingdom as the never-ending battle continued to current-day Duat. The evil three had attacked once again in an effort to get their fill of souls. Their plan was quickly thwarted by the watchful eye of Anpu. He thrashed his staff at the attackers, battling the onslaught on their return attacks until Heru entered the fight with a stifling ki blast. The two gods stood back to back, facing their challengers.

"Are you all right, brother?" Heru asked.

"I'm fine. Let's vanquish them," Anpu said.

The two charged their energy and broke out to opposite sides, running in a circle around their enemies. They ran so fast that they appeared to vanish, creating a large cloud of sand to distract their targets. The evil three took their defensive stances, confused by the actions of the gods.

"What the hell are they doing?" Wivu said.

"I think they're afraid. They aren't even trying to attack anymore," Lamia said.

Suddenly, Wivu was knocked to the ground. Mabaya and Lamia looked at him in shock.

"What happened?" Lamia shrieked.

Lamia was then tossed into the air and quickly came crashing down in front of Mabaya. Witnessing her fall, Mabaya attempted to charge his energy, his heads curled into their strike positions, but his powerup was quickly broken by a barrage of strikes that sent him tumbling toward the ground. The evil three were tossed around like debris in a tornado, taking hit after hit from the angry gods. The gods changed the direction of their attack, running at the three and quickly tossing them in the air toward each other. They took aim at their targets in the sky and charged their power.

"MAAAAN-SAAAA-MUUU-SAAAAAAA!!!"

From their hands emerged a large, golden, braided ki blast that blazed toward their enemies. The light blasted over Duat like lightning, fading to reveal that they had vanished.

"They're gone," Anpu said.

The two powered down, each releasing a deep sigh. Anpu grunted as he cradled his arm, his golden blood dripping from his covering hand.

"You're hurt!" Heru rushed to Anpu.

"Lamia managed to stab me with Montu's dagger when they attacked. The wound is deep, but I'll be fine, brother," Anpu strained. "We lost a few more this time. How is Ojore progressing?" Anpu asked.

"He shows promise in his ability, but with all things new, I must give him time to get adjusted. I can't afford to let up on him, but I can't push him too hard," Heru said.

"You'd think the murder of his family would be enough."

"It is enough, but for him it's something more. It is my belief that he is afraid."

"Afraid of what?"

Heru looked out at the masses of souls thinking of all the places they had all come from. He sighed and took a seat on the dark sands, and before him appeared an image of Ryan. He examined it with Anpu, paying attention to its spiritual details.

"Ojore didn't walk the same path as you and I. In his mind, he is more human than god, and that mental deficiency is no fault of his own. The sands of time have shown us the indoctrinated treatment of people of color for thousands of years, and he too is a victim of this. Our presence to him is merely an infatuation, something so bizarre that it piques his interest. He hasn't yet grasped the concept of being a god, and though he knows the truth, even with the promise of revenge, it still hasn't fully registered to him."

"Do you believe the ancestors were wrong to choose him?" Anpu asked.

"No, the ancestors would never give this responsibility to someone incapable of wielding this power. It does not mean to him what it means to us, at least not yet. He is still distracted with human concerns at his age," Heru advised.

Anpu checked his wound and formed something to wrap it. The exhausted god was wary to trust Heru's belief in the young god but was left with no choice other than to support the supreme decision of the ancestral gods.

"Do you believe he'll ever rise to power?" Anpu asked.

Heru looked at Anpu, his expression trying to hide the truth he felt inside.

"We can only hope," Heru sighed. "As much as I would like to interfere, my powers are limited, and in order to keep his trust, I must allow him to live to some degree."

The image of Ryan turned to him sitting still in meditation. His aura began to circulate around him, forming the shape of the red dragon.

"I've felt his spirit, and though he is introverted and angry, there is one thing that I believe will help bring him to the point of transition."

Next to Ryan appeared a separate image of Aaliyah standing alone. Anpu's eyes widened, and he dropped his arms in awe.

"Hathor!" Anpu gasped. "She lives!"

"This girl is called Aaliyah. I too was stricken by her beauty. Everything about her reminded me of my beloved."

Tears filled the wells of Heru's eyes. He shook his head and quickly wiped them away.

"It is my belief that when a man has something of his own to defend that a man finds his purpose. With this in mind, I will encourage him to court her in hopes that she will serve as the missing link that brings him to understanding," Heru stated.

Anpu smiled as he looked at Heru, smiling at Aaliyah's image. He remembered the love that the two once shared and felt encouraged by his brother's words.

"Love does make a difference sometimes," Anpu said.

Heru left Duat and traveled back to join Ryan in the Spirit Realm. He found him shaking with fury as he struggled to contain the overwhelming powers dwelling within. Ryan strained, veins bulging from his hands and neck. His eyes glowed a sinister red, and from his mouth echoed the breaths of the savage beast inside of him. Suddenly, his aura began to weaken, and he dropped to his hands and knees, gasping for air.

"Dammit!" he gasped. "I feel like I—like I almost had it!"

Heru looked down at Ryan, resting his own hopes for the universe upon his shoulders, a responsibility that only time could prove to confirm or deny.

"Relax, Ojore. You've done well today. Rest now, we will start again tomorrow," Heru said.

Ryan rose to his feet, confused. "Really, I feel like I, like I haven't done more than I've been doing."

"You may not now, but in the coming weeks, you will begin to see your progression and eventually capitalize on it. You know that you have a goal, but not yet what that goal is, and finding out what that goal is will be left to your own determination. Fear nothing and press forward, Ojore. The main person you must trust is yourself," Heru advised.

The two brought their fists to their chests again and bowed.

"You have the power to make things happen and produce change, Ojore."

We returned to the Life Realm; fortunately, the difference between time and space was different there. Trying to concentrate our energy had only taken up a few hours, but it felt as if we had been there for the majority of the day. We took a quick shower just before Camille and Reginald got home. The bastard had already been drinking. We could hear him arguing with Camille about dinner in their bedroom. We just wanted him to go away.

Their bedroom door opened and closed, and we sensed Camille's presence in the kitchen. We left our room to check on her, hoping her day was better than ours had been. We peeked around the corner and found her at the sink filling a pot with water. She looked normal, but we felt a disturbance in her energy.

"Hey, Ma. How was your day?" we said.

She turned, surprising us with a normal expression on her face as if she had been completely unbothered. The feeling was beyond unsettling.

"Hi, baby." Camille smiled. "Today was a day like any other, phone calls and angry customers mad because I can't fix their situation without a payment. How was yours?"

As much as we wanted to ask, we thought it would be better to play along with her façade just to help her through the moment. She'd had a rough day, and coming home to that asshole wasn't going to make it any easier.

"Just another day in the neighborhood," we replied.

Weeks had gone by, and the Illegit Family had begun to establish and grow in their new district. The once-powerful resistance under Diaz quickly fizzled out, even gaining the attention of media outlets as their decline made headlines in the metro area. Attempts to gentrify the area were blocked by the threat of retaliation from all three of the district leaders, leaving Face free to market to the people of the area. With the help of Deuce, Porter, and Simmons, he set up business fronts to assist with laundering his funds. He took the nightclub where he murdered Santos and remodeled it, changing the name to Dark Face.

The three district leaders redistributed territory, evening out ownership in the metro area so that they all could benefit from other social events that took place in the city, sitting them at the forefront of some development projects that had been introduced into the city's budget. The money poured in like golden waterfalls on a warm horizon. In an effort to keep an eye on his business, Face bought a high-rise in the middle of downtown, reducing his suburban property back to what it was originally intended for.

As the Illegit business grew, so did the Illegit Family. Recruitment efforts had expanded in the Illegit district in order to make the fronts appear as legitimate businesses. From time to time, Face or Deuce would drop in and offer opportunities to the employees to bring in more money working in one of his warehouses. The men were clear in their description of the terms, sometimes facing rejection from wary employees. Ultimately, the success pouring through the pipeline prompted Face to make additions to his own family to ensure his legacy would carry on. On the opening night of Dark Face, he held a meeting in the office just before opening the doors to the club. Mixed faces from all three districts filled the room, ready to throw money with smiles and bottles in their hands. Face stood proudly at his desk with his woman by his side.

"Gentlemen, it is not fate that has brought us to this point. No prayer or miracle could have gotten us here. It is simply the grit of our existence that gives us the will to pursue the takeover! This is the year of the takeover! Next is domination, and with domination comes a generation that can't escape the grip of the chokehold we've put on them!"

The men hollered in agreement, shaking their bottles and tossing money in the air. Face looked at Hong and Deuce, and they nodded and grinned back at him. The sentimental side of Face reared its head for a moment.

"De'Angelo always talked about this moment. We'd be sittin' off in the cut waitin' to make our next move, and he'd talk about the day he and I would get our moment to rule with the big boys."

He looked at his woman and placed his hand on her belly. His sinister grin cut across his face as he looked into her eyes. She smiled back at him, and the men in the room went wild once again. Face raised his glass of champagne in the air, prompting the men to raise their bottles. Nassar raised his cigar in the air as he sat on the couch with his tired knees.

"For De'Angelo, for all our fallen brothers, and for our future. Let's make some money together!" Face shouted.

The lively party continued with days and nights of money moving from place to place. Eager to maintain the prose of the family name, some Illegit members expanded their business fronts, but also their warehouses where they stored and distributed their material. The young members were held to the same standards as the others, charged with a specific task and threatened with death if they didn't fulfill their purpose.

Among those recruited was Omar, who was approached one day while visiting one of the fronts while getting something to eat. Against his better judgment, he took the job, hoping that he would eventually get lucky enough to stumble upon what he needed. The job paid him well, but not enough for him to make all of the money he needed to secure the full amount of his debt in the time he had. In his desperation, he approached one of the overseers of the warehouse he worked in, hoping to get an answer for something more.

"Wassup, man," Omar said.

"Waddup, bruh? You showin' up tomorrow?" the overseer asked.

"Yeah, yeah, I'll be here." Omar nervously looked around. "Quick question. How can I get some more, uh, lucrative work?"

The overseer looked at Omar from the side and played oblivious to his question.

"What you talkin' 'bout, man? This all we got."

Knowing asking too many questions could possibly get him killed, Omar faced his fear and pressed forward with his questions.

"Look, man, I used to be in the game a long time before all this shit was possible. An operation this big has other things goin' on. I ain't no snitch, I got a daughter that's about to graduate and some shady people on my back. I'm just tryin' to make a move to make moves, dig what I'm sayin'? Just help me out, bruh, please?" Omar pleaded.

The overseer looked at Omar, slightly irritated by his request, but he could hear the pain in his voice as he spoke. He looked around and shook his head, hoping he wouldn't regret his decision.

"Shit. Aight, man, follow me. I'ma make a call and see what I can do, and keep ya damn mouf shut. I don't need everybody comin' to me for favors."

Omar hid his grin and followed after the overseer, hopeful that his new position would put him somewhere that he could prosper.

Back in the Spirit Realm, Ryan stood before Heru, ready to begin the next phase of their training. Ryan had progressed to a point where he could replicate Heru's abilities displayed in their battle against DeMarcus and his brother's goons. Although he did not yet equal him in strength, Heru had the confidence that he was ready to go out on a mission to test his might.

"You have impressed me, Ojore. Your root and sacral chakras are in perfect alignment, bringing light to your solar plexus. Once in alignment with your heart, you'll be close to unstoppable. Your progress in the past weeks shows promise that you will exceed the expectations of the ancestors," Heru said.

"Thank you. I told you I wouldn't fail you," Ryan replied.

"It is not me that you have to worry about failing, Ojore. Trust in the power of your third eye and pay attention to the signs. I must advise you of some things before we set out on your mission tonight. You will be in total control of yourself and your abilities. You will decide what you will and won't do. Though I will be with you, I won't be able to interfere. Essentially, you'll be on your own, so be cautious of what you get yourself into. I trust that your better judgment will guide you."

Heru stepped up to Ryan and looked him in the eye as a proud father would approach his son. He placed his hand on Ryan's shoulder and grinned at him.

"This is the first of many journeys. The wrath of the ancestral gods rests in your hands. You are destined for greatness, Ojore. You are the Menacing Red Dragon, God of War. Let us depart from this place; the night awaits us," Heru charged.

Our essences joined again, and we traveled through time and space to the Life Realm. We awoke in our bed, lying there in case anyone grew curious about our activity. We put on our black sweatpants with the matching black hoodie, this time choosing black boots over tennis shoes. We felt that this night might call for more durable footwear. We didn't have a mask, but we had an old black bandana that we used to keep our hair back from when we had our afro. Hopefully it would serve us well in hiding our face.

We would prove Reginald right tonight as we set ourselves up for a window departure. We walked the house and made sure they were asleep before we left. We stacked the pillows and clothes up to create a shape of our body in the bed in case he decided to peek in, and we even decided to leave our cell phone just in case they decided to get crafty and try to track us. We didn't care about getting caught because Reginald had worsened to a point of drinking heavily every night. After 8:00 p.m., we were virtually nonexistent to him; it was Camille we were worried about. After their arguments, she'd look for something to do to keep herself from falling apart. We had to think of something better soon to keep her off of us.

We removed the screen from the window and hid it between the mattress and applied tape to the middle and sides of the curtains to keep them closed. Before we departed, we grabbed the Buddy and put it in our pocket. We hopped out of the second story window, clinging tightly to the wall, and let our window down to where we could fit our fingers underneath to get back in. We dropped to the ground and landed like a ninja, and the experience suddenly became all too real. We hated sneaking out; there was too much prep. We wasted 15 minutes just getting everything together.

"It's time for us to get moving," Heru said. "Wield the knife and seek out your target."

"Right," Ryan replied.

We took the Buddy from our pocket and closed our eyes as we concentrated on the energies coming from it. The majority of them felt farther away, surrounding the strongest at a distance, which would put them somewhere downtown. There was one that caught our attention, one that wasn't too far away. It felt alone and easy.

"I've got one," Ryan said.

"Good. Now you can't power up here because you might wake your neighbors. Go over to that wooded area there to awaken your powers."

We snuck through the houses, careful not to step in the vicinity of our neighbor's motion lights. The gentle winds of the night gave us the perfect amount of noise to hide our footsteps. We journeyed into the woods, far enough away from the houses to go without being heard, and rose to power.

"Now concentrate, Ojore."

We closed our eyes and planted our feet into the ground, feeling our pulse booming in our muscles as we prepared. We emptied our mind and focused on our rage. Instantly, our body strained as the furious energy we possessed flowed freely within us. Our mouth salivated as thoughts of murder and revenge consumed us. Our canines extended into fangs, and we desired to sink our teeth into our target. We were engulfed by hate as our eyes rose from the darkness of brown to the rage of red. We growled and swiped our clawed fingers through the bark of a pine tree. The empowering groans turned to heavy breathing as we successfully completed our transformation.

"Now go. Find your target and do what you must," Heru commanded.

We ran from the woods and headed to the street, anxious to see what our body could do before we had to fight. We hit the asphalt running almost as fast as we had run from our previous high school. It was different being in control this time. We could feel our body working, no wear, no resistance, just pure rage coursing through our veins. All five senses were on high as we ran down the street. We passed storefronts and dodged cars dashing toward our target. We could smell his blood in the air, and we wanted it on our hands.

We ran and ran until we finally reached a motel across town. The place was quite dilapidated, something off the radar for your common criminal. We observed the parking lot and snuck past the front office, making our way to the backside of the building. We reached into our cargo pockets and pulled out the new cutoff gloves we had purchased, quickly ducking behind the ice machine at the sound of footsteps coming by. We adjusted our bandana over our nose and put on our hood as we crept toward our target's location. We could hear all kinds of sounds coming from the rooms, but our senses were focused on the third door down. We kept our head low, taking advantage of the busted outdoor lights.

We got up on our target's door and heard the sounds of a squeaking mattress. A woman was moaning the name of her suitor as the headboard banged against the wall.

"Oh, Blood Hound, give it to me! Harder, baby! Harder! AH!"

We quickly scanned the parking lot and noticed a motorcycle sitting out front. From the handlebars hung a half shell helmet and a muzzle. We observed the bike's tag, which read in bold characters, *BLD HND*. This was our target. We could smell his blood through the stench of shame and cigarette smoke coming from the room. We pulsated with rage, anxious to tear the door down, but instead forced ourselves to the other side of the parking lot. We wanted a good clean kill, one without civilian casualties in the crossfire. Besides, no one would stay in a place like this for too long, especially not for sex. He'd be out in a moment.

We watched the window of the room for a few minutes, and soon we noticed the glare of light coming from the corner of the curtain. Someone was getting ready to leave. We ducked low behind the cars and waited for our moment. Time seemed to slow with our anticipation, and our muscles were charged and ready to attack. Our tongue scraped against our fangs, nearly bringing us to drool as we watched the door like a rabid dog. We heard keys jingle and flinched. Logic and emotion were at war, and we had to quickly find a medium to stay calm.

The lights went out, and the door creaked open, and a man and woman emerged from the room. Our eyes sharpened, trying to catch a glimpse of the back of his vest...*A-Town Violators MC*. We had heard the name before. He quickly put the vest on over his jacket and started putting on his muzzle and helmet. The time to attack was now.

"When are you gonna stop by again, Blood? I miss you when you're gone too long," the prostitute flirted.

"You and I both know you've got plenty of men to choose from. I'm just the only one that pays upfront," Blood Hound laughed as he fastened his helmet.

The fallacious woman walked up to him and wrapped her arms around his neck, drawing him nearer to her face.

"You say that, and yet you keep coming back. Just admit it." She slowly kissed him. "You like everything I do to you."

The intimate moment was quickly interrupted by the sound of a motorcycle being knocked to the ground under the roar of our wrath. We locked our eyes on Blood Hound, searching for his fear.

"What the f–"

Blood Hound pushed the woman away from him, and she fell to the ground in shock. He tried to reach into his jacket, but we immediately lunged at him and pushed him hard through the half-open doorway. Our bandana had rolled down and freed our teeth to bite if we felt it necessary. We took a heavy breath and looked to our side at the woman, still fearfully lying on the ground. She looked up at us and cringed as if we had pointed a gun at her.

"Run," we grunted.

Before we could turn our head, we felt a sudden sting in our chest, followed by another just below it. Our eyes widened as the world turned sideways, and it became harder and harder to breathe as the milliseconds passed. The sting remained constant, but wait...that sound, what...he had already hit the ground...he was...he wasn't...that sound...it was...

"He-Heru...help me," Ryan strained.

Ryan could feel his energy quickly fading as he squirmed on the ground. Tears rolled from his eyes, and he began to choke on the black blood caused by the bullets that entered his chest. The terrified woman crawled over to him and watched the black blood spill from his mouth. His chest rose one last time, slowly falling as his eyes rolled back and closed.

"He's dead! Blood Hound, he's fuckin' dead!"

Blood Hound emerged from the room, limping with his gun drawn.

"Yo, shut the fuck up," he whispered. "I know he's dead–I shot 'em."

The two nervously looked around, making sure no one else was outside watching them. Blood Hound walked over to observe the lifeless body but couldn't make out the face as it was still covered by the hood. The woman went into shock, tears falling from her eyes at the sight of the dead body.

"Shit, we gotta get up outta here," Blood Hound said.

He snatched up the woman by the arm and shushed her crying. "Look, calm down. Get your keys and get out of here, now! Don't call me for at least a week. Go, go now, hurry up!"

The woman rushed into the room and grabbed her keys and purse as Blood Hound struggled to pick up his 800-pound bike. The left side had taken a bit of damage, but he was still able to ride it safely. The woman turned out the lights to the room and fled to her car, trying to light a cigarette. Blood Hound started his bike, and the two quickly sped off into the darkness, leaving the cold body behind. The mission was a failure.

CHAPTER 13

IT TAKES A GOD

THE TERRIFIED PROSTITUTE drove sporadically down the street, failing to hold her composure. Her blinding tears caused her to have a near miss as she barreled through a stoplight, accidentally dropping her cigarette on her knee. She had seen many things and heard many stories in her line of work, though none of her experiences could prepare her for what had transpired before her eyes that night. The car rattled as she hit the brakes to pull over to the side of the road. She put her head on the steering wheel and cried out of fear.

She replayed the event in her mind, seeing the red eyes of the man dressed in black, the vicious pose he'd taken after he knocked over Blood Hound's motorcycle. She was awed by the power he'd displayed pushing Blood Hound through the doorway, but her fear didn't cause her curiosity to fade as she pondered the strange character. His actions did not match up to the things she had heard about in the past. The usual ending to the story would be that anyone involved would be killed, no witnesses left behind, not unless they were fortunate enough to escape. This man, however, allowed her an opportunity... he'd turned to her and told her to run. He knew what he came to do and didn't want her to get caught in the crossfire. His debt was personal.

She sat in the car for a moment, trying to calm herself down. She picked up the cigarette she'd dropped, threw it out of the window, and lit up another. She softly rocked back and forth, remembering the flood of blood leaking from his mouth.

Why didn't he come after me? she thought as she puffed the cancer stick. She wiped her eyes and looked in her rearview mirror, contemplating going back to the scene. Her conscience weighed in on her shoulders as she saw blue lights coming toward her in the distance. This man had spared her, a treatment she believed she was not deserving of. The lights passed her, and after a moment, she took one final puff of her cigarette. She dried her eyes one last time and flicked her cigarette out of the window, exhaling the white smoke as she put the car in gear. She faced her crossroad head-on and made a U-turn.

Meanwhile, the phone rang at the motel's front office. The night manager frantically tried to reassure the visitors that everything was under control while at the same time trying to give the 911 operator a description of what had happened. Overwhelmed with the calls, the manager locked the door to the lobby and hid in the manager's office so that she could speak with the operator in peace.

Most of the residents were reluctant to leave their rooms, avoiding the crime scene on the backside of the hotel. The spilled blood had gone as cold as the shadows surrounding it. Several police sirens blared far in the distance, making their way to the motel, the police not knowing if they'd be heading to a shootout or a homicide. The body of the young man had still gone undiscovered, lying motionless in the outdoor walkway.

The black blood dripping from his mouth slowed to a stop and began to dry along with the blood coming from his chest. From the two holes in his clothing popped out the two .50 caliber bullets that were fired at him. They rolled off of his chest and stopped in the cracks between the concrete sidewalk and the speckled wall. His body jolted, and suddenly his chest began to rise and fall again. The boy awakened, coughing and trying to catch his breath. He gripped his chest where he had been shot, still feeling a small bit of pain. He opened his eyes, trying to identify his surroundings, but his current fixation made everything around him seem hazy.

"He-Heru. I-I need you. I need help."

He wiggled his toes and moved his legs to make sure the rest of his body was in one piece. The exhausting haze kept him on his back as he struggled to calm his breathing. He reached his hand up to the cloudy crescent moon, hoping something would reach back.

"The ground is not a place for a god to lie, Ojore! Get to your feet at once!" Heru commanded.

"It hurts...my chest," Ryan wheezed.

"You cannot get caught here, Ojore! Get to your feet and leave at once!"

The fast approaching sounds of the police sirens grew louder, giving us a small window of opportunity to get out of there. We had to get to our feet quickly, or else it was going to be even worse news than getting shot. We rolled on our side and reached up to grab hold of the corner of the window seal to pull ourselves up. We staggered to our feet, and our legs felt like jelly as we tried to take our first steps. We held on to the walls of the building until we could see the main road and realized the cops weren't far away.

"Keep moving, Ojore! They will storm this place and find you if you don't get out of here," Heru said.

We had only taken about forty steps and already we were out of breath. We had to get to the trees on the other side of the street as quickly as we could, or we'd absolutely be caught. We gave it all we had, limping by the cars into the bright streetlight. We could see the blue lights of the police cars cast across the storefronts at the corner of the street; the cops were too close for comfort. We thrust our legs forward as if we were traveling knee-deep through a trail of mud. Just as the first cop car cut the corner, we made it into the woods. We pulled our bandana back over our nose and secured our hood. Given the distance we had to travel back home, we watched the scene from the shadows for a moment to give our legs time to readjust.

The night manager unlocked the office and allowed the responding officers to enter, telling them the details from the calls she had received from the other guests. More cars arrived at the scene and were directed around back to the scene of the crime. The officers were baffled at their investigation, finding nothing but some dried black stuff on the walkway along with the two bullets that had come from Ryan's chest. The officers chose to ignore the black material, mistaking it for some kind of dirt or residue from the rundown motel, but they took the two bullets as evidence in hopes to find the shooter.

Several officers began to walk the premises, knocking on doors, looking for answers and a possible lead on the shooting but were unable to get much information from the reluctant guest. While the cops marked the area around the bullets, the now calmed prostitute pulled into the motel and made her way to the back. Her eyes widened at the sight of the police lights, and she contemplated leaving again until she realized that there was no ambulance on the scene. The parking spots near her room were blocked off, so she parked her car on the far side of the parking lot and lit up another cigarette, waiting for the confidence to walk to her room.

She got out of her car and locked the door from the inside to prevent the horn from beeping with the remote. She flicked her cigarette and put her head down as she nervously walked back to her room. She squinted as she got closer to the bright lights, trying to keep her mind off of the dead body she knew was lying up ahead. She tried to focus on her door, but as she approached the cars, her mind went into a panic. To her surprise, the body of the slain man was gone, and the police had blocked off the area including a small section that included the door to her room. The woman's mind began to run wild with thoughts of being arrested, thinking the police might link her to the crime if they found the bullet casings in her room. She regretted not picking them up before she left.

There were two officers by her window looking for bullet holes to match the bullets found on the walkway. The woman crossed her arms as the chill of her fears ran down her spine. She had no idea what to do or what to say but chose to go into her purse for another cigarette to calm her nerves.

"Ma'am, I'm gonna need you to go back into your room. We're investigating a crime here," an officer said from behind.

The woman turned and faced him, and quickly her lies came together.

"I-I can't. I can't get back into my room. Yo-you guys have it blocked off. I-I just got back here. That's my car right over there, see? Uh, can you let me back in my room, please?" She shuddered.

The cop looked at her and saw that her eyes were puffy and her hair was unkempt. He took pity on her and called over to the other officers.

"Hey, guys, you mind if this lady goes in her room? She just got here, and she's tired."

The two officers looked at each other and allowed the woman to go into her room. One of the cops guided her around the crime scene to her door. As she searched her purse for the key, she looked over to the spot where the body had lain, the police lights disguising the black material on the ground. She found her key and opened the door, the police lights shining over the shell casings on the floor by the bed. She quickly stepped into the room and tried to close the door.

"Wait, ma'am, one sec." The officer stopped her.

"Yes, what is it?" she nervously asked.

The officer looked into her eyes as he raised his pen and notepad.

"You wouldn't happen to know anything about what happened here tonight, would you?"

Her heart dropped at the sound of the question, her mind flashing back to the horrific scene that had taken place right before her eyes. She wanted to ask where the body was but knew that it would lead to a long night of interrogation. She knew there was no way an ambulance could have gotten to the scene without her seeing it first. Her mind shifted back into fear, believing the downed man had gotten up.

"No, no, I just got here." She shook her head.

"Okay, ma'am, uh, if you can, please stay in your room until we can wrap things up here."

"I-I will. No problem."

She had to get out of there. She feared the vicious man would come back looking to finish what he started as he searched for Blood Hound. She emptied her drawers and threw her clothing and belongings on her bed and started packing her bag. She vowed to get as far away from the motel as possible first thing in the morning.

We had made it a little way down the street. We were walking much better, and things weren't as hazy, but we were still exhausted. We needed to get home, but we weren't going to make it by walking. We couldn't summon a rideshare because we'd left our cell phone at home, probably still the best choice we had made that night. The pain in our chest had subsided. We felt the spots where the bullets had hit, and they felt perfectly normal, but our hoodie and shirt were ruined. It was going to be fun asking Camille for money to replace them, or maybe not. We couldn't let her see our clothes in this condition, and we didn't even feel like coming up with an elaborate enough lie.

"Can you tell me what you did wrong, Ojore?" Heru asked.

"Can I tell you later?" Ryan sarcastically responded.

"No," Heru grunted. "Your ignorance caused you to fail your mission! If you were mortal, you'd be dead! I'm so disappointed you lost total control of your emotions!"

"Understandable," Ryan wheezed, "but uh, I don't know if you realize this or not. We ain't exactly down the street from the house. You mind helpin' me get home?"

We leaned against a road sign for a moment to catch our breath, looking back at the blue lights in the distance that we'd narrowly escaped. Our legs were getting too tired to walk.

"I told you, I can't interfere," Heru grunted. "When the ancestral gods awakened your powers and bestowed their wrath upon you, it made your body impervious to foreign control. I can only speak with you this way because of the bonding of our essence. In short, you are on your own."

Our mind at war, we tried to power up again but couldn't muster up the strength to concentrate. Essentially, dying had taken everything from us. We contemplated what to do. The house was entirely too far to walk to in our current condition, and even if we could walk, we wouldn't make it home before Camille and Reginald woke up. Just as we were about to sink to the ground, we spotted a bicycle sitting on the side of a fast-food restaurant. We crept up to the scene and sensed someone close by. One of the employees was outside smoking a cigarette while scrolling on his cell phone. We didn't have the energy for another fight, so we slowly walked up to him...at night...dressed in all black...having no idea what our face looked like.

"Hey," we softly called over to him.

"Hu-oh, shh-"

The worker tripped and fell back into the wall. He looked more shaken up than we were. We had to keep him cool.

"Relax." We put our hands up. "I'm not trying to rob you."

The worker quickly looked us up and down, fear stapled across his face.

"What do you want?" he squealed.

"Look, I'm far away from home, and I need a ride. What's it gonna take for me to get your bike?"

The scared man examined our face and relaxed a bit.

"You look like you need it more than me, man. It's yours."

"Thanks."

We quickly hopped on the bike and rode off into the night, hoping that the trip wouldn't take too long now. The worker watched us as we rode off, his hand waving in the wind. Another one of his co-workers came outside to take the trash to the dumpster.

"Yo, you got another cigarette, man?" the co-worker asked.

"Yeah. Hey, tell that idiot Andrew some guy just stole his bike."

We rode for miles and miles through the night. The only thing that made the trip easier were the numerous hills we were able to go down, allowing our legs time to rest. We kept pushing for what seemed like an hour and a half, and finally, we reached our subdivision. We stashed the bike in the woods and walked to the backyard and immediately realized that our problems were just beginning. When we left the house, we hadn't intended on dying, but we did. As a result, we'd lost a vast majority of our energy. We had no idea how we were going to get back into our room. We hated Reginald for being so clever.

We looked up at the second-story window and scratched our head. We couldn't walk through the backdoor and use our key because we'd set off the alarm. Fortunately, the upstairs windows didn't have sensors on them, but that wasn't going to help us in this scenario. All of the tools were locked up in the garage, and there was nothing in the yard big enough to climb up that would support our weight. We angrily paced back and forth until we looked into our neighbor's backyard. On the side of their shed was a ladder that looked just long enough for us to reach the window. We snuck over to their yard and grabbed it, but it was a lot heavier than we expected. We had truly lost a lot of power, but we had to muscle it over to our window because dragging it was not an option.

We carefully placed the ladder below our window and took off our boots and placed them over our shoulders to keep the noise down. Step by step, we made our way up the ladder, hoping this thing wouldn't fall because of the uneven grass. We made it up to the bottom of the window seal and ran out of steps, so it was on us the rest of the way. We planted our feet, but our shaky calves challenged our faith in the ladder as we pushed the window open. Fortunately, the window gave us just enough space to slip through. We pushed the curtains open and carefully put our boots through the window, making sure they didn't crash to the floor. Next, we prepared ourselves to slip through the window, the task calling for upper body strength we weren't sure we had. If we could get the right amount of push from the ladder, we could make it; however, one wrong move could cause us to knock the ladder backward and possibly us right behind it.

We grabbed hold of the window seal and mustered the last of the strength in our arms to pull ourselves up, using the last of our legs to push off the wall. We slipped perfectly through the window and guided ourselves flat on the floor. We'd made it. The worst of our night was over; we just had to make sure we woke up and put the ladder back unnoticed in the morning. We picked ourselves up and went to the bathroom.

The light revealed the wreck that we truly were, looking as if we had gotten shot and risen from the dead. The holes in our hoodie told the story of the greatest comeback in our history, both of them located just over our heart. The bottom of our pants was covered in dried mud from walking through the woods. The most harrowing detail was our face. There was black stuff that had dried all around the sides and faded stains on our teeth. We moved closer to the mirror, trying to examine and identify the foreign substance when suddenly there was a knock at the door.

"Ryan, are you okay? I heard noises," Camille said.

Apparently, we weren't as discreet as we thought. How did she get to this side of the house without us sensing her coming?

"Yeah, Ma, I'm good. I was, uh, sweating a lot in my sleep. I got up to take a shower," we lied.

"Okay, baby," she yawned. "I'll turn down the AC to cool your room off. Good night."

"Good night."

What the hell was this shit on our face? This couldn't be blood. It'd be cool if it was, but nah. We remembered coughing up blood, we could smell it, we could taste it, but this wasn't it.

"Heru, what is this stuff?" Ryan asked.

After a moment of silence, we realized that we wouldn't get the answer we were looking for, and we were too tired to care anymore. We stripped and got into the hot shower, noticing the black stuff was on our chest and torso as well. We thoroughly washed ourselves, allowing the hot water to soothe our tired muscles. With each second that passed, we started to get weaker and weaker. We got out and quickly dried off, using mouthwash to clean our mouth due to the lack of strength needed to stand at the sink.

We staggered back into our room and fell across the bed, barely having the strength to get underneath the covers. We quickly found the power we needed to get up, realizing we had forgotten to turn off the light. We got up one last time and put on our usual nightwear and turned off the light. We got comfortably under the covers and checked our phone. It was 3:47 AM, and we normally got up at 7:00, but we had to get up earlier to put our neighbor's ladder back. We'd made it through the day on less sleep before, but we were going to need every minute based on the way we felt.

"Can you please answer my question, Heru?"

"Rest, Ojore. We'll talk tomorrow when you take your lunch," Heru said.

"The god speaks." Ryan chuckled to sleep.

The worst part of waking up was trying to wake up. The majority of our strength had returned, and we were back to feeling nearly normal, but there were no words to express how exhausted we were. We successfully got the ladder back to our neighbor's house just before they prepared to leave home. We hopped back through the window with ease and got ready for the day. We walked to school, replaying the events of the night in our head, trying to figure out where we'd gone wrong.

We dragged through the first three periods. We thought Mr. Rose was going to help us, but he thought our tiredness was some form of artistic expression and instead used us as a model for the class to paint. Mr. Tukes was kind enough to make us a cup of coffee from his personal coffee maker, but unfortunately, he didn't have any cream or sugar because he liked his coffee black and proud. Lunch finally came, and the next lesson began.

"So let's talk about last night," Ryan said.

"You made a mockery of yourself," Heru replied.

"I'm aware of that, but can you tell me what I can do better?"

We looked across the courtyard and noticed Terrell coming out of the building. On the other side, we saw Aaliyah with Terry and his crew. We were still in disbelief that she was with him. She was putting on a good act with her fake smile, but she wasn't fooling us.

"You talk too much, and you're too cocky for where your powers are right now. You may be stronger than all of the mortals in the world, but you lack the strength and skills to survive under more dangerous circumstances. Not saying that this experience hasn't made you smarter and stronger, but for example, the woman that was on the ground. There was no need to tell her to run. She wasn't capable of doing anything, and she posed no threat," Heru said.

"Wait, wait, I was just trying to get her out of there. I didn't want her to get hurt."

"And look at what it cost you."

We sighed, tossing our napkin into our tray. We really died last night, and nobody knew. How artistic would it be to go to class and tell the story of death? How could we paint that into a picture? Could we do the math behind it, or was there a science to it?

"I hope last night was a learning experience for you," Heru said.

"Of course. I don't want to make a habit of asking people to borrow their bike, but there's more I want to know. What happened to my body? Was it like the same thing that happened when I got beat up?"

"Essentially. I didn't want to tell you this before you went out because I didn't want you to get careless. Nothing in this mortal world can kill you," Heru sighed.

We turned away from the other students as we got a rise of curiosity from the statement.

"What do you mean?" Ryan asked.

"You are a god, and as a god you are stronger than the majority of things that stand against you. In your current state you can be hurt by these mortal creations; however, they can't kill you, nor do they have lasting effects. To answer your question from last night, the black substance on your face, teeth, and chest was in fact your blood. The blood of gods is usually gold, but because you have not yet reached your supreme level, your blood is black. Once you unlock your true power, a few changes will be made to your being, including the color of your blood," Heru advised.

"Oh, well, I guess that's kind of cool. Something to work toward," Ryan said.

"Something you should unquestionably be working toward, Ojore. You now have healing powers that work independently of your consciousness. Last night your powers healed you after you succumbed to the bullet wounds to your chest. Because the damage would have been fatal if you were mortal, you died, essentially, but there is a small benefit to your mistake. Each time your body heals itself from significant damage, you get stronger than you were before. You may not notice it, but it's there, and your body will do the majority of its healing while you sleep when the damage is significant. As time goes on, you will get stronger and be able to withstand more damage, but once you unlock your true powers, you'll be untouchable to all things mortal. I don't recommend relying on your healing powers to help you because you'll progress much faster in your training," Heru advised.

"Trust me, I'm not trying to get shot again. It felt like it pierced through my heart. Any idea how long I was out?" Ryan asked.

"Because your powers are always working subconsciously, your healing powers immediately began to work on you. The total time it took to revive you was about three minutes in the Life Realm."

"Three minutes, hmm. That ain't so bad, I guess," Ryan said.

"A lot can happen in three minutes, Ojore, and though they might not be able to kill you permanently, you don't want to have to deal with an unnecessary process. They say that the strongest of gods have the ability to heal themselves instantly. I, myself, am capable of this, along with Anpu, but before you start to feel invincible, understand that you can be killed. It takes a god to kill a god, and Set's children are pure evil. Once they've learned of your existence, they will likely come for you. Their hands and ki-blasts are more than strong enough to take you down easily, but in order to kill a god, they have to use the weapon of a god. As I mentioned before, Lamia stole Montu's weapon when she murdered him, which allowed them to vanquish many of the other gods. If they get to you now, your training will be in vain. I push you as hard as I do because I refuse to see you suffer that fate," Heru explained.

"But wait, you said I was stronger than them, and if you and Anpu have been fighting them all this time, why haven't you killed them?" Ryan asked.

"You are stronger than them, Ojore, but not in your current state. You won't be able to defeat the three of them until your powers have manifested to their full potential. As far as your other question, there are many reasons why Anpu and I have been reluctant to kill them, the greatest reason being that they have closed our access to travel from the Life Realm to the Spirit

Realm in our physical form. We know what they did, but we can't get to the area where the stones are to change it. If we kill them now, I fear that we may never get out of Duat."

"And you need me to get strong enough to defeat them to get you out. Got it."

"The task is not as simple as it seems, Ojore. Your task in this world does not end at the expense of my freedom. You have a divine purpose to fulfill. It was no accident that fate chose you to be the God of War. You have a power that reaches far beyond comprehension, so I beg you not to take this lightly."

"I don't," Ryan said.

We looked over to Terrell and saw him looking pitiful while eating alone. Over the past few weeks, we had sort of become friends, but we only talked in passing or in class, seeing as we were still standoffish for the most part, so we didn't engage too much. Maybe it was the effect of these powers or my skate with death, but we wanted to be friendly today.

"Let's talk about this more later," Ryan said. "I think I'm gonna go talk to Terrell."

"We will. I know that you are introverted, but it is my belief that he may benefit from having a friend such as yourself," Heru said.

We grabbed our tray and tossed it in the trashcan and walked over to Terrell. He took the last bite of his sandwich and started to go for his fries as we approached.

"Mind if I sit with you?" we asked.

His mouth full, he motioned to us to take a seat. We sat on the plastic bench and pulled our sketch pad from our bag. We still hadn't been able to decide what we were drawing exactly, but whatever it was, it appeared to be coming along well. We analyzed the image for imperfections to look busy, still battling being standoffish. This was a trait that was hard to break from.

"How's your day been, bruh?" Terrell asked. "You looked really tired earlier."

Our conversations were never about anything more than classwork, or at least that's what we limited it to. We forced ourselves out of our reclusiveness and fought to engage in conversation.

"It was a long night, you know. Couldn't sleep. Stuff on my mind with these colleges," we lied.

"I know what you mean. My mom has been on me about going to college since my dad died. She was like that with my older brother, too, but she was on him so tough, he joined the military. Now she just worries about him all the time."

This guy wasn't kidding; he really was too realistic. It's not that we couldn't handle the conversation, but we understood why others couldn't. We didn't want to get too far into detail about this guy's life, but he kinda left us without many options to keep the conversation going.

"Your dad died? Recently?" we asked.

"Oh, no, it was years ago. Whenever people talk about college, it just reminds me of him because he was big on school. He had a Ph.D. and everything, swore to everyone that me and my brother would be scholars. I guess it's just a little harder for me because I'm at that point in life now," Terrell said.

So that's it, he's not weird, he's traumatized. He truly does need a friend.

"Damn, man, uh, I'm sorry to hear that."

"Oh, I'm okay, man. I've had time to adjust," he reassured us. "What made you come sit with me today?"

A moment to be honest but not too honest. We didn't want him to feel like this was some kind of pity party. This was an attempt at being genuine.

"Nun, you know. Just saw you sittin' here and decided to come over. It's not like we don't ever talk," we said.

We couldn't leave him with an open statement. With his wit, he'd likely hit us with something we couldn't easily answer to.

"So in other news, have you said anything to that girl you told me about?" we asked.

"C'mon, man, are you serious?" Terrell turned and scoffed. "That girl doesn't even notice me."

"Well, maybe it's because she hasn't noticed you noticing her. I told you to shoot your shot. If you miss, you live to shoot someone else," we laughed.

"And live with the pain of rejection? Are you okay, man? Maybe you aren't accustomed to the physical pains of love, but I don't wanna be that guy that walks around with hurt. Nobody wants to be that guy," he grunted.

"True, but you're okay with being that guy that never said anything and lives his life in love with a woman that has no clue of his existence? You sound like a hopeless romantic thespian," we chuckled.

Terrell crossed his arms.

"It's a safe place. It might be awkward, but it's safe. At least I'm not stalking her."

Terry and his crew of jocks approached our table, Aaliyah standing behind them. They did all the stereotypical bully stuff, popping their knuckles and their necks. Terry towered over Terrell as he sat at the table, and Terrell just sat there, not even making eye contact.

"Yo, Terrell, I'm thirsty. Gimmie ya milk," Terry demanded.

"Babe, leave that boy alone," Aaliyah said. "I'll buy you something to drink."

Terry turned to Aaliyah, and instantly our rage spiked. Our eyes sharpened on his head.

"Woman, leave me alone. I know you'll buy me something to drink, but I want his!"

We focused so hard on Terry that we forgot anyone else was standing around. His friend Leo saw our face and immediately got on the defensive.

"Yo, why you lookin' at my boi like dat? You wanna do somthin'?" Leo charged.

Our eyes rolled over to Leo's bean head. He was the shortest of the group, but he had the most mouth out of all of them. Amazing how confident people act when they feel protected.

"This ain't the time or the place, homie. I ain't no skinny Frank," we said.

Our rage burned like a wildfire, and a bean head was on the grill. Our calves began to jump with anticipation, and our mouth began salivating.

"C'mon guys, we don't have to fight," Terrell said.

Leo quickly turned to Terrell, adding gas to the blaze.

"Man, shut up! Ain't nobody talkin' to you!"

Terrell lowered his head in submission. We were about to break this guy's jaw. We could make good use of ten days of OSS, but it turned out to be his lucky day. The bell rang, and it was time for 5th period. He didn't know how lucky he was. Terry grabbed his shoulder and pulled him away from the table.

"Come on, bruh, it's Friday. Coach said if we get in trouble again, he's gonna bench us, and he's serious this time," Terry said.

Leo sucked his teeth and looked us up and down as he backed away.

"He ain't ready for it no way," he reassured himself.

The crew walked off with Aaliyah trailing behind. She looked back at us, ashamed of what had transpired. We figured we'd hear about it when we saw her later. Terrell nervously grabbed his tray and gathered his belongings.

"You didn't have to do that for me," Terrell said. "Now they're gonna bother you."

"They ain't finna do shit to me," we grunted.

We could hear the grit in our tone and took a few deep breaths to calm down. We ran our hand over our head and exhaled.

"Look, you don't need to be lettin' anybody talk to you like that. You're a man, a real man, strong and dignified. They only come at you like that because they're all together, and they ain't gonna do shit at school because they don't wanna deal with the consequences. You gotta know your enemy."

"Look man, I'm not you. They've been coming at me like this for years, and standing up to one of them isn't going to make all of them stop," Terrell said.

"Don't you get tired of that shit?" we asked.

"I don't want to talk about it. Can we just go to class?"

We examined Terrell's face. He had been humiliated enough for one day, and us talking to him now wasn't going to help. We exhaled a deep sigh and put our rage back on the leash.

"Yeah, c'mon. Let's go."

We had never been much for bullying, especially not back in the day. Our anger used to get us in trouble at school, trying to fight battles for others. Terrell didn't have it in him to fight, nor did he want anyone to fight for him. He was truly hurting inside. Maybe this was why he never went for that girl. We got to class, and he just sat there looking miserable again. We wanted to say something more to him, but we'd done enough damage and were afraid that making him face the situation might bring him to tears. Sixth period was exactly what we expected. Aaliyah came to class and approached us with shame written on her face. We already knew where this conversation was about to go.

"Hey, Ryan," Aaliyah said.

"What's goin' on," we replied.

She laid her backpack on the table and humbly sat in her seat looking down at the floor. We raised our brow and waited for her to come out with it.

"I, uh, I want to apologize for what happened earlier," she said.

"Apologize for what?" we inquired.

Aaliyah sighed. She was about to lie to herself.

"Terry and his friends can be very intrusive sometimes and–"

"So why are you apologizing for him?" we interrupted.

"Well, I just want to keep things neutral, and–and I know that he's not going to say this to you," she said.

We sat our pencil down on our sketch pad and turned to her. It was time to plant a seed.

"Let me explain something to you, sweetheart. You have never done anything wrong to me since I've been here, so I'm not mad at you, but one thing I won't let you do is apologize to me for what somebody else did. It's not your place to apologize for what they did, and honestly, I could care less if they apologize or not. Their actions are not a reflection of who you are, so apologizing for them is unnecessary, and it won't do anything to remedy the situation, and that's fine. But I noticed what you did do. You offered to get him a drink, and you didn't even have to do that."

"I was just trying to defuse the situation," Aaliyah said.

"Yeah, I get that, and that's sweet of you, but don't be foolish, sweetheart. I also saw how he came at you for speaking up. You shouldn't let him talk to you like that. Why are you with him anyway? I feel like you deserve so much better. Someone that actually wants to hold your hand around people."

Aaliyah glanced up at us and then gazed off into space. We had an open door to her emotions and made sure she heard everything we said.

"Look at me," we whispered to her.

Her beautiful brown eyes stared into ours in desperation, and we stared back with the confidence of the ancestral gods, a stare that no mortal man on this earth had been able to withstand since the dawn of her time. Her heart was wide open. We grabbed her soft hand with our warm right hand and covered it with the left. Our eyes locked on, and our voice lowered to the perfect tone with the right amount of twang in our accent.

"You are a queen, a goddess if you will, and therefore, you should be treated as such, and if that ain't what you're gettin' in ya relationship, maybe you need to reconsider who ya wit'."

She stared into our eyes, speechless. We could see her emotions ready to spill over. She gripped our hand tighter, almost as if she wanted to pull us in. She heard us, all right, she heard everything we said.

"Aight, y'all, turn to page 469 in your textbooks. Today we're gonna be talking about the male and female anatomy and the reproductive system," Colb said.

She blinked and came back to reality, not realizing the seed had been planted, watered, and just needed a little sunshine. It was only a matter of time. She reluctantly let go of our hand and got her textbook from her bag. She turned to the page as we scooted closer to her, glancing at us when she thought we weren't looking. Class went on, as usual, talking about the reproductive system with a bunch of horny teenagers.

The final bell rang, and the other students rushed out of class, but like us, Aaliyah was taking her time getting her things together. We packed our sketch pad in our bag and put our jacket on. Before we could put on our bag, Aaliyah walked up to us and placed her hand on our shoulder.

"Hey," she said nervously.

She looked at her shoes and took a breath, then looked up into our eyes again.

"Thank you," she said sweetly as she lowered her hand.

We looked back at her and dimmed our eyes, slowly looking her up and down. We found the right tone of voice again and returned fire.

"You're welcome," we said, followed by a tiny grin.

She took a step toward us and quickly wrapped us in her arms. Her body was oh so soft, gentle with the right amount of firmness. We were instantly hypnotized by the pleasant essences emitting from her glorious hair. We hugged her back with the pride and strength of the gods, for nothing is more welcoming than a good strong hug, and we'd just stolen a key. We let each other go and adjusted our clothes, Aaliyah mostly having to adjust her face before she met up with Terry.

"Well, I guess I'll see you later," she said.

"Yeah, you will. By law, I have to keep coming to this place." We grinned.

She exhaled a smile, shyly looking back at the floor again.

"I'll see you tomorrow. Bye, Ryan."

Aaliyah turned and walked away, and we watched her every step out of the door. Colb began cackling at us as we walked up to the front of the classroom. The expression on his face was one of excitement and instigation.

"I saw you back there putting ya moves on 'er, man. I thought we was finna get a live demonstration in here for a minute."

"Nah, man, it's not like that," we laughed. "I was just giving her some advice."

"That didn't look like no advice to me, lil' bruh. Look, I got some rubbers in the car if you need 'em now."

We both burst into laughter. Talking to Colb was like post-game commentary.

"Look, I don't care what you say, that girl wants you, and her lil' stupid boyfriend is about to take a loss," Colb said.

"Nah, nah, man, well, maybe! I'll see you tomorrow, Colb." We grinned.

"Aight, boy. Be safe."

We exited the classroom laughing, Colb still at his desk cackling on as we made our way down the hall.

"Showdy said she wanna rock yo' Timbs, G-Rock!" Colb's voice echoed loudly down the hall.

We got outside and began the trek home as we scanned the parking lot for familiar faces. Terrell had already left—the day had taken its toll on the poor guy. We continued walking and went virtually unnoticed by Terry, Leo, and the crew. They were too busy babbling with each other to even know we were there. Aaliyah sat on the back of Terry's car, keeping her distance from him as we passed by. We could feel her eyes watching us, and before we took the corner, we looked back and waved at her. She quickly waved back and turned away, afraid of being caught by one of his idiot friends.

We were trying to put together a scheme on the way home. We couldn't allow ourselves to be caught up in a situation like last night again, so we had to come up with something that would allow us the time we needed out of the house at night. It would be a stretch, but hopefully, Camille would go for it, and Reginald wouldn't care to say anything. We waited for Camille to get home and caught her in the garage, pretending to be happy about the good news we'd gotten at school.

"Hey, Mom, I got a job!"

"A job? A job where?" Camille asked.

"It's a warehouse job over there off of exit seven. One of my teachers at school is a night manager at the place, and he talked to a few people and got me in," we lied.

"That's great, baby. When are you supposed to start?"

We played bashful with her as we walked in the house. This was the part that mattered. Her mind was occupied with the frustrations of the day and the urge to relax. If we could get a yes from her while she was distracted, she wouldn't be able to go back on her word.

"He said I could start as soon as possible, but I had to get your permission first because of the hours."

"What are the hours?" she asked.

"Well, it varies, but some nights might be late nights with me getting off at...two in the morning, roughly." We squirmed.

Camille looked at us with the *I don't wanna tell you no, but seriously* mom look, and we immediately went to bargaining.

"It won't typically be during the week. He said that shift usually happens on the weekends, and that's if they have the business. It does happen during the week sometimes, too, but—"

We quickly put on the puppy dog eyes for appeal. This had to work.

"—Mom, I'm a senior, and graduation is just over the horizon. I know you've got a lot going on with the bills and everything. This job could help me pay for my college expenses."

Her entire face lit up with excitement.

"You got an acceptance letter?" Camille asked.

"Not yet, but I'm waiting for a response, and when I get it, trust me, you'll be glad you said yes."

Camille clenched her hands and shrugged off the weight. She gave us the *you clever bastard* look.

"All right, but if you start slipping, I'm making you quit," she agreed.

"Yes!" We jumped in excitement. "I'm gonna go call him now and figure out when I can start."

We took off to our room and closed the door.

"I can't believe that actually worked," Heru said.

"I told you not to underestimate me, Heru," Ryan said. "If there's anything I've learned in my years, it's that my mom doesn't ask questions, and she's pro-anything that has to deal with the progression of my future."

We spent the next few days traveling to the Spirit Realm for training. We were determined to get stronger, but more importantly, we wanted to avenge our death. Dying kind of heightened our determination and gave us more of a reason to focus. We tested ourselves, pushing our limits to the max until we were able to achieve a new level each day. We didn't care about anything else but getting him back, constantly replaying what we saw in our mind to plot our attack.

"A-Town Violators M/C, I know about that club. I think they have a clubhouse downtown not too far from the stadium. I'm sure that's probably where he is most nights," Ryan said.

"If they are a club, then that would mean there may be multiple members of this club, potentially meaning there may be a lot more threats you'll have to worry about," Heru warned.

"That just means I have to change my approach for this task. You leave that part to me," Ryan said.

A few days passed, and we were ready for our second attempt. We came home after school and changed into some black cargo pants, black boots, our workout gloves, and a black hoodie with a red T-shirt underneath. We looked at ourselves in the bathroom mirror and noticed a few changes in our face. We looked a little rough around the eyes, we were a bit gritty with the facial hair that was beginning to grow in. We left a note on the kitchen counter letting Camille know we'd probably be home late and to leave a plate for us in the fridge. It was too early to run all the way to the clubhouse, but we didn't want to sit and wait for darkness to fall because we wanted to be gone before anyone else got home. We decided to walk back to the school to see what was going on.

We walked to the practice field and ducked off by the trees and observed the football team taking turns trying to kill each other. The coaches were shouting at the players, desperately trying to get them ready for the next game. We noticed Terry in the distance getting a sip of water on the sideline. If he continued with his reckless behavior, we were going to add him to our hit list—Leo too. We hated seeing the way they treated people, but we had our own battles to fight. As much as we didn't want to get caught up with meager issues, we couldn't help but care to some degree.

Nightfall finally covered the city, and we snuck deep into the woods. We wielded the Buddy once more and felt for Blood Hound's energy. We noticed that some of the lesser energies we had felt were fading away, but the two big ones were still strong. We truly wanted to go after them, especially the second one because it felt so familiar, but correcting the mistake we'd made was more important. We found Blood Hound's energy. He was far, but not so far that we couldn't reach him.

"He's in the same direction as the clubhouse," Ryan said.

"Then he'll likely be there. Are you sure you are ready for this, Ojore?" Heru asked.

"I have no choice but to be."

We concentrated our energy, and that familiar fury flooded our body. We felt stronger and more powerful than we had before; even our teeth and claws felt sharper. Our desire to kill was at an all-time high, but we were more in control of our energy, still a little afraid of the power that we felt. We dashed from the woods, hoping we weren't seen by anyone on the practice field.

We feared we might be seen running, so we decided to stick to the back roads instead of taking the freeway. We were running a whole lot faster than we were last time—any faster and we'd need wings to fly. We jumped over cars and dodged a few busses, and soon we were hopping from rooftop to rooftop under the moonlight. This feeling was invigorating. Men would dream to have the power we possessed, but we had to quickly remember we weren't invincible. Not yet, at least.

After about twelve minutes, we found our way to the clubhouse. We hid across the street adjacent to the building and observed the area for a minute. There were several motorcycles parked outside the clubhouse, but none that looked like Blood Hound's.

"His bike's not here," Ryan said.

"He may still be there. Feel for his energy," Heru advised.

There were rough and brawny looking men inside and outside of the clubhouse. Loose biker chicks roamed the property, looking for someone to give them some attention. We could feel Blood Hound's presence somewhere inside.

"He's definitely in there. I'm gonna have to go inside to get him," Ryan said.

"Prepare yourself, Ojore. I sense a lot of negativity from this place," Heru warned.

"I told you to leave this part to me, Heru. Watch me work."

We quickly crossed the street and walked up to the open entrance of the clubhouse, putting our hands in the front pocket of our hoodie to hide our claws. As soon as we walked in, we immediately caught the attention of just about every guy inside. We quickly scanned the room, but there was no sign of Blood

Hound. He had to be in here somewhere. One of the bikers walked up to us, and he didn't look as friendly as the ones on TV.

"You look a little lost, ki–What the hell is going on with your eyes? Y'all see this shit?"

This was one of the few moments being made a spectacle of wasn't going to work for us.

"Uh, they're contacts. I have a costume party to get to," we lied.

"You got some long-ass teeth. Who the hell are you supposed to be, a vampire or somethin'?"

"No." We scrunched our face. "I'm something much worse than that. I'm the Red Dragon."

"Is that right, Red Dragon? What the hell do you want?"

"Uh, you might be able to help me. I was looking for Blood Hound. Is he here?"

The energy in the room instantly went from bad to worse. The biker in front of us stared us down while some of the others got up from their tables and surrounded us. We could sense the multiple energies closing in, but none of them were Blood Hound's. He was hiding in here somewhere, and we needed him to come out.

"What you want with Blood?" the biker questioned.

"One of his girls told me to meet him here, for what exactly, I don't know, but she told me I was supposed to be picking something up from him for her."

Our ears jumped at the sound of a gun cocking behind us. We watched the eyes of the biker in front of us closely, and we could feel the others slowly moving in. A lot can happen in three minutes, and we needed an answer in less than half of that.

"Look here, boy. I don't know where you come from, and I don't give a damn. I'm gonna tell you once, and it better be the last time I have to tell you. Get the hell outta here and don't ever come back."

The man looked us square in the eyes and didn't blink as he spoke. Given the feeling behind us, we knew he was giving us his version of mercy. We looked down at the floor and began backing away.

"Aight, aight," we submitted. "Just tell him one of his girls is looking for him. I was just here to get something for her."

We turned around and pretended not to see the angry men around us. Pretty sure we would have ended up in somebody's ditch under normal circumstances. We walked outside, feeling mocked by the energy we felt. We knew he was hiding in there somewhere.

"They're protecting him," Heru said.

"Obviously, but I'm not leaving until I see him," Ryan said.

"What do you propose we do?" Heru asked.

Just in front of the clubhouse was an old office building that had been converted to an afterschool care facility for inner-city children. The building itself was four stories high, which provided the perfect place to perch in the night sky.

"We're gonna wait him out."

We walked to the other side of the block that the building sat on, making sure that none of the Violators had followed us. We casually stood on the corner for a moment and watched the traffic drive by, looking as inconspicuous as possible. Once the final car passed, we looked up to the top of the building, squatting down to make sure we gave ourselves the right amount of power. Our legs shot off the ground and propelled us high in the air toward the building. We caught on to the ledge and pulled ourselves up on the roof and looked back to see how far we'd traveled.

"I was holding back. I probably could have jumped over this thing," we said.

We crouched down and walked over to the other side of the building and hid in the shadows while watching the clubhouse. Blood Hound wasn't getting by us tonight, and we didn't care how long we had to wait. Multiple bikers came in and out of the clubhouse, lining both sides of the street with their bikes, but strangely, none of their energies were linked to the energies we got from the Buddy. We had to figure out who these other energies belonged to before they faded away.

The night air cooled the city off but didn't bother us in the least. Apparently, one of the benefits to our powers was personal climate control. The burning rage we had inside kept us at the right temperature. We grew angrier as the hours passed waiting for something to happen. If anything, we understood the importance of taking our training to the next level. After a while, bikers began to head out in numbers, and we kept our eyes glued to the exit. Another thirty minutes went by, and there were five bikes left, but none of them looked like the one we'd knocked over the other night, and there wasn't a car in sight. Blood Hound had to get here somehow, and we knew it wasn't on the back of someone else's bike.

The bikes were spread out with two of them in front of the building, two a little farther down, and one located toward the end of the street. We didn't know who was riding which, but we knew they were guaranteed to move tonight. We could sense Blood Hound's energy in motion and continued to watch the exit. Suddenly, the side door creaked open, and two bikers walked out with trash bags in their hands.

"It's him!"

Our teeth gritted as we peeked over the ledge and watched the men throw the trash into the dumpster. They stood by and talked for a minute, and our rage overflowed with impatience.

"Leave," we whispered.

Blood Hound stretched his arms in the air and yawned, finally bringing himself to shake hands with the other biker. The two let go, and Blood Hound headed down toward the other bikes. Our eyes widened, and we stayed in place watching both men walk in separate directions. Blood Hound had already walked past the first two bikes, but we didn't know which of the remaining bikes he was walking to, and we had to wait for the other biker to go back inside to make our move.

The side door slammed closed, and Blood Hound was on the street alone. We crept toward the back end of the building and continued watching him from the ledge. He passed up the next two bikes, leaving the last one on the end. He dug into his pocket, and we heard the jingle of his keys. We hopped from the top of the building and landed in the playground, breaking the pavement beneath our feet. Startled, Blood Hound turned around and drew his pistol, frantically looking around for something to shoot, but he saw nothing. He took a deep breath and continued walking.

We watched and waited for him to get to his bike, the sound of his keys sliding into the ignition triggering us to finally make our move. We scaled the fence and landed in the grass and slowly crept up behind him, ready to pounce at any moment, but we didn't want to take him by surprise. We wanted him to know we were there.

"I've been waiting for you all night," we grunted.

Blood Hound quickly turned around and aimed his gun, but he was too slow. We instantly dodged to the side and sprang on him, knocking him down and smacking his gun away. He rolled over and tried to get to his feet, but we snatched him by the ankle and tossed him over the fence on the far side of the playground, hearing a splashing sound when he landed. We hopped on top of the fence and watched the pathetic biker struggle to his feet. He saw our silhouette in the streetlight, and his eyes were filled with terror.

"Blood Hound," we grunted.

"Wh-who are you?" He shuddered.

"Aren't you going to run?"

He froze in place with his mouth open, so we dropped down from the fence and began walking toward him. Blood Hound turned and took off toward the other side of the block, too terrified to realize the backside of the facility was completely fenced in. He made it to the fence, which was equipped with barbed wire on top and too high for him to climb over, but that didn't stop him from trying. He frantically tried to climb it, but his muddy boots continuously slipped on the chain links. We grew bored with his failed escape attempts and dashed over to him.

"Is this the same fear my uncle had in his eyes when you killed him and his son?" we growled.

Blood Hound turned and pressed his back against the fence and put his hands up. We had never seen someone look at us with so much fear in their eyes.

"Come on, man. I ain't killed nobody!" Blood Hound hollered.

"Lies!" we roared.

We lunged at him again, this time snatching him by his arm and throwing him toward the center of the field. His shoulder was undeniably dislocated. He landed in the soft red clay with his face skidding across and stopped on his back. We jumped through the air and landed on top of him, digging our knee into his chest. His painful groans were silenced as we slapped him across the face and grabbed him tightly by the throat. We moved in closer to his face and firmly pressed our claws into his neck.

"Look at me. Look at me real good," we grunted.

The terrified biker winced and squinted his dirty eyes open. We'd hurt him pretty good, but we couldn't cause too much damage. Not yet. Our breaths were beastly with a deep rumble in our chest. We opened our mouth and flashed our fangs at him, letting a bit of drool fall on his face.

"I'm gonna ask you a few questions, and you're gonna answer them. Tell the truth, and I just might let you live. A few weeks ago, a man was killed in his home, and you...you were there...and you weren't alone," we grunted.

"I don't know what you're talking about," Blood Hound strained.

We pierced his neck with our claws, and he squealed. His blood warmed the tips of our fingers.

"Okay, okay! I've been in a lot of people's homes. You gotta be more specific."

"Carey Scales. He and his son were murdered right next to each other."

"The snitch?" he coughed.

We angrily squeezed his neck tighter and made him gag.

"Show some respect for the dead, you bastard, and what do you mean snitch?" we asked.

"That's all the boss said about him," he coughed. "Said we had to take care of him. His son was just...collateral damage."

"And your boss, who is he?"

"Come on, man. He'll kill me if I talk."

We pressed our claws deeper into his neck and spread out our fingers.

"And what makes you think I won't if you don't?" we threatened.

He gasped for air, and his eyes spread wide open.

"Face! His name is Face," Blood Hound strained.

"What's he look like?"

"Tall, white face paint. Always wears black."

It was him, the spirit we'd seen when we first wielded the knife. We now had a name to the face. We snatched our claws from his neck and pulled the Buddy from our pocket.

"This look familiar?" We whipped out the blade.

"That's his knife," he coughed.

We angrily grunted, trying to piece together the murder and how the knife was connected.

"The police said they were shot. Did you pull the trigger?" We pressed the blade under his eye.

"No." He winced. "It was...it was Face. He shot 'em!"

"He shot both of them?" Our eyes sharpened.

"He shot the man," he coughed. "Another guy shot the kid."

"Who was he?"

"I had only seen him a few times. I-I don't know his name."

Upset by his answer, we angrily jammed the Buddy into his thigh. We squeezed his throat tighter, turning his scream into a quiet gurgle. He aggressively thrashed his head left and right in the dirt.

"I'm serious! I don't remember his name. I swear," he groaned.
"What's he look like?"

Blood Hound took a second to catch his breath. A couple of tears ran down the sides of his face and mixed with the blood on his neck.

"Slim...medium build...light-skinned...and he has a fade." Blood Hound winced.

We dug the very tip of the blade into the outside of his eye socket.

"You just described half the Black men in Atlanta," we growled.

"I'm sorry! That's what he looks like!" Blood Hound cried.

The description matched the other spirit we'd almost recognized. We'd figure out who he was eventually. We grunted loudly with frustration, but we had enough information from him to make our next move. It was time to go home. The light from the streetlights cast a shadow of the trees over our face.

"Do you know who I am?" we asked.

"No," he grunted.

"Do you remember what happened the other night?"

The look in his eyes gave the telltale signs of a gruesome remembrance of the past.

"The motel?"

"Exactly," we grunted.

We squeezed tighter on his neck and ran the knife down his shirt to his chest.

"You shot me twice the other night. It would only be right for me to do to you what you did to me."

We rapidly stabbed him twice and twisted the Buddy in his chest.

"And unlike you, I'm gonna watch you die."

We collapsed his trachea in our fist and made him choke on his own blood as more blood poured from the open wounds in his chest. We stood over him and watched until he bled out onto the red clay dirt, and then he was dead. The rage in our heart boiled over wildly from our first kill. It felt so good, so euphoric to get revenge. But it wasn't enough. We needed something more, something to add insult to injury, something to make it look like we didn't do it. He had on a pair of spiked arm bracers, something we felt might be useful in future battles. We removed them from his wrist and walked away, leaving his body in the red clay dirt only a few feet away from the children's playground.

We hopped the fence and looked around to make sure no one had borne witness to what we had done. The street was quiet; not even the sound of crickets flooded the air. Something glaring on the sidewalk caught our eye. We walked over to the grass and picked up the heavy piece of gold. It was his gun, a gold-plated Desert Eagle. This was the gun that he'd shot us with. Those two large bullets that took us down and left us lying on the ground helplessly. We remembered from our previous lessons that one of the evil gods stole the weapon of Montu and used it to kill him and other gods and felt that it was only customary that we do the same with his weapon.

We turned our head with our sights set on his bike. It was a sport bike, sleek and more rousing than his other bike. It was red and black, equipped with his leather jacket lying across the gas tank and his helmet hanging from the mirror. The keys sat ready to be engaged in the ignition—it had our name all over it. The leather jacket was perfectly worn-in and equipped with a few bonus gifts inside the pockets. We picked up the helmet and something fell to the ground. It was his muzzle. We picked it up and immediately fell in love with its beauty. It was made of gator scales with spikes in the top and bottom corners. We quickly fastened on the muzzle and fit it to our face, ending our search for a new disguise. We found that the helmet was modular and opened the front to put it on.

"Why are you taking this machine, Ojore?" Heru asked.

"Running fast is fun, but discretion is essential to our survival."

Dressed in his gear, we revved the engine and took off flying down the street. We got to the corner and stopped in front of the clubhouse catching the eye of the four remaining bikers walking out to their bikes. We revved the engine once more, and they waved back to us. We evilly grinned behind the guise of our new helmet and darted down the street away from the hidden crime scene.

We sped home, testing the limits of our new motorcycle on the freeway and clocking speeds of over 200 MPH, dipping low into curves. It brought back the memories of the days we'd spent with our uncle when he taught CJ and us how to ride dirt bikes a few years before. We were on the fast track to avenging their deaths as we rocketed down I-75. We soon got to our exit, and our common sense kicked in again. We suddenly remembered that we couldn't bring this machine home with us, especially not this late.

We cruised slowly down the street leading to our subdivision and quickly devised a plan that we knew would work. We rode the bike all the way to the front of our subdivision and turned it off. Fortunately, the development was built on a downward slope, giving us the incline needed to let the bike roll down to our house quietly. We coasted past the dark houses and rolled onto the sidewalk in front of our house, stopping the bike right at the property line between the two houses. We quietly rolled through the low-lying grass and parked it behind the house under our window. It would be safe there until tomorrow when we attempted part two of our scheme.

We hurried to the front door and made our way inside, kicking our boots off at the door. Camille had left the alarm off for us, so we armed the system for the night and quickly scurried to our bathroom. Our hands were covered with Blood Hound's dried blood. We felt like we were on an all-time high, finally receiving a taste of what we had so desired for so long. We looked in the mirror and witnessed a brand-new person—no, a god. We removed our bloody gloves along with our clothes and took a well-deserved shower, giving our hands a good scrubbing. We reached out of the shower and started to grab the Buddy, but then decided to let the blood stay.

We exited the shower, eyes brown, teeth and fingernails normal again. We grabbed our clothes and immediately put them in the wash as we would be using them again soon. We went into our room to put on our usual sleepwear and then went to the kitchen for the plate waiting for us in the fridge. Veggie lasagna, our favorite. We warmed our food in the microwave and sat at the table in the dark to feast. The aftereffects of our vengeful euphoria had made us tired, and we retreated to our room after our meal. We plugged the charger into our cell phone, cut out the lights, and got snug between our sheets.

"You did quite well this evening, Ojore," Heru congratulated.

"Thank you." Ryan grinned. "Oh, it felt so good to tear him apart."

"Indeed. We'll discuss the details we learned from him later. I am aware of the effect of your powers, but I must caution you to remember that the God of War is an advocate for peace. Do not lose your way with your newfound abilities."

"I gotta admit, it is invigorating and still scary. I'm hoping not to lose it either."

"Hear me, Ojore. If you fall victim to evil, I will rid this world of you myself."

"You know my heart," Ryan chuckled, rolling onto his side. "Goodnight, Heru."

We drifted off to sleep anxious to start the new day and continue the hunt. Blood Hound's vague description didn't offer us much clarity on the second mysterious spirit, but we weren't pressed. We'd get around to killing him eventually.

Frantically standing on the dark sands, Blood Hound found himself on the brink of insanity. His unsettled spirit panicked at the sight of the numerous souls scattered around him. Nothing felt to him as it normally would as he turned left and right, desperately trying to find something familiar.

"Christian G. Johnson," Anpu's voice rumbled.

Blood Hound turned to the sight of the God of Death perilously towering over him wielding his pike. He froze in place with his eyes locked onto the piercing eyes of Anpu.

"You are the first unworthy soul to face death by the wrath of the God of War. Your heinous actions have brought you to Duat to commence your spiritual journey and be judged by the weight of your heart. For now, your judgment stands pending, but trust that in due time your official judgment shall come," Anpu declared.

Anpu's terrifying glare brought Blood Hound to his knees, crying for mercy.

CHAPTER 14

STANDING FOR THE WEAK

WE WOKE UP the next day and stretched with a smile to the glow of the morning sun shining into our room. Our bed, so warm and cozy, begged us to stay as the sheets seemed impossible to climb from under. We lay in bed basking in the moment but knowing that soon our morning pleasure would have to come to an end. After a few more moments in our piece of heaven, we got out of bed and went to the bathroom to prepare ourselves for school.

As we got dressed, we looked on the floor of our closet at our thrifty leather jacket and helmet. We wanted to wear them to school so badly, but even more, we wanted to wear our new muzzle sitting at the top of the closet like a precious stone. We headed downstairs to the laundry room and got our clothes out of the dryer, wanting to wear last night's armor with honor, so we put on our victorious red hoodie and went to our room to find our red tennis shoes to match. We grabbed our cell phone and our backpack and headed outside to the back of the house to see our two-wheeled monster.

"I've got to think of a name for you." We grinned.

We knew that riding our new bike could bring us a destructive amount of unwanted attention, so we decided to leave it at home, but more importantly, we knew we wouldn't be able to keep it at home, so we had to figure out a place to hide it until it was time for us to use it again. Shouldn't be too hard to find a place, at least not out here. There were some undeveloped buildings not too far away that were left behind after the recession. We could take it there and park it and just run to the house.

We popped in our headphones and practically danced on the way to school playing air guitar and beating on our air drums. As we got closer, we pulled out our phone and decided to catch up on social media. We weren't really social, as we mainly used ours for art stuff, but we liked to check up on the news from time to time. We opened our page and immediately we stopped, astounded by the first headline we saw.

"*Man Found Slain on Playground at Metro-Atlanta Youth Center*. Oh shit, that's us!" Ryan said.

"What's us?" Heru asked.

"It's a news article about what we did last night."

We quickly paused our music and pressed on the screen for the article to load.

"The APD has reported a man has been found dead on the fenced-in playground of the Metro-Atlanta Youth Center. Thirty-four-year-old Christian G. Johnson was found this morning around 5 a.m. with multiple stab wounds to his neck, chest, and leg. Authorities are currently investigating how the victim's body made it over the twelve-foot fence blah, blah, blah...currently have no leads to the murder...The victim had allegedly just left his motorcycle club located next door to the youth center, mm-hmm... One club brother alleged seeing him off as he rode home on his motorcycle, but authorities have been unable to locate the victim's registration to report the vehicle as stolen," Ryan read.

We burst into laughter, holding our sides. It couldn't have been a more badly constructed situation. Our first victim was dead, and he wouldn't be missed.

"The bastard was riding a stolen motorcycle, and we stole it from him. HA! How 'bout that. Footage from the property's surveillance cameras were checked and revealed shadows of the altercation, however the incident, including the placement of the victim's body, were found out of range. We got away scot-free."

"Good. We were lucky this time, Ojore. You must be mindful of your appearance in the future," Heru advised.

"Don't worry, I took his muzzle to cover up. All I need now is a bulletproof suit of armor, but can you believe that the bike was stolen? That guy wasn't shit!"

We continued on our peaceful stroll, playing air guitar as we jammed to our music without a care in the world. Today was going to be a good day at school; the only problem was that we couldn't brag to anyone about what we had done.

Face posted by the window in his high-rise looking aimlessly about the city, his mind scattered like cirrus clouds. The early morning had awakened him too soon, and the irked gangster could not go back to sleep. He held his cell phone in his hand, quickly answering it as it rang with Deuce on the line.

"Yeah...I know... Come to the spot, I'll be here."

Deuce later arrived to find a slightly disturbed Face burning sage in his living room. The two quietly sat in dismay trying to piece together the news. The grim details of the incident left them with no clue as to who the guilty culprit could be, and the genocide of Diaz's organization from the districts made retaliation inconceivable.

"It makes no sense that this happened," Deuce said.

"Yeah, among all other things," Face sighed.

The smoke from the burning ashes drifted around them as they sipped their drinks. Their unsettled nerves begged for something to bring them back to peace. Face pulled up the article on his phone and reread the details of the murder while Deuce searched his call log.

"I talked to him a couple days ago. He was sayin' somethin' about having to shoot somebody," Deuce said.

"Yeah." Face snapped his fingers. "He said somebody ran up on him at a motel on the southside, knocked over his bike 'n shit, but he said he shot'em tho."

"Did he sound sure?"

"Apparently not. Ol' girl he was messing with told him when she got back to the scene the body was gone, but no ambulance ever came, and there was no blood. Just some black shit on the ground."

Face pulled up the phone and reread the details of the news article.

"Maybe the killer's one of them military tactical robots or somethin'. Either that, or he had on a vest. Even still, I think it was somebody Diaz knew, had to be. We cool wit' everybody else, so who else could it be?" Deuce wondered.

Face shook his head after reviewing the article and grunted. There were so many things about the situation that weren't adding up.

"Hmm, this article says that there was a slightly bloody footprint found near his body, and his neck had cuts in it that looked like claws," Face said.

"What the hell?" Deuce cringed.

"Same thing I was thinking. Then it says that they can't see any signs of forced entry to the property anywhere, but his body was found in the middle of the playground. They said that the footprint with the blood had stepped in the mud then disappeared 15 feet from the fence," Face said.

"So was dude air-lifted out of there or somethin'?"

"No, but supposedly his club brothers saw him ride off, which makes this all very confusing. Like, how in the hell can something like this happen and neither of them see it or hear it happen? I can't... like, I'm thinking his club had something to do with it, and they're hiding his bike."

Face palmed his head and rubbed his forehead in confusion. In the back of his mind, he feared that someone was retaliating against him for all of the destruction the Illegit Family had caused. He remembered going over names with Hong and thought there might be someone they had forgotten.

"You know which bike he was on?" Deuce asked.

"It doesn't say. Far as I knew, he only had a chopper. I need to talk to Hong. This ain't adding up," Face replied.

"You do that, and I'll go by the clubhouse later and see what I can find out. Might give us somethin' to go on. I'm finna go get somethin' to eat, I'll be back. Oh, yeah, did you find your knife?"

Face felt his pocket, the question reminding him of his other issue. He sucked his teeth in frustration.

"Man, hell naw, I'ma have to ask Ke-Ke if she saw it," Face replied.

"Aight, I'm out."

Deuce left with haste as the morning hunger growled in his belly. Still unsettled by the morning news, Face pulled up his call log and swiped over Hong's name. He walked over to the window and looked out at the beautiful morning warming up the city.

"Good morning, Face. How are you?" Hong answered.

"I've had better days. One of my boys died last night," Face replied.

"Oh, I offer my sincere condolences, brother."

"Thanks, but I think you can help me figure out who killed him. Remember that list of names we went over with Nassar? I think we might have missed one."

Today had been so smooth. We never would have thought that killing a man could bring us so much joy. Maybe that's why serial killers smile in the courtroom. Could also be why every-one here is so different. Since we couldn't talk to anyone about what we'd experienced, art continued its reign as our favorite class of the day. We started out painting his facial expression as we choked him out, but it proved to be a little too graphic for the crowd, so instead, we tried to paint the image we had been drawing for a while. *Still not sure how we're going to draw it, but however it comes out, it's going to be red.* We'd been kind of grinning all day, and a lot of people had noticed. We tried to tone it down, but as soon as we thought about last night, that sinister grin returned with a vengeance.

We got to 6th period, and things were different with Aaliyah. She wasn't flirting, but she was clearly nervous as she tried to ask us the *I'm interested* questions on the sly. She kept playing with her hair, nervously looking away when she asked her questions and was trying even harder to hide her smile when I answered. She couldn't even look at us when we grinned back at her. Ol' Terry was gonna be out of our way soon.

"Growing up, my grandma played a lot of R&B, so old school, like Barry White, the Isley Brothers, Anita Baker, Patti LaBelle, you know, the greats. My mom played a lot of R&B too, but she mainly listened to all the '90s stuff, so Jodeci, Dru Hill, Silk, En Vogue, TLC—"

"I love TLC." Aaliyah's eyes sparked.

"Yeah, *CrazySexyCool* was great, but my favorite is Jodeci and Dru Hill. Like, she'd play their songs, and you'd think whatever they were singing about happened to me." We laughed.

"No wonder you're so sweet to me. Your mom played all the right music," Aaliyah said.

She tried to slide that one in there. In short, she had been watching us, and she knew we weren't this kind to everyone else. She thought she was special... She was, but we weren't going to tell her that.

"So how come you don't have a girlfriend?"

Shocked by the question, we grinned as she tapped her foot on the stool waiting for the answer.

"I mean, it's not that I don't want one. I just haven't come across anyone that's ready for what I bring to the table." We grinned.

"Oh, I see." Aaliyah lowered her head.

"And also, the girls I do like usually have boyfriends, and uh, I don't believe in messing up happy homes, ya dig."

Her face came back to life as she quickly turned her head to hide her smile. She was cute, real cute. We already knew what the next question was, and we were going along with everything she was throwing at us.

"So who are the girls you like?" She stroked her hair back.

We looked at her with a playful smile, and her eyes lit up like Christmas lights as she stared back. She turned her head, trying to hide her expression, but we couldn't miss the curvature of her round cheeks.

"That's classified information, my dear," we laughed.

"Okay, okay, I'll give you that." She grinned. "Well, can you at least tell me what kind of girls you like?"

"Pretty ones." We grinned.

She laughed hard and quickly tried to pull herself back together. She hid her face behind her hand, but her smile peeked through at the bottom. Colb looked up from his desk and raised his brow with a grin, watching us work. The other students looked over at us all mad n' shit. They were just hatin'.

"Seriously, tell me," she begged.

"Why you wanna know so bad?" We locked eyes with her and lowered our voice. "Ain't like you like me."

She closed her eyes and grinned with her head tilted to the side. We wondered what she was going to say, and from the energy in the room, so were a few other people. She cleared her throat and carefully chose her words, trying not to admit the obvious truth.

"I'm just asking out of curiosity." She grinned.

We squinted our eyes and made a silly face at her, watching her smile grow larger and larger.

"Mmm-hmm, whatever you say, George," we joked.

She continued laughing, and from the corner of our eye we could see Colb laughing at his desk. Some of the other girls looked away in disgust, but they just wanted some attention.

"Tell me." She slowly ran her hand down our arm.

We looked her up and down and grinned at her as we leaned back against the counter. We looked away to think so we could give her a real answer, something she would take away and hopefully see in the mirror one day.

"I like a woman that's confident enough to be herself in this world. People today are so hyped up about keeping it real and not being down with fake shit, but we forget how to be real people sometimes," we said.

"Yeah, you're right about that," she agreed.

We connected with her eyes again and said a few words with inflection to make sure she got the answer she wanted to hear.

"Like, if you were my girl, I wouldn't want you to act like a girlfriend, I'd want you to just be you. Like, don't give me your representative; the person you are is who I fell in love with, not this façade that you put on to seem pleasant to other people. I want your actions to come naturally and not because we have a title. I mean, of course, I like affection just as much as the next guy, along with other things, but aside from that, I like a woman who isn't afraid to talk to me, you know. Communication is key, and if we can't talk to each other, there's no need for us to be together."

She looked down and shook her head in agreement. We were scoring big points.

"But I think the biggest thing for me is always personality. A lot of girls think that rude shit is cute. I ain't with that. Give me the respect that you expect from me. There are so many girls out here trying to control guys with these requirements that they can't even live up to—"

"But they expect you to do it? Been there," Aaliyah interrupted.

"So you feel what I'm sayin', right?"

"I feel exactly what you're sayin'," she flirted.

We had to pretend that we didn't catch her comment, but no one else watching pretended with me, especially not Colb, clearing his throat all extra loud.

"But, yeah, like me, I make it simple. I describe myself as a hand in poker. I'm a Royal Flush and I'm all in, put all my cards on the table so you see what you're dealing with. I'll love you, and you're not gonna think it, you're not gonna guess, you're not gonna hope, you're gonna know that I love you, and everyone around you is going to know it too. I'll be there for you, I'll care for you, I'll spoil you, and all you gotta do is act right. Simple, right?"

She looked at us mesmerized with love in her eyes. We knew what we were doing.

"Sounds pretty simple to me. You said, not think, not guess, not hope, but you gon' know I love you, girl." Aaliyah smiled.

"Exactly, and even more than that, I wouldn't want to be with a girl that wasn't willing to grow. The sad truth is that a lot of girls don't love themselves the way they should because they don't get that real love at home. It's a beautiful thing to see a woman who loves herself because she radiates that beauty to other folks around her," we added.

"Yeah, you're right about that; a lot of girls don't, and it's so sad to see," she said.

We connected with her brown eyes again, and this time we made it personal.

"Like you, I know you know you got it. That's obvious."

She grinned and made a funny face to deflect the compliment.

"I mean, I'm all right. I ain't all that," she said.

"Really?" We scrunched up our face.

"I mean..." She shrugged her shoulders.

"Whatever, girl. You wake up pretty every day."

She looked away with a grin and straightened her face as the words set in. She was no longer searching for an answer but listening to the words she had always needed to hear. She didn't realize that we had opened the door to her honest emotions, and we had walked into a small mess that we were prepared to clean up. Our first order of business: blow her head up with the truth.

"I don't really see myself as all that. I'm just average," she said.

"Girl, whatever. Every time you look in the mirror, it probably fogs up cuz the room gets hot when it sees you." We grinned.

She looked at the lab table and grinned, fidgeting with her hands and swinging her feet.

"I mean, look at you, you got the personality down to a T. Everybody likes you. You're the girl our parents describe when they talk to us about what to bring home," we added.

She brushed her hair back. "Really?"

"Well, at least that's what I think. You're the perfect blueprint of perfection."

She looked at us with a certain glow in her eyes, that certain glow that tells you everything about how a girl feels about you. Colb was peeking over his laptop, grinning from his desk, our only fan in the room secretly cheering us on.

"No one's ever said that to me before. Thank you," she said.

"No need to thank me, baby. I'm just telling the truth." We smiled.

We had her full attention. She didn't care about the classwork anymore. She smiled softly, looking into our eyes with tenderness.

"You've got those big, beautiful eyes that can make a man stop in place and turn to stone. Your smile is the sunshine at sunset, still bright, but absolutely breathtaking, captivating, and beautiful to look at. You got *all* that hair, and it's *all* yours, and when I see it, I just wanna run my fingers through it," we doted.

"You do?" Her face lit up.

"I mean, you know, I ain't tryin' to catch a charge, so I keep myself at bay," we laughed.

She giggled, and it sounded so soothing to our ears, and that smile was doing something to us. We had to watch our words on the next feature to avoid sounding like a pervert.

"But seriously, from head to toe, you look like an African goddess, like Hathor, the Goddess of Love. Everything on you is shaped just right, perfectly proportioned."

There was a passion that had developed between us during the conversation, and we were both drawn into the moment. She looked at us with bedroom eyes, and we stared back with a devious grin. We leaned in a little closer to each other. We could smell her essence of natural hair products and scented lotions, and the blood began to flow from the depths of our feet to everywhere in between.

"But my favorite thing about you is that deep, dark, chocolate skin. I love it. I look at you sometimes and I wonder if you melt in warm temperatures."

98.6 degrees, to be exact.

"Your skin looks like silk because it has that shine to it, and depending on what color you have on, it makes it so irresistible. You don't play fair, like you don't have to do nothing but show up, and you can have any man you want, all because of that skin. And you know it. M-m-m. My darling, you are simply mesmerizing," we doted.

She bit her lip and quickly switched to a grin in hopes that we didn't see her, but we caught every bit of that bite. We looked at each other like we wanted to give the class a lesson in anatomy, but we were quickly pulled apart by the sound of the final bell. She released a deep exhale to bring herself out of the fantasy we were creating; a trip to the bathroom to dry off might be necessary before she met up with Terry. We both took our time packing our bags to leave, our eyes were having their own conversation.

"You got some serious game, Ryan." Aaliyah grinned.

"I don't spit game, Aaliyah. I just tell the truth." We grinned. "Everything I said was based on facts that we clearly both know."

She bit her lip again and looked away. Neither of us had ever wanted to stay at school so badly.

"Besides, I told you that you were a goddess the other day, so I know you already know I see you for what you are," we said.

She started to say something back and quickly retracted with a huge smile on her face.

"You know what, I'ma leave before I say something." She blushed.

"Say what you need to say, sweets." We grinned.

Her mouth fell open, and her eyes widened with a mixture of shock and joy. She gathered herself, still tugging at our curiosity.

"What?" we asked flirtatiously.

"Nothing, it's just"–she grinned, looking down at her feet–"my dad used to call my mom 'Sweets.'"

"Well, maybe he saw in her what I see in you."

She grinned, trying very hard not to bite her lip again with us looking, but her eyes told us the whole story.

"I think I like that," she said softly.

Her eyes flashed back to us, wide and glowing. Her aura lit up around her, pounding the blood through our heart like a super-sonic boom. She needed to leave before it got heavy.

"If you like it, I love it...Sweets." We grinned.

Her face lit up again, and she smiled. That smile was all the game she needed.

"Let me get out of here." She giggled, placing her hand on my shoulder. "You're a real player, ain't you?"

We looked softly into her eyes and exhaled with a grin.

"I'm just a guy."

"No, you're much more than that. Love yourself, Black man."

She gave us a hug, and it was slow and a lot stronger than the last one. She smelled so goddamn delicious. She got on to us, so close it took everything in us not to grab her booty. We slowly pulled away from each other, our lips nearly touching as our heads returned. Our eyes got caught staring at each other again, and we found ourselves locked in this undeniable passion with desires that screamed for fulfillment.

"See you tomorrow, same time, same place?" we flirted.

She batted her eyes and put on her sensual voice.

"I'll be here, and I'll be on time." She winked.

She walked away, leaving us with a grin that was the tell-tale sign of infatuation. Such an unsettling disturbance was happening beneath us and we had to quickly fix ourselves before we could go. She looked back before she walked out of the classroom and caught us looking right back at her. We smiled at each other with the confidence that we had left a mark on each other's mind. She left the room, and Colb skipped from behind his desk to make sure she was far down the hall. He looked back at us with a ton of innuendo in his gaze.

"Showdy said she wanna rock yo Timbs, G-rock!"

We slyly laughed, trying to downplay the scene, but we knew deep down inside that we wanted more to come from this conversation. Flirting with her just wasn't enough.

"Look, man, I told you I got some rubbers in the car, and it's lookin' like you gon' need 'em real soon if you know what I'm sayin'!" Colb said.

"You ain't sayin' nothin' I don't already know, but she gotta leave her dude first," we said.

"Man, forget that dude." Colb batted his hand. "You need to gon' 'n get dat before it's too late."

We looked up at Colb with confidence and raised our brow.

"I'ma say this, and then I'ma dip out. It ain't gon' ever be too late for me. Remember that," we said as we walked out of the classroom laughing.

Colb's laughter traveled with us down the hallway as we made our way to the first floor. We walked outside and put our shades on with a grin to match the sunshine. We looked over into the student parking lot, and there she was waiting for us to walk by. Terry and his boys were so unaware that they didn't even notice us smiling at each other. As we walked by, we blew her a quick kiss, and the look on her face was priceless. The idea of flirting with her was fun, though we sometimes wondered what was keeping her with her idiot. No matter; we had bigger fish to fry anyway. She'd come to us in due time if she was as smart as we thought she was, and if not, we got to flirt with a pretty girl.

We got home and quickly readied ourselves to commence part two of our scheme. We sat our stuff in our room and grabbed the jacket and helmet we'd stolen and headed downstairs to the back of the house. It sucked not having a fence because hiding this thing the way we hid it was hard enough. The majority of the residents in the neighborhood kept a similar schedule, except for our next-door neighbor. The retired vet seemed to never leave his house unless it was Sunday, making things a little more complicated for us. We didn't care so much that he saw us on the bike but were more afraid that in the rare moment that they saw each other, he might mention it to Camille.

We came out of the back door to our sleeping beast. She was so sexy with her black and red curves. We zipped up our jacket and strapped on our helmet and put the visor up and discovered that it had a shade that you could slide up and down. We put the shade down to hide our face and stepped around to the front of the house to see if anyone was outside. The neighborhood appeared deserted.

"Hey there, neighbor!"

Our heart dropped to the ground, and we slowly turned to find the man next door waving to us.

"Ignore him, we have things to do," Heru ordered.

"I can't ignore him, it's my neighbor. Not saying hello to him is more disrespectful than trying to hide this bike," Ryan whispered.

"Then make it fast!" Heru ordered.

We started walking back toward the bike and waved at him. Fortunately, he was getting in his truck to leave, so we rushed to the back of the house and peeked around the corner until we saw him go past. We really needed to work on focusing on people's energy. Being able to feel the energies of everything around us had tasked us with learning how to focus our senses on specific things. We hopped on the bike and jetted out of the neighborhood before anyone else saw us.

We rode less than a mile down the street to an undeveloped building that we learned had been sitting for years before we moved to the area. The spot was perfect for hiding the bike because only one portion of the building was complete, giving it the right amount of weather protection. The area itself looked like no one had set foot on the land since they had stopped building, as there were mini pine trees growing around. We pulled around to the back of the building and found a door to the completed side. We forced the door open and found nothing but dilapidated building material and an old hammer. We pushed the bike inside and parked it in a corner. We happened to find a wheel lock inside of the bike's rear seat and locked the front wheel, and we brought along a small duffle bag to keep our helmet and the jacket secure. We couldn't risk Reginald going through our room again and finding a damn thing.

We dipped through the trees, heading back to the house, a route we'd make for ourselves during the nights we'd hunt in the future. We got back to our room and lay on our bed to prepare ourselves for our training session in the Spirit Realm.

"What's the lesson for today?" Ryan asked.

Later that evening, Deuce made his way to the Violators' clubhouse. The building reeked of mourning and alcohol as the club dealt with the death in its own reckless way. Deuce met with the president, vice president, and a few other members of the club to try and piece together the previous night's incident.

"Some kid came in here asking for him last night around 7:30. It was weird, though. He didn't seem like the type that would come to a place like this," the vice president said.

"What he look like?" Deuce asked.

The members chimed in with the traits they remembered about the strange visitor.

"He was young."

"'Bout average height."

"Black sweats, hoodie."

"And he had red eyes!"

"Yeah!" they all agreed.

Deuce's face turned to confusion as he tried to imagine this suspicious person in his head.

"Red eyes?"

"I think I heard him say something about contacts, but yeah, his eyes were red," the vice president said.

Deuce laughed to himself, entertained by the description. Nothing about what he was being told seemed to add up.

"Like, it's not funny. I just find it hard to believe some red-eyed dude done walked up in here. He couldn't have been alone," Deuce said.

"He definitely did, but our guy J.D. said he said that one of Blood's girls sent 'em to pick up somethin' from him," the president added.

"His girl?" Deuce raised his brow.

Deuce thought back to the phone conversation he'd had with Blood Hound about the incident at the motel.

"Yeah, I was back here wit 'em. He was tellin' me about some guy he shot at a motel on the southside," the president said.

"The motel? He told me about that, too." Deuce lit up.

The story seemed to be coming together as they tried to link the separate incidents together.

"Right. Now I only assume this must be the girl he was talkin' about cuz I've only met one girl before, she's basically a prostitute. I went by the spot today lookin' for her, but ain't nobody seen the bitch. I think she had somethin' to do wit' it."

Deuce rubbed his chin, playing the phone call back in his head. He remembered Blood Hound telling him that the guy came out of nowhere and flipped over his bike but said nothing that incriminated or gave even a little suspicion to the mysterious prostitute.

"I feel you, but I don't know. Way he was talkin' the other day, he didn't suspect a thing with her. Even said he told her not to call him for a week. He's been seeing that girl for a while," Deuce said.

"Hell, the crime scene itself don't make sense, but he's dead," the president said.

The men sat in their seats riddled with unanswered questions and overwhelming confusion. The president chugged the remainder of his beer and tossed the bottle in the trash.

"Even worse, the cops are gonna be watchin' this area even more than they were before, and we can't even force our way over there to investigate the scene because of the cameras. They even got his gun, a gold Desert Eagle." The vice president shook his head.

"Damn," Deuce sighed.

"It's a messed-up situation all way round this thang," the vice president said.

Deuce looked at his phone and read a text from Face. He rose from his seat, texting him back.

"I gotta get out of here, Face needs me for something. You guys just lay low. I'ma be your new point of contact, so make sure your boys have my number," Deuce instructed.

"Gotcha," the president replied.

Deuce quickly shook hands with the men in the room and hastily left the clubhouse. He rushed past the row of bikes toward the end of the block to his car, but his hurry was halted when he noticed the yellow police tape tied to the fence. He stepped through the bikes to the other side of the street and stood before the taped-off section to look through at the other taped-off area on the playground. He shook his head and exhaled with sorrow as the reality hit him in the chest.

"He's really gone."

He slowly walked the rest of the way to the car, trying to understand how everything happened. He looked at where they told him his bike was parked and panned over to the top of the fence and wondered how Blood Hound could have possibly made it to the other side. The conversation didn't lower his suspicions of the bike club, but he couldn't figure out any motive to link them to it. He hopped in his car and pulled off as he called Face to follow up on the events.

"They tell you anything worth listening to?" Face asked.

"Man, they just as confused as we are," Deuce sighed.

"I felt like that was gonna happen. I talked to Hong earlier. We met up and went over everyone, and we didn't miss anything. Everybody was accounted for."

Deuce turned on to another street, passing by a cop car heading in the opposite direction. He watched the rearview to make sure that he was not being followed.

"Damn. Well wait, they did say somethin' crazy happened that night. They said some kid, older kid, came up in there askin' for Blood and they made him leave. Said he had red eyes or somethin'."

"Red eyes?" Face questioned.

"They all chimed in on that. Other than that, they described him as a regular guy. Said he came up there lookin' to get somethin' from Blood for one of his girls, but the pres said he ain't been able to find'er."

"That sounds suspicious."

"Yeah, but at the same time, I know about the girl he was messin' wit', and he's been on that for years. This ain't some money-hungry chick, and if she was, Blood woulda been put her to work for us."

Face paced around his high-rise, sipping the liquor he'd stolen from Diaz's house. He stopped to look about the dark city, wondering what could be happening on the dirty city streets, hoping that it wouldn't affect the progression of the Illegit Family.

"His death remains a mystery," Face grunted.

"I even walked by the crime scene. Bruh, ain't no way he got over that fence on his own. Somethin' big got 'em over that. I wanna say the bike club has somethin' to do with it, but I can't see why," Deuce said.

Deuce pulled into a gas station and parked in front of the store.

"Whatever the situation is, we can't dwell on it too long. I doubt this will turn out to be anything major, but meet me back at the spot. We've got some stuff to go over with Hong and Nassar about the next move," Face said.

"Aight, I'll be there in twenty," Deuce confirmed.

The two ended their call, and Deuce headed inside the store to get something to drink. The unsolved death left the men uneasy, but there was no time to waste on unsettled emotions. Face stepped away from the window and plopped on the couch, unsatisfied with the events of the day. He feared that Blood Hound might have been set up, and a setup to someone that was a major key in his operation could potentially be damaging if it was not quickly dealt with. He made a call to Porter and Simmons and put them on the case, although there were no leads on the savage murder.

Thousands of miles away in their hidden pyramid, Mabaya, Wivu, and Lamia feasted upon the bodies of travelers who had been caught far from where they had been instructed to go. The savages sat around the fire, ripping flesh from the bones of their meals, their hands and mouths covered in blood like a child at a barbeque. Mabaya stared into the fire while chewing his food with an unsettled curiosity on his mind. Lamia peeked over to him as she unraveled her meal from her tail and prepared to swallow it.

"What angers you now, Mabaya? Was your meal unsatisfying?" Lamia asked sarcastically.

Mabaya cut his eyes over to Lamia and grunted with disgust.

"Quiet, fool, your statement only sickens me more," Mabaya said. "It appears neither of you have pondered on what I've pondered."

Wivu and Lamia looked at each other, curious about their brother's mindset. Mabaya licked the blood from his hand as he rose to his feet and started pacing around the fire.

"Thousands of years have passed, and the battle of us and them continues. Two fighting against three is what it has always been. No victory, no defeat. Another day to battle again is what we all leave with, yet we all crave something more," Mabaya said.

"You know why we haven't killed them yet, Mabaya?" Wivu said.

Mabaya swiftly turned and stared at Wivu with piercing eyes.

"It isn't about them being dead, Wivu, can't you see that?" Mabaya roared. "Can't you see what's been happening? I find it hard to believe that neither of you see what I see."

Lamia cautiously set down her meal in fear that her brother would soon become violent. Wivu angrily rose to his feet and locked his eyes on Mabaya as he stepped up for another battle among the siblings.

"Is it a battle you wish to have with me?" Wivu threatened.

Mabaya flailed his arms in the air and grunted at his brother's misunderstanding.

"My battle is not with you. However, you've proven to me that you are oblivious to the situation I speak of."

"Explain yourself, brother," Wivu said.

Mabaya continued pacing around the fire, his face filled with a rage resting below the surface.

"Each time we face them, they are both together, attacking at the same time. They start together, and they finish together. Lately, the first to attack has only been Anpu, and he does not begin fighting at his best. For thousands of years, I've observed everything about his unbeatable fighting techniques. He has not been showing his true power until he is joined in battle by Heru," Mabaya said.

Wivu curiously stared at Mabaya, seeking to understand his brother's observation.

"What are you saying, brother?" Wivu asked.

"Anpu is merely toying with us, buying time for Heru to finally join him. Heru is up to something," Mabaya said.

"What could it be?" Lamia asked.

"That is the question," Mabaya said. "Our negligence will lead us to a dark place if we do not figure out whatever it may be."

Wivu began to laugh at his brother's frustration. He sat down and licked the flesh of his meal from the bone.

"You worry too much, brother. In these thousands of years, neither of them has ever stood alone to defeat us. They've been trapped in Duat for so long Heru has probably finally broken. His mind is wearing down, and soon he will meet defeat. Worry not, brother, this may actually be good for us," Wivu said.

Mabaya angrily stared at Wivu, his eyes wide with the intention to attack.

"Do not be fooled, Wivu. We must be cautious."

Lamia grabbed her dinner and carried him away from the fire as her brothers continued to argue. She didn't care for the demeaning words of Mabaya, nor did she put any thought into what he spoke of. She found herself a spot away from them and proceeded to swallow her food whole.

WARZONE

WE HAD BEEN working extra hard in the Spirit Realm, and it appeared to be paying off. We had gotten significantly stronger since our first kill, a strength that would intimidate the brawniest warriors across the galaxy. The key now was controlling our abilities on different levels. We had refrained from simple things like shaking hands as we had reached a point in our strength that we could easily bend solid steel like toilet paper. We had to replace the doorknob on the front door because we had grabbed it too tightly and crushed it coming in from school one day. At night we would sneak out and pull trees out of the ground at a local construction site just to test our strength. There was an added security in our minds being so strong, but what we really needed was time to adjust to normal things with our newfound power.

We were walking down the crowded hall to the cafeteria with Terrell making small talk about class and other assignments that would be coming up soon. It turned out that he wasn't as bad once you got around his trauma, and we had become good friends, bonding over certain interests we shared outside of school. We still hadn't extended ourselves to hanging out with him though, as our standoffish nature blocked any urges for extended human friendship, but we knew how to be nice. He'd introduced us to Ms. Lisa, the kind lunch lady who managed the cafeteria. She was like the elder Black woman that adopted all the kids she liked as her niece or nephew, though she didn't have any children of her own. She always made sure he ate whether he had money or not, a privilege that she believed should be granted to everyone.

One morning we went to Ms. Lisa's office with Terrell so that he could load money into his lunch account. She sat at her computer looking up his file and smacking the monitor because the system was moving slow.

"Come on, computer," she said. "I swear they gave me one of the first computers the school ever had, they do me so wrong. Nephew, you know how to fix this?"

All the boys were Nephew, and all the girls were Baby Girl. Due to our standoffish nature, we just assumed she was only talking to Terrell. A notification popped up on the screen, and he read the quick text.

"It says you've got system updates, that's probably what the problem is. Try updating and restarting the computer and see what that does for you," Terrell suggested.

"You know, that's what I was thinking, but they never want us to install anything on these computers. Thank you, nephew."

As she moved the mouse to restart the computer, we noticed an engagement ring on her finger, but there was never a mention of a husband, much less a boyfriend that she might have been seeing. We could always sense a certain kind of brokenness in her and just assumed it was some kind of depression. Today we decided to put an end to the assumption and figure out what the real issue was.

"How long have you been married, Ms. Lisa?" we asked.

The computer screen blacked out and reset as she looked down and admired her ring. We could sense a change in her emotions as the sparkling diamond glistened in her eyes.

"Oh, I'm not married, nephew, but this was the ring my fiancé gave me," Ms. Lisa replied.

She suddenly felt so sad. Usually, women dote over their rings and the man that gave it to them. We had to know more.

"Your fiancé—you never told us about him," we replied.

"Yeah, I always assumed you were married already," Terrell added.

Ms. Lisa looked at us, and we could see the hurt. There was a story behind this ring stemming from a dark place in history. Ms. Lisa slowly rose from her seat and closed her office door. As she sat back in her seat, she rested her chin on her hand, and her emotions intensified. We as well as Terrell grew extremely concerned as the loving glow on her face transformed into a gloomy frown. She looked up at us, her eyes glossy and her emotions hanging from the ledge of a waterfall.

"I'm gonna tell y'all a story I haven't told anyone here," Ms. Lisa said.

Years ago, Lisa Samuels had the best day of her life. Cloud nine couldn't begin to describe how she felt that evening as she skipped through the park with her beloved George. The smile on their faces told the story of a fairy tale that had come true. She raised her left hand toward her face as she stood under the streetlight and watched as the diamond shimmered in her face. The ring ensured a promise that would lead her and George down the path of matrimony, something they had both desired from the time they'd met.

The evening skies grew darker as they walked back to George's car hand in hand. He had placed his jacket around her shoulders to warm her from the evening chill. She squeezed his hand in excitement, anxious to tell everyone about their engagement.

"I've got to call my sister and my mother and my...Oh my goodness, honey, I love you so much!" Lisa doted.

"You deserve it." George grinned. "I'll do anything for you, my love."

Words that resonated in her heart each time he spoke. The wind blew a bit harder, and he pulled her close and wrapped his arms around her. They looked at each other and smiled as they passed under the streetlight, their love making them unaware of the other pair of eyes watching them. A man crept from the bushes holding a gun at his side watching the happy couple engage in a kiss. The romantic George hoisted his lady up in his arms as she giggled with joy in the safety of his arms. As he brought her down, Lisa snuggled in close to her man with her eyes closed, hoping for another kiss, but to her surprise, the protective George nudged her behind him with his eyes locked on the gun aimed in his direction.

"Give it up, chump, don't make me use this thing!" the armed robber threatened.

The robber's finger sat on the trigger with the hammer cocked and ready on the cold steel revolver. As George stood before Lisa, he remembered seeing this same man sitting on a bench by the lake. The robber knew what they had and wasn't leaving until he had it. The frightened Lisa quivered with fear as she watched her protector slowly reach behind his back and pull out his wallet.

"Just give him whatever he wants, honey," she pleaded to George.

"It's okay, baby, everything's cool," George said, holding up his wallet. "Here, man, come take it, it's yours."

George stood motionless, watching the man's eyes while in the back of his mind, fearing that the robber might come for his lady's ring next. He wasn't going to allow him to steal her joy, nor would he allow a stranger to take what he had worked so hard for. He could hear Lisa's breaths of terror behind him and knew that he had to act quickly. The mugger slowly approached George, his jittery hand shaking the pistol. His breaths were heavy, matching the dark circles around his stressed eyes. George held his composure as the gun drew closer to him, loosening up his fingers to make it easier for the mugger to grab his wallet.

As he stepped within reaching range, the mugger focused his eyes on the brown leather wallet, taking his eyes off of George's free hand. George quickly tossed it behind the mugger's back, and as he turned to follow the falling wallet, George grabbed hold of the gun and attempted to snatch it from the mugger's hand, but the mugger proved to be stronger than he anticipated. The two began to wrestle over the gun, sending Lisa into a heart-wrenching shriek. She watched in terror as her man desperately fought for his life. A shot fired off into the air as they wrestled for control of the gun. Lisa ducked and screamed for help as George dipped low and tackled the mugger to the ground.

The men rolled around in the grass, grunting with all of their might, neither one of them letting up. They dished out punches and knees, trying to force the other to give up. Lisa stood terrified, unable to move. She wanted to jump in and help her beloved but was afraid that her action might cause trouble for both of them. The men tumbled onto the walking trail, and another gunshot rang out. Lisa froze, her eyes wide open as she watched the mugger quickly rise to his feet and fearfully look down at his first victim. He grabbed the sides of his head and twitched as he gazed at the sight.

"Oh shit, oh shit! It wasn't supposed to happen! Not like this," the mugger groaned.

He took off without looking back, abandoning his gun and disappearing into the dark woods, leaving Lisa standing scared under the streetlight. She could hear the straining breaths of her beloved as he lay on the cold hard ground. She broke from her stillness and slowly walked over to George, lying on his side. She saw the small pool of blood forming from his torso and immediately her tears began to fall. She dropped to her knees and turned him over on his back, propping his head up on her thighs.

"Honey, no! Oh my God, oh my God, oh my God," she freaked out, digging in her purse for her cell phone.

George opened his eyes and reached his hand out. She took hold of it, the diamond still shimmering from the glow of the streetlight. His jacket fell from her shoulders, and a cool breeze passed through his soul. She struggled to dial 911 as her tears clouded her vision. She squeezed his hand tightly, begging him to stay with her. Her brave warrior shook violently, keeping his eyes focused on her.

"My man's been shot! Please send help! Stay with me, Georgie, don't leave me, honey," Lisa cried to the operator.

The operator tried her best to keep Lisa calm, but she became more and more hysterical as she watched George's blood flow from his shirt. After advising the operator of their location, she set the phone on speaker and followed the basic instructions the operator gave her.

"You need to apply pressure to the wound. Do either of you have a jacket or something?" the operator asked.

Lisa immediately remembered his jacket and reached back to grab it. She rolled it up and pressed it on his wound, keeping her eyes on his.

"Baby, I love you. Please don't leave me, not like this, please don't go," Lisa pleaded.

"Ma'am, I've got officers dispatched to the park with EMTs close in tow. They should be arriving in less than two minutes. Stay with me until they arrive," the operator confirmed.

Her dripping tears soaked into his bloody shirt as she pressed the jacket on his wound. The lovely two locked eyes, and George began to cough, creating a trail of blood leaking from the side of his mouth. He placed his hand on top of hers and felt her ring still safely on her finger and grinned.

"It's gonna be alright, Georgie," she cried. "They're coming, and they're gonna save you."

George raised his bloody hand to her cheek, and her tears mixed with his blood. She leaned in as he stroked her hair back behind her ear and shushed her as he stared into her eyes.

"I-It's all right, baby. It's alright." He shuddered.

He caressed her face, and she fought to compose herself, fearing that these might be their final moments together.

"I-I'm grateful, grateful th-that you chose me," he whispered. "I'll al-always be... in love with you."

Seconds felt like minutes as the two waited for the ambulance to arrive. Lisa could hear the sirens far in the distance, placing all of her hope on them getting there before it was too late.

"Y-you always been so, so good to me. I-I...you deserve more than I could ever give. You brought j-joy to my life, the a-apple of my... my eye. I'm just, glad...I-I got the chance...to love you."

George's hand slowly slipped from her face and crashed to the ground. His eyes closed, and his head turned toward the shadows. His chest fell as his last breath escaped from his body, and his soul departed from the Life Realm with the gentle breeze. Lisa screamed in agony as she swept up his lifeless body and held him tight, begging for her beloved to come back to her. Moments later, police and EMTs arrived on the scene to find the bloody and distressed Lisa clutching to the only man she ever truly loved.

Ms. Lisa grabbed a napkin and wiped the tears from her eyes. We and Terrell stood quietly in shock, listening to the story. We were almost sorry we'd even asked.

"He died in my arms right there in the middle of the park. I was so torn up, the cops and the EMTs almost had to forcibly remove me from him. I told them what happened, and within a few minutes, they had a helicopter flying over the area. They caught the guy trying to carjack somebody when the police found him. I've worn the ring just about every day ever since."

Neither one of us knew what to say. We weren't prepared for that story or any story like that. It was one of the most painful stories we had ever heard. We just sat there quietly.

"You know, it's funny that you asked that question today. Today would have been his 53rd birthday, making this the 15th year that we would have been together. I made a routine that I commit to each year, no matter what the weather is. I get off work, and I take the ring to get cleaned and polished professionally. Then I put on a nice dress, get some nice flowers, and I go and visit his grave for a while." Ms. Lisa smiled.

We had to find his soul. We just knew he had to be somewhere in Duat missing his beau.

"He was the only man that ever loved me," she wept. "And no matter how long it's been, I miss him more and more each day."

The bell rang, signaling the start of 1st period. She quickly gathered herself and dried her eyes, forcing a smile on her face.

"I'll write you boys a hall pass. Don't worry about your account today, nephew, we'll take care of it another time. And, uh, keep this story to yourselves. I don't want everyone coming to me feeling sorry for me. I'm okay," Ms. Lisa advised.

"Yes, ma'am." Terrell nodded.

"Of course," we agreed.

We left her office with our passes and walked through the empty hallway to our classes. The only silver lining to the story was that she got some kind of justice, but we wondered why she'd never tried to move on. Terrell looked at us, and we shook our heads not knowing what to say to each other. Later that day, we were leaving for lunch with Terrell. He seemed bothered the entire time. For 17-year-old kids, we were stressed like 40-year-old men going through a divorce and erectile dysfunction.

"I know I'm gonna fail this econ test," Terrell said. "I haven't even tried to study for it. I'm starting to see the benefits of going to the military."

"I think you just got the wrong teacher. Dr. Stegall has me understanding the stuff I see on the news," we replied.

"Nah, bro, you're just smart. Honestly, I think I'm just burnt out from my mom being on my back so much lately."

Terrell wore his stress on his sleeve like a dirty jacket on a cold fall day. We worried that if he ever had a breakdown, he might not be the same guy anymore, just some angry, socially awkward being with violent tendencies, or maybe he'd just cry. Either way, we were friendly enough to care about him.

"It's gonna be aight, bruh. Moms stress us out trying to do what they think is best for us," we said.

Suddenly, Terrell was struck in the back of the head with a half-empty water bottle from behind. He grabbed his head, and we both turned to find the culprit was none other than Terry laughing with his boys, walking away from the lockers we had passed. Students burst into laughter at Terrell's expense, cosigning the embarrassment written all over his face. Our eyes locked on Terry, but just as we took a step in his direction, we noticed Aaliyah walking behind him.

"Why did you do that? You could have really hurt him," she scolded Terry.

Terry found justification in his actions as he usually did, arguing with her in front of people to protect his small masculine ego.

"Because I wanted to throw it at him! You gon' snitch on me or somethin'?" he bucked.

An intense fury tingled in the tips of our fingers, and we balled our fist at our side. We just wanted to hit him and bash his head into the lockers and watch his blood leak into a pool in the middle of the hallway. A hand grabbed our shoulder, and we turned to see Terrell looking defeated telling us no.

"Don't worry about it, man. It's...it's just high school BS. It'll be over soon."

We couldn't take it anymore. We refused to watch as Terrell continued to be bullied. There was only one thing we could think of to do.

"Dammit, bruh! Look, cancel whatever plans you had after school. Wait for me in the parking lot, you're hangin' out with me later. We ain't havin' this shit no more!"

We walked off in the opposite direction to prevent ourselves from chasing after Terry with our pulsating rage, but more importantly, we had angrily extended ourselves to be social with a new friend. His defeated mentality set him in the ranks of being subservient, and we refused to allow his mistreatment to go any further. We thought back to the days before we left Friendly Heights swearing to ourselves that Byron would be the last person we'd ever befriend as we dealt with all of the crap we were both going through at the time with school, but here we were about to stand up for our...friend.

"Let go of your inhibitions, Ojore. A good god cares about the well-being of others. I know that you are quite withdrawn from normality, but this friend of yours needs you, much like my kingdom needed me," Heru said.

We stopped walking for a second and sighed away our frustration. We realized there was only one way to resolve this issue, and being angry about it now would block us from getting to that point. We had to dig a little deeper; we had to use our mind. The rest of the day went by smoothly. Aaliyah had reached a point of comfort with us in flirting each day. She didn't even bother to bring up what Terry had done; she just focused on seizing the moment she had with us. A mischievous option posed itself as a possibility in our new scheme, but we felt that it would only be a distraction...that is, of course, unless what we were feeling was real.

The final bell rang, and the dark-skinned goddess hugged us with a smile as she said goodbye. Colb cackled with us out the door as usual, and we quickly made our way to the parking lot. Aaliyah watched us as we walked to Terrell's car. We eased ourselves in the passenger seat, trying our best not to break the handle or slam the door. We waved goodbye to her as we drove off, and she watched us as we made our way down the street. She didn't seem to even care about being caught anymore.

We traveled to a subdivision of townhouses on the other side of the highway we lived by. It was a small neighborhood with only one turn and one place to enter and exit. We pulled into his driveway, and he got out to check the mail before using the side panel to open the garage.

"We can hang out here for a while, I guess," Terrell said. "My mom's gonna want me to get to studying when she gets home."

We stepped inside of his clean home, and suddenly we felt like we did the first time we went to Byron's apartment. Everything was so...put together. The living room was fully decorated, and there were pictures of a younger, happier looking Terrell with his father. We could sense his emotion; he was retracting. We snatched our eyes away from the photos and turned to look at him, but he was already watching us.

"So we going to your room or staying down here?" we asked.

"My room. I'd prefer Mom meets you before I have you in her living room," he laughed.

We followed Terrell to his room, and over the next hour, we allowed him the verbal release he so needed. He revisited the emotions tied to his father's death several years ago, citing the mental breakdown his mother experienced that changed the dynamic of her parenting toward him and his brother. He told of the arguments his mother and brother had had after he revealed that he was going to the military. He explained his social awkwardness as a means of keeping people away from his demented mess.

"I just try to keep my distance from everybody, like, it's not fun, man. I just wanna get the hell out of here. You see what she's done to me. Like, she guilt-trips me into doing what she wants, and she uses my dad and my brother as leverage on my emotions." Terrell shuddered.

His eyes were heavy with stress and worry as he began to pace back and forth. We feared he might burst into tears at any moment.

"And I wanna say no sometimes, but I'm scared she'll kick me out because she threatened to kick my brother out when he said he was going to the military. Like, my only other family is in Knoxville, and I don't want to go there. I just, I just—"

We quickly stepped to him and carefully placed our hands on his shoulders. His eyes were glossy, so we had to think quickly to keep him from crying.

"It's aight, bruh. It's aight, relax. Have a seat for a second. Breathe," we instructed.

He slowly sat on his bed and closed his eyes to take a deep breath. This guy was truly hurting inside.

"You see I ain't really got no friends, like, you're the only friend I got," Terrell said.

"I know, wait, I mean…I didn't mean it like that, but yes, I'm your friend." We sighed.

His only friend. That could only mean we were the only person he trusted. Shit.

"I think it might be a good idea for you and your mom to get counseling, and if not the two of you, you at least need to talk to someone at school more qualified than me. They might be able to help you more than I can."

Terrell turned to us with relief in his eyes, a look that we had never seen come across his face.

"No, bruh, like, you're perfect. I know I look terrible and everything, but just having someone to vent to goes a long way. I've never been able to talk to anyone the way I just, well, spilled my guts to you about my life. I know I'm weird, I say shit that doesn't fit the conversation half the time, but that's because I talk about what's on the surface. Once you get past that, I'm pretty normal—well, almost anyway."

"I mean, that's how I look at the situation," we replied.

"It's simple, man. My dad died, and my mom lost her mind trying to figure out how to be a single mom. She wanted the best for me and my brother, but the best was her best, and her best wasn't what we needed, nor is it who we are."

Terrell released a deep sigh of relief, exhaling his truth.

"She didn't mean to hurt me. She didn't mean to push my brother away, she just…she did what she thought was right. She wants us to have the future my dad promised he'd give us. And that's forgivable."

Terrell leaned back and plopped across his mattress. He stared aimlessly at the ceiling and released another sigh of relief.

"You don't know how long I've been holding that in. I feel so much better."

"Good, and now you need to say it to your mom," we said.

He quickly sat up and began rubbing his forehead.

"Nah, man, I can't say this to her. She...she won't accept it the way I want her to."

"And how exactly does she plan to stop you? You gotta make it clear to her that she's the source of your dysfunction," we said.

"Yeah, only for her to remind me that I'm a Black man, and as a Black man in modern society I have to be strong and carry the weight of the world on my shoulders at all times, and all that unfair shit we're subjected to," Terrell deflected. "I'm just gonna focus on graduating out of this house. I've gotten this far."

"When's the last time you heard from your brother?" we asked.

"It's been months. He doesn't really respond much. I think he might be a little more messed up than me."

The story of his home life didn't seem like it was going to get any better, but he reassured us that he understood what he was dealing with. We decided it was time to bring up our real issue, so we dressed up our statement nicely in order to make sure he didn't get the idea that we thought he was weak.

"Well, hopefully that'll fix itself in time. Look, Terrell, you're... you're a cool guy in my book. You're just dealing with a lot of shit, and I...I can't allow my friend to just go through shit alone. I'm here for ya. If you need me, of course. I try not to get involved in family matters, but as far as everything else in life, I'll go to war for you," we said.

"Thanks, bruh," Terrell sighed. "I really appreciate that."

"Which brings me to my next subject. What the hell is up with Terry?"

Terrell sighed and sank. A different layer of his stress appeared on his face.

"Ugh, I knew this question was coming," he groaned.

"And I need you to come with that answer," we replied.

Terrell stood from his bed and walked over to his closet. He reached inside, pulled out an old shoebox, and set it on the bed. Inside were a bunch of old papers and cords from old video games from his younger years. He sifted through the junk and pulled out a picture of two preteen boys.

"That you and your brother?" we asked.

"That's me and Terry in 6th grade. We used to be best friends," Terrell said.

The smiling faces in the picture told the story of two young boys that looked as if they'd be lifelong friends in their matching blue shirts. They were happy, almost even innocent.

"What happened?" we asked.

Terrell put the picture back in the box and closed it with a sigh filled with sorrow. We felt his energy drop again. He picked up the box and started to take it back to the closet.

"We kinda went through the same thing; he lost his dad, too. I lost mine first, and he was there for me as much as he could be, but neither of us anticipated him losing his dad so soon. I was still really messed up from my dad dying, and I...my mom just kinda made that situation a lot worse than what it should have been. I couldn't be the friend he needed like he was for me when he was going through it. We were young and immature, and we lacked social understanding of trauma. I believe he resents me for it, but he just won't acknowledge it," Terrell explained.

"So why do you let him get away with treating you like a second-class citizen?"

"I don't know, bruh. A part of me feels bad for him, which is stupid now, and the other side...I just don't want to fight because a fight with him is a fight with his new set of friends," Terrell sighed.

Terrell was stuck in a whirlpool of emotions he wasn't equipped to deal with. We had to help him in some kind of way that could possibly free him of some of his demons.

"What if I kicked his ass for you?" we suggested.

"What? C'mon, man, fighting him is just gonna make things worse for you," Terrell said.

"I ain't worried about all that. Look, I told you I'm your friend, and as your friend, I wouldn't be a friend if I just sat idly by and watched some guy and his friends get the best of you. You're a strong guy, Terrell, but you gotta believe that shit just like I believe it. I can't make you as brave as I am, but I can make sure nobody messes with you from this point forward," we said.

Terrell looked at us with a case of shock on his face as if we had said something to him in a foreign language.

"You—you think I'm strong?" Terrell asked.

"Yeah. Look, man, strength ain't about how hard you can hit, or how much weight you can lift. You just sat here and told me your whole life story, and you were honest about it. That takes strength, that takes bravery. I don't even talk about what's going on in my world, and here you are willing to tell it all for your own mental health. You got real strength, bruh. You're stronger than me."

Our kind words of affirmation sank deep into his cerebellum and touched his heart, creating a smile on his face that no one had seen from him in a long time. He appeared to be at a loss for words as he grinned.

"Bruh, you...you don't know how much I needed to hear that. You're trying to make me cry, man?" Terrell said.

"Nah, I'm tryin' to keep you from cryin'. It ain't easy for us, man. The world already hates us for no reason, so anything else added to that fire just tears us down even more. We've gotta lift each other up, like brothers. That's from the heart," we said.

He tried to shake our hand, but we gently pulled him in and went into a bro-hug. His energy began to calm and settle to a more normal state. He was going to be okay, and now he knew it. He looked up at the clock on his wall and realized his mom would be coming home soon.

"I gotta get you out of here before my mom comes home—she's really trippy about company—but bruh, I appreciate everything, like, this conversation has really helped me, you don't even know," Terrell said.

"It's no problem, man. I'll tell you what, meet me in the cafeteria in the morning. I've got a plan to get rid of Terry, but I'll need your help with it."

"I'll call you once I'm in the parking lot." Terrell smiled. "How far away do you live?"

"Don't worry about it. I'll walk. I got some things I wanna see on the way home anyway. Come lock me out."

We gently shook hands with Terrell as we headed out the door, relieved that we didn't break anything in his house. It was relieving to see him smile at the end of the day. He'd have a bright future ahead of him if he could get the right help.

"You did good, Ojore," Heru said.

"Yeah." Ryan grinned. "It felt like it was the right thing to do."

We walked out of the neighborhood, feeling the crisp winds blow across our face as we prepared our minds for this evening's training. We decided to employ some of the tactics that we'd learned over the last few weeks. We closed our eyes and listened to the sounds of the world around us. We saw the energies of all of the life forces surrounding us, from the slow winds to the running water of a nearby creek. There were birds all around, perched in trees and flying through the air, not to mention the tons of cars passing by on their way home from a long day. We could sense the emotional stress of the drivers around us, possibly from the slow pace of traffic before them. We sensed deer hiding deep in the woods, waiting for the perfect time to come out and cross into the open field down the street. We could feel the rise and fall of emotions from the patrons at the gas station as they filled their gas tanks. We could feel everything in the world revolving around us from the distant sun to the ancestors watching us, waiting for manifestation.

The energies created mystical colors that formed into images of the living world around us. The world was more beautiful than itself. We could see value in life as we had not seen it before. Nature boomed around us like an overcrowded city. It was a sight to see, but we wanted to free the creatures dwelling in its circumstances.

We reached our neighborhood and finally opened our eyes. The visual reality was slightly depressing as the array of colors became mediocre in the afternoon sun. We walked inside to the smell of Camille's spaghetti—another stressful day at work for her. We kicked our boots off at the door and walked into the kitchen to greet her. We didn't need our spiritual vision to sense how stressed she was; she wore it like a fresh face of makeup.

"Hey, Ma," we said.

She slowly turned to look at us, and we instantly wished she hadn't. Camille was good for putting on a fake smile over the years, but she wasn't even trying anymore. Ever since Carey and CJ were killed, she'd been trapped in her depression, and by the way things looked, she'd be there for a while. The only thing worse than that was feeling like the strongest man in the world but being powerless to help the woman we loved the most.

"Hey, baby, how are you?" she replied.

We couldn't even smile and pretend to be okay seeing her like this.

"I'm okay, just another day at school. I went by Terrell's house to help him with his econ test. How was work?"

"Stressful as usual." She mixed the sauce. "Please text me if you do anything after school because it scares me when you're not here when I get home."

"Oh, sorry about that." We rubbed our head. "I definitely meant to."

"This world is getting crazier and crazier each day. If it ain't some young kid being killed by a racist cop, it's a young kid being killed by some random idiot," she said.

"And I promise I'll do everything to make sure that you don't have to experience that."

She looked at us with 'the Black mom side-eye,' and we grinned. She still had some life in her.

"When's the next time you go to work?" Camille asked.

"Oh, it'll be sometime this week. He's trying to get some extra hours for me to come in, but he said he had to get approval for the hours from the district manager. I'll know something tomorrow for sure," we lied.

"Okay, I was asking because Reginald was asking where you were the other night. Can I ask you a question? I feel like I already know the answer."

Dammit! What could this question be? Did she find our bloodstained clothes? Did she see the bike? Did our neighbor talk to her? Was she becoming suspicious of our behavior? Something had to have tipped her off.

"Are you using drugs?" Camille asked.

We closed our eyes and burst into laughter with a great sigh of relief. We went from about to crap our pants to picking ourselves up off the floor.

"C'mon, Ma, really? Me on drugs? As if I needed anything else to further drive me away from people." We laughed.

"I had to ask. Reginald went searching through your room again, swearing up and down he smelled something, but he didn't find anything."

That bastard went through our room again. We felt a vein stricken in our neck, and we were rushed with anger.

"What is he in my room for? Like what is he really expecting to find?" we grunted.

"Calm down, baby, I watched him. He was going through your stuff like a crackhead looking for a rock they hid. He used to do stuff like that back in the day, so he automatically assumes that you do it, too," Camille explained.

"But that doesn't give him the right to search my room, especially when I'm not here! I don't care about what he did back in the day. He ain't my daddy, and I don't take after him."

"But he is the man of the house," Camille added, "and his rules are his rules. Frankly, I'm tired of arguing about it with him."

We remembered back to when we came home the other night and heard them arguing in their room.

"Is that what y'all were fighting about the other night?" we asked.

Camille sighed and looked away from us in distress. Our brave warrior goddess had met her match with an enemy she wasn't prepared to quarrel with. It was time to end this conversation.

"Look, Ma, I'm not on drugs. I'm not doing anything illegal. That ain't what I do, I know you know that. I'm trying my best to make this easy for you, but if he doesn't stop what he's been doing, it's going to get a lot worse. I stay out of your arguments, I ignore his drunken rants, but just like you, there's only so much I can take."

We stopped to give Camille a hug and sensed the sadness she was hiding inside. This process wasn't easy for either of us.

"I love you, okay? This year hasn't been so kind to us, but I know it'll get better in time," we said.

"I love you too, son," Camille sighed. "I'll let you know when dinner's ready."

Camille's cell phone vibrated on the kitchen counter. We passed it to her and noticed she'd received a text from Reginald. As she read the text, her energy changed from sad to curious.

"Everything good?" we asked.

"Yeah, Reginald's just staying late at work. Gives me more time to relax," she said.

We felt that there was something strange about the text, but our intuition was calmed by Camille's grace for relaxation. We went to our room and put down our things and readied ourselves for dinner. After we ate, we took a shower and got into bed. We traveled to the Spirit Realm knowing exactly what we wanted to train on.

Ryan and Heru stood upon the rough sands surrounded by a dense white mist. The two warriors faced each other, Ryan charged with the determination to master his skill.

"What is it that you desire, Ojore?" Heru asked.

"I want to control my strength, and I don't want to leave until I've got it," Ryan replied.

Heru grinned, pleased with his student's request. He extended his hands, swiveled them around, and formed a thin, hollow glass ball. He rested the ball upon his fingertips and held it before Ryan's chest.

"Take hold of the ball," Heru instructed.

Ryan reached for the glass ball with both of his hands and tried to carefully take it from Heru's fingers, but it shattered into pieces the moment he touched it. Heru formed another glass ball in his hands and took a step back.

"You must first focus on what it is you're trying to do."

He bounced the ball up and around, from hand to hand and even on his arms.

"You must understand how strong you are when you are gentle."

He tossed the ball up into the air.

"Use the power that you have."

The ball came down and landed softly on Heru's fingertips.

"But take only what you need."

Ryan reached for the glass ball once again, fueled by his burning desire to master his power.

Across town, Face lay back on his bed, holding his woman in his arms. He'd been rubbing her belly for a while feeling the exciting kicks of his unborn child, but the dread of losing his once murderous friend still toyed with his mind. The baby kicked his palm, and he grunted without joy.

"What's wrong, bae?" Ke-Ke asked.

"Nothing, baby, I just—"

"Still thinkin' about Blood Hound?"

"Yeah," Face sighed.

He continued rubbing her belly, hoping the baby's kicks would take his mind away from the pain but knew that if it hadn't worked by now that it wouldn't.

"It's gonna be aight, bae," Ke-Ke said.

"I know, baby, it's just...Blood Hound's been down with me since juvenile. This was a tough one, especially with De'Angelo gone. He was like my other brother," Face sighed.

Ke-Ke leaned to the side and turned to kiss Face's cheek and reached up to play with his long locs.

"I think you should go out and celebrate with your boys, bae," Ke-Ke said.

"What?" Face grunted. "Hell nah, I'm not leaving you alone to celebrate, especially while you're pregnant."

Ke-Ke repositioned herself and lay on her side. She cuddled up next to Face and reached for his hand, placing it back on her belly.

"Boy, I will be fine. I'm pregnant, not needy. Besides, I'm tired of seeing you moping around here all sad 'n shit. Call up your boys and go hang out this weekend. Throw money, get drunk, do whatever, just bring yo ass home in one piece."

"Yes, ma'am," Face laughed. "I guess it wouldn't be a bad idea to take a break. I'll plan something this weekend, try to see if I can get Deuce to put something together at the club, like a farewell party for Blood."

"See, you got the right idea, bae. Now rub my belly and smile, dammit." Ke-Ke smiled.

Face scooted closer to his beloved; her warm belly felt soothing to his hand. He rested his head on the soft pillow above her head, and he quickly remembered something was missing.

"Oh, yeah, babe, I've been meaning to ask you. Have you seen my knife?"

We woke up the next day ready for our physical exam. We brushed our teeth as we normally did, rinsing the toothpaste from our lips and washing our face in the mirror. We twisted up our hair, debating whether or not we'd be going to the barbershop to get faded again. We just wanted to look good today. We went to our drawer and picked out our black cargo pants and then went to the closet and picked out a red T-shirt. We wanted to take our muzzle with us so badly, but we couldn't risk anyone identifying it.

The Georgia mornings had become particularly nippy as the fall had finally started to set in. Because of our powers, the temperature never really bothered us, but we couldn't walk around in just a T-shirt and jeans in 40-degree weather, so we grabbed the skull cap that Carey had bought us a couple years back. It still smelled like the air freshener he would spray in his car. Today was going to be a step toward avenging his death. We grabbed the Buddy, our shades, and our black jacket and headed to the door to get our boots. We walked through the cold feeling the warmth of our rage. Seeing our breath in the wind was like the dragon before he blew his fire. There was so much power in the palm of our hands that we couldn't wait to unleash.

We sat in the cafeteria and ate some fruit as we awaited Terrell's arrival. The anticipation of today's scheme had us hopeful for a successful end. This was a different kind of rage. It wasn't personal; it was justified. As excited as we were about today, none of it was for our own gratification, per se, but nonetheless, we wanted to do it. Terrell texted us, letting us know he was in the parking lot, and we felt a charge run through us that put a sharp grin on our face. We texted him back and told him to meet us at the back of the vocational building and headed out the side door of the cafeteria.

"You couldn't have told me this somewhere else, you know, somewhere warm, like my car or something?" Terrell asked.

"Yeah, I may have gotten a lil' ahead of myself," we said. "I wanted to make sure nobody overheard anything because this plan has to work."

Terrell raised his shoulders to keep his neck warm in the morning chill. As his teeth chattered, we realized that we were virtually unaffected by the weather. We didn't even have our jacket zipped up.

"Aight, let's take it inside. Just go with it when you see him, and I'll take it from there," we said.

As we walked back to the vocational building, we could sense an uneasy feeling coming from Terrell. We had to keep him on board with us.

"Do you really have to do this? I mean, you're basically asking for a war," Terrell said.

We stopped and looked at Terrell with a straight face that turned into our sinister laugh.

"I'm the God of War," we replied. "Besides, after what I'm gonna do, they'll be no war to fight."

We kept walking and left Terrell confused standing in place. There was a part of the plan we hadn't told him.

"What exactly are you planning on doing?" Terrell chased curiously.

"Don't worry about all that. Just do what I need you to do so I can do what I gotta do after school, ya dig." We entered the building.

We left Terrell at the door staring at us strangely as we strutted down the hall. We walked to 1st period channeling the patience of a monk. The game was set; we just needed time to move at the pace we wanted to. We went through our first two classes eagerly watching the clock. In art class, we painted an image that was a silhouette of a man being held by his neck by a dark and shadowy figure. The provocative image got the attention of Mr. Rose, who curiously admired the sadistic painting.

"I can definitely say that I find the brush strokes quite amazing," Mr. Rose said. "I can see the man in the air, but what do you call the thing holding him? It doesn't appear to be another being."

We looked at the inspiring instructor and practiced our freedom of expression.

"Revenge."

Fourth period came, and we had just about had it with time. The anticipation had gotten to us, and we became more and more aggravated waiting for the fourth lunch bell to ring. We sat at our desk, watching Mr. Tukes apply life lessons to simple mathematics and apply his formula to our lives. We possessed an exponential power that could multiply astronomically to levels that no mortal would ever begin to reach. The division of our ancestral past led us to a place where we only knew a mere fraction of our history. There is no formula to calculate what percentage of information we know or don't know, but we were no fool to adding what we had learned to manifest in our conquest. The lies of history were left in parenthesis with hopes of solving all of their mysteries at a later time, but for now, we were focused on solving our X factor.

The lunch bell finally rang, and we quickly made our way to the cafeteria. We got our food and went to our usual chill spot and waited for Terrell to show up. We scarfed down our food like an uncultured savage in the woods, the meal jump starting our energy. We shifted gears mentally, and we were eventually joined by Terrell. He was still feeling reluctant to go along with our scheme, but we refused to let him back out.

"You ready?" we asked.

He looked across the yard and spotted Terry and his crew. He sighed a deep concern for the outcome, but his concerns were not ours.

"You sure you still wanna go through with this?" Terrell asked.

"It appears you're afraid to."

"I'm not afraid." Terrell shrugged. "I just feel like there's a better way. I mean, what about Aaliyah? Can't you talk to her about it first?"

We looked over at Aaliyah aimlessly looking at everything except for Terry. She didn't want to be over there with him, and the expression on her face solidified that she didn't know why she was even there anymore.

"Aaliyah can't do anything more than we can by talking to him; you've seen that. Terry is an emotional terrorist, and there's only one way to deal with people like that," we said.

"C'mon, bruh, we don't need this kind of drama at school. Don't y'all two have a class together? Just talk to her," Terrell pleaded.

We looked back over at her and caught a glimpse of her looking at us. She quickly turned her head, suspecting Leo may have caught her looking. We grunted at the feeling that came over us. A heroic feeling. She wasn't a mere damsel; she was indeed a goddess in rare form, but she needed to be shown how a goddess is to be treated...and we were the only gods qualified to show her...but we couldn't...not yet.

"As beautiful as that goddess may be, she can't undo the wrongs committed by Terry," we said.

"Wait, what? Why are you talkin' all methodical?" Terrell asked.

"You must go after her, Ojore," Heru demanded. "She needs to be loved by you!"

"Oh my goodness, will you shut up," Ryan grunted.

Terrell sat back in his seat and looked away from us, intimidated by our response.

"My bad, bruh, I just don't want no trouble," Terrell said.

Our emotions surrounding Aaliyah were still quite unequal. While a part of us valued her as a friend, there was a part of us that desired something more, something that was obviously there. We weren't bought and sold on pursuing anything with anyone at the time. Maybe a part of us was just in denial. *Who are we kidding, we're tired of seeing her fine ass being mistreated by that idiot every day!*

"No, not you, I...ugh...I want to keep Aaliyah out of this. She's an innocent party, and getting her involved will only make things worse. She's dealing with enough as it is. She doesn't need anything else to get in her way," we stated.

"I don't even know why she talks to him," Terrell said.

"Neither do I," Heru added.

Ryan grunted at Heru, urging him to keep quiet.

"You know, you should talk to her, bruh, I think you'd be good for her," Terrell said.

"What?" we shrieked.

"Listen to your friend; he is wise," Heru said.

We looked back over at her, catching her captivating profile from the side. Suddenly we were rushed with great feelings of denial with no real explanation.

"I'm just sayin'. I've seen the guys she's dated before, and it was one bad decision after another. I'm not sure what her situation is at home, but I think a guy like you would be able to show her what real love is," Terrell stated.

Our defenses immediately rose and blocked out everything good about Aaliyah. The thought of us dating felt toxic, at least we wanted it to for the moment.

"Nah, man, I...I got too much going on right now," we denied. "A pretty girl like that would want all my time and my money."

"Shii—Terry ain't got no money," Terrell snapped. "His mama got him that car. From what I understand, he don't even take her out on dates. That's got you written all over it, man."

That evil thing called desire played in our head. This thought wasn't a part of the plan for the day.

"Bruh, look, you're trying to distract me. We doin' this like I said. Just be ready," we instructed.

"Aight, man," Terrell conceded, "but I know real love when I see it."

We sighed and carried our tray to the trash, once again looking at her beautiful face. We could see the sheen of her skin and the glow of those glorious eyes in the sun from a mile away. The lunch bell rang, and it was time to head to 5th period; the fantasy ended for now, and we put our focus on our original scheme. We and Terrell had developed a routine after lunch. We took the long route to our drama class because foot traffic from the cafeteria made it nearly impossible to get to class on time. Sometimes along that route, Terry and his boys would post up in the hallway and occasionally accost Terrell. We hadn't had any encounters with them so far today, so we were banking on them to say something now.

We walked through the crowded hallway and spotted them a few yards ahead. We pushed Terrell closer to the side they were posted on, receiving a little push back from him. We gave him the 'angry mom intimidation stare,' and he quickly altered his route in their direction. We saw Terry notice Terrell from the corner of his eye, Aaliyah standing right by his side. He was definitely going to take the bait.

"Aye, Terrell, tell yo fine-ass mama I'll be over after practice tonight," Terry laughed.

The bait was taken. Everyone in his corner laughed except for Aaliyah. She chose not to engage with his immaturity, but instead sank back and dropped her eyes in shame. It was time to add a little spice to the mix and cause a continental shift in Terry's target audience.

"You know, Terry"–we stepped up–"you talk a whole lot of shit about his mom, so much that you've inspired me to write a song for you. Give me a beat, Rell."

Terrell began beatboxing the beat we'd rehearsed, gaining the undivided attention of Terry and his band of idiots. Aaliyah's eyes had lit up from the moment we'd stepped up to Terry, but she wasn't ready for what we had prepared.

"She's so damn fine, on the cloudy days. When deez hoes outsi-e-ide, I don't go out to play. Well, you'll learn to-day, who's ma-kin' me feel this way..."

Aaliyah was trying to hold in her laughter as the boys watched us in disgust. We and Terrell stood back to back and continued our song.

"Yo girl," we sang.

"Yo girl," Terrel sang.

"Yo girl!" we all sang.

"I'ma fuck yo girl!" We pointed in Terry's face. "Yo girl!"

Terry immediately jumped at us and was quickly snatched back by his boys. We stood motionless, staring the brazen fool in his eyes. Aaliyah kept glancing at us, trying her best not to smile as she tried to calm him down. The big fool was raising his voice in anger, gaining the attention of the teachers standing in their doorways down the hall. We had to shut him up before he ruined our plot.

"Let me go, bruh, let me go!" Terry jumped. "He wanna talk hard, I'll let him say dat shit again, c'mon!"

"Terry, calm the hell down," we said calmly. "We both know that neither of you can risk getting in trouble again, so let's talk like gentlemen."

Leo appeared ready to swing as he looked back at us, trying his best to keep Terry at bay. Terry grunted loudly as he gathered himself, losing the attention of the teachers that were watching for any possible altercation. Aaliyah tried to hold his arm, but he ripped it away from her, trying to look tough in front of us. His actions only made kicking his ass more appealing.

"You lucky they holdin' me back or I'd knock yo lil' ass out," Terry threatened.

We grinned confidently in hopes that his statement would prompt them to let him go, but they didn't. They had a game Friday they couldn't afford to miss.

"Well, clearly you wanna fight, whether it be to defend ya girl's honor, or maybe it was my song. Preferably, I think the latter, but this obviously ain't the place to do it. How 'bout y'all meet us after school, 3:15 down the street at the soccer field? It'll give us the right amount of time to fight, and you guys can get back to the school by 3:30 for practice, or the hospital, wherever you decide to go after," we teased.

"You's a bold muhfucka, ain't chu? Y'all hear this lil fool talkin'?" Leo bucked.

Leo was shorter than all of us; who in the hell was he calling *lil*'? He literally looked up to us.

"I mean, I'll fight all of you one on one. Matta fact, you can be second. Wassup?" We laughed.

We dangled the sweet bait in their furious faces and waited for them to bite. Our heart beat fast with anticipation as we sensed their disturbed energy. Leo wanted to fight, but not alone. Terry definitely wanted to see our black blood all over his hands but for the wrong reasons. We just needed them to agree.

"Ryan, c'mon. Y'all don't need to fight," Aaliyah interjected. "You have enough going on as it is."

Aaliyah's gentle reasoning was quickly cut short by Terry's quick temper. He turned his head and looked at her as if he wanted to hit her with all of his might. Our eyes locked on him, and our muscles prepared to drop him.

"What the hell I done tol' you 'bout gettin' in my goddamn business?" Terry grunted.

For the first time, we saw fear in Aaliyah's eyes, and it set off a bomb in the back of our head. Her eyes widened as she backed into the lockers and dropped her head in submission. Our confident grin transformed into a menacing scowl. We looked up into Terry's disgruntled eyes as he turned to us and said the words that would cause a cataclysmic change in all of our lives.

"Three-ten, and you better make sure ya mom's there to identify you when I get done with you. I'm finna beat the shit outta yo ass," Terry threatened.

We stood boldly in the center of the hallway watching as Terry's idiots followed behind him. Aaliyah slowly stepped from the lockers to follow them, and we gently grabbed her hand. She looked at us with her glossy eyes, and we stared back, daring her tears to fall. She dropped her head in shame and softly pulled her hand away. We'd see her later.

"It worked," Terrell said. "You got what you wanted. Now what?"

We watched as Aaliyah made her way down the hall with her head down. We wanted so badly to run after her and make sure she was okay, but our sinister scheme would remedy her emotions better than our words would.

"You just be at your car at 3:05. Let's get to class," we said.

The entire time we sat in 5th period, the only thing we could think about was him making her cry. He'd made her cry. He'd hurt her feelings. He'd made her sad. He'd yelled at her, and we knew it wasn't the first time he had done it. The veins in our arms popped to the surface, and we could feel our hands choking the life from his thick neck. We were breathing heavier, finding it harder to calm down than usual. We looked at the clock, and time seemed to be going even slower than it had been this morning. We became so irritated that we grunted loud enough for the entire class to hear. Mrs. Cowart and the rest of the class turned to look at us, and once again all the attention was on us.

"Is there something you'd like to share with the class, Ryan?" Mrs. Cowart asked.

"No, I, uh, thought about something I have to do after school and...I'm sorry. Long day."

"Well, I hope it gets better for you." She raised her brow.

We might not have been for all the attention and fame, but it wouldn't be terrible if an audience showed up to watch us demolish the village idiots and their leader.

"Everything will be fine at 3:10 by the soccer fields down the street," we replied.

"Oh, God." Terrell palmed his head into his hands.

Curious, Mrs. Cowart engaged with us to find out more.

"What's happening at 3:10?"

All the ears in the room were tuned in to our frequency, and Terrell was broadcasting live on the air.

"He's gonna fight Terry and probably his friends, too. I tried to talk him out of it, but he won't listen to me," Terrell blurted.

The class went into a stir of wonder and excitement as they were all anxious to see a fight. Mrs. Cowart looked off into space, nodding her head side to side. She stood in place for a moment to think and then quieted the classroom down.

"Let me say this. I don't care what it is you are fighting about, but you're a very creative student, and you've got your whole life ahead of you. Don't allow anyone to ruin all that you have going for you, not even Terry. I know who you're talking about. You're at a very pivotal place in life, and one bad decision could ruin everything for you," she stated.

Our sinister grin formed, followed by our evil laugh.

"I have no idea what you're talking about, but I'll be sure to let you know how it goes, that is if you don't find out before you see us tomorrow," we replied.

Mrs. Cowart shook her head and walked back to her desk as the class reveled in their ideas of how the fight was going to go. Some believed we were crazy enough to win, and others thought that we were crazy to be going against Terry while all of his friends were with him. They then brought up Aaliyah, and again the question of why she was with him came up. The fury in our chest was ready to make a mockery of his face to defend... defend her honor, but her honor wasn't ours to defend.

Class dismissed, and we gathered our things to go to 6th period. Terrell quickly got up and rushed toward the door.

"3:05, Terrell!" we hollered.

Terrell quickly stopped at the door and looked back to nod as if he'd been caught red-handed trying to escape. He dropped his head and left the classroom slowly. Just as we got up to leave,

Mrs. Cowart cracked the door after the last student exited and approached us with concern heavy on her shoulders.

"I don't advocate violence, and I would never pit two young brothers against each other; however, I will say that you were smart to have this fight off school grounds because they'll arrest and suspend you if you fight here. Whether you win or lose today, just make sure you get one in for me—I mean, for theatre." Mrs. Cowart grinned.

We both laughed, and she patted our shoulder in approval.

"And hit him hard," she added.

"I'll try not to break him." We grinned.

We walked into 6th period and fist-bumped Colb at his desk. Aaliyah was already sitting quietly with her hands on her head staring into the black slate countertop. She looked pitiful. We and Colb looked over at her, and neither of us liked what we saw.

"Aye, you need to go fix that," Colb advised.

We walked to our side of the desk and moved our stool closer to Aaliyah. She didn't move; she just kept staring at the countertop looking embarrassed, like she wanted to cry. We put our hand on her shoulder, and she gave no response, but we could feel the hurt from her energy. Her glow was darkened by her anxiety. We slid our hand down her arm and up to her hand and gently pulled it toward us. She didn't pull away, but she was afraid to show us her pain. We held her soft hand and gave her a moment to calm down.

"It's okay, Sweets, you don't have to hide from me," we said. "We know he hurt your feelings."

Her eyes glossed up, and we could see a tear forming in the well of her eye. We watched it, dreading to see it fall, but she quickly reached up and wiped it away with her other hand.

"I try so hard to love him," she sniffled. "I just don't understand."

She was distraught. We refused to allow her pain to continue any longer. We were taking Terry out today.

"I think it's time for you to stop trying," we said.

She looked over at us with her lips folded in, and even in her saddest moment, her glossy eyes were still glorious. Her spirit couldn't handle any more drama for the day. We scooted closer to her to keep our conversation quiet, hoping we could give her something to go on.

"Look, I know that this isn't the easiest situation for you to be in, but you did your best. You have to accept that. My uncle taught me that we can't afford to dwell on things we can't change because we lose the time we'd have with other things. It's a hard pill to swallow, but you can't get the benefits of the medicine if you don't take it," we stated.

Aaliyah looked back down at the desk, trying to think of where it all went wrong.

"I just don't know why he acts this way. Here I am, damn near about to cry because of him, and for some reason I don't want you to fight him," she said.

"Well, I can tell you now, the fight is inevitable. I want to break his jaw for my own personal reasons. Not only that, but when he got loud with you in the hallway, it took everything in me not to bust his lip."

She lowered her head, and a small smile appeared on her face.

"I'm not the kind of guy that turns a blind eye to wrongdoing, and more specifically, I was taught that as a man you defend your women, and you're my friend, so by technicality, you're one of my women." We grinned.

Aaliyah's smile grew, but she didn't look at us. She was blushing again. She cleared her throat and tried to cover her mouth to hide her smile, but we already knew we'd won.

"I understand that you have your reasons for wanting to fight him, but I believe there are better ways to resolve everything," Aaliyah said.

"That may be true, but I'm not looking to resolve anything. I'm looking to end it. I mean, with all due respect, my dear, the best thing you can do is talk to him about it because my decision has been made. It may not be what you want, but in my opinion, it's what everybody needs to see," we said.

She looked over at us with concern and almost became the most unattractive person in the room.

"Do you really think you can win?" she asked.

We closed our eyes to prevent our face from turning at the sight of her. In one second, we cursed her out in forty thousand different ways in our head. Some of the things we said were so funny, a smile appeared on our face. Very quickly, we had to remember that she only knew us as Ryan, not the Red Dragon. We exhaled our frustrations with a smile and tactfully answered her question.

"Don't let the smooth groove fool you, my dear. I may not look like much, but I'm not the guy you want chasing after you on a dark street at night," we replied.

She quickly looked us up and down and attacked us with trivial denial again.

"But... he's so much bigger than you. I just don't want you to get hurt," she pleaded.

We looked away, and our sinister laugh sounded off. She had no idea she was talking to a god. The classroom phone rang, and Colb went over to answer it, glancing at us as he took the call.

"He may be bigger than me, but he can't do what I do," we said.

We leaned back on the countertop and widened our legs, giving her a dirty look.

"Just wait, I'll show you exactly what I'm talking about."

Aaliyah grinned and shook her head. Although we were glad that she wasn't about to cry anymore, we questioned if she was worth pursuing. Her doubts were particularly discouraging, though, at the same time, we had to make ourselves aware that she was not privy to our capabilities, nor were we going to openly admit to her what we could do. How do you go about telling a girl that you killed a man with a knife because using your hands would have been worse?

The clock flipped to 3:00, and the final bell rang, giving us a few more minutes until showtime. The class cleared out, including Aaliyah, who was running to find Terry before he left. As we got to the front of the classroom, Colb stopped us with a deeply concerned look on his face.

"Remember that phone call I got earlier?" Colb asked.

"I take it that it was about me," we replied.

"That was Mrs. Cowart. She told me what happened in class today, and I assume that's where you're headed now."

We looked at the time. It was 3:01. We had to get out of there before Terrell tried to leave us.

"Yeah, that's where I'm going." We inched toward the door.

"Wait." Colb reached out his hand. "Just hear me out. Terry and his boys, that's a lot."

"Nothing I can't handle." We inched further.

"I'm not saying you can't. I'm asking if you think you'll need help."

We stopped in place, confused by Colb's statement.

"Help? Can't you lose your job for that?" we asked.

Colb stood from his desk and quickly walked over to us to make sure his voice wasn't heard.

"I'm just sayin', if you need me to roll up, I got a ski mask in my truck. I can pull up and break it up with quickness. We can make a safeword so I know when to move."

Once again, Colb riddled us with laughter at the end of a school day. The crazy part was that he was dead serious.

"I owe that big-headed bastard and his friends an ass whooping for the prank they pulled on me last year. They better be glad it was covered by my insurance," Colb said.

"Colb, I appreciate it, but I got it, bruh. Don't worry, I'll avenge you. I gotta go."

We quickly shook hands with Colb and headed toward the door.

"Good luck, lil' bruh, and if all else fails, go for his balls," Colb said.

We lowered our head in laughter and hurried to the parking lot. The hallway clock read 3:03. We had to hurry because Terrell's uncertainty gave us nothing to rely on. We made it outside and saw Terrell putting his backpack in the backseat of his car. He looked over and saw us and waved as we ran over to him.

"I thought about what you said earlier, and uh, I just wanna say, if it all goes to shit, I'm jumping in," Terrell said.

We grinned at him and shook his hand. Our boy's nuts had finally started to show up.

"The bravery, bruh, that's what I'm talkin' 'bout!"

We quickly looked around after we hopped in the car and noticed that Terrell and his idiots had already left. There was an unusual sum of cars headed in the direction of the soccer fields, all students from the school. It looked like the word had gotten out about our fight, guaranteeing everyone would see what we were going to do, and then it hit us.

I need to transform.

How were we going to transform and hide everything? We had to hide not only our eyes, but our fangs and our claws. Fortunately, we'd brought our full-fingered gloves and a pair of shades, so we'd be good, so long as we didn't talk much through the fight. We had to make sure we kept our shades on. Our red eyes would certainly set the whole crowd off.

"We need to get this over with quickly," Heru instructed.

We pulled up to the parking lot, and there were already over twenty cars parked, with a decent-sized crowd forming near one of the goalposts. The moment of truth was right before us. Terrell parked his car and looked at the time. It was 3:08, and we had less than two minutes to get ready. We looked over at the five idiots and saw Aaliyah trying to reason with Terry about fighting us. It looked like she was losing the argument.

"You know, if you change your mind and don't want to go through with the fight, I'll still be your friend," Terrell said.

We looked at him crazily as we removed our seat belt. We had to think of what to do before we got out of the car.

"Go ahead and go down there, tell them I'm coming. I need to transform first," we said.

"Transform?" Terrell questioned. "Boy this is real life, that stuff only works in cartoons."

"Just go." We forced him out. "I'll be down there in a sec."

"Aight, I'll tell them. Lock the door when you get out."

Terrell exited the car and shook his head as he walked toward the field.

"This fool done lost his mind, and I agreed to jump in and save him. What the hell." Terrell shook his head.

Once he was a good distance on the field, we dipped low in the seat and concentrated our energy. The beautiful transformation pulled our sleeping powers to the surface, and we began to feel normal again. We wiped the saliva dripping from our savage mouth, tasting the blood of our target in the air. We put on our gloves to hide our claws, and they had just enough thickness to keep the sharp tips from breaking through the fabric. We put on our shades to cover our eyes, checking ourselves out in the mirror to make sure everything was covered before we got out. We walked down to the soccer field looking like a Boss God about to punish a rare challenger.

As we reached the crowd, we were careful to make sure we didn't reveal our hidden secrets. The crowd opened up and allowed us to make our way toward the middle. On the opposite side stood Terry and his idiots, looking back at us as if they had all planned on moving on us at once, the challenge we really wanted. Terrell walked over and put his hand on our shoulder as we stared at the challengers.

"If any of them move, I'm jumping in," Terrell said.

"I don't think you're going to have to do anything. Just look after Aaliyah for me," we replied.

"Aaliyah? Why would I look after her?"

Aaliyah held Terry's jacket as she engaged in a verbal battle with him about the fight. She was desperate to keep the action from happening.

"Terry, c'mon! Just go back to the school and go to practice," she pleaded.

"Man, hold my jacket and watch the fight," Terry rudely replied.

"This is stupid, just let it go and go to practice," she yelled.

Terry stepped to her and forced his finger in her face. Aaliyah leaned backward, fearing he would hit her.

"You know what's stupid? You! If you don't wanna be here, give my jacket to one of the boys and take your ass home," Terry roared.

The crowd roared with ooohs and screams of embarrassment as Aaliyah walked to the side in shame. She lowered her head and stood there, beaten and mentally abused. The power pulsated from our chest and down to the tips of our fingers and toes. We wanted to sink our fangs into his face and leave a mark that would never be erased. We wanted to hear his bones crunch at the sound of our feet trampling his body. We were going to do all this and more, and then we remembered we couldn't kill him in front of all of these people.

Terry popped his knuckles as he put on his football practice gloves and looked over at us laughing, Leo cosigning their slick comments as they looked at us with our shades on.

"You ready to get ya ass whooped? You know I gotta get back to the school, so we gon' make this quick." Terry grinned.

"You know I'm ready, but I'll sweeten the deal. If you can knock off my shades, I'll drop my guard and give you 30 free shots, you and your boys. Knock my shades off and y'all can jump me," we taunted.

The boys laughed at us, thinking they had been given a free opportunity to be ruthless. Terry laughed and agreed to the seemingly easy terms and conditions of the fight.

"Aight, and if I don't break 'em, I'm keepin 'em," Terry replied.

The stage was set. The crowd stepped back to give us room to fight. People were pulling out their smartphones and deleting old pictures to make room for the video on their memory cards. There were a few guys in the crowd taking bets as to who would win, most of them believing that we were going to get jumped. We rotated our wrists and balled our fists as we both slowly stepped toward each other. We didn't bother to put our guard up; we just walked toward him like a superhero impervious to the bullets being shot at him.

"Remember, Ojore, keep your energy concentrated on his energy at all times," Heru said.

"I'm not gonna hurt him too bad, Heru, just enough to make him regret waking up today. Mostly body blows he'll feel every time he moves," we whispered.

The voices in the crowd rumbled as we got closer. The cameras had full coverage of the fight from all angles. Terrell stood behind us, ready to move. Aaliyah looked on, slightly shaking as she balled up Terry's jacket in her arms. Leo and the other idiots cheered on Terry, not realizing he was walking into a trap. He noticed we didn't have our guard up and confidently dropped his, shouting to the crowd and declaring he was about to kick our ass. He spread his arms and gave us an invitation to commence the battle.

"C'mon, bitch, hit me!" he shouted.

Our eyebrows ducked behind our shades, and we dashed at him with a four-punch combo to his ribs that stunned him. The crowd roared as we nearly backed him into his corner. He didn't even try to swing for fear of taking another one of our punches to his ribs. The goal was to keep him away from where he felt safe. We slapped him across the face, sending him rolling to the ground, but he quickly rose to his feet, looking at us and trying to figure out what had hit him. Leo and the idiots were in such shock, they forgot to jump in and save Terry from this ass whoopin' he so desperately needed.

We walked over to him like a shaded villain as he tried to sidestep around us.

"Kick his ass, bruh!" Terrell shouted.

The crowd went wild as we stepped toward Terry and continued delivering a barrage of punches to his chest and body, hammer-fisting his shoulders and making his arms useless in battle.

"I'm gettin' all dis shit on tape, bruh," someone yelled.

It had only been a few seconds, and the battle was already over. We rushed Terry and slapped him back and forward across the face. We could see the pain-filled tears in his eyes begging us to knock him out, but unfortunately, we weren't done yet. We snatched him by his shirt and held him in place, power-punching him deep in his gut, his face telling the story of a man whose only wish was to breathe again. We roared with each hit, each punch more powerful than the last.

"Two—three—four—five!" the crowd counted.

We back-slapped Terry, our hand sending him spinning to the ground before Aaliyah's feet. Aaliyah simply looked down at him without pity, revealing her anger toward him. Leo and the idiots hadn't moved from the spots they had been standing in since before the fight had started. Terrell jumped up and down from the sidelines, hyping up the crowd. We yanked Terry by his shirt and snatched him up to his feet. He stood hunched over trying to protect his damaged ribs. We knew he wouldn't be able to take much more, but we didn't care. We were going to make him take every hit we threw today.

We smacked him up, down, left and right, and kicked him into the crowd of people standing behind him. They suddenly came together like the ropes of a boxing ring and caught him before he fell. He tried to grab on to them for safety, but they shouted at him and yanked his hands away with all their might.

"No! You gotta fight," they yelled.

They forced him back into the circle and pushed him right toward us. We hit him with two dazing backhanded slaps from left to right, and suddenly came a message from our sponsor.

"Enough, Ojore! End him with your Super Dragon Uppercut," Heru ordered.

There was a move we'd learned in our training that had become a personal favorite, so much so, that we'd given it a name. We looked at Terry, still standing, but in terrible shape. We quickly studied his chin, marking the spots where we planned our final punches. We dashed at him with what we had left to finish him. We swung with a hard right cross to the jaw, sending his face flying right, but he was quickly stopped short as he was hit with a left cross that snatched his head back to the left. We crashed our fist into his jaw two more times, giving him a whammy of crosses from right to left.

The defenseless tyrant was broken but not yet defeated as everyone watched him in awe as he took every bit of the ass whoopin' we delivered to him. His body stood before us waiting for a gust of wind to blow him down. The crowd watched intently as we dipped low and quickly charged for our final punch. We roared, getting louder and louder as our power reached completion. We aimed our fist right under his jaw and jumped into the air with the most powerful uppercut anyone had ever seen. We took to the air, our body spiraling around as the force of our uppercut sent his rising body back toward his corner. It was as if time slowed down while we were high in the air. We witnessed all the starred eyes beneath us watching the amazing feat. Their eyes were in disbelief as they watched the God of War easily vanquish his foolish challenger while catching it all on video to remember as proof of what happened that day.

Terry's beaten and bruised body slammed hard to the ground. He was out cold. The crowd went wild, jumping up and down and forcing their cameras in Terry's face to record his most embarrassing moment. We'd finally given him what he needed.

Aaliyah forced her way in front of everyone and threw his jacket beside his beaten body.

"It's over, Terry!" she screamed as she walked off the field.

We wanted to run after her, but it wasn't over yet. All eyes were on us as we stepped on Terry's chest to walk toward the other four idiots. They were still looking down at Terry's motionless body lying on the ground. He snored as his blood leaked from the side of his mouth like drool. We'd definitely broken something in his mouth with that uppercut. The idiots were proving to be smarter than we thought, still standing in their same positions. One of them still had his hand in his pocket from before the fight began. Leo had no words as we bravely walked up to him, staring him down like an unworthy peasant. We weren't concerned about the others; they didn't look like they'd survive one backhand slap, and we couldn't hold back our true strength much longer.

"Any of the rest of you bitches wanna fight today?" we said straight to Leo's face.

They all remained silent, and a couple of them backed up a step.

"I thought so. Let's keep it that way." We looked over our shoulder. "Terrell, what time is it?"

Terrell eagerly pulled back his sleeve and looked at his watch. "3:12," he hollered.

We turned back to Leo, who was staring at us like a child caught doing something they shouldn't have been.

"Looks like you've got just enough time to get him to the hospital. Be sure to tell him what happened when he wakes up, and also make sure he knows I'll do it again," we threatened.

We boldly turned our back and walked off like a hero, our jacket like a giant cape blowing fiercely in the wind. The crowd was still hyped, taking pictures with Terry as he lay on the ground. The era of his terrorism was ended by the unlikely warrior with no history. Terrell ran up beside us with an excitement that we had never seen from him.

"Bruh, you were sensational! Like something out of a movie! You kicked his ass and made it look easy, like, you're not even breathing hard! And that uppercut at the end, you were in the air! Like, if it were an alley-oop, you would have uppercut him and slammed the ball all in the same jump! You got it, bruh, you definitely got it. Ain't nobody gettin' stupid with you after this!" Terrell exclaimed.

We grinned along at his commentary. Needless to say, it felt great putting someone in their place, but we couldn't escape the energy we felt from Aaliyah as she made her way away from the scene. We stopped and looked in her direction and spotted her just outside the park wondering if we should go after her.

"Not now, Ojore. She needs a moment to herself," Heru said.

Terrell stopped and looked at us, not realizing that we were looking at her.

"What's wrong, bruh? Don't tell me you're feeling bad about beating him," he said.

"No, I'm just worried about her," we said.

Terrell looked over at Aaliyah walking away, but because of his excitement, he could have cared less about her.

"You just kicked her, well, now her ex-boyfriend's ass, and she had to stand there and watch it happen. She's probably just embarrassed, but forget about that, bruh, you just did some phenomenal shit!" Terrell said.

We walked to the car and took one last look at the scene. The crowd was still surrounding Terry, and he still hadn't gotten up. We decided it would be best for us to leave in case things took a turn for the worst. We were careful to use the right amount of power for all of the hits, but there was no way of gauging how much his body was able to withstand. We looked around for Aaliyah when we pulled out of the park, but she was long gone.

"I'm not gonna lie to you, bruh, I really didn't think you were going to beat him, especially not like that. You did to him what I wish I could have done to him a long time ago. This might sound crazy to you, but I feel liberated. Thank you!" Terrell said.

Terrell dropped us off at the house and honked the horn with a smile as he drove off. He leaned back his seat with an eased state of mind, ready to embark on his new days of freedom at school. There would be no more threatening, there would be no more grief, no more having his lunch stolen by bullies that exercised their strength in numbers. Everything was going to be easy now. He could go to school and not have to worry about what was going to happen to him. He happily waved at pedestrians as he drove by, blasting one of his favorite songs through the busy streets. He pulled into his neighborhood and began riding slower to impress the kids playing outside. The ashy black paint on the side of his car shone like pure gold in his mind. He turned right onto his street and turned his music down, remembering his mother's warning about his loud music, but as he got closer, he noticed a Humvee sitting on the street outside of his house.

"Is MJ home?" he whispered to himself.

He slowly pulled into the driveway and got out to inspect the Humvee, wondering what the reason was for the surprise visit. He checked the date on his cell phone and realized that it was far too early for his brother to be back home. He quickly found his house key and made his way toward the door anxious to solve the mystery, but the door was already unlocked. He twisted the knob and rushed inside to the living room and immediately stopped in his tracks. Before him stood two men dressed in their formal military attire facing his mother on the couch leaning forward with her head down. Terrell stood confused as the straight-faced men turned and looked at him, neither of them being his brother. A soft whimper from his mother's mouth bounced on his eardrums.

"What's wrong?" Terrell fearfully asked.

Mrs. James slowly raised her head and sat upright, revealing a folded flag resting in her lap.

Thousands of miles away, the young Michael James had been riding in a convoy with his fellow soldiers. They were riding to another base located another 30 miles south of their current location. It had been a long day; the sun was cooking the desert plains, and the ride was only the beginning of what would be a long day of work.

"I mean, my mom ain't really all that bad, it's just, well, after my dad had his heart attack, she just changed on us. Like me and my lil' brother went from having the freedom to live to being treated like robots. She never cared that much about college or whatever—hell, I learned more about college from watching TV commercials. She just wanted what was best for us, but she went about it all wrong. I know my lil' brother's probably going through it like hell by himself, but my mom lo—"

Out of nowhere, the convoy was blown apart by enemy rockets fired from hidden warmongers. The rocket intended for James' convoy exploded in the sand inches away from the Humvee, but the force of the blast sent the vehicle violently flipping over and over again. The doors on the side of the explosion blew off, ejecting James alone from the Humvee and into the hot sands. He lay motionless, dark clouds of smoke surrounding him. He slowly began to open his blurred eyes to the cries of some of his fellow soldiers. He turned to his side to get up and saw the legless body of one of the female soldiers in his convoy. Her body had been ripped in half by the power of the explosions.

He muscled his way to his feet, staggering through his delusion. He couldn't feel anything as he stumbled through the shrapnel in the sands. Bullets whizzed by him, striking other soldiers scattered around him. The trails of black smoke darkened the sky and formed a blinding path that was like walking down a dark corridor to doom. The disoriented soldier didn't raise his gun; he just kept walking, each step bringing him closer to home.

He was left without a chance at regaining his complete balance as another rocket landed in the sands a small distance away from him. The powerful blast swept him from his feet and tossed him through the air into the hot desert sands. He landed face first, his weakened state taking his ability to catch himself. He slowly raised his head from the sands and with all of his strength, muscled his way to his feet. He didn't bother to pick up his gun, nor did he even know it was there. He just continued staggering through the desert, stepping over the dismantled body parts of the members in his convoy.

The screams that once rang in his ears were silenced by the sounds of single gunshots. Tears fell from his eyes without the cries to match as he struggled to stay on his feet. The black smoke formed a dark wall in front of him, leaving him no way to go forward, but he didn't stop. The brave soldier was destined to see his mother and brother again. He remembered his promise to Terrell, to not leave him alone in this world the way their father left them, but his ability to keep that promise was soon taken from behind his back.

He heard three bangs go off in his ears and felt something touch his back in three different spots. The soldier found it harder and harder to stand and broke down to his knees. His hands dropped to his sides, and he blankly stared into the black hellfire of smoke and shrapnel before him. A masked enemy armed with a loaded machine gun aimed at James' head, wondering why the unarmed soldier was still up. He rushed up to him with the butt of the gun and knocked him hard to the hot sands. James, still alive, didn't try to pick himself up this time. He had walked as far as his beaten body would allow, but his torture had not ended yet.

The enemy had been given distinct orders to hunt and kill by any means, a mission objective they had fulfilled almost to completion. The masked enemy grabbed James by his shoulder and flipped him on his back and aimed the barrel of his gun in his face. Sand stuck to the tears on James' face, his eyes blurring in and out as the harrowing image looked down at him. The enemy slid his mask down and exposed his face, and James' eyes widened as he looked into the eyes of his assassin who was a man who he had met at his base only a few weeks before.

The rogue soldier put the gun barrel against James' forehead as he reached up to him with his weakened arm. The fresh smell of gunpowder from the barrel entered James' nose as he made a feeble attempt to get away. Without concern or sorrow, the rogue soldier pulled the trigger on his machine gun, breaking the promise that Specialist Michael James had made to his brother Terrell James, leaving him suddenly in a warzone like their father had left them.

CHAPTER 16

KILLING IS A TECHNIQUE

TERRELL WAS INCOMPLETE. Terrell was destroyed. Terrell was broken. He came to school the very next day after he found out his brother was dead. He told not only us, but the entire class, and probably the classes before what happened. Terrell fell apart again, and again, and again throughout the day. Everyone wondered why he'd come to school, but no one told him to go home. They didn't call Terrell's mother. They didn't send Terrell to the counselor's office. They let Terrell sit in class and cry. All. Day. Long.

We stayed close by his side as he told everyone what happened. Seeing him cry took us back a few months before when we were incomplete, broken, and destroyed. It had been a while since we had traveled to Duat to see Carey and CJ. They hadn't done much but cry in confusion when we visited, and after a while, the emotional strain became too much for us to handle. For the most part, it's what made us focus so hard on our training. We had gotten so much stronger that we built a wall of rage around us to hide from our pain. We talked to Terrell after school, and versus trying to relate our stories, we told him it would be best for him to take the rest of the week off of school. He looked us in the eyes with all of the anguish he carried looking for a logical reason.

"What am I going to say to my mom?" Terrell asked.

We didn't know what to say to him. We refused to lie to him any more than the world already had. His brother had lost his life fighting another man's war under the guise of fighting for his country that was stolen from his own ancestors. Our heart broke for our friend, reopening the wounds we'd thought were healed over. We were hurt, more hurt than Camille or anyone else in our family. We of course hadn't heard a word from Fi-Fi or her husband, and Hank and Alpharetta had been particularly silent as well. It wasn't fair that we would soon graduate without our cousin. We used to compete academically, athletically, every way two cousins could go head to head. We were a team, two young men destined to bring honor to the family name, and he was dead along with his father, our coach.

We got home from school and locked the door to our room and cried. We had to bleed the pain from that wound. We still had a mission to fulfill, and carrying that weight wasn't going to make anything easier for us. In order to avenge them, we had to let them go. Our powers didn't feed off of sadness—they fed off of rage, hatred, and anger. Sadness was a form of weakness, and with it in our system, we were weakened. We traveled to the Spirit Realm for our training, but this time we took a different approach before we began.

Ryan and Heru met upon the rough sands of the Spirit Realm standing on opposite sides of a pond with a small waterfall. The pond was surrounded by dense greenery as if the land had been preserved by the gods for eternity. Heru held an empty golden scuttle, and he began to walk toward the clear water pond.

"Enter the water, Ojore," Heru instructed.

As Heru entered the ankle-high waters, Ryan curiously approached the pond, wondering what today's training entailed. Heru lowered the small scuttle into the water and filled it up, and suddenly the sounds of African drums began to play, hidden in the background as Heru raised the scuttle before him.

"Great ancestors, past and present, we come to you in honor of your great sacrifices. We wish to bring peace among the lands and restore the goodwill of the gods within the people."

The drums began to beat harder and louder as the essence of the ancestors surrounded the land with their energy.

"We beg all of you for your continued guidance and ask once more for your abundant strength as we journey through these ominous times on these rough sands. Empower us with your legacy that we might avenge the anger of Mother Earth."

Ryan closed his eyes and lowered his head. He could feel the spiritual beings around him recharging his might. His internal wounds began to slowly close as he raised his head toward the sky.

"Ra!"

Heru poured a short drip of water into the pond.

"Auset!"

He continued to pour as he called out names.

"Asar! Hathor! Montu! Be with us on this journey! Deliver us and bring us back!"

The sky began to change color, leaving behind twisted trails from where the clouds had traveled. Ryan stood still with his eyes closed, tears rolling down his cheeks as he accepted the healing from the ancestral spirits.

"Call out the names of your beloved ancestors, new and old, Ojore."

The drums banged louder and louder as the spiritual energy in the realm grew. His eyes closed and his face scrunched from the infuriated healing inside, Ryan called out the names of those heavy on his heart.

"Carey! CJ! Michael," Ryan shouted.

Heru poured out water for each name called, granting healing to the young warrior. His energy fully restored, Ryan's fiery aura shaped his body, and he began to charge his power.

"We thank you, ancestors! We beg your mercy as we endeavor to new heights! We shall be victorious," Heru called out.

Ryan's power peaked, and he roared with his eyes toward the sky. He released his weakness and accepted his birthright as the God of War. The strength of Montu stomped within his spirit, the love of Hathor nurtured his heart, the eye of Ra gave him a vision, the leadership of Asar empowered him, the care of Auset gave discernment to his thoughts, and the deaths of Carey, CJ, and Michael gave him purpose.

Heru lifted his hand into the air and the waters of the pond rose above them. He dropped the water on top of Ryan, sending him deep down under the clear waters. The waters brought calmness to his spirit, equalizing the tension and frustration of his heart. His chakras flowed back into alignment as they each grew in strength. He allowed the calm waters to hold his body peacefully, slowly opening his eyes to see the light. Ryan found himself in his normal state, facing a proud Heru on the rough sands of the Spirit Realm.

"We perform libation to give honor to our fallen ancestors as they always dwell with us in spirit," Heru said.

Ryan bowed his head toward Heru, who smiled with the belief that the young god was ready to ascend to another level. He approached the Red Dragon with delight as he commenced their training.

"Your powers are linked directly to the wrath of the ancestors. It is important that you always remember them to be the source of your power, for without them, you would be nothing. Many have died for the sake of your freedom. Honor them for their sacrifice, and onto you, they will bestow a power beyond mortal measure. As the God of War, you have many more abilities that you will discover on your journey. Being fast and strong is only a small portion of your responsibilities, and it is my belief in you that compels me to give you more knowledge. Today I want to teach you something that I believe you will infinitely master in due time," Heru said.

Heru's body began to glow with a light golden aura, and from his hands formed two orbs of radiant energy. He closed his hands, and the orbs dissipated, giving his hands the same radiant glow. Ryan looked on without blinking, intrigued by the light show.

"Even as a god, there are enemies that may prove to be more powerful than yourself, and in those moments, you will use this tool to assist you in vanquishing your enemies. This technique is known among the great gods as the Mansa Musa Blaze, and with its great power you are to be diligent with respect to your use of it," Heru said.

Heru turned his back to Ryan as he stared deep into the space of the Spirit Realm. His energy concentrated, he planted his feet in the rough sands and envisioned a target before him.

"Every god has an essence, and each essence is different from the other. In time, you will discover your essence, and your powers will reflect what your essence is. I will show you mine," Heru said.

Tiny sparks of energy formed around Heru as the light energy of his hands beckoned to be released. He motioned his hands as he had done many times in battle, and his arms and chest pumped with energy. A gritty groan escaped from his mouth, and he chanted the word to produce his infamous blaze.

"MMMMAAAAAAAANNNNNNNN-SSSSSSAAAAAAAAAAAAA-MMMMMMUUUUUUUUUUU-SSSSAAAAAAAAAAAAAA!!!"

An enormous beam of energy exploded from his hands and flew across the endless Spirit Realm at rapid speed. The radiant golden light blinded Ryan as it blew around the rough sands like a violent hurricane. The force of the blast nearly blew him away, but he fought and maintained his footing. The golden beam of energy traveled far away from the two gods, and the peace of the realm was soon restored. Heru continued to look in the direction of his blast, dropping his hands and standing upright as he mentally assessed his technique. He closed his eyes and took a deep breath, releasing the tension in his muscles from the impact of the blast.

"You try," Heru said.

Ryan anxiously stepped up and planted his feet into the rough sands and exhaled his excitement. He focused his energy and prepared to send a blast out as far as Heru had.

"Wait, show me what you did," Ryan said.

"Of course," Heru agreed. "First, you cup your hands to your left side, facing the opposite direction."

"Like this?" Ryan motioned his hands.

"Yes, just like that. Next, you will bring your hands straight out in front of you, keeping them horizontal with your arms fully extended and your hands closed."

Ryan did as he was instructed, extending his arms and hands with laser-like precision.

"Good. Now cup your hands to your right side, again pointing your hands in the opposite direction."

Ryan followed the words of his instructor, displaying perfect form with the swaying of his hands. He looked to Heru to make sure he was doing it correctly and received a nod of approval.

"Now you'll force your hands to the front and release as much energy as you can muster into a devastating blast. The power release you will experience will go far beyond any punch, kick, or staggering blow you can deliver to your enemy. Give it a try," Heru advised.

Ryan again exhaled his excitement and calmed his nerves to focus his energy. He aimed his eyes into the endless abyss before him, concentrating his energy for the blast. Once he felt ready, he chanted the word and swayed his hands just as his spiritual guide taught him.

"MMMMAAAAAAAANNNNNNNN-SSSSSSAAAAAAAAAAAA-MMMMMMUUUUUUUUUU-SSSSAAAAAAAAAAAA!!!"

His charged scream echoed into the empty abundance of the Spirit Realm, but nothing came from his hands. Confused by the lack of action, Ryan looked to Heru for an explanation.

"What happened?" Ryan asked.

"Try again," Heru advised.

Ryan refocused his energy and planted his feet. After taking a few breaths, he attempted the blaze again.

"MMMMAAAAAAAAANNNNNNNN-SSSSSSAAAAAAAAAAAAA-MMMMMMUUUUUUUUUUU-SSSSAAAAAAAAAAAAAA!!!"

Again, his scream echoed through the empty abundance, and again nothing happened. Ryan grew frustrated with the technique, his arms pulsating with his charged fury.

"Why isn't it working?" Ryan grunted.

Heru calmly crossed his arms behind his back and closed his eyes, feeling the invisible waves of energy flowing around him. He took a few deep breaths, listening to the ancestor's messages and began to grin. He opened his eyes and lowered his head before the frustrated Dragon.

"This task is nothing I expect you to master overnight, nor do I expect you to master it anytime soon. Your chakras are coming well into alignment, but you still lack the strength in your third eye to perform this technique," Heru advised.

Ryan lowered his head in frustration as his hard work hadn't come with the payout he expected. The wise Heru sensed his student's tension and attempted to encourage his spirit.

"The anger in your power is a blessing and a curse, Ojore."

"What do you mean?" Ryan grunted.

"The power of the Mansa-Musa Blaze was created not by the strongest of the ancient gods. It was an ability harnessed by those that rivaled you in power at your current state."

Ryan raised his brow in disbelief.

"There were once dark gods that plagued the lands, murderous and savage with their attacks on the people. Due to their unfathomable strength, some of the strongest of the great gods were defeated by these powerful dark gods. Their appearance spelled the end of days for many societies of the time, for no god could outmatch them. Just as all hope seemed lost, there arose a god. The wise ancestor knew that his power would never rival the power that these dark gods possessed, but in his desperation to save his people, he discovered how to harness energy not only from deep within but also the powers of divinity. The result was the Mansa-Musa Blaze. He used this attack to vanquish the dark gods that threatened his people and then went on to teach this technique to the other great ancestors until the world was rid of the deceitful pest.

Your problem is not that you lack the power; you lack the concentration. To you, being powerful is about strength and how hard you can punch, when in actuality, it is being centered and spiritually elevated. You have significantly progressed in your chakra alignment, but you must give a different approach to your thought pattern in order to align your third eye with your other chakras. There is nothing more for me to teach you, but until you master this concept, which we can only hope will happen soon. Remember, your evolution is dependent upon you," Heru advised.

Ryan looked at the claws protruding from his fingers and released a grunt of frustration.

"What more is there for me to do?" he asked.

"There is something you must overcome in order to progress to the ultimate level of your destined abilities.

Heru turned and stepped away with grief. His faith in the Red Dragon began to waver.

"Something to overcome? Is this supposed to be a damn riddle or something? We don't have time for this," Ryan said.

"I am unsure, Ojore. The ancestors have not given me specifics as to what you must overcome, but they have advised that the answer lies within you. I know not what direction to go in with you at this point, but for now, we practice what we have already learned," Heru said.

We tossed and turned as we slept that night, seeing images of our family at Carey and CJ's funeral. There were so many sad faces, so many hurt feelings, and at the end of it all, we were the strongest person in the world but unable to save them. We couldn't evolve to save them; we couldn't save ourselves from this powerful, white-faced spirit in our dream. He and his blank-faced accomplice pointed guns at us and ended us with a hailstorm of bullets.

We woke up angry as hell Saturday morning trying to figure out what it was going to take to make a change within us. We sat at the kitchen table eating an unsatisfying bowl of cereal, desperate to figure out this mystery. We were already wild with power, so would it take us being softer? Would it take a sacrifice? Did someone have to die?

"I think I know what it is," Ryan said.

"I'm listening," Heru said.

"You said the ancestors told you that the answer lies within me, and you also said my powers are linked to the wrath of the gods. Wrath is an emotion linked to anger. Anger caused by the wrongdoing of someone else toward them. This whole thing has been about revenge. Every time I hold that knife, I mainly see that guy, Face, and everyone else is irrelevant."

"What is your idea, Ojore?"

"I think all I have to do is kill Face and I can evolve," Ryan said.

"You may be correct, Ojore, but I believe your evolution may require a little more depth," Heru said.

We heard the twist of a doorknob, and from their room, Camille emerged in her robe and slippers. She looked rougher than usual, as if she hadn't gotten any sleep the night before.

"Who were you talking to, baby?" Camille asked.

"Uh, nobody. I was, uh, rapping," we lied as we sipped the almond milk from the bowl.

We finished our breakfast and quickly made our way back to our room. We looked inside our closet and picked up the stolen muzzle we so desperately wanted to wear.

"I want to go after Face tonight. Wherever he is, I need to find him and kill him. I've gotten strong enough to handle myself well if anything should arise, so it's time to stop playing around and take him out," Ryan said.

"Be cautious, Ojore. There are still mortal creations that can severely hurt you. You are not yet at the level in which you will be unaffected by these things," Heru advised.

"I don't recall saying I was afraid. I know what I'm up against, and if I have to die a thousand times before I do it, then that's just what it is. I have a desire to kill this man, and it won't rest until it's done. We gotta make a move tonight."

"So be it," Heru said. "Tonight, we seek the one known as Face and avenge the deaths of your loved ones."

We didn't do anything else for the rest of the day. The house was quiet with a few openings and closings of doors from time to time. Our rage calmly pressed against the surface of our skin, desperately waiting for the time to come for us to leave the house. We watched the fall sun prepare to set in the west and decided it would be best for us to leave at a time that wouldn't allow too many questions to be asked, but the only problem was Reginald and Camille were both at home. We hoped Reginald wouldn't trip about us leaving for work, but he was a different kind of bitch made. The threat of him searching our room already had us hiding stuff that didn't even need to be hidden.

We decided to put on our black cargo pants with a red T-shirt and stuffed the Buddy in our pocket as we grabbed our keys from the nightstand. Tonight was a black boots kind of night because we'd be taking out the motorcycle we'd stolen for the first time. With a grin on our face, we reached up to the top of the closet and brought down the dope muzzle. It still smelled kind of new. We took the spiked arm bracers and stuffed them in the side pockets of our pants to put them on later. We took our phone off the charger and checked to see if we'd missed anything, but there was only a text from Hank we'd ignored. There was nothing personal against him, but having him back in Georgia was kind of weird. Even with all the changes in the family, his closeness just didn't seem to make anything better, but I didn't want him to leave again. Alpharetta tried to keep up with us as much as she could, sending a text or a call every now and then, but I could never really tell her anything. She was notorious for turning small talk into an overexaggerated psychological dysfunction. It was great not having to listen to her and Camille arguing, but in some way I kind of wished they still were. Camille at least tried to smile then.

We walked to Camille's door and softly knocked and waited anxiously for a response. We heard her footsteps coming toward the door and took a step back as she cracked the door open.

"What is it, baby?" Camille grumbled as if she had just woken up.

"I'm about to go, I forgot to tell you I had to work tonight, but I'll be back early in the morning," we lied.

"Please be careful and talk to your boss about a set schedule for you. I don't feel comfortable with this randomness. You're still a high school student." She sighed.

"Don't worry, Mama, I'll talk to him."

Camille reached out of the doorway and grabbed our arm, clearing her throat.

"Make sure you straighten up your room before you go," she whispered.

A subtle warning for the pending search that would take place once we left the house. Camille never stopped trying to protect us from the harm she'd brought us into.

"I did. The only thing that changed was the bedsheets," we replied.

"Okay. Mama loves you."

"I love you, too."

As her door closed, we took note of the several beer bottles sitting on the counter in the kitchen. It appeared that Reginald had gotten himself drunk, making it that much easier to get out of the house without a single question being asked about transportation. We were still angered by the thought of him being in our room, searching through our things, and violating our personal space. We mostly feared him messing up any of the artwork we created. He wasn't a fan of anything that we did, and many a time we'd heard the story of sabotage from a stepparent. We needed this school year to speed up.

We made our way outside and quickly ducked off into the woods to power up. Our senses heightened more and more with all the training we had gotten in, hopefully putting us closer to this evolution we had to master. Shooting beams of energy from our hands had been a lifelong dream, a dream that we were destined to make come true. Our eyes red, our fangs sharp, our fingertips clawed, and our wrist spiked, we ran through the trees, making our way to our hidden motorcycle. We got to the building and found everything just as we had left it. We started the bike up and revved it to listen to its roar.

"I'm gonna call you Rage," we said.

We put on our gear and checked the time, knowing it was still early. We couldn't allow anyone to see us like this, so we decided to go to the one place that could give us motivation for what we planned to do tonight. We took to the highway, committing to no less than 120 mph, riding like time was running out. It had been months since the case turned cold, so it was no surprise that the house had been renovated and put up for sale. We sat across the street in front of Carey's old house admiring the fresh coat of paint, remembering the police tape that had been there only a few months before. We remembered the days when we would run the block riding bikes with CJ, the hot summer days when we all did yard work until our skin was completely tanned, and we'd never forget the days in the garage where we attended man school while lifting weights. What hurt the most was the fact that they didn't get to live to see the god we became.

We kept our helmet on the entire time we sat out there—fortunately, no one passing by thought anything suspicious. The training intensive weeks had hardened us; there was nothing more inside to pull sadness from. Avenging our family was the blood-boiling rage that woke us up every morning and lulled us to sleep at night. We remembered seeing the blood on the floor and walls and felt a charge rise from our feet through our fingertips.

"We should not stay here much longer, Ojore," Heru said. "It's about time that we commence the night's mission."

We pulled out our cell phone and realized that we had been sitting for three hours.

"Damn, I didn't realize so much time had gone by," Ryan said.

We whipped out the Buddy and closed our eyes to concentrate on the energies that remained.

"The strongest one is Face. We'll go after this one, and then go after the other guy," Ryan said.

"So be it," Heru replied.

We revved up our engine and sped off into the night, ready to take out our next victim.

The night was picking up as Face and Deuce comfortably made their way through the city in the back of a luxury SUV. Face's cell phone rang nonstop with people calling in desperation to get into the club, and Deuce was busy on the phone barking orders at security to ensure that everything went off without a hitch. Tonight was a much-needed night for celebration for the two tyrants as the road to maintaining order over their district had proven to come with a few tedious tasks. This night of joy would give them the rest they needed to keep the chokehold they had on the streets.

"I don't care if they got a badge and a gun, I said don't let 'em in unless they aim at you! Now we'll be there in ten minutes. Hol' it down." Deuce hung up the phone.

"I'm on my way, I should be there in a few...I know what it feels like, but I'm not driving.... You should've worn a thicker coat...Yeah, I know, they're all in line. Look, I'll see you when I get there, it won't be much longer. Bye," Face hung up his phone. "Woo! People, I tell you."

"I know, right," Deuce laughed.

"These folks be yellin' at me like I don't murder people! Like, who do they think they're talking to?" Face joked.

"Right," Deuce agreed.

The SUV turned down the busy city streets, riding slowly through the night lights. The sidewalks were full of pedestrians, some experiencing their first night under the city lights, others ready to continue their lives with another reckless weekend. Miniskirts, halter tops, and spandex were the outfits of all the women up and down the sidewalks, leaving nothing to the imagination for the men that pursued them. The club was only a few blocks up the street, and already Face could see the line wrapping around the corner.

"Looks like we got a good crowd tonight." Face smiled.

"Hell yeah. We better have a good crowd after that damn payoff. I tell ya, bruh, it's hard runnin' an honest business," Deuce joked.

"Ahh! All I wanna do is get a drink in my hand, smoke a lil herb, and booty watch all night."

"You do that. I gotta be on securities asses for that shit that happened a few weeks ago. How in the hell does a whole fight break out and nobody knows about it?" Deuce grunted.

Face and Deuce pulled up to the club, and immediately their entourage surrounded the SUV. Security made their way to the vehicle and gave them the red-carpet treatment, escorting them and their crew of Illegit members through the doors of the club.

"Aye yo, bro, it's me! It's me, aye man, they trippin', can I get in wit' y'all?" one patron hollered from the line.

The club was packed with patrons dancing their drunken night away. Flashes of light were all over the place with girls taking selfies every three seconds. The club had only been open for a few hours, and already there was a loser at the bar buying drinks for every pretty girl that gave him attention. Each section was packed with people on their cell phones documenting their nights on social media, faking it for attention.

Security escorted the Illegit group to the VIP section already furnished with bottles on ice and an appetizing spread of hors d'oeuvres. Deuce made his way to the kitchen to yell at the cooks to keep everything in order as they had just bribed the health inspector the week before. Face posted up with his Illegit Family, looking down upon the regular patrons of the club like broke peasants. He reached into his jacket pocket, pulled out $10,000 in hundred-dollar bills, and rose to his feet.

"Aye yo, shout out to my boi Face and the Illegit Family in dis bitch. I see you, bruh," the DJ called out.

Face waved over to the DJ and walked up to the balcony of the VIP and began tossing the money through the air. The patrons went wild trying to catch the hundred-dollar bills as they reached the dancefloor, some being so desperate as to push others away from the money they sought. Face poured himself a drink and sat on the plush leather couch, and before him appeared a hand passing him a freshly rolled blunt. His night was about to get lit.

We rolled through the city streets, observing the people walking up and down the sidewalks. There were men and women in cars blasting music and hanging out of windows as if they'd never been anywhere before. We'd never understood what was so fascinating about Downtown and Midtown; it was just a bunch of clubs and restaurants. There were only so many songs to dance to and only so many that a DJ would be willing to play. We didn't even listen to the radio anymore. It was a concept of rolling fun and depression that we could never understand. It was the same party, just a different crowd.

We rode down a busy street, and we could feel the pulses of energy beating through us as we approached a busy nightclub. The line was wrapped around the corner of the building, so we knew this had to be the place. There didn't appear to be a place where we could park that would make for an easy escape, so we decided to park at the parking garage adjacent to the club. We sat at the top of the garage looking down on the building, trying to find the best way in. We spotted an alley that led to the back of the club and hoped to find a door that we could break into.

"He's definitely in there," Ryan said. "I've gotta be smooth with this one. I can feel some other energies in there with him, too."

"This mission will require stealth and heightened senses, Ojore. Beware of your surroundings and blend with the crowd," Heru advised.

"Damn, I should probably take this stuff off then."

We removed our motorcycle jacket, the spiked bracers, and the muzzle we so desperately wanted to wear. If we were going to blend with the crowd, we had to look more like the fools standing outside. We hoped that the cover of darkness inside would be enough to get us close to our target. We decided it would be best to leave our golden gun with the bike. Its bulky build would have made it hard to hide once we were inside. Hopefully, the smell of motor oil and engine exhaust we'd picked up didn't call us out. We looked up into the night sky and observed the moon hide behind a cloud, giving us clearance.

"Time to move," we said.

We ran to the edge of the building and jumped from the top of the parking garage down to the roof of the nightclub. The patrons were so distracted by the night chills and selfies to notice us launching through the sky. We landed on the roof with ease and scurried into the shadows to hide from possible onlookers watching from the skyscrapers. We looked over the edge of the building and noticed a man standing at a door beneath us on his cell phone complaining about how his night was going. He had a gun on his hip that would quickly be ours, an easy target with an easy entry.

"They got me out here like this on my first night, like, why ain't nobody tell me to bring a jacket? I'm thinkin' I'ma be inside the joint, but nah, these assholes put me outside in the back. Like, ain't nobody comin' here! The homeless ain't even comin' back here. Kinda shit is dis!"

We felt kind of sorry for the fool, but we knew that he was the kind of guy that would do his job in hopes of receiving better treatment. He had to be taken out. We continued to watch him as he complained, waiting for the right moment to attack.

"It's gettin' colder and colder out here. I bet they don't even give me a warm cup of water... This gon' be my last time doin' this shit...I don't know when I'm getting off, I might just leave dis bitch."

We hopped down from the roof and spooked the security guard as we landed in front of him.

"Shift change." We smirked.

We delivered a swift punch to his abdomen and backhanded him to the ground. He was out cold. We took his gun and dragged his body to the dumpster and left him beside it, covering him up with a few trash bags to make him blend in like a homeless person. The backdoor creaked open as we snuck inside, the gun tucked on our hip under our shirt. We passed by the restrooms and saw a few girls carrying their drunk friend to the bathroom. The poor girl had made a mess on her dress, and it was all down the back of her leg. This place was already outrageous, and it was barely eleven o'clock.

The pulses of energy got stronger and led us toward the dancefloor. We had to be careful as we could feel eyes in different directions looking at us. We couldn't tell if it was the security guards or just some girl or guy sizing us up; either way, we couldn't afford to get caught. We looked across the dancefloor, and all our senses focused on a man sitting up in a balcony area. It was him, it had to be him. We just had to get closer to him. We started to make our way to the center of the dancefloor under the neon lights. The colors of our clothing hid us from the glowing effect of the black lights. We were getting closer and closer until we were suddenly interrupted by the hype of the DJ.

"Err-body to da dance floor! It's dat new joint from dem bois! Let's get it," the DJ shouted.

Immediately the crowd shifted as patrons bombarded the dance floor, jumping and throwing their hands in the air. Some of the men were pushing one another around as they jammed to the hardcore beat blaring through the speakers. We were tossed around with the crowd like a small boat caught at sea during a hurricane. We kept our eyes on Face, never letting him escape our view. We quickly got irritated with the weed smoke and drunken ignorance around us, but we had to remember to remain calm so as not to blow our cover. We slowly made our way through the vexatious tidal wave, and before us was the opening staircase to the VIP section.

It was particularly strange that the entry to the VIP section was unguarded; there wasn't even a regular employee roaming the area to make sure the wrong people stayed out. We looked back and didn't see anyone watching us, so we slowly made our way up the stairs to the private section. His energy grew stronger as we crept up the stairs, concentrating the rage in our muscles to keep us moving steadily. We walked up a few more steps, and there he was.

Face was riding high over the horizon on cloud nine as he sat still on the plush seat. The mixture of alcohol and marijuana took him to the happy place in his mind that slowed the pace of the environment. His head bobbed as he looked out into the club, enchanted by the bright neon colors. He smiled as his eyes widened while he attempted to count every color he saw. The bright colors eventually became too overwhelming for him to count as the crowd shifted like tidal waves, and he burst into laughter and dropped his head back on the headrest of the seat.

"This shit feels so good," Face mumbled to himself.

High out of his mind with his legs and arms spread wide on the seat, Face was completely defenseless against anything that came his way. The Illegit patrons in the VIP were too distracted with money being tossed around and fallacious women to pay attention to their leader, leaving an easy opening for an attack.

We could hear our heartbeat as we slowly approached the white-faced fool. The bastard wasn't moving; he was just sitting there with his head turned up to the ceiling. Our eyes cut into him, remembering the bloodshed of our family at his hands, and the rage steadily built within us. He was weak and wide open for destruction, and no one had even noticed we were there. We reached for the pistol on our hip and continued stepping toward him. We were going to put this one through his forehead, just like they did CJ. The sounds of the club blended into one solid silence, and all that we could hear were the pounding beats of our heart.

We stopped in place, standing only a few feet away from our target, our steady rage anxious for the evolution to come with the kill. We slowly raised the gun from our hip, and the bastard raised his head, smiling at us without concern. His shades had fallen off, and we looked into the depths of his soul and found nothing but an endless line of hurt and destructive behavior. Our hand was nearly high enough to shoot him right in the middle of the forehead. He didn't move. He kept smiling. The gun was in the perfect position. We took aim. This was for CJ. This was for Carey. This for Camille's tears. This was for Hank's regrets. This was for....

The worst shit ever heard in life...a shotgun blast from behind. A blast so loud that the DJ stopped the music, and everyone cleared the dance floor and bum-rushed to the exits. Patrons were pushing each other out of the way, some even trampling others as they frantically ran for their lives. Security quickly flaked and escaped to the outside, pretending to secure their perimeters as they hid among the crowd. The streets were flooded with distressed patrons, some crying, some desperately trying to find their friends, and others nursing the injuries they'd received. Several police cars arrived on the scene and began forcing patrons across the street to block off the area while some patrons took to social media to document the horrific event live.

Deuce grabbed the inebriated Face while wielding his sawed-off shotgun, stepping over his immobilized target. He enlisted the aid of the remaining Illegit members and ordered them to carry Face to the back door of the club while he called their driver. There wasn't much time before the police would storm the building, giving Deuce only a few moments to scan the area. He sifted through ashtrays, extinguishing leftover blunts and spilling liquor on the seats and floors to purposely make a mess of the area and discovered Face's shades sitting next to the loaded 9mm lying on the floor. He picked up the gun and stuffed it in his coat while he looked down at his kill. Under the guise of the dark lighting, black blood spilled from the holes in his back and chest creating a mixed pool of bloody liquor on the floor beneath him. The seats and tables were spattered with black blood and guts, hiding the hole in the wall left by the traveling slug. Deuce snatched up Face's shades and carefully stepped over the body, making his way to the back and caught up with his team as their ride arrived.

"Get us the hell out of here now," Deuce ordered.

They dipped through the dark alleys, narrowly missing the homeless sleeping and walking by the back doors of closed businesses. They finally made it to the street, nearly swiping a few cars that were approaching the intersection. The driver sped toward the freeway, checking his mirrors to make sure the police weren't following him. Deuce strapped the drunken Face into his seat and held him up, hoping that the bumpy car ride wouldn't end with Face vomiting on him.

"Are we going back to the high-rise?" the driver asked.

"No, get on 20 West. I'll tell you where to go from there," Deuce advised.

The driver dipped and dodged around cars, flying down the highway to their destination. Face groaned as he came in and out of his high, struggling to keep his head up. He rested his head on Deuce's shoulder and uttered gibberish until he fell asleep.

"Just sleep, bruh," Deuce said as he pulled his cell phone from his pocket.

He made a quick call to Ke-Ke but got her voicemail as he nervously scanned the highway in the rear window.

"Ke-Ke, it's Deuce. Face is fine, but we had some shit go down at the club tonight, so call me when you get this message."

He hung up the phone and began making another call to Porter and Simmons to get them on the case as quickly as possible. He gave orders to the driver as they got farther away from the city, causing Face to groan more from the hollering in his ear.

"Relax, bruh. Here, put on your shades. You cool now." Deuce planted the shades.

Face turned and laid his head back on the seat and felt the shades on his face.

"I'm cool," Face uttered before drifting back off to sleep.

Finally, Porter picked up the phone with his usual poise and greeted Deuce with all of his methodical energy.

"Joker, Joker, it's Deuce, Deuce, but this ain't spa—"

"Porter, chill, this ain't no house call," Deuce interrupted. "I need you and Simmons to get to the club immediately. Somebody tried to kill Face!"

Back at the club, the streets were lined with intoxicated patrons and police cars running around as if they had just entered a warzone. Unsure if the shooter was still inside, the police waited for the SWAT team to arrive as they fought to block the news crews from commencing their live reports. Inside, the neon lights were still going. Flipped tables and chairs blocked the path of walkways riddled with spilled food and drinks. A smeared shoe print told the brief story of the hysteria that had plagued the night club only moments before.

Over in the VIP, once crisp, clean dollar bills were now stained and floating around in the black, bloody liquor pool.

Ryan's body lay lifeless on the dirty floor, his face drenched with undrunk alcohol and blood leaking from his mouth. The gaping hole created by the slug tore through his spine and ripped its way out of his chest. The forceful blow had carried his body two feet before he crash-landed on the floor. Despite the incredible strength he had gained, the Red Dragon had once again been killed by the worldly creations of man.

Embers began to spark inside of the hole as bones and internal organs reshaped and reformed. The scattered guts disintegrated into ashes, leaving no identifiable trace of their expulsion. The black blood dried on the surfaces it touched, separating from the spilled liquor, and we suddenly opened our eyes in a daze, already aware of what had happened. We grunted and groaned as we struggled to pick ourselves up off of the dirty floor. We rose to our feet, holding on to the rails of the balcony to keep our balance. Beneath us was an open dancefloor, lit, and live without anyone to occupy the space. The gun we had was gone, and there was a large hole in the front and back of our shirt. We'd failed. We'd failed majorly, and we didn't have time to discuss what had happened because we knew we had to get out of there.

We sat down and slid down the stairs from the VIP because our leg strength hadn't replenished enough for us to handle the pressure on our knees yet. We sat at the bottom of the stairs and caught our breath for a second, gripping our chest as our blood pressure built back up. Just as we got back to our feet, we sensed the presence of several people entering from the front.

"APD! Come out with your hands up!"

We had to hurry up and get out of there, but we couldn't remember our way to the back door. We frantically staggered through the hallways at the back of the club, the SWAT team quickly closing in on us. We could hear their footsteps getting closer and closer, followed by the fearful reminder of the guns they had. Just as the armed squad found their way to our location, a stroke of good fortune found us in the form of an emergency exit. We dipped out of the door, and an alarm went off throughout the club, disguising the sound of our footsteps. We grabbed the door handle and slowly closed the door, knowing we wouldn't be able to outrun the cops if they saw that it was open.

We leaned against the wall to catch our breath again and noticed our leg strength was coming back faster than before. Part two of our failure was the death walk back to our motorcycle, which was conveniently located across the street from the club at the top of a parking garage with a ton of cops and well-dressed terrified club patrons in the middle of the street.

"Shit."

We paced back and forth for a second, trying to figure out how we were going to get past all of these people. The cops had blocked off parts of the intersection and weren't allowing anyone to cross. There was no magical escape route or even a sewer to travel through to get across, and if they caught us back here, we were doomed. We took off our sticky gloves to rub our head and realized we reeked of alcohol and gunpowder. Suddenly, we had an idea. We knew there had to be dried blood on our face because of the black stuff soaked into our holey shirt. We already looked like shit as it was, so it wouldn't be too hard to pull off our crazy stunt. We staggered around to the front with a delusional expression and crept up behind a cop guarding the area, but he quickly turned and spotted us.

"Got a dolla, officer?" we asked with our hand out.

"Hey! Across the street, dammit, that means you, too!" the officer shouted.

"I just need a dolla."

We pushed our way through the crowd, hearing the cries of the distraught partygoers. They were all hugging each other and crying with amateur reporters taking their experience live to social media. We made our way through the crowd, asking people for dollars each time they offered to help.

By the time we got to the bottom of the parking garage, we were able to stand upright, which was great because we had to travel up six flights of stairs, and the elevator was broken. We fought our way to the top, wishing going up was as easy as going down. After taking two more breaks, we finally made it to the top. We looked over the edge and stared at our failed attempt filled with shame. Face was still alive, laughing at us, laughing at Carey and CJ as he had before he killed them. The slug through the back didn't compare to our embarrassment. We walked away from the ledge, trying our best to hold it together. We rode home at a reasonable speed, canceling the celebration of dips and leans, our ego reduced to that of a law-abiding citizen. We couldn't tell if it was the wind or our emotions, but a tear escaped from our eye as we rode down the highway. Our evolution had gotten that much further away.

CHAPTER 17

CHANGING THE GAME

THE MORNING SUN transitioned to its afternoon position in the sky, no longer shining over Face as the fearsome killer slept like a baby in his king-sized bed. The room was quiet and peaceful with the sounds of birds chirping outside the window. Face's cell phone began to vibrate once again as he'd missed the first seventeen calls. The tyrant began to come out of his sleep, his head moving left to right as he groaned. He opened his eyes, reaching for his phone, and quickly ignored the call and rested his head back on the pillows. The sound of someone clearing their throat echoed through the room, and Face quickly realized he wasn't alone. His eyes shot open, and he quickly sat up and looked about the room.

"'Bout time you woke up." Deuce scrolled through his phone.

"How long have you been sitting there?" Face asked.

"Long enough to know that you're a little handsy with yourself when you sleep," Deuce snarked.

Face threw the covers off of his body and realized he was still in the same clothes from the night before. His hair was wild and unkempt, and his face paint was smeared and blotchy. He grabbed his cell phone, shocked that he had over 17 missed calls, the most important ones from Porter and Simmons.

"Shit, I gotta call my girl back. She gon' be mad as hell I ain't come home last night," Face grumbled.

"You good. I called her for you last night and this morning," Deuce said.

Face stretched and yawned with his spirits lifted as he prepared to live a brand-new day, but there was only one problem that slowed his progression.

"Last night must have been dope," Face said.

"Oh, it was dope all right. You clearly had a lot of fun," Deuce snarked.

"Oh yeah, I...I don't really remember much of it. Like, why did we come back here when the high-rise was downtown? You know my girl stayin' wit' me now?" Face asked.

Deuce lowered his phone and gave Face a blank stare.

"Well, you know, I didn't want drama to follow us home."

"Drama? Oh, you had some women. I gotcha," Face joked.

"That's right, Face. I had so many hoes, I had to shoot 'em off with the sawed-off," Deuce snarked.

Face laughed but immediately stopped, noticing Deuce's angry mug. He tried to jog his memory for anything that might have occurred the night before, but he couldn't pull anything. His cell vibrated with a text from Simmons that added to the tension in the room.

Call me ASAP. We need to talk.

Face slowly set his phone down, afraid to ask what the text might be about. He looked up at Deuce, who also set his phone down and stared back.

"I didn't do nothin' stupid last night, did I?" Face asked.

"You really don't remember anything about last night, do you?" Deuce tilted his head.

Face remained silent, sitting in the bed, embarrassed as Deuce looked off and laughed away his frustration.

"Somebody tried to kill you last night, and I shot him," Deuce said.

"What?" Face jumped.

"Yeah, right there in the VIP."

Deuce grabbed his jacket from the other side of the sofa and pulled out the gun he picked up from his victim. He showed it to Face before placing it on the coffee table.

"With the gun of one of the guards, mind you. He got his ass up there, and I have no damn clue how in the hell he got past security, but somehow I managed to catch his ass right when he got to you."

"What the hell was I doin'?" Face asked.

"You were gone, bruh. Whatever you smoked or drank had you on yo ass. You were sittin' on the couch thingy, you had your head laid back, your arms spread across the headrest with a big ass smile on your face. You looked up at the bastard right when he had it aimed at your head."

"He was 'bout to shoot me in the head?" Face trembled with shock.

"Yeah, man. Lucky I got there when I did. I put a goddamn slug in his back and got us the hell out of there. Had to get the boys to carry you out."

"Carry me? I—" Face scratched his head. "Bruh, I smoked the same weed and drank the same drink we always drink, like, how do I not remember this?"

Face's inability to remember the evening's dramatic events threw him. The thought of a man holding a gun to his inebriated head sent his mind into a whirlwind of dismay. He rubbed his forehead, getting his face paint on his hand, and dropped his hands on the mattress in frustration.

"Did you get a good look at the guy before you shot 'em?" Face asked.

"Nah, I just busted 'em, figured Porter and Simms would take care of that for us. That's probably them that's been callin'. You need to hurry up and call 'em back."

Deuce rose from the couch and headed toward the door.

"Aye!" Face called out.

Deuce looked back at Face after passing the threshold.

"We can't tell Ke-Ke about this," Face said.

Deuce crossed his arms and sighed away his frustration.

"I already spoke to her today, and I left that part out. I'll tell you what I told her, and we'll just run with that, aight? I'm finna get somethin' to drink, you need to get yo funky ass in the shower," Deuce said.

Face lay back on the bed and stared at the ceiling, trying to come to grips with the situation. He grabbed his phone and called Simmons back and was immediately bombarded with a million questions.

"I been...well I...I know it's after 2 o'clock...look, look, look, I'm at the hiding spot, just meet me here. Aight."

Face got out of bed and began to undress to take a long hot shower. As he removed his shirt in the mirror, he noticed spatters of black stains on the shoulder. He examined the stains in the mirror, unable to identify them, and assumed it was dirt from all the moving they had done the night before. He tossed the shirt into the trash and hopped into the shower to cleanse himself of his evening. He exited the shower and wiped the steam from the mirror and stared at himself, face to face with that damaged man in the mirror. He could hear his brother's voice chastising him as a boy for being sloppy with his work.

"You make a mistake like that in the real world, and they'll have you killed," De'Angelo's voice echoed.

He didn't bother to apply his face paint. He just got dressed and grabbed a pair of his shades. Even though his assassin had been killed by his best friend, his confidence was still very shaky, fearful that he might be being sought after by the same people that sought after Blood Hound. He couldn't put his finger on who it could be, considering he didn't keep enemies long enough for something like this to occur, usually killing them off at the height of opposition. His stomach in a knot, Face went downstairs to look for something to eat. A short while later, Porter and Simmons arrived, quite perplexed with Face for returning their calls so late. The four men went down to Face's office to discuss the unfortunate events of the prior evening.

"The hell you mean he wasn't there?" Face shouted.

"No one was found in the club when the SWAT team did their sweep. There wasn't even any blood found up there, just some black stuff that looked like dirt. The shit was spattered everywhere like blood, so we sent a sample of it over to forensics so once we get the results, we'll let you know," Simmons advised.

Face angrily turned to Deuce, staring at him with daggers in his eyes. Deuce carefully watched Simmons as he pulled up the surveillance from the club's cameras. The footage displayed a wide shot of the dancefloor with the VIP section at the top. The bright neon lights lit up the bottom of the screen, allowing Face to show up perfectly on camera.

"You said you shot him, Deuce!" Face grunted.

"I did shoot him! I shot him right in the back!" Deuce defended.

"Then why didn't they find him? Tell me th—"

"Hey! Just watch the goddamn tape," Porter interrupted.

Simmons pressed play, and the party was live once again. Face could be seen taking a drink and smoking at the top of the screen. Simmons fast-forwarded the video and paused it when an unidentified man showed up at the bottom of the screen.

"Keep your eye on this guy," Simmons advised.

The man was unidentifiable, as the camera caught him from the back of the head. He walked across the dancefloor and was suddenly tossed as the crowd jumped like a tidal wave, and soon the man was lost. Simmons fast-forwarded the video a few seconds more, and Face was shown dropping his head back on the headrest. Simmons played the video normally, and a few seconds later the strange man appeared, sneaking into the VIP.

"There he is again. Now what I don't get is that you had all these other people up there with you, how in the hell did they not see him?" Simmons said.

"That's exactly what I was trying to figure out," Deuce added.

The unidentified man stopped and raised the gun at Face, who slowly raised his head.

"And this is where he put the gun to your head. I wonder why he didn't pull the trigger then. I don't know, but he took his time, and then this happened to the poor fella," Simmons said.

The unidentified man's body jolted forward and slammed to the floor as Deuce rushed into view. The crowd scattered like roaches as Deuce commenced a quick sweep of the area and started spilling bottles of liquor on the floor.

"See, I told you I shot 'em!" Deuce bucked.

"Yeah, you definitely shot something," Porter said. "We found the hole the slug left in the wall."

"So how in the hell did the SWAT team not find him? It's not like he just got up and walked away," Face said.

"Keep watching," Simmons said.

The video continued with Deuce ordering a few Illegit members to carry Face to the back of the club. They picked him up and headed down the stairs as Deuce stuffed the dropped handgun into his jacket. Simmons fast-forwarded the video a few minutes and pointed to the top of the screen.

"Now watch this shit."

The shocking video showed the unidentified man start to move and very slowly rise to his feet, hanging onto the railing for dear life. Face's and Deuce's jaws dropped to the floor in dismay as they witnessed the man miraculously come back to life.

"What-in-the-hell!" Face started.

"Y'all better be playin'," Deuce grunted. "This ain't the time for no joke."

"This is one hundred percent not a joke," Porter said. "This man got up and walked out the back of the club before SWAT saw him. Show 'em the other camera."

Simmons pulled up a second camera screen, and coming down slowly from the top was a crippled man, staggering down the hall like a gunshot victim. He held on to the wall to support himself as his legs appeared that they would give out on him at any moment. The four men's eyes were glued to the screen as the man neared the camera by the exit. Simmons paused the video with a clear freeze-frame of the man's face. His face was smeared with black dirt with a large build-up of blackness around his neck and chin. The black substance covered his shirt, exposing the large hole in the front. The man was beaten just beyond recognition.

"Look like anybody you know?" Simmons asked.

"Nah." Face shook his head. "He looks like every other Black guy in Atlanta."

"I don't know a Black guy anywhere that can survive a slug in the back," Deuce said. "He have a vest on or somethin'?"

Simmons zoomed in on the image and focused on the shape of the man's torso. They all looked closer and examined the screen but didn't see anything significant about the man's shape.

"He looks pretty normal to me, and if he does it's a real thin one," Simmons said. "Hell, I can pretty much see the full shape of his chest."

Face ran his hand across his forehead and nervously scratched his scalp while Deuce hastily left the room. Simmons took screenshots of the image and saved them to his laptop to keep as evidence. Porter sighed, rising to his feet, and looked over at Face.

"I don't know what demon you pissed off, but this ain't no regular rival you're dealin' with, kid. If what we are seeing is real, and this guy got up and made it out of that club, then chances are either he or someone else is gonna strike again, and you gotta be ready," Porter advised.

"I've never seen shit like that in my life, and we've seen it all," Simmons said.

Face nervously fumbled his fingers as he rocked from side to side. The imperfect killer had been reduced to that of a scared child lost without his parents.

"W-what do you suggest we do?" Face asked.

"What *you* need to do is simple. Get with Deuce on this and beef up security. I suggest bringin' some of them Illegit boys to wherever you are at night, 'specially 'round your girl. You might even wanna call your boy Hong and see if he might know something—then again, it could be his doing. We got Diaz out of the way, so we know it ain't him, either that or there's some mysterious fourth person that's rivaling against you. As for me and Simmons, we'll handle the police shit. We gotta make this tape disappear," Porter said.

Deuce re-entered the room with his sawed-off shotgun and held it over Face's desk. He cocked the fore-end back, and an empty shell fell from the ejection port.

"I shot 'em, Face. I know I shot 'em! I was too close to miss!" Deuce proclaimed.

Face nervously looked up at Deuce and then exhaled back into his chair, balling his fists together against his forehead.

"Relax man, I believe you, I just...we got some real shit on our hands, bruh," Face said.

Simmons closed his laptop and began to put it into his carry bag.

"Well, look, we gotta get to work on this while it's still hot. Deuce, I've sent you a copy of the images we got. Hopefully, the images are clear enough," Simmons said.

"I can run 'em by some of the boys and see if they recognize him." Deuce laid the shotgun on the desk.

"All right, let me know what you find," Simmons said. "Porter, you think you can sweet talk this back at the station to see if we can get facial recognition?"

"Shouldn't be hard to do." Porter shrugged.

"Okay, we gotta move. I got an email saying forensics has been cleared to investigate, and we gotta get on it before they do. I'll call you guys if we find anything while we're there," Simmons said.

The detectives made their exit, but Porter stopped at the door and looked back at Face.

"Remember what I told you, Face. Don't take this shit lightly."

Deuce plopped into the chair in front of Face's desk and sat back, trying to hold in his frustration. Face looked at his cell phone; there was another missed call from Ke-Ke. He sighed and tossed his phone onto the desk.

"I gotta call my girl."

"And tell her what? We need to figure this shit out before we call anybody," Deuce grunted.

"I know, I know, I just...this is some crazy shit to wake up to."

Another shirt ruined, another chance lost, and another day trying to figure out where we went wrong. We had been up for a few hours, staring back at the ceiling, angrier at ourselves than we were the last time this happened. We hadn't spoken a word to each other since we woke up, replaying everything in our minds that occurred last night. We were right there in front of him with the gun to his head. Why didn't he die? Even if we did get shot, he should still be dead anyway. They say killing gets easier after your first one, so why was this so hard for us? We replayed it in our mind over and over and over again, and finally, we realized what didn't happen.

"Why didn't I sense him coming up behind me?" Ryan asked.

"Because you were focusing too hard on one person when there were multiple things around you that also needed your attention," Heru replied.

"That shouldn't have stopped me from sensing him, though. I thought I could sense danger."

"You can, Ojore, but you were so focused on your objective that you were reluctant to watch after yourself. You channeled your energy on Face, forgetting that there were other energies around that are also linked to the blade you carry, hence why the force of energy you feel from it is so powerful. You separated the entities in your mind, focused on one, and forgot the rest, a tactic that led you to failure," Heru explained.

"Well, why didn't you tell me?"

"Because you must learn from your mistakes, Ojore. Though the duty as your spiritual guide has been bestowed upon me by the ancestors, I must still train you for the war that is before us. I will not always tell you what to do, nor will I always help you when you face danger. Montu faced many battles without the aid of myself or any of the other gods, and through it all, he reigned victorious until his tragic demise. Understand that in this period of time, you aren't facing the challenges he faced in battle. You may fall, but you will rise again against this threat. My duty is to prepare you for the threat that can take you away from this world. I can train you into a warrior, but only you can be the God of War."

We scoffed and banged our head against the pillow. We grabbed our phone and looked at the time knowing we needed to get up. We dropped our phone on our chest and exhaled our frustration with the understanding that we had to learn to stand on our own feet and that we were strong enough to do it.

"I believe you may need a little more training before you venture out again," Heru recommended.

"No." Ryan rose from the bed. "I don't need any more training. What I need to do is stop holding back. There is so much power within me, and I keep tiptoeing around it because I'm scared to use it the way I truly want to."

"What is it that you wish to do with your powers?"

The room was silent for a moment as the question was ignored.

"Once you can answer that question, I'll allow you to rest. For now, we begin our day," Heru said.

We finally got out of bed and started our day, unbothered by the others that lived in the house. We carried the anger from the chip on our shoulder all day. We didn't smile, we didn't meditate. We did try to work on this thing that we had been drawing for a while, ultimately making a few more lines here and there. The clock hit six, and we decided we needed to leave before it got too late. We put on another pair of black cargo pants with a red shirt and a light black jacket to go under our motorcycle jacket. We then reached to the top of our closet, determined to make use of our muzzle tonight. We headed toward the door for our boots while shooting a text to Camille that we were leaving for work. We weren't making time for conversation.

The evening sun began to hide behind the tree line as we dipped through the woods, our eyes sharper, nose wide open. We got to our motorcycle and suited up, riding around town for a while as we waited to be cloaked under darkness. Tonight, the energy from the knife would lead us to a two-story house in an old community just outside of the city. We didn't recognize this energy like we did the others, but we were taking him out anyway. We rode past the house, scoping out the property, and sensed multiple energies on the inside, but didn't see many cars outside. Something was going on in this house, and it wasn't a party. We parked the bike a little way down the street and removed our motorcycle jacket. We rolled up the sleeves of our light jacket and put on the spiked bracers, ready to inflict damage on whoever got close. Our golden gun stuffed in our pants, we snuck through the backyards of the other houses and made our way to the target house.

We stood in the backyard for a moment, observing all of the lights in the windows and found that the house had a basement with a side door, giving us even more ground to cover. We went back and forth about how we wanted to handle this hunt and decided since we were technically going in blind, there was no need to practice stealth. Even though we had a gun with us, we wanted to try and do this without the distraction of a weapon. We strapped on our muzzle and popped our knuckles.

"Are you ready, Ojore?" Heru asked.

"I am the God of War," Ryan replied.

"Show no mercy."

Our eyes red, our teeth sharp, and our hands craving blood, we commenced the heinous attack, aggressively kicking in the side door. The room quaked with fear as half-naked men and women scattered away from the flying door. It flew into a table with a mountain of cocaine on top and made a dust cloud for us to hide under. The gunman watching the room immediately aimed his pistol at the doorway as the others cleared the room screaming, alerting everyone upstairs. He eased toward the doorway, ready to fire at anything that moved, but the poor fool was too distracted to realize that we were right behind him.

"What happened?" We disguised our voice.

He kept his gun aimed at the door, still looking for something to shoot.

"I don't know, bruh, the door just flew in! It was like an explosion or somethin'," he replied.

"I guess I knocked at the door too hard."

"Yeah, I—"

Shocked by the change in our tone, the man quickly turned, ready to fire, but he instead was met with a devastating punch to his face that sent him spinning to the floor. His gun flew across the room, and we watched his body squirm. He was finished. We sensed more people coming and made our way to the door leading upstairs. We listened to the thump of the footsteps and realized that only one person was coming down. We flattened ourselves against the wall and waited for them to cross the threshold. His gun entered the room and readied our hand. At first sight of his neck, we extended our arm and snatched him by the throat. Our claws dug into his neck, making holes big enough for our fingers to slip in through. He dropped his gun and tried to reach for our hand as he gagged on his own blood while we flexed our fingers, cutting through his trachea until we could feel his spine. We flipped our middle finger, and his body jolted and immediately went limp. We let him go, and his body dropped to the floor and bled out.

We had to hurry upstairs before anyone else came down, so we skipped up the stairs and dashed through the basement doorway, finding ourselves by the open front door. It appeared that all of the men and women from the basement had been smart enough to make a run for it. There were small chemical vats on top of wooden crates with all kinds of tubes lying around. It appeared that there was some kind of drug operation going on, but we weren't there to investigate. Our senses heightened when we heard the sound of a gun cocking. He was hiding at the corner, waiting for his chance to fire, a chance we weren't going to give him.

We kicked over a stack of crates and dashed to the other side of the room. The sound of the fallen crates lured the man from behind the wall with his gun drawn, scanning the room. He looked through the doorway and then down to the floor, thinking we had been caught underneath the fallen crates, but we were hiding behind a table in the dining room across from where he was. We grabbed a small container with a clear liquid inside and hurled it at him as hard as we could. The container burst into pieces on impact, and the man began to scream in agony as the liquid in the container burned through his clothes and skin. We dashed toward him and violently kicked him down the stairs. His beaten body tumbled down to the basement, his neck breaking as he smashed into the steps.

We heard the sound of someone running toward the stairs leading to the second floor and decided to meet them halfway. We jolted down the hall to the base of the stairs and hit the light switch on the wall, crouching down in the shadows with our eyes sharp as we waited for a silhouette to appear from the top. Our next victim hurried from the top of the stairs, unaware of the pending danger awaiting him. Just as he got to the middle of the stairs, we leaped from the shadows and tackled him into the stairs, breaking through some of the wood. The impact disabled him, but it didn't stop us from punching him as hard as we could in the chest, breaking his rib cage and forcing the bones to pierce his heart. We punched him a few more times, and finally, his eyes rolled back as he coughed up blood. We left his body stuck within the stairs and continued our way up to finish the job.

There were four doorways at the top, and we could feel someone hiding close behind some of them. We stood in the middle of the hallway, listening to their nervous breaths as their minds boggled, trying to figure out what the hell was happening downstairs. The floor creaked as their bodies trembled at the sound of our footsteps. They were terrified. Suddenly, the door behind us swung open, and a woman ran out from the room, hollering and swinging a crowbar at us. We toyed with her, easily dodging the slow attacks as we smiled behind our muzzle. She swung and missed once more, and we knew she didn't have any more swings left in her. She made a mad dash toward the stairs but wasn't quick enough to get away from our far-reaching hand. We snatched her by her hair and yanked her face-first into the wall, dragging through the old sheetrock. We forced her toward the stairs and sent her violently crashing through the oak wood banister, followed by the sound of a loud thud on the old hardwood floors.

We stepped over to the broken banister to gaze at the mess we'd made downstairs when suddenly we heard the floor creak. We quickly turned to see what the sound was, and that's when we saw the two flashes appear from the darkness of the open doorway. We fell into the wall, struggling to stay on our feet as our breath left our body. The bullets were lodged deep in our abdomen, and we could barely even release a whimper before hearing footsteps pound toward us. We staggered to our feet, clenching our side, trying hard to catch our breath. Now would have been a perfect opportunity to use our gun. Our strength was dwindling, and if we didn't get out of there soon, we'd probably die again.

From the doorway appeared a tall muscular man, pointing a gun at us. The evil stare in his eyes told the story of past murders in cold blood, but if he was going to kill us, we weren't going to make it easy for him. We grunted and charged at him, not realizing how weak we had become. Before our punch could make contact, he slapped us across the face with his pistol and sent us crashing back into the wall, something we could have avoided if we had just fired back. With our black blood leaking from our eye, our energy faded more and more.

The swole killer took his time, each punch feeling harder than the last. He was breaking us, and we couldn't stop him because of the severe pain in our torso. Every time we were about to hit the floor, we'd get hit with another punch that would send us back into the wall. We couldn't even lift our arms to block his punches, literally getting our ass beat worse than when we demolished Terry. His deep, sinister laugh echoed through the hallway, and suddenly the strong giant snatched us by our neck, our feet dangling beneath us as we were being choked with our back against the wall. Why didn't we go for our gun? This was it. We were about to die again.

We slowly raised our arms, trying to knock away his powerful hands, but our power was weaker than it would have been if we were still mortal. Our energy continued to slip, our pain level increased, and the room got hazy and dark. The sounds of the house began to blend into one solid sound of impending death while our hands slowly dropped to our side. We couldn't even feel the grip he had on our neck anymore. Our hand was right by our gun, and we didn't even have the power to reach for it. Just before we slipped off the edge of our consciousness, a strong voice broke the frequency of the white noise blaring around us.

"CONCENTRATE!"

Concentrate. We had to concentrate. The gunshot wasn't killing us; this man, this mortal man was. The pain of the gunshot had distracted us enough to misguide our focus, leading to the most taxing beatdown we'd ever had. As a kid, we would stand at the bus stop during the wintertime, some mornings the low being in the 20s. We had no choice but to stand in the cold as our parents had to be at work by a certain time, and waiting for us would not allow that to happen. Our bones trembled, our teeth chattered, and our fingertips hurt as the blood vessels felt as if they were freezing over...and we survived it. We survived it each and every year. We survived it each and every year because we'd learned to ignore the cold. We ignored the strong cold winds pushing us around as we walked home just as we ignored the pain in our hands to perform a secret handshake with our closest friends. We ignored the stifling cold as if it weren't there. We didn't need our gun, we just needed to concentrate.

Suddenly, the pain in our gut wasn't relevant. Our eyes started to open up again, and the blurry image of a large man choking us came into frame. We felt the rage rushing through our body, and we concentrated our energy into our right arm. We slowly raised our hand and grabbed hold of his wrist, and the strong giant grunted as he tried to squeeze harder. We repositioned our neck and found a spot that gave us a chance to get in a good breath. We inhaled, and we could feel our body recharge with energy. Our eyes refocused, and with our menacing red eyes, we stared directly into the eyes of the giant. We got a firm grip on one of his forearms and inflicted the strength of a wild boa constrictor, digging our claws into his forearm and squeezing as hard as we could. The hallway echoed with the sound of his bones shattering, leading to our quick release followed by his agonizing scream. The Red Dragon was back in the game.

The stupid man leaned to the side, trying to nurse his arm, neglecting the opportunity to go for his gun, and we immediately took advantage of him. We charged at him, punching him in his shoulder and dislocating his good arm, and his gun fell to the floor. We kicked him into the wall, and he broke through the sheetrock into the next room. We quickly pulled our gun from our waist and showed its golden glory off to him.

"Do you have any idea how much these things hurt? Let me show you."

We fired two .50 caliber shots into his gut, and he screamed in pain. We laughed at his suffering as his red blood spilled from the front and back of his shirt onto the hardwood floors. We crept up on him slowly like the Grim Reaper ready to take another soul as the frightened gangster took his last breaths.

"How do you want to die today?" We aimed the gun at his face. "Should I take my time and watch your eyes pop out of your head while I strangle you like you did me, or should I make it quick and spatter your brains all over the floor?"

We looked into his eyes and saw tears rolling down his cheek. "I'll let you decide."

The crippled giant struggled to breathe as he stared at the menacing figure before him. We lowered the gun and inched closer to him, wrapping our hand tightly around his neck and staring into his bulging eyes. His feet kicked around, but without his arms, he had no way to escape our might.

"Did you laugh at my uncle's tears when Face took his life? Did you watch the bullet spatter my cousin's brain on the wall? Tell me how it went. I know you were there."

We squeezed his neck tighter and watched the whites of his eyes spot red. We could feel his pulse becoming weaker, and his energy started to fade as bloody vomit spilled from his mouth.

"You deserve a death more heinous than this, but I don't care about you enough to waste my time with you. I hope they find you with that same look in your eyes."

We flexed our grip and heard the bones crack in his neck. His feet stopped moving, and we couldn't feel his energy anymore. We let him go and stood over his body. The energy from the Buddy weakened as its second victim made his way to join Anpu in Duat. We removed our muzzle and wiped the black blood from over our eye. Our rage calmed as we closed our eyes and exhaled.

"The difference between life and death is a matter of your concentration, Ojore," Heru said.

"I see that now," Ryan replied.

"How are you feeling?"

"I'm okay." Ryan clenched his side. "It doesn't hurt as much, but it stung like a bitch a minute ago."

"As I've advised you before, your healing powers are working independently of you. In time, you will learn to concentrate your energy to where you'll be able to heal your injuries instantly. The injuries may still be present, but the bleeding has stopped thus far," Heru said.

We raised our shirt and observed our bloody side. Our shirt and skin were stained with our dried, black blood formed by the two nasty bullet wounds, but the bleeding had stopped. We could feel the lead bullets inside of us, but it felt like they were slowly shifting back toward the entry wounds.

"This healing stuff is insane," Ryan said. "How long do you think it'll take to finish?"

"It is likely that your wounds will completely heal while you are sleeping. Your healing process is a particularly slow one, as you have not yet learned to concentrate on the process, but there is no need to worry. Your injury is contained, and you are safe," Heru advised.

"Good. I'm gonna look around."

We began to search the four rooms in hopes of finding something of value to our mission. The place was an obvious trap house, so someone would be coming by soon to check up on things. We checked the first room, but there was nothing except old supplies spread all over the floor. The second room had a putrid smell with a small cot in the corner. It appeared that someone was sleeping on their side under a thin sheet, but upon further investigation, it was the dead body of a dope fiend. Our face cringed as we caught a big whiff of the body's stench when we pulled the sheet back.

"Must have been their tester," we said.

We quickly exited the room and closed the door behind us with hopes that we'd be able to free the fiend in his next lifetime. We entered the third room, which was set up like an office with a desk and shelves. We took our time going through everything, dumping the contents of the drawers onto the floor and looking over everything on the shelves, but we found nothing.

"What is it that you seek, Ojore?" Heru asked.

"There's gotta be something here," Ryan said. "This is a dope house, and if it's anything like the movies, there might be something I can use."

We didn't find anything in the office, and there was only one room left. We slowly opened the final door of the dim room and noticed that there were several tables along the walls. We went from table to table, skimming through their contents for something of value.

"What more could there be for you to behold? You possess the power of the God of War given to you by your ancestors," Heru said.

"I don't know; that's why I'm looking. I said there might be something of value to me," Ryan replied.

We searched a few of the tables and found nothing but drugs and some more old supplies. We tried to think of a possible use for some of the stuff, but a chemistry set wasn't something we put on our Christmas list. We searched a few more of the tables, and still there was nothing. Frustrated with our search, we flipped a table and kicked its contents across the floor. Annihilating our target simply wasn't enough, especially since it wasn't the target we wanted. We turned to walk out of the room and happened to spot a black duffle bag sitting on the floor underneath one of the tables. Probably some more supplies, we thought as we scooped it up from the floor. We found the bag had significant weight to it and that we didn't hear any shuffling of glass or plastic material.

"What does the bag contain?" Heru asked.

"Let's find out," Ryan said.

We unzipped the bag and reached inside, running our fingers across what felt like stacks of paper. Our eyebrow raised with curiosity, and we started to get a little excited.

"This can't be what I think it is," Ryan said.

"What might it be?" Heru asked.

"I know this isn't what I think it is."

We picked up the bag and carried it out of the dim room into the hallway. We looked away from the opening of the bag as we reached inside to pull out one of the many stacks of paper inside. We nearly went into shock when we looked back at our hand.

"Holy shit...holy shit...and the bag is full, holy shit...I gotta get the hell outta here!"

We'd hit the jackpot with this kill. There were thousands, maybe even a million dollars in this bag. Drug money, untraceable money, money somebody would never see again. We strapped the heavy bag to our back and headed out of the house the same way we'd come in. Just as we made it to the basement door, we sensed a small bit of energy coming from the gunman we'd taken out on the way in. We slowly approached him to see if he posed any kind of threat, even going as far as to kneel by his face to see how messed up he was. He kept opening and closing his eyes, likely without being in control of the motion.

"Are you going to allow him to live?" Heru asked.

The extra weight on our back made us quite generous for the evening. This man posed no threat, and with the punishment he'd received this evening, more than likely he'd be looking for a new line of work if he were ever able to recover.

"I'll let him live. I need to get this stash home," Ryan replied.

We hurried back through the backyards to our motorcycle and blared our pipes fast down the street on our way back to our hiding spot. Once we arrived, we parked the bike and turned on the light on our phone as we stripped off the bag. We reopened the bag, gazing at the magnificent array of cash crammed inside.

"How much do you think is in there?" Ryan asked.

"I am not sure, Ojore, but it is my belief that it is too much for you to count in one night on your own. What do you plan to do with it?" Heru asked.

We picked up a stack of cash and fingered through the bills. One stack alone was enough to help Camille pay off all of the debts she had outside of the house.

"I'm definitely gonna give my mom some money to help her out. Reginald thinks he runs shit because he helped her get the house, but this is gonna change the game," Ryan declared.

We fantasized about the things we would do with the money. A vacation was definitely in order. We could see Alpharetta on a cruise ship with some strong man waiting on her every beck and call. Maybe with this money, Camille would have the confidence to leave Reginald for good. We zipped the bag up and proceeded to walk out of the door with it until we had a startling realization.

"I can't take this home!"

There was no way this bag would go unnoticed in that house. With Reginald's random searches, this bag would probably be found within a matter of minutes of us getting home. The money was safer in the trap house than it was at my house. We could see him sifting through the bag stealing our money and doing something stupid like buying beer with it.

"Where will you keep it?" Heru asked.

"Can't we travel to the Spirit Realm and stash it there somewhere?" Ryan joked.

"If only life were that simple, Ojore. I believe it shall be safe here. Your machine has gone untouched in the time it has been here, so the same should go for your newfound wealth. I would suggest making some modifications to the outer area to ensure that no one but you can get in; otherwise, this area is safe."

We set the bag back on the floor as we looked around at the condition of the space. It would take us a little while, but we needed to do everything we could to secure the area.

Later that night, a call was made to Deuce while he and Face were trying to get things handled with the night club. They immediately retreated from the hideout and headed into the city to the dismembered trap house to meet one of the shaken Illegit Family members who went by the name Big sitting outside the house in his car. He was smoking a joint and rocking himself back and forth in the driver's seat. As his bosses approached his vehicle, he was hesitant to roll the window down for fear that he'd be punished for having to call them as the bearer of bad news. The pair immediately noticed the man's unusual discomfort and launched their investigation.

"What the hell happened?" Deuce asked.

Big put out his blunt before he addressed the men, still afraid to make eye contact.

"Uh, it was...it was a massacre in there," Big stated.

"That's not telling me what happened," Face replied.

Big cringed with fear and started rubbing his forehead in nervousness.

"Uh, i-it's...it's dead people in there! Everybody's dead," Big blurted.

"What? Man, get out the car!" Deuce ordered.

Big hesitantly got out of the vehicle, keeping his eyes focused on the ground and putting his hands up as he stood with his back against the door.

"I don't want no trouble, boss. I was just doin' my job," Big whined.

"Man, put ya goddamn hands down, relax," Deuce ordered. "You called us out here and said it was an emergency, so I assume you already been in the house, right?"

"Yeah."

"Okay, tell us everything you saw."

Big took a couple of deep breaths and ran his hand down his face. He was still shaking, and his calves were trembling. Deuce scoffed and opened the car door, allowing Big to plop into the seat. The frightened gangster put his face into his hands, and Face and Deuce looked at each other, feeling that there was something strange going on.

"Me and Dre got here at the same time. We were coming to get the money to bring it to Hong's people for the laundering, and when we pulled up, you know, um, we saw that the front door was open. I called ol' boy that runs the house, and he didn't answer, so me and Dre decided to go in."

Big paused for a moment, and his shaking got worse.

"And then what happened?" Deuce asked.

Big started to move his head from left to right, and tears filled the wells of his eyes.

"I ain't never seen no dead body before, man, especially not like that," Big cried.

Face and Deuce groaned with frustration. Big's story had taken long enough to tell, and the bosses were already stressed from the day's events. Face grabbed Big by his jaw and forced him to look into his shades.

"Look here, hold your shit together. You wanna be a part of this family, you're gonna see a lot of dead shit, and hopefully, you won't see yourself, you understand? Now, where's my money?"

Big's eyes widened as the question he feared answering most had come up.

"I-I-I don't know."

"What?" Face shouted.

"I don't know! I didn't make it past the front door. I couldn't handle what I saw in there! Dre went in. He said it was crazy in there. He said it was folks dead right by the front door. It's some dead guy that got beat into the staircase, some trick got pushed through the banister and ol' boy look like somebody shot him and strangled his big ass," Big squealed.

"Hol' on, hol' on...you tellin' me Drax is dead?" Deuce asked.

Big looked down and nodded his head. Deuce stepped away for a brief moment and threw a misguided punch in the air.

"Goddammit!"

"The money?" Face questioned.

"Right! He said he got upstairs and didn't see the bag Drax told 'em 'bout, so he went to the basement. He said the tables were flipped, and coke was all over the floor, but the guard, or whatever, was still alive. He was messed up too, so Dre took 'em to the hospital. He was mumblin' somethin', but we couldn't figure out what he was sayin'," Big explained.

Face crossed his arms and paced back and forth while Deuce called Dre to figure out where he was. Big sat nervously, still refusing to make eye contact with his angry bosses. He trembled as he heard Deuce giving an explicit tongue lashing to Dre in fear that he might soon be joining the others inside the house.

"Someone tried to kill me, Drax is dead, and now my goddamn money is gone. If I don't get some good news soon, I'm gonna start killing everybody," Face said to himself.

Big's sphincter clenched tightly, hearing every word that Face spoke, causing him to rock even harder. He kept his eyes glued to the pavement and tried his best to stay quiet.

"Aight, stay there. We on the way." Deuce hung up the phone. "Dre is at Atlanta-Metro, said the guard is messed up but he can talk. Let's roll."

Deuce hurried back to the car, but Face remained in front of Big with his arms folded. Big could see Face's feet turning toward him and closed his eyes, afraid to see what terrible fate awaited him.

"Big, Big...BIG!" Face shouted.

Big shrieked and fearfully turned his head away from Face and threw his hands up.

"I'm sorry. Please don't kill me. I swear to God I told you everything I know," Big pleaded.

"Chill out, man, you're making me nervous," Face said.

"Sorry." Big quickly lowered his hands.

"It's a lot of crazy shit goin' on, young cat like you needs to be careful. Get the hell out of here and lay low for a while, but make sure I can reach you if I need you, understand?"

"Y-yes, sir."

Face nodded his head and walked back to the car. Big sat motionless in his car as the pair pulled off, still afraid to move. His shaking still hadn't stopped as he nervously wiped his tears away. He slowly reached over for his blunt but found that he couldn't keep his hand steady enough to light it. The shaken boy rested his head on the steering wheel and cried.

Face and Deuce quickly arrived at the hospital and headed inside to find Dre in the waiting area. They took a brief walk down the hall as Dre explained his side of what took place at the massacred trap house. Their stories aligned, lowering the suspicion of foul play, but they still desired to know what happened.

"So when I found him in the basement, it was coke 'n shit all over the floor, the tables were turned over, the door to the outside was all the way across the room, it was like a storm had hit or somethin'. I picked 'em up and got him in the whip and brought 'em here," Dre explained.

Deuce rubbed his chin, piecing together the story in his head. Face's phone rang with a call from Hong, and the night began to get worse.

"Shit!" Face looked at his phone and answered. "Hong... yeah, I know you didn't get the money...I don't know, probably. We're trying to figure that out now. Let me call you back in a few minutes."

Face hung up the phone and quietly rubbed down the tension in his forehead. The other two remained quiet while he took a moment to gather himself.

"You said...he can talk, right?" Face asked.

"Uh, yeah, you just gotta give 'em a second to get his words together," Dre replied.

"Good, I got time. I got all the time in the world," Face grunted.

Dre led the men back to the guard's room while he was being checked by a young nurse. She was reviewing his vitals when the gangly man walked into the room and was completely startled by Face's white paint. Face reached into his pocket while shushing the young girl as her eyes locked on his shades. The guard's eyes shot open, and he began to breathe heavily as he lay in his bed, setting off the monitors as his blood pressure shot up.

"My dearest, I believe there is a patient down the hall that is in need of your gentle care."

The young nurse was immediately calmed as Face grinned while sliding a hundred-dollar bill into her shirt pocket. The shaky girl quickly took the money and exited the room. The terrified guard frantically tried to reach for the remote to summon a nurse when Deuce realized their presence was causing him to lose it.

"Calm down. Calm down, you're safe. We just wanna ask you some questions. Relax, breathe a little bit, we don't need you havin' a heart attack. Be cool," Deuce assured.

The men gave the traumatized guard a few moments to calm down and proceeded to ask him questions about the night. The side of his face was swollen from his temple to his jaw from the earth-shattering punch he'd received. They listened attentively to the man's slow and slurred speech for clues that might solve their mystery.

"It all happened...so...so fast. I was...sittin' by the...the stairs, and sudd—suddenly...it was like...an explosion. The door...it flew in, hit the table. Coke was...everywhere. Next thing I know...I'm on the...the floor. Couldn't move," the guard slurred.

"Did you happen to see anything?" Face asked.

"Uh, yeah, yeah. A man...young man. Black bag...he looked at... at me."

"What did he look like?"

"H-he had...he had...red eyes," the guard said.

Face and Deuce looked at each other, confused as the man's vague description didn't quite match the young man that they had seen in the club footage but did remind them of the visitor the bikers had advised them about.

"You sure he had red eyes?" Face asked.

"Yes, and a...a red...red muz-muzzle," the guard slurred.

Face took a deep breath and exhaled his frustration. He looked over to Deuce, who simply shrugged his shoulders, just as confused as he was.

"Aight. I want you to call us when you get outta here, and make sure I can get in touch with you if I need to, you understand?" Face stated.

"Yes," the guard replied.

"Same goes for you, Dre. I told Big to lay low until we figure this out. You two better not be lying to me. I swear I'll kill you and your families if I find out you had something to do with my missing money," Face warned.

"I swear to God, I don't know nothin'!" Dre pleaded.

"And if you learn somethin', you better make sure you tell me, got it?"

"Yes, sir."

Face and Deuce headed back to the car and sat in silence. Face removed his shades and stared at the sunlight peeking in the other end of the parking garage. His blank expression signaled to Deuce that he was ready to murder.

"What'chu wanna do?" Deuce asked.

"I wanna find my money, Deuce. I wanna find my money and take it to Hong like it was supposed to be delivered, and then I wanna find the red-eyed bastard that took my money and pull his eyes out of his head with a corkscrew and serve them to him on a plate. He's got five million of my goddamn dollars in that bag, and I want my five million back now!"

Deuce started the car, and the treacherous pair left the parking garage. Face sent out a text to his trustees advising them of the missing money and offered a generous reward to whoever found the mysterious red-eyed thief. The game shifted gears, finding the Illegit Family at war with a new and unknown nemesis.

CHAPTER 18

TERRITORIAL AND POSSESSIVE

IT WAS THE calmest week we'd had in months. It was as if a weight had been lifted from our eyebrows because the resting scowl that we were born with hadn't found itself on our face at all. We weren't going around smiling at school, but we were definitely feeling something different for a change, and everyone at school noticed. The masses were still riding on our victory over Terry, but that small victory meant nothing to us. Math had become our favorite subject to study after school because we'd been back to our hideout each day counting the money we'd stolen, and so far, we'd counted over two and a half mil, making us the quiet millionaires that no one would ever know.

We planned on giving something to Camille at some point in time, but we had to be cautious of Reginald. His behavior had gotten a lot worse in the past week. They had argued every day since last Saturday, making this the sixth night we hadn't left the house out of worry for Camille's safety. Though their constant bickering was slowing us down, the energy levels on the Buddy remained about the same, which could only mean they were either still looking for us, or no one important had died yet.

"Tomorrow will make seven days that we have not sought out your enemies, Ojore. We are losing valuable time," Heru said as we roamed the halls.

"You know why we haven't been out, Heru. I can't leave my mom at night with that shit going on," Ryan replied. "Can we talk about this later?"

"No, we must discuss this now," Heru insisted. "It is my suggestion that we start our attack sooner as it will allow you to be at home during those pivotal moments of Reginald's presence," Heru advised.

"Fine, that's cool." Ryan nodded. "Whatever you want."

"Humble yourself, Ojore. Do not allow your newfound wealth to distract you from obtaining your goal. Each day we miss is another missed opportunity."

We scoffed as we walked by another student, who gave us a strange look. We quickly straightened our face and shrugged our shoulders to distract them from the spiritual dialogue as we schmoozed down the hall.

"I'm not distracted. I got this, trust me, and can you please stop talking to me when I'm in the hallways? I keep getting looked at."

Yeah, things had been very different around the school since we'd taken down Terry and his idiot squad. He'd been out of school recovering all week, and it appeared that nobody missed him, not even Aaliyah. She had been different, too. On the surface, you'd think she was going through the lighter end of breaking up because she wasn't smiling as much, nor was she really interacting in class like she normally would, but she wasn't shy when she got around us. She began joining us during lunch with Terrell, telling us what we believed to be the private details of her life. We took the moments to wipe away the dirt covering the windows to her soul. She wasn't sad at all, more so relieved as the understanding mixed into her reality.

"I made a lot of stupid decisions when it came to the guys I dated in school," Aaliyah confessed. "I only dated Terry because...

well, with everything I told you about my childhood, I just wanted to feel protected, so I went for him because I thought he was big and strong."

She looked away embarrassed by her words and lowered her head, trying her best to own up to her ill-managed decisions. We didn't judge her at all. Like us, she was still learning.

"I feel like I lost a piece of myself in this relationship. Like, I don't miss him, but I, I feel so incomplete."

We sipped our drink, knowing there was nothing that we'd be able to say to instantly make her feel better, but we refused to leave this beautiful goddess in this place of despair that the world had left her in.

"I mean, I'm no expert when it comes to relationships. As you can see, I stick to myself as it is anyway, but one thing I do know is that you're not incomplete. My uncle, he, uh, he would say stuff to me sometimes that always made sense because he'd remind me of how old I was, and that things would get better in time. Sweetheart, we're 17, and being 17, we're still in the learning stages of this love thing, you know. Hoping to make all the right decisions is like hoping that someone treats you right because that's how you treat them. It's risky as hell, but we do it anyway. An incomplete person wouldn't be able to sit here and be honest with themselves about the poor decisions they made because that's a complete thought. You have to be well put together to see your shortcomings, and you've gotta be solid to acknowledge them."

We sensed a special calmness from her whenever she was around us this week, but the battle inside us continued on the matter of drawing her close. She was still using those *mezmereyez* against us, and she was winning, too, but it wouldn't work. We weren't the kind of guy she really wanted, at least not to her knowledge. Sure, we could give her everything she'd ever need in life, but she wouldn't want us. Besides, it would take an incredible amount of understanding for her to love what we were. One side felt that she was worth the fight, and the other felt that she wasn't worth the heartache, especially after what had happened when we'd said good-bye to Kristine.

Colb passed a few looks at us during class, trying to figure out what had gotten into Aaliyah. Despite the jovial pervert that he was, he was always very concerned about the students he liked. We just let him know she was going through it, and she'd be okay in time. Her face carried a look of distant gloom, but spiritually she was on the brink of evolution, breaking away from the mindset that had cursed her over the past few years. It's a shame that she had to go through so much at a young age, but the ancestors were kind to her, allowing her to see the truth and be freed before she was exposed to the real world.

The final bell rang, and we walked together to her locker to get one of her books for her economics homework. Maybe it was the cloudy sky and the cool weather we were having, but we sensed an edginess in her spirit on the walk to the parking lot. We could smell the rain coming as we walked to the corner, Aaliyah staring at the spot where she'd once stood aimlessly waiting for Terry to acknowledge her. There was no break in her face as she reviewed her memory of past time wasted, but her spirit was uneasy as we stopped on the corner to go our separate ways.

"Do you have an umbrella?" we asked.

"Nah, I forgot it today. I'll be okay though. One of the benefits of being natural is that I don't have to fear the rain." Aaliyah grinned.

She wouldn't look us in the eye suddenly, nor would she start to walk away. She was pretending to be calm, but we could sense her discomfort. She didn't want us to go.

"I guess that is a benefit, isn't it?" We smirked. "You gonna be okay walking by yourself? I could walk with you if you want."

She looked at us and inhaled deeply and then looked away and nodded her head as she exhaled. That pretty girl couldn't hide from us. She needed a shoulder to lean on, and that shoulder was only available to her during school hours.

"Yeah, I'll be fine. I know a shortcut through the woods, so I'll beat the rain," she replied.

Maybe if we just asked her, she would actually say something.

"Aight, that's wassup. Hey, you sure you're good?"

She took a deep breath and exhaled as she looked off in the distance. After all that she had told us, she was now trying to keep something from us. She looked at us with those brilliant brown eyes, empty of embarrassment, shame, and tears, and told us what was going on.

"Yeah, I'm fine. I...It's just gonna be a long weekend." She grinned.

We reached out to hug her, and she held us tightly, stealing what she felt was her final moments with us. We inhaled the scent of her sweet perfume, and a calmness ran down from our head to the tips of our toes. Sprinkles of raindrops touched our foreheads and signaled to us that the heavy rains would come soon. We didn't want to let her go, but we had to give her the chance to gain the strength to tell us to stay. Not only that, but we were afraid of getting attached. Losing a pretty girl hurts worse when she's as fine as this one.

"I'll see you Monday," we whispered in her ear.

We peeled away from each other, and once again she tricked us into looking into her eyes. There was so much energy between us that fighting it only prolonged the war inside.

"Be safe this weekend," Aaliyah said with care.

"I will. Now get out of here before the rain starts hittin' hard." We grinned.

She took off, waving good-bye as she headed toward the woods, her delightful essence still wrapped around us, gently tugging us in her direction. As badly as we wanted to follow, we had work to do, and we couldn't sacrifice any more time, especially with the current climate. We turned away and began our stroll to our hideout, our grin finally showing itself since no one else was around.

Terry quickly wiped the angry tears from his bruised eyes as he and his boys watched Aaliyah walk into the woods. The five of them had skipped school today and were now hiding out in Terry's car a short distance down the street from the school. The beating Terry had taken from Ryan resulted in them all getting kicked off of the football team, the coach making good on his warning. With no games for them to play on Friday nights, the five-star squad decided to make up their own game. Their first opponent would be Aaliyah, outmatched five to one.

Leo looked over at Terry from the passenger seat, his eyes sheened from the pills they had all taken earlier. The boost in his testosterone urged him to make a move as he tapped his foot and rubbed his thigh, but no move could be made until the ringleader gave the word.

"What'chu wanna do, T?" Leo asked as he readjusted himself.

Terry's eyes followed Aaliyah until she disappeared into the trees where no one knew she would be. Terry pulled his keys out of the ignition.

"Let's go get a touchdown."

The rowdy boys filed out of the car with a hazardous malice pumping through them. Aaliyah unknowingly continued her stroll into the woods, picking up her pace when she felt more of the raindrops splash on her head. She couldn't help but feel foolish for not telling Ryan what was truly on her mind. So many times she'd confidently told others how she felt, but with the week of confessions, her shame barred her from the openness she'd once had. The rain started to pick up, and the cooler temperature in the woods sent a chill down her back. She stopped for a second to zip up her jacket when she heard laughter a short distance behind her.

"Aaliyah!" Terry hollered from the hill.

She turned to see the team of fiends staring at her in between the twisted maze of trees, and her unaided heart was

Aaliyah screamed, "Get away from me!"

Terry stepped toward Aaliyah, his four minions following on his heels. Aaliyah slang mud at the boys as her last-ditch effort to keep them away. A splash of mud landed across Terry's face, and his psychotic smile morphed into his feared death stare. Aaliyah blocked her face and clenched her legs together to prepare for the impact of his boot as he stomped toward her. She closed her eyes, too scared to scream for help.

The heavy rain hid them from the public eye. It hid the sound of them screaming at each other. It hid her unanswered cries for help. It hid the sounds of mud splashing behind them. It hid the sound of tree branches crashing to the ground, but it didn't hide the sound of our roar fading in as we dropped down from the treetops. We came flying down, delivering a destructive dropkick to Terry's chest as he turned to discover what animal had made the roar. He flew into the fence over Aaliyah's head, the fence chiming loudly as the chain links slammed against the aluminum post. He bounced off the fence into a small tree and splashed into the mud puddles forming at the bottom.

We hit the ground, immediately darting at Leo, finishing him with a rising uppercut. We sent him flying into the twisted bushes with a swift spin kick and broke off a tree branch on our way down. We roared as we swung the branch and broke it over the back of one of the three remaining fiends. He went flying off the hill, tumbling into the muddy waters awaiting him below. We hit the ground and charged at the final two, side-kicking one into the other. We caught them as they were falling down and slammed their heads into each other's, knocking them out cold.

Curious as to why she hadn't been hit, Aaliyah hesitantly peeked from behind her guard, and to her surprise, bore witness to Terry barely on his knees being jacked up by a familiar-looking man. Her eyes moved left to right and saw that the other four fiends had been reduced to lawn décor, and she immediately tried to wipe the rainwater from her face to identify the mysterious hero.

We looked into Terry's bruised eyes with a violent glare, fighting back the urge to rip his body into pieces. We could have sunk our claws into his neck and ripped out his trachea, we could have punched a hole through his chest, we could have killed all of them together, but we refused to murder them in front of Aaliyah. Once again, this girl served as their saving grace from the sadistic rage we were holding inside, but we had to make sure Terry was powerless against Aaliyah in the future, so we took from him the strongest weapon he had.

"Stay away from my goddess!" we grunted.

We cocked back our hard fist as we jacked him up by his throat before the hill. We had to remind ourselves several times to use control over our actions, our face scrunching up with even more frustration the longer we kept him in our hand. We roared as we released our fist from its restraint and sent it flying freely toward his open mouth. Our fist landed on his jaw with precision, shattering bone and teeth into pieces as his body ejected from our grip. He flew from the top of the hill and splashed into the large mud puddle awaiting him at the bottom with his dumbass friends to break his fall. We stood victorious at the top of the hill looking down on Terry's beaten body, and we wished it was what we had done the first time. There was no time for us to bask in our victory; our injured goddess was in need. We relaxed our powers and turned to her to offer our aid.

Aaliyah's heart burst with relief as she opened her eyes and saw Ryan walking toward her. Her eyes leaked tears of joy as he approached, removing his jacket to shield her from the calming rain. Just before he knelt at her side, he uttered three words to her that ignited the passion she had desperately been trying to hide from him.

"You okay, baby?"

We knelt down and threw our jacket around her, looking her body over to make sure she hadn't been hurt.

"I–I'm okay," Aaliyah whimpered. "I think my ankle is sprained, and I cut my hand on the fence."

We took her by the hand and quickly examined the cut. It wasn't deep, but it needed to be cleaned up.

"It's gonna be alright, baby. I'ma take care of you," we promised.

We looked up and immediately were locked into the passionate eyes of our beloved. Her energy entranced us, drawing us in toward her soft, luscious lips we'd once pretended we didn't want to kiss. *My Heart Belongs to You* by Jodeci started to play in the back of our mind, and before we could pull away, our hand reached out and gently caressed her soft cheek. We both met in the middle as the raindrops fell onto our soaked heads. We closed our eyes and engaged in the most anticipated kiss we'd been depriving each other of. Her passionate desire traveled through her lips and ignited an inferno of passion we had been holding back for months. She grabbed the collar of our shirt and pulled us closer, sending jolts of passionate magma coursing through our system. Thunder clapped in the sky, and we both slowly pulled away from each other. We stared into each other's eyes, acknowledging the passion between us to be genuine. She bit her bottom lip, and we released a deep groan...there was more than just a kiss between us.

"C'mon, let me take you home."

We picked her up from the cold, wet ground and carried her the rest of the way home, her loving eyes gazing at us as she threw her arms around our neck. We entered her empty home and carried her up to her bedroom, placing her down gently on her bed. The rain had completely soaked our clothes, but we weren't in a rush to get out of them. We knelt down and helped Aaliyah take off her shoes while she removed her jacket and tossed it into the corner. She reached down and caressed our face just as we finished removing her shoes, entrancing us yet again in her *mezmer-eyez.*

"Do you need anything?" we asked, trying to break from the desire.

"All I need is you," she slyly replied. "Can you get the peroxide from the bathroom? It's under the sink."

There was an intense pressure weighing on our chest as we stared back into her eyes. No one else mattered to her at that moment, and nothing in the world concerned her more than what was happening between us. We found ourselves without words, but there was still a portion of us that was trying to run. We hurried to the bathroom to get the peroxide to clean up her hand. She still had on her wet dress, and we wondered why she hadn't changed, considering we had just traveled through the cold rain. We knelt before the soaked goddess, dabbing her hand with a cotton ball. She didn't even flinch as the peroxide stung the shallow cut. She had her sights locked on our helpful face as we tried our best to pretend that we didn't know what she was feeling. Her eyes filled with desire, she grabbed our wet collar and pulled us closer to her sweet face, and our heart skipped a beat.

"I can't let you leave in those wet clothes," she whispered.

There came a moment in time where everything we had learned, everything we had tried, and everything we had experienced suddenly meant nothing to us. The words of the old school music vibrated from the subconscious thoughts in our mind, giving us the understanding of the four-letter word that many no longer believed in. When two souls intertwine, the spiritual link birthed from their interaction aligns them into one entity, making one strong where one is weak, healing one's heart where it is broken, and solidifying the cosmic energies empowering them to conquer each other in an explosive satisfaction that they can only get from each other.

A few hours had passed, and we were quietly getting dressed while Aaliyah slept. Once we had all of our clothes on, we concentrated our energy and emitted our body heat, allowing us to dry our clothes within seconds. We sent a text to Aaliyah's phone, kissing her on the forehead as we snuck out of the house. The passionate interaction put the icing on the cake for the week, starting off our weekend with a bang. We strutted home jamming to our favorite songs, breaking it down in the rain like a '90s R&B singer.

Things were quiet when we got to the house. The rain had caused many delays in traffic, and both Reginald and Camille were stuck out in the midst of it. Earlier in the week, we'd bought some more clothes for our nighttime adventures, and seeing that we had ruined a good amount of our shirts and hoodies, we thought it would be best to set ourselves up with a wardrobe exclusively for the Red Dragon. We put on our new black cargo pants with our black composite toe boots. They felt great, and we knew they'd be great for kicking people in the ribs. We put on one of our new hoodies, something that matched with our pants. It was black, and it had a dope design stitched in red. We liked it so much, we'd bought an extra one just in case we got shot again.

We checked our phone and noticed we hadn't received a response from Aaliyah. She must've still been asleep. We almost forgot that it had already been one hell of a day, but even more, we still couldn't believe we did it. We still had the scent of her perfume dancing around in our nose. There was something significant about her touch, the way she looked at us before she placed her lips on ours. We couldn't allow ourselves to get distracted with her in our thoughts, but the taste of her essence remained on our lips. Our muzzle in hand, we checked out of the house with a grin, heading to dismantle our next target, hoping that the euphoria of the kill would keep us floating.

The rain picked up, creating a soothing resonance outside the window. Aaliyah rolled over, snugly wrapped in her comforter, and extended her arm to the other side of the bed. Subconsciously, she felt that something was different and slowly her eyes opened to a dark screen on her charging cell phone with the notification light blinking. She slowly stretched her limbs and retrieved the phone and checked the message Ryan left her.

Hey Sweets, I had to go. Sleep tight n text me when u wake up.

She smiled as she read his text and sweetly planted her face in the mattress where he'd once lain with her and caught his scent in the sheets. She deeply inhaled the musk of his manhood, rolling over with a smile as she stared at the ceiling. She exhaled a happy sigh of relief as she sat up in the bed and scooted by the window. She opened the blinds to look outside at the rain and found that her father hadn't made it home yet. Soothed by the sound of the rain, she opened her window and wrapped herself back up in her comforter, thinking about what she and Ryan had done, exposing herself to her feelings about him.

She played love songs from her cell phone, singing the lyrics with her hero in mind. She reimagined the entire fight, plugging in what she thought might have happened when she'd had her eyes closed. She remembered how strong Ryan's arms had felt when he picked her up and carried her home and how safe he'd made her feel after he took her shoes off. She gripped the sheets and ground her body against the mattress with her eyes closed, reimagining everything that happened after they'd kissed again. She could still feel his hands caressing her face and running down the small of her back. Suddenly, her mind shifted, and she opened her eyes and put a thought into the universe.

"I want to be with him."

She looked over at her reflection in the mirror, her hair wild and frizzy from the rain. She could see a familiar look in her eye, that look that had gotten her into trouble a few times over the years, but this time there was something different about it. She smiled confidently in her thoughts as she held up her phone, feeling nervous at how to respond to his text. Glancing over her emojis, she leaned by her window and played with the thought of having his last name.

We found ourselves savagely breaking down another trap house, but this time it was a little different. There were no half-dressed people packaging cocaine; it was just a bunch of boys hanging around, smoking weed, and drinking up. They clearly weren't aware of our arrival, nor were they prepared for the brute force we issued to them after we broke through the front door. The darkness of the skies allowed us to be creative with our kill tactics. We knew there would be guns, but we refused to allow the threat of bullets to stop us from finding who we were after.

We snatched up a guy standing nearest to the front door and quickly dragged him outside, his disloyal gang unwilling to follow after him to find what was beyond the threshold of the broken porch lights. They heard him beg for his life, and shortly, everything went quiet. The foolish gangsters watched the open doorway with their guns drawn, listening to the sounds of the rain. We just so happened to get lucky with our catch as we found his shoulder holster equipped with two pistols and four extra clips. We felt this setup might prove to be useful for this situation, so we stuffed our golden gun in our hoodie and stole the poor fool's weapons. We hated using guns, but until we learned how to shoot ki-blast from our hands, they would have to suffice.

We could sense the majority of the men standing in the living room and aimed the cannons toward the window. We opened fire, feeling their energies panic sporadically or fall completely. The first two mags emptied, we ducked underneath the window seal and reloaded. We could hear the groans of the men we hit as they bled out on the floor and readied ourselves for the second attack. Just before we reentered the house, our cell vibrated in our pocket, and we just knew it was Aaliyah. We didn't have time to check the message, but the thought of her turned our mission into an adventure pretending that she was trapped inside the house, and we were coming to save her.

"I'm comin', Sweets!"

We barrel-rolled to our feet and shot at anything that moved as we entered the house. The Red Dragon had come to slaughter everyone inside as we stared down the sights of our pistols with our red eyes. We kicked down doors to bedrooms, gunning down anyone inside whether they posed a threat or not. We could feel a few more energies scattered about the house. They were either scared and hiding or waiting for their chance to attack.

Suddenly, the lights clicked off, and gunshots rang out from another part of the house. We dropped to the floor and groaned as we watched for the direction of the blinking blast from their guns. Shortly after the lights clicked on, and to the two shooters' surprise, their target was gone. They panicked, looking at the floor before them, not realizing that we were standing behind them with the loaded cannons to the backs of their necks. We ejected a bullet from each gun into their spines, offering a small chance of survival for them at point-blank range.

We could hear someone breathing behind the couch near the front door and crept over to show off our new toys, careful not to step on the dying men scattered across the floor. With each step we took, the breaths got heavier and heavier until we were directly behind the person we'd heard. We jumped over the couch and landed in front of them, shoving our evil eyes in their face. He shrieked like a frightened schoolgirl, kicking his feet into the floor and pushing himself away from us. We allowed him to get up and run, and he dashed out of the doorway screaming for help as he ran down the block. Before we could turn our head, another gunner emptied their clip at us. Our eyes shot open, watching the bullet holes in front of us form in the wall. His gun clicked and cocked back after the final bullet rang out, and we found ourselves in disbelief as we discovered that the violent banger couldn't shoot. We slowly turned our head around like a perched owl and took aim at him with one of the guns, firing one bullet between his eyes. The white wall behind him splattered with red blood, and his body fell to the floor to join the other dying fools.

We crept through the house, sensing one more energy hiding somewhere inside when suddenly, a folding chair was flung at us from across the room. We aimed at the mysterious chair thrower standing confidently against a wall, his hands open and ready to duel.

"C'mon!" he hollered. "Put the guns down and fight me!"

We grinned behind our muzzle at his invitation for battle and tucked the pistols into their holsters. We kept our guard down and slowly walked toward him like the villain in a horror film. He ran up to us, throwing haymakers and sucker punches, but only fell deeper into his cinematic demise as we dodged and blocked his misguided attacks. We pushed him into the wall, but the fool refused to accept his fate, still trying to fight the losing battle. He charged back, swinging a tall floor lamp, the near misses costing him shots to the ribs from our new boots. He fell to his knees holding himself, and boy did we make him wish he had been smart enough to run.

"You didn't give my uncle a chance to run, did you? No, you helped beat him and watched him cry as his son was murdered in front of his eyes."

The foolish gangster wheezed for air, his head drooping down to the floor. He rested his head on the rug, his struggle to breathe worsening as he flattened his body along the floor. We placed our boot on his head and looked down on him for being so pathetic.

"If you're fortunate enough to live another lifetime, I encourage you to run when you see me."

We stomped his head into the floor, and his blood splattered across the room like a grape run over at the grocery store. His blood reminded us of the mud we'd run through as we destroyed the athletic wastes of sperm earlier that day. Rather than play around in the puddle of blood like we wanted, we immediately ransacked the house, searching for anything of value.

On the other side of town, Face and Deuce were meeting with Hong at his underground casino. They were discussing the five-million-dollar loss they'd taken in the previous week, Face fearing the money would be a total loss. Hong tried his best to understand the story the men gave, but there was one detail given that didn't make sense to him.

"There is no way that one man did all of that alone." Hong stroked his hair.

"A part of me feels like I'm being lied to," Face agreed, "but looking back on the situation, my guard was pretty messed up, and the hospital isn't gonna take just anybody who says they're sick. He's still in there recovering."

Deuce poured himself a drink at the minibar while reviewing text messages from previous days on his phone.

"Yeah, and I had a few street teams out there lookin' for somebody who fit that description, but ween found nobody," Deuce said. "You'd think the red eyes shit would make it easier, but folks don't even take you serious after hearing that."

Hong stroked his hair and grinned at Face's frustration as he kicked his feet up on his desk and reclined back in his chair.

"It appears you are being haunted by the angry ghost of our friend Diaz," Hong laughed.

"That's not funny," Face scolded.

"On a serious note, it is my suggestion that we keep this between us and leave Nassar out of it. It took a while to convince him of your worthiness, and he does not know you the way I do. I fear he may not want to conduct business with you if he finds that you are already having problems," Hong said.

Face dropped his head back and looked at the ceiling, releasing a loud groan.

"I gotta find my damn money. It's gotta be somebody on the inside, man. I know it," Face said.

Deuce received a text and suspiciously stepped out of the office as he replied.

"I'll be right back."

"Everything good?" Face asked.

"I'm 'bout to see."

Face sat back in his chair, turning his head left and right as the office door closed. Concerned for Face as he twiddled his hair, Hong decided to make Face an offer to help set things right.

"I can help you make your money back," Hong said.

"What do you mean?" Face raised his brow.

Hong opened the desk drawer and pulled out a black ledger book and a pen. He opened the book to the current month and placed his fingers on a date two weeks from the current day.

"I was going to wait to do this because I wanted you to get used to how things work in the districts, but you have proven yourself to me over the years, and it seems you've hit a point of desperation." Hong tugged his hair.

"I'm listening."

"Of course, you know the districts serve merely as a hub for the state, but my family has extended their reach beyond the borders of the state, and we're all around the nation. It is time, I believe, that I get you introduced and well versed with the family. I have a shipment arriving in California two weeks from now that will be risky to bring here because of federal operations, but if you can get a few of your men to retrieve it from the docks and bring it to me, the payout will be substantial," Hong offered.

Face grinned, and his evil laugh gurgled from his throat. He extended his hand to Hong, and they shook with a smile.

"Thank you," Face said.

Deuce nervously reentered the room, releasing a sigh as the conversation he had did not end well.

"Just make sure you find out who stole your money," Hong joked.

The men laughed together as Deuce approached them with anxiety. There was more bad news to be delivered.

"We got a problem," Deuce interjected.

The men turned to him, Face fearing the irony of losing something else just after receiving something that might progress him forward.

"What the hell is it now?" Face grunted.

Deuce sighed and rubbed his forehead as his vibe became more and more disturbed. He regretted giving his cell number to some of his Illegit Family.

"Another house got hit."

"What?" Hong tugged his hair.

"Goddammit!" Face banged his fist on the desk. "When?"

"Less than an hour ago," Deuce said. "One of the guys that was there is gonna meet us downtown by the Ferris wheel. We gotta roll now."

Face angrily grabbed his jacket from the chair and stormed toward the office doors.

"I'm tired of this shit, man! The hell is going on out there? Hong, I'll call you when I figure this shit out."

The two shot across town, anxious to meet with the responder. Face rode in the backseat with his gun lying across his lap, blending in with his black clothing. His anger rose higher with each moment that passed, contemplating whether he would kill the poor man if he didn't answer the questions to his liking. They made their way through the city streets unenthused by the city lights and festivities going on around them. They fast approached the Ferris wheel, Deuce recognizing a familiar face as he pulled up. He rolled down the window and hollered over to the frightened young man.

"Get in the back!"

The man got in the back seat of the dark tinted car, not paying attention to Face sitting on the other side of the seat as he closed the door.

"The hell is your name?" Face scolded.

"Oh, shit!" the young man shrieked, quickly spotting Face's gun aimed at him.

The young man scooted his body all the way up against the door, his fear returning to him as if he were in front of the red-eyed killer. Deuce kept his head facing forward and headed toward the damage site just outside the city.

"Your name?" Face grunted.

"Corey! Corey Cole!"

"Relax, Corey, you're making me nervous, and I have a gun in my hand. I wouldn't want my finger to slip and spray your blood all over my leather seats," Face said calmly.

Corey took a few deep breaths and eased himself comfortably back in the seat.

"That's it. Relax. Now put your seatbelt on," Face instructed.

Corey nervously fastened his seat belt, keeping his eyes on the barrel of Face's gun aimed at his side.

"Tell me what happened tonight, Corey."

Corey's nervous breathing warmed the cabin of the car as he wiped the sweat from his forehead. He quickly tried to recall everything he could remember from the house, afraid that his nervousness might bring him more trouble.

"Um, we, um, um, I, we–"

"What happened tonight?" Face roared.

Corey quivered and nervously clenched his hands together. He no longer felt the need to try and cover up the situation because he figured he would be dead soon either way.

"We were havin' a party at the house and–"

"A party?" Deuce hollered as his eyes pierced through the rearview mirror.

"Y-yeah. I mean, yes, yes, sir."

Face slowly removed his shades as he grasped the already ill-explained situation, his gun still aimed at Corey's torso.

"You son-of-a bitches had a party...when y'all were supposed to be workin'... and did not invite me?" Face scolded.

"They ain't een invite you, Face. They said to hell wit' dis Illegit shit," Deuce instigated.

Face sank his head into his hand and started to gently shake as his stress level rose. Suddenly, he jolted toward Corey and snatched him by his locs, painfully forcing the barrel of his gun up Corey's nose.

"Do I look like a goddamn clown to you?" Face roared. "I just lost five million dollars, and you bastards are having a party? I'd kill you if most of you weren't already dead!"

Corey closed his eyes, his heart pounding through his chest. His hands were up, shaking due to his forced surrender.

"I asked you a goddamn question, boy," Face roared.

"No, sir?"

"Do-I-look-like-a-clown?"

"NO, SIR!"

"So why you playin' wit' my money like it's a goddamn circus? You lucky we in this car or I'd put a bullet in your face," Face threatened.

"Now keep talkin'," Deuce added.

Face drew back his pistol, still angrily staring at Corey. Corey was so shaken that the fear numbed him. His head sank down, and his words became monotonous, matching his blank expression.

"There was a party. We were smokin' and drinkin' and shootin' dice. The door broke down and somebody got dragged outside. Everybody started shooting, and then everybody started dying. I hid behind the couch, and some dude with red eyes jumped—"

"Red eyes?" Face interrupted. "You get a good look at his face?"

"He had something covering his face, like a muzzle, and he had on a hood," Corey said. "But the skin around his eyes was light brown, so he's probably Black."

Face thought back to his beaten guard in the hospital and remembered how clear he was about the man with the red eyes. He feared that Hong's joke might be true.

"Why didn't he kill you?" Face asked.

"I-I ran. I was scared," Corey confessed.

Face sighed and looked out of the window, trying to hide his fear. He stared at the passing buildings and exhaled a deep breath.

"What'chu thinkin', man?" Deuce asked.

Face shook his head, unable to answer the question.

"Just drive to the spot. We need to see how bad it is," Face said.

The men soon pulled up to the spot, and Deuce immediately noticed that the front door was missing. They parked on the opposite side of the street and observed the dark house. It appeared that no one else had been by, nor had the police been called.

"We goin' in?" Deuce asked.

Face hesitated to answer, fearing that his red-eyed nemesis might still be lurking inside. He looked at the distraught Corey and mustered up the courage to enter the house.

"Hell yeah, we goin' in. Corey, you stay in the car, and you better not try to leave. I'll find you and I'll kill you, understand?" Face threatened.

"Yes, sir."

Face and Deuce crept over to the house, carefully watching their backs. They pulled out their cell phones and pulled up the flashlights and entered the house. The two were rocked into disbelief, discovering the morgue of bodies laid out across the living room. Not one living soul was found in the house, and every room had been trashed just like the last house.

Corey sat in the car reevaluating his young life and felt that he wasn't cut out to be Illegit. He pulled out his cell phone and sent a text to his mother begging her to let him come back home. Just as he was about to get out and run away, Face and Deuce emerged from the house with their guns in hand. They walked over to the car and opened Corey's door, signaling for him to get out.

"It's a goddamn slaughterhouse in there," Face said. "You're sure that it was some dude with red eyes that did all this?"

"You sure you ain't have nothin' to do with it?" Deuce scolded.

"Yes, sir. I wouldn't lie to you," Corey replied.

"Good, because we'd kill you and your family, too. Now, here's what's about to happen. You're going home, you're gonna stay there until you get the word from me that it's okay to come back to work. Keep your mouth shut and stay out of trouble. If you see anything, you call, got it?" Face instructed as he and Deuce got in the car.

"Yes, sir."

"Now get outta here."

The fearful two pulled off, leaving Corey in the dark streets still shaking from the events that had transpired in the car. He soon realized his trip home would be harder to do as he'd left his cell phone in the backseat of the car. He looked at the cars aligned on the street and ran across one that he liked. He quickly rid himself of his terror and headed back into the dark house to find the body that had the keys to the car he wanted.

Getting back on the interstate, Face and Deuce contemplated their next course of action. Face had finally calmed down and regained his composure as images of the bodies he'd seen flashed in his head. This was the second house in a week to get demolished, though the loss wasn't as financially traumatic, being only a few hundred thousand. Though Hong had given him a silver lining for his finances, the loss was still a loss, and they were no closer to solving the mystery as to who the red-eyed vigilante was.

"Are Porter and Simmons done with the club yet?" Face asked.

"Man, hell nah." Deuce sucked his teeth. "They talkin' 'bout Internal Affairs investigating the office 'n shit, so it's gon' be a while 'til they can do other shit."

"Dammit, man. We gotta figure this out," Face said. "We can't afford to keep taking Ls like this."

"I know, but you got other shit on ya plate right now. I'ma drop you at the high-rise so you can check on ya baby, and I'ma see what I can do about this."

Face smiled at the thought of his beloved Ke-Ke and the baby boy they'd soon bring into the world. He felt that as long as they were safe, everything would be okay.

"Thanks, bruh, but don't stress yourself out too much. Hong made a deal with me that's gonna get us paid real soon, we just gotta stop shit from happening until then," Face said.

After a weekend of phone calls and a few confessions, Monday morning came with a few changes that were quite unexpected. The journey to school was a little extended today as we were escorting a special someone. The walk was a little different as there was an extra hand to hold. It was almost unbelievable as we approached the school because nothing was official until everybody saw it. Here we were with Aaliyah, hand in hand with the most beautiful girl in the world, us, the quiet guy that liked to draw, holding hands with a goddess. It was a publicity stunt; there was no way she could actually be this into us.

We approached the threshold of the cafeteria, the place where everybody hung out for breakfast in the morning, and she still hadn't let go of our hand. We had to make sure this was real, that this wasn't some sick game she was playing with our emotions.

"You sure you really wanna do this?" we asked.

She hit us with that bashful smile, that mystic glare of love reflecting in her eyes. If there was a look that made us any surer that she was serious, it was that one. No longer was it just a smile that she gave everyone; it was the smile she gave us. She wasn't being just a friend to us anymore—she was our girlfriend.

"I've never been more sure of anything in my life," Aaliyah sweetly replied.

Her soft words attacked our heart, and that cheesy smile we'd worked so hard to hide emerged from the hellish depths of our soul where we'd buried it in middle school. We crossed the threshold into the cafeteria, and suddenly it was all eyes on us. *Face forward, don't smile, okay grin, look cool,* we told ourselves as we took the first five steps. Aaliyah walked showing off her confidence—either that or she must have sensed how nervous we were because she went from just holding our hand to cuffing our arm and locking our elbows as the eyes of the other students followed us. She made it clear that we were her man. The goddess had finally found her god.

CHAPTER 19

BETRAYAL OF THE FAMILY

THE PAST COUPLE of weeks had been quiet around the house, days sometimes going by without Camille uttering a word toward us. The most conversation had was them having short arguments about bills and his alcoholism, but we didn't have time to focus on the silence between us. We were in our room preparing our clothes for tomorrow evening's slaughter. The new hoodies had proven to be durable in the wash and even better at rejecting blood stains from our victims. We were putting new laces in our boots as we learned an informative lesson about our history.

"Anpu and I have fought many battles against the terrible three, and though we've yet to defeat them, the toughest battle I've faced was with their father Set," Heru said.

"What was so tough about him?" Ryan asked.

"Though Set was evil, he was still a god and my uncle. He had been around long before I recognized my potential. To be truthful, Set could have easily killed me like he killed my father, but his dishonor is what essentially led him to his death."

"What did he have against your father?"

"We may never truly know the reason, but from what I observed, I would think it had something to do with power. It is unbelievable how deep sibling rivalries may go. I suspect that there may also be a rivalry between the terrible three, but they are linked by their father's evil ways. It's what keeps them bound."

"Tell me about it," Ryan chuckled. "Antonio tried to kill me when I was a kid. You and Anpu almost met me a whole lot sooner."

We finished lacing one boot and tried it on to make sure the fit was perfect. We then laced the second boot the same as we did the first.

"Yes, it is fortunate that you were the one that survived," Heru said. "The distance between you and your father is understood; however, I must question why you never speak of your sister."

"Because I don't have any siblings," Ryan laughed. "I'm the only child here if you haven't noticed."

There was an awkward silence as we tried on the second boot. We stood up and stepped around to assess how it felt to walk around with them on our feet. The added weight gave a more solid movement to our kicks.

"I should have invested in composite toe boots a lot sooner, the cushioning, too. I could fight in these for days," Ryan said.

"Ojore, are you unaware of your sister?" Heru asked.

We lowered our foot to the ground, an awkward expression turning our face. We were Camille's only child, but we hadn't seen Antonio in a little over a decade. Of course, it only takes nine months to birth a child, but there had never been a discussion between us and Camille about siblings. There was a conversation we'd had in the car with her eleven years ago about wanting a little brother, but that went no further than a conversation.

"What sister?"

Another awkward silence fell over the room as we anxiously waited for an answer to our question.

"Lie down, Ojore. We will discuss this in the Spirit Realm," Heru said with sorrow.

The high-speed travel across the universe didn't seem fast enough as we transitioned to the Spirit Realm. Our mind overflowed with curiosity, our biggest concern being Heru's saddened tone. Upon entering the Spirit Realm, Ryan's fiery aura formed and carried him down through the misty skies to the rough sands to meet Heru. As he touched down, he noticed Heru was standing before him with his back turned, an unusual behavior for the Sky God. He could sense Heru's anxiety, and his curiosity began to scare him a little.

"What's going on?"

Heru turned to see Ryan's curious eyes and lowered his head, heavy with sorrow. He sighed, for he knew that there was no way he could bring himself to delay the conversation. He raised his hand and from the sands formed two stone benches across from each other.

"Sit with me, Ojore," Heru said.

The two would normally sit upon the rough sands enraptured by their auras as they meditated, but the intensity of this conversation called for the elder god to require a real seat. The two sat down, Ryan reading Heru's strange body language as he adjusted himself for the nature of the conversation. Unable to patiently wait through Heru's silence, Ryan aggressively jumped into the delicate matter.

"So Antonio has another kid I didn't know about?" Ryan asked.

The troubled god lowered his eyes, unable to look at his young pupil.

"Yes, Ojore. Antonio's seed sowing didn't stop after your birth, unfortunately. He went on to conceive just one more," Heru answered.

Ryan palmed his head and rubbed his chin, trying to piece together a timeline in his head that would explain when his sister may have been born.

"So why didn't you tell me about her when you met me?"

"It was my assumption that you possessed that knowledge."

Ryan angrily grunted his frustrations, the flames of his aura sparking up around him. Heru sat attentively, his eyes resting on the rough sands beneath them. Ryan took a few deep breaths and calmed himself, showing progression in control of his powers as his rage reached a new maximum.

"I'm not mad at you. It's just...after all these years, Antonio... still pisses me off to this day. Like, I keep finding his mishaps over time, whether it be a flaw with me or this. I just...I just can't win with him," Ryan explained.

"Your frustration is understood, Ojore."

Ryan stood up and began to pace back and forth to walk off his anger, his aura calming with him. He walked back to the bench and sat down, rubbing the back of his head.

"I'm okay, I'm okay. So where is she? I wanna meet her, and please don't tell me she lives in Decatur, because if we were that close to each other all of this time, I'm really gonna get pissed," Ryan groaned.

Heru remained silent, his eyes glued to the rough sands. Ryan looked at Heru in awe, throwing up his hands in disbelief as he smiled.

"You can't be serious right now," Ryan laughed. "She lived that close to me? Might as well go find her now."

Heru lowered his head and sighed as the pain in Ryan's humor breached his heart.

"You can't."

The energy in the realm changed. Ryan glared at Heru with misunderstanding, his spirit disturbed from being told no. It was not often that Heru told him that there was something that he couldn't do.

"What do you mean I can't? She's my sister!"

Heru raised his head and focused his eyes on Ryan's. He swallowed the pressure in his chest and prepared himself for the worst.

"Because of the psychological oppression the world presented to her, the young goddess wasn't strong enough to win her battle with depression. Sadly, she saw fit to take her own life."

Heru's words echoed through the Spirit Realm and bounced around inside of Ryan's head. His last breath escaped his body as if his soul had been taken. His mouth fell open, and his eyes were in shock as found himself frozen in place. Tears rolled down his cheeks as his brain deciphered his mentor's words. Heru closed his eyes, feeling the strain tearing at his pupil's heart.

"Suicide?" Ryan whimpered.

"Yes."

Ryan dropped to his knees and dug his hands into the rough sands. His emotions unraveled as he broke down. A sibling's love that he never knew had come and gone without his knowledge, and the hurt of discovering her tragic end fractured his spirit. How could he not have known? Why didn't anyone bother to make him aware? Could his presence in her life possibly have helped her divert her from her demise? So many unanswered questions for an unknown soul.

"It's not too late, Ojore. I can take you to her," Heru said.

Ryan's body shook as he attempted to gather himself. He battled with Heru's offer in his head, understanding that the meeting wouldn't be a heartfelt reunion. He looked up at Heru and dried his eyes, the two with sorrow heavy on their hearts.

"Take me to my sister."

Heru helped Ryan to his feet, and the two traveled over to Duat where Anpu awaited their arrival. The two gods met Anpu on an open plain of the dark sands, and standing close behind Anpu was a shy teenage girl. They walked from opposite sides of the plain and met in the middle, the two young siblings nervous about their first meeting. The shy girl peeked from behind Anpu as Ryan fought hard to hold back his tears. Anpu gently took her by the hand and eased her from behind him.

"It is okay, this man will not hurt you," Anpu assured her. "He is your brother, Ojore, the God of War."

The young girl stepped from behind Anpu and revealed herself to her brother, who was shocked to see their uncanny resemblance. Her eyes were almond-shaped just like his with a similar facial structure, leaving no room for denying that they were siblings. Ryan slowly approached the young girl while she nervously fumbled with her fingers.

He extended his hand to her. "Hi. I'm Ryan, your brother. What's your name?"

"Remember, she can't speak to you here," Heru reminded.

The nervous girl was reluctant to reach out and shake her brother's hand. She lowered her head and stepped backward toward Anpu. Her eyes were distressed, and Ryan could sense a hint of fear from her spirit. The young god couldn't understand her discomfort.

"She was known as Janay. She was only 15 when she found herself here," Anpu said.

Ryan looked at his distraught sister and found that they carried a similar pain.

"What happened?" Ryan asked.

Anpu placed his hand on Janay's shoulder to comfort her, and Ryan took a few steps back to give her space. He struggled to keep still, resisting the urge to hug his beloved sister.

"Antonio's negligence affected Janay from a very young age. She spent her younger years wondering why he did not love her as a father should. Her life lacked a positive male figure, and as years passed, her sorrow evolved into an unraveling depression, and that depression was one day pushed to its limits by Antonio's ignorant irresponsibility."

"Don't forget what I told you about your father. He'd lie to get into heaven if he could," Janay's mother said to her as she exited the car.

"Hey, my sweet baby! Daddy missed you," Antonio lied.

Janay smiled, trying not to fall for the evil antics of her father that her mother warned her about. It seemed his sinister charm was still effective in the midst of her teenage years.

"You and your damn mother with this child support shit. What do you even really need? I should have given her the

damn money for the abortion like my boys said. What the hell was I thinking?"

Janay relived the pain she carried from her childhood, a pain that manifested from the hurt of a love that was never provided. A hurt that manifested into a deep depression.

"If it were up to me, you'd be better off dead. You and your brother! All the two of you have ever done is take my goddamn money from me! And your mothers, the goddamn bitches, they don't deserve one red cent!"

Her father's words echoed in her head daily as a constant reminder that he would never love her the way that she deserved. His unkind words led her to her mother's medicine cabinet, where she found some leftover pain medication from a surgery her mother had had. Without care or supervision, each one of the pills painfully slid down her throat, dissolving and attacking her vital organs until they were rendered defenseless by Antonio's evil words echoing in the darkness surrounding her spirit.

"Janay, I'm home...Janay, girl why didn't you put the meat in the sink like I asked you...Janay...Oh my God, Janay! Janay! Wake up, baby, no! Please, Lord, not my baby! No! Janay!"

"He corrupted her spirit from the inside out. His constant disapproval caused her to take herself away from the world before she could learn to love herself. The most unfortunate thing in this matter is that she came here in search of peace, only to find devastation. It is as if the cycle of torment is an endless one for her."

The harrowing story forced the tears from Ryan's eyes, his senses homing in on her resistance.

"And when she looks at me, she sees him."

"Wipe your eyes, for you know that you are a greater man than your father will ever be. You are the God of War, a prestigious title, an honor greater than any mortal honor that can be bestowed upon you," Heru declared.

Ryan feared his frustration might frighten Janay, so he took a brief moment to capture himself. He wiped his eyes and straightened his face as best he could before he stepped across the dark sands and knelt at his sister's feet. Her eyes widened, shocked by his submission as she looked into his teary eyes.

"Janay, there's so many things I want to say to you right now, things that would take an eternity to tell you. First, I want to make something very clear: I am not Antonio. I don't love Antonio, and I will never treat you the way Antonio treated you. The only thing he and I have in common is blood and light skin. Blood doesn't make you a father. There are several qualities that go into making a man into a father, and he possesses none of them. I've lived my entire life wishing I had a brother or sister to love and protect just as my uncle did me, and I've lost him just like I've lost you. Even worse, I didn't even know I had you when you were here," Ryan cried.

He dropped his face into his hand and wailed out loud, exhaling whatever pain he felt inside. Heru approached him and placed his hand on his shoulder again, bringing calm to the resting wrath Ryan struggled to hold inside. Anpu observed Janay as she stood motionless before her grieving brother.

"I love you, little sister. I love you very much. I will live for you, I'll live every day for you, and not only will I live for you, but I will right the wrongs of history and set you free from this place. I will bring peace to your soul so that you may live among the gods and goddesses like you deserve."

The warrior god rose to his feet and dried his eyes with a newfound motivation. There was a new flame in his heart that had come from the deep trenches of her hurt. Her pain was now his pain, his revenge was to avenge her untimely death.

"Thank you, Anpu, for bringing her here for this. She needed to see that there was someone in the world that truly cared for her," Ryan said.

"It is the work of the ancestors that brought us here, Ojore, but be encouraged, for her mother still lives," Anpu replied.

Ryan's eyes widened as the small ray of hope gave him a chance to gain more understanding.

"She does? Where is she? I'll go wherever she is!"

"Stand still, and I will give you the knowledge you seek," Anpu said.

Ryan planted his feet and observed as Anpu put his middle and index fingers together. From the tips of his fingers formed a small golden orb that he raised to his forehead.

"With this power, I bestow this knowledge upon thee before me to see things the way that they should be."

The golden orb was now charged with miniature jolts of energy traveling around it. Ryan closed his eyes as Anpu placed his fingers upon his forehead, allowing the knowledge of the orb to be absorbed by his brain. His eyes shot open with a golden glow as the knowledge settled into his mind.

"I can see it. She is alive, but she is unhappy. She is distressed. She needs my help, immediately."

He closed his eyes, and they returned to their natural state. A new mission had been added to his workload, but he was still curious and full of questions that his sister was unable to answer. He hoped that meeting his sister's mother would give him greater insight to who she had once been.

"Come on, Heru, I gotta get back home. I have a lot of work to do."

The two began to walk off, Ryan still in wonderment of the life of his baby sister. He despised not meeting her while she was alive, for he would never know what her voice sounded like. They would never have the opportunity to bond as other siblings had, nor would they have the opportunity to grow together.

"Wait, Ojore. Do not leave yet," Anpu called out.

Ryan and Heru turned to see Janay running toward them. She stopped just before Ryan, looking into his eyes. He immediately opened his arms, and she flung her arms around him and bore her face into his chest. He wrapped his arms around his dear sister, allowing his pain-filled tears to flow.

"It's okay, little sister. I'm here, and I'm not going anywhere."

Hours passed, and we transitioned back to the Life Realm, awakening to sounds of pots clanging. We proceeded to the kitchen in hopes of getting the remainder of our questions answered by the one person that was notorious for not giving us the full story.

"Hey, baby. You sleep good?" Camille asked.

"Yeah, you know me. I love my midday naps," we said.

"Trust me, I know. I came in there to ask you what you wanted for dinner. If it weren't for the fact that I could hear you breathing I would have thought you were dead."

We knew that Camille was strategic at dodging questions that she didn't want to answer. She even said they used to call her the politician when she was in high school. The best thing we could do was get the answer that would best suit our needs and run with whatever we got.

"Mama, I ... need you to ask you a question, and I need you to be completely honest with me."

She looked at us with deep concern as she turned the water off and placed the pot on the stove. There was no way she could have prepared herself for what we were about to ask her.

"What is it, baby?"

We looked into her eyes, and she looked back in the way that a child would look at their parent when they knew they were in trouble. Her marriage was hitting hard against the rocks as it was, and we were the only thing keeping her sane. We could tell that she feared our question might rattle the cage of our relationship.

"Did you know I had a sister?"

Camille immediately dropped her eyes into the sink. We sensed the shift in her spirit and knew that she had been deceiving us.

"You knew? And you didn't tell me? Why? Why wouldn't you tell me this?"

"Baby, wait, listen. Let me explain," Camille pleaded.

"Yeah, you definitely gotta explain this one to me. I wanna hear this."

Camille dropped everything in the sink as her eyes filled with tears. She came and joined us at the table and placed her head into her hands as she gathered herself.

"She was born about two years after you. Back then, things were still crazy but a little different. Antonio was upset with me because I told him that I didn't want to be with him. That man was insane, like, after you were born, he would bring his new girlfriend along with him to pick you up because he thought he was making me jealous. I tried to get to know the girl since I knew he'd have you around her, but after a while, things changed. A short time after your first birthday, I saw her at the mall and she had a baby bump, but she was particularly unpleasant when I walked up to her. She was going off about him being her man, and I just needed to take you and get the hell on, and all kinds of BS," Camille explained.

"What does that have to do with you not telling me I had a sister?" we asked.

Camille sighed and picked her eyes up from the table. She looked at us with regret as she struggled to piece together her statement.

"There were so many reasons why I didn't tell you, Ryan. I was young, I was so young, and I was only doing what I thought was right. Antonio has this way of manipulating people and preying on their fears. My biggest fear at the time was you getting caught up in the same web of lies that he tricked me with. I didn't want him to try and use your eagerness to meet your sister as means of having control over you. We had enough going on as it was, and after that stunt he pulled at the pool that time, I knew I had to protect you from him."

An answer we couldn't argue with. A lifetime of emptiness because of the ignorance of one man. We hadn't seen him in over a decade, and the rage we held aside for him resurfaced. We retreated to our room and wanted to cry, but our tears were cut short as our sorrow quickly evolved into rage, a rage that could only be satisfied by our bloodlust for revenge. We were going to kill Antonio tonight and bring an end to his mental misery once and for all, but then our cell phone rang.

"Hey Ryan, it's your granddad. Have you got a minute?"

We sat on our bed a bit disgruntled by the timing of his call. We wanted to hang up, but Hank never called for no reason.

"Yeah. Wassup, Granddad?"

"Well, I just wanna chat with you for a moment. Your mom called me a moment ago, and she sounded pretty upset. It seems that you found out about your sister." Hank tiptoed.

He knew, too. I've never understood how families can keep secrets for generations, such as the entire existence of another person. Why were they lying to us? What else were they lying about?

"Yes, sir."

Hank released a long sigh and whispered a short prayer to himself. It was strange for him to call us like this. We had become used to his reasoning in the background, but we found him standing at the forefront trying to defend something.

"Listen very carefully, grandson. Do not blame your mother for this. The truth is, she wanted to tell you about your sister a long time ago. In fact, we all wanted to get to know the little girl, but your father...he was a bad man, a very bad man, and I wouldn't have been able to forgive myself if something were to happen to you because of him. You're too young to remember, but there were times when I had to console your mother because of something stupid that he may have done just to upset her, and it upset me," Hank explained.

"But what was the point in lying to me about it? I would have understood if you just would have told me," we said.

"And I'm sure that's true, but I'm from the old school. Sad to say, that's just how we did it back then. I didn't want her to have to deal with what could have happened with Antonio, and I wasn't going to stand for him corrupting my grandson, but I will tell you this. I planned on telling you about her one day. I had a few connections over in the police department, some old army buddies of mine. I asked them to keep an eye on the bastard for me," Hank stated.

"Yeah, he's been really quiet," we replied.

"Well, long story short, the call I made wasn't just a phone call. They paid him a visit on my behalf."

Hank took a deep breath and exhaled slowly. He sounded as if he was about to deliver yet another devastating blow to our ears.

"Antonio's been paralyzed from the waist down for nearly a decade."

Our eyes burst open with shock.

"Granddad!"

"Look, nobody messes with our family. That's the lesson I instilled in your uncle, and that's the lesson I hope he instilled into you. Like I told you, don't blame your mother. She did the best she could, and from what I can tell, she's done a fine job. Now you keep that information between us, nobody else needs to know," Hank advised.

"Yes, sir." We smiled.

"Now, I'm gonna get off this phone. You go talk to your mom and let her know everything's all right. Have a good night."

We ended the call and tried to wrap our head around what we'd learned. We would have never thought that Hank had it in him to do something of that magnitude. Following the lieutenant's orders, we knocked on Camille's door and beckoned her to the kitchen to sit down. We talked to her for hours about the history that we'd never known.

We started our next day early to make sure we had time to do everything that we wanted to do that day. We first went to check on our money to ensure that everything had gone untouched.

Afterward, we borrowed Camille's car and went to the grocery store to find the freshest bouquet of flowers we could find. We traveled back to the Eastside to a cemetery located just off of the highway. Doves were flying around from a burial taking place on the other side as we began the search for her tombstone. Of all the things we would have been searching for, it sickened us to have to find her like this. We approached her tombstone, reading her name with grief.

"Janay Dennison."

The bastard signed her birth certificate. We knelt before her tombstone and laid the flowers on her grave. Slowly, the tears began to flow again.

"Your death will not be in vain, little sister," we promised.

A while later, we gathered ourselves and said our good-byes. We went back to the car with one more place to go. Just outside of Atlanta was a psych ward, a building so disguised by the city that you'd think it was another restaurant. We parked at a local parking garage and walked into the facility. The energy in the building was so awry, it made us a little uncomfortable. There were so many thoughts, so many voices asking too many questions. We could sense the energy of the staff, and they didn't care much for their patients. The security was so relaxed that we gave false credentials just to see what would happen, and also because we weren't yet old enough to be there without an adult.

"Hello, sir. Who are you here to see?" the attendant asked.

"Jenise Graves."

The attendant checked for the name in the system and looked back at us.

"And your name, sir?"

"Uh, Arnold Graves. I'm her nephew. I'm going off to college soon, and I wanted to see her before I left," we lied.

The attendant gave us a dirty look as we smiled back at her and reached for a clipboard.

"Uh-huh. Well, I'm gonna need you to fill out this form and I'll check with the doctor to see if she's available for visitation."

No one had been here to visit her since she had been admitted. It was almost as if her family had forgotten about her after Janay passed away. We filled out the form and waited until our name was called to go back with a doctor to escort us. There were so many voices asking questions, so many thoughts we couldn't yet understand.

"Mr. Graves, good afternoon. I'm Dr. Brock. I understand that Ms. Graves is your aunt?" He extended his hand.

"Uh, yes, she's my aunt." We shook his hand. "I haven't seen much of her since my si-cousin Janay passed away."

"I understand. Well, let me take you back to where she's set up, and I'll give you the rundown of her situation."

The kind doctor led us to a large room where a few other patients were sitting around watching television and staring at us quietly as we walked through the room. They all appeared to be well functioning individuals in our presence, but we couldn't ignore their submissive energies as their thoughts bounced around in our head.

"Well, this is strange," Dr. Brock said. "They're never this calm when I walk in here. Hmm, you must have good luck."

"Maybe it's just a good day," we replied.

"Maybe. Ah, there she is over there. Now as I was saying before, she hasn't said a word to our staff in months, so I wouldn't expect much of a conversation from her."

She sat in a lounge chair with her arms and legs flailed out, her hair wild and tangled around her head. Her expression detailed the state of suspended grace that she had been in since Janay's death. The doctors had practically given up on her, especially since no one had been by to visit. We walked over to her and quickly scanned over her spirit. Her essence was drained. We pulled up a chair in front of her while the doctor observed and took notes. The surrounding patients had all turned to us and were sitting attentively, a phenomenon the staff had not seen before.

We observed her face. Her eyes were dimmed and unfocused as if she was high on medication. We could only hope that if she looked at us, she wouldn't be frightened by the resemblance we shared with Antonio. We straightened our face and widened our eyes to ensure that she could get a good look at us.

"Look at me."

Her tired eyes slowly moved from their corners, and she blinked to clear her focus. She immediately gasped and clenched the blanket resting in her lap as if she'd been startled. Her eyes were open wide and locked onto ours. Intrigued by our interaction, the doctor jotted down his notes and continued to observe her sudden reaction.

"Relax, I'm not going to hurt you."

We could sense a great deal of fear coming from her, but she wasn't trying to run. Her eyes hadn't moved from our face, and we could feel them looking over every detail of our facial structure.

"She does not see you as you appear, Ojore. She sees you for what you are," Heru advised.

It all began to make sense. The doctor's words about the patients echoed in our head with a new understanding. The others surrounding us could see it just as well as she could. They knew what the doctors didn't. Jenise slowly relaxed in her seat, her eyes still moving about our person, observing us.

"Do you know who I am?" we asked.

She nodded her head, letting us know that she understood, but we needed the doctors to know she was all right.

"I need you to use your words so that I know you really understand."

"Yes, I know you," Jenise uttered.

The doctor's eyes shot wide open, and he nearly dropped his clipboard.

"Who am I?"

"God."

The doctor found a seat and continued to observe as he wrote his notes down while ignoring the other attentive patients. He pulled out his cell phone and began to record our interaction for his notes.

"That's right. I am the God of War, and I'm here to protect you from harm," we whispered to her. "Listen to me carefully, Ms. Graves. Janay is in good spirits. She is safe, and soon her spirit will be set free. It is time for you to get back to normal so that I can get you out of this place. The sooner you get everything together, the sooner I can get you. Do you understand?"

"Yes," Jenise replied.

"Good. Everything is going to be all right. I'll check on you once each week until they decide to release you. You have absolutely nothing to worry about, okay?" we assured her.

Jenise sat up straight in her seat and appeared more attentive than she had ever been. She combed her fingers through her hair and tried to make it neat. She then began adjusting her clothing and looked to us for approval. We stood up from our chair and extended our hand to her.

"I'll see you soon."

She took hold of our hand with gratitude and looked into our eyes with tears forming in the wells. She had been freed from the dungeon of her mind.

"Please, when you see her, tell her I love her," Jenise whimpered.

"I will." We smiled.

The doctor was rubbing his head, awed by what he had seen. We rose from our seat and approached him, trying to glance at his notes.

"You have my information. Please call me with her progress."

"Y-Yes, I'll–I'll do that," Dr. Brock agreed.

We proceeded out of the visitation room, and a guard escorted us back to the front to sign out. The doctor had no idea that he had just been a victim of our power of persuasion, as his verbal contact with us in the future would violate so many laws.

No sooner than we left the room, the mixed energies and end-less questions bounced around in our head again. We left the building and sat in the car for a moment, trying to understand what had just happened.

"How did she recognize me? How did all of them see who I really am?" Ryan asked.

"Sometimes the mentally insane aren't. They are able to see the spiritual influences that reside on this Earth. Help her, and I'll see to it that she is your Earth mother. Now let us not waste time trying to understand the irrelevant. We have more work to do, I will ensure that you keep your promise to her."

We drove home thinking about what Hank had told us earlier. A part of us wanted to find Antonio just to see what he looked like in his paraplegic state, and the other side still wanted to finish the job. We settled on the fact that he would be suffering for the rest of his life, a life that he would likely live alone. With Janay gone and us departed, he'd likely die alone, too. We had long forced ourselves to accept that our life was much better off without him, and this situation was the reassurance to be okay with it. We called Aaliyah and met up with her at an ice cream parlor she had told us about before. We met in the parking lot and ran into each other's arms. She looked at us after she kissed away the frustration in our eyes.

"I can't understand why your mom wouldn't tell you about your sister. That's, wow. I'm really sorry to hear that, baby," Aaliyah said.

"Don't be. It's not your fault. I only wish I could have met her before she passed," we said.

"Oh, babe."

Aaliyah leaned on our shoulder and tried to comfort us with her tenderness. Just her looking at us eased our pain, but we kind of played up the hurt to steal more of her affection.

"It was a lot of information to take in, but my granddad gave me an understanding that made sense to me. I guess I just gotta let it set in," we said.

"I don't understand the older generations sometimes. It's like they live off lies that grow and devastate people and then wanna offer some weak-ass excuse after they realize how damaging the lie was 40 years later," Aaliyah stated.

"Yeah, that's what I was thinkin', but after learning the full story, I wasn't as mad. I had just left from seeing her mom when I called you."

"Really? How is she?"

"She was so torn up by Janay's death it landed her in a psych ward, but she'll be out in a little while," we said dryly.

Aaliyah looked at us, slightly disturbed by our blunt delivery.

"You really are taking this well, I see." She nervously grinned.

"Doing the best I can at least."

She caressed our cheek and leaned in to kiss us. She took her time pulling away and slowly took our soul right along with her. Where had this woman been when we were going through our depression? She grinned at us with that special glare in her eyes, and we had to remember to focus on what was important.

"You wanna go back to my house? My dad left me with the car, and he'll be at work for a few more hours," she hinted.

A tempting offer, an offer so tempting that refusing it hurt about the same as finding out we had a sister.

"As lovely of an encounter as it may be, I have to decline. I gotta bring my mom back her car and help her with some stuff with my grandma before it gets too late. Can I take a rain check?" we lied.

She looked at us, trying to calm those sexy raging hormones, and curled her face.

"Okay, but you owe me a date," she grunted.

"This don't count?"

Aaliyah playfully punched us in the arm, and we tickled her back. We wrapped our arms around her, catching the invigorating scent of her perfume on her silky dark skin. The woman was a walking pheromone, and we had to get in charge of our desires to focus on our mission for the evening. We got into the parking lot and kissed good-bye. She drove off, sticking her tongue out at us, taking along with her the promise of a romantic evening. We got in the car and drove home to quickly change into our uniform for the night. We shot a quick text to Camille and left her keys on the kitchen counter before making our way through the woods to our motorcycle.

Tonight, our rage craved something bigger. We wanted something that was going to satisfy our displeasure from the past two days. We needed a lot of blood on our hands to make us feel better. We decided to focus on the second energy we'd recognized from the Buddy as we were anxious to keep up with the theme of discovering the unknown. As we rode across town, we remembered the lesson Hank had spoken about protecting our family. We could only hope that he would be proud of us if it was ever revealed that we were responsible for all the deaths taking place.

We traveled to the outskirts of town and rode past a facility that looked like a warehouse. We scanned the parking lot as we passed by and immediately noticed a van that looked familiar. We parked a short distance down the street and walked back through the woods to the warehouse, trying to remember where we had seen the van before. We placed the thought in the back of our mind and adjusted our muzzle for slaughter. No guns with us tonight as we wanted to challenge ourselves by using whatever elements were around to aid us in our attack. Whoever didn't run tonight was going to die along with the energy we were after.

We hopped a fence and crept up behind a guard smoking a cigarette outside of his vehicle. We pulled out the Buddy and prepared to pounce on him and take the pump-action shotgun hanging from his shoulder.

"Don't you know smoking's bad for your health?" we grunted.

The spooked guard turned around, fumbling to grab the handle of the shotgun and was immediately met with the blade of the Buddy being shoved through the bottom of his jaw. We jacked him up by the handle of the blade and twisted it around, and blood gushed from his nose and mouth. We dragged his body behind the cars parked by the fence and took everything he had on him.

We ducked low and searched around the facility for a way in, the mysterious energy getting stronger. We figured we would fare better using stealth for our operation and found a ladder that went up to the roof of the facility. At the top were dirty glass windows that gave us a good view of the activities going on inside. Large crates and boxes were being moved around with materials being processed from gas tanks. We figured a gunshot to one of those tanks would cause a great deal of destruction, but someone was creeping up behind us. We felt the cold steel of a gun pressed firmly against the back of our heads.

"Drop the gun, hoe," the man said.

This wasn't the person we were after, but he was going to die just the same. We put the shotgun down by our side and put our hands up, slowly rising to our feet. We turned around slowly and stared down the barrel of a 12-gage boomstick. The dim lighting gave the gunman a clear view of our eyes above the muzzle.

"You dat dude they been talkin' 'bout, the one that's been knockin' off all the houses, huh?"

Our slick grin formed behind our muzzle.

"Yes, it's me. I am the Red Dragon."

He made a grave mistake allowing us to our feet. He should have just shot us and tossed us off the roof.

"You's a real slippery dude, you know. You got the big boss trippin' hard about you." He puffed his cigarette.

"Yeah. It's a shame you won't be able to tell anyone about me."

We dipped low and pivoted into a spin kick and broke the man's knee, sucker punching him in the face before he could hit the ground. We snatched him into the air and turned to the glass, looking to see which pane would break easiest. Inside, the men were hard at work creating and packing loads set to go out the following day. The ear-shattering sound of broken glass interrupted the steady workflow as an unconscious man fell to the concrete floor. Several men ran toward him and watched his squirming body bleed out. They looked up to the glass ceiling and spotted our silhouette in the moonlight.

"If you don't wanna die tonight, get the hell out," we roared.

All eyes shifted to us as we cocked the shotgun and aimed at the gas tanks on the wall. With one pull of the trigger, a slug blazed from the barrel toward the danger zone. With one hit, the entire wall blew open, setting off a shockwave that shook the entire building. Mass devastation filled the building as many of the unfortunate victims were blown to bits in the explosion, the remaining survivors trying their best to escape to the parking lot. We dropped inside of the warehouse and went on the hunt—our target was still very much alive.

We crept below the smoky haze that filled the building, knowing that the cops would definitely be showing up soon. We kept our eyes peeled for the exit, watching for anyone that may have been trying to escape. Bullets went flying past our head, barely missing our ears. We dropped down and crawled behind crates that were burning and sensed the direction of the gunmen. We fired back, each slug finding its target through the fire, but as we lowered the barrel of the shotgun, we saw someone that looked familiar running out of the building. We immediately jumped through the fire to the other side and rushed to the exit to find the mysterious van peeling out of the parking lot. We hurried back down the street to our motorcycle, gunning down anyone we saw who was leaving the building. We focused on our target and kept our distance from him as we gave chase in the night.

Something felt familiar about this energy. We felt like we knew it, and we knew it well. We pounded down through the city streets until they turned to single-laned roads and led to a cabin hidden deep in the woods on the outskirts of the city.

We parked the bike near a ditch by the street and crept through the woods, following the path of the long driveway. Our target was definitely inside, probably terrified from the explosion that had forced him here. All of the lights were on as we observed the house. There were several men inside loading weapons and hollering to each other. We spotted the van, and vague memories appeared from instances where we remembered seeing it, but we couldn't remember who it belonged to. We aimed our shotgun and began blasting through the windows of the house, hitting whoever got in the way.

We ran toward the front door and waited for some fool to run out. The door swung open, and we quickly snatched and stabbed the first person to come out, but he wasn't our target. We could sense a few more energies inside and figured it would be best to ravage the place until we could find him. We had to figure out who this guy was tonight, but we had to be extra careful because letting him escape was not an option.

We burst through the open doorway, sending slugs flying in all different directions. One poor fool took a hit dead on and flew out of a window. We caught the movement of another man running around a corner and fired at him, but fortunately for him, the slug missed. Another man tried to attack us from behind with an ax but was met with a spinning back kick to the chest. He dropped the ax as he crashed into the cabin walls, failing to catch his breath as he gasped for air on the wooden floor. He attempted to crawl away from us as his red blood dripped from his mouth. We picked up the ax from the floor and raised it into the air, our focus on his heart. We slammed the ax through his back and broke the handle through to the floor.

We continued our hunt, catching wind of the loud banging on the backdoor. Someone was trying to escape, but they weren't going to get far from us. There were two energies left inside, and both would be falling by our hand tonight. We slowly crept to the back of the house, where all of the commotion was coming from.

"Whose retarded-ass idea was it to put this damn lock on the door?" one man shouted.

"I don't know, man. Just get this shit open," the other man replied.

That voice, the first one, sounded familiar. We had to put a face to the voice for clarity. We found ourselves a short distance down the hall, watching them as they desperately attempted to break the lock. We charged the fore-end and felt a ripple of their energies wiggle with fear. They both turned to look back, our target locking eyes with us. We almost recognized him... No, it couldn't be.

"Just shoot the fuckin' lock," the man screamed.

The other man shot off the lock, and our target pushed through the back door. The other man wasn't as fortunate as our target, catching a slug to the middle of his back before he had the chance to run. His blood splattered all over the wall as his body ricocheted off the door jamb and fell through the open doorway. The words of our target echoed in our head as we tried to match his voice with others in our head. That accent, the twang on the words, the untrustworthy slyness in the tone. There was only one person who we could think of that it could be, and we didn't want it to be him. We pulled out the Buddy and grabbed it by the tip of the blade as we marched toward the backdoor. We spotted our target trying to make his way toward the dark woods ahead and flung the Buddy toward him. We hit perfectly, the blade traveling through the back of his leg and out of his knee. He bounced and rolled on the ground, groaning in agony as he lay in the dirt.

We crept up on him slowly as he tried to crawl away. We sensed his energy, and suddenly, the moment became all too real. We dropped the shotgun on the cold hard ground as our rage rose to new heights in a matter of seconds. Never in our lives had we felt a feeling that bore so much pain. He was in our face, around our family, in our uncle's house. We pulled down our muzzle and removed our hood to reveal our face in the darkness, our shadow from the house lights darkening his path. He turned over to see our black silhouette and our glowing red eyes standing over him. His soul was stricken with fear that only a god could deliver.

We grabbed him by the ankle and took hold of the Buddy, twisting and pulling slowly as we removed it from the back of his knee. We ignored his screams as we were far from through with him. We were going to make him suffer through the night. We grabbed his ankle and dragged him back into the house as he screamed for help that wasn't coming. He kicked around, trying to get away from our grip, and with each kick, we squeezed tighter, eventually crushing the bones in his ankle. We still hadn't turned to allow him to see our face in the light as we prepared to venture down the dark stairs to the basement. We knocked him out to give ourselves time to prepare him for his execution.

A short while later, we had our target bound by his hands and hanging from the ceiling. We pushed his body around to allow him the opportunity to wake up before we rocked his rib cage with bone-shattering punches and kicks. He hollered as our bullish punches crippled his pain sensors as he battled with the aches from his busted knee.

"Wake up, bitch!"

Kenny hacked and gasped for air as his body aimlessly swung around. Blood, sweat, and saliva dripped on the floor as he nervously looked around, trying to determine what had taken place while he was out. The sounds of his groans only angered us more as we continued our one-sided attack. We hit him harder to the sounds of him choking on his own blood as he hacked it up.

"Ten years you've been around this family! We trusted you! You killed CJ! You killed both of them, you bastard!"

We unleashed a combo of devastating blows until he stopped screaming. He wasn't dead, but he was certainly hurting. We could hear him struggling to breathe and decided to let him know who we were before he tried to pass out. We grabbed his swinging body and turned it toward us.

"You recognize me, bitch?"

Knocking him out had made him slightly delirious, and the current attack on his ribs wasn't making it any better. We decided to give him a break from the abuse to make sure he knew who he was dealing with.

"Maybe this'll make it easier for you."

We jumped up and kicked him down from the makeshift hook, his shoulder breaking his fall. We stood over his body and gave him a second to recoup. When his breathing sounded normal, we continued with our onslaught. We jacked him up by his collar and brought him close to our face.

"Do you know who I am?"

Kenny focused his eyes on us and was immediately overcome with guilt. Tears formed in his eyes, and he started crying the way he should have been crying at the funeral.

"What's my name?" we shouted.

"Ryan," he whined.

"That's right, it's Ryan. Nephew to your former best friend Carey and cousin to his son CJ. And you killed them!"

We threw his tied body into the folding tables across the room, knocking down the glass jars and tools sitting on top of them. We rushed over to him and dragged him out of the mess.

"Nah, I ain't done with you yet, bitch," we warned. "You're gonna tell me everything I wanna know before I kill you."

We dragged his body back to the center of the room and tied him to a chair to keep him up. The rib attack had depleted his core strength.

"They trusted you. My uncle allowed you into his home. He allowed you around our family, his son. He took you in when you got here from New York, you grimy son of a bitch!" We hammer-fisted his bad knee.

Kenny wailed in pain and flailed his body until the chair tipped over. We grabbed him by his neck and picked him up from the floor, backhand slapping him after we propped him back up.

"Why? Give me a damn good reason why! And why CJ? He had nothing to do with any of this!"

We gave him a second to catch his breath, anxious to hear his explanation, though no reason would suffice. We watched his swollen face bleed the blood that should have been his splattered on the walls. We had to quickly gain control of our rage because we wanted so badly to punch his heart through his back.

"You ready to talk?" We cracked our knuckles.

"You gotta u-u-under-stand, man, he snitched. He was—he was 'bout to mess everything up," Kenny groaned.

"And look at you now, about to die at his nephew's hand. Was it worth it?"

A question we really wanted an answer to.

"Nah, man, you don't get it." Kenny struggled to catch his breath. "There's a whole operation going on here that you don't even know about."

"You mean the one run by the guy Face that wears the white face paint, and the entire drug and weapon operation going on? Yeah, I been the one sabotaging his houses for the past few months," we grunted.

Kenny's eyes opened in shock as he looked over our face again, noticing our one trifling detail.

"You! You're the—the guy with the red eyes? You killed all those people. He's been looking for you."

"Yeah, he better be. I'd tell you to tell him I'm looking for him, but you're dying tonight. You know, I've always felt something strange in your essence. I never could trust you the way that they did, and I'm glad I didn't. I never would have let you get that close," we growled.

"Look, I-I didn't wanna do it," Kenny said.

"Then why the hell did you?" we charged. "He was an innocent child! Seventeen years old with everything going for him, and you... you pulled the trigger on his dreams in front of his own father. You are the embodiment of the ultimate betrayal! Now go ahead, answer my question. Why, Kenny, why did you do this to my family and then lie to our faces with your weak condolences at his funeral? Tell me why."

Our beastly breaths shook him to his core as we stared into his eyes. Kenny was a worm, a parasite looking for a way to come up at the expense of anyone that would fall for his tactics. He wasn't hard, a man by no means, just a weak fool at the end of his rope.

"I was scared."

"Of?"

"It was gonna be the end for me! Look at me, man! I ain't never had shit. I dropped out of high school. I ain't got no real skills. I can't get no job. Why the hell you think I came to Georgia in the first place?" Kenny sobbed.

We looked down on his pitiful tears, exercising no empathy for his lies. There was no such thing as forgiveness for what he had done. We went back and forth in our minds for a moment wondering if we should turn him in to the police or just kill him now.

"Tell me something valuable and I'll let you live," we offered.

"I'll tell you anything, what do you wanna know?" Kenny sobbed.

"Is Face working with anyone else I should be concerned about? And don't lie to me. I'll know if you're lying."

Kenny thought for a moment, and suddenly it was like a light bulb went off in his head.

"Yeah, yeah, he's got two guys he's working with. It's uh, an Asian dude, I think his name is Hong or somethin', and some old guy that looks like one of them Arabs. I think they said his name was Mr. Nassar or somethin' like that. They, uh, they took out some Mexican dude a few months back, and Face was supposed to be takin' his place on like their board or somethin'."

"Their board?" We raised our brow.

"They, like, run the city in different parts."

"Districts?"

"Yeah, somethin' like that, and Face was supposed to be the new guy takin' over for the ol' guy they killed," Kenny said.

As janky as he was, Kenny was giving us some valuable information. It actually might be worth keeping him alive for a while. It seemed that the Buddy only provided targets to obliterate related to the scene of the crime, but the newfound information gave us a new mission objective. We weren't just going to kill Face—we were going to destroy his entire organization.

"Is that all?"

"Oh, uh, and he's got these two cops workin' for 'em, uh, Porter and Simmons. Yeah, they're detectives. They been lookin' at all the shit you been doin," Kenny advised.

"Is that so? I guess I'll have to wait for them to come when I have time to waste. Is that all you got?"

Kenny looked up at the ceiling struggling to buy himself more time in hopes that we would set him free, but he couldn't think of anything else.

"That's, that's all I got."

We paced back and forth for a moment as we finalized our decision. We wanted to bring closure to our family and put their minds to rest. We wanted them to know that the murderer they were after had been caught and brought to justice, but we also knew that it would bring our family a greater hurt if they knew it was Kenny. The same Kenny they'd trusted and invited to family events. The same Kenny that Alpharetta treated like a son to fill the void of her missing daughter. We couldn't trust the justice system to do its job, especially with two cops that could possibly pull strings in his favor. Hank had taught us a valuable lesson the other day: Sometimes revenge is better when it's done in the dark.

"Remember at the funereal, when you stood in my grandmother's face and gave your fake-ass condolences?" we asked.

"Yes," Kenny said.

"You lied. You lied not only to my grandmother, but you lied to me, my mother, my aunt, my grandfather, my uncle, and my cousin. You lied to my entire family, an unforgivable offense, and I lied to you when I told you I was gonna let you live."

Kenny's eyes shot wide open in fear. His tears returned as we yanked him up by his collar and made him stare into our red eyes.

"I'm going to beat you. I'm gonna beat you until I don't have the power to break your bones anymore. I'm gonna break you, not only for the lives of my uncle and my cousin, but for everyone I'm sure you've betrayed. And don't worry, I'm gonna use your phone to record it all, so when they find you, they'll know it was me. They'll know the Red Dragon got his revenge, and they'll tell Face I'm coming for him next."

We grabbed his phone from his pocket and dropped him back on the floor. We went over to the fallen tables and picked one up and found something to prop his phone up with. We unlocked it and opened the camera and noticed a familiar face in the last photo taken. A picture of him and Carey posing behind his van, a picture that CJ likely took at their house. It reminded us that we were at war, that we had a reason to be merciless, and we weren't going to spare anyone no matter how destructive the path got.

"This is for you, Unc."

We replaced our muzzle and hood before we switched on the camera and positioned it to where the murder would take place. We hung Kenny from the ceiling again, and for the next hour, we made him our personal punching bag. We practiced punches and kicks that we hadn't had the chance to attempt on others because of all of the guns. We beat him and beat him until our face and hands were covered with his blood. We shattered every bone in his body from his feet to his head, and we got it all on camera.

Before we departed, we checked upstairs for a cell phone charger and happened to find one in the living room. We plugged up Kenny's phone to make sure the battery was fully charged when whoever came by the house discovered the mess we'd left behind. We stopped and sat on the basement stairs and took a moment to assess ourselves. Killing Kenny was the best option for us, and even though it wouldn't bring our family back, we felt better. We wished we could have included our family in this beatdown, but they would have wanted to bring him to the police. There was still a void in our heart. A few tears fell from our eyes in mourning of our uncle and cousin. They hadn't deserved to die, nor had they deserved to die the way they did. They never should have had the amount of trust they had for him.

We left the house as it was, lights on with bodies all around. We had come out tonight with the purpose of spilling blood, but we still felt empty. We yearned for the blood of our enemies on our hands, but we had to make sure we got everyone, including the ones that Kenny told us about. A new objective in mind, we raced home to make preparations to dismantle Face's organization and anyone that got in our way in the process.

CHAPTER 20

FIND THE GUY WITH THE RED EYES

W E HAD BEEN pretty quiet today. We weren't as active in school, and those that cared seemed to notice. We tried our best to deliver our feelings to our canvas in art class, but the colors meant nothing to us. The emptiness we'd taken home the other night seemed to have a lasting effect. The boring lines on our canvas gave us nothing to pull from as Mr. Rose looked over our shoulder and noticed something wasn't right.

"Ryan, it seems you've lost that special grit you seem to put into your work. Is everything all right?" he asked.

"Yes, yes, I'm okay. Uh, I have a few things on my mind that are clouding my artistic eye."

Whatever that meant. We just weren't feeling life that day. We knew the feeling would pass, but we didn't want to live in the moment either. We roamed the hallways in between classes looking like we weren't dating the prettiest girl in school, even though the thought of that could make anyone smile. We sat in our other classes working on the thing we'd been drawing for months. We had been making some progress with it, but it still looked unfinished to our standards. Lunchtime came, and Aaliyah and Terrell sat with us, trying to find us through the cloud of gloom that hung over us.

"Man, sorry about your sister, bruh. This world is so messed up," Terrell said.

"Thanks. I'm just trying to let it go for now, but the pain's still fresh for me, you know," we replied.

Aaliyah placed her arms around us and kissed us on the cheek. Even on our worst day, that woman could still give us something we could feel.

"Well, it's like you said, babe, your granddad already took care of it, so don't dwell on it. I think the best thing you can do is develop a relationship with her mom and get to know your sister through her," Aaliyah said.

"Yeah, Aaliyah's right. That's a whole 'nother side of the family you can get to know. They might look at you like they looked at your sister and hook you up before you go to college or something," Terrell said.

"Shut up, Terrell," we laughed.

"I'm just sayin', man. You can't keep walking around here lookin' all crazy. People are gonna look at your girl like she's the problem."

We all burst into laughter. It was a strange feeling, but it had been a while since we'd had more than one friend that made us laugh like this.

"Speaking of which, I should probably tell you guys what I did this weekend," Terrell said.

"You got a job?" Aaliyah joked.

Terrell smiled at Aaliyah's joke and looked off into space. Whatever he had done this weekend was something serious, we could sense it. We could only hope it wasn't something as bizarre as what we did this weekend.

"You're funny, Aaliyah. Nah, I, uh, I visited my brother's memorial on Friday, and it kinda did something to me. So I talked to my mom, and of course, she gave me a hard time, but I went to see a recruiter Saturday. I'm gonna join the Marines to honor my brother."

"Wow, that's huge, and very noble of you, too," Aaliyah said.

"That's wassup, bruh. Just don't let them brainwash you into one of those soulless machines that they dump on the side of the road after they get hurt. I've seen how they do the veterans over by the VA hospital in Atlanta," we said.

"Yeah, I know what you mean," Terrell said. "I don't know what I'm gonna get into when I get there, but whatever it is, I'll use it to pay for school so I can keep my mom quiet."

The bell rang, and it was time to go to our next class. Aaliyah hugged and kissed us once more before we and Terrell departed to our drama class, but it wasn't long before we fell back into our trance of darkness. We had to shake this feeling. Killing Kenny just wasn't as satisfying as we had hoped it would be, maybe because we had hoped that it was a stranger.

"Hey, man, word of advice, it gets a lot easier with time. Don't be afraid to take a little time to yourself. I know she'll understand," Terrell said.

If only he knew what the real issue was, but his message was much appreciated. We continued to ride the wave of our emotions for the rest of the day in hopes that the next hunt would cure our dysfunction.

Porter and Simmons had been on the job for hours trying to cover up for Face and the Illegit mishaps. They lost out on the warehouse explosion because the fire department beat them to the punch. With the loss of the warehouse, Face's drug and weapon trafficking had been reduced to a halt, and his only means of moving anything would be through Hong or Nassar. Several phone calls had been made, trying to locate anyone that might have been working at the site, but the bodies found in the parking lot led the county officers into launching an investigation to figure out what happened and who the property belonged to, forcing Face to lay low.

The detectives later found themselves at the ransacked cabin checking around the property for a body count, a process they had become accustomed to in their recent investigations. The smell of blood and decomposing bodies filled their lungs as they walked through the house.

"Axed 'em in the back. That had to hurt," Simmons said.

"I'm gonna stop saying whoever this is and start saying what. I've seen too many empty shell casings since the last two places. I'm starting to think this is one of those killer robots," Porter said.

They walked toward the back of the house and noticed the doors to the basement and back doors were open. They looked at each other, knowing their discovery was about to take a turn for the worse.

"Where do you think we should search first?" Porter asked.

They made their way down to the basement, quickly discovering Kenny's broken body hanging from the ceiling. A pool of his blood was drying on the floor, complementing his battered face. While Porter took note of the body, Simmons scanned the room and called Face to update him.

"Whoever did this must have really had it out for him. Shit, he just shot everyone else," Porter said.

"Yeah, his face says it all," Simmons uttered as Face answered his call. "Hey, Face...Yeah, bad news. The cabin's a bust."

"He broke every bone in this boy's body. Simms, you see this shit? Everything on this boy is broke," Porter gawked.

"I'm on the phone with Face! Sorry, that was Porter...Same as always. Everyone's dead, not even a random person standing in the woods."

Simmons fumbled around the fallen tables, sifting through the broken equipment, but found nothing. He looked up by the standing table and noticed a wire traveling upward from the socket and traced it to an object sitting on the end of the table.

"Is that a cell phone?" he whispered to himself. "I think I found something."

He walked over to the table and discovered the cell phone propped up and plugged into the charger with the screen facing the wall and the camera pointed toward the hanging body.

Simmons looked back and forth from the camera lens to the hanging dead man and wondered if the two were connected.

"It looks like...Porter, come look at this. Face, let me call you back. I think I've found something." Simmons ended the call.

Porter joined Simmons by the wall, still in awe of the imperfect murder.

"They're gonna have fun cleaning that shit up. What you got?" Porter asked.

"A cell phone but look at how it's positioned. Strange, right?"

Porter looked at the phone and traced the lens back to the hanging body and was immediately shocked by the minor discovery. He looked up at Simmons and looked back at the phone.

"You think there's something on it?"

"Only one way to find out," Simmons said.

Hours flew by, and the detectives met with Face and Deuce at the high-rise to look over what they had discovered. They started it over and over from the beginning to get a good glimpse of the seemingly unstoppable menace with the red eyes. Simmons had already taken a still from the video, but because of the muzzle and hood the perpetrator was wearing, he was unable to send off the photo for facial recognition.

"This is our guy, the guy with the red eyes everyone's been talking about. The video's over an hour long, but the beating goes on for longer. He maxed out the space on the memory card," Simmons said.

The men continued to restart the video, observing the fraction of a face they had for the red-eyed murderer in the dim light. Face's anger grew by the moment as he reflected on his current losses, struggling to place the blame on this one unidentified man. He slammed his fist on the table, startling the other men in the room.

"Turn it off. I don't wanna see this shit," Face grunted.

"We need to see it," Deuce said. "This is the guy that's been causing all our problems."

"Really, Deuce? You really believe that shit?" Face rose from his chair in an angry fit.

Tensions were high for the white-faced gangster with his unidentified menace still at large. With each day that went by, he grew more and more intolerant of the irrefutable facts surrounding his situation. It wasn't real to him anymore, and he refused to believe it was happening the way that it was being presented to him.

"You really believe that this, this guy, who's probably wearing contacts, this one man, you really think he took down the houses, full of people with guns, by the way, sabotaged an entire warehouse operation that's gonna break our pockets? I don't even know how much money he's stolen from us at this point, and do you even realize how many of our people we've lost? You really expect me to believe that one man, this red-eyed bastard, is solely responsible for all of this shit? You gotta be outta ya goddamn mind if you think I believe that shit!" Face hollered.

"Well, what the hell else do we have to go on?" Deuce asked.

"I don't know, goddamit, but I know he's not working alone," Face groaned.

Face paced around the living room, the other men quickly jumping out of his way to avoid any confrontation. Face grabbed his pistol from his desk for comfort and continuously loaded and unloaded the magazine.

"And I still haven't found my goddamn knife!"

"You lost that thing months ago," Deuce said.

Face turned to Deuce, trying his best not to raise the gun to him. His eyes were filled with anger as they stared at each other with daggers in their eyes.

"Deuce, you're tryin' me. You ain't finna sit here and tell me that one man is capable of all this! All these young boys we've recruited done got smart on us," Face said.

The room was silent for a moment as Face thought of what to do to save his operation. He didn't want to risk any more of his

Illegit soldiers, but protecting his investments was turning out to be a struggle for business. He walked back to his chair and sat down to go through his phone. A text came through from one of his Illegits, and he released a sigh of relief.

"Finally, some good news," he said. "The boys we sent to Cali are on the way back. They got the shipment, and they should be here by Thursday evening."

"I'll call Hong and let 'em know," Deuce said.

"No, I'll call Hong and let him know. What you need to do is reach out to every member of this family and let them know that there is a red-eyed bastard on the loose that needs to get handled with extreme prejudice. Hell, offer a reward if necessary. I want that bastard's head on my desk!" Face instructed.

Deuce flailed his arms and walked toward the window to make the calls, but the unsatisfied Face felt that there was more that could be done. The crazed villain wanted to make sure he weeded out any possible loose ends that might attempt to sabotage him even more.

"Wait! It seems like every time something happens there's always a lone survivor that talks about the guy with the red eyes. This time, there wasn't! There's absolutely no way that he could'a got that body up there by himself. It's too high off the ground. I find it odd that he had the time to sabotage our warehouse and make it out to the cabin in the same night. Nobody's that fast! I believe whoever's helping him knew we were catching on, so they helped him stage this little video. From now on, when anything happens, I don't care how big or small, anything, if they so much as mention the guy with the red eyes, they're dead!" Face declared.

Deuce nodded his head and slowly backed away, turned by his leader's dysfunction. Face went on grumbling in anger to himself as the detectives wrapped up their findings. Face's discomfort was becoming a problem for them, fearing that the current wave of destruction might lead to more trouble. They left Face alone to wallow in his frustration and headed back to their car.

"It's about to be a bloodbath in the streets," Porter said.

We were feeling much better these days. The pain of loss goes away quicker when it's too late to say good-bye, but she'd always have a place in our heart. Maybe once we freed the souls in Duat we could bring her back somehow. The good vibes charged our aggression to continue our hunt as we prepped our motorcycle for tonight's ride. Nothing like someone else's blood on your hands to get the black blood pumping. We wanted to find the other men that Kenny had spoken of, but we had no way of figuring out who they were.

"I should have asked him for more information, a location, or something," Ryan said.

"Remember, Ojore, whatever it is that you desire, put it out into the universe, and it will come to you," Heru said.

"You really think the universe is going to show me someone I want to kill?"

"You are the God of War, and you fight for a divine cause ordained to you by the ancestors. There's nothing that the universe won't do for you."

We looked up to the ceiling in a playful manner and flung our hands up as high as we could and sarcastically called out to the universe.

"Oh, great universe, 'tis I, the Dragon of Red. Please, I beg ye to find me the ones spoken of by the late Kenny, whom I killed in vengeance for my family," Ryan laughed.

"It shall be so," Heru declared.

We began our hunt that evening, traveling toward an energy that felt far away. We blazed down I-20 westbound passing between cars and 18-wheelers with ease, but suddenly we noticed that the energy we were after felt like it was coming closer to us. We quickly got off of the highway and waited for the energy to make its way toward our location. Whoever we were after was moving fast, possibly traveling into the city—either way, we were ready to take them down along with anyone they may have had with them.

We posted up at a gas station that overlooked the interstate just outside the city and watched as the cars passed by. The anticipation pulsated through our body the closer the energy got to us, and suddenly we started to feel that emptiness again. It had been lurking in the dark corners of our mind waiting to catch us when we felt our best. To make matters worse, we still couldn't figure out what we needed to do about our chakra alignment. What if how we felt was wrong? What if exacting revenge wasn't the right thing for us to be doing? What if it didn't help us evolve? What if the goal was to let it all go and forgive, and we had been failing the whole time miserably? Was forgiveness the moral behind the wrath of the gods to obtain our third eye alignment? What if we got so beside ourselves that we lost all control tonight? Wait, what was that?

We looked to the highway and spotted two 18-wheelers passing by, and our target was in one of them. We didn't have time to think anymore; it was time to kill. We revved up Rage and pounded down the highway behind them. They were traveling somewhere, somewhere big with all they were hauling. We didn't see any markings on the truck, so we weren't sure where it was going. We stayed back and cruised behind them as they led us through the city. We neared an old factory, and the trucks turned into the property while we went farther down the street and made a U-turn into a property that was full of luxury cars. We wouldn't have thought twice about the cars, but they were all mysteriously parked in front of a closed building. We parked the bike on the side of the building and crept across the street to find our target.

We hopped the fence and observed the trucks through the trees. They were backing in at the docks to the building, and parked off to the right was a small shuttle bus. We looked a bit closer and noticed several men and women dressed in formal wear walking up a loading ramp to a roll-up door on the other side of the old factory. Something was going on, but we couldn't figure out what. These people didn't look like the ones we had taken out before, but they weren't regular people either.

"Something isn't right about this, Heru," Ryan said.

"I can sense it, too. These people don't appear to be affiliated with Face's barbarians," Heru replied.

We continued scanning the area for clues and spotted an Asian man wielding an assault rifle walking around the trucks.

"Well, that ain't normal," Ryan said.

There was definitely something big happening at this place, but because of the group of people we saw, we were afraid that we might end up hurting innocent people. We stayed in the woods observing the property, trying to buy time for our decision, but truthfully, we felt that we had gotten beside ourselves. It was as if after all the murdering we had done, we had finally developed a conscience.

"What are you waiting for, Ojore?" Heru asked. "Your target is in there waiting for you."

"I know, I, uh, I'm just gonna wait for him to come out. There's a lot of innocent people inside, and I just wanna make sure I get him," Ryan lied.

We were lying, and we didn't know why. Something came over us that had shaken the wrath of our foundation, and we were losing our touch. We didn't know what we wanted anymore.

"The blood of the innocent is not a concern for the God of War, Ojore. We are at war with a powerful enemy, and if we let up on our stance with this enemy, we will lose this battle for sure! You are on a mission, and those that aren't intended to be hurt won't be if they are intelligent enough to get out of the way," Heru stated.

We started to feel the battle between our emotions and our morality. We weren't sure what side we were on, but the rage was winning as it flowed through our body and tingled our senses. A part of us began to feel that we couldn't trust Heru for encouraging our dark behavior, but we were soul bonded. We then remembered that he no longer had control over our actions and started to question who we were. Were our powers slowly turning us into the villain? Why was our desire for revenge changing us? Why did it feel so good to destroy? What kind of god were we becoming?

It was time to go get that blood we wanted on our hands, starting with the guy with the machine gun. We pulled out the Buddy as we stealthily crept from the trees, watching his every move. He wasn't actually paying attention, just messing with his cell phone and scrolling through his social media. He was just some guy they gave a gun to. We decided to step out in plain view because this guy clearly wasn't a real threat. He was innocent, but he had a really big gun.

"Hey, who are you?" The man aimed at us.

"Whoa!" We threw our hands up. "Do you even know how to use that thing?"

"Shut up, fool! Do not insult me, or I will show you how it is used," he threatened.

"You obviously don't know how to use it."

We flung the Buddy at his face and caught him directly in the eye, sending the blade through his brain. His body staggered for a moment, and then he fell backward, squirming on the ground.

"You're supposed to shoot first," we snarked.

Now we had a gun and the Buddy. We hopped on the loading dock behind the parked 18-wheeler and peeked around the corner to see what was going on. A few armed men were monitoring the workers unloading the trucks. They didn't appear to be much of a threat, but we could sense more energies than what we saw. Our target was on the move somewhere within the facility, but strangely, his essence felt beneath us. We had to quickly figure out how to navigate the facility, and judging by the size of the gun we had stolen, this might turn out to be a particularly difficult task.

We hopped down from the dock and crept over to the empty shuttle bus and noticed the keys still in the ignition. After a quick glance at the building's roll-up door, we immediately thought of the perfect distraction. We shifted the bus into neutral and pushed it away from the building in order to keep the engine noise down. Once we got the bus far enough away, we hopped inside and prepared ourselves for one of the craziest stunts we would ever attempt. We kept the sliding door open, sizing it up to make sure we jumped the right way. We gave the building one last look and revved the engine to give the workers inside the only warning they were going to get. We floored the gas pedal and barreled toward the building, switching on the cruise control at 60 MPH. Inside, two armed guards were standing by the door, one of them receiving the word to take the shuttle to the parking lot to pick up new visitors.

"I'll get on it." The man ended the call. "Hey, it's your turn to drive the shuttle. I'm tired of seeing people tonight."

"Fine," the other worker scoffed. "This job has made you lazy. You used to be ready to work all the time."

The angry worker hastily turned to the garage door to raise the rolling door, but just as he was about to press the button, he was distracted by the sound of a powerful diesel engine roaring on the other side. He looked over to the loading docks and saw the men were still unloading the trailers. He immediately grew suspicious and turned to check the shipment log. Suddenly, the factory was shaken by the force of the shuttle bus crashing through the door, instantly killing the two guards. The men unloading the trailers ran for cover as the other armed men scattered like ants to get out of the shuttle's way. The shuttle flipped on its side and crashed into stacks of large shipping crates sectioning off the work floor.

We rushed inside while the dust was still flying up and began our violent killing spree, and any innocent soul that was in the way would be added to the frenzy as bonus points. We sensed the locations of the eight men in the factory and commenced a shootout. The first three were easy shots, seeing as everyone was distracted by the sight of the crashed bus. We ducked behind a few shipping crates and tracked the locations of the other five men, one of them directly on the other side of the crate we hid behind.

Hidden below the factory was Hong's underground casino, business booming as usual. There were dozens of rich and corrupt patrons in attendance, gambling their millions across several different tables. The environment provided a live band and alcohol to keep the inebriated guests at bay. Hong was busy in his office with one of his guards and four of the Illegit's finest preparing the payment that would be delivered to Face when the walls suddenly shook, followed by a few crashing sounds. They all looked up at the ceiling, their faces filled with shock at the sound of gunshots.

"What the hell is going on up there? Go check it out and get back to me immediately," Hong ordered his guard.

The guard quickly bowed and rushed out of the office into the loud vibe of the casino, the booming music and drunken excitement keeping the guests unaware of the action upstairs. He rushed to the stairway, advising two more guards to come with him. Meanwhile, we were dodging bullets from across the factory. We had shot down a few more of the other guards, leaving two more for us to get rid of. We rushed back to the broken garage doorway and ducked around the corner outside. We noticed the flipped bus with its gas tank right in our view. We took a breath and rushed back inside and unloaded on the gas tank until the bus exploded. Our idea worked perfectly, the explosion engulfing the final two guards in its flames. We wanted to destroy everything in here before we left; it all had to go. We started to feel that emptiness inside again, and our lack of control over it was driving us insane.

Suddenly we were struck in the arm and chest by bullets from three guards coming out of a doorway. We quickly dashed behind a shipping crate to catch our breath for a moment. The heat from the fiery blaze soothed us as we hid until we couldn't feel the bullets anymore. We stepped back from the shipping crate and then rushed into it, sending it sliding into one of the men across the room. The other two guards dived out of the way as the unlucky target was crushed against the wall. Distracted by the death of their co-worker, we blasted them and sent them on a one-way trip to meet Anpu.

We checked the men for more ammo and punched them for shooting us as our rage raised higher. We found the door they'd come out of and followed the stairs down to the basement of the factory. We could hear a loud commotion on the other side of a door: a band, people, and laughing. We started to get beside ourselves again. We felt weak, as if our deadly touch had been handled. We could hear Kenny crying in our head about how terrible his life was, we could hear Terry snapping at Aaliyah, we could hear all the speeches Camille gave us after she dealt with the repercussions of her bad decisions, and we didn't care. We couldn't feel anything, and then we could. We felt the wrath of the gods, the anger of the ancestors, the cold shoulder of revenge.

We roared, sending a ground-shaking rattle through the stairwell. We kicked in the door and just started shooting at anything moving. All the pretty colors around meshed together as the bloodshed spread all over the room. There were dozens of people in the crowded area, and they all had to get a piece of us. We could feel our target to the right somewhere above our head and started to walk around, looking for a flight of stairs. People were passing by us running for their lives. Some of them got away as we were firing back at guards firing at us, but the others were much less fortunate. Bullets flew by, narrowly missing us, and we continued nailing our targets with precision. We had so many feelings but felt nothing.

Scared in his office, Hong watched his men grow slim in numbers from the monitors in his office. He and the other four Illegit Family members contemplated what to do as the chaos unfolded beneath them. All they could hear was gunfire and the random screams of people dying, desperately trying to get away.

"Man, I told y'all we shoulda skipped that last stop!" The frightened thug shivered.

"If it's who I think it is out there, ain't but one of us gettin' out alive," another thug said.

Curious as to who the men were referring to, Hong interjected himself into their conversation as he grabbed a sword from the wall.

"Who could it be?"

The big and rugged men turned to Hong with fear in their eyes, sending the once calm Hong into worry. He gripped his hair, hoping the answer to his question wouldn't come with the same scenario as his troubled friend.

"Yeen heard 'bout all them boys who got slaughtered at Face's spots? You know, the dude wit' the red eyes? He's been out here knockin' off the family."

Hong's eyes widened, and he strongly tugged his hair with stress, remembering the stories Face had told him about. Could the attacker be the same threat that Face was referring to, or was it just another angry rival family looking to sabotage his casino?

"I ain't goin' out like no punk!" one of the thugs declared.

The foolish man strutted out the office door and stood by the railing of the walkway, firing his weapon to taunt the hidden threat.

"Aye, Red Eyes, where you at, homie? Come holla at me!" He fired.

Suddenly, three gunshots blasted through the man's chest. He staggered back into the side of the doorway and stumbled forward, falling over the railing to his death. The men in the office quickly drew their guns and aimed toward the doorway as Hong ducked behind his desk with his sword. The spoiled boss had been pampered for so long, he began to panic without the protection of his guards. As they continued to watch the doorway, the men noticed that the gunfire had stopped.

"It's quiet out there. Maybe he's dead."

"If he's dead, then who shot Joe?"

Our target eliminated, we were curious to find out who else was upstairs. The theme of Asain culture around the casino gave us a clue to who the property belonged to, not to mention the morgue of armed Asian men we'd created upon our arrival. We jumped up from the bottom floor to the walkway, where we spotted three more men, but we could sense four. It all started to make sense.

"Hong is here."

Hong was definitely here. He was the fourth presence that we felt. The universe had delivered on its promise. We landed on the walkway and quickly dashed behind the wall to escape the bullets being fired at us.

"Take him out! Take him out," Hong screamed as he fled from behind his desk.

The crafty criminal had a false wall built into his office and quickly escaped from the chaos with his sword in hand, leaving the others to defend themselves against certain death. We quickly dashed past the door, sending a horizontal row of bullets to the back of the room. We heard the screams of the men as they hit the floor and then dashed into the room to finish the job. We fired mercy shots into their heads and sensed Hong somehow getting farther away from us, traveling upward. We stepped toward the wall where we sensed his energy when the shoulder strap of a bag caught our leg. We looked down and spotted two bags filled with money...yet another jackpot.

"We gotta come back for this."

We sensed Hong getting farther away from us but had no idea how he'd managed to get out of the office. There was no way he could have gotten past us without getting shot, and he was only distancing himself with each second that passed.

"I don't know what to do," Ryan said. "Maybe it's a false wall, but how do I find the right place?"

"Ugh, Ojore, how many times must I remind you? You are the God of War. Just kick through the walls," Heru advised.

"Oh, yeah. Sorry." Ryan shrugged.

"You are losing your touch, Ojore."

Angered by his factual words, we kicked the wall, and a portion of it fell inward, revealing a hallway leading to a flight of stairs. We traveled up the stairs, following Hong's energy, fueled by our ancestral rage. We recanted images of our past, words said to us by our deceased loved ones, and we began to wonder if they would even want us to do all of this for them. Would Carey be happy about us avenging him, or would he shame us with his disappointment? We grew tired of trying to be the bigger person and decided to be the bigger killer. We just needed these feelings to stop messing with us.

Hong was somewhere close, and wherever he was, he was alone. We continued up the stairs until we reached a lone doorway that led to the roof. Without caution, we opened the door and searched the area with only our eyes, and suddenly something dashed in front of us. It was almost as if time slowed down as we watched a sword come within inches of our face, a grunt of evil intentions traveling through the soundwaves close behind. We quickly raised our gun in defense to block the attack, but to our surprise, we had run out of bullets. Hong dashed by us, jumping over the fixtures on the rooftop.

"Come and get me, Red Eyes!" Hong shouted.

Hong ran to the edge of the building and began making his way down the ladder leading to the backside of the building. We slowly walked over to the edge, and those doubtful feelings loomed over us as we stared into the dark area. We couldn't determine right from wrong anymore; we just wanted to do what felt right to us.

"You'll die trying to catch me, Red Eyes!" Hong hollered.

The quick villain had already found him hiding in the darkness awaiting our descent down to his battleground. We tossed the empty gun and jumped off the roof, crash landing on the rocky ground. Hong's maniacal laughter echoed around dark corners as we followed his energy. We could hear steel being pushed around, his dark eyes watching us.

"That's it, a little closer," Hong's voice grunted.

We heard the sound of a match being lit and saw a small flame fall into darkness with a sudden big plume of flames on top of a small hill. The inferno fell sideways and rolled toward us. We jumped over it with ease, infuriated by Hong's games.

"Show yourself!" we roared.

The foolish Hong laughed at our anger, not realizing the threat that we truly were. His lucky swing had gained him arrogance but cost him common sense. We heard the click of a switch, and suddenly we were surrounded by the blinding lights of construction equipment. We covered our eyes as they readjusted to the light, and that was when Hong decided to make his move. He rushed us with his sword and slashed us across the shoulder. We roared from the sting of the cold steel into our arm while Hong carefully cleaned the blood from the blade with his hair. We turned and looked at him with a menacing rage in our eyes. He didn't deserve death with a smile. He flung the blade around in the air like a samurai, striking his attack pose at the end as he glared into our eyes.

"Come on!" Hong confidently hollered.

He motioned his hand toward us as a taunt to bring the battle to him as he waved his sword around. We removed our hood and pulled off our muzzle, hissing at him, our fangs dripping for another kill. The impatient fool rushed toward us, ready to unleash his most fearsome attack, and we were going to give him the chance to do it.

He swung his blade in every direction, and we dipped and dodged out of his way. We taunted him by staring directly into his eyes. With every missed swing, we could see the desperation in his soul. Hong wasn't crazy; he was terrified. He believed the stories he had heard about us, and he knew this was his last shot at survival. He knew it would be a dishonor to his family to lose. He knew he was going to die, though we applauded him for not going out like a punk. We let him keep going for another minute, and his swings weren't as strong and swift as they had been before. The brave fool had gotten winded but refused to give up...and then we remembered he'd cut our arm. We grabbed him by the wrist and squeezed tightly until he dropped the blade.

"You cut my arm," we growled.

We slammed our fist into his gut, and with it we took the last bit of breath he had. We raised him into the air, and his body wrapped around our fist.

"I've been having a few bad days lately. You should have just surrendered."

We slammed him to the rocky ground and watched his body quiver as the shock bounced him around. We kicked him in his side and watched him skid across the ground into the old brick wall. He wasn't dead, but he was in crippling pain. We walked toward him and knelt to watch him struggle to catch his breath. He raised his head and looked into our red eyes and started to grin as we stared back. We were done playing with him now; it was time to get the information we needed and go home.

"Listen closely, I will only say this once. I am on a mission to find specific people. You weren't one of them. I know you possess information that I want to know, and if you give it to me, I'll let you live," we said.

Hong grinned and coughed as he processed our request. Strangely enough, the brave fool was still defiant.

"You...you American fool. All you people do is betray your own. I'll never help you," he grunted.

You people? What did he mean by 'you people'? We rose to our feet and stomped thru his knee and immediately reached down and ripped off his calf. He screamed in agony and burst into tears from the unbearable pain. His screams calmed us enough to go on with our investigation.

"Perhaps you didn't hear me the first time; I tend to speak in a low tone. You have information that I want, and if you care to live, you're going to give it to me. Understand?"

"Whaddya...whaddya want?" Hong hollered.

"I want you to calm down and answer my questions. Who is Mr. Nassar, and where can I find him?"

Hong strained his eyes, looking at us as his tears fell. We knew more than he had anticipated.

"W-what do—what you want with Nassar?" he asked.

"What I want with him isn't your business. Where I can find him is what you're going to tell me."

We examined his pockets and noticed the shape of a cell phone in his pants. We didn't want to take the chance of him lying to us under pressure; he had already proven to be willing to die. We'd learned something about guys like this from all the movies we saw and hoped he was the same. Maybe we could trick him with his own honor system. We ripped open his pocket and snatched his phone.

"Well, it looks like I'm just going to have to give him a call myself, huh?" we said.

"No, no, please! I'll do it. Allow me to make the call; it is the honorable thing to do," Hong groaned, reaching for his phone.

That was easier than we thought. We handed him back the phone and crossed our arms, wondering if he was actually going to do it.

"Put it on speaker phone," we advised.

The phone rang for a moment, and finally, the voice of an elderly man came to the line, humbly greeting Hong as if he were one of his own.

"Hong, my boy. I hope all is well with you, friend. It is later than usual for your call," Nassar said.

The weakened Hong began to cry, his dishonor crippling him more than the pain of bleeding out from the loss of his leg. He looked at us as he raised the phone to his mouth, regretting his decision to make the call. We stared at him with a straight face, waiting for him to say the wrong thing.

"Mr. Nassar, I have failed you," Hong hacked. "The man with the red eyes, he is coming, prepare yourself. Tell all of your men. Tell them that—"

We took the phone from him and stepped away to finish the conversation, taking the pressure off of his ripped leg and allowing his blood to flow.

"Tell them the Red Dragon is coming. Tell them they will die trying to defend you. I know where you are now. I can feel your presence, and soon you will feel my hand crushing your heart while I look into your eyes. Hong and his men died trying to defend themselves. I suggest you take a lesson from his failure before I arrive. I'm coming for you, old man."

We dropped the phone and stomped it into pieces, leaving the elder shaken with our harrowing words. We picked up Hong's sword and looked over at him, fading from the blood loss. We walked over to his broken body and decided to take pity on him.

"You fought an honorable battle until the end. For that, I applaud you; however, there is one grave mistake you made. You cut my arm, and when you cut my arm, you cut through my hoodie. I liked this hoodie. I liked it a lot, and because of that, I'm going to kill you."

We took his sword and forced it through his chest and into the wall. His body went into convulsions, and blood began to spill from his mouth. His head slowly sank into his chest, and soon he stopped moving, his eyes still open as he took his last breath. We rose to our feet and looked down at the mess we'd made. Were our powers corrupting us? We felt fine while we tortured him to death, but now seeing him dead before us... We weren't the Red Dragon; we were a monster on a rampage. We loved it and hated it at the same time.

We made our way back to his office to grab the money bags, smelling the scent of blood and gunpowder in the air. We stepped out of the office and headed up to the loading docks upstairs, ignoring the innocent bodies lying around on the floor. They weren't our concern. We reached the front where we'd entered, and those old feelings of emptiness continued to kick us around.

We were going to set everything on fire, burn it all, but those people, they were probably bad people. They still deserved for their families to know what happened to them. Something was wrong with us. We had never been this sympathetic, even before the powers. We checked one of the bodies and found his cell phone, and called 911. After giving them a false name and reporting everything we saw, we ended the call and threw the phone into the back of one of the big rigs. We went outside and quickly set both of the trucks ablaze, watching the flames resemble the rage flowing through us. The blaring fire engines in the distance alerted us that it was time to go. We crept back through the woods back to our motorcycle, and hurried home.

We took a hot shower to wash our black blood off of us—another hoodie ruined. Strangely enough, we felt as if we weren't healing fast enough. We were anxious to rest, but we couldn't lie down until we picked the bullets out of us. We could feel a powerful disgust surrounding us. It grew more robust with each breath we took as we took our time massaging the bullets to the surface and pulling them out with our fingers. It was painful to do, but it was even more painful to see. The powerful disgust started to become overwhelming as our black blood tainted the water swirling down the drain. We stopped to look at one of the bullets, realizing how easily we could have died if we were still mortal. It was crazy to think of, but after being shot so many times, it was hard to believe that Carey and CJ had died from only one of these. We dropped each bullet on the shower mat and sat down to let the warm water mixed with our tears. Something was very wrong inside.

"Heru, what is this—this feeling," we breathed heavily. "It doesn't feel good."

The feeling was terrifying. We could feel it touching us. It felt like there was more than one.

"I feared this would happen," Heru groaned.

It was as if the disgust were in our minds and on our skin. We could feel its frustration; it was angrier than us. A disgust so powerful that goosebumps rose from our skin.

"It is them, the dark gods I have warned you about," Heru said.

"They found me?" we shrieked.

"Not exactly, Ojore. Something I seem to have forgotten," Heru sighed.

The disgust filled our chest with terror. This couldn't be. What were they going to do?

"As your chakras come into alignment, so grows the strength of your divine energy. Much like you have the ability to feel the energies of everything around you, they also have the ability to feel you. How could I have been so careless? I've forgotten to teach you how to hide your energy. My years in captivity have blinded me. Ojore, you must try and concentrate."

"Concentrate on what?" Ryan shook.

"You must concentrate on internalizing your energies to hide them. The less they sense of you, the less you will feel them," Heru explained.

"What about you? Can't they feel your essence, too?"

"No. Though our essences are aligned, my energy is confined by the dimensions of Duat. I am afraid you are alone in this circumstance," Heru sighed.

We closed our eyes as we sank into the tub. They were all over us, touching and prodding. For the first time since we had gotten our powers, we were truly scared.

The mental torment continued for the next couple of days; we just couldn't seem to shake it. We had declined training with Heru, as our trust in him had started to dwindle. We knew he could sense it, but it was as if he was avoiding the subject, too. It's even harder to distance yourself when you have a girlfriend that loves you. The heartbreak of sensing her energy after she had tried everything to make us smile. We didn't mean to make her feel useless, but whatever was on us was more than she'd be able to fix.

Life at home had taken a turn for the worse. The arguments had become louder and more violent. Reginald had been winning the arguments through intimidation and fear mongering. The night before, we'd heard him threaten to kill her, and shortly after, he'd left the house with Camille crying in her room, and tonight was no different.

We had killed so many people, people that we thought were bad in the name of revenge. We were afraid to grow; we were afraid of becoming a merciless killer without rival or consequence. Were we being encouraged by the good of our ancestors, or were we doing the bidding of a demon? Had we become a demon corrupted by our own power? Could it be that we were descendants of murderers, and that was the true reason why they were locked away in Duat? It couldn't be...could it?

This shit had to stop. Heru and Anpu had awakened us to so many things... Why wouldn't we trust them? Why wouldn't we believe their truth with the evidence of their stories all around the world? What the hell was making us feel this way? Where was our heart? Seventeen had never been this bad. We lay on our bed in the darkness of our room, listening to the tongue-lashing Camille and Reginald were giving each other. We soon realized the arguments were only one-sided, Camille desperately defending herself from Reginald's outlandish accusations. He'd married Camille thinking he had found a puppet because she played into his little game, and Camille, as sweet as she was, believed that her tenderness would soften him up and he would change for the better when in all actuality, he was destined to get worse. No matter what she did, no matter what she said, she was wrong. He took advantage of her kind weakness. She was still that little girl damaged by the sharp tongue of her mother.

They continued to get louder and louder, and we could no longer just lie still. We sat up on the bed with beads of sweat running down our forehead. We were angry, gritting our teeth as our fangs pressed firmly against our bottom lip. We dug our claws into our sheets as we released the heavy breaths of wrath boiling in our soul. We wanted them to stop. We needed peace and quiet, and we weren't going to get it.

"You goddamn bitch! I do everything for you! I pay the goddamn bills, I take care of your goddamn son, and I'm the reason you live in this goddamn house!" Reginald hollered.

"Reggie, I'm sorry. It's just been a long day, and I'm tired. If you want something to eat, just order it, and I'll go pick it up," Camille replied.

His alcohol abuse warped his brain and turned him into the enemy. Tonight was the night it was all going to take a turn for the worse. We could hear their voices in our head, all their arguments, all their bickering. We could feel our rage pounding through every muscle in our body along with our mouth salivating for another kill.

"You gettin' smart wit' me, bitch?" Reginald bucked.

We sensed a sudden change in Camille's energy. She was more scared of Reginald than she had ever been. Our eyes sharpened, our senses were heightened, and time stood still as her fears became our reason.

"N-no, I was just saying that–"

"I done told you 'bout gettin' smart with me!"

Reginald swung his fist without giving it a second thought. He punched Camille in the face and sent her crashing into the wall, and then we lost it. We broke from our room, coming around the corner roaring like the dragon from our dreams, ready to tear Reginald limb from limb. We bore witness to too many things in less than a split second. Camille was on her side, lying on the floor, and the wall had a brown mark from her face smearing makeup on it, and Reginald was standing over her with his fist cocked back, ready to hit her again. All bets were off. There was no mercy, there was no taking it back, there was no room for apologies. Reginald was about to die. We dashed toward him and jammed our fist into his gut, causing him to piss his pants and throw up all the liquor he'd drunk within the last hour.

"Don't touch my mother!" we roared.

We twisted our fist in his gut and grabbed his shoulder, tossing him into the glass kitchen table and menacingly stomping our feet as we walked toward him. Our rage craved blood; our fangs desired death. We had wanted to do this for so long, and the only thing that used to stop us was now barely conscious and lying on the floor. The shattered glass was stained with his blood from the impact, and the fragile steel frame broke into pieces. Dazed, confused, and barely able to breathe, Reginald rolled around in the broken glass, trying to figure out what happened. We could hear his voice in our head from the annoyances of how he wanted the dishes in the dishwasher, to every bit of belittling he had done to Camille. We remembered when she'd told us that he had searched through our things when we weren't there. It had all led up to this moment.

We grabbed him by the throat and forced him to look into our eyes. We wanted to make sure he learned what real fear looked like. He had bullied the joy from Camille, a joy that used to greet us tenderly with hugs and kisses, a joy that taught us that tomorrow would be a brighter day, a joy that could have possibly helped us get through the emotions that we were going through at the moment. He'd killed our joy, and we were going to return the residue of anguish he had left behind.

"Die!" we roared.

We sank our claws into his neck and squeezed tightly to watch his eyes bulge from the sockets. We cocked our fist back and aimed for his large, balding head. We had never realized how much hate we'd built up inside toward him. He should have been the first person we killed. We released an ear-shattering roar and fired our fist at his head as hard as we could. The impact was so powerful, the flesh and bones of his neck disconnected from his body. His head bounced on the floor and hit the wall, splattering blood around the kitchen. We'd done it. We'd killed him...finally.

We roared through the house once more, releasing the stress we had been holding in for so long. Our body started to shake while the warm blood from his neck stained our hands. We forgot where we were for a moment. That final punch had taken a lot from us; we'd put everything into it. The one task that we were ordained to do from birth was to protect our mother, and we had been failing miserably at it.

"Your mother, Ojore, go to her," Heru said.

We shook our head and snapped out of it. We let go of Reginald's headless body and grabbed a dish towel from the sink before we tended to Camille. She was still on the floor trying to get up. We eased her to her feet and guided her over to the couch. We ran to the freezer to get her an ice pack for her bleeding mouth. She was crying, and her embarrassment wouldn't allow her to look us in the eye, but we had to make her do it. It was the only way we'd be able to explain the mess we'd made.

"I tried. I tried so hard, I just—"

"Relax, Mama. It's okay, look at me. It's gonna be okay," we said.

"No, no, I can't. You were never supposed to see me like this," Camille sobbed.

We gently grabbed her wrist and forced her hands down and knelt before her. We had to let her see us.

"Mom, look at me."

Camille slowly raised her head as tears dripped from her chin. We wiped her teary eyes and slowly revealed our face to her. Immediately, her spirit turned on us, fearing the image of what her only son had become. She pushed our hands away and kicked herself up on the couch, backing away from us. We feared the punch had made her delusional, but we had to let her know we were real.

"No, no, no, no, no!" Camille hollered.

"Mom, relax!" we pleaded. "Calm down. It's me, it's Ryan."

The frantic Camille took control of her breathing and slowly eased herself back on the couch. We both stared at each other for a moment, us trying to look as innocent as possible. We had to let her see us this way, let her know who we truly were. A moment went by, and she began to slowly examine our face like a mother would. She was still frightened by our demonic appearance. She looked into our red eyes and noticed the stress hiding underneath them. She moved our lips around to see our sharp fangs shining from the top and bottom row. She looked down and grabbed our hands to examine our claws and saw Reginald's blood stained across our arms. We immediately locked eyes again, and then she slowly turned her head into the kitchen. She saw the blood splattered on the wall and dripping from the window seal.

"Where's Reginald?" Camille asked.

We looked into her eyes and thought of Reginald's headless body hidden behind the kitchen island. His eyes were still open looking at us from the cold kitchen floor, still showing that angry scowl toward Camille.

"Mama, I got a lot of stuff I need to talk to you about."

We took our time telling her everything, even going all the way back to the accident and telling her what actually happened. It was the toughest conversation we had ever had with Camille because we had never been so honest with her before... we never could be before now. She cried on our shoulder, ashamed that she had lost touch with her son. We reassured her that she hadn't done anything wrong. Camille was a good wife, and as a good wife, she put her marriage first. Whether or not it was to the wrong person, she'd done the best she could with what she had. She hadn't forgotten about us; she'd just gotten lost in the idea of something she wanted so badly.

We helped her into her room, and she lay down on the bed. She looked up at us and held our hand, and we looked back, sensing her energy. She was going to need a lot of time to heal from this mistake, but we would be by her side every step of the way.

"I love you, Ryan, and please don't ever believe anything different," Camille said.

"I love you, too, Mama, and no matter what I believe, I'll never believe that you don't," we replied.

We kissed her on the forehead and walked out of the room, closing the door behind us. We had a huge mess to clean up in the kitchen, and with Camille out of the way, we'd be able to easily fix this. After cleaning the kitchen, we wrapped Reginald's head and body in large garbage bags to keep his blood from dripping all over the house and carried him to his car. We took him out of the bag, propped him up in the passenger seat, and let his blood leak all over the car. We took his head out of the bag and tossed it in the back seat and got in the driver's seat to put Reginald's death into play.

Reginald was a middle-aged man that had issues that stemmed from his childhood, issues that he never seemed to get over. In his young adult years, he and others had quickly learned from his experiences with alcohol that he had anger issues. Over time, he became more abrasive and disheartening to the women he dated, especially to one Camille Scales. He treated her as if she were a doormat until he decided that he wanted to redecorate.

One night in a drunken stupor, he punched her in the face and stormed out of the house to his car. He swerved across lanes, trying to drive to some unknown destination, and mysteriously made it to the highway. He pushed his engine, speeding up to over 100 MPH. He swerved again, and his car scraped against the guard rail, bouncing him to the other side of the highway. It flew off of the low soft shoulder and crashed hard into the thick Georgia pine trees. The impact crushed the front end of the car, decapitating him as his body flew through the windshield. Sparks from dismantled engine parts fell on the dry straw and met with the leaking gas tank, and seconds later, the car exploded causing a brush fire. Minutes later, several fire and police units arrived on the scene to block traffic and attack the blazing inferno.

We hid in the trees and watched him burn from the other side of the highway. We knew he was already dead… we just wanted to make sure he wasn't coming back. We wanted to make sure people saw his car swerving as we drove down the street to the highway. We took advantage of the night and put the car in cruise control to successfully jump out of the window before the crash. No one saw us do it, nor would anyone believe it if they had seen it. Reginald wouldn't be missed by anyone, not even his own family. No cop was going to question why he left the house when his signature was swelling on the side of Camille's face. No one would forgive him because he was dead, and there was nothing to redeem. His funeral would be small and boring, just like his existence.

We headed over to our hideout and retrieved the bags of money we had stolen and brought them home. We peeked in on Camille, who was fast asleep, ignoring the phone calls coming in from the police about her husband's accident. We had to take care of her, and it wasn't something that was going to be fixed overnight. She needed time to rediscover herself and believe that she had the power to move forward, but that wasn't something she was going to get from us. We tossed our dirty clothes into the wash and showered off the tainted blood from our body. As usual, we put on our boxers and basketball shorts and lay down on our bed with millions of dollars sitting next to us on the floor.

We were a lot calmer with Reginald out of the way, but his death only put a bandage on the real issue pressing us. There was more we needed to experience, more that we needed to explore, but first, we had to figure out what more was.

Anpu's watchful eye glared over Duat, his concern focused on Ryan's progression. He watched the trillions of souls glow in the darkness and began to wonder if this would be their eternity. He closed his eyes and sighed, trying to relax as the exciting development of the new God of War had become taxing on his mind. His faith was strong, but his hope was beginning to dwindle.

"I know you worry, Anpu," Heru said.

He slowly approached his brother from behind, both of them stressed from the situation.

"He is all that we have left. We have no choice but to believe in him, but I fear his age may be a problem," Anpu sighed.

"I do not believe his age is a problem for us. This is a matter of time. He is being forced to learn at a pace that far exceeds the time we were given to manifest our energies. In my opinion, he is doing exceptionally. He is learning how to better hide his energy, a tactic that will hopefully buy us some time with him. It is my hope that since he is not yet as powerful as them, they will disregard his energy," Heru said.

Heru looked about the glowing souls surrounding them, remembering how long it had been since they had been free to walk the earth.

"I can feel his energy. His alignment is almost there, but there's a battle going on within him. We can only hope that he comes out on the right side," Anpu said.

Heru stood silent, his thoughts at war with his logic, "He has to find his heart."

CHAPTER 21

A MATTER OF CONVERSATION

AFTER SEEING HIS daughter off to school, Omar went back into his room to prepare for his day. He checked the calendar on his phone to keep track of the upcoming due date for his debt as he counted the money he had already saved. He was still short by a few thousand, and with Sid and Murry coming to visit soon, his mind scrambled to find a way to get the money he so desperately needed. He grabbed his jacket and headed to the door, mixing his paranoia with determination.

The past few months hadn't been so great to Omar financially. The losses taken by the Illegit Family slowed the workload and put the devoted father into a money crunch. He couldn't go back to the warehouse because it had been destroyed in an explosion after being attacked by the guy with the red eyes. He had even tried to get a loan from a bank, but his weak credit history left him without leverage. Omar had been instructed to always park his car a short distance down the street from the trap to retain the peace in the area. He walked up to the house, scanning his eyes around the property to ensure the place hadn't been raided in his absence. He made his way inside and proceeded to be checked by the gunman overlooking the house.

The observant Omar had been a good employee during his time in the trap, gaining the trust of some of the Illegit members of the house. He worked in the room where they packaged up the now small shipments that went around to some of the gang's staples, and the observant Omar had also noticed that every Wednesday the funds generated from sales would be prepped and ready for pickup in a big black bag held onto by the gunman near the door. The black bag could have anything from a few hundred thousand or more, depending on how well business was going on a particular week, and with that thought in mind, Omar fathomed the thought of risking it all.

He went about his day as normal, processing whatever strain of drug was placed in front of him. He remained alert, his eyes attentively watching who and what came through the room he was in. The passing hours wore on his mind as he quietly stressed about his finances. With Aaliyah starting college in the fall, Omar felt it was his responsibility to support her financially through it all, just as he had for his late wife. He'd already been beating himself up for diving back into the lifestyle he'd once lived, but his inability to put his pride to the side unraveled him into a toxic mental overkill.

There was a knock at the door, and the gunman got up to open it. Omar's eyes went to work, observing two men walk into the room, both of them carrying several bags along with the notorious big black bag hanging from one of their shoulders. The men proceeded to an open table and dumped the money on top and started to do their count. Omar listened to the numbers they called out between each other and fantasized about what he could do with the amounts. With $100,000, he could pay off his debt with Sid and Murry, and with $350,000 his possibilities were endless. Shortly after counting all of the money, a call was made to confirm the amount that would be picked up later in the evening. Omar watched as the men placed the money into the large black bag and set it on the floor next to the gunman, who caught Omar's eyes looking strangely at the bag.

"You lookin' at the wrong thang, ol's school." The gunman brandished his weapon.

"S-sorry, I was...sorry." Omar lowered his head.

His fantasy of taking the money and running remained a fantasy, for another loss for him would lead to him and Aaliyah being out on the street or worse. He went back to quietly doing his job and kept his head low, allowing the voices of doubt and worry to take full residency in his mind. The sounds of a motorcycle blaring by in the distance took his mind down the highway of despair. A short while later, Omar neared the completion of his workday and started to text Aaliyah when a sudden loud boom shook the house. Everyone in the room looked to the door as their hearts fell to the floor. They were all aware of the attacks in previous weeks, and anything out of the ordinary was perceived as a threat.

The gunman drew his weapon and inched toward the door to listen to the sounds on the other side. His facial expression revealed that nothing good was happening down the hall. The men in the room had a choice: wait for death to come to them or make a break for it in hopes of a chance for survival. Omar stepped to the back of the room, his mind in a different place than the others. Desperation nestled its way into his brain and consumed him. In the wake of his wife's death, Omar had vowed that he would take care of Aaliyah by any means, even if it meant risking his own life to ensure her survival.

The observant Omar watched as the others crowded the door, using their fear as a distraction. He kept his eyes on the head of the gunman as he quietly pulled a hidden pocket knife from his jacket. He blocked every other solution out of his mind, waiting for the right moment to go through with his new plan.

"I can't sit here and wait for this shit to happen, I gotta get the hell outta here!" one of the men said.

"Me, too!" another agreed.

Suddenly, several gunshots went off down the hall, and the room went into a panic. The workers bum-rushed the door and nearly trampled over each other trying to get out. The gunman quickly jumped out of their way, watching them as they fled from the room, but he missed the observant Omar, who was watching him as he crept from the back of the room. The panicked gunman picked up the money bag from the floor, leaving himself open, and that's when Omar seized his fantastical moment. He pounced on the gunman and wrestled him to the ground while stabbing him in the neck. The frightened gunman was powerless to defend himself as the blade cut into his jugular and caused him to choke on his own blood. Omar's desperate effort turned him into a murderer, saving himself from a fate that he would have shared with the others if he hadn't acted.

He held the gunman down until he finally stopped moving, leaving the bloody knife in his neck, and quickly took the bag of money from his arm. The blocked sounds returned to their normal tone, and he could hear the gunshots and screams from men dying down the hall. Omar broke from the room and nearly tripped at the sight of one of the bodies of his Illegit superiors on the floor. He hurried down the stairs and nearly fell again trying to duck from the stray bullets flying through the house. He slipped through a puddle of blood from one of the men he worked with, his heart skipping a beat from the sounds of the terror taking place only one story above him. He pushed himself off the wall and kept moving. He had to make it to his car; he had to make it home to his daughter. He had to make sure she was safe, and he had to make it out of the house with the money.

The sounds of a demonic roar shook the house, and Omar could feel fear pulling at his soul. He finally found the open front door and broke out as fast as he could to get to his car. He was so close to achieving his goal, so close to being free, and then a dark and shadowy figure suddenly appeared in front of him as he stepped under the spotlight of a streetlight. Frightened and defenseless, Omar quickly turned and tried to run in the opposite direction, and to his surprise, the dark shadowy figure appeared in front of him.

"Give me the bag," the dark figure groaned.

Omar clenched the bag to his chest, unwilling to surrender the prize he'd worked so hard for, but without a weapon, he was powerless to fight. *I should have grabbed that guy's gun*, he thought to himself as he inched away from the dark figure.

"Please, my brother! I-I'm in a bad way right now. I owe some dangerous men some serious money, and my, my daughter, she needs money for school, like, this is my last hope. I've got nothin', this is all I got. I need this, please!" Omar pleaded.

The dark figure slowly stepped into the light, and Omar shrank as he stared back at the guy with the red eyes. They pierced through Omar's soul without regard to his meaningless words, the red-eyed man flexing his hands to sink them into Omar's neck.

"Give me the bag or I'm going to kill you," the red-eyed murderer swore.

Omar had vowed to his late wife that he would ensure the care of their daughter by any means, but the only stipulation was that he was to remember that he had something to live for. Within minutes of stealing the bag of money, Omar found himself surrendering the funds to the red-eyed menace, placing himself right back in the same worrisome place he'd started in.

"You made a wise decision, now make another one before I change my mind," the red-eyed guy grunted.

He slowly disappeared into the darkness, leaving the broken Omar standing alone under the streetlight. He dropped his hands to his sides with his body feeling empty from the robbery. In a matter of a few minutes, he had lost his job, his last hope, and now he was in the process of losing his mind. The sound of a motorcycle blaring in the distance snapped him out of his funk. He reached in his pocket and checked his phone and saw a text from Aaliyah.

K. ily!

Omar slowly walked to his car, losing his emotional battle as rain began to sprinkle over the neighborhood. He plopped into the driver's seat, and before he could start his car, he planted his face on the steering wheel and burst into tears, knowing there was nothing more he could do. He knew Sid and Omar weren't going to take what he had, and they weren't going to give him more time to get what he needed. After a while, he dried his eyes and drove home, fortunate to have escaped with his life.

He got home that night and sat in the driveway for a while, afraid to face his daughter and tell her what happened. Aaliyah's birthday had just passed, and the 18-year-old was excited to prepare for her next journey in life. With graduation in three months and college starting in six, the two had spent some time over the weekend buying supplies she would need for her dorm. Omar thought of her acceptance letter hanging on the refrigerator and lost his nerve. He texted Aaliyah and told her he had a few runs to make and backed out of the driveway without a destination in mind.

The next morning Omar lay awake in his bed listening to the sounds of Aaliyah preparing for school. He had been staring at the ceiling hoping to get an idea of what to do, but he realized he didn't have the drive anymore. He was no longer the man he had once been with the unstoppable hustle, falling into the role of the tired old man the Illegit members used to make fun of. He heard Aaliyah's footsteps heading downstairs and quickly hurried out of bed to catch her before she left.

"Li-Li!" he hollered from the top of the stairs.

"Yes?" Aaliyah answered.

Omar made his way down the stairs in his pajamas, nearly tripping over his own feet. He approached his beautiful daughter with his eyes riddled with stress and a smile, leaving Aaliyah to think he had just woken up. He'd failed his greatest creation, a truth his pride refused to let him tell as he looked into her brown eyes.

"Um, I'll uh, I don't have to work today, so, uh when you get home, uh, maybe we can go look for more college stuff for you, you know, i-if you want." He cleared his throat.

Clueless to his demise, Aaliyah smiled and agreed to the generous offer.

"Yay! I was hoping you'd get some time off soon," Aaliyah said. "Maybe we can go to the outlet mall and find the comforter set I was looking for."

"Yeah, yeah, we can do that." He grinned.

He looked at his daughter and was amazed at how much she had grown over the years. Her smile reminded him of the bright and jovial smile her mother had once had, a smile he had once been willing to do anything to protect.

"You are a very beautiful young woman, Aaliyah. Just look at you—all grown up, looking like your mother when I met her. She would have been so proud of you."

Omar's voice cracked, and Aaliyah immediately clung to her father to keep him from crying. She kissed him on the cheek as they hugged by the door, happy that her father was crying for a good reason. Omar hugged his daughter tightly, uncertainty written across his face as he looked out the window. Aaliyah looked up at him and smiled.

"Aw, Daddy, you didn't even cry like this when I actually turned 18," she laughed.

"I know." Omar smiled as his tears fell.

Aaliyah went to the kitchen to grab a napkin for her father while he looked out of the window at his car. She returned, and he wiped the tears from his face, struggling to hold back the truth.

"I should be home around 3:30 so we can leave as soon as I get home to beat the traffic," Aaliyah suggested.

"Yeah, sounds good. I'll be ready." He nodded.

He wanted so badly to tell her the truth but couldn't bring himself to speak it. He looked at her with his tired eyes and said the only thing he felt mattered.

"I love you, baby."

"I love you, too, Daddy. I'll see you later." Aaliyah headed out the door.

"I'll lock up. Be safe."

He watched her from the window until she turned the corner and headed back upstairs to his depression. He sat on his bed feeling just as empty as he had in his car the night before. He lowered his head and rubbed his beard, and as he raised his head, his eyes spotted the black pistol he had sitting on the dresser. His emotions subsided, offering him one solution to solve his personal problems. He walked over to the dresser and grabbed the gun, examining it in his hand. He looked in the mirror and saw a lesser version of himself holding the gun. His mind settled on his thoughts as he dropped his hands and turned away from the mirror.

Our days were getting a little better. We had been traveling to the Spirit Realm to see Janay and relaying Jenise's words to her. She was doing better, too. The doctors were still reluctant to release her because it had been so long, but they assured us that if she kept on the path she was on, they'd release her eventually. Aaliyah was still faithfully by our side. We had to give her a lowkey gift for her birthday to keep her dad from getting suspicious. We hadn't met him yet, and from what we've learned, a good gift at a young age usually leads to a bad first impression.

We did as much as we could do to keep a smile on her face, a few small gifts here and there, and words of affirmation every day. We yearned for more of her physical touch, but the desire to kill always seemed to kick harder. The school day ended, and we were walking home holding hands as we usually did. She had a certain excitement about herself, smiling more than usual, or at least more than she had been since we got into our funk. Her energy felt different. Maybe she'd gotten another acceptance letter.

"Have you heard from any of the colleges you applied to?" Aaliyah asked.

We knew it; she'd heard from another one of her top three. This girl was going places.

"Nothing yet," we replied.

"No worries, baby. A man of your talent, I know you'll be hearing something soon."

She paused for a moment and looked up at the trees with a smile. There was something else on her mind, something big, at least it was to her. She had a knack for telling us everything on her mind, so we waited for her to bring her thoughts to light.

"Do you think we have what it takes to survive in college?" she asked.

She was beating around the bush... and two can play that game.

"For me, I'll see when I get there. For you, I know you'll be phenomenal."

"That's not what I meant, baby," she giggled. "I mean us. Do you think our love is strong enough to survive for four years?"

We took a moment to think about her question. We had only been together for a few months, and already we were about to face a make-or-break situation. She had been the voice we needed to hear to keep us from sinking deeper into ourselves, a woman that any man would be foolish not to want by his side. She showed promise and potential, and there was one other thing about her that we knew.

"I know I don't want to endure this life without you, and I know I don't want to have you as just my friend. True enough, we don't know what the next four years is gonna throw at us, but I know one thing—"

We stopped and gazed into those beautiful *mezmer-eyes*, our breath taken away as they glistened in the sunlight.

"You're the kind of woman that I'd want to marry."

Her face lit up, and once again we saw our brown girl turn red. Her smile made us smile, for we truly believed the words we'd said to her. Aaliyah provided that missing element from our life that we longed for. There was love, there was tenderness, there was passion—all that was missing was the fantastical wedding before the ancient gods.

"Oh, babe! You really wanna marry me?" Aaliyah asked.

"I think you already know the answer to that, Sweets." We smiled. "What made you ask me that?"

She clenched our hand a little tighter and stepped in front of us. Was she about to propose? She looked into our eyes full of confidence and sincerity and said something we would never have guessed.

"I want you to meet my dad."

Our eyes shot open. She was serious.

"Your dad? Today?" we asked.

"Yeah, he's off today, and we're supposed to be going to go look for stuff for college, and with him finally getting a day off work, I figured this would be the perfect opportunity for you guys to meet, that's if you think you're ready," she said.

We were shocked that she asked, considering we didn't anticipate meeting him until prom which was months away. This was all happening so soon, but we couldn't say no, not to our goddess. We had been around the toughest of criminals, but nothing could have prepared us for the moment of meeting her father.

As we neared her house, the intensity of the moment grew. We saw his car parked in the driveway and realized how on the spot Aaliyah had put us. We weren't prepared to answer questions, and we weren't dressed the way we would have liked to have been, not to mention the awkward face we make when we're faking a smile. We couldn't imagine this going well, nor would we imagine it going bad. We had just ransacked a trap house and survived the night before, but as long as we stuck to the subject of high school, we'd be safe. Aaliyah hurried in front of us to put her key in the door and looked back with a huge grin on her face. Her excitement told us that we were the first guy she'd ever brought home. She unlocked the door and paused.

"You wait by the door, and I'll get him," she said.

She slowly opened the door, trying to hold in her excitement as she entered the house and called for her father. We crept in slowly behind her and stood by the door, trying to hide how nervous we were. Hank had taught us that we should shake hands firmly and look whoever we were talking to in the eye. We turned toward the window, trying to figure out what to say if he were to ask us about college when suddenly, our concentration was broken by the sound of the most terrifying scream we had ever heard in our entire lives.

"Aaliyah!"

We quickly turned and saw half of Aaliyah's backside in the doorway of the kitchen and immediately rushed to her aid. She was inching her way out of the kitchen with her hands up to her face and bumped into us as we approached, causing us to look down. What we saw was a familiar red substance splattered on the floor. Aaliyah fell into our arms crying as we slowly looked up at the kitchen table. No...no, it couldn't be!

Last night, we ransacked a trap house and killed everyone inside. We'd chased a man outside and demanded the bag of money he was holding. He'd pleaded with us to let him have it, that he needed it to pay his debts, that he needed it for his daughter, that he had nothing left. We should have let him keep the money.

Omar dropped his hands to his side with his gun in hand and went downstairs to the kitchen. The troubled man couldn't scrounge up the energy to eat anything. He sat at the table for hours going back and forth about the idea that had popped into his head. He no longer had the drive, he no longer had the desire, he no longer had a reason. His depression and anxiety joined forces and told him what to do. They lied to him and told him Aaliyah would be better off without her father to support and protect her. They told him that he had failed as a father. They told him he was better off dead.

Omar cried as he sat at the table and agreed with his depression and anxiety and carried forward with his plan. He went upstairs and took all of the money he had been saving and piled it safely on Aaliyah's bed with a note to ensure that she wouldn't miss it. He went back to the table and grabbed the black pistol and chambered a round. Tears rolled down his cheeks as he said a prayer asking for the protection of his daughter. He raised the cold pistol and placed the barrel in his mouth, shaking as he closed his eyes one final time.

His body was in a chair and slumped over the kitchen table, leaking blood to the floor. His brains were splattered across the walls and floor of the kitchen from the bullet exiting out of the back of his head. His eyes were slightly open, looking at us with that tired desperation from the night before. We recognized his face, we could hear his voice, but we couldn't feel his energy. The walls closed in on us, and we couldn't breathe. We replayed those moments under the streetlight in our head again and again. He had nothing left, he was in debt, he had to take care of his daughter. If only we would have listened. If only we would have just given him the money.

We dragged Aaliyah outside and called the police. Within minutes, several squad cars and an ambulance pulled up to us sitting outside crying on the steps. The cops closed off the street as several neighbors peeked from their front doors to see what was happening. We held Aaliyah tight and blocked her eyes as they wheeled his body outside. She broke down crying in our arms, and we remembered that she had once told us that she didn't have any more family. We were literally all she had. The cops pulled her away from us for a moment to ask her some questions, and we sat on the stoop observing her and trying to gather our thoughts.

"Why didn't I know it was him? Why couldn't I sense his presence and know it was her father?" Ryan asked.

"You had never met him before. You had no way of knowing it was him," Heru said.

"That makes no damn sense. They're related, shouldn't they share some sort of, like, spiritual bond that lets me know who they are? He was her dad, man," Ryan freaked.

"Ojore, contain yourself! You know that every living being carries its own energy, and those energies are unlike any other. This was not your fault! Remember this important fact: You let him live; he chose to take his own life."

Heru's words cut the tension we were carrying. We could have met him today. We could have seen his face, we could have remembered him, we could have found a way to help him, we would have helped, but he made the decision to commit suicide. As tough as it was to accept, we weren't responsible for his death. The situation didn't leave us much time to dwell on our issues as the cops neared the end of their investigation. Aaliyah's neighbors crowded the front of the house from the other side of the police tape, offering their condolences, kind enough to place candles on the sidewalk in his honor.

The final squad car left, and after a while, Aaliyah's crowd dispersed back into their homes. We walked back to the stoop of the house and sat down under the sunset. She leaned on our shoulder, and we placed our arms around her, feeling her quiet tears fall on our hand. We sat in silence for about twenty minutes, wishing we could take her to the Spirit Realm to see him just to give her some type of closure, but it wouldn't solve anything.

"Where am I gonna go? Where am I gonna stay? I don't have any family. I don't wanna stay with any of my friends, I just don—"

She burst into tears again. We held her close and kissed her forehead thinking of what we could do. It would have been a simple task to take her home and tell Camille what happened, but we had to keep our secret. We couldn't let her know who we really were, what we really did, and we definitely couldn't tell her where we'd run into her father.

"Baby, it's okay, it's okay. Listen, listen, I got an idea. We can get you a hotel room and you can drive your dad's car to school," we suggested.

"I don't have any money. My dad wouldn't let me work, and I don't have anything saved up," Aaliyah cried.

We lifted her chin and made her look into our eyes. The sweet girl even cried pretty. We hoped to never see her distraught like this again.

"Who said anything about money? Just listen to me. Let's go upstairs and get as much of your stuff as we can. I'll take care of the rest."

We helped her to her feet and held her close when we crossed the threshold of the house. Everything felt strange, like walking into a morgue. We entered her room, and she immediately saw the money sitting on her pillow. There was a note sitting next to the small fortune that read *It's yours. I love you.* The final gift he would leave her.

"This was the money he was saving to pay those guys he owed," she whimpered. "What do I do?"

She looked at us with her troubled eyes, and we couldn't free ourselves from the guilt. She was hurting because of our negligence. That old familiar feeling began to come on us again. We had to move quickly and get her out of here.

"Put it in your bookbag and hold on to it. We need to get your clothes."

We packed her clothes and essential items into laundry bags and an old suitcase and put them in her dad's car. Exhausted from her tears, we helped her to her car and locked up the house. We wanted to get a hotel room for her, but first, we had to go home and get some money. It would have been better for her to stay with us so we could keep her under our protection, but Camille was still unstable after all that had happened. Things had been quiet since Reginald's cremation, and she allowed his family to keep the urn. She hadn't said much lately, and now wasn't the time for us to spring something like this on her.

We parked in the driveway and left Aaliyah in the car to go inside. Camille was in her room napping after a long day, so we kept quiet to make sure we didn't disturb her peace. We got back in the car, and Aaliyah was fighting sleep, admiring a picture of her and her father from years ago. We dried her eyes and kissed her cheek and proceeded to drive to a local hotel. We got her the best room in the building with the idea to keep her there as long as she needed it. As we walked back to the car to retrieve her belongings, it hit us that we were truly all she had left. We were too deep in our own mind to realize that she didn't have a group of girlfriends that she hung out with, and we had never really talked about friends because we were all that mattered to each other when we were together. The anxiety we felt began to get heavy on us, and we felt like we were starting to drown.

When we got to her room, Aaliyah placed her picture on the bedside table and lay across the bed. She was exhausted. Her eyes were puffy from all of the tears, and she even felt spiritually drained. We helped her undress and left her to rest while we got the rest of her stuff from the car. We were so consumed with anxiety as we played the blame game in our head. We needed to go after someone. It seemed that everyone was dying except for the people that we wanted to kill. We wanted Face's blood on our hands, along with anyone else that was involved with him, and we were going to go get it all tonight.

We got back to the room and placed her clothes in the closet. She opened her beautiful, cried-out eyes and looked up at us as we sat on the bed next to her. The stress we both displayed as we looked into each other's eyes only made the situation worse. We placed her hand on top of hers and kissed her forehead, preparing ourselves to leave.

"Can you stay?" Aaliyah asked.

A question we weren't prepared to answer in the least. She sat up and rubbed her eyes before using her magic to direct our anger into compassion.

"I know it's...I-I just don't wanna be alone right now," she sobbed.

We instantly wrapped our arms around her, and she bore her face into our chest to cry. We couldn't leave her like this. She needed us by her side more than anything right now. We pulled away from her and kissed her forehead and looked into her eyes.

"Of course, Sweets. You know I'd never leave you like this."

We kissed her back down to the mattress to make sure she lay down. A saving grace she was for our enemies, as they'd live to die by my hands another day while our rage sat just beneath the surface on reserve. We removed our boots and our jacket and turned off the light, allowing the glow of the streetlights to color the room from the window. We lay in the bed next to her still trying to convince ourselves that we weren't wrong for what we did. There was so much going on in our minds, so much work that needed to be done. We weren't completely put together, and our goddess was falling apart.

"Can you hold me?" Aaliyah asked.

We had to let it go for now. We rolled on our side and spooned our goddess, wrapping her tightly in our arms. She was asleep before we could even tell her goodnight.

"I love you, Sweets."

That night we traveled to the Spirit Realm, fighting shame with principle. We couldn't help but feel terrible, but our actions were unjustified. As the ancestors guided Ryan down to the rough sands, he spotted Heru waiting for him with his arms folded. His aura engulfed his body and slowly withered away as he touched down. He looked up at Heru, doing his best to maintain a straight face. The slightly annoyed Heru simply shook his head, struggling to find compassion.

"Are you absolutely sure that you want to do this now?" Heru asked.

Ryan lowered his head to the sands and rubbed away a tear forming in his eye.

"Yes."

Heru sighed. His factual statements would not remedy the situation to his liking. He paused and set his emotions aside to gauge the situation from an immortal perspective.

"If you feel you must do this now, allow me to caution you before I take you to him. You have not fully recovered from your own issues with Janay, and I fear that this may only make things worse for you if you do not see and understand it in the way that I have prescribed. His death is not your fault, Ojore. It would be different if you were to have killed him, but you did not. He made the decision to take his own life, and he proceeded with the actions to do so; therefore he is responsible for his own death. You let him live, giving him the option to choose his own fate. It was not a choice that you or I or the ancestors could change. The only thing that you're in control of is you."

Ryan kept his eyes on the rough sands in commitment to his decision. He heard the words of his elder and hoped that they would find their place in his mind before he met with Aaliyah's father.

"I'm ready to see him now," Ryan said.

Heru's logistical understanding wouldn't allow him to conceive Ryan's emotions, but despite his feelings, he journeyed to Duat with Ryan. They arrived to find Anpu standing on the dark sands with the empty Omar on the open plain. He still appeared to carry the stress from his earthly worries as the pairs stood far across from each other. Ryan nervously struggled to find the courage to speak to his girlfriend's father. He feared that the meeting would set them apart, and he'd never obtain his approval.

"This is what you wanted, Ojore. You must face your fears just as you face life—fearlessly," Heru advised.

Ryan swallowed his pride and raised his head high as the two left their guides and walked to meet each other in the middle of the dark sands. They stood before each other, granting mutual respect. They saw the stress in each other's eyes, Omar shedding a tear as he recognized the young man before him. The souls of Duat had no voice, granting Ryan the perfect opportunity to be honest.

"Hello, Mr. Latrell, my name is Ryan," he said nervously. "I'm your daughter's boyfriend."

Omar turned his head and raised his brow, scanning the young punk and stressing about his daughter. He balled his fist and straightened his back as if he were ready to attack.

"I'm also the guy that robbed you at the trap house the other night."

Omar's expression changed, and he lowered his fist to his side. More of his tears rolled down his cheeks as he tried to control his anxiety. Ryan's fiery aura engulfed him and transformed him into the image that Omar knew as the guy with the red eyes. Omar's eyes widened with fear as he backed away from the menace, but he was stopped by Anpu, who placed his hand upon his shoulder.

"I'm not here to hurt you. I wanted to talk to you about Aaliyah."

Omar stood up straight wiping his tears from his chin. Ryan nervously cleared his throat, trying to find the right words to heal Omar's broken spirit. The two faced each other, sympathizing over the one girl they loved the most.

"I think it goes without saying that I wish I would have let you keep the money. Our meeting would have happened under better circumstances. You know, Aaliyah wanted me to meet you today. She...she was so excited. She told me right after school because we were talking about college, and she asked me if I thought we could make it all the way through, together, and I told her...I told her she was the kind of woman that I'd want to marry. She looked so happy," Ryan said.

Tears formed in both of their eyes. Omar looked off in the distance, trying to keep his composure. Ryan lowered his head toward the dark sands and wiped his eyes.

"I wish she wouldn't have found you that way. I can still hear her scream in the back of my head. She was so frightened. I tried to console her the best I could, but when I saw it was you, I broke down, too."

Omar shamefully turned away and covered his face to hide the tears falling from his eyes. Ryan wiped away his tears and looked at Omar as seriously as he could.

"Mr. Latrell, I am the God of War, and my war was not with you. The situation that caused this is bigger than both of us, but it doesn't remove my responsibility. I want you to know that Aaliyah is safe in my care. For the time being, I've set her up in a hotel, and I'll even buy her a car to make sure she can get around when she goes to school. I'll protect her, I'll love her just as she tells me you loved her mother. She'll never have to worry about anything, and you've seen what I'm capable of, so you know I'm serious. Your daughter loved you, sir, and I will do everything in my power to ensure that your effort is recognized by the world, and that she excels to be everything you hoped that she would and more," Ryan promised.

Omar turned back to Ryan, and the two faced each other as men. Suddenly, Omar sprang toward Ryan and hugged him, and they held each other for a moment and sobbed. Omar's hug served as a symbol of his approval over his daughter's choice, and with it, he released the darkness that plagued him. His spirit became brighter like some of the other souls, and he appeared to be at peace with himself. Omar smiled as they pulled away from each other, putting his trust into the god before him. They shook hands, and Omar nodded his head, grateful for his daughter's protection.

We woke up early the next morning, and the reality of the situation hit us all over again. Aaliyah was lying next to us sleeping peacefully as we sat up in bed. Her things were all around the room as we had left them the night before. We checked our phone and didn't have a call or text from Camille, but we had to get home anyway for school. We typed a quick text to Aaliyah and quietly snuck out of her room. We transformed outside once we were in the clear and dashed through the woods to the house.

Camille had already left for work, but we still needed to talk with her later. We took a quick shower and scrubbed the dried tears from our face, allowing the warm water to soothe us as we remembered the conversation we'd had with Mr. Latrell. We wished we could tell Aaliyah about it and how happy he had been when we'd parted, but it was something that we would have to keep to ourselves. We walked to our room to get dressed and looked at our muzzle in the closet, giving rise to our rage again. A furious rage filled our hearts with a desire for blood on our hands. We didn't care what was right or wrong anymore; all we cared about was revenge. We put on a pair of cargo pants and grabbed a hoodie as we stuffed our feet into our composite boots. We snatched our muzzle from the top of the closet and shoved the Buddy in our pocket as we headed to the garage, rejecting our first chance to eat.

We flew across town, driven by our unstoppable rage. We no longer cared if anyone saw us on the motorcycle. All that mattered was that we had the blood of our enemies on our hands. It had been a while since we'd threatened the man known as Nassar, enough time for him to beef up his security in anticipation of our arrival. It was time to deliver on our promise and show up to make him feel our fury. Our wrath guided us to a mosque that sat just outside of the city. We were baffled that an evil businessman would be at such a profound place, but we proceeded with our criminal intent regardless. We decided our muzzle and hood wouldn't be necessary for this mission—everyone was going to die. We began our rampage with an ear-shattering roar to alert

Nassar and his men that we were outside and stormed toward the building like a one-man army.

The elder Nassar was surrounded by several of his men praying in his private quarters as the powerful roar shook the room. They all looked to the door in shock, ready to face the revelation the elder had prepared them for. Nassar remained seated as they all rose to their feet like soldiers.

"Protect the elder!" one of Nassar's men shouted.

The unarmed men filed out of the room, ready to challenge the guy with the red eyes in the name of their leader. The last man left the room, closing the door behind him, leaving Nassar to sit quietly. He himself didn't believe that one man could cause such destruction, even with the death of his beloved friend Hong, but he chose not to call in his task force to assist his defenseless soldiers. Before he could reach for his cell phone, the old man heard the gut-wrenching sounds of his men being reduced to fallen warriors. There were sounds of glass breaking and tables being destroyed, followed by the hellish roar of a beast that seemed to be getting closer and closer. Nassar sat motionless on the floor, listening to the painful sounds as he closely watched the door.

The elder became nervous without his cigar to smoke, and he began to sweat profusely as the painful sounds echoed in his head. He lowered himself into his prayer position and prayed for the souls of his men in honor of their sacrifice. He continued to pray until suddenly there was silence. He raised himself from the floor and sat up straight, his teary eyes glued to the door. There were no more screams, there were no more objects being broken, but the terror hadn't stopped. He could hear the sounds of a man breathing heavily on the other side of the door. He watched as the doorknob slowly twisted and the door creaked open from its latch. It was him: the man with the red eyes.

We were even more enraged to find that Nassar had lived to be so old. We'd anticipated more of a challenge finding him, but his pathetic unarmed soldiers made the task easier than raiding one of Face's drug houses. We sensed his fear from outside; he wasn't ready to die. He nearly had a heart attack as we stood in the doorway with his men's blood dripping from our fingertips. Saliva dripped from our fangs while we thought about how we wanted to break him apart. We took one step toward him, and he gave us what we thought was his final plea.

"You have kept your word in finding me," the weary Nassar stated.

"I'm not the kind to waste my words," we grunted.

We could see the rise and fall of his chest increase as we got closer to him. The beads of sweat on his forehead ran down his cheek into his beard as his lips trembled with his words.

"Y-you, you are...a very powerful man. Y-you serve great p-purpose," he continued.

"And I have a greater purpose for killing you," we growled.

The terrified elder froze in place as he neared his demise. We readied our hands to take our time ripping his flesh from his bones. He closed his eyes and slowly bowed his head, appearing to accept his unavoidable fate.

"Y-you, you are...y-you are a very troubled man. I-I am sorry... for your pain."

We stopped in place. It was as if an invisible barrier sprang in front of us. We looked at Nassar. Our claws craved his blood on them, but our mind wouldn't allow us to move.

"Your pain...it is unfair. Your rage i-is justified. I-I understand your emotion."

The tension in our forehead increased, and our shoulders tensed up. Our rage rested on the surface of our skin, causing our hands to shake. We breathed heavily, battling our emotions with logic. He was trying to distract us, but we couldn't sense any ill-intentions coming from him... but why were we listening to what he was saying?

"I know what you are...here to do, but I worry your actions may not bring you the peace you desire. I beg you, talk to me." Nassar beckoned.

Our hands shook from the tension breaking away from our body. We closed our eyes, and the thoughts of everything we were dealing with rushed through our mind. Aaliyah's loss was our loss, Camille's pain was our pain, and we yearned to hear our sister's voice. We'd never see our cousin's graduation day, nor would he ever get to experience the adult joys of life. Carey had done the worst of the best he could, for his son, for both of us. He'd never grow old enough to see the manifestation of his sacrifices. Nassar slowly reached out his hand to us, and suddenly the dynamic of power equaled in the room. We felt a shift in his energy; it was genuine. Our rage settled, and our fist shook as we angrily stared back at him, willing to fulfill his request.

"Talk to me." Nassar shed a tear.

We closed our eyes and released a deep exhale, taunted by the peace we so deeply desired. We slowly knelt and sat on the floor across from Nassar, our eyes locked on him, watching his every move. We placed our rage on a short leash and allowed the old man his chance to speak to us.

"I am grateful for your mercy. I sense that there is a problem, a problem that...that you desire to avenge. I know your quarrel is not personal with me, but I wanted to offer a different perspective on how to look at the situation," Nassar said.

We listened to the old man speak, wondering where his words would leave our feelings. We were carrying so much pain and covering it up with our rage. Destruction was our muse, and we saw nothing wrong with it because it's what we'd wanted all along. To be left alone is to be free.

It all seemed to begin when Ryan was a young boy. He shared his kindred spirit with the children of the neighborhood, always smiling, but there's always the one kid that comes around and changes things. He and his best friend Byron were outside showing off their skills at throwing spirals with a football. Ryan, the tough competitor he was, threw the ball as high as he could to ensure Byron wouldn't be able to catch it. The ball soared over Byron's head and crashed to the ground a few yards behind him, bouncing into a roll that led him to the street.

Byron went to recover the loose ball, but as he made it to the street, he found that his football had been recovered by three bigger, unknown kids that were roaming the neighborhood. Byron asked for his ball back, but the kids refused and taunted Byron, keeping the ball away from him. Ryan heard the frustration of his friend and ran to his aid, finding that the three bullies were pushing the poor boy around. They knocked him off his feet and mocked his cries as Ryan ran up to defend him. He fearlessly demanded the ball back as he helped his friend to his feet but was immediately met with excessive force from one of the boys who punched him in the face and knocked him to the ground.

The foolish boys laughed at Ryan as he struggled to pick himself up from the hot pavement. He turned his head in a daze to see his best friend curled into a ball holding his ribs in pain. He felt a warm liquid drip onto his hand and looked down to see the blood that had leaked from his nose. He slowly rose to his feet and watched the drips of blood roll off his fingers and onto his new shirt. His eyes focused on the blood as tears filled the wells of his eyes, but he had no urge to cry.

His thoughts began to process ten times faster, and an incredible anger flooded his senses. His hands started to shake as he balled them into fists and brought them to his face. His heavy breaths turned to unhindered grunts of anger to the sounds of his best friend's painful groans. The unplayful bullies grew concerned about his strange behavior and slowly approached him to satisfy their curiosity. They grabbed him by his shoulder, and in the blink of an eye, everything went black.

There was a loud ruckus outside the apartment, and a young boy's voice screaming for help echoed through the breezeway.

Fearing her son might be in danger, Camille rushed outdoors to save her only child. The boys were not in the place they'd advised they would be, prompting her to follow the harrowing sounds of anger coming from the street. The grunts grew louder and louder as Camille dipped between the parked cars to find the auspicious feat.

Two of the bullies lay on the ground, one face down and motionless while the other rolled around, groaning. The last was probably the most terrifying thing Camille had seen her son do in his youth. He had one hand gripping the throat of his final victim, roaring at him with every blow he delivered. Blood leaked from the boy's nose and mouth while he flailed his arms, trying to block the surprisingly stifling punches, but his efforts were unsuccessful. Camille shouted to her son, desperate to end the rampage, but after catching a glimpse of the darkness in his eyes, she feared he was too far gone.

Ryan switched his attack, joining his hands and strangling the foolish bully. His arms were locked, and his fingers dug into the thick neck of his victim. He dug his knee into the boy's sternum with his eyes wide open. The sinister look in Ryan's eyes terrorized the boy's spirit and caused him to wet his pants. Ryan growled like an animal in the wild as he looked down at his foolish prey. Camille ran over to her son in desperation and pried him off of the boy before he passed out. He went wild with screams, flailing his arms around like a crazed animal, his hands craving more of his enemy's blood smeared over them.

We quietly exited the room closing the door behind us and made our way through the mosque, observing the destruction we'd created in our haste. The background noise in our head was settled as we finally accepted the things that we couldn't change. We made our way outside, and the bright light of the sun shone on our skin bringing a genuine peace to our spirit. Geared up and equipped with knowledge, we started up our motorcycle and followed the road that took us home. Once we arrived, we sat in the garage for a moment gathering our thoughts. There were so many things we'd gained perspective on during our conversation with the old man that brought us to the next level of understanding. There was a purpose behind everything we had done and would do, we just had to get to a point of comfort with it all. There was so much that was said, so many feelings, so many emotions, but now we knew that we'd be okay with time.

The morning was still young, the time placing us somewhere around 2nd period, so we decided to head to school. The staff at the attendance office didn't seem to care for our excuse for being tardy. A simple 'I'm a senior,' and it was an all-access pass to any class. We got to our AP Lit class thinking nothing of the night before. We knocked at the door, and a few seconds later Mr. Stevens opened it. Once he saw it was us, he placed his hand on our shoulder and looked us in the eye.

"Hey, do you mind talking to me after class?" he whispered.

"Uh, yeah, no problem," we replied.

Instantly, we could feel a shift in his energy and an even greater shift as we entered the classroom. It hadn't occurred to us that word of Mr. Latrell's suicide had gotten around, and with Aaliyah not being here today, all of the attention would fall on the person closest to her. We took our seat, feeling the eyes of sorrow from the other students as we passed by. We started to miss our baby but couldn't muster up the energy to text her. She hadn't texted us, so we assumed she was still sleeping, but ultimately, we had just made some form of peace within us, and we didn't want to disturb hers.

Class ended, and we walked up to Mr. Stevens' desk as the room emptied. The troubled man took off his glasses and rubbed his forehead. Mr. Stevens was a good man. He cared about his job, and more importantly, he cared about each and every one of his students. He didn't take well to the news of his star pupil, and her not being at school today put him in a very dark place.

"When I read the email this morning, I was speechless. I've had some pretty harrowing situations happen to some of my students, but this...this just breaks my heart. How is she doing?" Mr. Stevens asked.

We didn't know what to say. How was Aaliyah doing after finding her father dead with his brains splattered on the walls, floor, and kitchen table? How would anybody be after the one person they love kills themselves? How in the hell were we supposed to answer this question? We lowered our eyes and sighed as her unpleasant scream echoed in the back of our mind. She wasn't okay... she was broken and probably contemplating the same fate.

"All I can tell you is that she's going to need a lot of time to get through this," we replied.

Mr. Stevens rose to his feet and hugged us. We needed it; putting on a face for the game wasn't always so easy. He placed his hand on our shoulder and looked us in the eyes just like our uncle used to when he'd say something that he really wanted us to listen to.

"I don't know what it's like to witness something like that, but I do know the importance of being that shoulder to lean on when someone's going through something. Please, Ryan, be her anchor, be the strength that keeps her strong. She's going to look to you to be there for her. I can see it in your eyes, I know you love her. Please...don't let her down," Mr. Stevens stated.

A kind charge from a man who led with his heart. We respected Mr. Stevens for all that he had done for his students. Aaliyah was his favorite. He'd helped her get scholarships and even helped her focus on her development in her writing. He even knew Mr. Latrell quite well. He treated Aaliyah like his niece and had done everything he could to make sure she would shine after graduation. He entrusted the responsibility of her heart to us.

The day went on, and a few others had come to us to offer their condolences and ask about Aaliyah. We didn't tell them much, nor did we reveal where we had taken her. It was strange being in this position, but we couldn't help but think it was preparing us for something we weren't ready to deal with, which we were still unsure of. The lunch bell rang, and Terrell joined us outside in the cool winter air. We didn't want to be around everyone in the cafeteria with all the questions; we would rather they just walk around moping like people at a funeral. There were only a few people in the courtyard, and we were far on the other side keeping our distance. The cold air was nothing to our skin, but Terrell struggled to stand with us.

"It's like the Grim Reaper is just on a killing spree." Terrell shivered. "First my brother, then your mom's husband—well, he doesn't really count—then her father! This shit is getting too close to home."

And let's not forget the plethora of men and women we've slaughtered over the past few months and the many more we intended to rid the world of.

"Don't tell anyone I told you this, but I was with her when she found him," we stated.

"You what?" Terrell's eyes shot open.

"Keep it down." We lowered our head to dodge the attention. "Yes, I was there. It was a very...we wish we hadn't seen it."

"Bro why did you..." Terrell lowered his voice, "why did you come to school today? After seeing something like that you need to go see a therapist or somethin'."

We blew steam from our mouth and looked up at Terrell from behind our dark truth.

"I've seen a lot worse."

There was a girl that had entered the courtyard as we were talking. She had on a thick coat with a hat and her face slightly covered as she walked over to us. Terrell looked up at her as she approached, and his energy became very nervous.

"You aight, bro?" we asked.

His eyes opened wider with each step that she took. We could hear his heart beating faster and faster, tripling the pace of her footsteps.

"That's...that's..." Terrell dropped his hands.

The mysterious girl walked up to us as if Terrell wasn't present. She fixed her hat and uncovered her face, revealing herself to us.

"Hey, are you Ryan?" she asked.

"Yeah," we replied.

She looked over at Terrell, nervous to speak on what was truly on her mind. She felt the same way we did as she stuffed her hands into her pockets. Terrell had gotten suspiciously quiet, his jaw locked as she stood before us.

"I'm Adrianna, Aaliyah's friend. Well, at least we used to be friends."

So that was it. This wasn't just an ordinary girl—this was Terrell's crush. She was a beautiful, fair-skinned Black girl with a slender, athletic build. She had freckles nicely speckled across her face with light brown eyes. Her hair was thick and natural, puffing out from under her hat, but what was that lingering under her eyes?

"Can I talk to you for a moment, privately?" she requested.

We looked over at Terrell, who looked as if his heart were stressed to its last beat. The poor boy had gone stupid in the mind over this girl and nearly pissed himself with her so close. He needed to get away from her until he grew the nuts to speak to her.

"Can you give us a minute, bruh?" we asked.

"Uh, uh, uh, y-yeah. I, uh, it's cold. I'll see you in class." Terrell quickly scurried off.

We were embarrassed for him. With any luck, he'd get it together someday. Adrianna stood by us trying to keep herself warm as a cold breeze blew by. *Used to be friends*...we didn't understand it. Her energy told us that she knew what had happened, but her eyes told us that she was affected by what happened as well. We paid attention to her breathing, ready to catch her if she broke into tears.

"What's going on?" we asked.

Adrianna released a deep sigh. "So... like I said before, she and I used to be friends."

It seemed impossible to me that someone would stop being friends with Aaliyah for any reason—the girl was simply too loveable. We had never seen Adrianna, not even in passing. She was never with Aaliyah when she was with Terry. There had to be something more, something deeper that led to this cold conversation in the courtyard.

"We had been best friends since middle school. Mr. O was like an uncle to me. She used to spend the night at my house all the time. We literally did everything together. We were like sisters. She got really close with my mom at one point, and that's when we learned the story about what happened to her mom."

Adrianna turned away from us and wiped her teary eyes. She readjusted herself and fought to hold herself together, taking a seat where Terrell had once sat.

"My mom once told me that I needed to watch her because she felt like Aaliyah was gonna go through something at some point without her mom being there. I really wish she wasn't right." Adrianna shivered.

"What do you mean?" We raised our brow.

"I wasn't sure about you when I heard she started dating you, especially after hearing about your fight with Terry. I figured you were just another meathead like all the other guys."

Aaliyah grew desperate to fill the void from her mother's missing love in her life, but she was also still suffering from the trauma of all that she had witnessed from her father's troubled past. Despite Omar's attempts to teach her everything he could, she still carried the fearful desire to protect herself from harm. Her unfinished mind operated on emotion, disobeying the logic that had fallen into the dark shadows of her thoughts. Time after time from middle school on to high, Aaliyah made poor decisions on the boys she chose to love, each one being worse than the last, and each time her best friend watched as she sold herself out for the love of the troublesome figures.

There was a dire need to feel something that wasn't there. There was a desire for someone to be present. She was good to them; her only hope was that they would in return give her the same love and affection. Instead, she repeatedly cried on her best friend's shoulder, trying to understand why it never worked. Time and time again, Adrianna came to Aaliyah's aid after getting her heart broken, and time and time again Aaliyah rejected Adrianna's logic once a new fool came along. A time came when Adrianna grew tired of seeing her friend get hurt. She stopped thinking logistically and began to think of Aaliyah with her emotions. After a fit of choice words, Adrianna separated herself from Aaliyah's ill-managed emotions, ending the sisterhood of their friendship.

"I couldn't stand watching her get hurt anymore; it just never got better. Even worse, she wouldn't listen to me when I tried to talk to her, so after a while I just let her go be stupid for these boys. I quit talking to her while she was dating one guy, and then when I heard she got with Terry, I just gave up on her altogether, but then you showed up out of nowhere. I haven't seen her smile like that, ever, and she smiles all the damn time. She glows when she's walking with you, like, you can fake being happy, but you can't fake the glow," Adrianna said.

She sighed as she nervously bounced her hand on her thigh.

"I didn't think anything like this would ever happen. I wouldn't wish this shit on my worst enemy."

Adrianna stood up and looked at us, her eyes red from fighting back her tears. She'd never stopped caring for her sister.

"I can tell Aaliyah really loves you, and it's a beautiful thing to see after all these years. Please...please don't break her heart, especially not now. She needs you more than anyone in this world."

We lowered our eyes and nodded our head, receiving the message that Adrianna delivered. Her emotions toward Aaliyah were still hurt, but there was enough logic left behind for her to let us know she still cared. She began to walk away in the winter cold, but we couldn't allow her to leave with her emotions so distraught.

"I can take you to her if you want to see her," we called over to her.

Adrianna quickly turned around and ran toward us. A couple of tears ran down her speckled cheeks, still fighting to hold back the waterfall.

"Please." Her voice cracked.

Her eyes were filled with desperation. She needed to see her friend. She wanted to be there for her sister. We needed to make it happen.

"Meet me in the parking lot after school. I'll be waiting by Terrell's car for you."

The bell rang, and it was time for us to go to 5th period. With a couple hours left in the school day, we could sense her excitement as her day would now end differently than anticipated.

"I'll be there, please don't leave me!" Adrianna pleaded.

"I won't. I'll see you after school. The parking area by the school's sign."

We had a little surprise for Terrell at the end of the day. We walked with him to his car after school and thought of everything we could to delay him for a few moments.

"Bruh, the tires look fine. I just got these, not even six months ago," Terrell said. "By the way, I meant to ask you what Adrianna wanted with you."

We looked at him with a grin as he stood up from checking his tires.

"Why don't you ask her yourself?"

Adrianna quickly walked up to the car, nearly out of breath after making her way through the building to find us. Her book bag in hand, she was ready to go on the journey we'd promised her.

"Sorry I took so long. The halls were pretty congested. Thanks for waiting for me."

Terrell's eyes shot open, and his heart nearly exploded as his crush stood before him twice in the same day. He froze in place with his keys dangling from his fingers. It was the best surprise we could have given him.

"I need you to take us somewhere if you don't mind. I'll drive, you two talk," we said as we grabbed his keys.

We tapped him on his shoulder to break him from her spell and got in his car. Fortunately for him, he had just cleaned his interior. We took the short journey across town, the two of them making small talk as we focused on the road. We made our way to the hotel and pulled up to the front, knowing that soon we would be in the front row of an emotion-filled theatre, so we released Terrell from his torment and sent him home. Adrianna followed us into the hotel to the top floor, where our goddess awaited our return. We got to her door and paused for a moment to brief Adrianna on how we should commence their meeting. We stepped in first to make sure she was decent, but found our baby sitting in the middle of her bed looking worse than she had when we'd brought her here. Her eyes were again cried out from the day, and her hair was wild and unkempt from nervously running her fingers through it. She looked so broken.

"Hey, Sweets." We stepped toward her.

She greeted us with her sad eyes, waiting for us to come closer, but we kept our distance to introduce the next guest.

"Needless to say, uh, everyone asked about you today. I told them what I could, which wasn't much, to say the least. I know you don't want to see anybody right now, but I brought someone with me that wanted to see you."

We walked back to the door and allowed Adrianna in. She entered slowly, her eyes immediately leaking with tears when she saw her distressed friend sitting on the bed. They both looked at each other, and their faces turned to saddened frowns of hurt and pain. Aaliyah opened her arms, craving the warm embrace of her sister.

"I'm sorry," Adrianna cried as she ran to Aaliyah.

Adrianna jumped on the bed next to her sister, and they both bawled in each other's arms. So many years of pain and frustration between them resurfaced as they mourned their loss. We turned away and focused our eyes on the floor to prevent any more tears from falling. The energy in the room was high, but we just didn't want to cry anymore.

"I'll be back," we said as we left the room.

We went downstairs and sat in the lobby to give them a chance to talk freely about everything. We reflected on our conversation with the old man and no longer cared why he desired to help us. We wanted to be better, we wanted to grow, we wanted to evolve, but we still had unfinished business. Today's venture was a necessary detour toward our progression, and hopefully from this point forward, we would make our aspirations come to fruition.

The conversation upstairs was going well as the two young women rekindled their sisterhood. They had experienced many different things in their time apart, both of them feeling guilty that they hadn't been there to protect the other as they once vowed. Adrianna dried her sister's eyes and looked around the room, refusing to leave her like this.

"I'm not letting you stay here another night. You need to come home with me where you belong. We still love you, never stopped," Adrianna said.

"I-I just—I don't want to be a burden on you guys after all these years," Aaliyah sobbed. "I've always been the problem."

"You're not a burden... you're my sister. I'm gonna be here for you no matter what the problem is."

They embraced and cried in each other's arms again. The love and care that they'd once had was empowered once more with all the right elements. They pulled away from each other, smiling as they wiped the tears from each other's face.

"C'mon, girl. Let's get your stuff," Adrianna said.

CHAPTER 22

CONSIDER US EVEN

THE PAST FEW weeks had been hell for Face and his business. He was hemorrhaging money at an alarming rate, and Hong's death practically destroyed any possibility of joint business ventures for the future. He and Deuce had been unable to reach Nassar regarding any new weapons, nor did they have the funds to purchase enough firepower to cover all of their remaining men. The one thing that remained consistent was the story given by the survivors of the savage attacks, and Face's punishment proved to be just as heinous as the guy with the red eye's wrath.

Face once again found himself in the basement of his safe-house with a defenseless and bleeding man before him. He and several of his men were engaged in the torturous interrogation of the lone survivor of the latest attack. They'd tied the poor man to a chair and beat him for hours in search of the truth. He'd pleaded with his captives that his story was legit, but they ignored his words, rebutting with harsh punches and kicks to the face and body. Unable to get the straight answer he desired, Face decided to increase his measures of torture.

"Who the hell took my money, dammit?" Face hollered.

The restrained man wailed from his pain as blood leaked from his mouth. He struggled to catch his breath, barely able to see out of his swollen eyes before being hit with another strong backhand slap to his face.

"I'm tellin' you the truth," the man cried out.

"Lies," Face roared.

The angry Face drew his pistol and put it to the man's bloody head as he tossed his shades and stooped down to his victim's face. His eyes pierced through the man's swollen and bruised eyes, sending an unraveling fear to his soul.

"You think I'm stupid, don't you?" Face asked.

"No, no, I don't I—"

"Yeah, you do! You think I'm brand new to this shit! He thinks we're rookies," Face laughed to his men.

A wave of laughter filled the room as the Illegit men laughed at their boss's crude humor. Face's grin quickly turned to a face-melting scold as he turned and pistol-whipped the poor fool.

"Do I look like a goddamn clown to you? This ain't no joke!" Face shouted.

The room instantly went silent. The hurt man struggled to raise his head from the staggering blow before having Face's pistol shoved into his cheek.

"Who the hell took my money? You better tell me now, dammit! I'm gettin' real impatient."

Teeth fell from the man's mouth as he bled from the new cuts on his face. The strikes of confessions past had beaten him in ways that he'd never predicted, and he feared sticking to the truth would only worsen things. Even worse, lying would guarantee an unhappy ending to his life. He battled back and forth with his mind, trying to figure out what to say, afraid to speak either of his thoughts.

"It...it was—"

"You better not say it! You better not tell me it was some dude with red eyes! You better not say that shit to me!"

The restrained man nervously lowered his head and remained silent, sending Face's inpatient rage through the roof.

After a moment of the man's silence, Face walked away from him, staring at the ceiling. He turned and looked at his victim and decided the interrogation was going nowhere.

"Cut 'em," Face uttered.

The tied man shrieked, and his bruised eyes shot open. He squealed, trying to shuffle his body free from his restraints after he witnessed a man approaching him with a pair of hand pruners. He screamed at the top of his lungs as his bloody pinky dropped to the floor.

"Stop your whining," Face scoffed. "You'd be in a lot more pain if I could find my goddamn knife."

Suddenly, the basement door slammed open from the top of the stairs, startling the crowd of men.

"Face! Face!" a man shouted as he tumbled down the stairs.

The surrounding men helped their fellow family member to his feet but soon jumped away from him after discovering blood splattered on his shirt with the letters R and D written on his forehead in dried blood. Deuce looked the man up and down, shocked by his frazzled appearance. The man was clearly in shock as he stood before the crowd to deliver his message.

"The Big House...i-it's gone!" the bewildered man cried.

"Whoa, whoa. Whatchu mean the Big House is gone?" Deuce questioned.

Deuce observed the man's body and realized that the blood on his face and clothing wasn't his own. The frazzled man fumbled his hands and shook his head as if someone was still after him.

"It's gone! I-it blew up," the man stuttered.

Face's jaw dropped to the floor as he stared at the crazed man in disbelief. Deuce slapped his palm on his forehead, knowing the sudden hit would cripple the Illegit Family's grip immensely. The shaking man pointed his finger at Face with his eyes wide open.

"He's coming for you! H-he told me t-to tell you he's coming!"

"Whoa, hol' up, calm down a second." Deuce grabbed the man. "Who's coming? Who the hell did this to you?"

"And what's up with them letters on your forehead?" Face asked.

The crazed man's eyes were riddled with fear, for the traumatic experience had shaken him to his soul. He drew back his hand and cuffed it to his chest. The other men surrounded him, waiting to hear the name of the villain responsible for the destruction. The man nervously looked left and right and then looked up at Face standing before him.

"Who was it?"

"It was a—"

The restrained man groaned from his bloody throne, catching the eye of the nervous man looking over Face's shoulder. He saw the lost member lying lonely in its own pool of blood on the floor, and his stomach tied into a knot. He glanced back at Face, and they locked eyes, the tension between them pounding like an irregular heartbeat. As the man's bearings returned, he found himself surrounded by his Illegit brothers, waiting for him to say the wrong thing.

"It was...It was..."

We charged through the front door of this big house like a SWAT team with a no-knock warrant, destroying everything in sight. Several men rushed toward us with their guns drawn, but none of them were given the opportunity to shoot. We threw wooden chairs at them and watched them shatter from the forceful impact. While the others were distracted by the flying objects, we dashed over to them and broke their wrists, snatching the guns from their hands. We violently threw our fist and swiped our claws through the unfortunate bunch, leaving nothing to be desired by their survival, but from the corner of our eye, we realized that one target had been missed.

"Call Deuce! Call Deuce," a man screamed, running for his life.

The terrified man darted for the next room and slammed the door behind him. There was nothing special about him, but he had something we wanted hanging from his shoulders. We went after him like a villain in an old school horror, sensing all the negative energies around us, the house looming with fearful predators. A door opened, and a crazed man charged at us with a taser, something different from the norm of bullets flying at us. We didn't give him the chance to swing before we backhanded him with our spikes. They ripped through his face and sent him flying into the wall, smearing blood across it as he sank to the floor. His blood dripped from our wrist, enticing us to seek more. We kicked the hallway door open, and it led to a flight of stairs and another closed door. We kicked the door open and hollered to everyone inside.

"Who wants to die?"

We heard footsteps shifting around and prepared for conflict, but then some wimpy voice cried out to us.

"I surrender! I surrender!"

He ran toward the door, flailing his arms in the air, but unfortunately, we weren't feeling generous. We rushed into the room, knocking him into a wall, and quickly spotted several men surrounding the door ready to fight, or so it seemed. A few of them put up their hands holding objects to strike us with, while the others took off running into a supply closet. Someone came up behind us with a gun, but the fool didn't think it was a good idea to shoot first. With a dip and a spin, we jolted behind the bastard and shoved the Buddy in his back while we choked him with our free arm. The other fools rushed to his aid, but we grabbed his gun-wielding hand and started shooting at them. They all dove to the floor to dodge the bullets, but one unlucky fool caught one to the heart.

We aimed his gun up toward the ceiling and fired the last few shots through the ceiling to send a message to the fools upstairs. There was a scream followed by the sound of someone tumbling down the stairs into silence. We grinned and pushed our unlucky victim off the blade and watched him fall to the floor.

"Who else wants some?" we offered.

The three remaining men jumped up from the floor and ran at us with their weapons of choice. The first ran up swinging a steel pipe. We dipped low into a sweep kick, sending him airborne. Before he hit the ground, we caught him and constricted our arms around him until we heard his rib cage crack. We tossed him aside like a lifeless ragdoll and charged for our next target. He ran at us with a crowbar, but the weight of it made him slow on the swing. We grabbed the open end and snatched it from his hands, propelling him toward us. Before he could catch himself, we shoved the straight end through the bottom of his jaw and raised him into the air. We shook him around a bit and then tossed him toward the last man standing.

He was bold with his approach, flexing his muscles as if he were going to strong-arm us. Before the overconfident fool could raise his arms, we jumped and dashed at him, slitting his throat as we passed by. He dropped to his knees, gagging on his own blood, allowing us to focus on the other four people hiding from us. We approached the doorway of the supply closet with the Buddy in hand and were met with four men aiming guns at us from inside. The bloody situation became a standoff as we all stared at each other from our opposite sides, neither of them having the courage to shoot us. Someone must have wanted us alive. They noticed the Buddy in our hand and the aggression in our eyes and nervously readied themselves to fire.

"We'll blow ya brains out if you take another step!" one of the men threatened. "Is he really serious?"

"Nah, he's just testin'. Don't be stupid!"

These men obviously hadn't paid attention to the stories told about us. They were all trembling as they aimed their guns, our grin heightening their anxiety. We slowly reached over to the light switch and flipped it off as we dashed into the room and closed the door. Bullets went flying around in the dark, penetrating the friendly flesh of the allied men in the room. The gunfire soon stopped, and all was silent for a moment. We turned on the light and exited the room untouched, leaving behind a massacre with foreign blood splatter all over us.

Before we headed upstairs, we noticed strange crates along the walls of the large room. Inside were smuggled guns, some of them appearing to be military-grade. We quickly thought of what was waiting for us upstairs and found one that caught our eye. We were lucky to find fully loaded magazines on one of the tables that matched the choice we made. We strapped it over our shoulder and proceeded to the stairs to retrieve what we believed to be rightfully ours.

We crept up the stairs, sensing a few more energies, and all but one of them felt indifferent. We reached the top end of the wall hiding by the creaky staircase and thought it would be best to get them to make the first move. We took off our hoodie and hollered gibberish as we tossed it into their view. Bullets went off like fireworks as the men emptied their clips at the piece of fabric, and we crouched down, clenching our gun to our chest as the bullets tore through the wall and floor before us. The bullets kept flying for a few more seconds and then slowly fizzled out. We now had to replace our hoodie, and even though it was our fault, we were going to make all of them pay for it.

"I'm out," a man shouted.

"Did we get 'em? Shit, I'm empty."

There was a smokescreen at the top of the stairs, providing the perfect cover. We sensed the location of the men and crept up the stairs, taking our time to aim at the blinded targets. We jolted from the smoke, firing one shot at a time, sending them each to a closed casket funeral. Before we could clear the room, the man with our prize jumped up and took off into a closet and slammed the door.

"Please, please leave me alone!" he shouted.

We ripped the door from its hinges, and he hollered like a pubescent child, kicking and screaming toward the wall.

"NO, NO, NO! I don't wanna die," he cried.

We aimed our gun at him, pressing the warm barrel against his forehead, and hissed. The aroma of fresh urine filled the air as he quivered on the floor.

"Get up!"

The panicked man slowly rose to his feet with his hands up, looking down at the floor.

"Look at me."

He looked into our angry red eyes and began to hyperventilate. He was going to pass out if we didn't calm him down.

"Please don't shoot me, please don't shoot me, please don't shoot me!" he cried.

"Do as I say, and you might live," we said. "You're going to tell me everything I want to know."

We lowered the gun, and he immediately proceeded to tell us everything Face had been up to since our attacks began. We had stolen around twelve million dollars from his gang, enough money to bring his operation to a screeching halt. The white-faced killer had been reduced to a well-guarded refugee as we learned that he had hired a task force that was made up of twelve contract killers that were recommended to him by his late friend Hong. He told us how Face had been running around scared, knowing that we would soon find him, a fear he had never seen from his boss before. We then made him tell us everything going on with the house, and it turned out that everything inside was the bulk of what the Illegit Family had left. We were going to destroy it all, every last piece of it. We said we wanted to destroy his organization, and here we were standing at the brink of destruction. The plan was set and ready to be carried out, but nothing could have prepared us for the gem the poor fool mistakenly dropped on us as our image tormented his soul.

"How far along is she?" we asked.

"I don't know, but she's pretty big, like, 'any day now' big."

Malicious thoughts entered our mind, and that sinister grin of ours appeared across our face. There was a deep rumble in our soul, shaking us from the darkest depths within. Images flashed into our head, and with each moment our thoughts grew darker. There were thoughts so dark we didn't believe that they were from the wrath of our ancestors. They were evil, but in our world of war, they were justified. *One thought at a time,* we told ourselves.

We grabbed the man by his collar and forced him from the closet. He slipped and fell into a puddle of blood from one of his fallen brothers and quickly jumped back to his feet, traumatized by the foreign stains. We dipped our fingers in the red pool and wrote our initials across his forehead.

"You're gonna be my property for a while." We grinned.

We followed him down to the basement to the supplies he'd told us about. Propane tanks were lined up against the walls along with vats of chemicals, similar to the ones in the first house we'd raided. We grabbed a few vats of the dangerous chemicals and commenced a walk-through of the house, dousing everything in sight. We traveled back to the propane tanks and released their gases into the air before exiting out of the basement's side door. We dragged our property to the street and took the bag from him as we stood outside, watching the house in silence for a moment. In light of all that had just occurred, we somehow forgot that we had dominion over whether our hostage would live or die. His nervous breaths started to make us angry...angry enough to let him live.

"You know where Face is?" we asked.

"I can find him," the man responded.

"Good, two more things. One, tell him I'm coming for him."

We aimed our gun at the window of the house.

"Two, tell 'em what you saw."

The fumes from the gas and chemicals filled the house with no way to air out the rooms. We shot our gun at the window, the bullets ricocheting around and causing sparks to fly in the house. The big house exploded to pieces with the sound of a loud sonic boom sending debris flying everywhere around us. The windows of the cars parked in front of the house immediately shattered as the shockwave rocked through the air. Our bloody assistant was knocked to the ground by the force as flaming debris rained from the sky. We stood motionless against the shockwave, staring back into the fiery blaze. The familiar inferno burned like the rage within our heart, but the destruction didn't equate to the rise we felt from the dark thoughts we'd had earlier. The large smoke cloud in the sky would alert the authorities to the location soon, but we weren't in a hurry to flee from the scene. We sent our assistant on his way to deliver our message in his beaten car and took to the woods to hide high in the trees. There was still more work to do, but we had to wait for it to arrive.

Face and Deuce frantically paced around the office, stressing over their huge loss. Porter and Simmons were already on the line with Face heading to the crime scene to investigate. A few members of Face's team had left and taken the two traumatized men to the hospital with hopes of getting the lost finger sewn back on. The story of the Red Dragon told by the crazed man was still too far-fetched in their minds, but with Hong dead and Nassar seemingly out of the picture, it was the only believable possibility. Everything from the club surveillance video to the video retrieved from Kenny's phone, along with the eyewitness descriptions from Illegit members pointed to a man with red eyes.

"What are we gonna do, Porter?" Face asked.

"I don't know what we're gonna do, but you need to get your team on this guy as quickly as possible," Porter said. "I don't know why you didn't take this more seriously when it all started in the first place."

"Well thanks, Dad, but now's not the time for a lecture. I gotta figure this out quick. I don't know what the hell's going on anymore, like, what the hell happened to Nassar? Is he dead or is the old bastard not talking to me because Hong's dead? I don't... UGH," Face groaned.

He angrily banged his fist on the desk. Deuce signaled to Face to end the call with the detectives before the conversation took a turn.

"Look, Porter, just...just call me when y'all figure out what's going on over there, and if you see any guns, please bring them to me. We stored the last shipment we got from Nassar there, and if they're gone, we literally have no more weapons," Face instructed.

"Aight, I'll call you."

Face ended the call and flipped his chair as he went back to pacing around the office. Deuce ignored Face's outburst while he checked the messages he had received.

"They got his finger sewn back on, but they said he lost a good amount of blood in the 'accident,'" Deuce said.

"Do I look like I give a shit about that now?" Face bucked. "I mean do I really because I could have sworn that other fool told us we lost the Big House today?"

Deuce twisted up his face and shoved Face's shoulder, and the two quickly threw up their guards, ready to eliminate their frustrations through fisticuffs.

"Look here, you ain't finna be talkin' to me like I'm one of these other fools! Y'on just pay me, I make money for the crew!" Deuce bucked.

The two stared at each other, waiting for the other to make a move. The heavy breathing between them gave light to the frustration they carried. Face soon retracted his stance trying to focus on what was most important.

"Look, man, I just need you to help me think. Our pockets are in deep shit right now, I got a deranged lunatic trying to kill me, and everyone who could've helped us is dead. I don't want your help, I need it," Face said calmly.

Deuce looked him up and down as he dropped his guard. He turned away from Face and released a deep exhale as he flopped onto the loveseat and began rubbing his forehead.

"This situation has us both spooked if you ain't noticed, but we can't worry 'bout the business right now. We's a little short on manpower, so I think the first thing you need to do is move ya girl around," Deuce suggested.

"You're right," Face agreed. "Hell, I only got her at the high-rise cuz she says she doesn't like being out here."

"Well, she ain't got a choice now, so call her and tell her pregnant ass to pack a bag. We need to make this move today cuz this shit is gettin' too close to home."

Meanwhile, the cul-de-sac of the former Big House was swamped with firetrucks and police. The firefighters had almost successfully extinguished the hellish blaze as a news crew reported from the scene with a helicopter flying overhead. Porter and Simmons discreetly pulled up to the scene, flashing their badges as they walked between the fire trucks and patrol cars. They attempted to bait a few officers for information, but because the flames weren't completely out, no one had been able to start conducting an investigation. A tow truck arrived on the scene to haul off the singed cars that remained at the property, prompting the detectives to get the tag numbers from each car. It wasn't long before the detectives snuck away from the scene just as they had snuck through it. They pulled off, leaving the work to CSI, the both of them prepared to tell Face that the house was a total loss.

They looked just as he said they would: corrupt. The Black cop walked around waving his badge with a smile as if he had actually done something, and the White cop looked like the kind of guy you watch out for when you're out in public. Their connection reeked of dirty money, but it seemed our luck hadn't run out with our destructive rage. We watched their car roll down the street and sensed their careless feelings as they left the scene. We couldn't allow them to escape from us, especially with our messenger on his way to his master. It would only give them a chance to figure out how to delay us further. The loud roars of Rage would alert everyone to our presence, so we had to be sneaky and quick with our departure if we wanted to win again. We quietly hopped out of the tree and discreetly pushed our motorcycle through the woods until we were far enough away to emerge from cover and start the engine. Our final mission objective for the day: Kill the dirty cops. With them out of the way, there would be no one to cover Face's ass when we destroyed shit–that is, if there was anything left to destroy.

The detectives traveled down the wooded highway listening to old school R&B on the radio as they drove back to the station. They had been working nonstop trying to cover Face's operations, but the corrupt duo had finally had enough of the Illegit foolishness. Porter reclined his seat to rest his eyes and blow off his frustration while Simmons pulled out his phone.

"You think I should call him?" Simmons asked.

"For what? it's not like we found anything. Besides, Face is done. I knew it was only a matter of time once his Asian buddy got murdered. Pretty soon, he ain't gonna be able to pay us and that's gonna' cause a problem. I say we tell him we're under investigation by I.A. and make a clean break while we can," Porter said.

Porter confidently put his shades on and laid his head on the headrest while Simmons dropped his phone on the dash. Their detective work was officially done.

"I guess you're right," Simmons said.

"When am I not? And we ain't gotta worry about the crazy bastard coming after us because we already got a mountain of evidence against him. He doesn't want the drama we can bring. We need to get as far away as possible from him before whoever's coming after him comes after us," Porter added.

Bullets bit through the vehicle and shattered the back windshield, causing Simmons to swerve. He regained control of the car and looked into the review, spotting a motorcycle quickly gaining on him.

"Shit! Porter, get your gun out! Porter!"

Simmons looked at his long-time partner and noticed blood gushing from the top of his head, nose, and mouth. One of the bullets had found its mark after passing through the trunk of the car, and the jovial Detective Antwan Porter became the brunt of his own joke.

"Aww, shit," Simmons shrieked.

He punched the gas and zoomed down the deserted road, trying to watch the motorized gunner behind him. He reached for his pistol with no idea how he was going to shoot back. The bullets came flying at the car again, and Simmons ducked his head, trying to avoid the lead stingers. They burst through the front windshield and shattered the glass, impairing the view for Porter to keep his speed. He desperately rolled down the window in an effort to see, but he quickly regretted the decision as bullets came blazing by, destroying the mirror. He dipped his head low to see as much as he could through the uncracked portion at the bottom and saw that he had approached the twisted turns of the dreaded trail. He slowed his vehicle and eased into the first turn, pushing the engine again once he got into the apex of the curve. No bullets came by him as he zoomed through, giving him the confidence to keep going.

We needed a little more space to make this trick work. We held off just a little to give him a chance to make it to the second turn. He wasn't going to take the time to shoot back, so we had all the time we needed to make the perfect shot. He went into the second turn, his back wheels slightly screeching as he drifted. We pulled the trigger, and a single bullet darted toward the car, tearing through the air, ready to destroy anything in its path. The bullet struck the rear tire and caused a major blowout as the car took the curve, sending shredded pieces of tire flying through the air. We could hear him scream as he lost control of the car and watched as the car went off-road and flipped over three times before finally landing on its roof. We quickly stopped our bike to avoid the wreckage and waited—we knew the crash hadn't killed him.

A few moments passed, and the coughs and wheezes from a disoriented Simmons sounded off from the twisted vehicle. He wrestled with his seatbelt to free himself from the ruins as blood leaked from his face and mouth. He struggled his way out of the wreckage, leaving the bloody body of his partner behind. The hard pavement made it harder for him to crawl away, and his fractured knees made it more difficult to move. His wide eyes and strained breaths spelled the critical end for the corrupt detective as he heard the ominous footsteps of someone coming up behind him. He didn't stop to look back but instead tried to move as fast as he could away from the sound. In his injured state, his desperation couldn't match his energy, and eventually his muscles gave out along the side of a wooden light pole.

We removed our muzzle and helmet and approached him slowly with death riding on our shoulder. To see him desperately crawling away brought a satisfaction to our rage like none before. He was pathetic. He had no heart, no dignity, just a weakling with a badge to make himself feel important. He wasn't even trying to fight for his life. We leaned over and flipped him onto his back and watched him struggle to breathe, a perfect time for a conversation followed by a quick eulogy. We grabbed him by his collar and sat him up against the pole. He stared into our red eyes, enchanted with terror as he realized his blue privilege wasn't going to save him.

"This little piggy followed my destruction...this little piggy should have stayed home...that little piggy went with you...and now, that little piggy is gone." We aimed our gun at his head. "And now this little piggy is gonna tell me what I want to know if he wants an open casket funeral."

Simmons began breathing heavily as the warm barrel stared him in the face.

"W-w-what—what do you wanna know?" he strained.

There was nothing that the little piggy could tell us that we didn't already know, for his death would send the message that we wanted to send. For some reason, we wanted to take the opportunity to learn something about our victim.

"Why did you become a cop if you were gonna work for a criminal?"

Simmons leaned his head back and laughed into a cough, finding humor in our curiosity.

"Open your eyes, kid. When you're a cop, you work for the bad guys. Face—he gave us a chance to do something great for our families. All the force would have done is give us a pension if we lived long enough to get it. There are people much worse in the world, people like you. You've murdered more people in the past few months than I've busted in my entire career. You're the real menace to society," Simmons responded.

We didn't like his answer. We lowered our gun and slowly tilted our head to the side, appalled by his blatant disrespect for true justice. We felt it rise within us again, that disturbing rage, that agitated rage that grew tired of psychotic diplomacy.

"A menace? You know what, you might just be right. I'm the worst kind of menace. Allow me to formally introduce myself. I am the Menacing Red Dragon, God of War. I was chosen by my ancestors to rid the Earth of scum like you who prey on innocent people. You hide behind a badge and bully innocent people using your 'privilege' to get ahead, only to get a promotion and do a slack-ass job at helping the people that you're supposed to protect and serve, like my uncle and my cousin. This isn't about stopping a crime boss; this is all about avenging the deaths of my loved ones that I'm sure you assisted in taking away from me. My path of destruction is simply me being a menace—a menace to an evil much worse than anything I could ever do. You either lost your way or you never had one. But no matter, I'm gonna send you to a place where there's only one path to take. You'll still have an honorable funeral, and your piglet friends will lie about how great of a guy you were, but you'll die knowing you ain't shit, and I'm gonna make you feel really shitty when I come to visit."

We raised the gun back to his head, and the pleading began.

"W-w-w-wait! W-what about Face? Y-you usually send someone back to him to warn him. D-don't you have a message you want me to give him?" Simmons pleaded.

"He already knows." We grinned. "Why do you think he sent you out here?"

We pulled the trigger and splattered his brains all over the place. Detective Rick Simmons served and protected his personal interest until his untimely and much-desired death. He left behind a legacy of battery and abuse of power, the souls of his victims now free from his scrutiny. We wiped down the gun and tossed it on the ground next to him. It had served its purpose for the day. We geared up and got back on our motorcycle to head back to the fiery scene, parking the bike a short distance away from the blocked-off street. We snuck through the woods and went back to where we'd posted up in the trees to retrieve the bag we'd stolen and took a moment to observe the crime scene. The firefighters had finally put the fire out, and the police were doing a walk of the area to search for evidence. We hopped down from the tree and snuck back to our motorcycle and sped off.

We came up to the turns again, and a car had stopped to check on the wreckage. We continued on, unbothered by the find, but the piglet's words remained in our mind. A menace? Did we really qualify as a menace? We wouldn't exactly define ourselves a hero with all the bloodshed that colored our path, but the answer to that question lay in the hands of whoever was saying it, so it all depends on what side of our wrath you were on. We took our findings home, but there was still something off within us. Something about his words mixed in with our rage, and we couldn't stop thinking about everything we had done.

Were we a menace with an insatiable appetite for destruction, and if so, why did it feel so good?

The nighttime came with a loud awakening of power within us. We grunted as we sat in the darkness of our room fiending for more bloodshed on our hands. We traveled to the Spirit Realm in search of an answer for our menacing urges. It was as if every dark, depressive thought Ryan experienced had switched to the most chaotic outcome. It challenged his common morality, justifying the gruesome thoughts that entered his mind. They had to be stopped, he had to eliminate all that he felt on the blade, or his appetite wouldn't be satisfied until he did; however, what he felt was something much worse than anything he had done before. The wrath of the ancestral gods reigned ruthlessly in his blood, driving him into a chaotic rage. Power surged through his fingertips, his chest pumped with fury, and his fangs dripped for the taste of hysteria on his tongue.

The Spirit Realm was dark, echoing with the voices of the ancient ancestors as the two gods met on the rough sands. Ryan stood before Heru heavy with his rage. Saliva spilled from the side of his mouth as his cynical laughs welcomed the grimy thoughts into his mind. Spirits whispered in his ear, coaxing him to follow his minacious feelings, but the young god craved the approval of his spiritual guide first.

"Heru, this is different," Ryan laughed. "Ooh, but it feels so right. Sooo right!"

Ryan's beastly breaths shook the Spirit Realm as his aura wrapped around him. Red bolts of energy electrified the dark sky, exciting his rage even more.

"You know what we have to do, Heru. You know we have to," the deranged god urged.

The red bolts of energy lit up the darkened sky as Heru looked into Ryan's eyes. Heru observed the looming visions processing in his pupil's mind, the darkness of his thoughts beckoning for his clearance. Heru had long wished for freedom, a gift stripped from him twice in life at the expense of those he loved. He had fought the war against a hellish opponent too many times before. His reasoning turned to desperation, sacrificing his moral code for the greater pleasure of murder. Heru had grown tired, his mind weakened by the millennia of captivity. It was war. He raised his head to the sky and listened to the whispers of the angry ancestors and glared back at the rabid God of War.

"It seems that the ancestors have a request they wish for you to fulfill," Heru said.

"You know we have to do it. You want me to do it, don't you?" Ryan grunted from the pulsating rage.

The Sky God battled with his morality, falling short of the example he projected to his people. The Divine Principles of Ma'at no longer seemed to matter as the darkness of war transformed his mind.

"I know that the request is an outrageous one for a mortal, but you are the God of War, and a part of maintaining peace is fighting the war. We are at war, Ojore. There are no rules to war; there are no innocent victims, only enemies on the wrong side. There's no place for emotions, only what must be done for the greater good."

"We must do what is necessary." Ryan grinned.

Ryan's cynical laughter brought Heru to a place that had long been disregarded. The ancestors angrily whispered in their ears, their thoughts growing darker and grimmer.

"They took something from me, Heru." Ryan twitched with a low growl.

Revenge was the bond of their spirits.

"Then you must take something closer away from him," Heru said.

The chaotic grin of the God of War gleamed through the Spirit Realm as the ancestors granted him the knowledge he sought after. His aura flared with a great fury as the ancestors shook the realm, exclaiming their rage, their dark disturbance felt in Duat.

"Go, Ojore! Go and get to your revenge!"

Ryan's aura shaped around him, forming a fiery dragon head with wings. He laughed maniacally, tasting his desire with his fangs as he darted back to the Earth Realm to fulfill the request of the ancestors.

Face paced around his hotel room talking to his beloved Ke-Ke as she transitioned into her new safe place. Fearful of the threat from the Red Dragon, the white-faced murderer had sent his men to retrieve his pregnant lover from the high-rise and transfer her to the safe house outside of the city. The lack of public knowledge of the property made him confident that moving her was the best option. He felt his presence in the city would only draw more trouble for them to deal with, but being apart was an emotional struggle for both of them.

"When can I leave this house, Face? You know I don't like being all the way out here. It's so dark outside. I hate this country shit," Ke-Ke complained.

"I know, baby, I know. It's just, it's kinda dangerous right now, and I need you and my baby in a safe place," Face replied.

"Dangerous?" Ke-Ke questioned. "I've been around dangerous shit wit'chu before—hell, we even shot a fool together. I ain't worried about this dangerous shit."

"And that's exactly why I put you out there. Baby, you're holding our future, and I'd like to see him one day, soon hopefully, all healthy 'n shit. I gotta keep you away from the danger to make that shit happen."

Ke-Ke's pregnancy appetite reached its peak, and her eight-and-a-half-month belly went on a rant.

"Ugh! I'm hungry, Face! All the food places I like are in Midtown! You gon' let ya' son starve out here, is that what you gon' do? I thought you said you loved me," Ke-Ke whined.

"Baby, baby, calm down, please!" Face pleaded. "Look, I'll send you some food. I'll send you whatever you want—matta fact, text it to me and I'll order it now."

Ke-Ke's whining ceased, and she grinned at Face's pleasant words as if they were flirting.

"Anything I want? You promise?" she asked.

"I haven't gotten a text from you yet," Face crooned.

The phone call immediately ended, and Face released a sigh of relief as he leaned against the wall. He was exhausted from his torturous activities from earlier in the day, but his anxiety wouldn't allow him to rest. He started to pace around the room waiting for his lover's text, but Deuce grew tired of hearing his footsteps as he rested on his bed.

"Bruh, sit'cho ass down somewhere, dammit. You gon' let that girl stress you out. She's pregnant, not disabled. She got a whole team of folks over there that can go get her somethin' to eat, but she callin' you? You don't see the problem wit' that?" Deuce groaned.

"Come on, man. She holdin' my baby, and we all the way out here in Villa Rica. You know how long it's been since I cuddled her and rubbed her belly?" Face yawned.

Face's cell phone went off with Ke-Ke's food request, and he began reading off the list. Deuce rolled over in his bed, frustrated from his lack of sleep.

"Ol' sprung ass," Deuce mumbled, covering his head with a pillow.

Face's team of assassins took shifts guarding his room at the cheap hotel. They established their perimeter and targeted anything that looked suspicious. They even went as far as to pay off the night manager to set up a guard in the front office. Nothing was going to get by their watchful eye. Confident in his security, Face sent his final text to Ke-Ke and inserted his charger into his phone.

Call me wen u get ur food.

Just as he was about to place his phone on the bedside table, he realized he hadn't gotten a report from Porter or Simmons.

"Yo, you heard from Simms?" Face asked.

"I ain't heard shit. Go to sleep," Deuce bluntly replied.

The exhausted Face lay back on his bed and stared at the ceiling. His paranoia made it impossible for him to fall asleep, and his stress only made him desperate to stay awake. He picked up his phone, anticipating the phone call from Ke-Ke, nervously fumbling it in his hands.

Ke-Ke finished using the restroom and slowly made her way to the sink to wash her hands. She smiled as she felt the kick of her hungry baby and rubbed her belly to soothe him as she made her way back to the bed.

"Whoo, relax, little boy. Mama's gonna feed you soon," she promised.

Several men were geared up inside and outside of the property, strapped and ready for any threat that might come by them. They were advised to shoot on sight, no matter if the uninvited guest was friend or foe. They circled the property, watching for anything out of the ordinary, but there weren't enough men outside to cover the property on all sides at once. The Illegit members had lost their luster with all of the deaths surrounding them, and they were either too paranoid to focus on the job or too distraught to take it seriously anymore. Some of them were just glad they had a gun.

We observed them from the woods across from the property. There were six men outside, all of them ill-equipped for the job. Face had left his beloved in the care of his worst. There weren't enough of them inside or outside to stop us, nor were they ready for the brutality we planned to unleash on all of them. We crept out of the woods, the Buddy sharp and ready to serve its purpose. Our alligator grunts quieted as we approached our first victim standing in the driveway.

We kicked a pinecone to the center of the street to get his attention. The nervous fool pulled up his gun and slowly marched toward the lone pinecone. We sensed his heart beating quickly and gripped our knife tighter and tighter the closer he got. He stepped into the street and quickly sighed away his nervousness after looking around and realizing there was no threat. We emerged from the darkness and snatched him from behind. A quick shriek escaped from his mouth just before we broke his neck, and we dragged him back into the shadows. It was time to cover our hands in their blood. The menace was activated.

"Yo, you straight over there?" a voice called from the top of the driveway.

The other Illegit members rushed around to the front of the property to see what the harrowing sound was.

"Where the hell is he? Yo' quit playin', man, where you at?" one of the men shouted.

Four, five, and six. We took his gun and strapped it to our back and then held him up and kept him as straight as we could. We eased his body into the light, keeping a close eye on the men in the yard.

"Man, this fool always playin'," one of the men scoffed.

We stopped in the street, our body still hidden by our decoy and the shadows. We were anxious to brutalize them, our senses raging, our rage boiling.

"The hell is he doin'?" another man laughed.

The show was over. We shoved his body toward the bottom of the driveway and jolted back into the shadows. His body crashed to the ground, and he lay there dead before his Illegit friends while we took aim.

"Oh, shit, that looked like it hurt."

We pulled the trigger and picked them off one by one. The first bullet ripped through the neck of one of the men and slung bits of bone and tissue out the back. Now we had their attention.

"What the hell was that?"

The second bullet went right into the heart of our next victim. The poor fool fell on his back, reaching out for someone to help him as his life slipped away. One of the members tried to drag him out of the way but ended up catching the third bullet with his teeth.

"Just shoot!"

The final three unloaded their rounds into the darkness, killing tree branches and any small animals that may have been rummaging around in the brush. The gunfire stopped, and we could sense several disturbed energies going into a panic inside the property. We meant to keep the gunfire down, but our rage flared up like a power surge, that blood lust ached for brutality, and the menace within was unleashed. We wanted to take our time giving individual attention to our enemies to let them know how special they were. We ran from the darkness and attacked the remaining three bastards with the butt of our gun before blasting their brains all over the driveway. We could sense them all inside. They were scared, they didn't want to die, but no one was leaving alive tonight. We kicked in the front door and roared through the house to let them know the Menacing Red Dragon had come to collect their souls.

Ke-Ke ignored the stressful kicks from her baby as her curiosity pulled her from the bed. She rubbed her belly as she waddled to the bedroom door to see what had caused the chaotic commotion. The sounds of agonizing screams and gunshots strained her mind as she clenched her cell phone to her chest. She opened the door and looked over the balcony to see a man with red eyes gunning down her security with one hand while choking another man with his other. He slowly raised his head spotting her watching him above the railing and began grinning like an evil lunatic.

"Hello, Kelana," we hissed.

We stared right through to her soul and shook the very foundation she stood on. She felt the burning sensation of our rage shoot through her body hearing our voice tell her she was next. We sensed her fear and began to laugh hysterically while we looked at her pregnant belly. The baby kicked, and she snapped back to reality, darting back into the room, screaming at the top of her lungs. Tears fell from her eyes as she fumbled with her cell phone, desperately trying to call Face for his protection while hiding in the closet. The call seemingly took forever to connect, but the weary villain quickly answered the phone, unaware of the heinous attack.

"You get your food, babe?" Face asked.

Her cries made it impossible for Face to understand her, but he could tell something was severely wrong.

"Calm down, calm down. Say what you said again." Face sat up from the bed.

"The red-eyed man is here!"

A disturbing chill shot down Face's body, and his chest was stricken with pain as he heard the screams and gunshots on the other end of the phone. The treacherous rampage hadn't stopped, and Ke-Ke was now defenseless against her attacker. Her horrific screams haunted Face's mind. Tears welled up in his eyes, and he nearly dropped the phone rushing to dress himself.

"Oh, God! Baby, I'm comin'! I'm comin'!"

He ran over to Deuce's bed and pulled him by the ankles to wake him. The frustrated Deuce rose from his slumber, ready to fight.

"Man, what the hell is yo problem?" Deuce yelled.

"Bruh, come on, we gotta go. It's an emergency!"

"For what?"

"He-is-at-the-house- wit'-Ke-Ke! We gotta roll," Face groaned.

"Oh, shit!"

The men dashed from their room, alerting the task force, and were soon jetting down the highway in two SUVs. Face had forced his driver into the backseat and darted down the dark interstate, dodging around cars at triple-digit speeds. Ke-Ke was still on the line groaning as her sudden fear sent shockwaves of pain to her belly. The stressed baby inside of her kicked around, giving her hellish abdominal pains, and the loud gun battle going on in her house made it impossible for her to calm down.

"Where are you, Face? Why aren't you here? I'm so scared," she cried.

"I'm comin', baby! Just stay with me, I'm comin'," Faced urged.

Face's task force checked their guns to ensure they were ready for the war that sounded off through the speakerphone. They were an elite team of assassins, some of them taking a break from their contracts to retrieve the pay offered by Face, but to their ignorance, Face no longer had the funds to pay them. The skilled mercenaries were walking into a death trap against a resilient enemy they didn't have the skills to defeat.

We ditched our gun as the thrill of bullets no longer excited us. Our hands were hungry for blood and broken bones. We dashed to the stairs and kicked one of the men into the wall. We snatched him by the neck and began bashing his head through the sheet-rock into the solid wooden stud until it broke. We released his bleeding neck and left him to tumble lifelessly down the stairs. There was someone else coming from the top of the stairs, con-fidently screaming threats at us as they reloaded their gun. We could sense their fear, their hands shaking as they struggled to replace the magazine. We dashed up the stairs and caught him by surprise, our red eyes and dripping fangs mere inches away from his face while our claws drained his neck like vampire teeth.

Several rounds went off, and soon everything went silent. Ke-Ke knelt on the floor of her closet, holding her stomach, afraid and trying not to whine too loud, unsure of the potential danger beyond the closet door. She couldn't hear any footsteps, and the agonizing screams had ceased.

"Babe, you there?" Face frantically asked.

"Yeah, yeah, it's quiet," Ke-Ke whispered. "I think he's dead. I-I heard a bunch of gunshots."

She got up and crept out of the closet, her curiosity compel-ling her to go and observe if the potential danger disrupting the house had been stopped. She held the phone to her ear as she slowly approached the door.

"Stay where you're at!" Face commanded. "We're still twenty minutes out, and I don't need anything happenin' to you."

Ke-Ke grabbed the door handle, giving Face no response as she slowly opened the door. She immediately fell to the floor screaming in distress at the sight of our menacing red eyes. We laughed like an evil villain as we ran our tongue along the tip of our fangs, staring deeply into her soul again. She dropped her phone as she kicked and grunted, trying to pick herself up off of the floor to run. We whipped out the Buddy and slowly pursued her, listening to Face scream for her through the phone.

"Come here, darling," we hissed. "I've been saving this one for you."

She spotted the knife, and her chest constricted, stressing her out so badly that we could see the frightful kicks of the baby. She found it.

"Babe! Babe! Answer me! Ke-Ke!" Face screamed at his phone.

Seconds later the call ended, and Face hollered into a whine, tossing his phone against the dash. He punched the gas harder, and the engine roared as they traveled down the dark highway. Deuce set his shotgun aside and attempted to call Ke-Ke again.

"It rang once and went to voicemail." His heart dropped. "I'll keep tryin'."

Tears quietly rolled down Face's cheek as his strained eyes focused on the dark road ahead.

Meanwhile, the panicked Ke-Ke locked herself in the bathroom, desperately trying to find something to help her barricade the door. Her extraneous efforts caused severe pain in her abdomen, and her baby frantically kicked around as if he too were running from the danger on the other side of the door. She clenched her belly, releasing laborious groans as she struggled to stay on her feet.

We knocked three times at the bathroom door and heard her frantically scurry away, her eyes watching the shadows of our feet at the bottom of the door. Her loud wheezes excited our rage, and we could smell the adrenaline rushing in her bloodstream. The menace was about to fulfill the request of the ancestors.

"Open the door, Kelana," we cackled.

We twisted and pulled on the locked doorknob just to hear her wince in terror. Banging on the door made her scream as she backed into the far wall. She held her belly tightly, crying from the pain, trying to calm herself. She knew Face was coming, but not knowing when he would arrive killed her hope. It was time to stop playing with her; we had a message to deliver.

"Your man is a merciless killer, Kelana. He killed so many people for the wrong reason. My uncle and my cousin died because of his ignorance. He took something from me that I can never get back, and now I must do the same. The ancient rule is an eye for an eye, tooth for a tooth. He took two from me, and I'm gonna take two from him."

We punched a hole straight through the door, and Ke-Ke shrieked as the broken wood crashed into the wall next to her. She stood frozen against the wall as we peeked through the hole at her, our enraged red eyes locking on to her with a hiss. She didn't have much fight left in her. Her heart was strained with fear, and she was sweating profusely. The pains from her belly were just as stressful as our presence, but her suffering wouldn't last long. We punched the door once again, and a huge chunk of it fell off. She screamed as we reached inside and unlocked the door, pushing the remaining piece open.

The wrath of the ancestors rocked the Spirit Realm. Heru stood in the ravenous darkness awaiting the grim action to be commenced by Ryan in the coming moments. He missed his beloved, he missed Montu, he missed his kingdom, he missed the past—a distant memory that carried an endless hurt.

"I'm sure there was someone in your life that told you to leave him, but you didn't listen, did you? No, you loved your menace, you loved the lifestyle, and you were captivated by the danger. Now, look at you. You've pissed yourself you're so scared… scared to see a real menace, and to think, the menace you love left you as prey to me. Where is he, Kelana? Why isn't he here protecting you?"

"Finish her!" Heru screamed from the rough sands.

We stared at her like a rabid beast, switching the Buddy into the overhand position. Saliva dripped from our fangs, and we hissed at her to watch her quiver.

She was in shock, staring back at us as if we were the God of Death. Her body was glued to the wall, nowhere to run, nowhere to hide, and no way around us. Her life flashed before her eyes as she realized she had fallen in love with the wrong man. We sensed her regret, and it seemed that the young woman wanted to die. She didn't even respond to the jolting pains in her belly anymore. We dashed toward her and placed our hand over her mouth as the Buddy stabbed through her pregnant belly and into her unborn baby. Her eyes shot open, and she winced from the pain as she locked on to our menacing red eyes. We showed her our soul, we made her feel our pain, we dumped our anger onto her and made her feel the weight of the load we carried. With a strong grip on the Buddy, we slowly twisted it around like a door key. Tears fell from her eyes as she reached up to grab our wrist.

"Face did this to you," we whispered in her ear.

We yanked the knife out and watched her fall forward on the bathroom floor, blood gushing from her belly, but our work was far from done. We still had a message to deliver.

Face and his task force flew down the dark street, their tires screeching as they pulled up to the house, spotting the bodies of the Illegit members lying lifeless on the ground. They all filed out of the SUVs armed and ready to shoot anything that moved.

One of his men checked the body and signaled to everyone that he was dead.

"Team two, check the outside and secure the perimeter. Team one, we're goin' in," the task force leader commanded.

The men turned on their flashlight attachments and hustled up the driveway, checking the other five dead men sprawled out across the yard. The empty shell casings indicated another failed gun battle, a waste of money spent on strong weapons. The teams split up with Face and Deuce heading inside with their guns ready. They crossed the threshold into the aftermath of a massacre. The walls were riddled with bullet holes, and bodies were scattered all over the place leaving bloodstains on the hardwood.

"Ke-Ke!" Face hollered through the house.

Face's call went without response. He and Deuce aimed their guns up the stairs as they traveled up to search for Ke-Ke. The house reeked of gunpowder and fresh blood, Face's mind fearing the worst as he stepped past the bloody broken stud in the wall. They reached the top of the stairs and noticed that the bedroom door was cracked open.

"Ke-Ke!" he cried out again.

Still no response. Face and Deuce looked across from the door and noticed another body riddled with bullets and an arm missing. They looked at each other frightened but shook off their fear and pressed forward. They rushed into the bedroom, aiming their guns in every direction with the task force close behind. The two aimed their guns at the closed closet and approached the door slowly. Face reached for the doorknob and yanked the door open, and Deuce shoved his sawed-off through the threshold, but there was no one there.

"I thought she said she was in the closet?" Deuce looked at Face.

Confused, Face slowly turned his head and noticed the glare of the bathroom light from around the corner.

"Ke-Ke!" he called once more.

There was still no response. Face shakily raised his gun as he approached the corner and peeked his head down the small hallway to the bathroom to find the broken door swinging on one hinge. He lowered his gun at the sound of his heart breaking into a million pieces. His knees felt weak as he struggled to keep his balance walking to the broken door. He pushed aside the swinging piece and dropped to his knees.

"Ke-Ke," he whimpered.

Before him lay the bloody dead body of his beloved Kelana with the front of her nightgown cut open. Her left hand covered her plump belly, and stabbed deeply through her hand was the missing Buddy. Carved along the bottom of her belly bled the bold word 'REVENGE.' Face had finally been reunited with his missing blade. He reached out his hand, but the weight of his heartbreak sent it down to the floor to hold him up as he cried. Deuce rushed to the broken doorway and was immediately stricken with pity as he witnessed the bloody scene.

"Is she...oh, shit." Deuce sank.

Deuce stepped away from the gory scene, unable to handle the harrowing sight. Face banged his fist onto the bloody tile floor, burdened with the thought of never getting the opportunity to meet his unborn child, to feel the grip of his hand around his finger, or to watch him grow into manhood misguided by his street teachings. He could feel the thick blade of the Buddy strike through his son's heart, a punishment deserving of a man who failed to protect his woman, and this time his big brother wasn't there to save him from his mistakes. He experienced the brokenness that he had left upon many people when their sons, brothers, cousins, and fathers didn't come home. The evil tyrant had been defeated...and then his phone rang.

The ring tone was nothing ordinary, but one that he had specially chosen for his woman. Deuce rushed back to the bathroom, sharing Face's curiosity as to who the call was coming from. Face quickly dried his eyes as he struggled to pull the phone from his pocket. Both of their hearts strained as they saw 'Ke-Ke' appear at the top of the screen. Face reluctantly answered the call and put the phone to his ear.

"Eye for an eye, tooth for a tooth. I'll see you soon, Face."

CHAPTER 23

ANSWERING THE CALL

THE ENERGIES ENTERING Duat sent an unruly disturbance through Anpu as he watched over the souls. They had arrived only moments apart, all suffering the same fate, the mark of war stained into their being. There was one that stood out to Anpu as he glared in disbelief, the eyes of the soul filled with more confusion than the others. Had the war become so gruesome to the point of no one being spared?

Heru stood still upon the rough sands as the ancestral wrath came to a calm. His eyes were closed, settling the dispute between emotion and logic. He dropped his hands to his sides, struggling to find a middle ground for what he had done as he felt the presence of Anpu approaching him from behind. There was a coldness that filled the air, a change that challenged man and god alike.

"How could you allow this?" Anpu questioned.

Heru lowered his eyes to the rough sands, his spirit cracked but not yet broken. The millennia had worn on the Sky God's strength.

"I did what needed to be done," Heru shamefully replied.

Anpu felt the pain in his brother's words. This was no ordinary war fought by an army of soldiers; this was spiritual warfare. The warrior's code followed by the gods was broken in a fit of brokenness.

"This is not the way," Anpu said.

"Then what other way is there?" Heru turned to Anpu. "What more can we do? How many more souls have to suffer before we are finally free?"

The middle ground of logic and emotion had been discovered between the two gods. Anpu was shaken by the wrath of Heru abandoning their moral code, and Heru struggled with his frustrations fighting to help Ryan evolve. Desperation was the thin line supporting their efforts.

"We cannot subject ourselves to the ideals of evil. We are better than them! Our ancestry is better than them, and our future depends on it," Anpu said.

Heru lowered his eyes, his mind overwhelmed with the disturbance of his anger. The ray of hope Ryan projected had nearly corrupted him in their time together, coupled with the pain of unforgiven losses. They all wanted to be free, they all craved vengeance, but there was a need for a leader to bring the new god to life.

"It's just... it's been so long, Anpu. So long without justice. We've fought this war on an uneven playing field. He is progressing, but with each day that passes, I lose hope. This war has changed me, it has hurt me, and I do not wish to feel this way anymore. I'm lost, brother." Heru sighed.

Anpu approached Heru and placed his hand on his shoulder, their spiritual battle scars showing clearly on their faces.

"You are not lost, brother. You are still here, fighting in this war just as you did before we were condemned to this life. You never surrendered to your enemy, no matter how divisive their tactics became, and no matter how dark the battle has gotten, they have not defeated you. We have something more to fight for, and though it is taking more time than we could hope, we cannot lose focus. We were once in his position, and we did not become who we are overnight. Great gods are not born, they are built by greater gods. We have to teach him the right way, or we tread the waters of losing him to the other side," Anpu said.

The two gods looked into each other's eyes and witnessed the pain they carried. The war for their freedom would continue, though the thin line of hope they had found gave them assurance that their freedom was upon the horizon. Anpu turned away from Heru, preparing to return to Duat.

"It would be foolish of us to think that he would be able to achieve evolution in such a short period of time."

His aura consumed him as he began to transition.

"But it's not impossible."

The past couple of days were pretty calm. We got everything out of Aaliyah's old house and put what we could into storage. She clung closely to us and Adrianna as a means of moral support, and we were happy that they were able to rekindle their sisterhood. We still hadn't introduced her to Camille yet as they both needed to grieve, and we needed to get our head clear as well. For whatever reason, we were delaying taking down Face. He was already defeated, and we had essentially taken the most important things from him. We needed to spend some time around the house anyway, seeing that continuing our killing spree wasn't out of our reach.

We rode around town with Aaliyah, trying to fill in where her dad left off buying her stuff for college. We went from store to store buying just about everything she looked at, but no amount of money spent could fill the void of her losing Mr. Latrell. We still tried our best, listening to everything she wanted to talk about, motivating her with words a father would say, and most importantly, being more than just a high school boyfriend. We were a delightful substitute as it showed in her smile, but every now and then, we'd find the tear trace of her sorrows. We parked in front of Adrianna's house, preparing to leave for the evening, her saddened face falling back into the shadows.

"It just sucks because no one's gonna be there for me at graduation," Aaliyah sighed.

"What do you mean? My family will be there for you just like they'll be there for me. Adrianna's too. It's a package deal, babe," we replied.

"That's different. Your actual family is gonna be there for you. I don't have a grandmother or grandfather, both of my parents were only children, and I barely know my cousins out of state. Graduation is gonna be terrible. I don't have anyone to take pictures of me, I just don't—"

"Babe, calm down. It's okay."

We leaned over the center console to hug her, and she released a deep exhale. We knew it was gonna take a lot of time, but we just wanted our goddess to be okay.

"I know the situation is tough, but you've gotta look at it a lil' different. The whole school knows about your situation. You're graduating, and on top of that, you're popular with the administration. Everyone's gonna be there for you. Folks you don't even know, college recruiters, famous people, radio stations, everybody. Yes, my family will be there for me, but they'll only be there as a small portion of everyone else that's going to be there for you. You're the star, Sweets, and everyone around you is within your orbit. It's all about you," we said.

She turned to us with her glossy eyes and planted a soft kiss on our lips. She sniffled, and we stroked her hair to soothe her tears.

"I love you so much," Aaliyah whimpered.

"I love you more, Sweets." We kissed her forehead.

These were the calmer days. She hadn't cried as much, but her tears let us know that she was handling it as well as she could. The task at hand wasn't hard, but we just weren't used to dealing with so much emotion. This kind of affection was new to us, but every time we looked into those brown eyes, it got a little bit easier. Moments later, our cell phone rang with a call from

Camille. It was unusual for her to call us at this time because she didn't normally get off of work until after five.

"Hey, Ma, wassup?"

"Hey, where are you right now?" Camille calmly asked.

"Oh, just out here chillin' with Aaliyah. We went to the mall after school."

Camille released one of her infamous deep sighs, the sigh that says something was terribly wrong.

"Okay. I need you to come home. We need to have a talk," she said.

A talk so important it couldn't be discussed over the phone. We could sense the discomfort through her words.

"Okay, I'll be there soon," we replied.

"I love you, son," Camille said.

Everything started to get strange. It wasn't uncommon for Camille to tell us she loved us, but nothing seemed good about the call, nor did her 'I love you' seem happy. We had to get home quickly.

"I love you, too."

We lowered our head, thinking of what it could possibly be. Everything was going so much better since we had eliminated the problems we were having, so what was this sudden disturbance in our peace? Why couldn't everything just be okay long enough for us to get better?

"Are you okay? Do you need me to drive you home?" Aaliyah asked.

"Yeah, I, no I, uh, I think I should walk. She didn't sound too good, so whatever it might be, I need time to mentally prepare for it," we replied.

We exchanged *I love you*s with our goddess, and after a long kiss good-bye, we walked home under the evening sun. Our mind ran rapidly trying to figure out what she was going to tell us. Naturally, we feared the worst.

"Keep your head to the sky, Ojore," Heru encouraged.

"I don't know if you've been paying attention to my life, but... Never mind."

We neared the house, and it was as if the energy of the entire neighborhood had changed. We walked in the house, sensing the distraught emotions of Camille as she sat on the couch in the living room. She was holding papers that were folded like a bill, and she had been crying.

"Hey, Ma." We sat on the couch. "What's wrong?"

She sniffled and wiped her eye with a tissue she was clinging to. She tried to fix her face before she looked at us, but her eyes were still bloodshot red from her tears. We placed our hand on her shoulder to console her, curious to know what happened. She looked down and bounced the papers in her hand and then set her hand still on her knee.

"What are those papers?" We glanced at them.

The papers were from the same hospital we had been at a few months before. We looked up at her awaiting a response. She took a moment to gather the courage to speak, unsure of how to explain everything to us.

"I'm sorry, baby," Camille said. "Mama had a rough day."

"What's happened?"

She released a deep sigh and looked toward the windows, and some more of her tears began to fall. Once again, Camille had surprised us with another level of hurt.

"Before I start, I just want to tell you how proud I am of you. For as long as I can remember, you've been there for me, you've defended me, and most of all, you've protected me, everything a good son would do."

"That's what I'm supposed to do," we replied.

Our heart beat irregularly as we tried to figure out how to feel. Camille was setting us up for something terrible. We kept glancing at the papers every time she turned her head, but her shaky hands wouldn't stay still.

"You're such a sweet boy." Camille smiled at us. "You know, after Reginald's funeral, I thought it would be a good idea to go to the doctor and get a full check-up. I finally went last week, and um, they found something unusual going on with me."

"Unusual? W-what do you mean?" We raised our brow.

Our concern grew deeper and deeper. We wanted her to just come out with it, but we weren't ready for the potential pain it was going to bring us.

"Well"—she cleared her throat—"they ran some tests on me and said they'd call me in a few days with the results once they got everything figured out."

She turned and looked at us with her teary brown eyes. There was so much sorrow on her face. This wasn't Camille talking, this was our mother. She grabbed our hand and looked into our concerned eyes, and we stared into her soul and felt the quiet brokenness that had been plaguing her for years.

"Ryan, I have stage four breast cancer."

The world went black, and we fell into an endless abyss of darkness. Her words echoed in our head and shattered against our hurt feelings, causing a pain in our chest equivalent to having one's heart torn away. We opened our eyes and found it harder and harder to breathe. Mom was pulling away from giving us a tight hug. She gently leaned us onto the backrest of the couch and tried her best to calm us down. With every second that passed, life grew darker and darker, destroying our hopes of ever seeing a brighter day. First our uncle and our cousin, and now our one and only mom, our favorite mom, the woman that had loved us, fed us, bathed us, and clothed us. She had a problem we were powerless to fix, and all we wanted to do was die.

"It's okay, son. I'm okay. I'm okay with this," she whispered in our ear.

"No, no, Mama, it's not okay, like, isn't there something, anything we can do? There are cancer cures everywhere! I can go find you something, just give me a few hours, I ca—"

She softly shushed us just as she used to when we were a kid. She grinned at our distraught face just like she used to when we were frustrated.

"It's too late for me, son. The cancer has spread too much for it to be reversed, but it's okay. I'm okay with this," Mama said.

Our brain couldn't process the thought of losing her. The thought of her not being around for our college graduation, never getting the chance to see her grandchildren, and dying young enough for the tragedy of her death to haunt us for years to come was inconceivable.

"What do you mean you're okay? Is that supposed to make me feel better? Am I supposed to smile because—you're okay with dying on me?"

She pulled us close and rested our bewildered head on her shoulder, slowly stroking her hand along the side of our head as she shushed us again. We could barely breathe as the news of her disease broke us down. How much power did we have as a god if we couldn't defend our mother from death?

"Don't think of it that way, sweetheart, think of it like this. In my time, I've made a lot of bad decisions, you know. There were times that I felt like I failed as a mother because you, well, I dragged you along with my issues. Your grandmother and I have seemingly never gotten along, and that only further put our relationship on the back burner because I had so many problems my damn self. I thought about it today. I thought about it for a long time before I called you, actually. I've made you suffer enough through this with me, and with this happening, I think you'll actually be better off without me," Mama said.

We immediately sat up and looked at her with tearful disgust.

"How can you say that?" We wiped our eyes. "Better off without you? How?"

Mom had never been so down in the dumps that she would say something so outlandish. This was beneath anything that we had experienced before. As angry as we had gotten with her over the years, we never wanted her to feel this way.

"Ma, like, who the hell would I be without you? First of all, you had me, okay, you could have easily aborted me. You put your friends and social life on hold because you chose to be a mother instead of a bitter baby mama trying to use a man for money. You grew up and handled your business. All those times you missed things when I was young was because you were working for us. You wanted me to have nice things—hell I thought we were rich when I was a kid. You sacrificed everything just to make sure you"—our tears began to fall and the pain in our chest punched through our rib cage—"you saw my smile. Need I remind you, the other fool tried to kill me. Ma, you—you did the best you could with what you had, and though that wasn't much, look at me! You gave birth to a god, the God of War to be exact, like, who else can say that but you?"

Mom smiled as she wiped away our tears again. We were still her baby boy struggling with learning how things worked and failing to understand why we couldn't fix them. She didn't want it to happen this way; she just wanted to be free. There was no way we would ever respect her decision, but she knew that our acceptance would come with time.

"No, son, this is where you come in. My job is done. I was listening to everything you told me that night, and from what it sounds like, my purpose has been served. I got you here, I got you this far, and now it's all on you to do what you have to do."

She sounded like she had been talking to Heru. We hated everything she said because she was right: It was on me now. We had to evolve. We had killed so many people and gotten so consumed in our own feelings that we'd forgotten what our original purpose was.

"It sounds harder than it actually is, Ryan. This is just a hurdle in your story, but you're a champion. You said that you were chosen to be the God of War. I believe you should be that. Be the hero to the world that you've always been to me. I can just imagine you with that big cape standing all menacingly at the top of a skyscraper." Mama smiled.

A tear slowly fell from her eye, and she grinned as she looked off into space, imagining us as a superhuman savior to the Earth. Mom always wanted us to be the best at whatever we did, and no matter the result, she always believed in us. She was so supportive, so encouraging.

"I've never been happier in my life. Just please, promise me one thing," Mama said.

"Anything," we agreed.

"Promise me you'll go to school and get a degree. It's the one thing I wanted and never did."

Mom always had a way of getting what she wanted from us. There was no way we could say no to her, and she knew it. We pulled her in for a hug, and she gently rubbed our back. Our mind was so scattered, we didn't know what to think anymore. We just wanted the power to reverse time. We wanted to repair all the time that passed when we were upset with her. We wanted to go back to the days when we were happy to see each other after a long day. We wanted to have that relationship with her that she didn't have time to have, but even with all of the money we had stolen from Face and his Illegit gang, there was no way to buy back the time we wanted.

The train of distraught emotions seemed to derail Face's motivation. He and his crew had spent the past few nights in hiding and staying at different hotels. The former predator had been conformed into prey as he struggled to cope with his excessive drinking, his guns next to his pillow looking back at him enticing him to end it all. Each night, he scrolled through his phone looking at the pictures Ke-Ke had sent to him as her belly grew to block out the harrowing images of her bloody body lying on the bathroom floor. Nightmares of his unborn child dying in his arms drove him into madness. Though his spirit had been broken, the nemesis had not yet been defeated. From the depth's anxiety came an idea that would bandage his broken spirit.

"I want 'em dead, Deuce." Face downed his shot. "I-I really wanna make him suffer."

The groggy Face sat before the coffee table and began to pour himself another shot. Deuce quickly approached him and snatched the bottle from his hand and took a sip for himself.

"You need to stay off the drank, man," Deuce said.

"Why he had to kill Ke-Ke? He coulda just, coulda just came after me...but no. The bastard killed my son!" Face shouted.

He rose from the couch and unholstered his pistol, aiming at his reflection in the mirror.

"He didn't have to kill her!" Face shouted. "Look at me. What did I do? What did I take from him?"

Face's paint was dried out and blotchy, leaving white stains on his black collar. His formal image had never been so spotty. Face was weak and yearning for the restoration of his power that lay in the hands of his late lover.

"Put the gun down, Face," Deuce commanded. "We're gonna figure this out, but we can't do that wit'chu gettin' drunk. Just chill, man."

Face lowered his gun, still staring sadly at his reflection in the mirror.

"We gotta kill 'em, Deuce. He has to die," Face sobbed.

"Man, stop cryin'. I know we gotta kill 'em, but we ain't got the manpower to do it. Shit, you see how he tore through all our shit," Deuce said.

Face plopped back onto the couch and placed his head in his palms. The angry killer was reduced to whining as the alcohol in his system softened his raw emotions. He and Deuce pondered for hours trying to formulate a scheme to rid themselves of the red-eyed shadow haunting them. Nightfall came, and Face finally sobered up as they transitioned to another hotel for the night. His mind clear and functioning normally, he settled on a thought that would grant vengeance not only for him but for everyone that had fallen victim to the Red Dragon's plague.

"So how do we get everyone there?" Deuce asked.

"Simple. I've got the contact numbers of a few people in Hong's crew, and one or two guys in Nassar's. I haven't called because I figured they were all under fire, but I can put a word out to them and get them to meet up with us," Face said.

"Aight, and where we gon' meet these people?"

"You know that abandoned hotel off of 85? It's the perfect place to pull this off. We ain't gotta worry about pedestrians, we ain't gotta worry about the cops gettin' there before we can roll out, and Hong actually put me in touch with a lawyer of his awhile back just in case we do get caught up in something."

"And if he don't come?"

"He'll come. I know he will," Face assured. "He still got Ke-Ke's phone, I know he does, just ain't got that shit turned on. He'll get curious, start lookin' for somethin' she might know, and he'll see the text. It's gon' be too good for him not to show up. If he can take out a warehouse full of folks, somethin' like this ain't gon' scare him away."

Deuce sarcastically looked at Face, disgusted by his outlandish scheme, but chose not to challenge Face as it was the only feasible idea that they had come up with. There was nothing more the duo could do, and with the start of a new month only days away, their time with their added protection neared its end.

"You really think that's gon' work?" Deuce asked.

"Look, if he wants me like he said he did, he'll show up, and we'll be ready. This time, I'm gonna shoot 'em myself to make sure he's dead," Face promised.

On the opposite end of space and time, Ryan sat with Heru on the rough sands of the Spirit Realm. Struggling with his concentration, Ryan had given up on his training for the evening. He didn't feel the desire to fight anymore, defeated by the thought of his mother choosing death over fighting for her own life. Concerned for his young pupil, Heru searched his heart to find the words to bring him comfort.

"She was correct, Ojore," Heru said.

"How? How was she right about wanting to die? Aren't there rules against suicide?" Ryan asked.

"She was correct about the task being on you. She has fulfilled her purpose as the ancient gods saw fit. You are the God of War."

"What does me being the God of War have to do with her dying on me?" Ryan snarked.

Ryan turned away from Heru, rolling with the downturn of his unstable emotions. The one person he loved the most didn't want to live anymore, and any words against his feelings were personal attacks.

"You can still help her," Heru said.

"How?"

Heru sighed and closed his eyes, inviting the ancestral spirits to join them.

"Look up," Heru said.

Ryan turned his head up toward the outer realm and glared at the infinite stars glazing through time and space. The stars began to move, creating an awesome light show among the galaxies. Shooting stars traveled across the sky in a thousand different directions, and within the blink of an eye, the stars took shape and formed into the bodies of CJ, Carey, and Janay. The three stood together looking down at their loved one yearning for peace to be brought to their souls.

"You've forgotten about them. They were your original purpose. They were what your fight was all about, but you've fallen victim to your own emotional dysfunction... and I have too." Heru lowered his head.

Ryan looked over to Heru, wondering what his elder meant.

"I was wrong to tell you that killing her was okay. My time here has corrupted me, and I will not make that mistake again. I apologize, Ojore."

"It wasn't your fault," Ryan said. "I wanted—at least that's how it felt—I wanted him to suffer like I did. I wanted him to feel what it's like to lose the two people closest to you. When that guy told me about her, I had already made my decision."

They stood silent upon the rough sands, the ancestral stars staring down upon them.

"That isn't who we are, Ojore. We are not deranged menaces murdering people. We are an example of just leadership."

"Yeah, well maybe we look at life a bit differently," Ryan said. "I'm not a hero to the people, at least not now. I'm psychotic, I'm hurt, and even more, I want revenge. I want him and anyone else associated with him to suffer for eternity. They took away my reason for living, and all I have left is a reason for them to die. We may have the same enemies, but we aren't fighting the same war, and I don't fight like you."

Heru looked into Ryan's red eyes and witnessed his fury. The young god had lost his tenderness and regard for peace. The destruction in his eyes told a story of annihilation, but there was something there that made Heru believe he still cared.

"Why does everyone keep dying? They won't come back like I will. I don't want to be alone out here, Heru," Ryan said.

"You won't."

Heru placed his hand on Ryan's shoulder, trying to find the words to comfort him. The two faced a pivotal moment in the young god's progression. The pain of loss was something they both had in common, but Ryan's past depression and discouraged feelings were something tough for Heru to battle with. The elder god's understanding of logistical principles differed from the young god's hurt feelings. Heru feared that Ryan's evolution would be further delayed if he didn't soon conquer his emotions.

"I understand that your mother's battle is an unfortunate one, but we are all relying on you to win this war. Her, the ancestors, all of us. Success comes at a small price, but if you fail, we all suffer. I know that it seems unfair, but you know as well as I that nothing comes without a fight," Heru said.

The two gazed into the stars above, seeing images of the ones they'd lost in battle. The ache in their hearts were lined with the tears of sorrow cried by their ancestors. Ryan looked into the eyes of his uncle, knowing he was not reflecting the man his uncle had helped raise him to be. There was no pride taken in his own work, only the satisfying displeasure of revenge.

"He has to die... I just don't know if I have what it takes to evolve," Ryan said.

The sounds of cars and trucks driving by on the highway soothed the soundwaves of our room as we stared at the dark ceiling. Who were we? Were we truly fit to be a god with our emotions? Was puberty plaguing us with this emotional dysfunction, or was it the underlying depression we had ignored for so long? How were we able to hunt and kill all of those people only to be disabled by our mother's desire to die? Would this feeling go away with age, or would we eventually grow to ignore it like we'd already done to ourselves? If we failed and we all died, she'd be with us forever in Duat, but who wanted to live there?

The shaky conversation came at the wrong time. She could have waited to tell us this, though there was no right time to drop that kind of information. We had to figure out how to work with it, which seemed impossible. We couldn't talk to Aaliyah about this, at least not yet. We'd talked to her earlier and she wasn't feeling well. Mr. Latrell was still in there, lingering in the back of her mind. We couldn't be around her like this; we'd just end up crying in each other's arms all night. It was best to let Adrianna handle her for now.

"Do not doubt yourself, Ojore. Remember, you were chosen for this battle," Heru said.

"Yeah, well, the ancestors could have chosen me at a better time," Ryan snarked.

"Still upset, I see. You are very fortunate, Ojore. Thousands of years have passed, but I remember when the elder gods were training me. Like you, my abilities didn't come naturally—they took time, but they knew it before I did, and they were patient. Be patient, Ojore. In time your answer will come clear," Heru advised.

We looked at our phone to see if Aaliyah had contacted us, but she hadn't. We sent her a goodnight text with the promise of seeing her sometime the following day. As we set our phone on our nightstand, we got the urge to check the phone we'd stolen from Kelana. We'd turned it off and left it in the drawer of our nightstand as a souvenir, seeing that we'd traded our knife for it. We hadn't touched it since the night we'd killed her, her dried bloodstains still scattered across the back. For some reason, we felt compelled to turn it on.

The phone powered up, and the screensaver was a picture of Kelana with Face holding her belly. He looked happy. We wished we could see his face now. Suddenly the phone vibrated, and a message came through from Face with several other recipients.

"Meeting tomorrow @3pm, abandoned hotel off 85N. Bring at least 50 of your men. We will avenge our losses."

We were confused as we read the message. Did Face mean for us to receive this? No sooner than we read the message, more people responded to the group text advising their attendance at the meeting.

"Are you going to go, Ojore?" Heru curiously asked.

There was a tingling sensation in the back of our mind. The ancestors were speaking to us with voices of encouragement, but we had to prove to ourselves that we wanted this life. We could sense hype in our energy, and there were no excuses that would allow us to deny the opportunity to finish our feud once and for all. The fact that it had lasted this long was educational, but we were missing out on things that were important to us. For the first time in life, we actually enjoyed school, we were in love with the most beautiful girl in the world, and life as we know it would take a dramatic change in the next few months. We'd made a pattern of avenging sidebar anger instead of tackling the main issue head-on, not to mention the fact that we felt like we owed it to our mom.

"I'll go, but I'm gonna get there early," Ryan said.

The next day, Face's plan was set in motion. In an effort to retain the remaining numbers of men in the Illegit Family, Face and Deuce decided that it would be best to only use their paid task force to carry out the plan. They loaded themselves into the black SUVs and merged onto the interstate, heading up 85N from their last hotel.

"I'm going the hell home today," Face said to himself as they passed his high-rise on the interstate.

It had been days since the tired tyrant had had a decent night's sleep on top of missing the warm cuddles of his queen. He imagined the torture he wanted to invoke on his nemesis and couldn't decide if he wanted him dead or alive. He remembered the precision of the Buddy sitting upright through Ke-Ke's hand stabbing into the body of his unborn son as he loaded his gun. He felt the pain of 'REVENGE' being stabbed into her gut as she bled out on the bathroom floor while he loaded his second pistol and decided that a quick and easy death was no longer suitable for the red-eyed bastard.

"Hey, tell the guys in the other car I want him alive, that's if the other guys don't get to him first," Face said.

"10-4," the assassin replied.

The only thing that pacified his boiling anger was the meeting. He had constantly checked his phone, responding to messages and making sure no one backed out of the plot. The unsettling anticipation kept the team on their toes as they exited the highway and approached the abandoned hotel. They circled the parking lot to ensure that no one else was occupying the area. Upon parking, the team commenced a full sweep of the gutted building, checking the stairwells and any vacant rooms for possible threats. Once the building was cleared, Face and Deuce exited the vehicles and were escorted into the building.

"Deuce, send a text and tell them all we're meeting on the 6th floor," Face said.

Deuce proceeded to send the message to the soon-to-be arriving families as they made the trek up to the 6th floor. The innards of the abandoned hotel were riddled with broken glass and graffiti. Left astray by a failed development company, the abandoned hotel still possessed forgotten crates of building material and supplies. Confirmation texts from their allies came through as they reached the 6th floor, and the Illegit assassins set up shop by the window to monitor any activity coming in and out of the property. The time was 1:53 p.m., the skies were clear, and the essence of death sifted through the air as the wait began.

We came around 285 and spotted the building as we merged onto 85. We could already sense that Face wasn't alone, and suddenly those feelings of nothingness came back to haunt us. We were exhausted from the back and forth of our indecisiveness, so much so that the desire to destroy was essentially taken from us. It felt like a chore coming here, and we even contemplated turning around and going back home once we got off the exit. We should've waited; we weren't ready for this.

"Ojore, you must focus. Your abilities are linked to the belief you have in yourself. You must not go in there unprepared. It is my belief that you can handle this better than you've handled everything else, but I fear that you may be in your own way. Be strong, Ojore," Heru warned.

"I'm fine," Ryan lied. "Once I get in there, I'll be alright, so don't sweat it."

We zoomed past the abandoned building, spotting two black SUVs sitting outside. It looked like the party hadn't started yet, so we were right on time. We pulled into the nearest open parking lot to park the bike and snuck our way back to the building through the trees. There was no need for us to wear our muzzle—if we were going to settle this, our face needed to be seen. We got to the backside of the building and hid in the woods for a moment. The first time we'd gone after this fool, he was drunk and disoriented, and somehow we'd still gotten killed. We sensed thirteen other energies inside with him, and if our former assistant's words were true, these guys were true assassins. It's one thing to fight a crew of drug pushing, gun-toting gangsters, but it would take more than our super strength to stop an assassin's bullet from fourteen people.

"What time is it?" Face asked.

"Two-seventeen," an assassin answered.

"Good, almost showtime. Now, these guys come in packs, but they ride in style, so you'll know them when you see them. They'll be here a few minutes early, or at least right on time. Most of them are en route now," Face advised.

Face nervously paced back and forth to the sounds of the cars zooming by on the interstate as he repeatedly loaded and unloaded his pistol. He craved having his knife in his hand but couldn't bear to possess another blade, still plagued by the graphic murder. He continued bargaining with himself over the red-eyed guy's life. Would he let him live out his last days being tortured to death in his basement or would they all engage in a firing line and riddle him to pieces with bullets? He started to grow a bit nervous about the arrival of the red-eyed menace, hoping that he would show after the reinforcements arrived.

We found our way inside of the building through the second-story window, and we could sense everyone gathered up above us. We snuck through the halls, hoping the sounds from the highway would help disguise our footsteps. We stayed low as we climbed up the stairwell, the bundle of energies getting closer. We started to second-guess ourselves, wishing we had been smart enough to take one of the guns we'd stolen with us, for there was no room for error here. We knew we had the power to stop them, but we were thinking too much about the possibility of him escaping. We approached the sixth floor and snuck out of the stairwell, sensing Face on the other side of the building.

"Hong's people said they 'bout 15 minutes away. I gotta hand it to you, bruh; this turned out to be a good idea. Last week you couldn't get nobody to sell you pipe dreams," Deuce said.

"Yeah, I gotta admit though, if I would have thought of this last week, I wouldn't have tried it. I literally had to be crazy enough to try some shit like this," Face replied.

We could hear vague echoes coming from down the hall. We could feel our heart beating through our chest with each step closer. Mom wanted us to be a hero; she'd really said that. We had to convince her to let us help her. We had to keep her around long enough for her to see what we accomplished in life. Those visits to Duat were so rough on the heart; we didn't want to go see her there. Why would she just wanna die like that, why not go out with a...

The hallway echoed with a loud bang, causing the men to duck and draw their weapons.

"What the hell was that?" Face hollered.

"Proximity explosive! Someone or something's in the building," one of the assassins said.

"Team one, let's check it out!"

Six of the men stormed into the hallway with their guns aimed at the smoky haze. Broken concrete and dust particles flooded the hallway, making it hard to see clearly what had happened, but one of the watchful assassins got a good look at the culprit beneath the smoke.

"Looks like we got somethin'!"

We opened our eyes, dazed as hell. The world was spinning, and we couldn't get our face off of the floor. It hurt to breathe, and we couldn't really see. We kept hearing sounds that we couldn't understand. It felt like an explosion. Was there an explosion? It felt like we'd crashed into a wall. It hurt so bad.

The assassins found their victim sprawled out and face down in the hallway. They quickly snatched him up from the floor and dragged him back to where Face waited with the other assassins and dropped him at the feet of his nemesis.

"Here's the unlucky bastard that set off my bomb. Can't believe he's still alive," the assassin said.

We struggled to pick our head up, failing to push ourselves up from the floor. We hadn't died, but we'd definitely scraped the surface of death with that hit. The explosion weakened us significantly, and we were still trying to catch our breath. The unlucky bastards had gotten us again.

"And he's a lively one, too."

We immediately opened our eyes and realized we were in the same room with all fourteen of the men. We looked at our hands, and a gut-wrenching feeling passed through us when we noticed our claws weren't there. We didn't feel the burning fury passing through us like we had moments before. We just felt...normal.

"Stand up," a voice said to us.

There was no way three minutes could have gone by that fast. We didn't move as our eyes traced the floor to the two sets of feet before us, and we immediately knew we had found ourselves in the belly of the beast with the sick and twisted monster himself.

"I said stand up, goddammit!" the voice said again.

Suddenly, everyone behind us gathered around, anxious to see the face of the bastard that they'd caught. Why would he be here, on this day and at this time if he wasn't invited? We couldn't think of a lie fast enough. We slowly rose to our feet, coughing up the dust from the dirty building. We kept our head down and focused on their feet; there was no need for them to see our face. We could lie and say we were some homeless wanderer—we already smelled like motor oil from the ride.

"Lift your head up," the voice said.

They wanted to see our face. We looked at our hands again and still had regular fingernails, so we knew our eyes weren't red. Our excuse could work. We were still in a little pain as we lifted our head. We strained our eyes and pretended to still be breathing heavily, and there he was, the infamous Face standing right before us with his gun in his hand. This must be Deuce standing next to him. We had to start looking pitiful if we were going to get out of this. Why was he looking at us so hard?

"Aye, man hol' up!" Deuce said.

Our heart pounded in our chest as Deuce looked us up and down and examined our face. He didn't know us. We hadn't been anywhere for him to know us, so why was he looking so damn hard? His eyes widened, and he pointed at us as if he'd figured out the puzzle to our identity.

"Yo, bruh, I know dis fool!"

No, you don't.

"It's him! It's the fool from the video at the nightclub! I shot you!" Deuce roared as he drew his sawed-off shotgun.

SHIT!! How? There was no way he could possibly recognize us from anywhere. Almost immediately we were staring down the barrels of guns wielded by fourteen angry men. Our calves kicked with adrenaline, but in our current state, we'd be lucky to make it to the stairs. We looked at Face's shades and saw our frightened appearance, the last thing many had seen before their own demise. They were all looking at us like they couldn't wait to begin exercising their best torture techniques. Face grunted as he aimed his pistol at our head, and we could feel the reopening of the gaping hole in our back from Deuce's sawed-off. What were we gonna do? Dammit, we should have waited to do this. Heru was right.

"Time?" Face grunted.

"Two-twenty-five," an assassin responded.

"Right before everyone got here," Deuce said.

Face took off his shades, his angry white face looking back at us with fury. His adrenaline pumped hard in his chest, and his hands started to shake. We almost wanted to smile, but we had to play this smoothly. For someone who made a living off of killing people, he seemed angrier than we were about his loss. The score was even, but now came the tiebreaker, and his team had possession of the ball.

"Somehow, I knew you wouldn't resist that text. I just didn't think you'd come so early," Face said.

Yep, we'd walked right into that trap.

Face lowered his gun. "No matter. I have guests coming, and we're all gonna take our time torturing the hell out of you."

We could feel our senses starting to return. They had us surrounded, but we felt we had one chance at getting out of here. One of the assassin guys was in our way. If he would just move, we might be able to juke out of the door. We'd only have one chance to get this right.

"Tell me, where are your red eyes now?" Face grunted.

Face locked eyes with us. There were 13 other men with gun barrels aimed at us. The men laughed at Face's crude humor as we slightly pivoted our feet toward the doorway six to seven feet away. Their laughter knocked off their aim by a few inches, giving us a very small window of opportunity. We committed to our turn and spun toward the door, sucker-punching the assassin in our way as we bailed out. The room exploded with gunfire, a few of them striking us in the back as we dipped down the hall.

Their gunfire ceased, and the assassins stood motionless, watching the doorway. There were no footsteps heard staggering down the hall, nor were there sounds of painful groans echoing from the sixth floor. They were unsure if their bullets had met their mark because there were no drops of blood on the floor, only dried black dirt.

"Go after him!" Face ordered his squad.

The shaken assassins remembered the harrowing stories told about the warpath of the red-eyed menace and were afraid to move. Thrown by their fear, the enraged Face raised his pistol and shot one of the unlucky assassins in the head to send a message to the rest of the team.

"I said, go after him!" Face grunted.

The assassins quickly cleared the room without question in search of the missing red-eyed killer.

"You three!" Face called out.

The last three assassins slowly turned back to answer him.

"Get us back to the truck, we're getting the hell out of here!"

We were out of breath, sitting on the floor hiding behind a large stack of building materials. We had several bullet holes burning in our back, and everything was starting to get a bit hazy. The run to the fourth floor had taken everything we had, and though we'd made it, it seemed that the run would be in vain. We were looking up at the cobwebs lined along the ceiling trying to breathe, but something had us scared. These were men that faced real war and loved it. The explosion had taken a significant toll on us, and the bullets took us even further. If we were found by anyone of them, three minutes of incapacitation could possibly turn into an unmeasurable amount of time of torture.

"Heru," Ryan strained. "You were...you were right. I should have waited. I'm gonna...I'm gonna die again."

"No, Ojore, I was wrong! You've done exceptional work, and you're not going to die! You have to concentrate! Whatever is plaguing your mind, let it go now," Heru advised.

"But the...my body, I can't–"

"Yes, you can, Ojore. You can and you will, but you've got to try! Come on, concentrate! Focus your remaining energy on your transformation!"

We took heavy breaths and slowly released them, ignoring the pain we felt. The vigor from Heru's positive thoughts rushed through us and transformed itself into rigor. We could hear their footsteps getting closer to the room, one of them fast approaching.

The assassin slowly entered the room with his gun drawn. His hands were shaky as he looked around the supply-filled room, keeping his eyes peeled for his target. He carefully stepped toward the window and happened to notice a trail of black dirt that traveled behind the stack of building materials by the wall. Though there was no blood on the floor, the stains captured the assassin's curiosity. He lowered his gun and followed the dark trail to see what might have made the stain.

We leaped from behind the materials and swiped our claws across his face, roaring like the flame burning inside of us. The fire was back. Distracted by his pain, the killer left himself open to our attack. We punched him as hard as we could and sent him flying into the concrete wall. The force of the impact was so strong it snapped his neck on impact. We sensed another assassin approaching and jumped toward the door. He ran up, wielding dual pistols, but before he had the opportunity to shoot one, we grabbed and broke his wrists and side-kicked him in the chest, sending him flying back into the hallway.

We now had possession of his beautiful .45 caliber pistols and thanked him by putting a mercy bullet through his heart. We jumped back toward the window to give way for the remaining assassins to make it into the room. We hid behind a stack of sheetrock and quietly waited for them to spread out as they entered. Once we felt them in position, we rose from the floor and sent bullets flying at them just as they had to us. We didn't discriminate on where we shot them as long as they were dead after the bullets hit. It was time to take the battle to them.

We ran out into the hallway, scraping our claws against the wall, reclaiming our title as predator. We were going to show Face the dangers of staring into our eyes by carving a new word into his forehead. We could sense more people heading our way and dipped into a room just before they hit the corner. As the three men passed us, we snuck behind them and followed them down the hall. At the sight of another open doorway, we snatched one of them and snapped his neck and jolted into a room with him. We laid his body down and quickly headed back to the hallway to take care of the others.

Meanwhile, Face, Deuce, and three of his assassins hurried down the stairs, anxious to get back to the SUV. His plan thwarted and his team significantly reduced in numbers, the troubled villain found his plan falling to pieces. The sounds of distant gunfire on the upper floors put his brain into a panic, worried that the bullets would soon turn on them if they didn't get away quick enough.

"Where the hell we gon' go?" Deuce asked.

"I don't know, but we gotta get the hell up outta here. Dammit, I should've shot 'em when I had the chance!"

"Relax, you two," an assassin said. "I've got a guy right outside of town that owes me a favor. We just gotta get there."

"I knew I liked you," Face said.

"What about the others?" another assassin asked.

"They got guns, and they better use them if they wanna survive," Deuce said.

The men made it outside and rushed toward the awaiting SUV while the driver felt for the keys in his pocket.

"Deuce, send a text to everybody. The meeting is canceled, and if they wanna know why tell 'em to call me," Face ordered.

Just as Deuce reached for his phone, screams rang out from the fourth story. The awful sight of a man falling from the building captured the eyes of the fleeing men as his body crashed to the ground.

"Was that one of our guys?" Deuce questioned.

We took aim from the window and fired a shot into his chest. The bullet ripped through his flesh and severed his spine before exiting with explosive fashion out of his back. He didn't see it coming... just the way he'd done it to us.

"DEUCE!!"

The assistant villain fell lifelessly to the ground. Face attempted to run toward Deuce but was blocked by bullets ricocheting off the ground by his feet. The assassins looked back toward the window and aimed their guns, ready to shoot back.

We jumped down from the fourth story window to the ground using the fool we'd tossed to break our fall as we landed. We rose to our feet and tossed our gun to the ground and looked across the parking lot at Face.

"OH, SHIT!" the men hollered.

We watched as the assassins scrambled to the doors of the SUV, Face slowly following after them as he bid farewell to his old friend. We felt a jolting sensation in our legs. Our rage was charged, our fangs were dripping, and our eyes were sharp. They were powerless even with their guns, and they knew we knew it. We started to walk toward the SUV as they peeled out of the parking lot, the sound of the spinning wheels putting a grin on our face. They hit the street, and we took off after them roaring with the fury of our ancestors.

They sped through the intersection, narrowly missing cars crossing the busy street. They dipped around slower cars as the engine roared up the onramp to I-85. We ran hastily behind them, jumping over a car crossing the intersection. The driver spun out and almost crashed into other cars sitting at a stoplight. We rushed up the onramp and saw them bogarting their way over into the fast lane. We dipped into traffic, dodging cars and trucks, nearly causing a pileup as we ran alongside 18-wheelers snaking our way around to them. We didn't care about being seen anymore. We only wanted to kill, and we were ready to kill anyone that got in the way of that.

"Where's he at? Do y'all see him?" Face searched through the back window.

"Nah, I think I lost him," the driver said. "I don't think he made it through that intersection."

They zoomed down the highway, dipping in and out of lanes, angry drivers honking their horns at them as they passed by. Unable to grieve the loss of his best friend, Face pulled out his phone and attempted to contact his guests.

"Dammit, I gotta call everybody! How long before we get to your boy's spot?" Face asked.

"About 15 minutes. I've already sent him a distress message, so he's getting his chopper ready," the driver said.

"He's got a chopper? Hell, yeah!" Face grinned.

They continued down the highway, the driver slowing to the speed of traffic to blend in with the other cars. The men relaxed from their fears and began to assess their weapons. The driver glanced at the rearview mirror and paid no mind to the man down the side of the highway. Suddenly, he remembered one striking detail that sent fear barreling deep into his gut...they were on the interstate.

"Oh, shit! It's him! He's behind us!" the driver shouted.

The men looked back and saw the angry foe chasing close behind them on foot. Face dropped his phone in awe, feeling a pain in his chest from the stress on his heart. He got down on the floor, reaching for his guns as he tried to gain control over his panicked emotions. The driver dipped through the lanes again, hoping to shake the nemesis, but he remained hot on their tail. His eyes widened as he peeked at the odometer and saw that they were traveling over 90 MPH.

"Shoot him!" Face hollered.

The two assassins readied their guns and took aim from the front passenger and rear driver side windows. They sent bullets flying at their vicious pursuer, each bullet missing its intended target as the skilled runner dodged each one. Traffic went into a frenzy as drivers slammed on their brakes, crashing into other cars and barreling into the median behind them. Face peeked over the seat, and to his dismay, the red-eyed man was still chasing after them with ease.

"You bitches can't shoot?" Face groaned.

"He keeps dodging!"

We'd let them run long enough; it was time to return fire. We charged the strength in our legs and jumped on top of the SUV.

We could sense Face directly beneath us, but he was too far in the middle for us to reach him. The shooters had already ducked their heads back inside to reload; we had to get rid of them quickly. The assassins quickly reloaded their guns and looked out of the back window to assess their target.

"Where the hell did he go?" one assassin questioned.

Face peeked over the seat and saw nothing but the stopped traffic getting farther and farther behind them. They looked out of every window, the driver even checking his mirrors to see if he could spot the missing culprit. Suddenly, an arm reached into the front passenger window, and the unlucky assassin was thrown from the vehicle. His body bounced hard on the hot pavement before being run over by a speeding car behind them.

"He's on the roof," Face hollered.

The assassin struggled to reposition himself to shoot upwards and was quickly grabbed by the back of his vest. The awkwardly shaped window made it harder to fit his body through the window as he thrashed and hollered to get free. Face cowered with fear and did nothing to help him, and the assassin was repeatedly yanked upwards with his head banging into the thinly padded ceiling until his neck broke. Face got down as low as he could and began shooting through the roof.

We jumped off the SUV, those last bullets narrowly missing us. With the shooters out of the way, all we had to do was get the driver. The SUV would be Face's grave. We wanted them to find him in a coffin of twisted metal. We ran closer to the back windshield, unable to see through to the other side.

"We gotta get rid of him before we get any closer to the place." The driver swerved across the lanes.

"I'm on it!" Face hollered as he crouched on the seat.

Sweating and afraid, Face prepared to fire, masked behind the tinted glass of the SUV. He refused to die by the hands of the red-eyed killer as many of his allies had fallen before. He firmly gripped his sweaty palms around the handle of his pistol, the sights of his gun aimed at the moving head with red eyes. He fired, the first bullet missing its mark and shattering the back windshield. The red-eyed runner backed off of the SUV a bit as he prepared for his second shot. He fired again, but his target spun around and dodged the bullet.

"Slow down a little!" Face hollered to the driver.

The driver let off the gas, and they began to drop in speed. The red-eyed runner got closer and closer to the slowing vehicle. Face took a deep breath and tightened up his aim, his nemesis locked dead-center in his sights. He exhaled and pulled the trigger, and the .45 caliber bullet boomed from the barrel of the gun and traveled out of the rear window. The solo bullet sliced through the air without warning to its running target as it fast approached him. A pothole in the road before the bridge snatched the attention of the red-eyed runner just before he could dodge, and the bullet struck him in the middle of his forehead. The glare of his red eyes immediately faded to brown, and his facial expression dwindled to oblivion.

"I got him!" Face shouted.

The SUV sped off, leaving the red-eyed runner in its dust. His failing body staggered to the side of the bridge and violently crashed over the sidewall. His eyes shut as his dying body plummeted down from the bridge into the murky waters of the river far below. The river swallowed his body and carried him downstream, and everything faded into blackness.

He could hear the sound of a thousand souls screaming in agony, the still air disturbing his skin. He couldn't feel any pain, but nothing seemed to feel right. He was caught in a web of emotional turmoil, trying to understand each of the millions of voices he heard spiraling around his head. His eyes shot open, and to his dismay, Ryan found himself surrounded by the dark sands of Duat. He looked around, scared and confused as this was not how he anticipated awakening after an unprecedented death.

Souls were scattered far around him, begging for someone to save them from their attackers, who appeared great in size far off in the distance. It was none other than the evil three, Mabaya, Lamia, and Wivu together feasting on the raw souls they captured. Ryan ran in their direction, anxious to thwart the attacks, but soon discovered he was powerless to defend the souls as his powers had been taken. He looked at his normal hands and saw that he didn't have his claws. He felt his mouth and couldn't feel his fangs. The insatiable wrath that once dwelled inside of him was no more, and for the first time in months, Ryan was a mere mortal. He dropped to his knees with head down, punching his fist into the sand.

"You want to help them, don't you, Ojore?" Anpu said.

He emerged from the dark gray gloom holding his staff as he stood before the defeated mortal soul, offering him no time to pity himself.

"Yes, but I can't. I can't do anything," Ryan replied.

"You're afraid, Ojore," Anpu explained. "You have the power to do whatever it is you please."

"I don't have it in me anymore. She's dying on me, Anpu. She won't let me help her. She's all I've got to live for," Ryan cried.

Anpu grabbed Ryan by the arm and pulled him to his feet.

"Stop lying to yourself, Ojore! Open your eyes and look around you."

Ryan opened his eyes to see flashbacks of heroism from his youth to the present. He heard the happy echoes of thanks that came from his defenseless companions that looked to him as a savior as his actions allowed them the opportunity to evolve in their own lives. A silent tear fell from his eyes as he battled the distant thoughts emerging from the depths of his mind. Quickly, the warm thoughts turned back to the harrowing torture of the souls by the evil three. The souls cried for someone to save them, for someone to set them free of their torment.

"Ojore, you know who you are. There is nothing confusing about your destiny, other than your lack of understanding of it. You have aged only seventeen years and have been given a responsibility that you don't fully believe you are ready to wield, but the ancestors would not have chosen you to be the God of War if you were incapable of manifestation," Anpu stated.

The distant souls reached out in hopes that someone would save them from their brutal demise. The evil three cast their weapons of torture about the souls, draining them of their energy, still refusing them their rite of passage. Carey, CJ, and Janay were picked from among the crowd, each of them mishandled by one of the evil three as they begged for their release.

"You are a lover. You cherish life, and you would give nothing less than your life to save the ones that you love. You stand for justice, upholding the laws of Ma'at in your own right. You care to see life grow and to punish those that seek to destroy it. Don't allow them to destroy the lives you fight to protect," Anpu said.

He was losing his battle against the evil three as the future of the Life and Spirit Realms rested on his shoulders. The pressures of graduating high school and defying the odds of the life expected for him collided with the responsibility of being a god and saving the universe from endless torture and death. The insecurity in his powers brought him extreme frustration. The voices of doubt filled his mind and beat him to his knees. He groaned with anguish, anxious to set his troubled mind free.

"That's it, Ojore, you're there! You feel it, don't you? That energy. Don't be afraid of it, that rage. It's who you are. The only thing delaying your evolution is you! It's all about you," Anpu encouraged.

Ryan continued to grunt, and his body began to shake, but he continued to hold back. He wrapped his hand around the neck of his insecurities, and they grabbed him back, forcing him to face himself. The difference between who he once was and what he had become spiraled around in his mind. The question of who he wanted to be had yet to be answered.

"Your energies are aligned with divinity, but you must accept their power! They aren't looking to us to save them anymore; they're looking to you! All things are possible, Ojore! Who you are is limited by who you think you are! You must believe in yourself!" Anpu roared.

Ryan's eyes shot open, and Anpu's words clicked in his mind. Ryan was a baby, born free and careless of the harms of society. His rage grew as he did, transforming him from youth into manhood. His fury hardened his spirit, and his compassion opened his heart for the spirit of the Red Dragon to align his chakras, as well as the essence of war within him. The ancestors cried out, giving their final plea for battle. Ryan closed his eyes as his body violently shook. He lowered his head and dug his hands into the dark sands.

"Who are you?" Anpu asked.

The Red Dragon's eyes shot fully open, red and glowing, his fangs growing with the disturbed grumble in his throat. The potential energy generating within him forced his veins to the surface as Anpu's words guided him to choose the path he chose to walk. Ryan was no longer a simple teenage boy.

"I AM THE GOD OF WAR!"

His body erupted from the dark sands into midair, and his fiery aura expelled from his body. He hollered as his energy-charged, shooting fire high in the skies of Duat while forming a large circle of fire on the dark sands. The body of the dragon formed from his aura and twisted through the air, spitting fire about the fiery circle until the flames were high enough to reach the Red Dragon. The Red Dragon spread his arms and legs wide as his body absorbed the energy from the blaze beneath him, and the dragon turned and flew through his chest and out of his back, covering a part of his body in flames. The dragon continued to fly through him until his body was completely wrapped in the essence of the beast.

The dragon opened its mouth and expelled flames in the shape of a spear that solidified into red crystals around the Red

Dragon, and soon all became silent. The flames below ceased to burn, and from within the egg-like sphere, the silhouette of the Red Dragon could be seen as red lightning bolts crashed into the dark sands. Anpu jumped to avoid the bolts as he observed the transformation in awe.

"Heru, he's done it!" Anpu celebrated.

Lightning bolts ejected from the sphere, cracking it open with each thunderous boom. Finally, the sphere fell apart, and the crystal shards fell into dust on top of the dark sands. Anpu blocked his eyes from the blinding light in midair, feeling the heat from its energy as if it were the sun. The ball of light lowered itself to the dark sands and dimmed as it formed into a fiery aura. Before Anpu stood the evolved Red Dragon with a new look.

His boots were red and black, complementing the golden metal shin guards topped with golden dragon heads. His black pants and undershirt were made of the dragon's scales. Around his waist was formed a large black belt accented with red flames and a golden dragon head on the front. Draped over his shirt was his black and red vest with the dragon curled around his neck. The vest adopted the red tribal symbol of the dragon head on the front with the red and black flames of the dragon on the back. There were golden dragon heads made of gold metal covering his shoulders with chains that linked across his chest along with golden spiked red and black bracers to cover his forearms with gold metal dragon claws to cover his knuckles. His muzzle transformed, taking the design of the dragon's mouth. His red and black headdress fit snugly around the crown of his head and flared out at the top with designs of the dragon's head.

The Red Dragon opened his sharpened eyes and observed the gift from his ancestors as his aura flared around him, forming the shape of wings across his back. Anpu knelt to the dark sands, giving praise to the ancestors, for the God of War was reborn, giving hope to the trapped occupants of Duat. He stared at the Red Dragon as he rose to his feet, weeping with joy as he ran toward the marvelous god.

"Ojore, you... you did it! You've evolved!" Anpu reveled.

"Your words, they helped," the Red Dragon said. "I know this is who I am."

"I'm proud of you, Ojore. I had to bring you here after you were killed because I sensed an indifference in your essence and determined it was what kept you from your evolution. Heru is waiting for you in the Spirit Realm. Because of your evolution, your spirits are no longer synced with each other," Anpu explained.

The Red Dragon observed his senses and realized he could no longer feel Heru's presence within him. He proudly looked at Anpu, happy that he was finally able to stand on his own.

"I swore that I would not fail you two, and today I will make good on my promise," the Red Dragon proclaimed.

He crossed his arm over his chest and bowed his head to his mentor. Anpu crossed his arms and confidently looked upon the transformed god.

"Who are you?" Anpu grinned.

"I am the God of War!"

CHAPTER 24:
HEART OF THE DRAGON

THE RED DRAGON'S body turned into flames and vanished from Duat, leaving nothing but sparks in his wake. He teleported to the rough sands of the Spirit Realm, where Heru anxiously awaited his arrival. The two gods greeted each other with gratitude, Heru showing pride in his graduated student. Tiny sparks of fire formed around the Red Dragon's head as his mask and headdress disappeared, revealing changes to his face. Small spikes took the place of his eyebrows, coupled with red scales around his eyes, and his eyes were sharper and more vibrant than ever before. He ran his fingers across his face, discovering the difference in his skin. His face expressed the light of his soul and the dark grit of his rage, the balance between night and day within him. The new god reeked of power, his profound presence felt far across the galaxy.

"You have chosen your destiny, Ojore," Heru said.

"I had to stop being afraid of myself. These powers, the rage, it's all a part of me. The ancestors saw me fit to have these abilities long before I knew anything about them. I had to realize that if they believed in me, there was no reason for me not to believe in myself," the Red Dragon replied.

A smile appeared across Heru's face as he witnessed his hope standing before him. He placed his hand on the Red Dragon's forehead, and his hand began to glow gold with radiant energy. The Red Dragon's eyes glowed as his body began to pulsate as he absorbed the raw power being gifted to him. Heru slowly pulled away, leaving a glowing gold ankh on his forehead that vanished into his scales. The energy settled, and the Red Dragon shivered as he opened his eyes, sensing a greater ability from his power.

"All of your hidden abilities have been unlocked. In time, you will figure out what they all are, but you still have further to go. Your powers are still growing, and over time you will see changes in your face, much like how I change when I transform. It may not seem like much now, but in time, you will see the glory of your transformation. Now go, do what you must do. I can't tell you what kind of god to be, but always remember who you are," Heru said.

"I'll never forget," the Red Dragon replied.

His mask and headdress sparked and reformed, and his aura formed into a dragon. The dragon snaked into the sky and traveled back across the galaxy to the Life Realm while Ryan's lifeless body drifted downstream, cloaked in the darkness of the murky water. The Red Dragon's essence descended upon Earth into the fast-flowing river and rejoined with its drowned body. Suddenly, the dark waters began to boil, and from the steam, I arose from the river with my blazing aura around me. The flames consumed me and healed my wounds and changed my clothing as I walked ashore. I looked around, familiarizing myself with my surroundings and remembered everything that had happened.

The river had carried me a good distance downstream, and Face had already made it far across town. There's no telling how long I was out, but I refused to let it stop me from destroying him today. I dashed back in the direction of the bridge, deter-mined to end the life of the ruthless tyrant for the sake of my people. I came up on the bridge, jumped back onto the highway, and began running just as I was before, only I was much faster than I remembered. My power pulsated through me as if I had fire-breathing dragons burning from each limb. I dipped and dodged around cars on the crowded freeway, leaving flaming footprints on the ground. I ran faster and faster until suddenly, my aura released a boom of energy, and my feet lifted off the ground.

Face and his last surviving assassin arrived at the gated compound and were ushered in by personnel expecting them. They were immediately identified and taken to Clancy, the assassin's friend and man in charge of the facility. While the friends talked, Face observed the compound, intrigued by how the staff ran like a well-oiled machine, everyone carrying a gun on their hip or shoulder. He nervously looked out of the window and observed the gated lot, fearing he would see the red-eyed maniac still running him down. Clancy approached Face and touched his shoulder, causing the panicked Face to jump and turn, ready to fight.

"Whoa, whoa, calm down there, buddy. I'm not gonna hurt ya. Name's Clancy, a friend of Five." Clancy extended his hand to shake.

"Five?" Face questioned.

"Oh, yeah. Nickname we gave him back in the service. I'll tell ya the story on the flight over. Come with me—the pilot's waiting." Clancy began to walk away.

"W-wait, where's Five?" Face asked.

"Oh, I put him on a different project. I got some new guys that'll take care of you in the hiding spot I'm taking you to. Hey, aren't you a friend of Hong's?" Clancy asked.

The two traveled through the facility to the nerve center to take the elevator to the helipad. Face had a million questions boggling through his head but was too afraid to ask anything. He readjusted himself, feeling for his pistols with his bicep—they were the only defense he had left. The men exited through the door to the helipad, the helicopter's rotors spinning as the pilot prepared for their flight. Clancy turned to Face to share one last piece of information with him.

"Just so you know, once you get on this chopper, you're leaving everything behind. If you've got any family you wanna reach out to, now's the time," Clancy advised.

"I'm good," Face said. "Everyone I know is dead."

Clancy nodded and proceeded to the helicopter, leaving Face to walk slowly behind him. The once fearless brute had been reduced to a fleeing refugee from a war that he'd started. He'd once grabbed men by the throat and tortured them in his three-story suburban hideout, but he now had nothing except for two pistols and the cash in his pocket. The fearful menace took his walk of shame with the pain of loss dangling from his shoulders. In an attempt to bring a ray of hope to his tragic day, he looked to the skies, hoping to see something beautiful in the clouds.

"What the fuck?" Face uttered to himself, dropping his jaw.

I was hovering high over some gated facility, and there he was about to escape in a helicopter. Just moments ago, he'd shot me in the head and left me to die in a river, and now the coward was trying to leave without finishing the job. I sensed the presence of others in the facility, but to me, they were nothing more than collateral damage—this was war. I tried to remember the hand formations that Heru had taught me to perform the Mansa Musa Blaze, but I wasn't sure if I had it right.

"I think he did it like this. Man-sa-mu-sa...WHOA!"

My hands sparked into flames, and a giant fireball exploded from them and barreled toward the helicopter. It wasn't what I was trying to do, but by the looks of it, it was going to do just what I needed.

Face spotted the fireball coming towards the building and tried to alert Clancy, but he couldn't hear his warnings over the roar of the rotors. Face scrambled to get back inside of the building, feeling the heat of the fireball on the back of his neck. The pilot noticed a bright gleam of light in his peripheral vision and looked out of the window to see the giant fireball just before impact. The helicopter exploded into pieces, and the entire side of the building erupted in flames from the fireball traveling through.

Everything was dim and hazy as Face opened his eyes. He was lying on his back watching the smoke rise to the ceiling as the heat of the fire brought him back to life. The poor fool had made it back inside of the building and avoided being caught up within the wreckage, but he would now have to find his way down from the top floor. He groaned as he slowly stood to his feet, feeling the pain from his body being slammed into the wall from the explosive impact of the fireball. He staggered down the hall, following a sign that pointed him in the direction of the stairs. As he staggered down the smoky hallway, he happened to look out of the broken glass window and quivered with fear as he saw the man that had just been in the sky staring back at him...and his eyes were red.

I made sure he saw me before he tried to run. If the smoke inhalation didn't kill him, his heart exploding as he ran from me would. I called his name and watched him fall over his misguided footsteps. I disappeared inside to join him as he journeyed through the flaming floors.

Face went into a panic as he struggled to run, breathing in the harmful smoke that darkened his path. He entered the burning stairwell and stopped as he thought he spotted someone through the smoke. The smoke slowly cleared from the top and he saw two red glowing eyes staring back at him. He froze as the eyes slowly glided toward him, and he realized this beast was not on his feet.

"How long did you make them plead, Face?" I grumbled.

He shrieked and took off down the stairs, burning his hand on the hot rail. It was lovely to watch the derailed nemesis experience what it was to feel fear. He wheezed as he made his way down, and I disappeared into the flames to surprise him again.

"He was seventeen, Face. Do you remember when you were seventeen?" I hollered.

"Leave me alone," Face cried.

He nearly tripped as he made his way down the next set of stairs. He looked back to see if he had dropped anything and the red-eyed demon was right behind him, tilting his head and staring menacingly.

"She didn't scream when I stabbed her the first time." I scowled.

He screamed and took off on his fourth wind. I continued the mental abuse, shouting at him and popping up in corners.

The red-eyed demon hovered down in the center of the rails, watching Face lose his mind trying to escape. He swooshed his hand in Face's direction, and Face tripped and tumbled down the stairs, landing on his side. Dazed again by the fall, Face struggled to his feet, hearing a hissing sound coming from behind. He turned over on his back and shrieked at the sight of the red-eyed villain brandishing his fangs and flicking his tongue at him. Face dug his heels into the floor, pushing himself away from the menacing terror, his heart nearly ready to give out.

"I'm going to devour your soul and the soul of your unborn child," I hollered behind him.

Face made it to the bottom floor and noticed familiar ground as he ran toward the unburning front. The terrified villain was out of breath as he reached the entrance, stripping himself of his smoking-hot jacket. He pushed through the hallway and got outside, making it a short distance before falling to his knees. The poor villain had nothing left. His body was hot and dehydrated, and his mind was corrupted and delusional. His hands pressed hard against the hot pavement as he struggled to catch his breath.

"Afraid and alone. I told you I was coming for you," I said.

Face slowly raised his head, barely able to throw his hands up. I dismissed my headdress, allowing the coward to see the true face of his killer. I stared at him, his white paint stained with blood and dirt, peeling from his face. This wasn't the same Face that murdered my uncle; he was just a shadow of a man who used to be fearless.

"I've taken everything from you. Your money, your future, your lover, and all that's left is you. You were given the opportunity in this life to be something more, and you chose to be less. You chose to be what they wanted you to be instead of living for yourself. You lived for the joy of bringing pain to others, profiting from the poison you injected into your own community, and you called it revenge. You proclaimed yourself as King, but just like the name of your gang, you were nothing. Now look at you, you're less than nothing. Quite frankly, you're not even worth killing. I was hoping that the smoke inhalation would have done the job for me, but you're a tricky bastard, the same tricky bastard that took the lives of so many men and women. You took them away from families that loved them, that grieved over them, but tell me Face, who's going to grieve over you?" I laughed.

Fear struck the nerves of the weakened villain, and he started to whimper.

"You see, everyone you've ever loved is dead or forgotten. When you die, your Illegit Family dies with you. I'll see to it that no one ever carries on the name!"

I planted my feet and took a stance to prepare my finishing move. I watched as Face lowered his hands in defeat, not even taking the chance to reach for his useless guns.

"Killing your family was for my revenge. Killing you is for everyone that never got the chance to say good-bye."

My form perfect and my energy charged, I locked my eyes on the beaten white face of my final target.

"MMAAAAAAANNNNNN-SSSAAAAAAAAA-MMMUUUUUUUU..."

My aura flared up with fire, whipping around wildly. I felt the unlimited power of the ancestors flowing through me. My war was finally over.

"SSAAAAAA!!!"

From my hands erupted a blazing hellfire that obliterated everything in its path into dust. Face's body dwindled from flesh to ash to nothing. The compound went up in an explosion as my blaze consumed every bit of matter it touched. I released my blaze and watched the tail of it disintegrate into a trail of fire before me. Where there was once a building was now a gaping hole in the ground surrounded by a large gate. I looked at the spot where Face had once knelt, and there was nothing there. I tried to sense his energy, but I couldn't feel anything.

"He's finally gone. It's over," I sighed.

I raised my fist to the sky and roared with pride, my aura blazing around me like a wildfire. I took to the skies and retreated from the location, hearing the distant sounds of sirens headed to the area. No one would ever know what really happened today, and there would be no mention of who had caused the destruction. Suddenly, my mother's calming words began to replay in my head—I could be a hero. Anpu was right when he said I fought for justice and punished those who sought to destroy it. There was nothing more in the world I wanted to do now, but I had to do it my way. Having these abilities was my calling, but I had a promise to keep first.

A few days passed, and I was in 6th period chatting with Aaliyah. She had been good these last few days, and she seemed to be getting better. With my killing spree finally over, I decided to put more time into us while I had the chance. My mother did the best she could to keep a smile on my face, and I wanted to do the same for my beloved. She'd had a dream the night before that had her smiling all day.

"He was happy, happier than I ever remember seeing him since my mom died. He told me everything was gonna be all right. Then he turned to the sunset and was like, 'You'll find someone that will love you even more than I did,' and I was like, 'Daddy, don't say that,' and he was like, 'Believe me.'" She smiled.

She placed her soft hand on my shoulder and hit me with that golden-brown goddess glare. I felt a sensation run down my back. I'd always fall victim to my pretty brown lover's eyes.

"Please...believe me," Aaliyah flirted. "And then get this, my mom shows up out of nowhere and tells me how proud of me she is."

"What!" I smiled.

"I know, right! Then they joined hands and walked off into the sunset. Like, I woke up crying because I was so happy. It's like they finally found each other in the afterlife and now they can be at peace," Aaliyah said.

"That's beautiful, baby." I grinned.

It had been a pleasure meeting Mrs. Latrell in Duat the other day. Anpu was gracious enough to let me know that he had found her, and we reunited her with Mr. Latrell after all these years. I got to see where Aaliyah got her eyes and her smile from as her spirit lit up with joy. Mr. Latrell was kind enough to reassure his approval of me with Aaliyah; he even hugged me again. I felt that it was only right that they had the chance to love again before everything got fixed.

"So, did you finish your drawing?" she asked.

"Oh yeah. Let me show you."

I reached in my bag and pulled out my sketchbook to reveal my masterpiece. I had worked on the piece for so long, I decided to make it a part of my uniform. It was the head of a dragon but with a tribal look. The sharp and curvy lines made it look dangerous, but the sleekness of its design had a special way of catching the eye.

"Oh wow, babe, this looks incredible! I love it. This would be a dope ass tattoo. You're not thinking of getting a tattoo, are you?" Aaliyah asked.

"No, baby," I laughed, "but I was thinking of getting a septum piercing."

"You what?" Aaliyah gave me the evil eye.

"I'm kidding," I laughed.

The school day ended, and I shook hands with Colb as we prepared to exit the classroom. He held on to my hand, and I motioned to Aaliyah to keep going as I turned to acknowledge his grip.

"I just wanna tell you I'm proud of you, Scales. You know, only a few months ago—hell, it ain't even been a year yet, and you... you really took care of that girl, man. That was very noble of you. I'm proud, man. I'm proud because I always hear women of color say we don't take care of them, and here you are doin' the damn thang, makin' us all look bad," Colb laughed.

"Thanks, Colb," I laughed. "I appreciate that."

"Hey, I gotta give credit where it's due," Colb said. "You got yourself a good one. Treat that girl right and she'll make a good wife to you one day. Hopefully soon."

Aaliyah as my wife—now there was a thought that made me smile.

"Yeah, real soon."

I caught up to Aaliyah in the parking lot talking with Terrell and Adrianna. He was doing better, too. Terrell had spent the last few months getting himself in shape for the military, and Adrianna had taken a liking to his weirdness. My boy finally got the girl of his dreams, and his happiness was written all over his face every time he saw her. His mom had come to terms with his decision, and she even got herself some counseling to help sort out her feelings.

"I leave two weeks after graduation, so I need y'all to dedicate y'all's summer to me," Terrell laughed.

"Damn, two weeks? You ain't gon' have time for shit, bruh," I said.

"That better mean we're gonna spend a lot of time together before you go," Adrianna sassed with a smirk.

Terrell looked at her, and an enormous grin appeared across his face. She had him wrapped around her finger, but I knew she was good for him.

"Just be safe," Aaliyah said, "and don't be a stranger when you come home."

"I will." Terrell looked at his watch. "Aight, I gotta get out of here. You guys be on your best behavior. No sex until you're thirty."

We all burst into laughter, the joy among friends flourishing between all of us. Terrell wrapped his arms around Adrianna, and they took their time kissing each other good-bye, her soft lips setting fire to his nervous system. He soon ran off to continue with his training before his big day. He was going to be a fine soldier someday. I just wished I could be out there with him to protect him.

"Well, babe, I was thinking we could head down to the outlet mall to get you some stuff for your dorm, Mr. Soon-to-Be Art School Freshman." Aaliyah smiled.

"Ooh, not today, Sweets. I've got something really important to do for my mom. In fact, I gotta get going," I lied, looking at my watch.

"Damn. Well, at least let me drive you home," she offered.

The girls dropped me off at the house, Aaliyah leaving me with a long kiss good-bye from her luscious lips. Saving the world would never be an easy task with her around, but every dark hero needs a beautiful distraction to keep the blood flowing. I ran inside to drop my bag then immediately headed out to fly.

"I'm on my way. How long do you think it'll take me to fly there?" I asked.

"That depends on how hard you're willing to push yourself," Heru said.

Now that our souls were no longer bonded, I had the power to speak with Heru and Anpu telepathically. I took to the air, flying high in the sky as my aura took the shape of a fiery dragon. I tested my limits, flying up and down doing spins and practicing sudden stops until I felt like I had it all under control. I had so many new abilities to learn, but I wanted to master my flying abilities as quickly as possible. My flight took me far across the Atlantic Ocean, seeing nothing but blue for miles. I flew toward the water and glided my hand through the waves, observing a pod of whales breaching. Dolphins dove in and out of the water around me, guiding me along our path over the deep blue sea. After flying for so long, I passed over the coast of West Africa quickly and carefully flying low between the buildings to avoid being seen by the locals.

I traveled over the immaculate cities and observed how they functioned so smoothly. These cities looked nothing like how they portrayed Africa on TV. They were very well established and even better looking than most American cities. I traveled across the Sahara, soaking up the heat from the desert plains. I even flew over a sandstorm that nearly blinded me. Finally, I reached a remote area of Egypt where Heru advised me I would be able to find the Gateway Stones.

"They aren't here," I panicked.

"They must be there," Heru grunted. "The platform of the stones was meant to be immovable!"

"Heru, I'm telling you, there's nothing here but sand! When's the last time you looked at this place?" I asked.

I looked around from the air and saw nothing but sand dunes for miles. Maybe the stones had been destroyed.

"You think they did something to them?" I asked.

"They couldn't have," Anpu said. "Otherwise, they wouldn't be able to cross over into Duat."

The stones had to be around here somewhere, but we didn't have a clue where to look. There was nothing but sand on top of sand on top of sand, and there was no telling how many sandstorms had occurred over the last three thousand years since they'd gotten locked in Duat. I lowered myself to the ground, and the force from my energy blew the sand away as I landed. I lowered my headdress and stood there for a second thinking. Suddenly the fireball went off in my head.

"I got it! The stones are buried under the sand," I said.

"They have to be," Heru said. "There's no other way."

"There's a lot of sand to dig through out here. You think the stones will be able to handle it if I blow through all this sand?" I asked.

"The Gateway Stones are stronger than any being in the universe. They will survive whatever pressure you apply to them," Anpu assured me.

"Good, because I didn't bring a shovel," I said.

I planted my feet in the sand, and with a vicious grunt, I charged my energy. My aura began to swirl around me, sucking the sand up into the air until a sand tornado formed around me, casting sand all around through the air. I looked to the ground, and large pillars began to appear. I forced my energy around it and cleared the land as I made my descent to the four pillars centered on a square platform.

"These are the stones? I didn't imagine they would be this big," I said.

"Yes, the Gateway Stones are quite large, but there is more to what you must do. Each stone is marked by a specific god with a specific element. You must match the elements associated with the elements in the four corners and push them there. The god on top must be facing outward in the cardinal direction of which the stone is placed. For instance, my stone bears the Wind element. It must be situated in the southeast corner of the platform. Move that stone first and make sure my symbol on top faces southeast," Heru explained.

I followed Heru's instructions and moved his stone to the southeast corner of the platform. Even for me with the power of a god, the stone felt as if it weighed a ton.

"This thing is a lot heavier than I thought," I grunted.

It took me a while, but I dragged the stone to the corner and turned it in the correct position. The stone locked itself into place, and a small tornado with thunder clouds formed around it. I sensed an enormous amount of energy coming from the windy stone; it even emitted enough force to blow me back a little.

"Now look for the stone that has Anpu on top. It has the element of Earth. Place it in the southwest corner," Heru instructed.

I pushed the heavy stone as best I could to the southwest corner, wishing there was an easier way to move the rest of them.

"There's gotta be a better way to move these things. Those evil ones must have worked together to move them so quickly," I grunted.

"It is likely that your theory may be true, Ojore. The Gateway Stones were designed by the ancient gods to deter any single god from moving them quickly in case of such a situation as Heru and I experienced," Anpu explained.

Twenty minutes had passed, and I finally had two stones moved into place. I set the Earth Stone in its proper position, and instantly vegetation began to grow from it. There were long strings of kudzu and vines hanging from a tree that took the shape of the stone and grew tall. Suddenly, a beam of energy shot across from the Wind Stone to the Earth Stone.

"Oh, crap, what's happening?"

"It is all right, Ojore. The stones wield enormous power, as I'm sure you can sense. Once you have all of the stones in place, they will bond with each other, forming a square of energy between them. Continue quickly," Heru advised.

I hurried back to the center of the platform and matched up the water element with the Water Stone in the northwest corner. On top of the stone was the goddess Auset. Once I positioned it correctly, strong waterfalls fell from all four sides of the stone. We could smell the freshness of the water and even took a sip as another beam of energy joined from the Earth Stone to the Water Stone.

"There's just one stone left," I said as I walked back toward the center.

"Yes, that is the Fire Stone. On top is my father, Asar. Place that stone in the northeast corner of the platform, but be warned, this stone will react differently with you since your powers are of its element," Heru said.

I approached the stone and gazed at the fire symbols engraved deeply into it. I heeded Heru's warning and walked around it, looking for any potential danger, but noticed nothing.

"It looks safe to me," I said as I prepared to move it.

The moment I touched the stone, it burst into flames and engulfed me in its blaze. The fire didn't burn me, but its heat was hotter than any temperature I could have ever reached. The fire put an intense amount of strain on my muscles, and I roared from the uncomfortable sensation it gave me. I started to sweat from the heat, the stone taking every bit of energy I had to move.

"It's hot as hell," I struggled. "It's heavier too!"

"Push through, Ojore! You are almost there! You have the power to do this! Don't give up," Anpu encouraged.

"It hurts to move," I groaned.

"Ignore the pain, Ojore! You must fight through this battle! Give it everything you've got," Heru coached.

I hollered from my pain, but I refused to be defeated by the overweight rock. I planted my hands and feet and roared as I charged my energy. My aura flared around me and gave me the strength to continue pushing. Power surged through my body as I strained and pushed the stone. The force was so strong that my vision blurred from the amount of energy being emitted by the stone colliding with my energy. I roared once more and forced all of my power into one final push. Luckily, it was all I needed. I adjusted the stone into the correct position, and instantly its flames disappeared from my body. The stone continued its inferno, and two beams ejected from it, connecting it to the Water Stone and the Wind Stone. Pushing this stone nearly left me powerless as I stood before it.

"The stones are now in place. You must now stand in the middle of the platform to reveal the chamber," Heru instructed.

I was drained. The walk to the center of the platform wasn't far, but I felt like I didn't have the strength to make it. I staggered back toward the center tile, which had the hieroglyphic of the gods standing above their element. I planted my feet on the tile, and suddenly separate beams of energy formed from the stones and connected to me. I roared as the beams charged me with so much power from the elements that I felt like I might explode.

"Focus the energy, Ojore! Raise your hands up in front of you," Heru instructed.

I strained as I raised my hands before me, and from the sands rose the hidden chamber of the Gateway Stones. The beams of energy disappeared, and the stones returned to their naturally rough state. My right hand now glowed gold and was filled with enormous power.

"Now, Ojore, enter the chamber and approach the handle to the lock."

I walked toward the chamber, observing the power in my hand. I felt like I could destroy the world—no, a portion of the universe with this power. There was nothing that would have been able to stop me if I had gone rogue with this energy. I entered the small chamber, and in the center was a dial made of stone coming out of the floor with a turning handle piece on top.

"Is this it?" I asked.

"Yes, Ojore, that is the lock! Turn it to the correct position and depress it into the floor to open the gateway," Heru exclaimed.

I grabbed the handle on top of the stone and turned it clock-wise until it stopped. I then took both hands and depressed the stone into the floor... and nothing happened.

"I did it, I think."

Suddenly, my heart jumped as I sensed three large, dark ener-gies behind me. I quickly turned, and from the opening of the chamber, I saw the silhouettes of the Evil Three standing before me. Their glowing eyes pierced through me as they observed the new god on the block unlike anyone they had ever seen. The girl hissed at me and flicked her tongue, and I hissed back, prepared to take them on. Just as I was about to charge my energy, I felt a familiar presence behind me.

"Stand down, Ojore. They don't want to die here."

Heru and Anpu were already in attack formation with their weapons in hand. The wrongfully imprisoned gods were now freed from the trenches of Duat. They charged their energies, and their bodies began to glow. They transformed into their god forms, and their bodies were cloaked with their golden armor. Their feathers and fur glowed like liquid gold as their eyes sharpened on the Evil Three. Heru readied his spear into the throwing position, and it began to emit his powerful energy. Before he could put his all into the throw, the Evil Three vanished from the scene without a trace. The freed gods calmed their energies as we exited the chamber, and for the first time in over three thousand years, they each took a breath of fresh air.

"It doesn't smell the way it used to," Anpu said.

"Many things have changed over the millennia, dear brother, but worry not, we shall be victorious in restoring order to the Earth," Heru said.

It was so different seeing them outside of Duat. The stress from being trapped for so long was still rough on their faces, but I could feel a special kind of joy within them now that they were free. Heru looked to the cloudless sky and felt the warmth of the desert sun. He released the tensions in his shoulders and exhaled a long sigh.

"I cannot thank you enough, Ojore. You've freed us from an eternity of demise. The souls of Duat will finally be able to receive their rite of passage. Soon, everything across the world will change with an entire generation of growth being brought into the lives of our people. You are truly the God of War."

I attempted to salute Heru, but in his excitement, he reached out and gave me a hug. Anpu smiled, glad to see his brother smiling again. Through it all, they had lost everything, but they still had each other.

"What are we going to do about the Evil Three?" I asked.

Their faces turned serious, and they both looked to the sky, trying to sense the energies of the nemesis but felt nothing in the surrounding area. Heru looked at me more seriously than he ever had before.

"It is important that we do not underestimate their power. They are capable of great destruction and will stop at nothing to break us down if we are not careful. We must begin the next part of your training immediately to get you prepared to battle them. You are stronger than all of them. Don't ever forget that. There are many things that we must take care of, but first we must move the Gateway Stones back toward the center and close the chamber," Heru instructed.

We commenced moving the four large stones back toward the center of the platform, and the chamber sank back down into the sands of the desert. The stones proved to be much easier to move because their energies had been exhausted. Anpu charged his energy and buried the platform deep beneath the sands again. We stood atop the dunes, satisfied with our work, our first task completed.

"Do you have any idea of how we're going to defeat them?" I asked.

Heru turned his head to the east, his eye glowing as he gazed far across the lands. His eye returned to normal, and he turned to Anpu and me.

"Follow me. I have something I want to show you."

We traveled a few miles across the dunes, the sand mimicking the waves of water I had just flown across. We came upon what appeared to be an ancient palace that had been long abandoned, an area that seemed to have even gone untouched by colonists. The two gods seemed to be calm as they guided me inside of the immaculate building, the walls decked out in hieroglyphics.

"These walls possess the stories that spark from the beginning of time of life on Earth, stories older than some of our own ancestors," Heru said.

We observed the walls and noticed images similar to Heru and Anpu, but with different headdresses. I couldn't believe that there were stories older than time on these walls; I only wished to have the ability to read them.

"As a part of our training, Anpu and I were to learn some of these ancient stories but were never allowed to enter this chamber to learn them as children. It was not until we had earned our powers and the respect of our positions that we were able to enter without consequence."

The walls told stories of great battles of good and evil that had occurred before time. There was so much detail within the art, so much meaning. Describing them as pictures on the wall was belittling to the artwork. Suddenly, Heru and Anpu stopped walking and turned to face me. A small grin appeared from the side of Heru's face as he looked pridefully into our eyes.

"Before the dark day of our entrapment in Duat, I came to learn of what was to come. The unfortunate side of these stories is that some of them are not measured in a specific frame of time, but the story of your victory was already written."

I followed Heru's eyes over to the wall beside us, and I was immediately thrown by the large, red dragon symbol engraved into the stone wall. Miraculously, it was shaped just like the symbol I'd drawn in my sketchbook. Every curve and point matched just as I had drawn it from my mind. It was no longer a coincidence that the idea came into my head—it was destiny.

"It has been prophesied by the ancestors that you, Ojore, are the chosen one to defeat the Evil Three. Anpu and I have been chosen to train you for your battles with them. We knew all about you well before you ever existed; we just didn't know when your time would come," Heru stated.

I felt a rise of power within me, happy that I had finally come to the right decision. This was my path, my future. I, the child of a single parent born in a society where nothing was expected from me, learned that today, well before the thought of me had even been imagined, I had been destined to be the God of War. I accepted the charge of my ancient ancestors with gratitude, and we all exited the chamber with enlightened spirits.

"Before we can get to your training, it is important that Anpu and I first set things back in order," Heru said.

Heru dropped his arms to his sides and looked up toward the sky. The glare in his eyes resembled the glare in my eyes when I'd accepted the call of the God of War. It was then I knew that he had an even greater responsibility to fulfill.

"It was my duty to protect the skies of Earth from harm until death. We as gods looked to Ra, the God of the Gods, for guidance and direction as his essence protected us all. With the many losses that we have taken, it is only right that I take on the sovereign duty of Ra and become God of the Gods to lead us into a new era of distinction," Heru said.

"Hail Heru." Anpu saluted with a smile.

I quickly saluted my new leader, thankful for his presence keeping us alive. This had been a tough journey for both of us, but the end results were beyond anything we could have expected.

"What about you, Anpu?" I asked.

"I am God of the Dead, and therefore my place is in Duat. With the gateway reopened, I will be able to usher the souls on their spiritual journeys to earn their rites of passage. I will be very busy for a while, though... I have over three thousand years of souls to sort through," Anpu laughed.

I stood before my mentors on the hot sands of the Sahara, humbled by their graciousness. Less than a year ago, I had been a depressed kid with anger issues, and now I stood on the land of my ancient ancestors as the new God of War. The gala event was paramount to my development as the burdens of my past ceased to exist. I was free.

"Before I depart, I want to give you this, Ojore."

Heru placed his hand over my right eye, and his hand glowed gold again. He retracted his hand and left a golden remnant of his eye that faded into my skin.

"Ra shared an eye with me to see everything that I saw and with me he shared everything he believed I should see. The same goes for you and me, Ojore. With this gift, you'll never be alone." Heru grinned.

We saluted each other once more, no longer as teacher and student, but as equals in the fight to restore peace to the Earth. I intended to fulfill the vow I'd taken as the God of War until the Evil Three were defeated by my hand, and I would leave myself no room for failure.

"I must get back to my duties. I will see you both in due time," Anpu said. "Should you ever decide to come to Duat, Ojore, concentrate your energy to open the portal. You no longer have to travel across the galaxy. It's as simple as this."

Anpu swiped his hand across the air in front of him, and a rip in the space appeared, flashing in several different colors. He stepped toward it and looked back to bid us farewell. He stepped into the portal, and instantly the colorful rip disappeared as if it had never existed.

"Take care of yourself, Ojore. Anpu and I will set things right within the Spirit Realm, and in due time we will continue your training. Be warned, it will be your combat training, and I do not intend on holding back on you," Heru said.

"I'll be ready," I replied.

"Good. In the meantime, be a god to your goddess and honor her with distinction, and most importantly, be the hero your mother wanted you to be." Heru grinned.

We saluted each other once more with respect to our new roles. There had been a point in time when I'd felt that Heru would lose faith in me, and now here we were about to embark on our next adventure.

"If you ever need me, I'll be above the sky," Heru said.

He crouched down, and his body dissipated into several thick, golden lines. The lines reshaped into a glowing golden falcon and expelled a burst of energy as it rocketed into the sky toward the sun and vanished. It was as if a weight was lifted from my shoulders. For the first time in a long while, the tension I carried was gone, and I was more relaxed than I had ever been. I don't know why I felt bad for doing it, but I decided the best thing for me to do was to heed Heru's words and go home to enjoy the things that made me happy.

A couple of months passed, and the world seemed to be getting back to normal. Aaliyah kept her face still in the mirror as Camille added the finishing touches to her makeup. The time had come for the two to meet, and their relationship flourished as Camille welcomed Aaliyah with open arms, bonded by their love for Ryan.

"The key is to always apply a basic, light foundation. It should look as natural as possible; that way all your other colors have the pop they're supposed to," Camille said, stroking the makeup brush.

She gave Aaliyah a good once-over, checking her face for missed spots and blemishes but saw nothing but perfection.

"And you are good to go, sweetheart! Check it out," Camille said.

Aaliyah opened her eyes and was struck with awe at her reflection.

"I look just like my mom did in her college graduation picture! Aw, thank you, Ms. Scales, this is perfect." Aaliyah smiled.

The two shared a warm embrace. Camille grabbed a tissue for Aaliyah and dabbed her eyes to ensure her tears didn't cause her makeup to run.

"It's all love, dear. Just my way of saying welcome to the family. I've never really met anyone Ryan has talked to, so him introducing you to me lets me know that you are truly special to him. Just treat him right 'cause he's the only child I got," Camille joked.

The two laughed as I walked into my mom's room, wondering what was taking them so long.

"Hey, what are y'all—"

Aaliyah turned to look at me, and once again, I was taken away by her beauty. The universe had taken its time putting her together.

"How is one capable of being so fine?" I asked.

We all laughed, and quickly the attention turned to me as I struck a pose in the doorway of the bathroom.

"I was born fine, baby, but you—where did you get that suit? You look so handsome." Aaliyah winked.

"Yes, indeed, that is a bad suit. See, he got his fashion sense from me," my mother added.

Perks of being a god—I could make my own clothing.

"Thank you, thank you, all I did was take a shower," I laughed. "We better get out of here soon or we're gonna be late."

Aaliyah and I grabbed our caps and gowns and got in the car with Mom. We held hands in the backseat as we rode across town for graduation. Everyone had their gowns open, trying to show off their fancy suits and dresses. I, of course, won the title for best dressed, and everyone stopped to gaze at the perfection known to the world as a suit, or maybe it was just how fine Aaliyah was in the dress I had bought her. Either way, we were all happy that this day had finally come.

There were several guest speakers, people that none of us knew, but their words reminded me of the wisdom given to me by Heru and Anpu. The many times I'd traveled to the Spirit Realm to visit Duat had opened my heart. Despite all the killing, I'd learned a real lesson in love. I learned how far I'm willing to go to see another person smile, and more importantly, I learned to love myself. I'd grown so much in such a short period of time—I wouldn't have recognized my old self if he were standing right in front of me.

Aaliyah prepared to walk across the stage to receive her diploma, still insecure about not having her family there for her. The principal called her name, and before she could take her first step, she was greeted with an uproar of screams and shouts from everyone in our graduating class as well as my mom, my grandmother, and my grandfather.

"That's my girl right there, shawdy," I screamed over the crowd.

The smile on her face was priceless. She hurried off stage to hide her tears of joy as she clenched her diploma tightly to her chest. Finally, the walks were over, and the principal gave her last remarks before congratulating us all. We tossed our caps into the air, and the crowd went wild, shouting for their graduates. After the ceremony, Aaliyah and I found my family outside in the courtyard waiting for us. My mom took one look at me and burst into tears, proud that she was able to see me make it this far. I introduced my grandparents to Aaliyah, and my grandfather couldn't wipe the grin off of his face as he admired her beauty. Just as we started to take pictures, I suddenly remembered there was something I had to do.

"Gimme just a sec. I'll be right back."

I disappeared in the large crowd of people, looking for someone who had come to see me that day. I finally found them and brought them back with me to introduce them to my family.

"Hey, everybody. I'd like you all to meet Ms. Graves, Janay's mom."

After much misunderstood review, the doctors had seen her fit to be released. With the money we stole from Face, we set her up in a nice place on the east side to restart her life. Heru advised me that he wanted me to bring her to him one of these days soon. I guess he saw something special in her.

Terrell and Adrianna found us among the crowd, and we all introduced our moms. Terrell's mom's face was drenched with tears knowing that in two weeks her son would be shipped off to some military base. She and my mom embraced, and we all came together to calm her tears. Aaliyah grabbed my hand and looked into my eyes with a smile. I smiled back, feeling our souls' bond through our touch.

"So what do we do now?" Terrell asked.

"I don't know, man. What should we do, Sweets?" I asked.

"Well, we're all 18 now. I say we hit the streets and celebrate while we can," Aaliyah said.

"I'm down for whatever," Adrianna added.

The four of us hit the streets that night, celebrating the sacred times of our lives. We'd experienced so much to make it so far in life that not one moment was ever to be taken for granted. Soon, we'd all be called to do different things in life, but the one thing that kept us humbled was the bond we had all made through friendship. There are times in life when we are called to go beyond our norms and evolve. There are those that live in fear of change, and those that embrace it. Who you are and what you choose to do determines your destiny... The ancestors chose me to be a god, but I chose to answer the call of a hero.

By power of fire and the blessing of the ancestors before me, I am the Menacing Red Dragon, God of War.

-THE END-

EPILOGUE

THE EVIL THREE *squabbled for years, hiding from Heru's eye as Mabaya's theory proved to be more than what they bargained for. Unable to feast on mortal souls, the evil demigods began to show signs of aging. The threat of the new god struck fear in their spirits, but the tricky fiends refused to have their plans thwarted by his arrival.*

They spent the next few years sneaking about the Life Realm, analyzing him and his actions. They learned his mannerisms and synced with his tone of voice. They exercised his walk and tried to match his vigor. The new god proved to be the ultimate warrior, but they found what they felt to be a weakness within his moral code. The new god was not immune to mortal feelings, and he cherished the life of the weak, unwilling to turn on them for his own sake. His selfless sacrifices affirmed with the evil demigods that he was emotionally unfit to be the God of War. Satisfied with their observation, Lamia was given the charge to vanquish their new enemy. Her goal: to eat his heart.

ACKNOWLEDGEMENTS

I WOULD LIKE TO *give a huge thank you to none other than the Queen of Storytelling, Ardre Orie and the entire team at 13th and Joan for seeing and believing in my vision and helping me make this mission possible. To all of my friends that saw the vision and vowed to be a part of it, this isn't a win for me, but a win for all of us. As I always said, once I make it, we've all made it. To my family, the road for me was never hindered by obstacles, but hidden by a dense fog giving no sight of a safe path to follow. Your teachings built me to survive the challenges in this world, and I will use what I've learned to champion all that is placed before me. To my ancestors, rest easy on the truth that your sacrifices were not in vain. In living this life, I've learned that I thrive off of negativity, and with that in mind, I want to thank all of the haters I've acquired throughout my life. It was your deleterious words that gave me the rage to not only write this book, but to also be nothing short of great at everything I do.*

Lastly, I'd like to thank Shanice Latrell. You found me at my worst and loved me until I became the best. My debt to you is one that will take an eternity to pay back, but I hope that my actions and the fulfillment of my promises will serve as a means of understanding the love I have for you.

This is only the beginning, we all have more adventures to come...

"Who you are is limited to
who you think you are."

Egyptian Book of the Dead

"Make your haters
your motivators."

Porsche Foxx

ABOUT THE AUTHOR

A NATIVE TO THE city of Decatur, GA, Ryan King Scales was destined to follow his childhood dream of being a superhero. He began writing adventure books at the age of 8 expanding the limits of his creative imagination until the struggles of life manifested into his greatest creation. His creative ability gained new heights in college where he majored in Fine Arts, as he has appeared in several movies and TV shows throughout his career. His ultimate goal is to be a world-renowned actor, writer, director, and producer. Red Dragon is actually one of the many nicknames he goes by and he believes that the Red Dragon is the higher self of his spirituality.

"Your dreams are the previews of your future."

— Ryan King Scales